PRODUCED BY **MAN OF ACTION ENTERTAINMENT** LOS ANGELES, CA, NEW YORK, NY

PUBLISHED BY **IMAGE COMICS** PORTLAND, OR

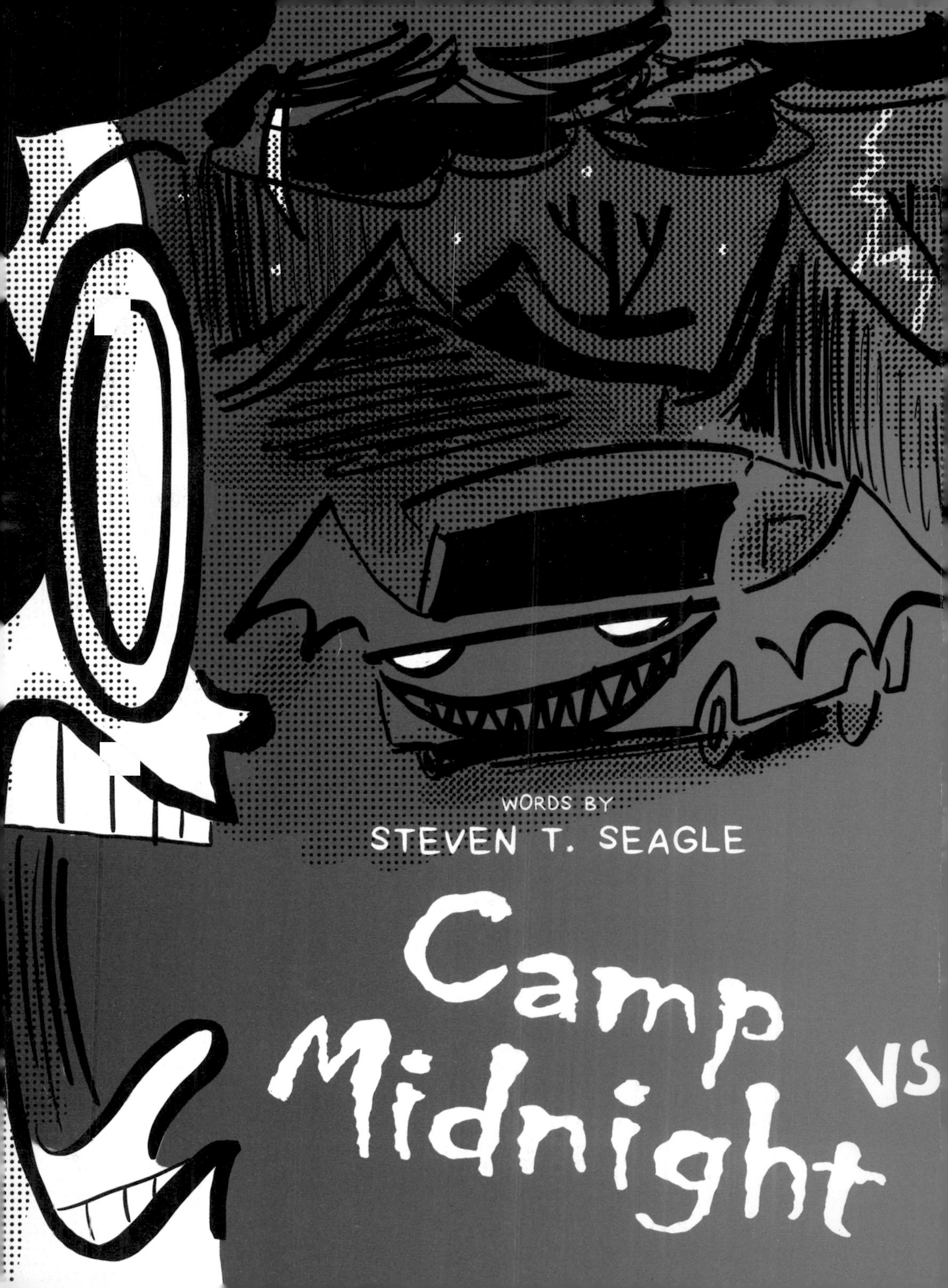
WORDS BY
STEVEN T. SEAGLE
Camp
Midnight
VS

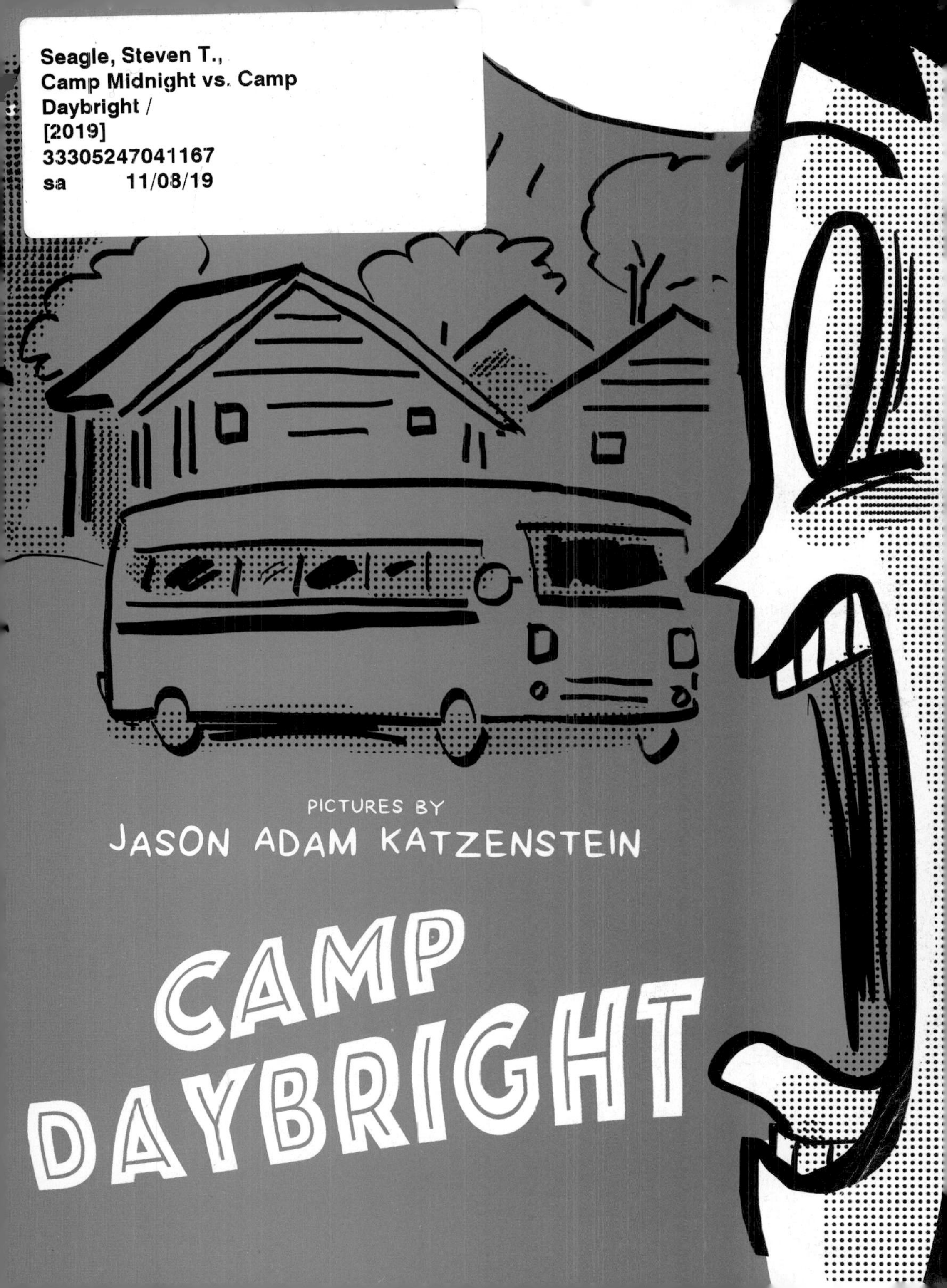
PICTURES BY
JASON ADAM KATZENSTEIN
CAMP
DAYBRIGHT

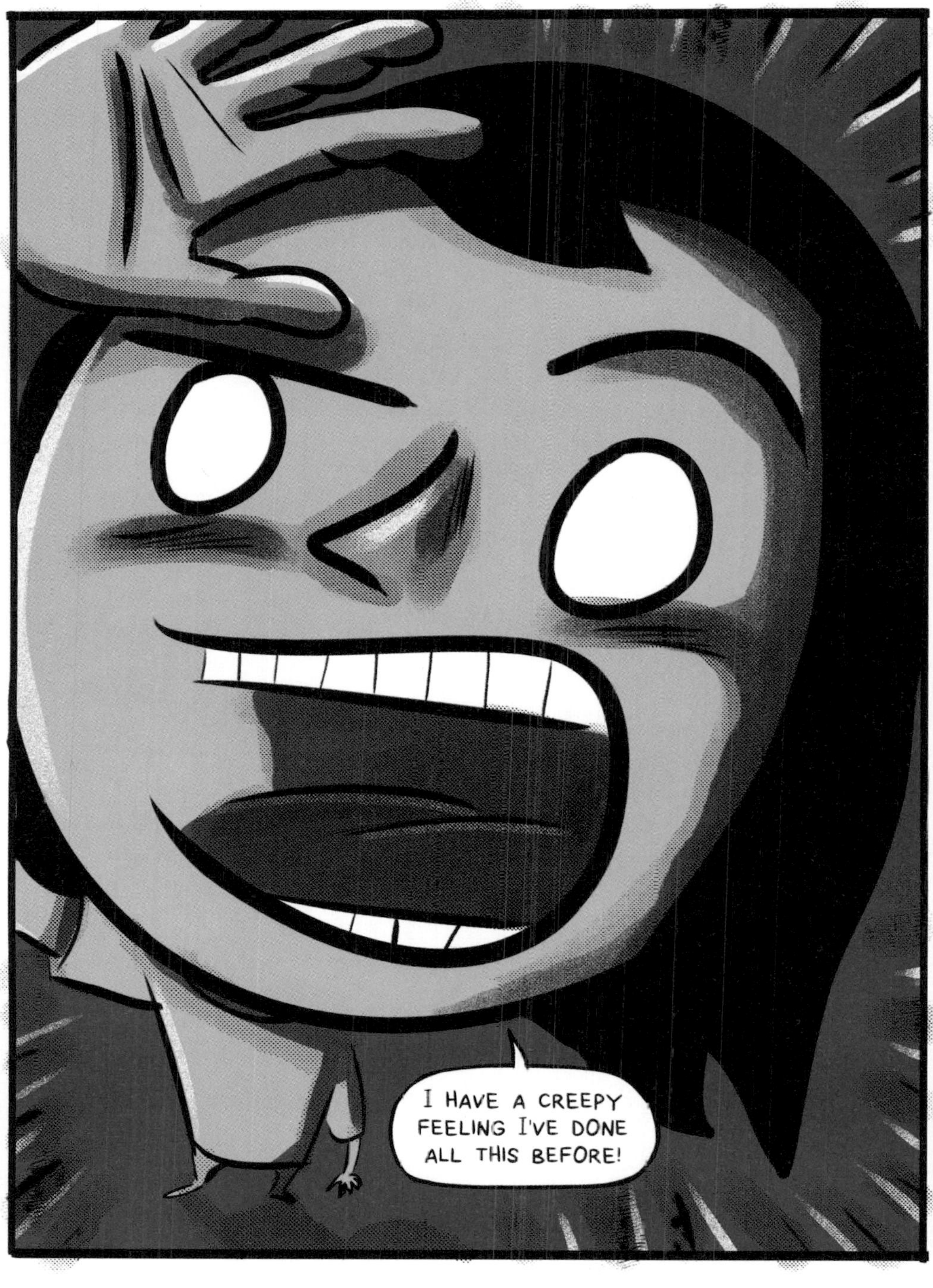
I HAVE A CREEPY FEELING I'VE DONE ALL THIS BEFORE!

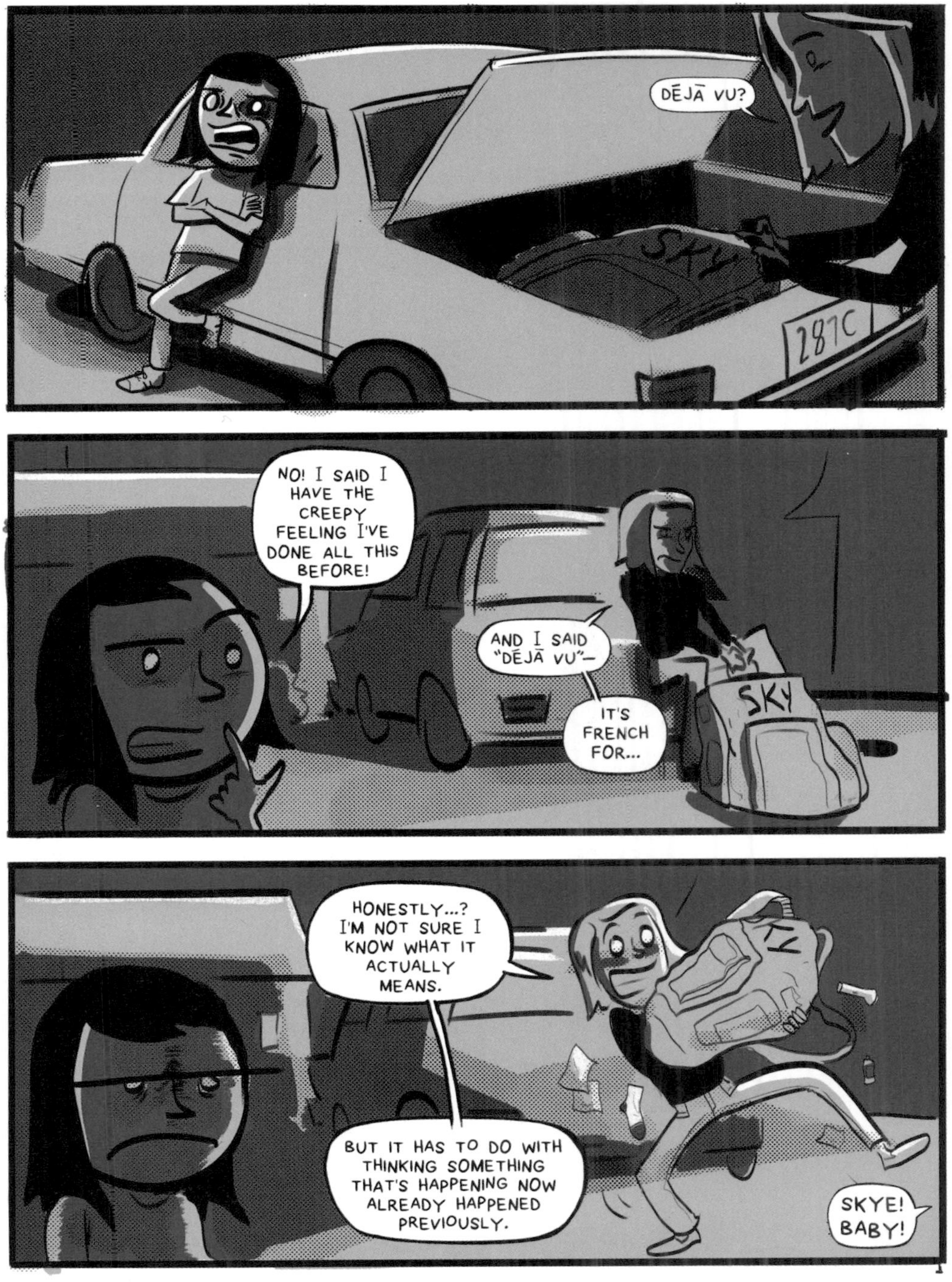
DĒJĀ VU?
SKY
287C
NO! I SAID I HAVE THE CREEPY FEELING I'VE DONE ALL THIS BEFORE!
AND I SAID "DĒJĀ VU"—
SKY
IT'S FRENCH FOR...
HONESTLY...? I'M NOT SURE I KNOW WHAT IT ACTUALLY MEANS.
BUT IT HAS TO DO WITH THINKING SOMETHING THAT'S HAPPENING NOW ALREADY HAPPENED PREVIOUSLY.
SKYE! BABY!

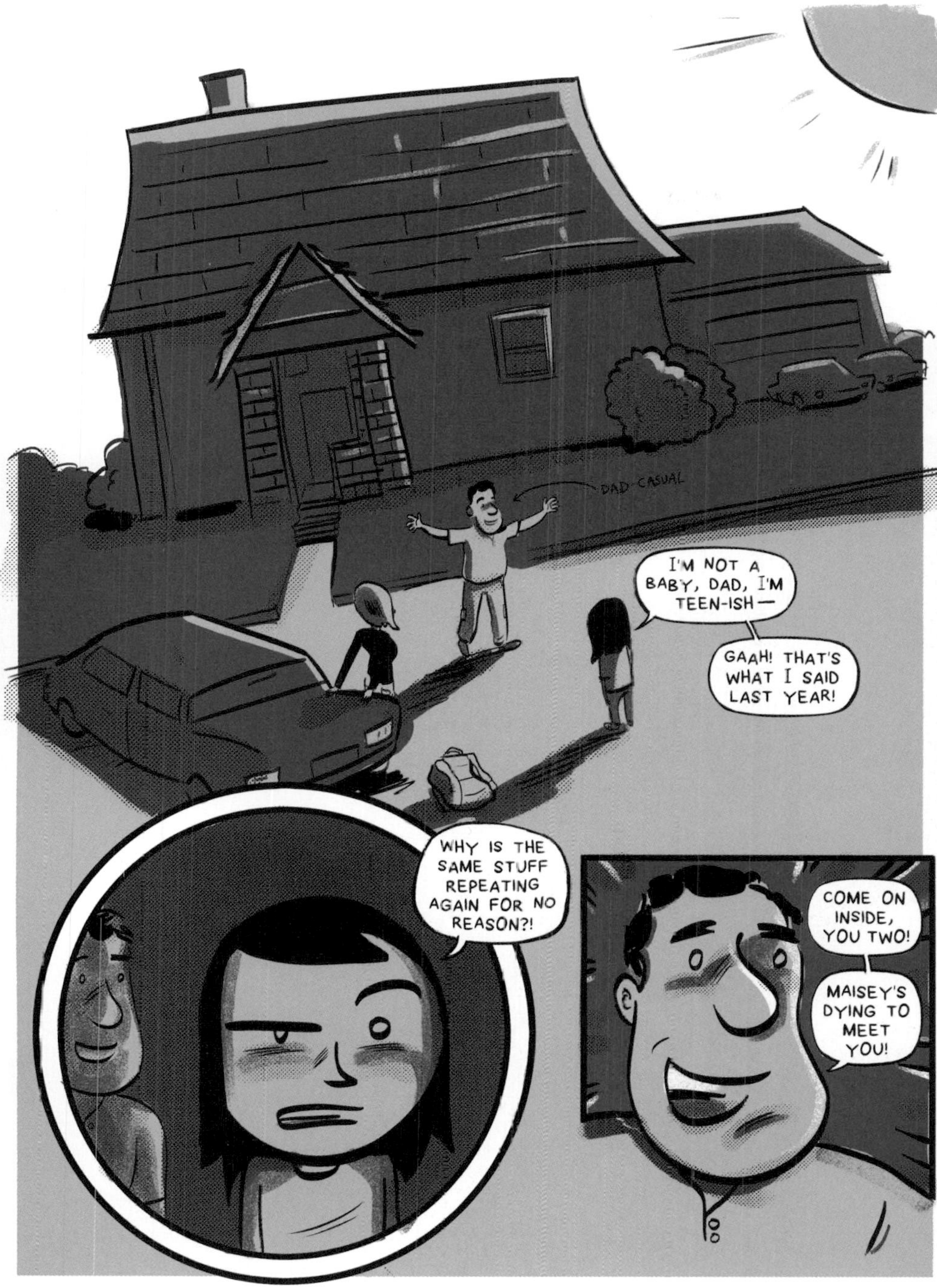

DAD-CASUAL
I'M NOT A BABY, DAD, I'M TEEN-ISH—
GAAH! THAT'S WHAT I SAID LAST YEAR!
WHY IS THE SAME STUFF REPEATING AGAIN FOR NO REASON?!
COME ON INSIDE, YOU TWO!
MAISEY'S DYING TO MEET YOU!

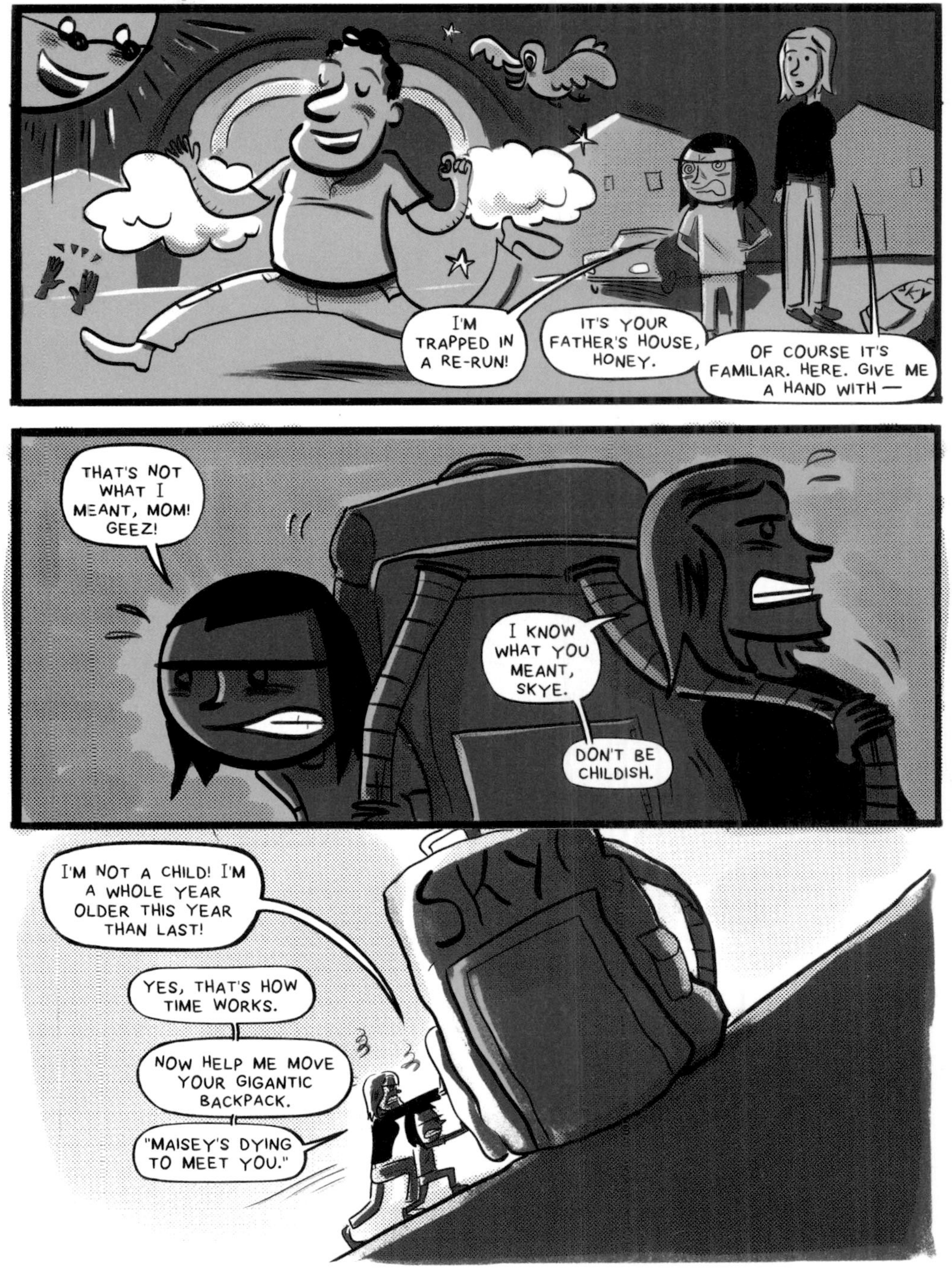
I'M TRAPPED IN A RE-RUN!
IT'S YOUR FATHER'S HOUSE, HONEY.
OF COURSE IT'S FAMILIAR. HERE. GIVE ME A HAND WITH —
THAT'S NOT WHAT I MEANT, MOM! GEEZ!
I KNOW WHAT YOU MEANT, SKYE.
DON'T BE CHILDISH.
SKY
I'M NOT A CHILD! I'M A WHOLE YEAR OLDER THIS YEAR THAN LAST!
YES, THAT'S HOW TIME WORKS.
NOW HELP ME MOVE YOUR GIGANTIC BACKPACK.
"MAISEY'S DYING TO MEET YOU."

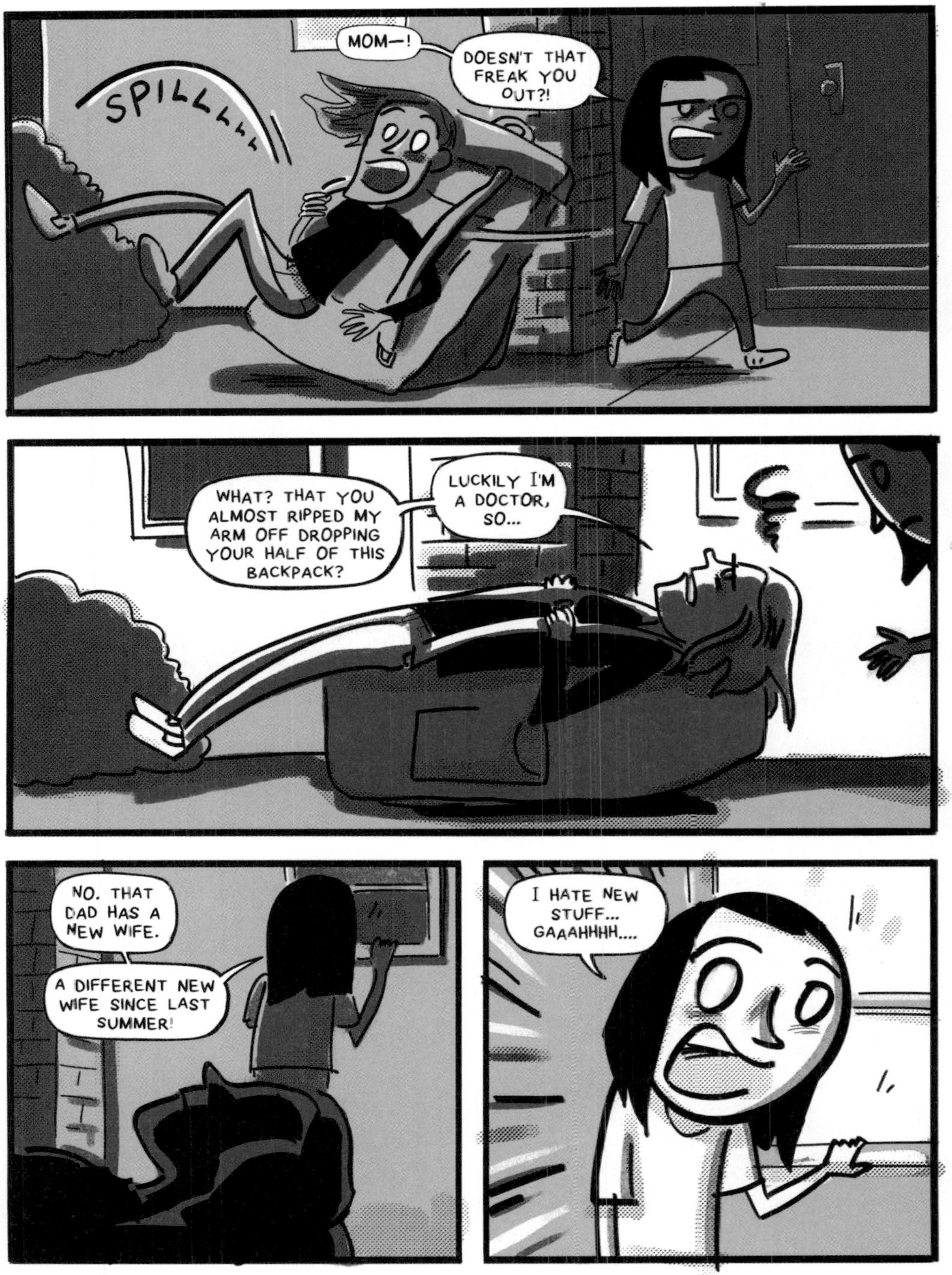
SPILLLLLL
MOM—!
DOESN'T THAT FREAK YOU OUT?!
WHAT? THAT YOU ALMOST RIPPED MY ARM OFF DROPPING YOUR HALF OF THIS BACKPACK?
LUCKILY I'M A DOCTOR, SO...
NO. THAT DAD HAS A NEW WIFE.
A DIFFERENT NEW WIFE SINCE LAST SUMMER!
I HATE NEW STUFF... GAAAHHHH....

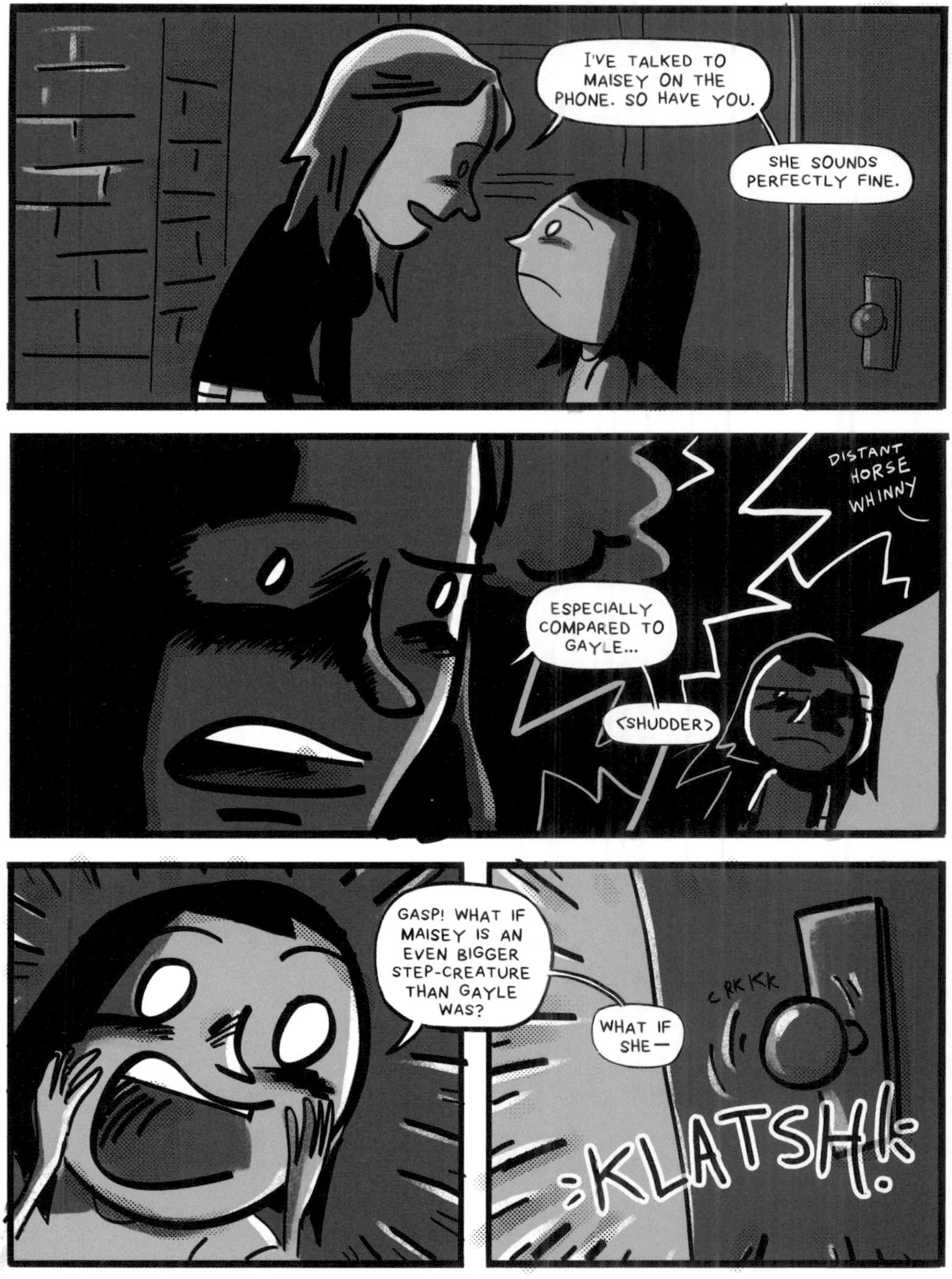
I'VE TALKED TO MAISEY ON THE PHONE. SO HAVE YOU.
SHE SOUNDS PERFECTLY FINE.
ESPECIALLY COMPARED TO GAYLE...
<SHUDDER>
DISTANT HORSE WHINNY
GASP! WHAT IF MAISEY IS AN EVEN BIGGER STEP-CREATURE THAN GAYLE WAS?
WHAT IF SHE—
CRKKK
KLATSH!

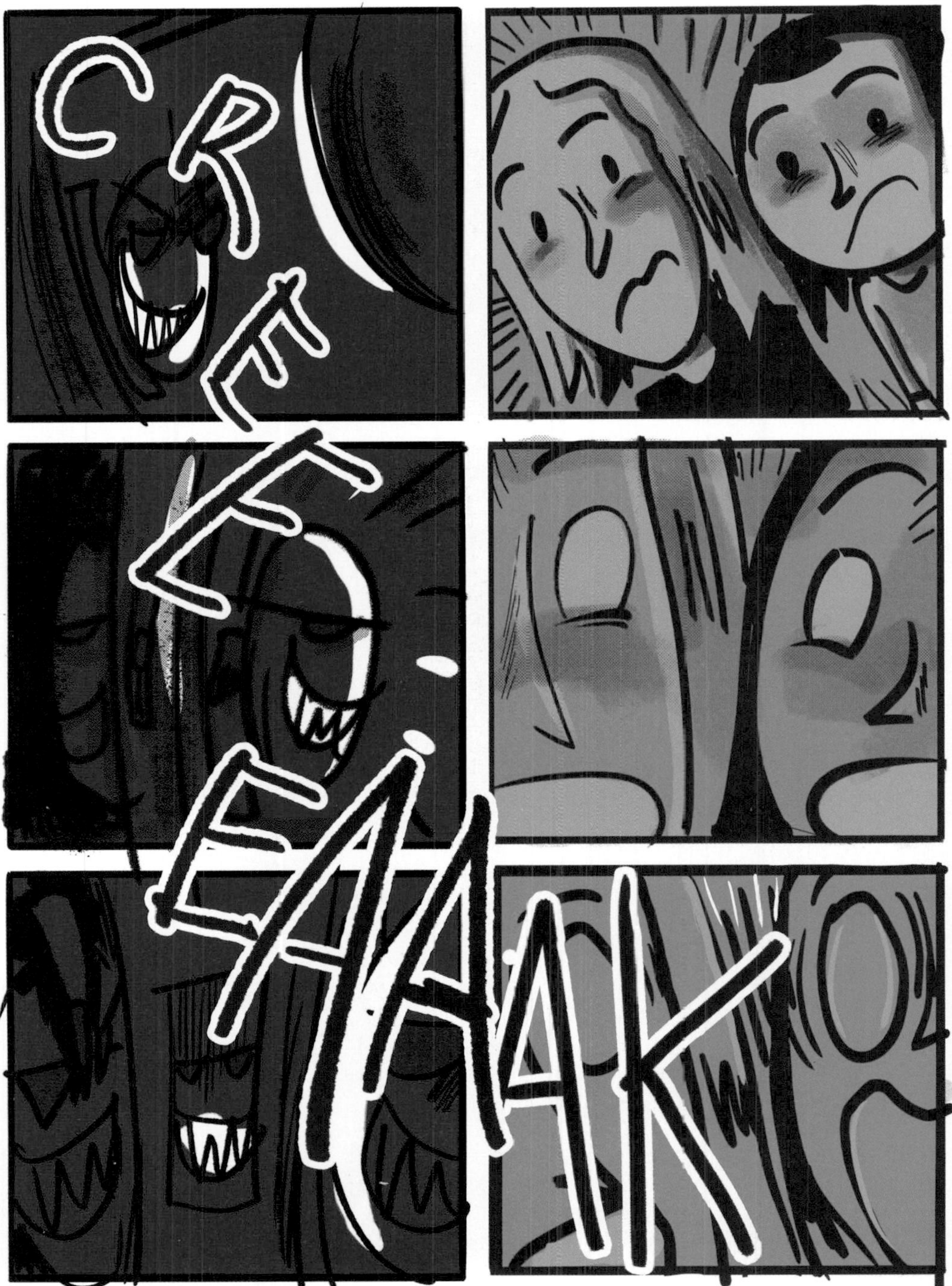
CREEEAAAK

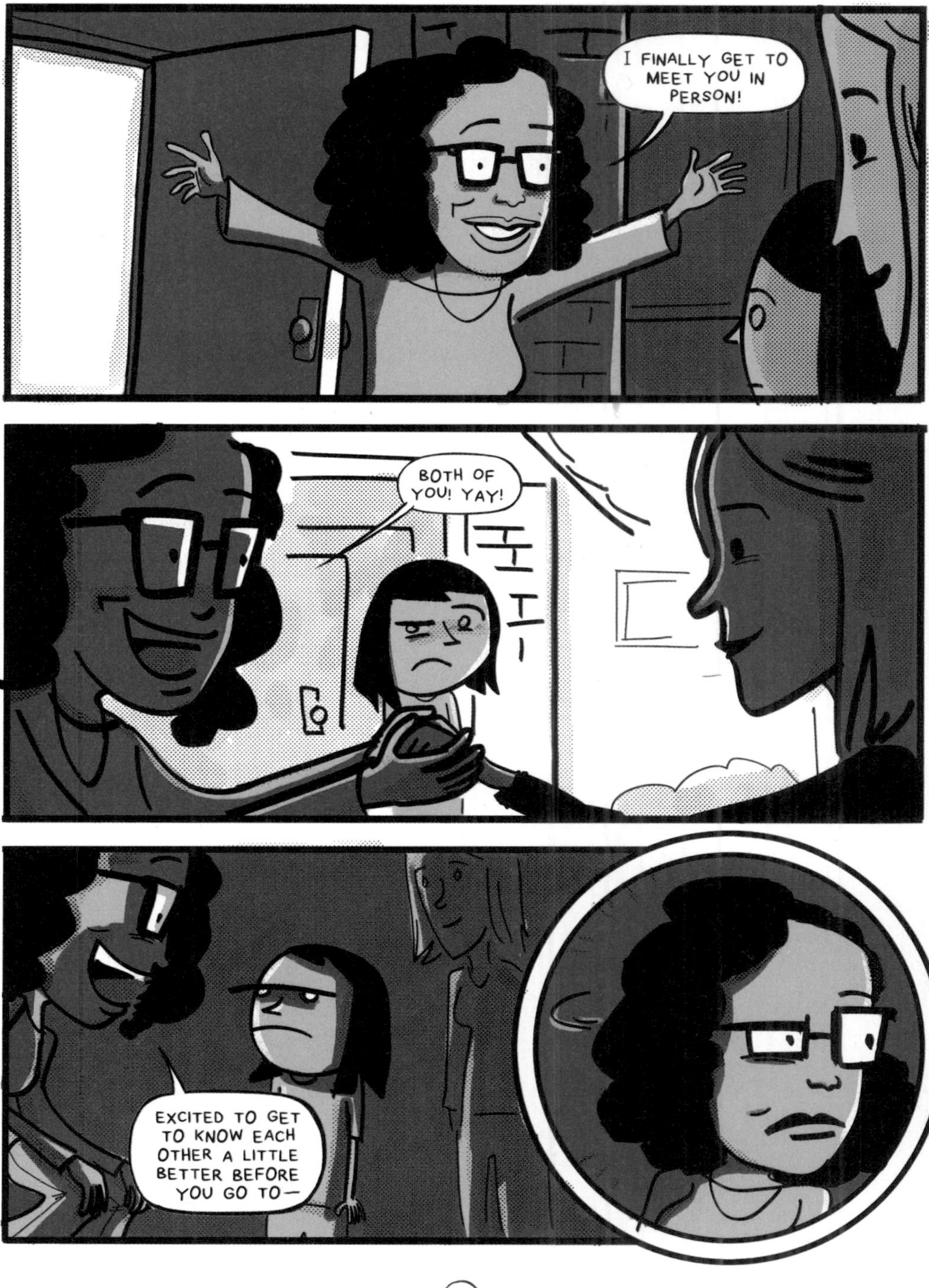
I FINALLY GET TO MEET YOU IN PERSON!
BOTH OF YOU! YAY!
EXCITED TO GET TO KNOW EACH OTHER A LITTLE BETTER BEFORE YOU GO TO—

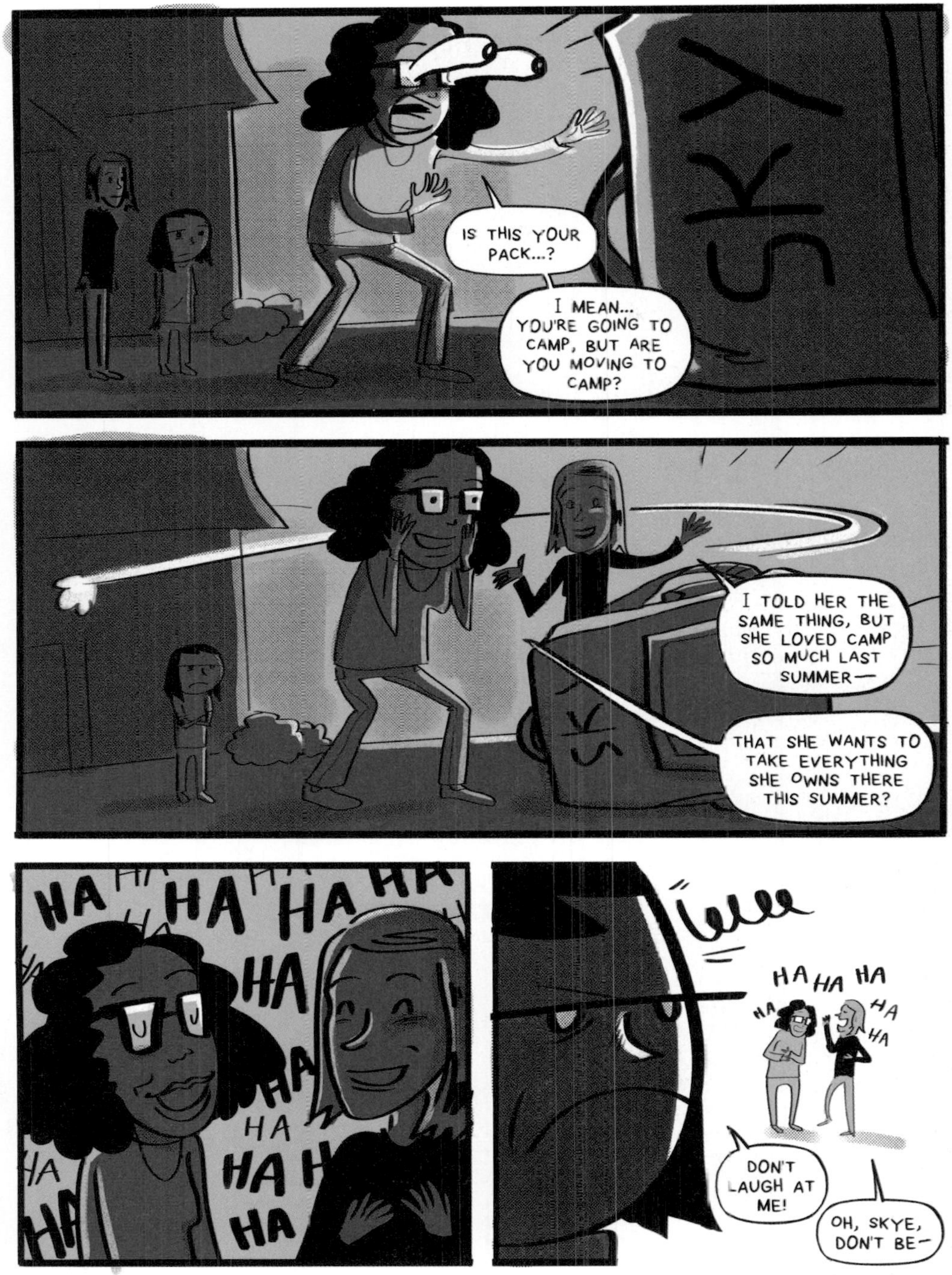
SKY
IS THIS YOUR PACK...?
I MEAN... YOU'RE GOING TO CAMP, BUT ARE YOU MOVING TO CAMP?
I TOLD HER THE SAME THING, BUT SHE LOVED CAMP SO MUCH LAST SUMMER—
THAT SHE WANTS TO TAKE EVERYTHING SHE OWNS THERE THIS SUMMER?
HA HA HA HA HA HA HA HA HA HA HA HA HA HA HA HA
HA HA HA HA HA HA HA
DON'T LAUGH AT ME!
OH, SKYE, DON'T BE—

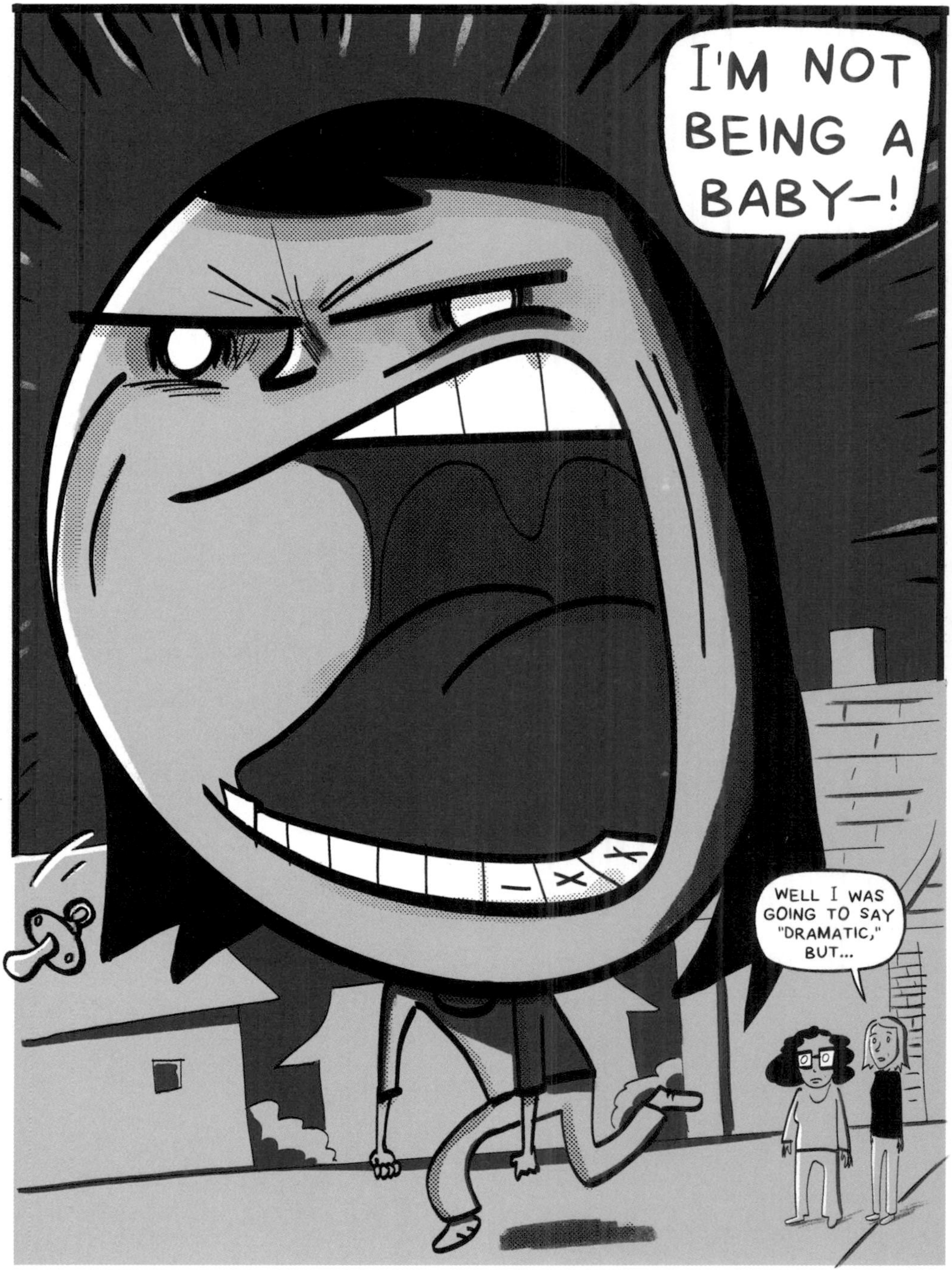
I'M NOT BEING A BABY--!
WELL I WAS GOING TO SAY "DRAMATIC," BUT...

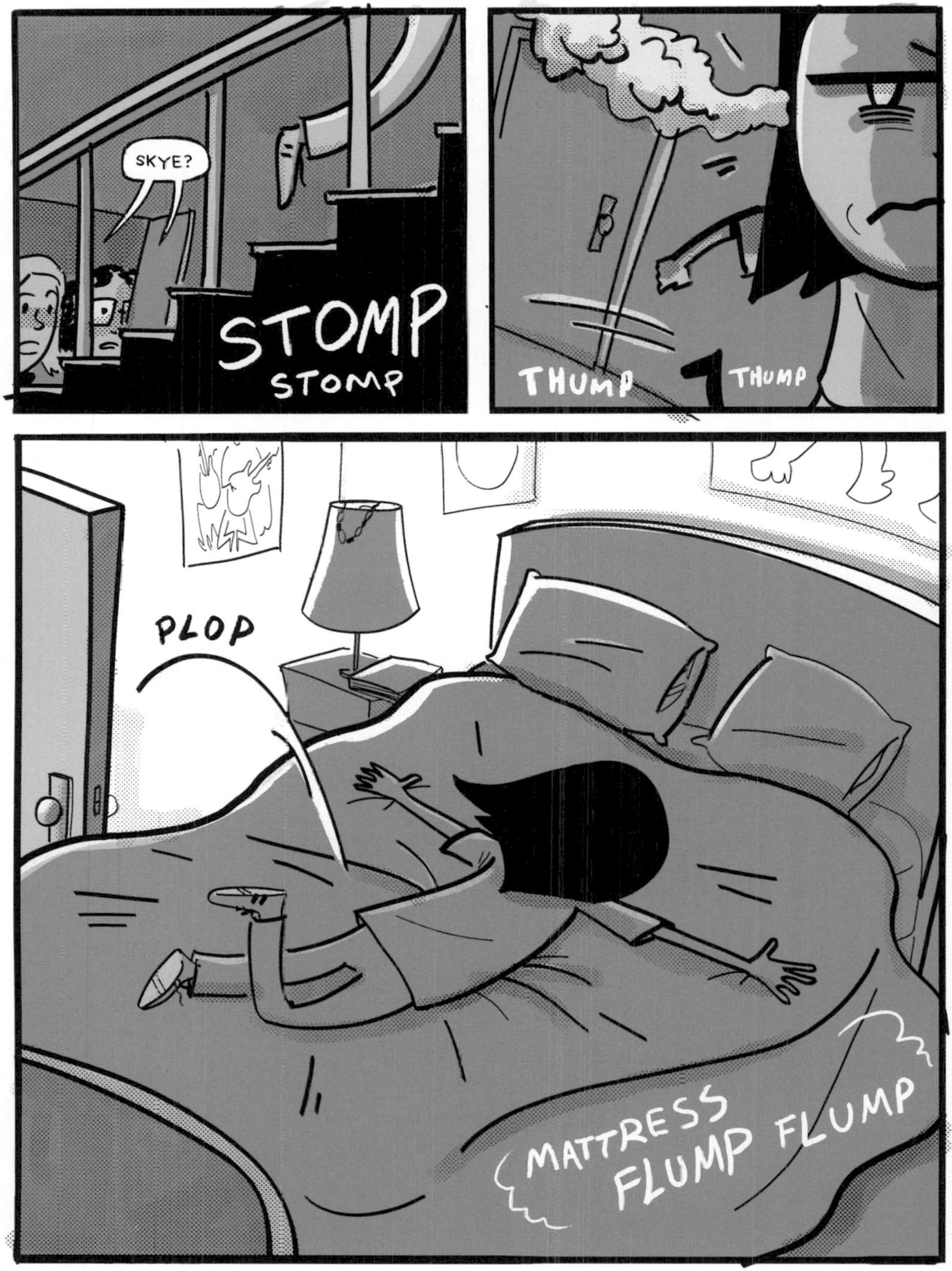
SKYE?
STOMP
STOMP
THUMP
THUMP
PLOP
MATTRESS
FLUMP FLUMP

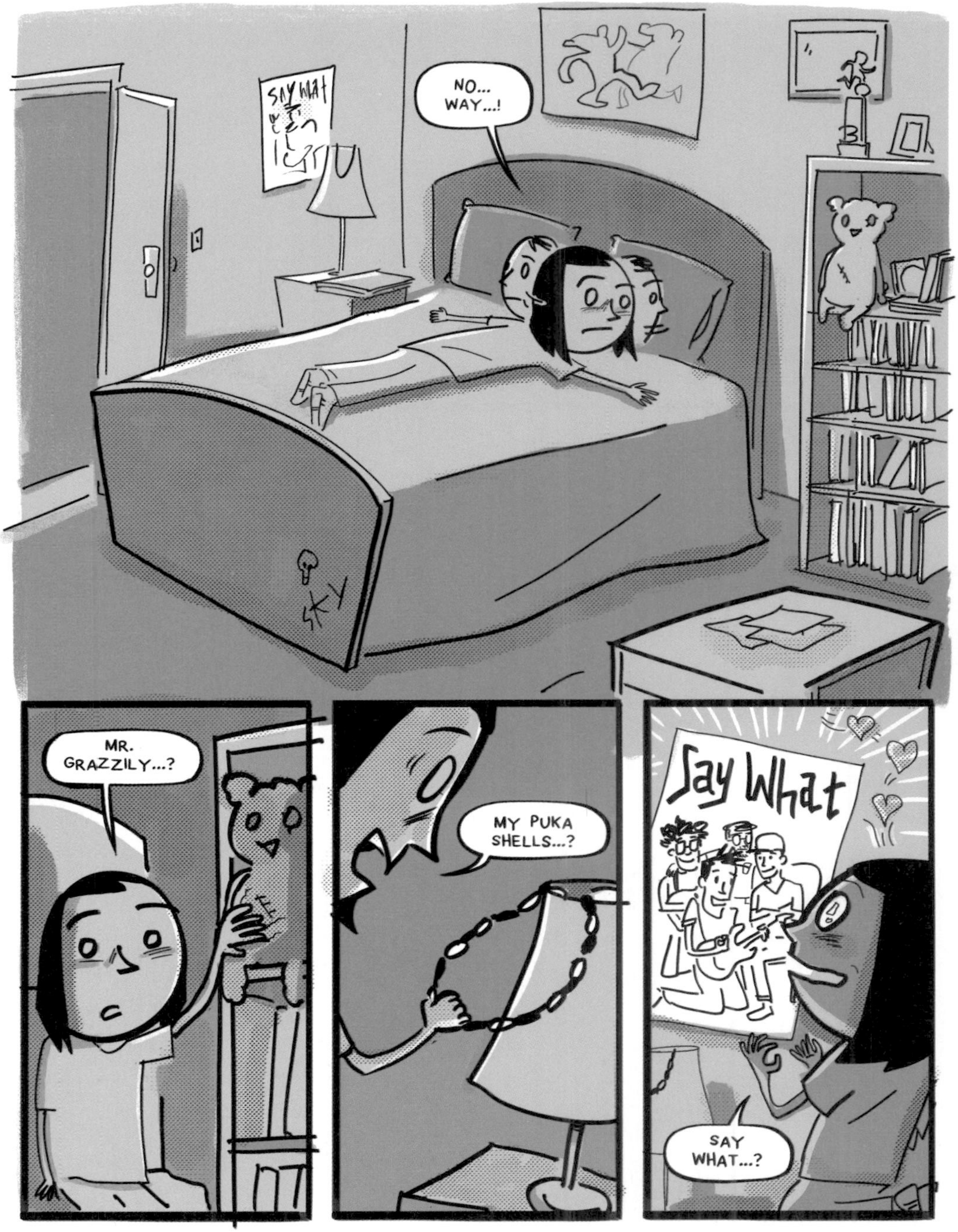
SAY What
NO...
WAY...!
SKY
MR.
GRAZZILY...?
MY PUKA
SHELLS...?
Say What
SAY
WHAT...?

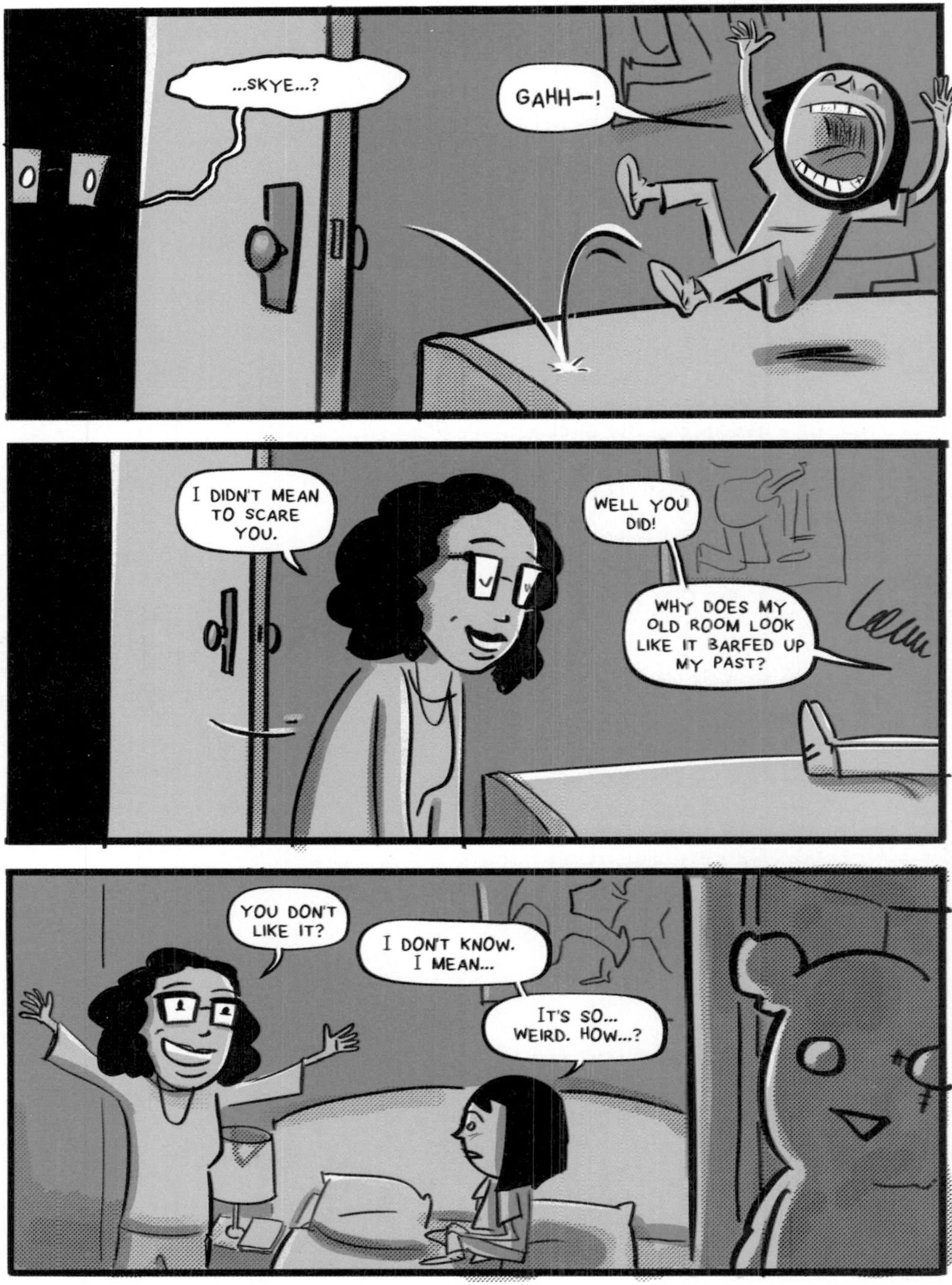
...SKYE...?
GAHH—!
I DIDN'T MEAN TO SCARE YOU.
WELL YOU DID!
WHY DOES MY OLD ROOM LOOK LIKE IT BARFED UP MY PAST?
YOU DON'T LIKE IT?
I DON'T KNOW. I MEAN...
IT'S SO... WEIRD. HOW...?

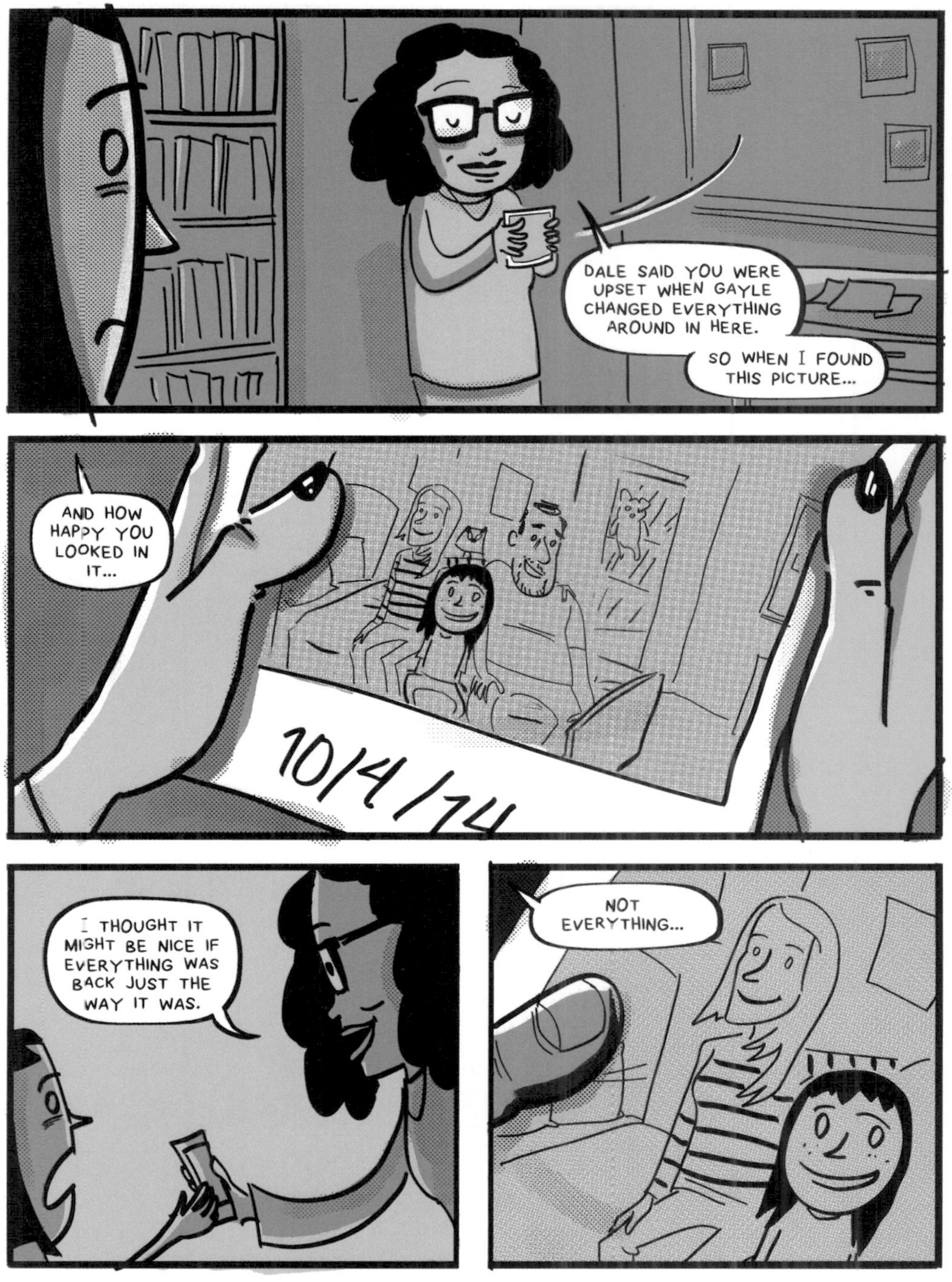

DALE SAID YOU WERE UPSET WHEN GAYLE CHANGED EVERYTHING AROUND IN HERE.
SO WHEN I FOUND THIS PICTURE...
AND HOW HAPPY YOU LOOKED IN IT...
10/4/14
I THOUGHT IT MIGHT BE NICE IF EVERYTHING WAS BACK JUST THE WAY IT WAS.
NOT EVERYTHING...

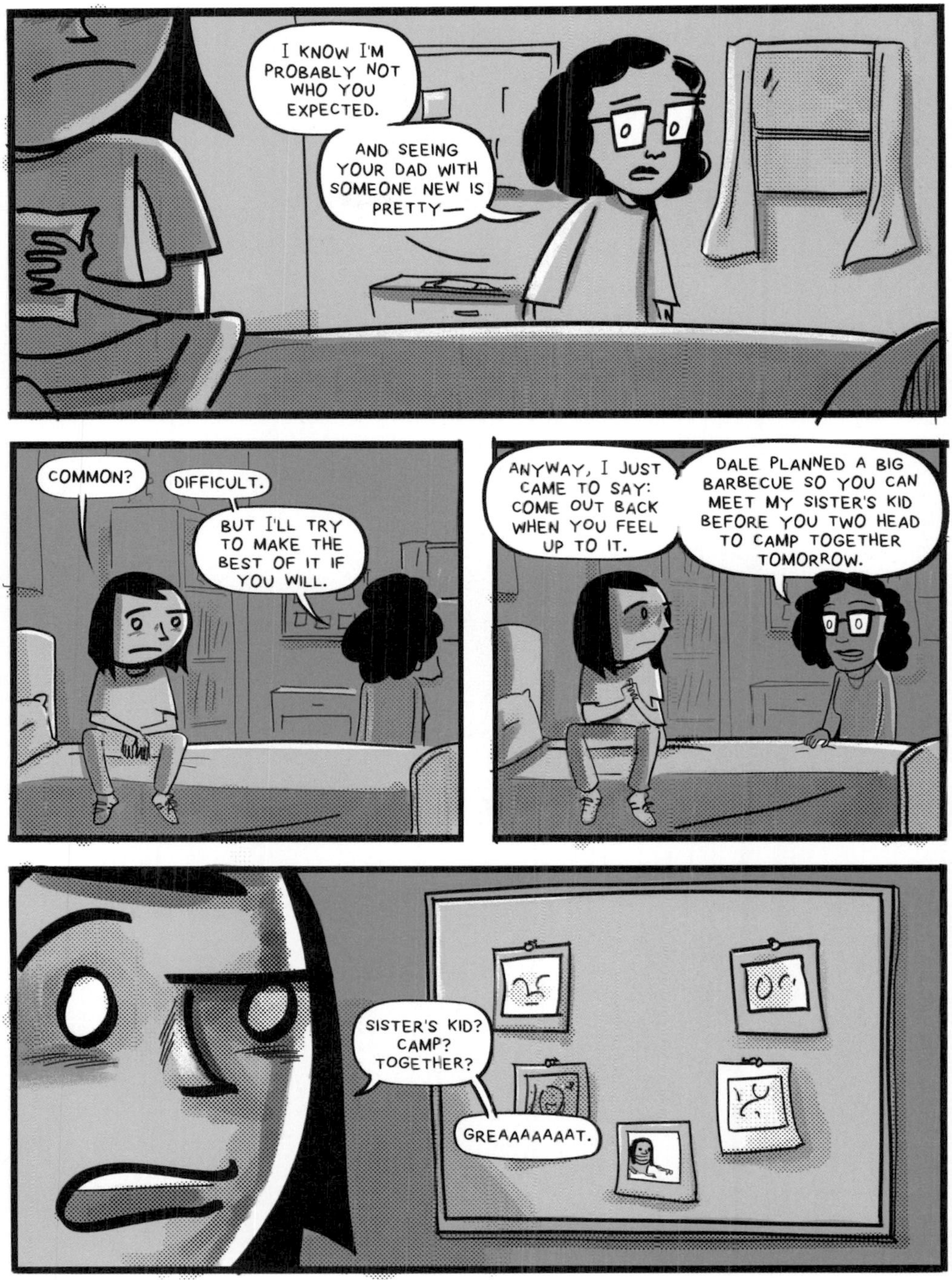
I KNOW I'M PROBABLY NOT WHO YOU EXPECTED.
AND SEEING YOUR DAD WITH SOMEONE NEW IS PRETTY—
COMMON?
DIFFICULT.
BUT I'LL TRY TO MAKE THE BEST OF IT IF YOU WILL.
ANYWAY, I JUST CAME TO SAY: COME OUT BACK WHEN YOU FEEL UP TO IT.
DALE PLANNED A BIG BARBECUE SO YOU CAN MEET MY SISTER'S KID BEFORE YOU TWO HEAD TO CAMP TOGETHER TOMORROW.
SISTER'S KID? CAMP? TOGETHER?
GREAAAAAAAT.

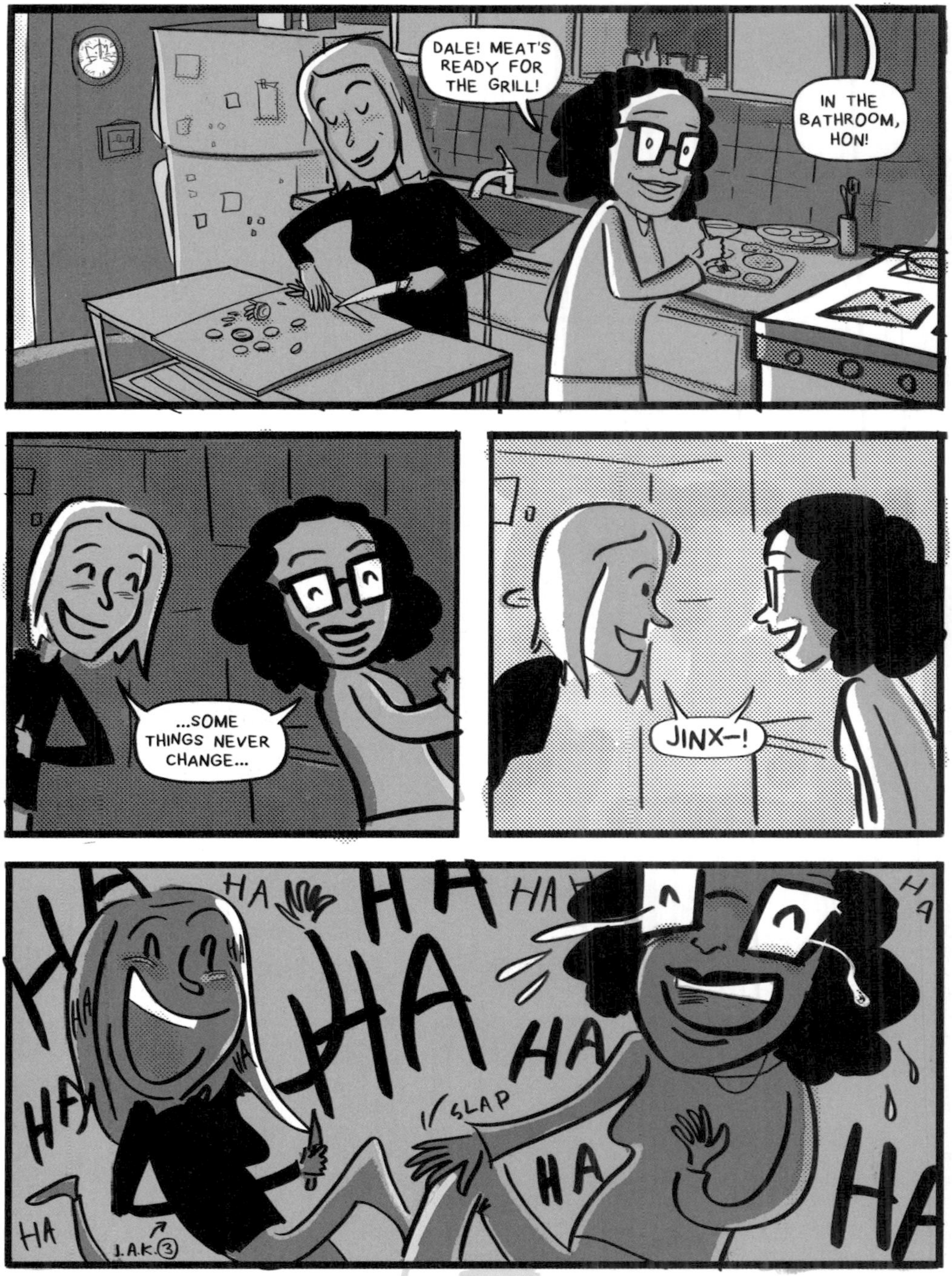
DALE! MEAT'S READY FOR THE GRILL!
IN THE BATHROOM, HON!
...SOME THINGS NEVER CHANGE...
JINX—!
HA HA HA HA HA HA HA HA HA HA HA HA HA
SLAP
J.A.K.③

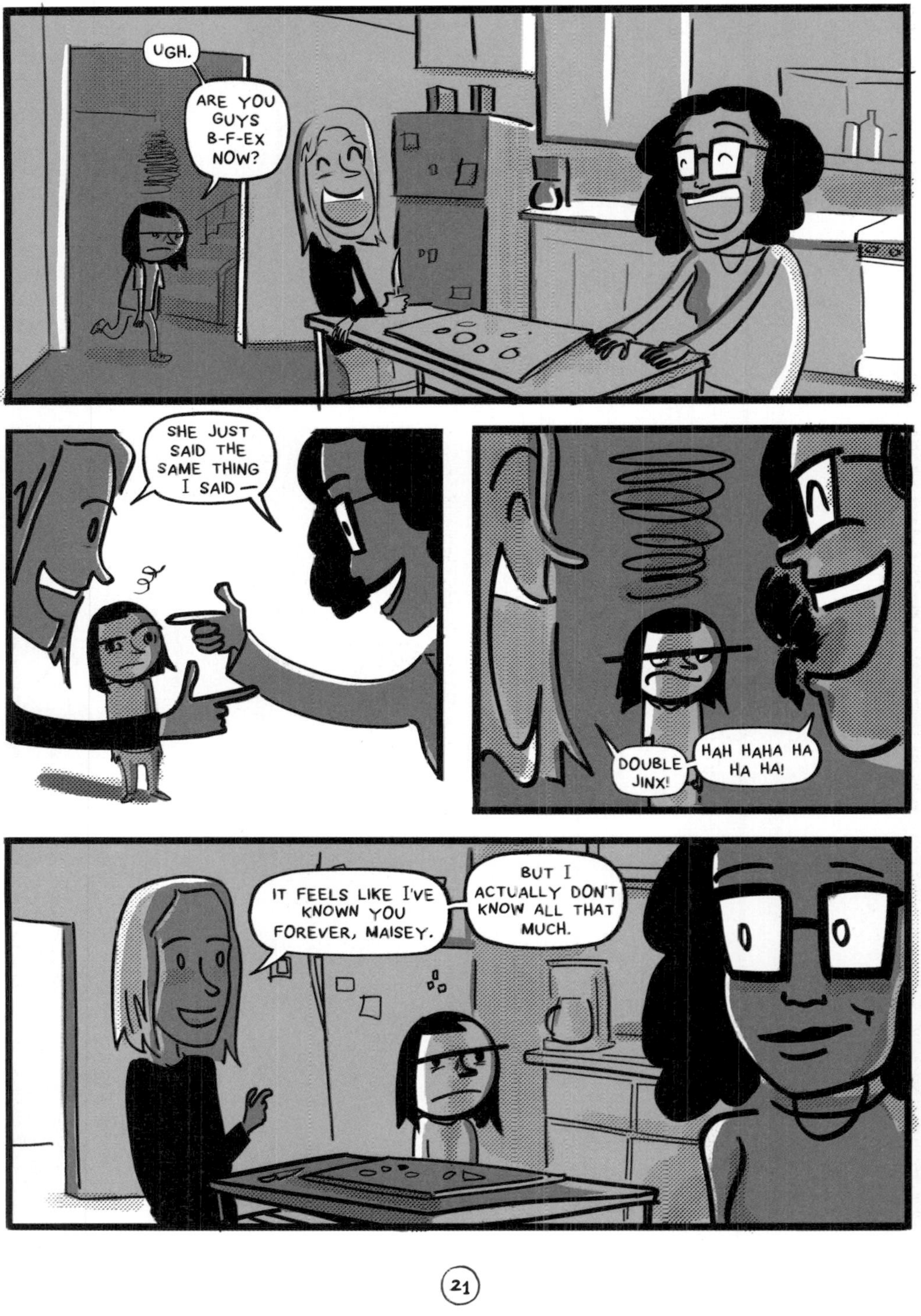
UGH.
ARE YOU GUYS B-F-EX NOW?
SHE JUST SAID THE SAME THING I SAID—
DOUBLE JINX!
HAH HAHA HA HA HA!
IT FEELS LIKE I'VE KNOWN YOU FOREVER, MAISEY.
BUT I ACTUALLY DON'T KNOW ALL THAT MUCH.

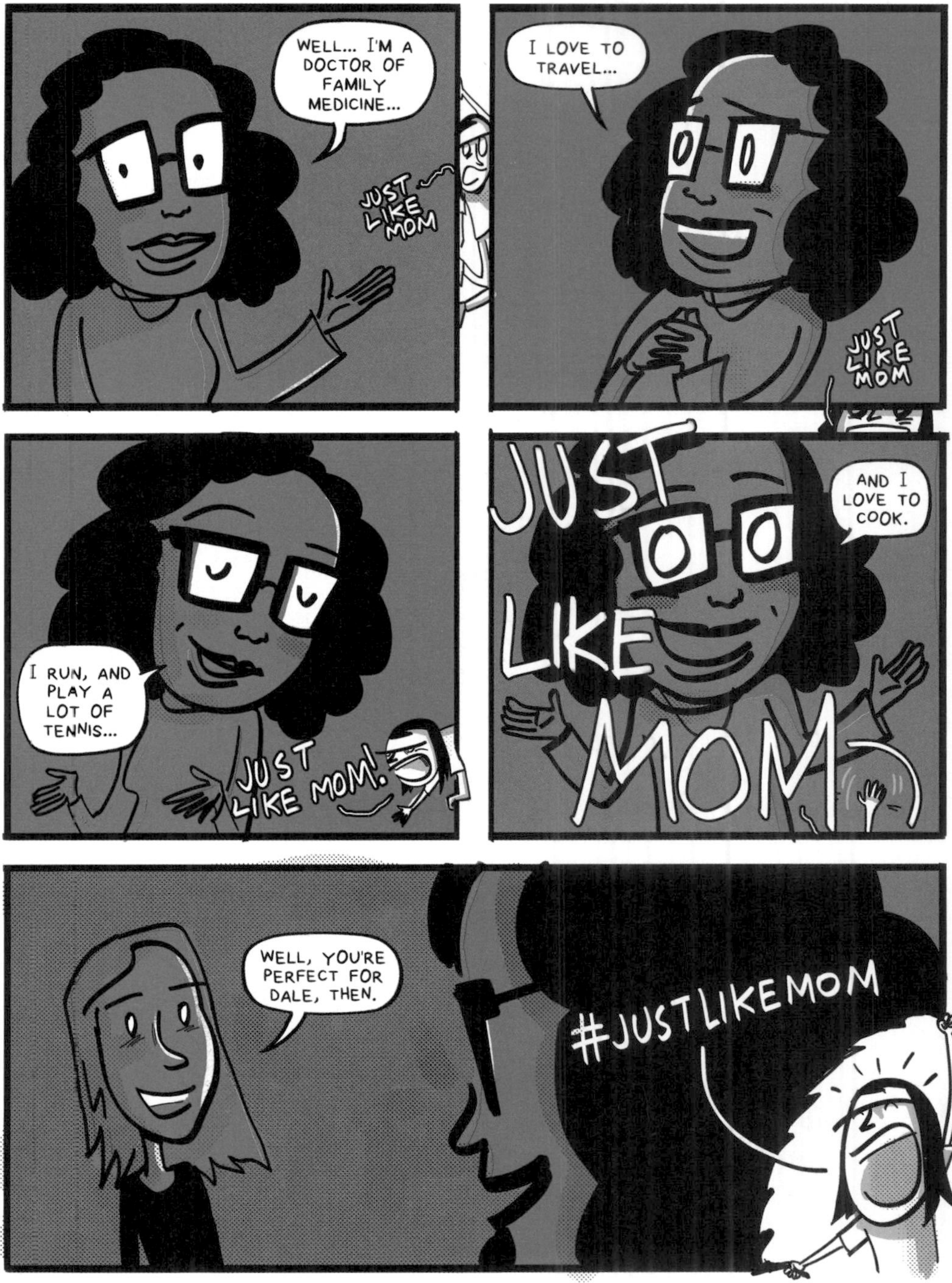
WELL... I'M A DOCTOR OF FAMILY MEDICINE...
JUST LIKE MOM
I LOVE TO TRAVEL...
JUST LIKE MOM
I RUN, AND PLAY A LOT OF TENNIS...
JUST LIKE MOM!
AND I LOVE TO COOK.
JUST LIKE MOM
WELL, YOU'RE PERFECT FOR DALE, THEN.
#JUSTLIKEMOM

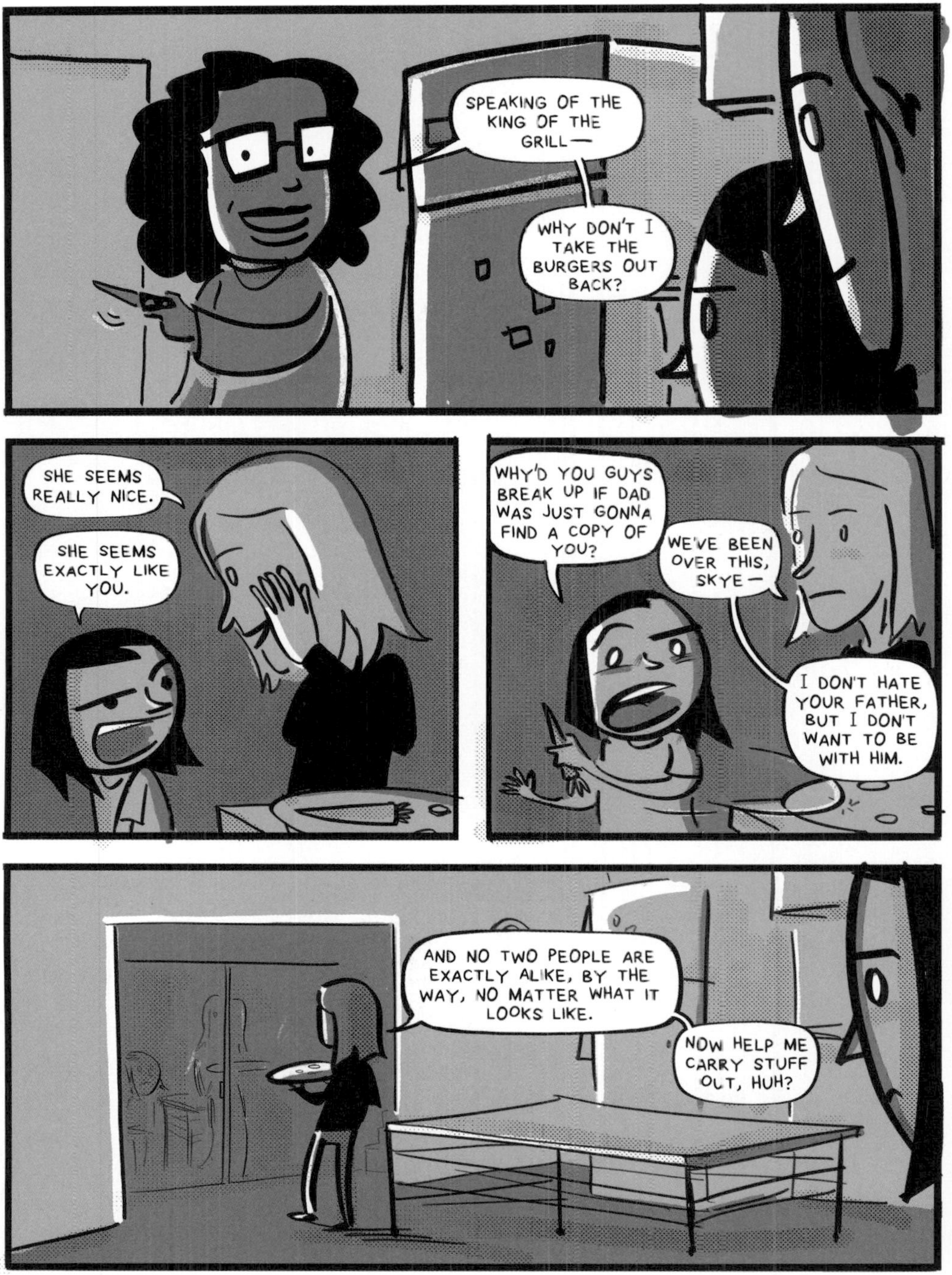
SPEAKING OF THE KING OF THE GRILL—
WHY DON'T I TAKE THE BURGERS OUT BACK?
SHE SEEMS REALLY NICE.
SHE SEEMS EXACTLY LIKE YOU.
WHY'D YOU GUYS BREAK UP IF DAD WAS JUST GONNA FIND A COPY OF YOU?
WE'VE BEEN OVER THIS, SKYE—
I DON'T HATE YOUR FATHER, BUT I DON'T WANT TO BE WITH HIM.
AND NO TWO PEOPLE ARE EXACTLY ALIKE, BY THE WAY, NO MATTER WHAT IT LOOKS LIKE.
NOW HELP ME CARRY STUFF OUT, HUH?

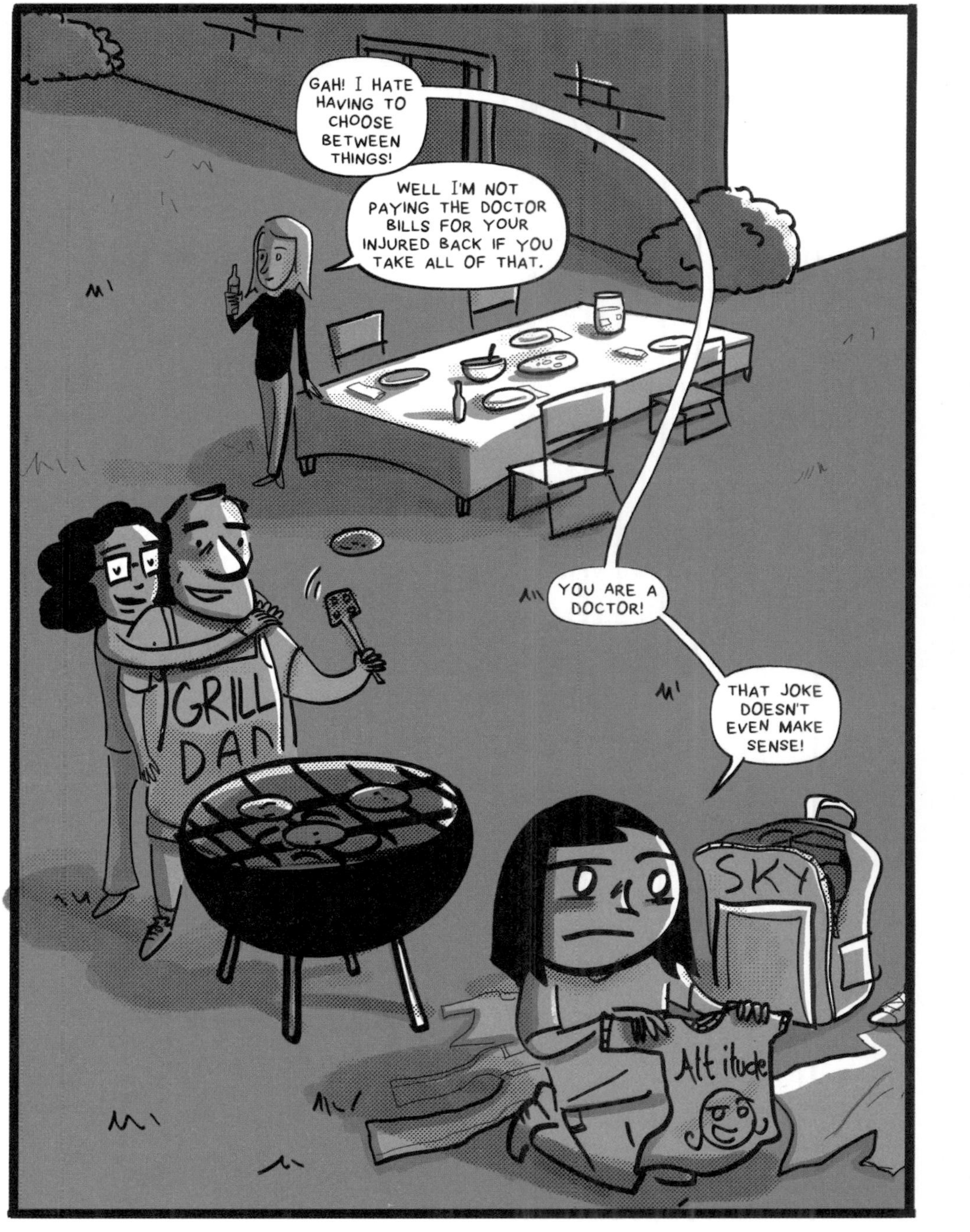
GAH! I HATE HAVING TO CHOOSE BETWEEN THINGS!
WELL I'M NOT PAYING THE DOCTOR BILLS FOR YOUR INJURED BACK IF YOU TAKE ALL OF THAT.
YOU ARE A DOCTOR!
THAT JOKE DOESN'T EVEN MAKE SENSE!
GRILL DAD
SKY
Alt itude

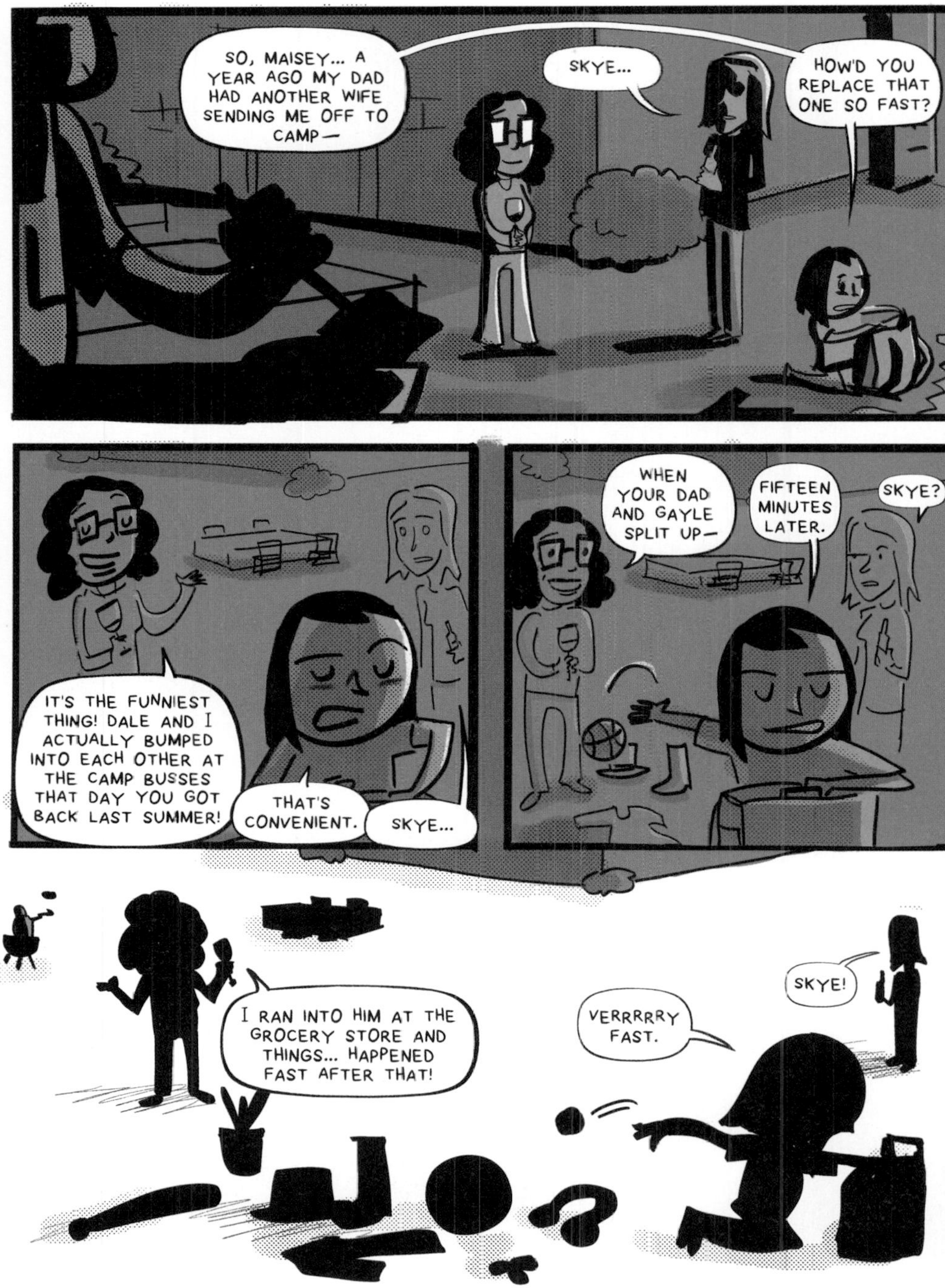
SO, MAISEY... A YEAR AGO MY DAD HAD ANOTHER WIFE SENDING ME OFF TO CAMP—
SKYE...
HOW'D YOU REPLACE THAT ONE SO FAST?
IT'S THE FUNNIEST THING! DALE AND I ACTUALLY BUMPED INTO EACH OTHER AT THE CAMP BUSSES THAT DAY YOU GOT BACK LAST SUMMER!
THAT'S CONVENIENT.
SKYE...
WHEN YOUR DAD AND GAYLE SPLIT UP—
FIFTEEN MINUTES LATER.
SKYE?
I RAN INTO HIM AT THE GROCERY STORE AND THINGS... HAPPENED FAST AFTER THAT!
VERRRRRY FAST.
SKYE!

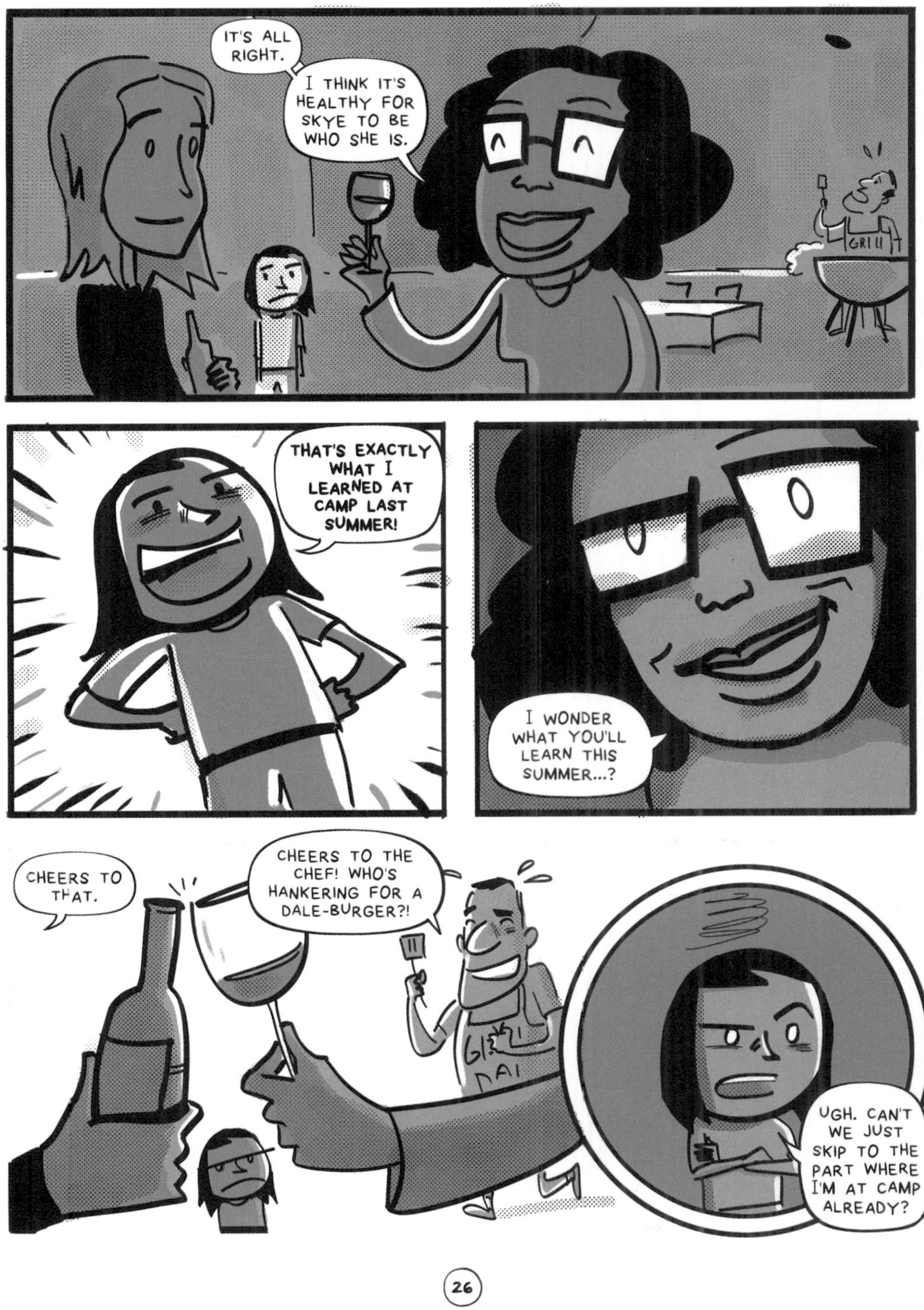
IT'S ALL RIGHT.
I THINK IT'S HEALTHY FOR SKYE TO BE WHO SHE IS.
GRILL
THAT'S EXACTLY WHAT I LEARNED AT CAMP LAST SUMMER!
I WONDER WHAT YOU'LL LEARN THIS SUMMER...?
CHEERS TO THAT.
CHEERS TO THE CHEF! WHO'S HANKERING FOR A DALE-BURGER?!
UGH. CAN'T WE JUST SKIP TO THE PART WHERE I'M AT CAMP ALREADY?

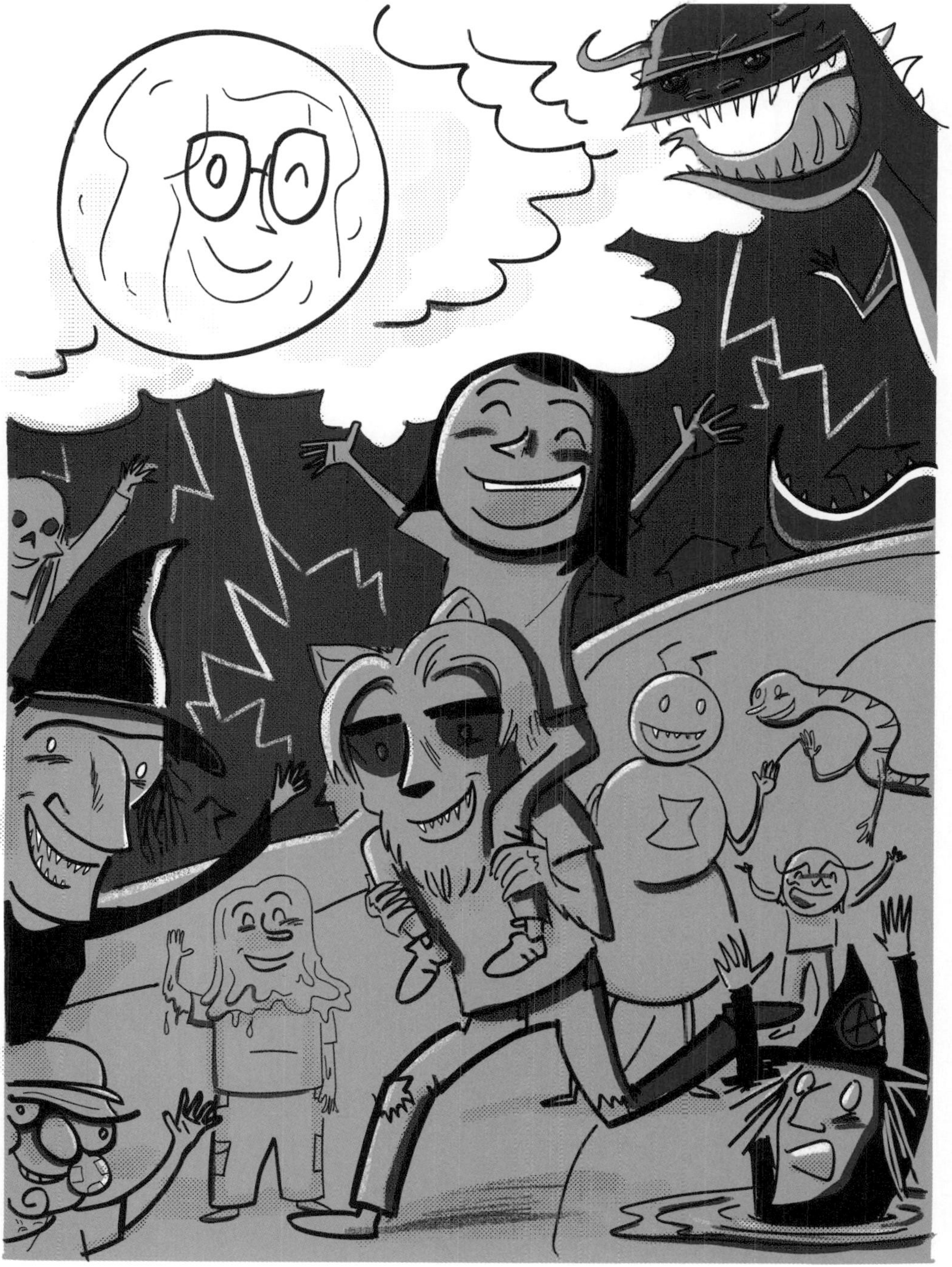

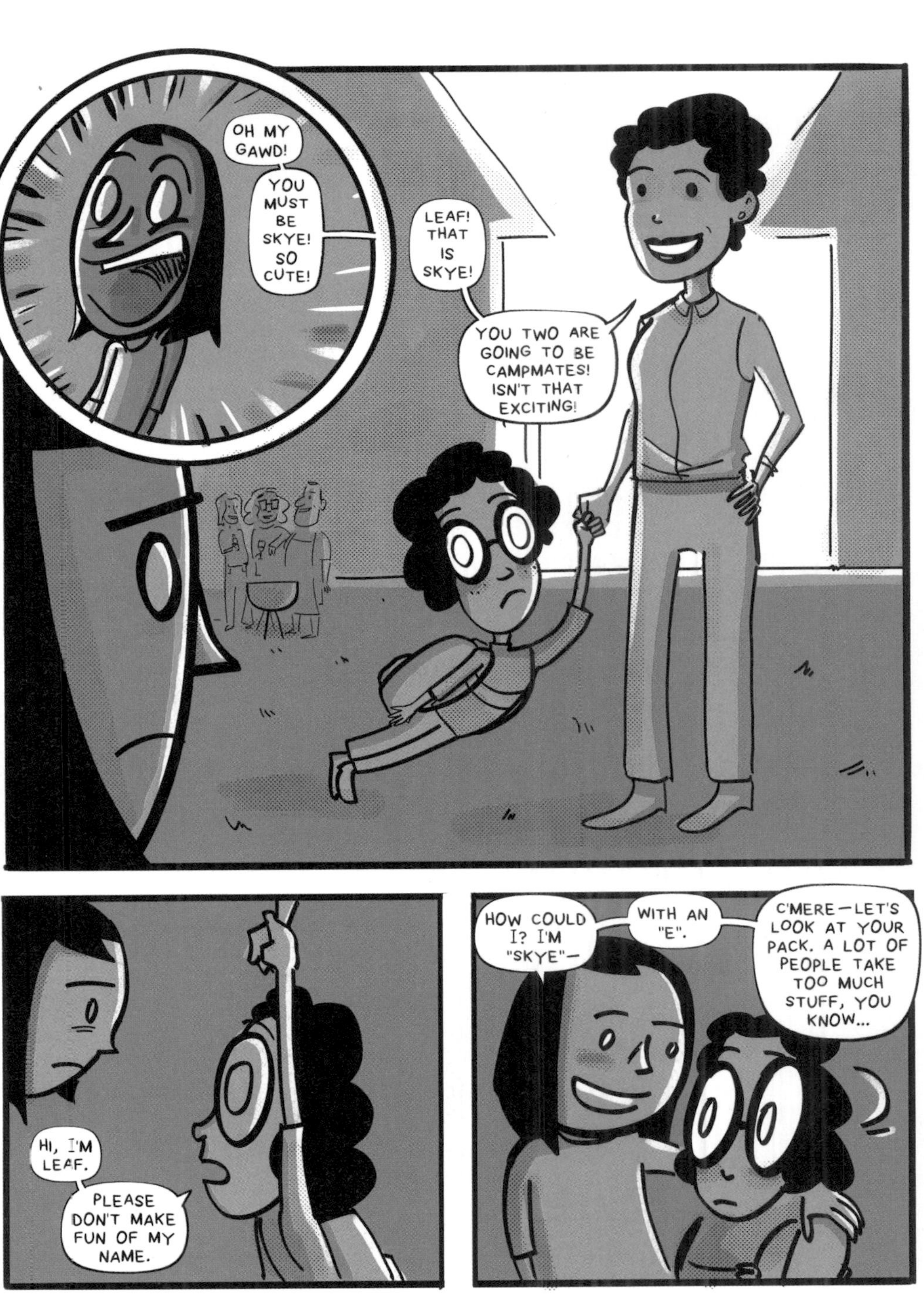
OH MY GAWD!
YOU MUST BE SKYE! SO CUTE!
LEAF! THAT IS SKYE!
YOU TWO ARE GOING TO BE CAMPMATES! ISN'T THAT EXCITING!
HI, I'M LEAF.
PLEASE DON'T MAKE FUN OF MY NAME.
HOW COULD I? I'M "SKYE"—
WITH AN "E".
C'MERE—LET'S LOOK AT YOUR PACK. A LOT OF PEOPLE TAKE TOO MUCH STUFF, YOU KNOW...

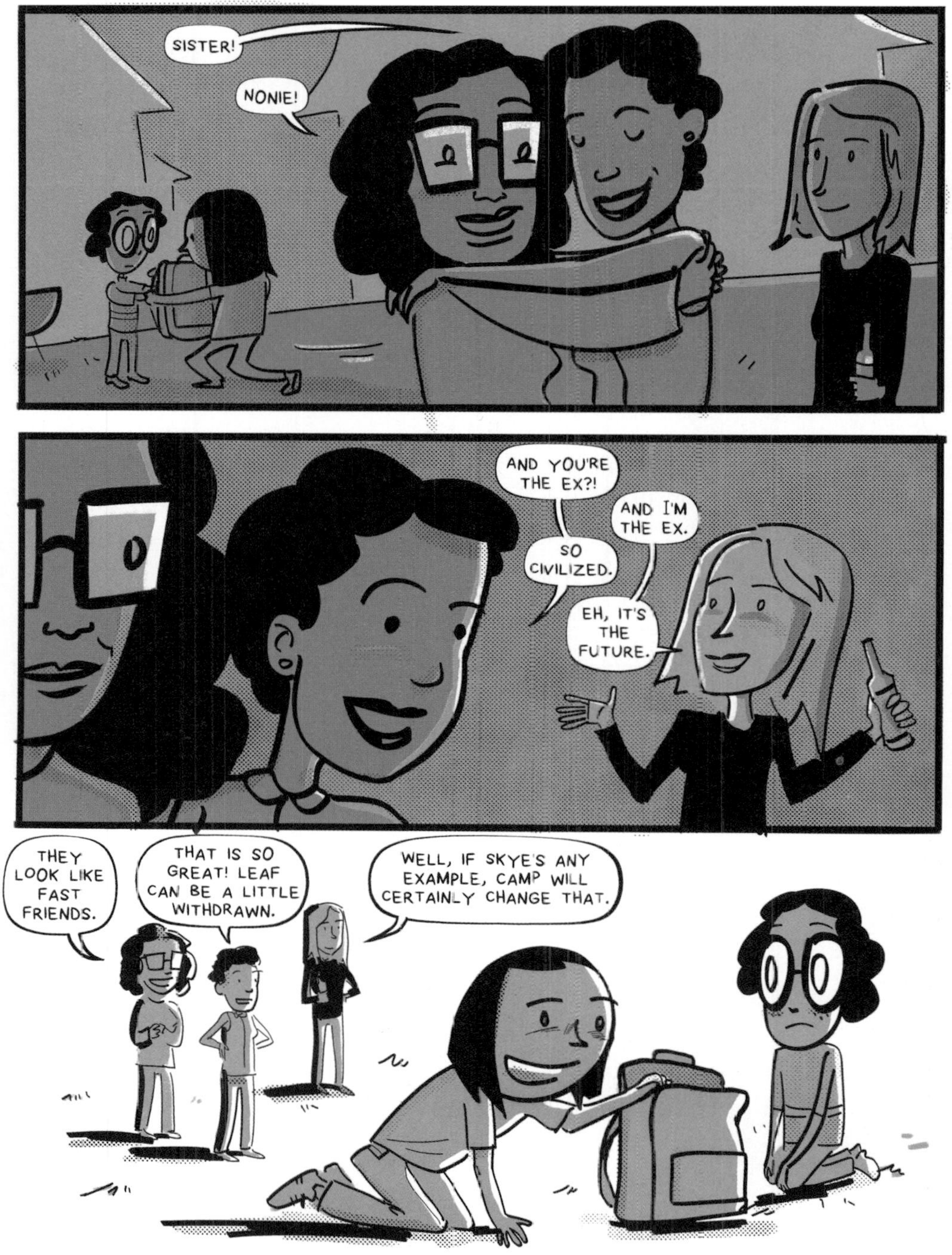
SISTER!
NONIE!
AND YOU'RE THE EX?!
AND I'M THE EX.
SO CIVILIZED.
EH, IT'S THE FUTURE.
THEY LOOK LIKE FAST FRIENDS.
THAT IS SO GREAT! LEAF CAN BE A LITTLE WITHDRAWN.
WELL, IF SKYE'S ANY EXAMPLE, CAMP WILL CERTAINLY CHANGE THAT.

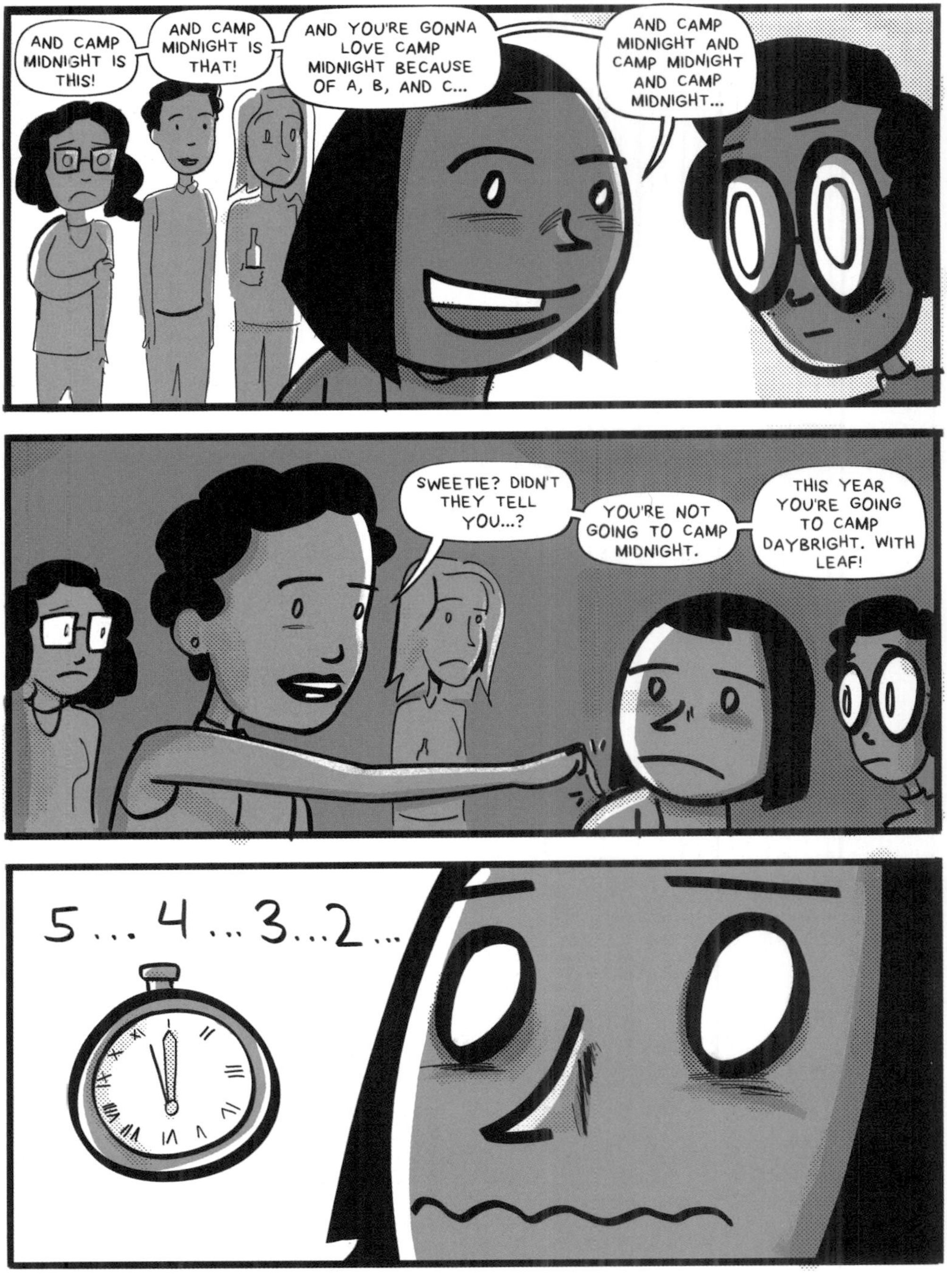
AND CAMP MIDNIGHT IS THIS!
AND CAMP MIDNIGHT IS THAT!
AND YOU'RE GONNA LOVE CAMP MIDNIGHT BECAUSE OF A, B, AND C...
AND CAMP MIDNIGHT AND CAMP MIDNIGHT AND CAMP MIDNIGHT...
SWEETIE? DIDN'T THEY TELL YOU...?
YOU'RE NOT GOING TO CAMP MIDNIGHT.
THIS YEAR YOU'RE GOING TO CAMP DAYBRIGHT. WITH LEAF!
5... 4... 3... 2...

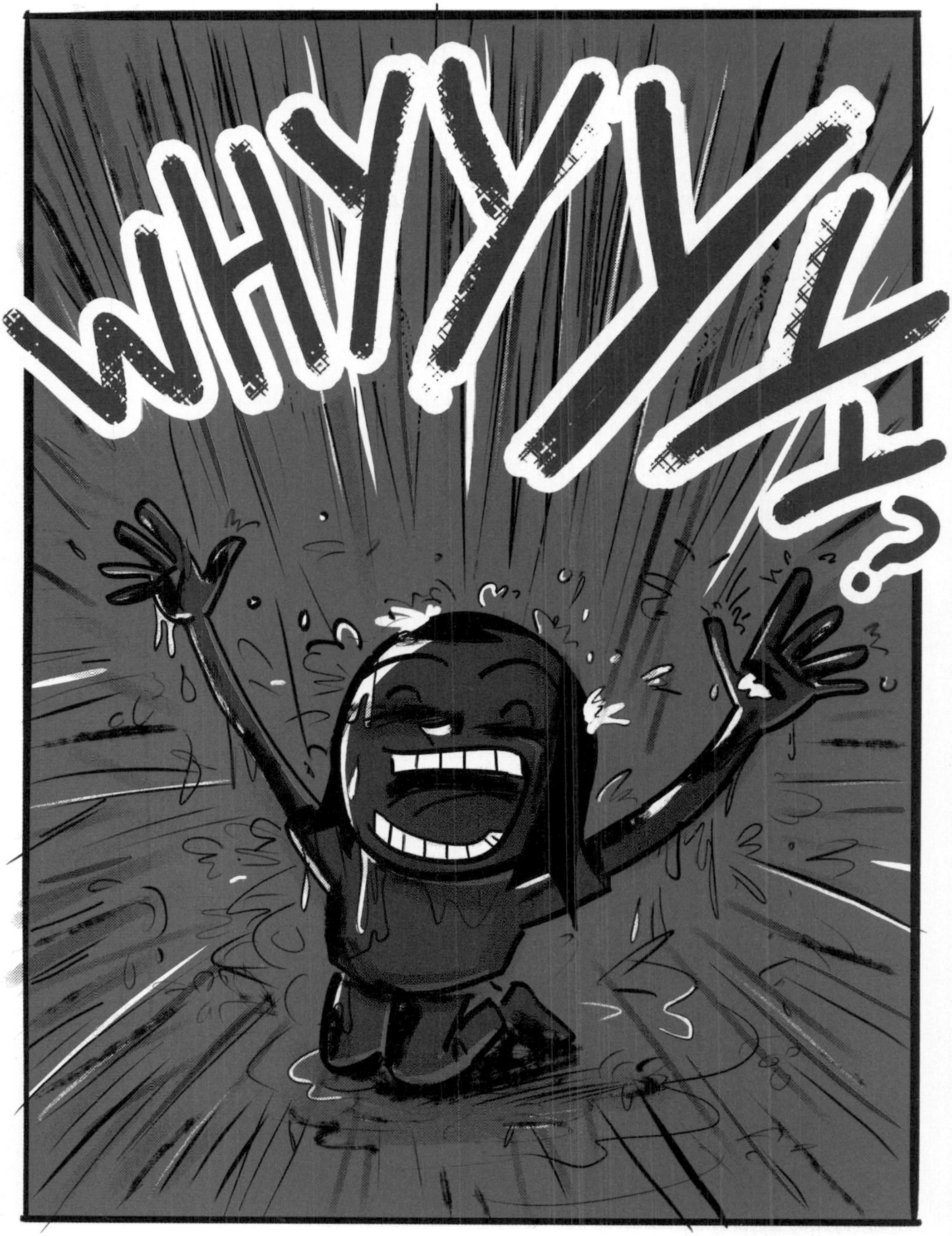
WHYYYY?

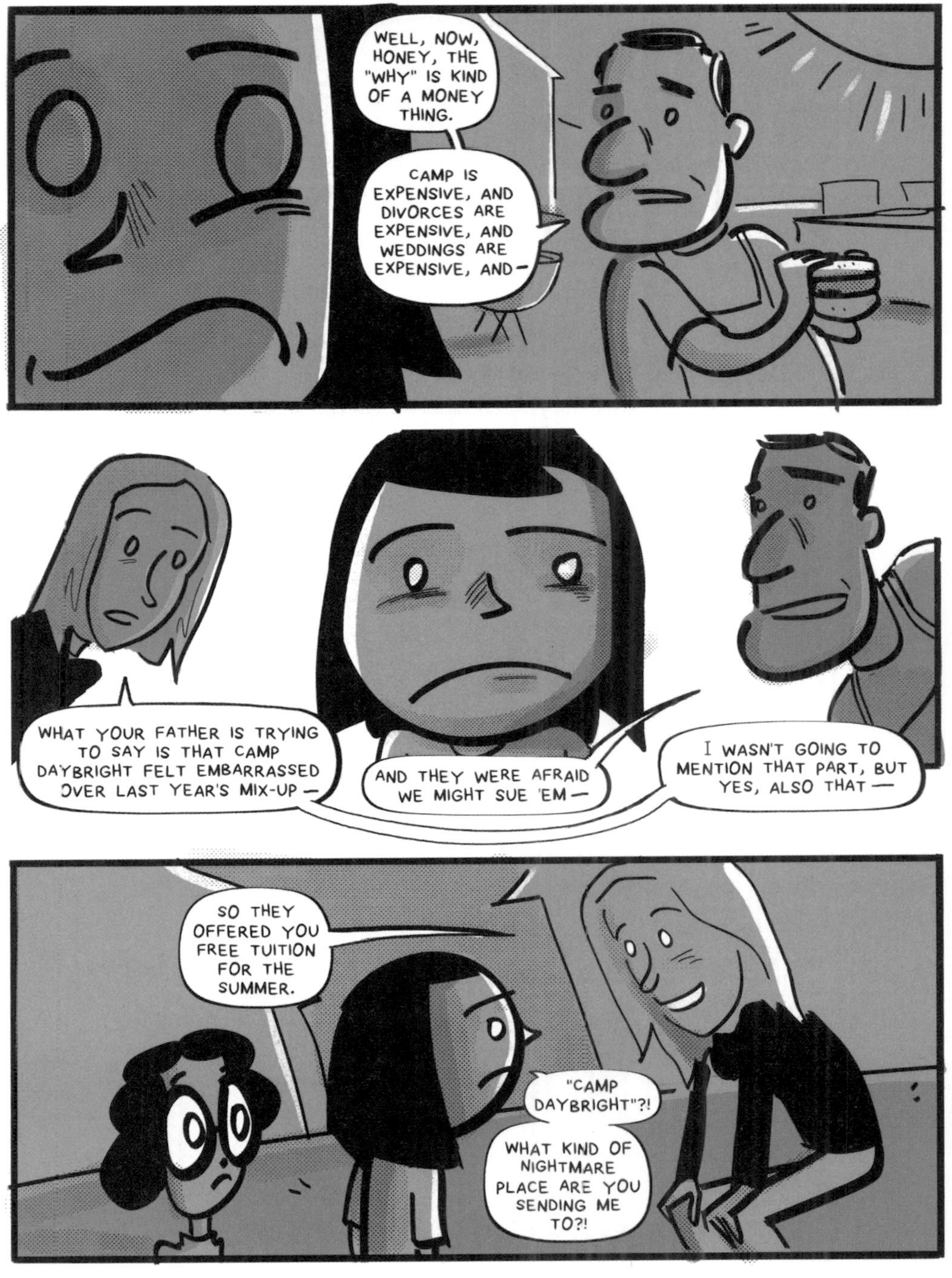
WELL, NOW, HONEY, THE "WHY" IS KIND OF A MONEY THING.
CAMP IS EXPENSIVE, AND DIVORCES ARE EXPENSIVE, AND WEDDINGS ARE EXPENSIVE, AND—
WHAT YOUR FATHER IS TRYING TO SAY IS THAT CAMP DAYBRIGHT FELT EMBARRASSED OVER LAST YEAR'S MIX-UP—
AND THEY WERE AFRAID WE MIGHT SUE 'EM—
I WASN'T GOING TO MENTION THAT PART, BUT YES, ALSO THAT—
SO THEY OFFERED YOU FREE TUITION FOR THE SUMMER.
"CAMP DAYBRIGHT"?!
WHAT KIND OF NIGHTMARE PLACE ARE YOU SENDING ME TO?!

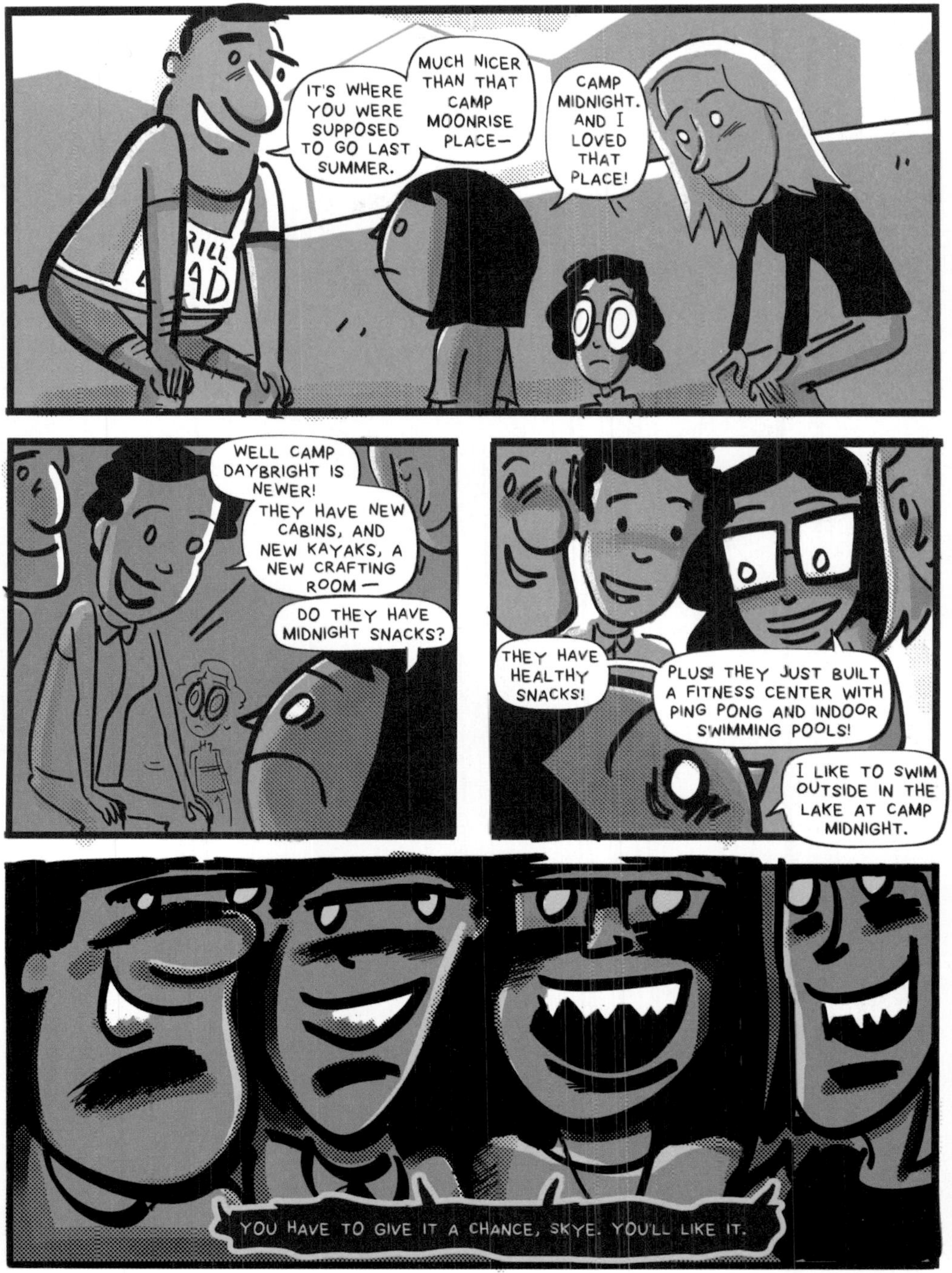
IT'S WHERE YOU WERE SUPPOSED TO GO LAST SUMMER.
MUCH NICER THAN THAT CAMP MOONRISE PLACE—
CAMP MIDNIGHT. AND I LOVED THAT PLACE!
WELL CAMP DAYBRIGHT IS NEWER!
THEY HAVE NEW CABINS, AND NEW KAYAKS, A NEW CRAFTING ROOM—
DO THEY HAVE MIDNIGHT SNACKS?
THEY HAVE HEALTHY SNACKS!
PLUS! THEY JUST BUILT A FITNESS CENTER WITH PING PONG AND INDOOR SWIMMING POOLS!
I LIKE TO SWIM OUTSIDE IN THE LAKE AT CAMP MIDNIGHT.
YOU HAVE TO GIVE IT A CHANCE, SKYE. YOU'LL LIKE IT.

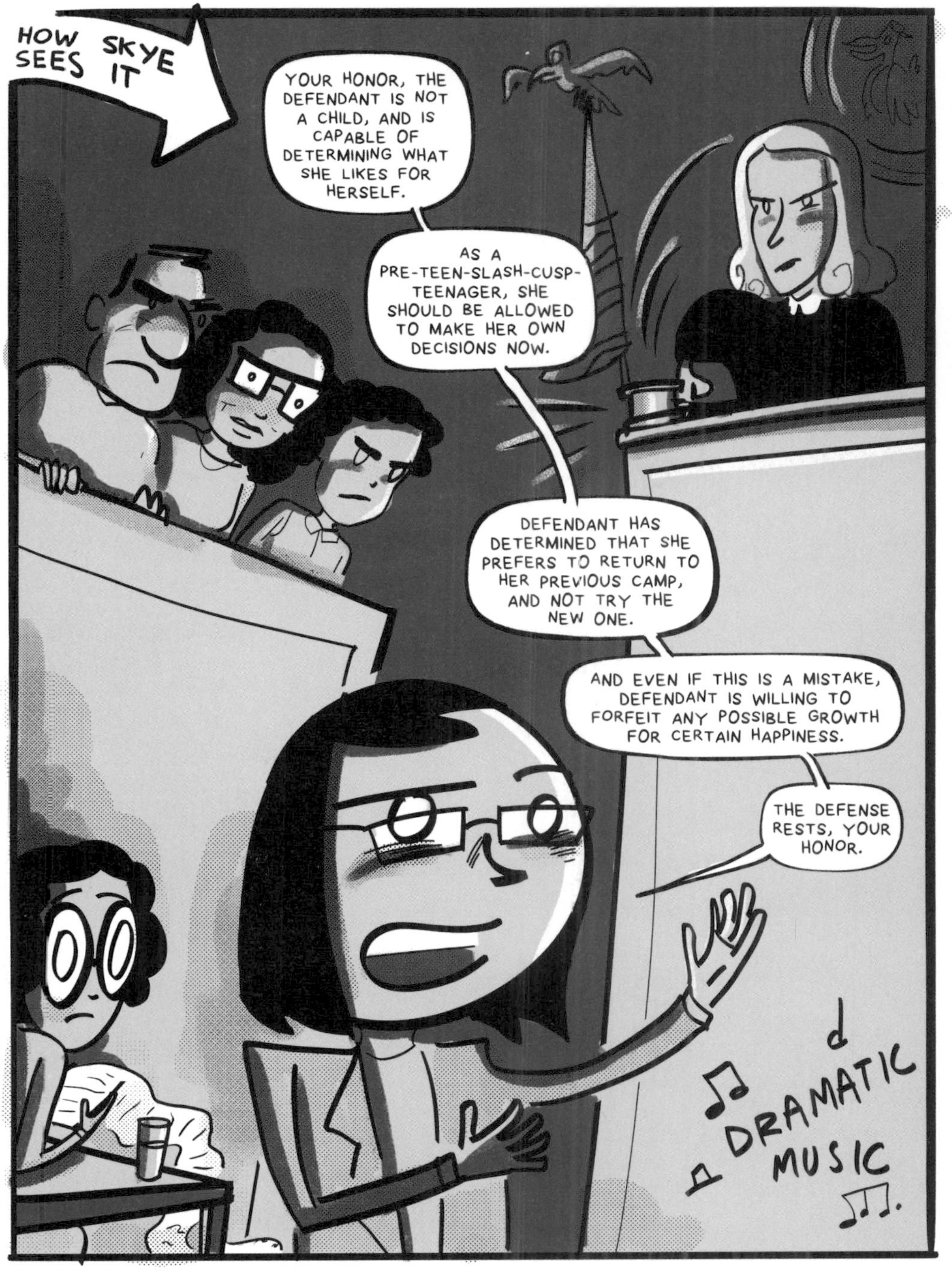
HOW SKYE SEES IT
YOUR HONOR, THE DEFENDANT IS NOT A CHILD, AND IS CAPABLE OF DETERMINING WHAT SHE LIKES FOR HERSELF.
AS A PRE-TEEN-SLASH-CUSP-TEENAGER, SHE SHOULD BE ALLOWED TO MAKE HER OWN DECISIONS NOW.
DEFENDANT HAS DETERMINED THAT SHE PREFERS TO RETURN TO HER PREVIOUS CAMP, AND NOT TRY THE NEW ONE.
AND EVEN IF THIS IS A MISTAKE, DEFENDANT IS WILLING TO FORFEIT ANY POSSIBLE GROWTH FOR CERTAIN HAPPINESS.
THE DEFENSE RESTS, YOUR HONOR.
DRAMATIC MUSIC

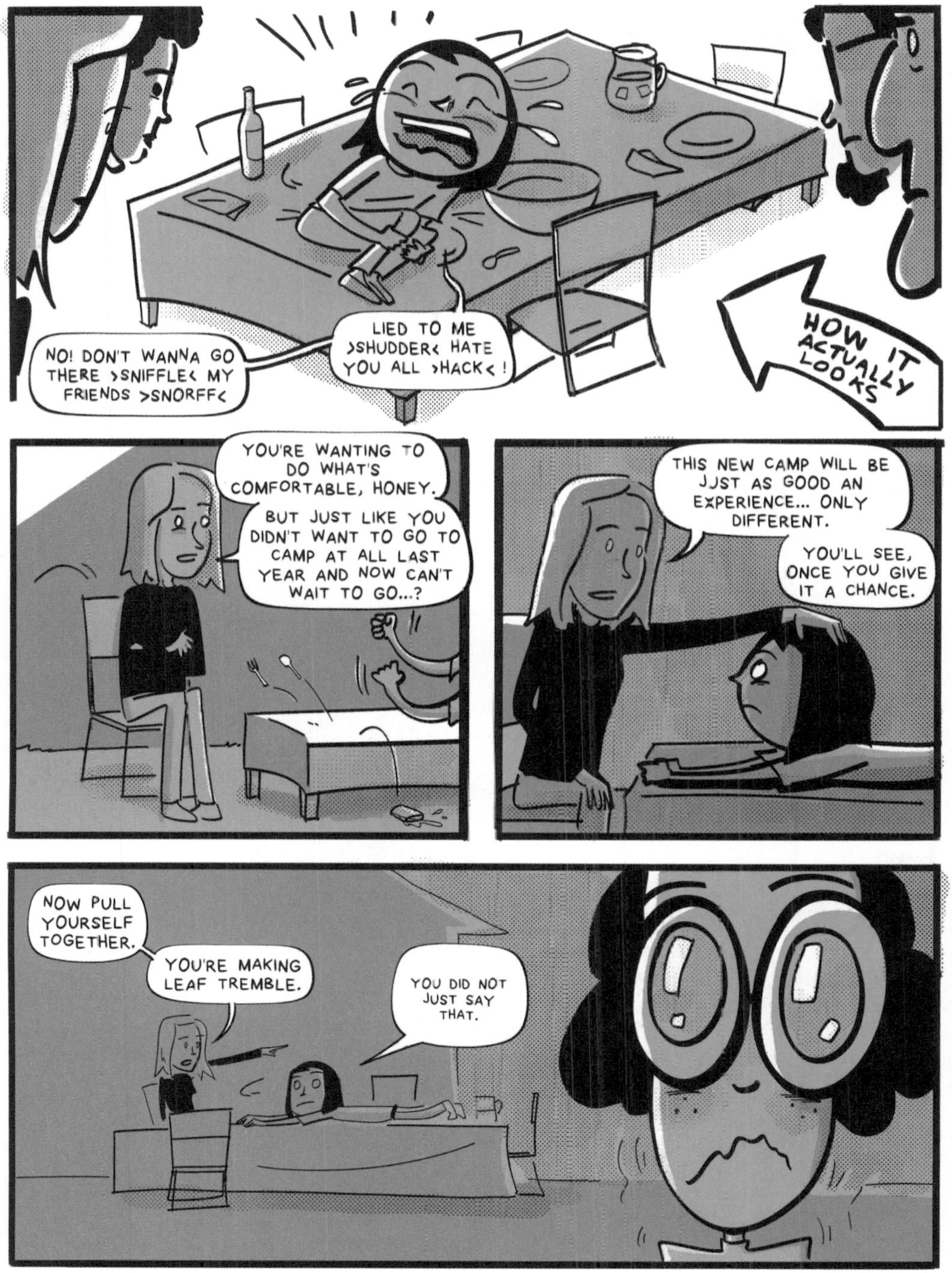
NO! DON'T WANNA GO THERE >SNIFFLE< MY FRIENDS >SNORFF<
LIED TO ME >SHUDDER< HATE YOU ALL >HACK< !
HOW IT ACTUALLY LOOKS
YOU'RE WANTING TO DO WHAT'S COMFORTABLE, HONEY.
BUT JUST LIKE YOU DIDN'T WANT TO GO TO CAMP AT ALL LAST YEAR AND NOW CAN'T WAIT TO GO...?
THIS NEW CAMP WILL BE JUST AS GOOD AN EXPERIENCE... ONLY DIFFERENT.
YOU'LL SEE, ONCE YOU GIVE IT A CHANCE.
NOW PULL YOURSELF TOGETHER.
YOU'RE MAKING LEAF TREMBLE.
YOU DID NOT JUST SAY THAT.

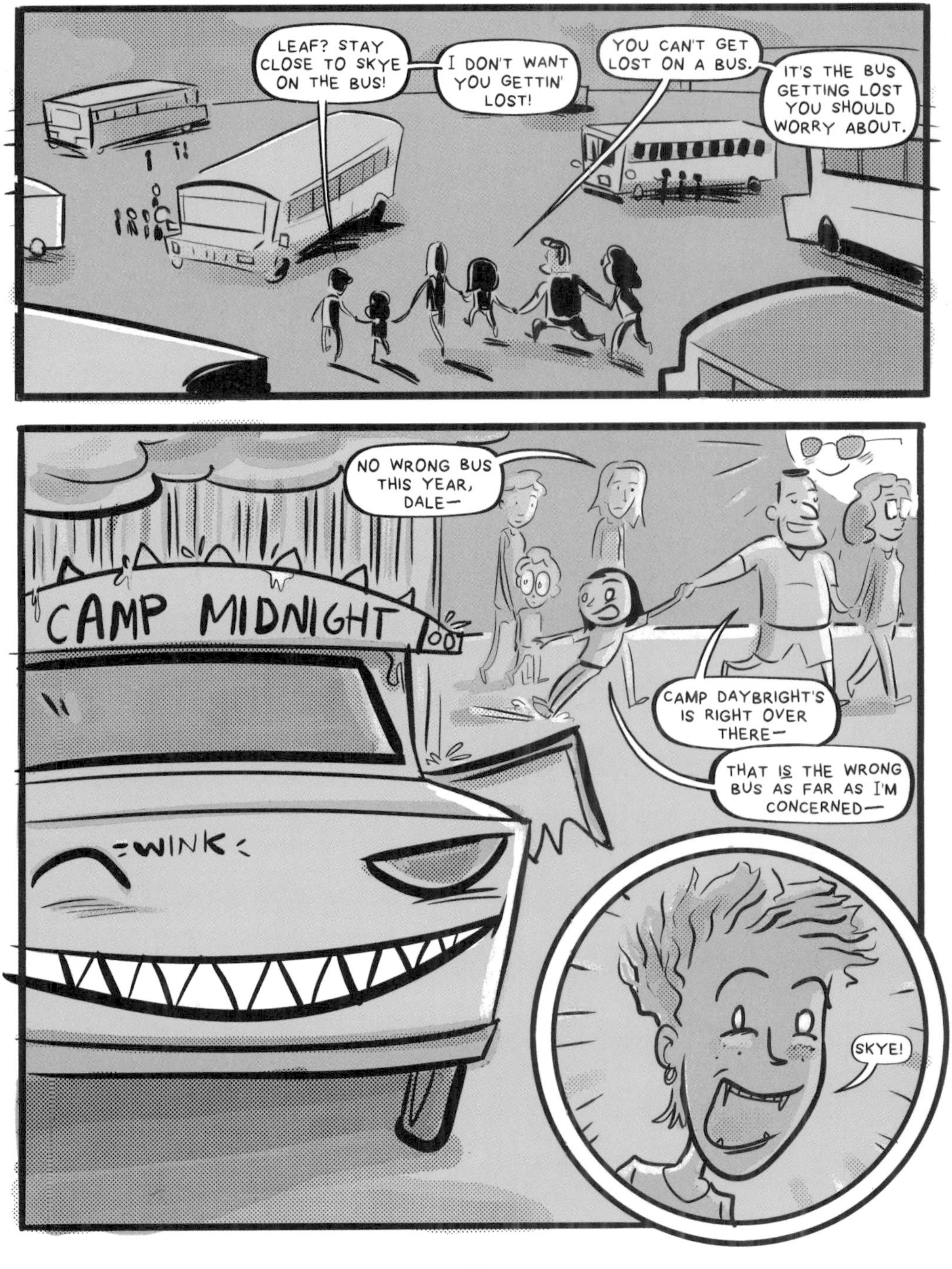
LEAF? STAY CLOSE TO SKYE ON THE BUS!
I DON'T WANT YOU GETTIN' LOST!
YOU CAN'T GET LOST ON A BUS.
IT'S THE BUS GETTING LOST YOU SHOULD WORRY ABOUT.
NO WRONG BUS THIS YEAR, DALE—
CAMP MIDNIGHT
CAMP DAYBRIGHT'S IS RIGHT OVER THERE—
THAT IS THE WRONG BUS AS FAR AS I'M CONCERNED—
WINK
SKYE!

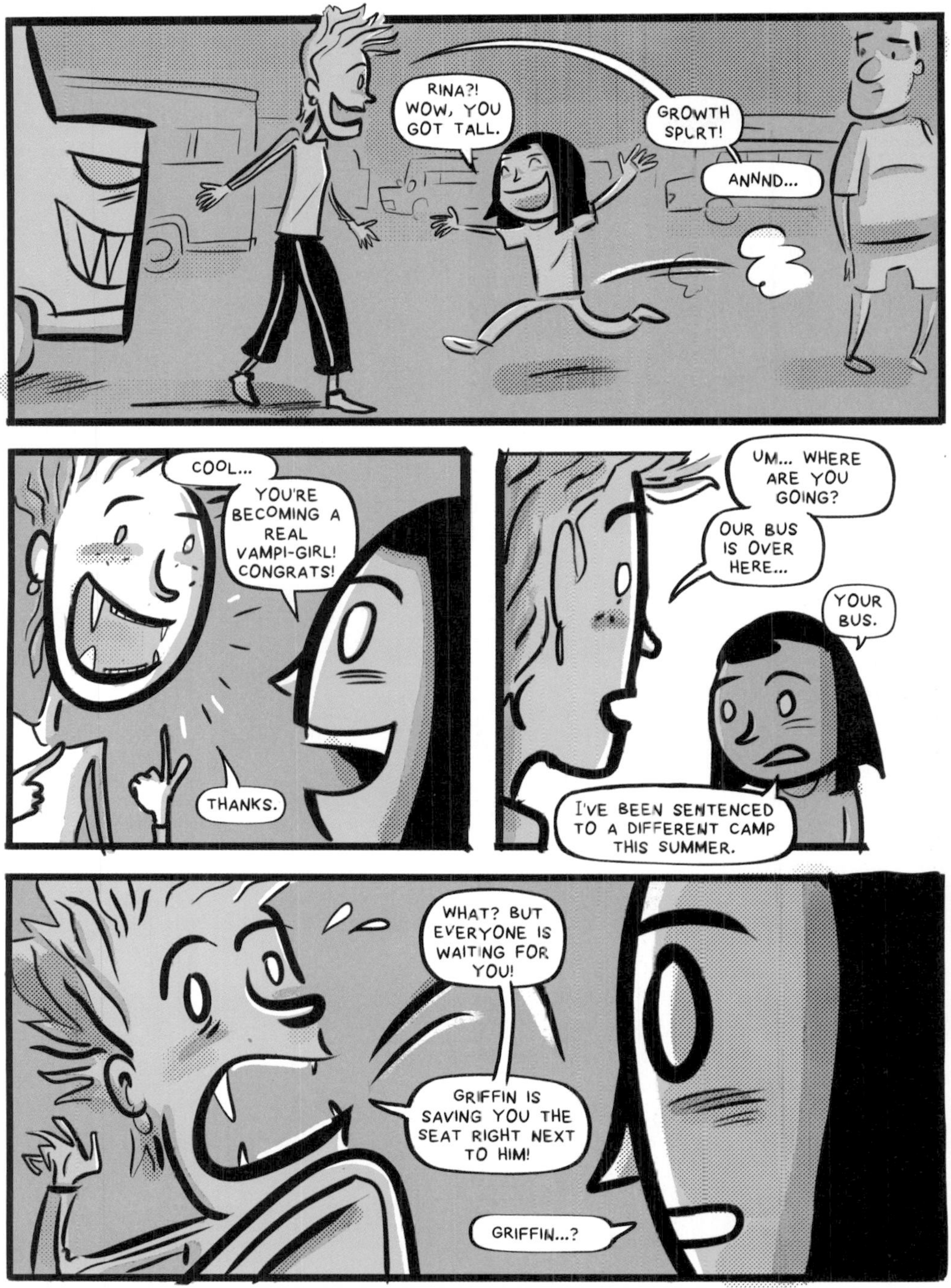
RINA?! WOW, YOU GOT TALL.
GROWTH SPURT!
ANNND...
COOL...
YOU'RE BECOMING A REAL VAMPI-GIRL! CONGRATS!
THANKS.
UM... WHERE ARE YOU GOING?
OUR BUS IS OVER HERE...
YOUR BUS.
I'VE BEEN SENTENCED TO A DIFFERENT CAMP THIS SUMMER.
WHAT? BUT EVERYONE IS WAITING FOR YOU!
GRIFFIN IS SAVING YOU THE SEAT RIGHT NEXT TO HIM!
GRIFFIN...?

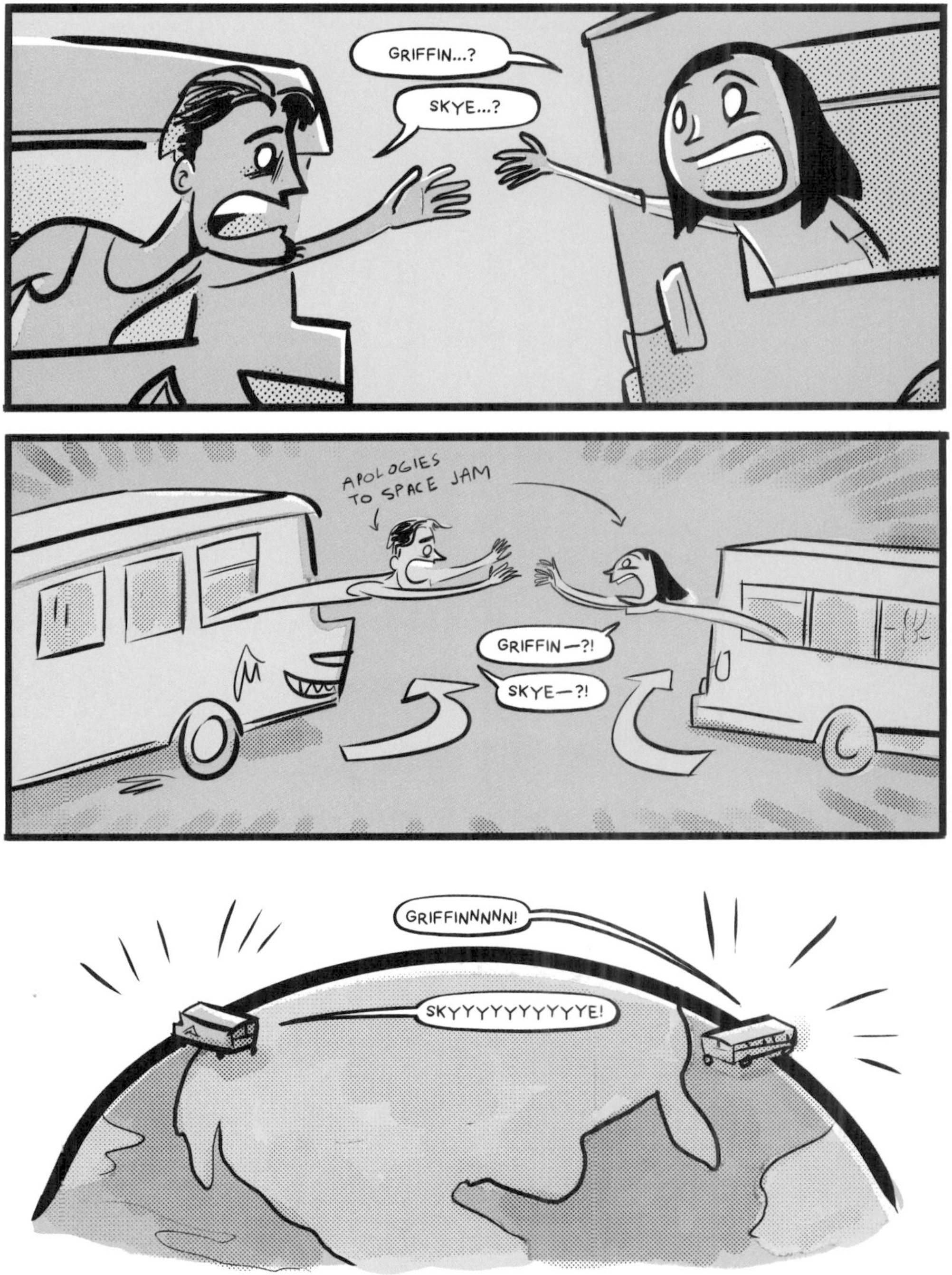
GRIFFIN...?
SKYE...?
APOLOGIES TO SPACE JAM
GRIFFIN—?!
SKYE—?!
GRIFFINNNNN!
SKYYYYYYYYYYYE!

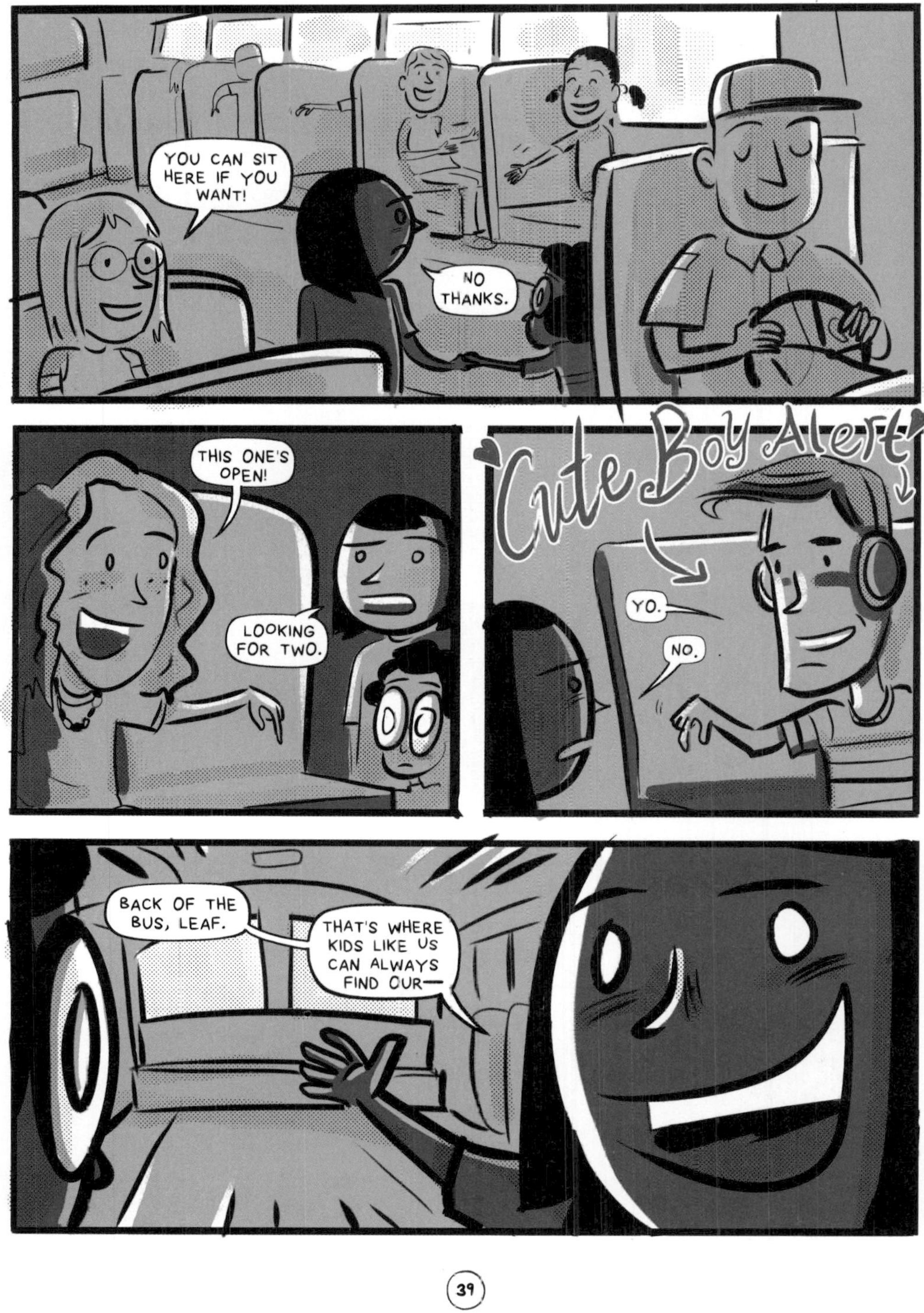
YOU CAN SIT HERE IF YOU WANT!
NO THANKS.
THIS ONE'S OPEN!
LOOKING FOR TWO.
Cute Boy Alert
YO.
NO.
BACK OF THE BUS, LEAF.
THAT'S WHERE KIDS LIKE US CAN ALWAYS FIND OUR—

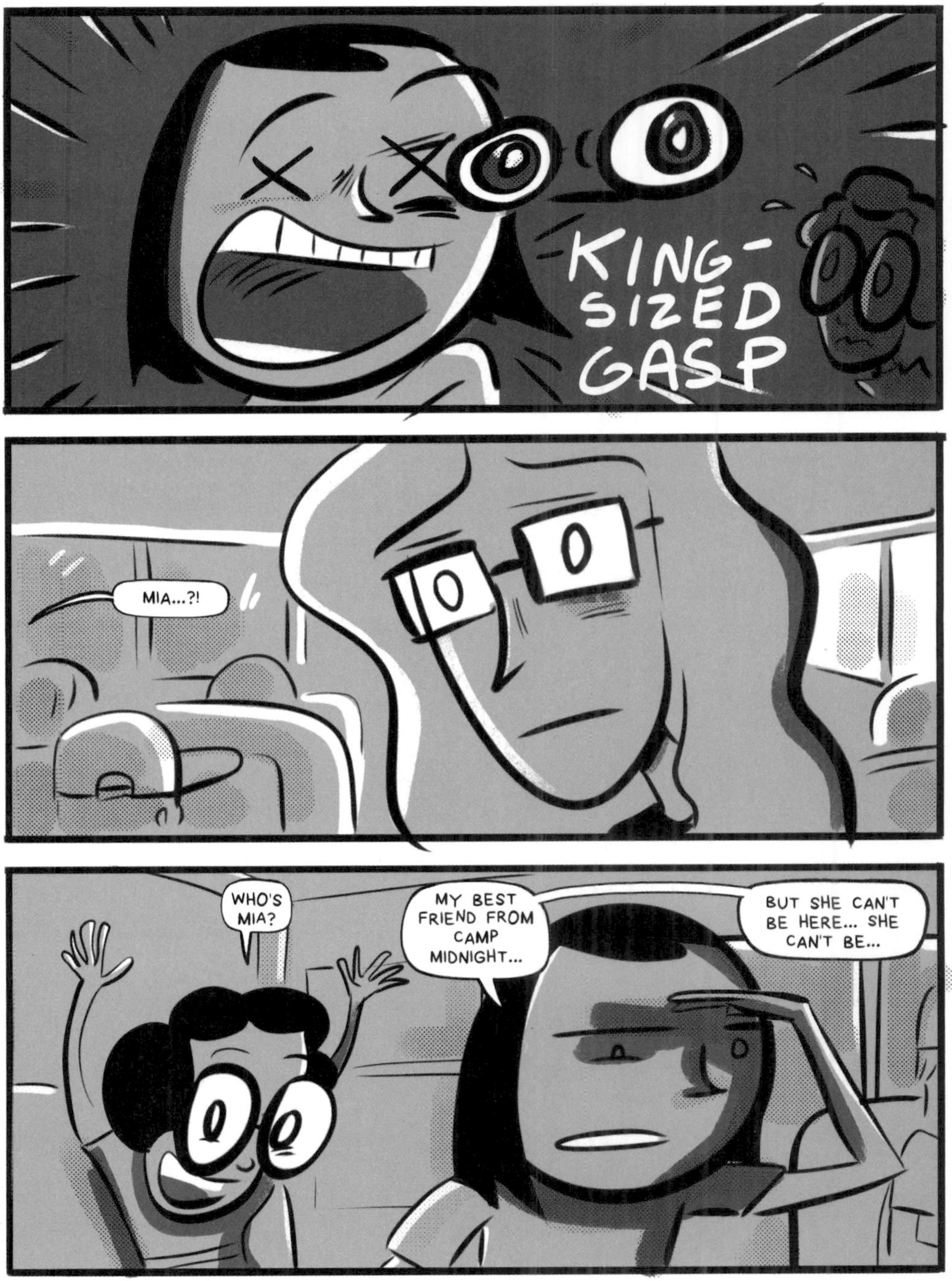
KING-SIZED GASP
MIA...?!
WHO'S MIA?
MY BEST FRIEND FROM CAMP MIDNIGHT...
BUT SHE CAN'T BE HERE... SHE CAN'T BE...

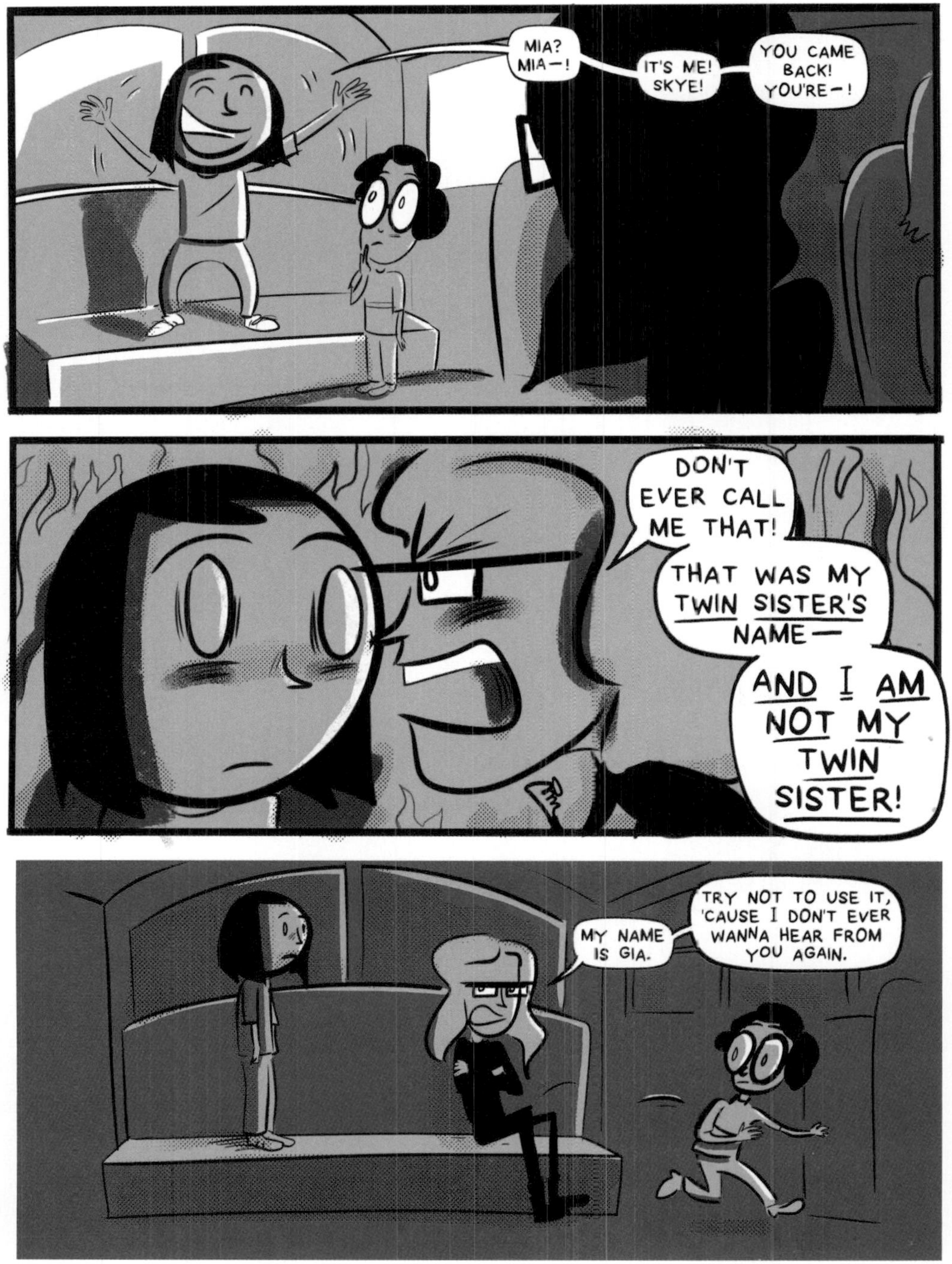
MIA? MIA—!
IT'S ME! SKYE!
YOU CAME BACK! YOU'RE—!
DON'T EVER CALL ME THAT!
THAT WAS MY TWIN SISTER'S NAME—
AND I AM NOT MY TWIN SISTER!
MY NAME IS GIA.
TRY NOT TO USE IT, 'CAUSE I DON'T EVER WANNA HEAR FROM YOU AGAIN.

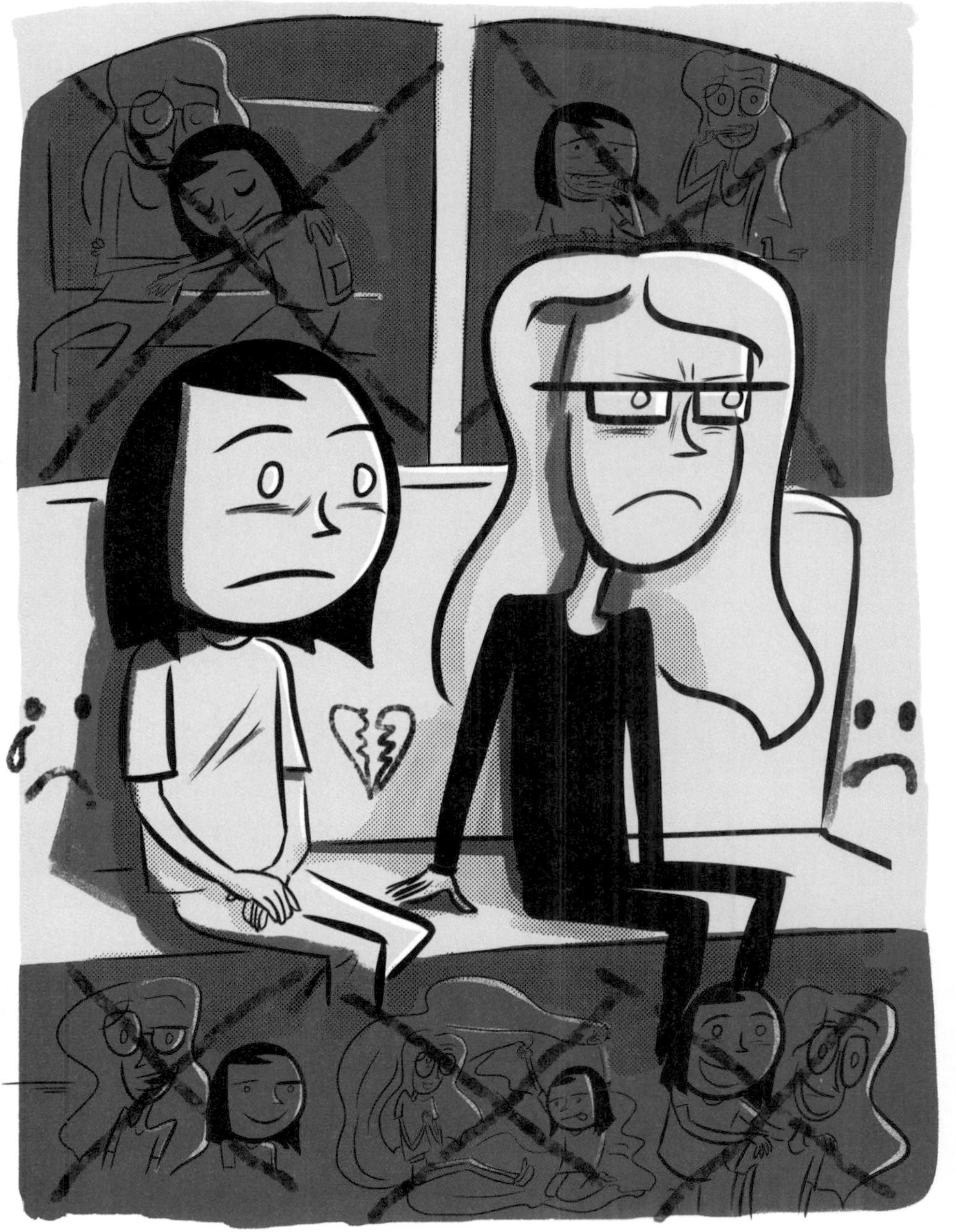

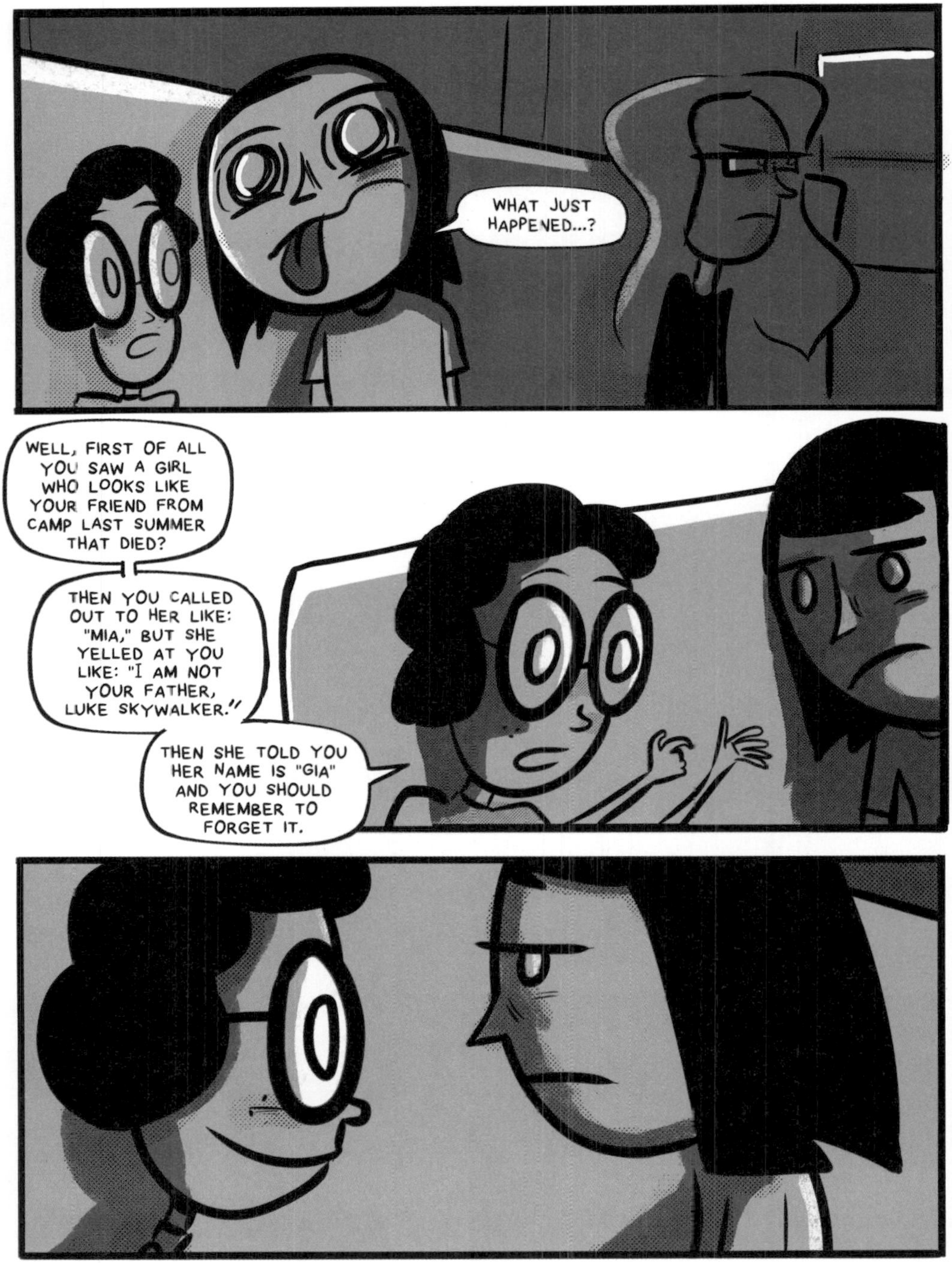
WHAT JUST HAPPENED...?
WELL, FIRST OF ALL YOU SAW A GIRL WHO LOOKS LIKE YOUR FRIEND FROM CAMP LAST SUMMER THAT DIED?
THEN YOU CALLED OUT TO HER LIKE: "MIA," BUT SHE YELLED AT YOU LIKE: "I AM NOT YOUR FATHER, LUKE SKYWALKER."
THEN SHE TOLD YOU HER NAME IS "GIA" AND YOU SHOULD REMEMBER TO FORGET IT.

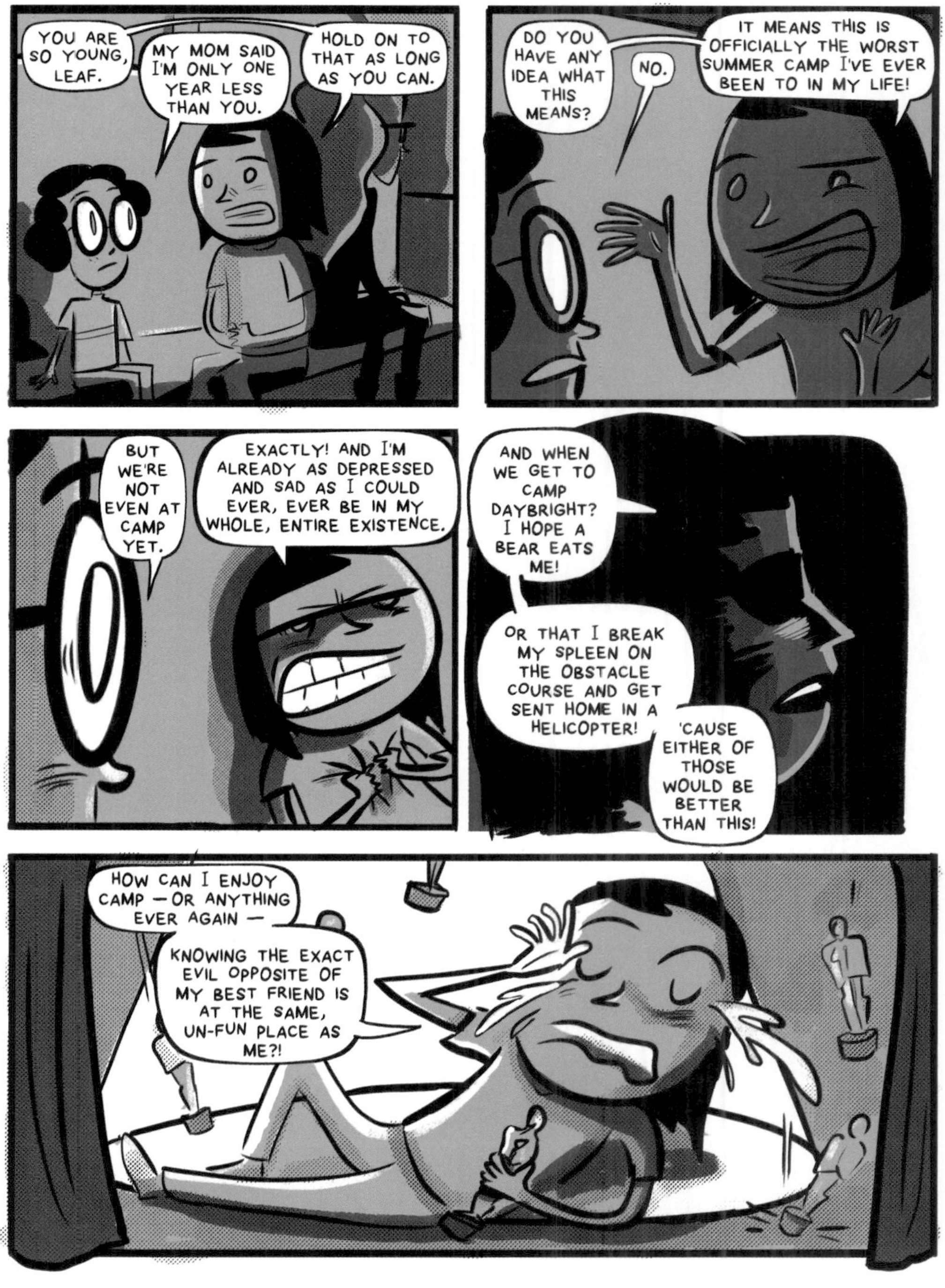
YOU ARE SO YOUNG, LEAF.
MY MOM SAID I'M ONLY ONE YEAR LESS THAN YOU.
HOLD ON TO THAT AS LONG AS YOU CAN.
DO YOU HAVE ANY IDEA WHAT THIS MEANS?
NO.
IT MEANS THIS IS OFFICIALLY THE WORST SUMMER CAMP I'VE EVER BEEN TO IN MY LIFE!
BUT WE'RE NOT EVEN AT CAMP YET.
EXACTLY! AND I'M ALREADY AS DEPRESSED AND SAD AS I COULD EVER, EVER BE IN MY WHOLE, ENTIRE EXISTENCE.
AND WHEN WE GET TO CAMP DAYBRIGHT? I HOPE A BEAR EATS ME!
OR THAT I BREAK MY SPLEEN ON THE OBSTACLE COURSE AND GET SENT HOME IN A HELICOPTER!
'CAUSE EITHER OF THOSE WOULD BE BETTER THAN THIS!
HOW CAN I ENJOY CAMP —OR ANYTHING EVER AGAIN —
KNOWING THE EXACT EVIL OPPOSITE OF MY BEST FRIEND IS AT THE SAME, UN-FUN PLACE AS ME?!

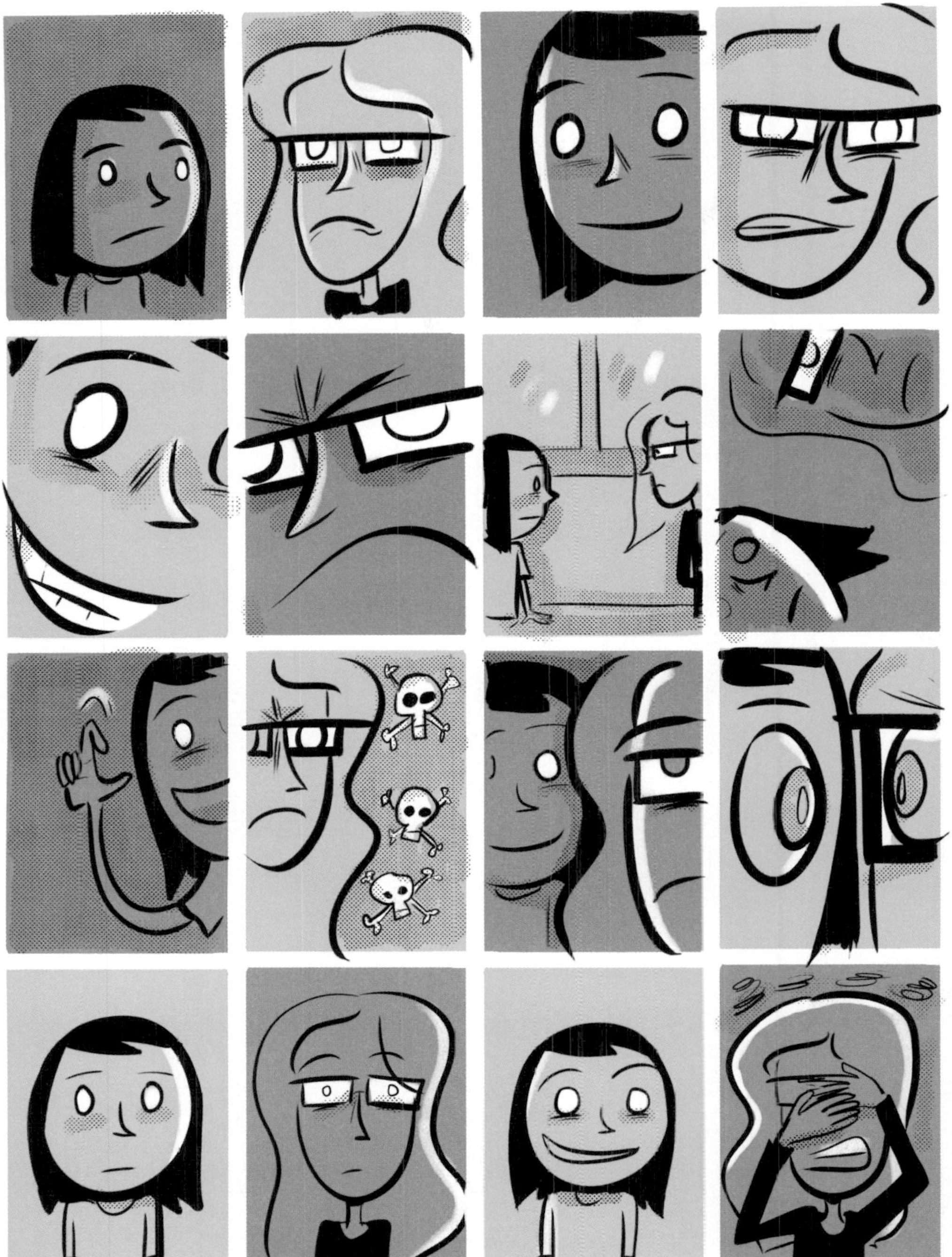

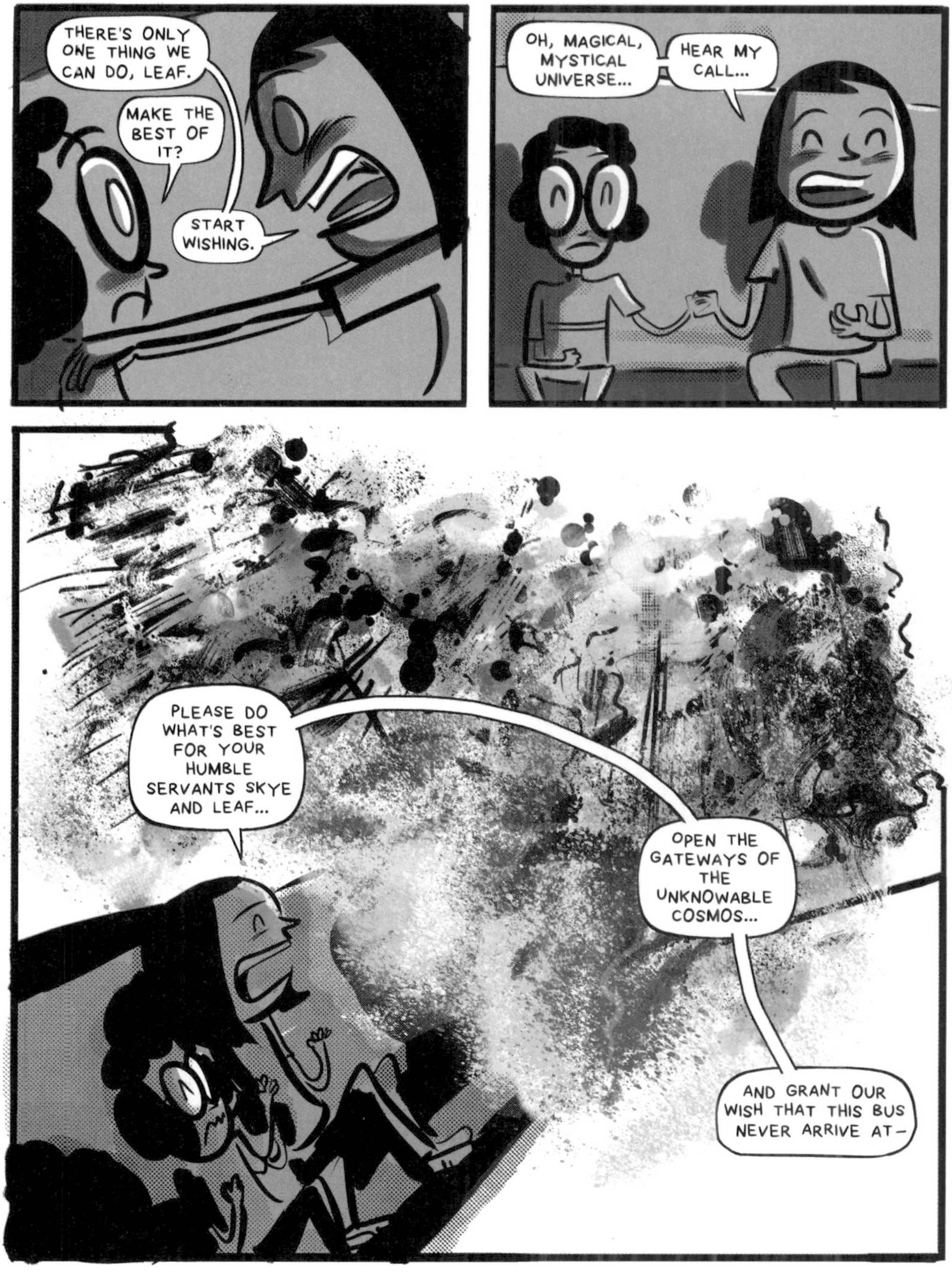

THERE'S ONLY ONE THING WE CAN DO, LEAF.
MAKE THE BEST OF IT?
START WISHING.
OH, MAGICAL, MYSTICAL UNIVERSE...
HEAR MY CALL...
PLEASE DO WHAT'S BEST FOR YOUR HUMBLE SERVANTS SKYE AND LEAF...
OPEN THE GATEWAYS OF THE UNKNOWABLE COSMOS...
AND GRANT OUR WISH THAT THIS BUS NEVER ARRIVE AT—

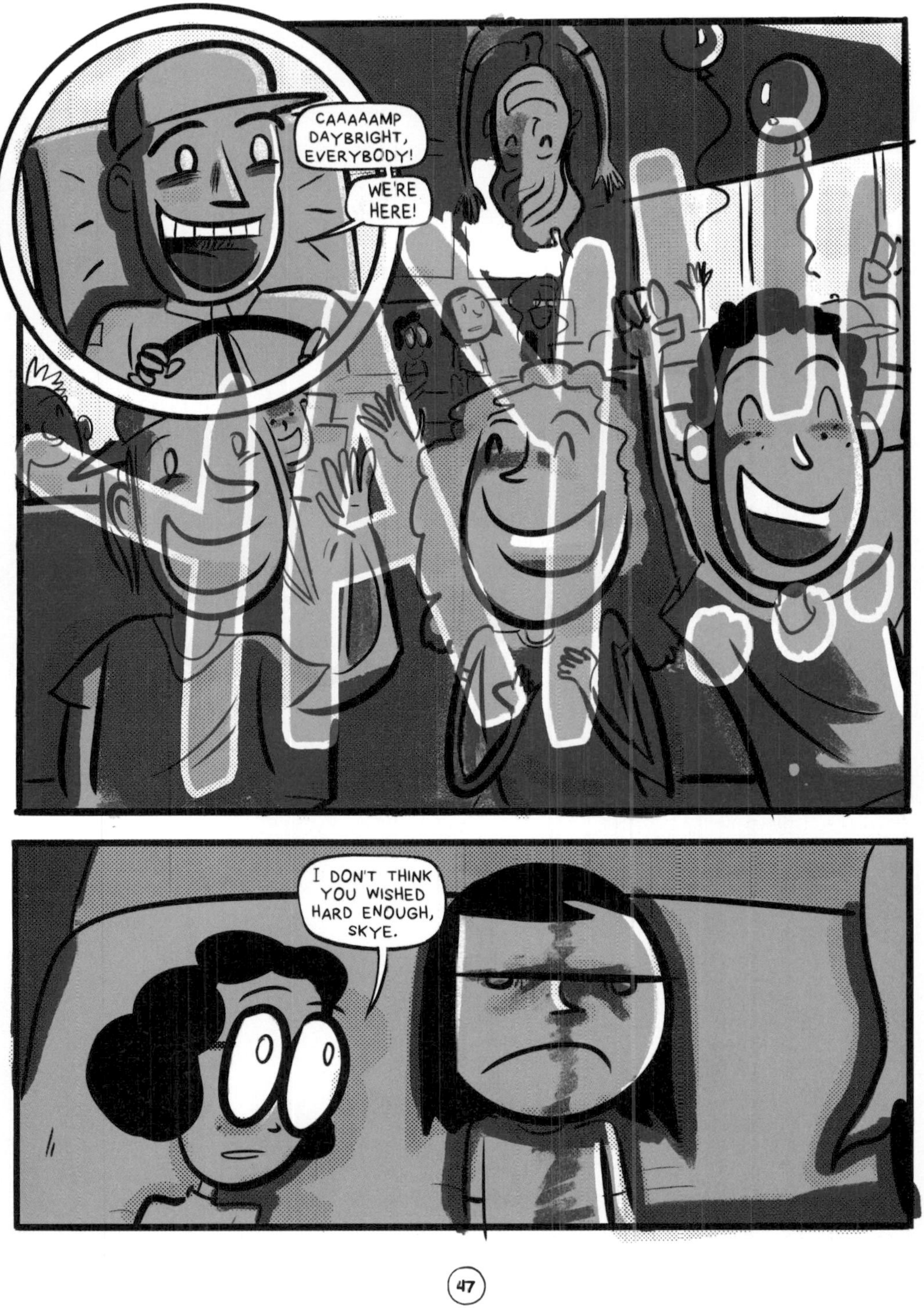
CAAAAAMP DAYBRIGHT, EVERYBODY!
WE'RE HERE!
I DON'T THINK YOU WISHED HARD ENOUGH, SKYE.

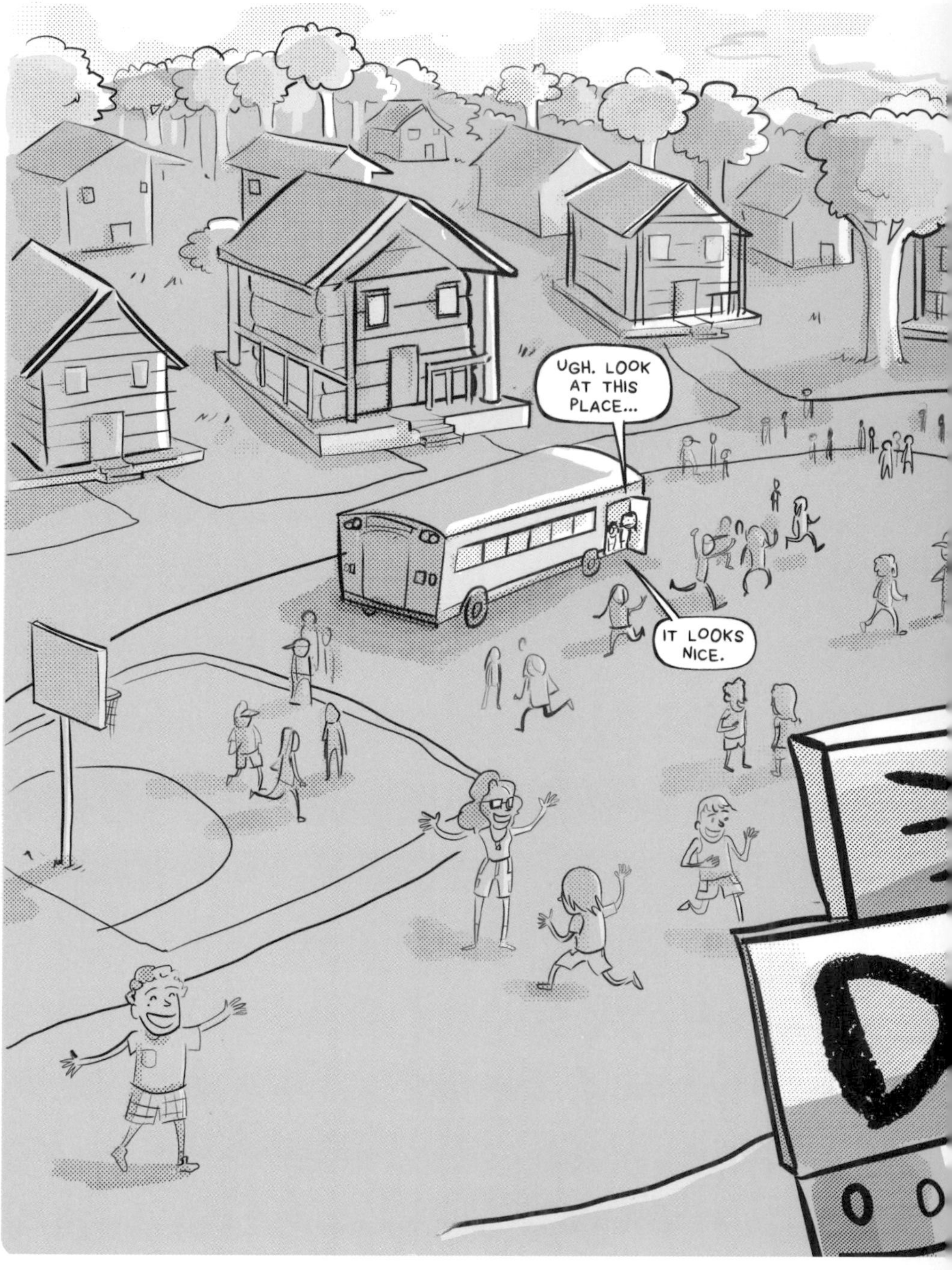
UGH. LOOK AT THIS PLACE...
IT LOOKS NICE.

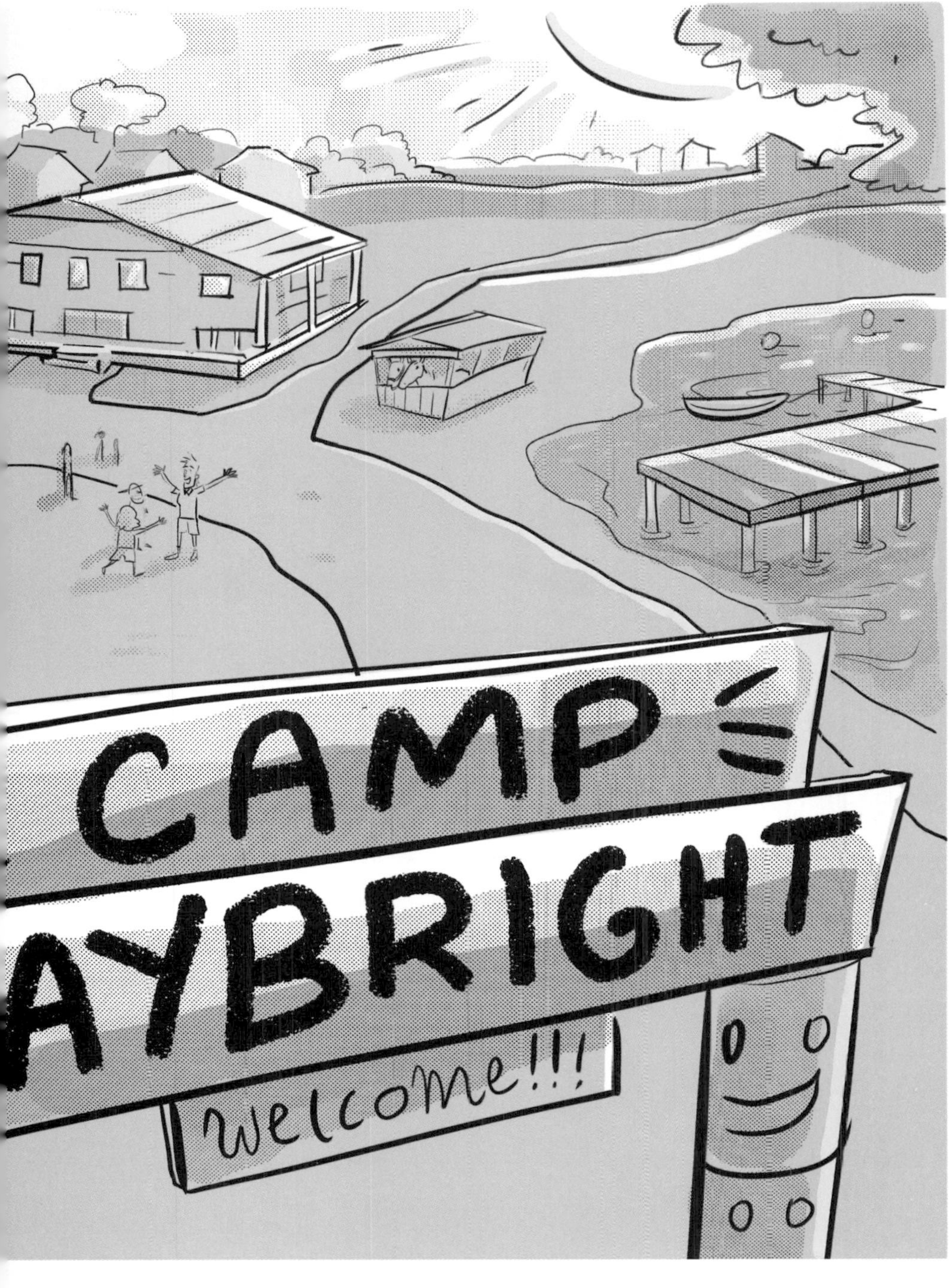
CAMP
AYBRIGHT
welcome!!!

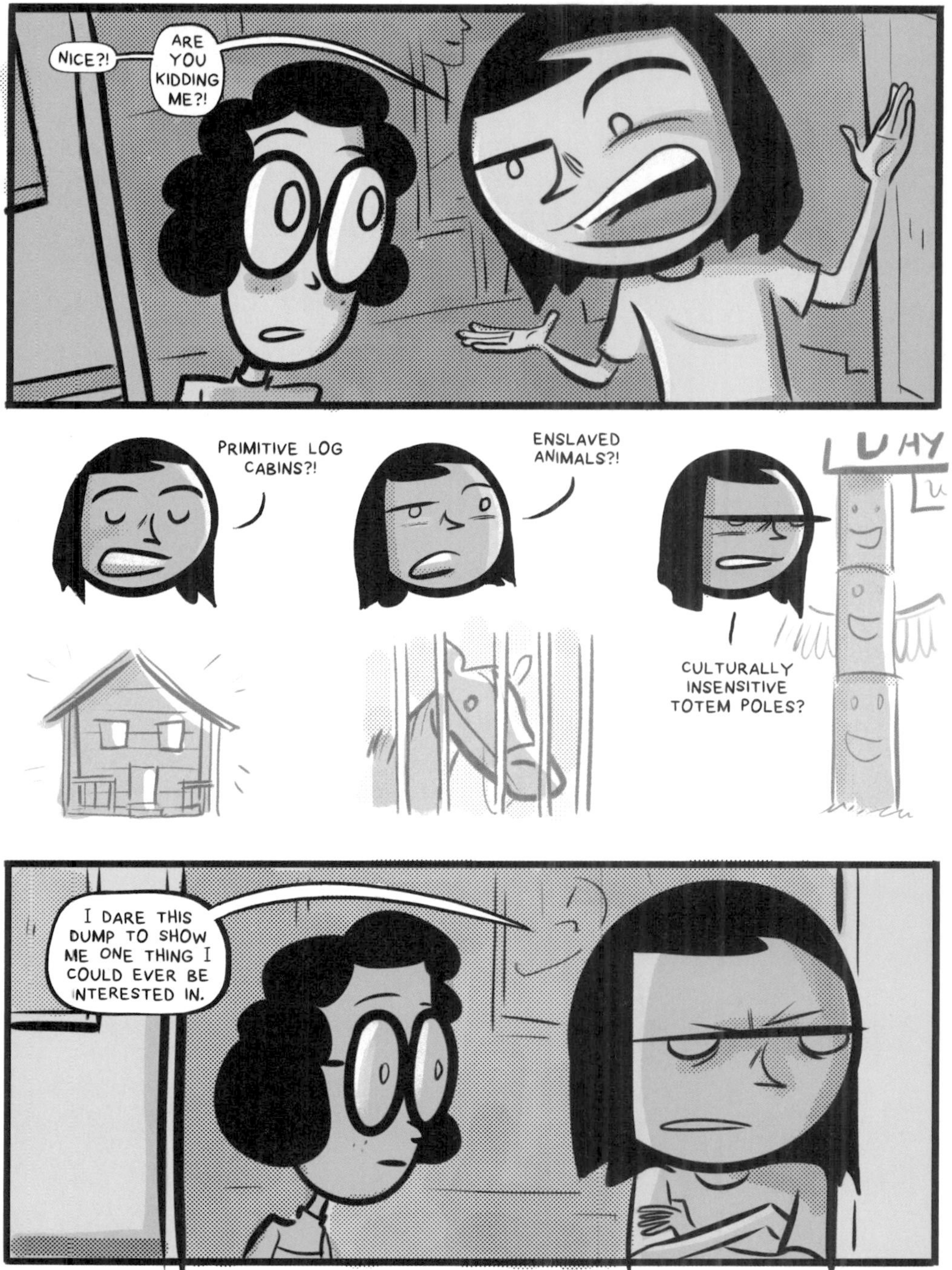
NICE?!
ARE YOU KIDDING ME?!
PRIMITIVE LOG CABINS?!
ENSLAVED ANIMALS?!
CULTURALLY INSENSITIVE TOTEM POLES?
I DARE THIS DUMP TO SHOW ME ONE THING I COULD EVER BE INTERESTED IN.

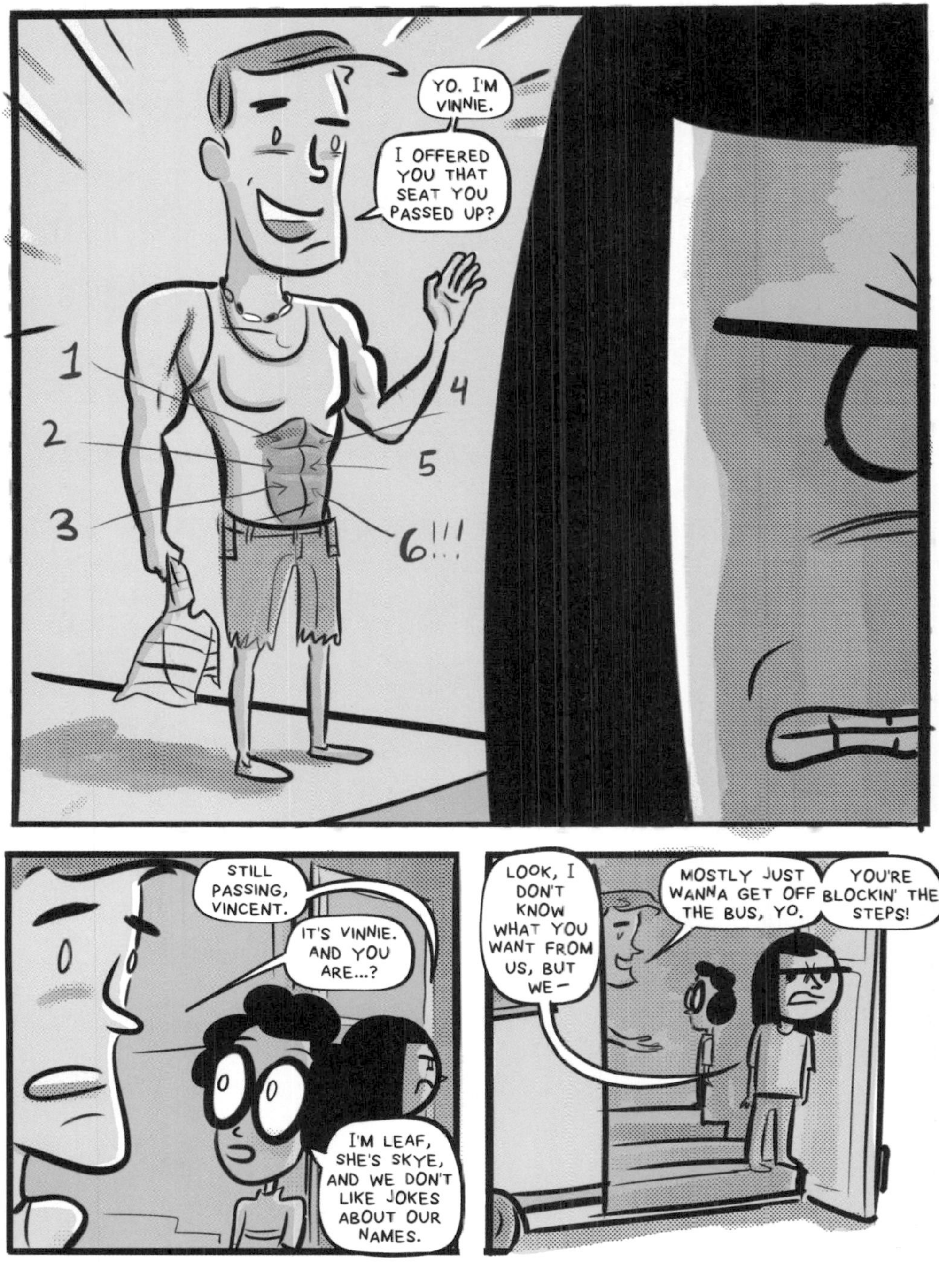
YO. I'M VINNIE.
I OFFERED YOU THAT SEAT YOU PASSED UP?
1
2
3
4
5
6!!!
STILL PASSING, VINCENT.
IT'S VINNIE. AND YOU ARE...?
I'M LEAF, SHE'S SKYE, AND WE DON'T LIKE JOKES ABOUT OUR NAMES.
LOOK, I DON'T KNOW WHAT YOU WANT FROM US, BUT WE—
MOSTLY JUST WANNA GET OFF THE BUS, YO.
YOU'RE BLOCKIN' THE STEPS!

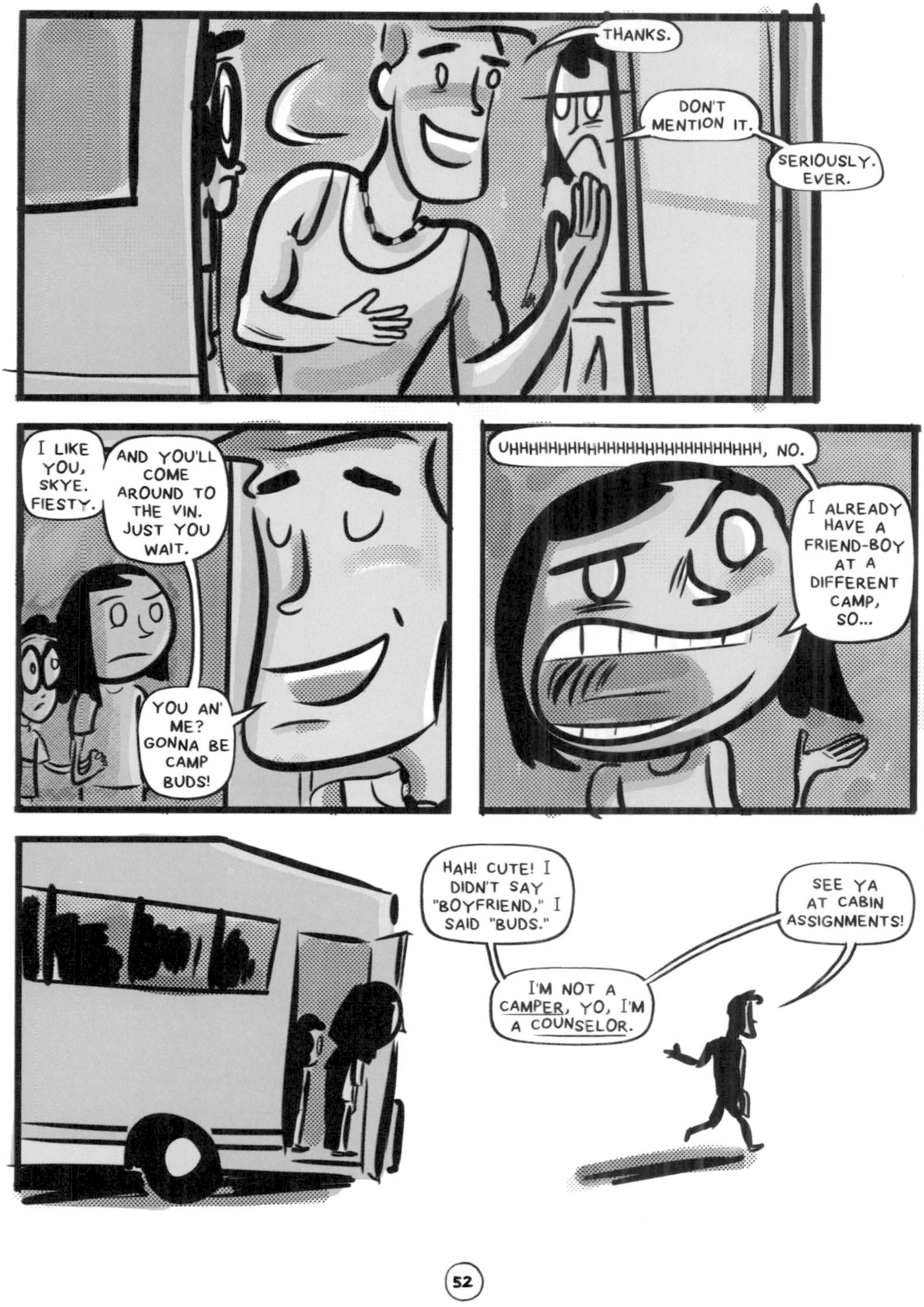
THANKS.
DON'T MENTION IT.
SERIOUSLY. EVER.
I LIKE YOU, SKYE. FIESTY.
AND YOU'LL COME AROUND TO THE VIN. JUST YOU WAIT.
YOU AN' ME? GONNA BE CAMP BUDS!
UHHHHHHHHHHHHHHHHHHHHHHHHHH, NO.
I ALREADY HAVE A FRIEND-BOY AT A DIFFERENT CAMP, SO...
HAH! CUTE! I DIDN'T SAY "BOYFRIEND," I SAID "BUDS."
I'M NOT A CAMPER, YO, I'M A COUNSELOR.
SEE YA AT CABIN ASSIGNMENTS!

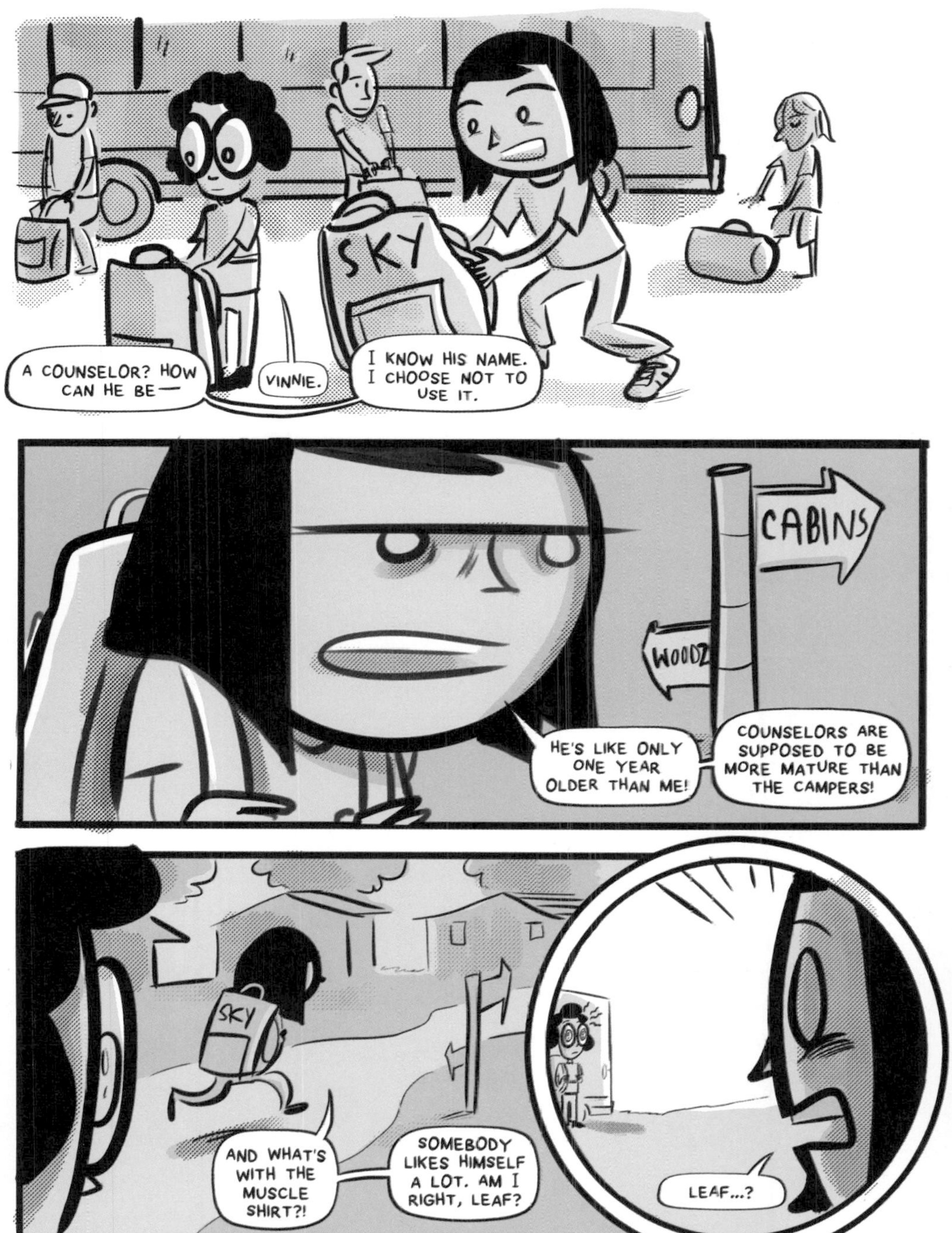
SKY
A COUNSELOR? HOW CAN HE BE—
VINNIE.
I KNOW HIS NAME. I CHOOSE NOT TO USE IT.
CABINS
WOODZ
HE'S LIKE ONLY ONE YEAR OLDER THAN ME!
COUNSELORS ARE SUPPOSED TO BE MORE MATURE THAN THE CAMPERS!
SKY
AND WHAT'S WITH THE MUSCLE SHIRT?!
SOMEBODY LIKES HIMSELF A LOT. AM I RIGHT, LEAF?
LEAF...?

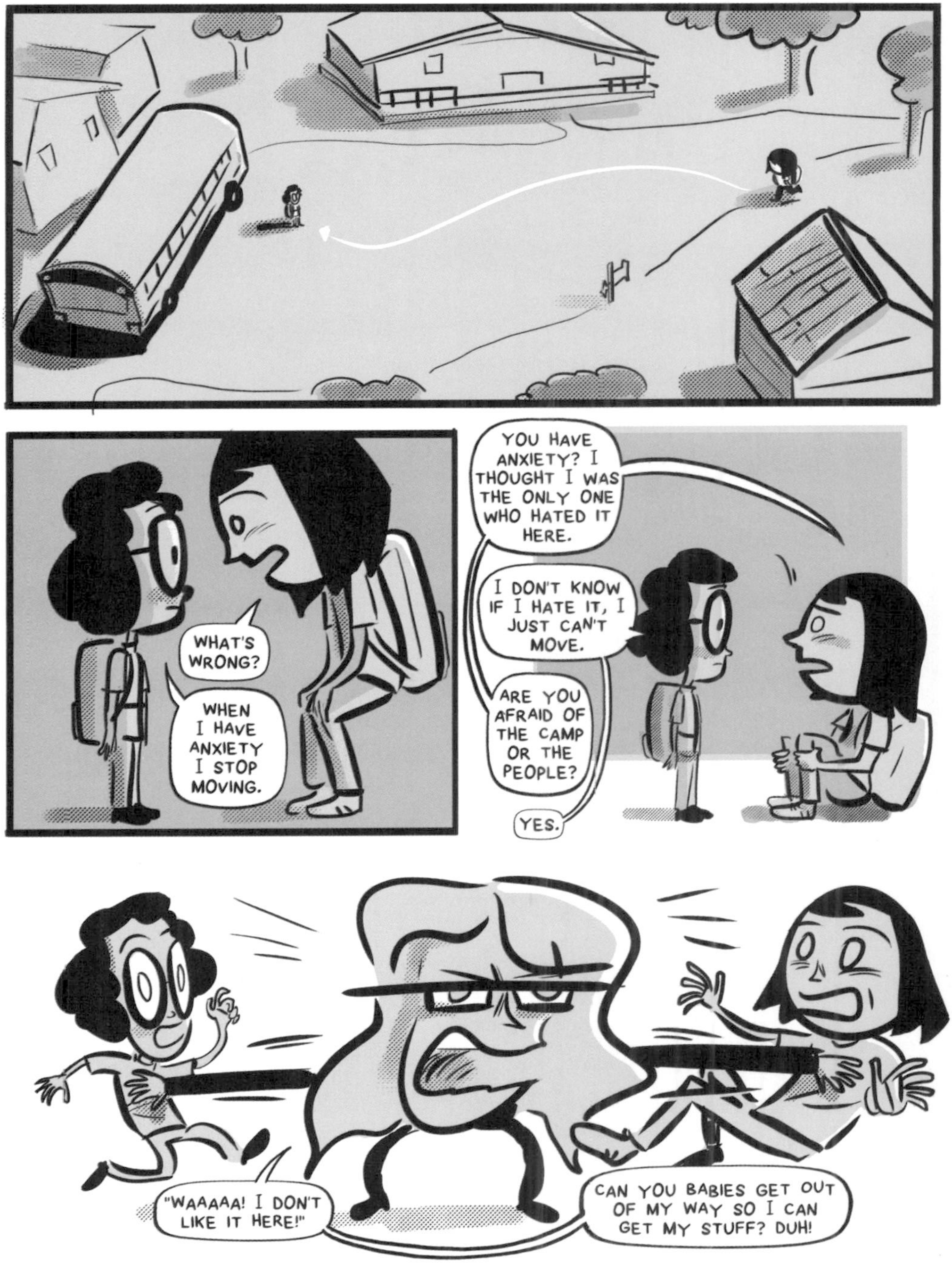
WHAT'S WRONG?
WHEN I HAVE ANXIETY I STOP MOVING.
YOU HAVE ANXIETY? I THOUGHT I WAS THE ONLY ONE WHO HATED IT HERE.
I DON'T KNOW IF I HATE IT, I JUST CAN'T MOVE.
ARE YOU AFRAID OF THE CAMP OR THE PEOPLE?
YES.
"WAAAAA! I DON'T LIKE IT HERE!"
CAN YOU BABIES GET OUT OF MY WAY SO I CAN GET MY STUFF? DUH!

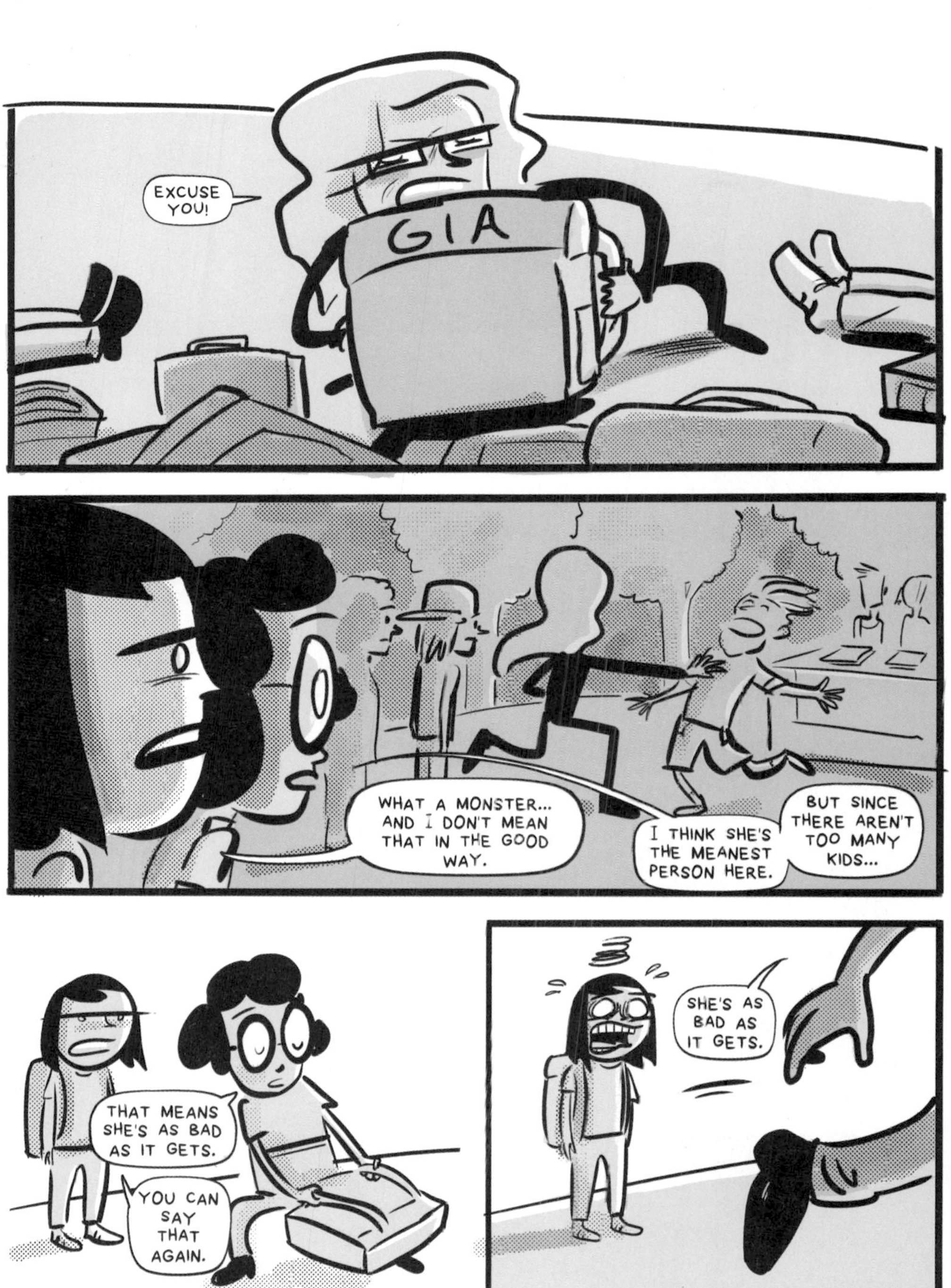
EXCUSE YOU!
GIA
WHAT A MONSTER... AND I DON'T MEAN THAT IN THE GOOD WAY.
I THINK SHE'S THE MEANEST PERSON HERE.
BUT SINCE THERE AREN'T TOO MANY KIDS...
THAT MEANS SHE'S AS BAD AS IT GETS.
YOU CAN SAY THAT AGAIN.
SHE'S AS BAD AS IT GETS.

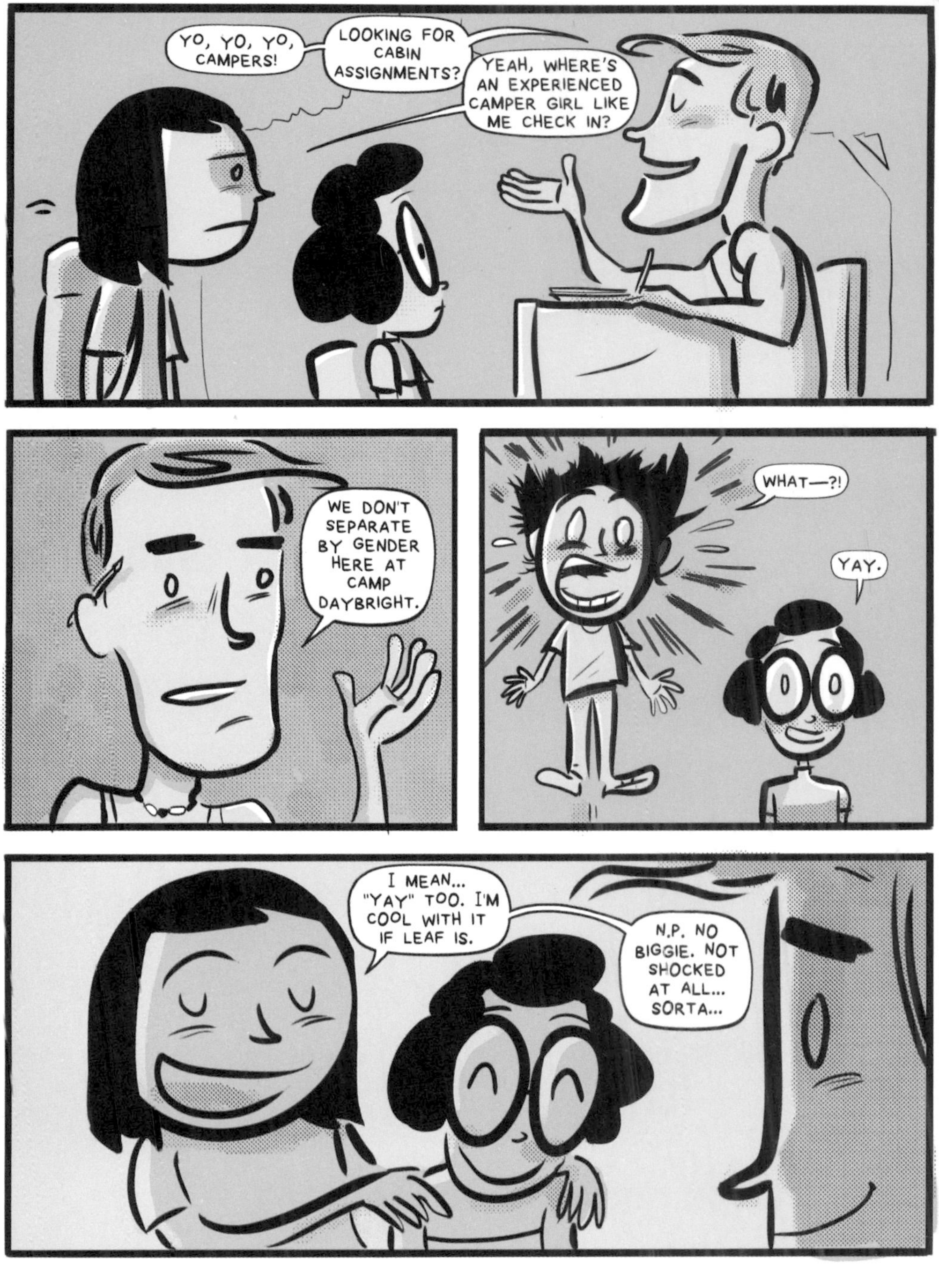
YO, YO, YO, CAMPERS!
LOOKING FOR CABIN ASSIGNMENTS?
YEAH, WHERE'S AN EXPERIENCED CAMPER GIRL LIKE ME CHECK IN?
WE DON'T SEPARATE BY GENDER HERE AT CAMP DAYBRIGHT.
WHAT—?!
YAY.
I MEAN... "YAY" TOO. I'M COOL WITH IT IF LEAF IS.
N.P. NO BIGGIE. NOT SHOCKED AT ALL... SORTA...

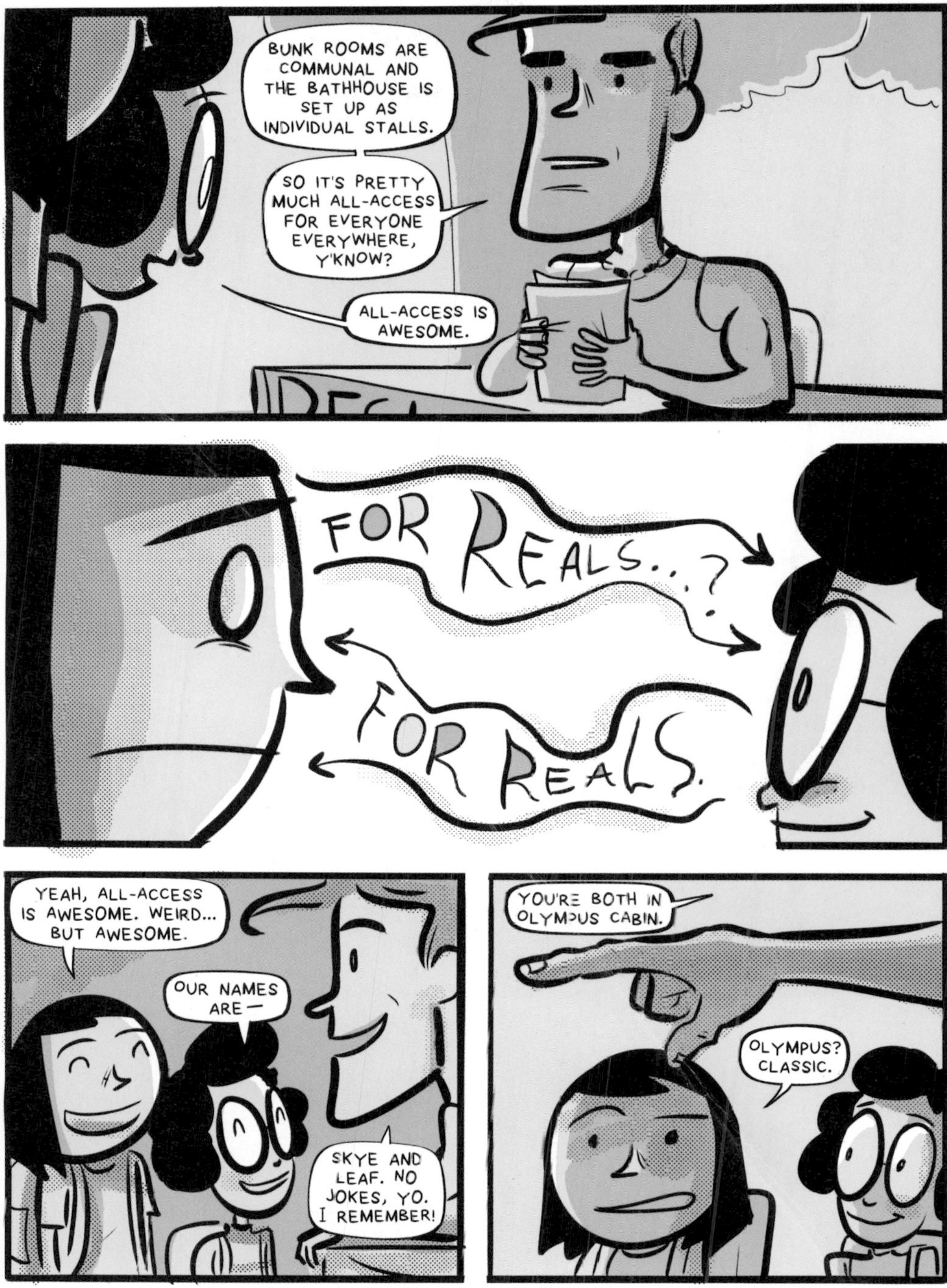
BUNK ROOMS ARE COMMUNAL AND THE BATHHOUSE IS SET UP AS INDIVIDUAL STALLS.
SO IT'S PRETTY MUCH ALL-ACCESS FOR EVERYONE EVERYWHERE, Y'KNOW?
ALL-ACCESS IS AWESOME.
FOR REALS...?
FOR REALS.
YEAH, ALL-ACCESS IS AWESOME. WEIRD... BUT AWESOME.
OUR NAMES ARE—
SKYE AND LEAF. NO JOKES, YO. I REMEMBER!
YOU'RE BOTH IN OLYMPUS CABIN.
OLYMPUS? CLASSIC.

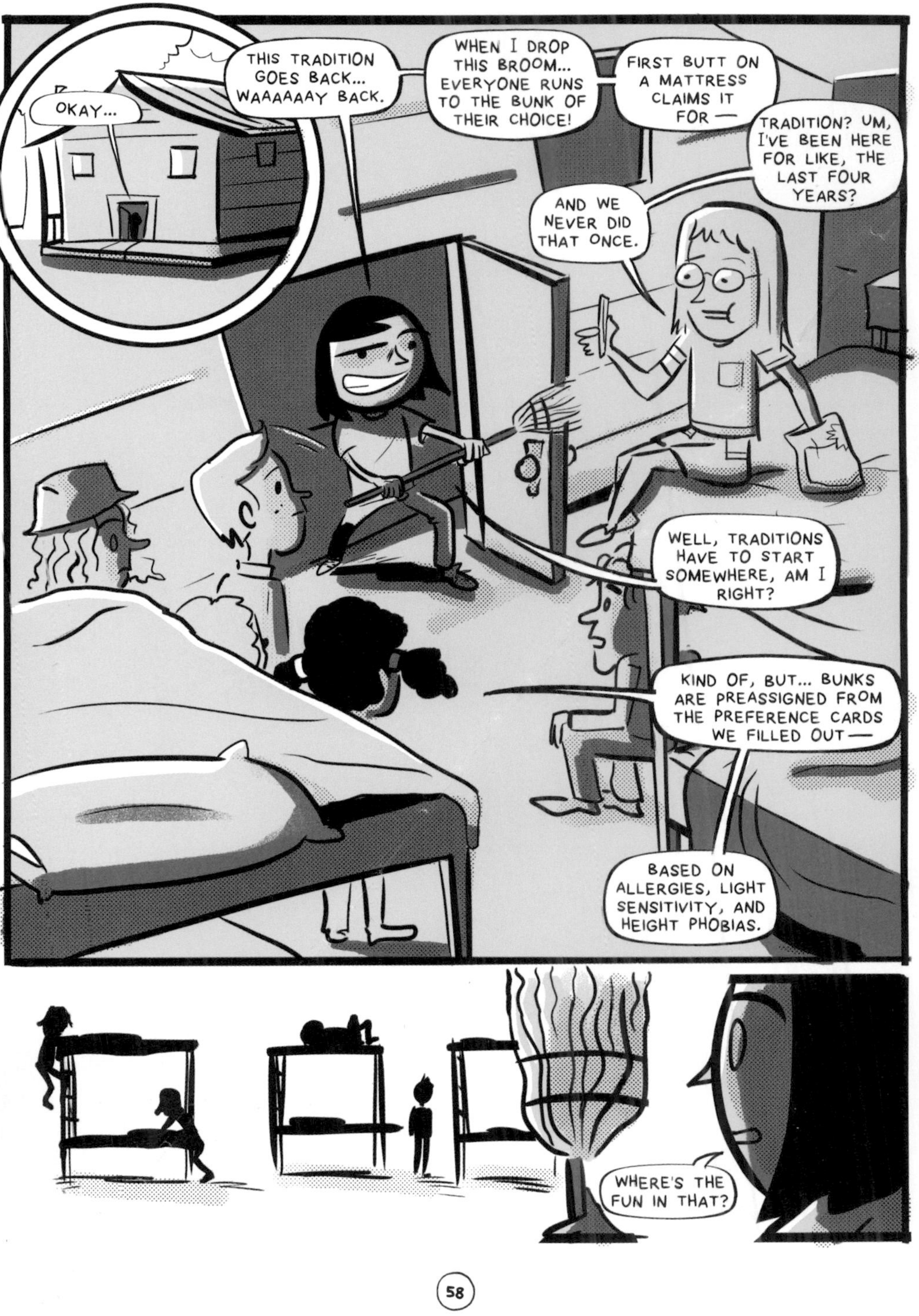
OKAY...
THIS TRADITION GOES BACK... WAAAAAAY BACK.
WHEN I DROP THIS BROOM... EVERYONE RUNS TO THE BUNK OF THEIR CHOICE!
FIRST BUTT ON A MATTRESS CLAIMS IT FOR—
TRADITION? UM, I'VE BEEN HERE FOR LIKE, THE LAST FOUR YEARS?
AND WE NEVER DID THAT ONCE.
WELL, TRADITIONS HAVE TO START SOMEWHERE, AM I RIGHT?
KIND OF, BUT... BUNKS ARE PREASSIGNED FROM THE PREFERENCE CARDS WE FILLED OUT—
BASED ON ALLERGIES, LIGHT SENSITIVITY, AND HEIGHT PHOBIAS.
WHERE'S THE FUN IN THAT?

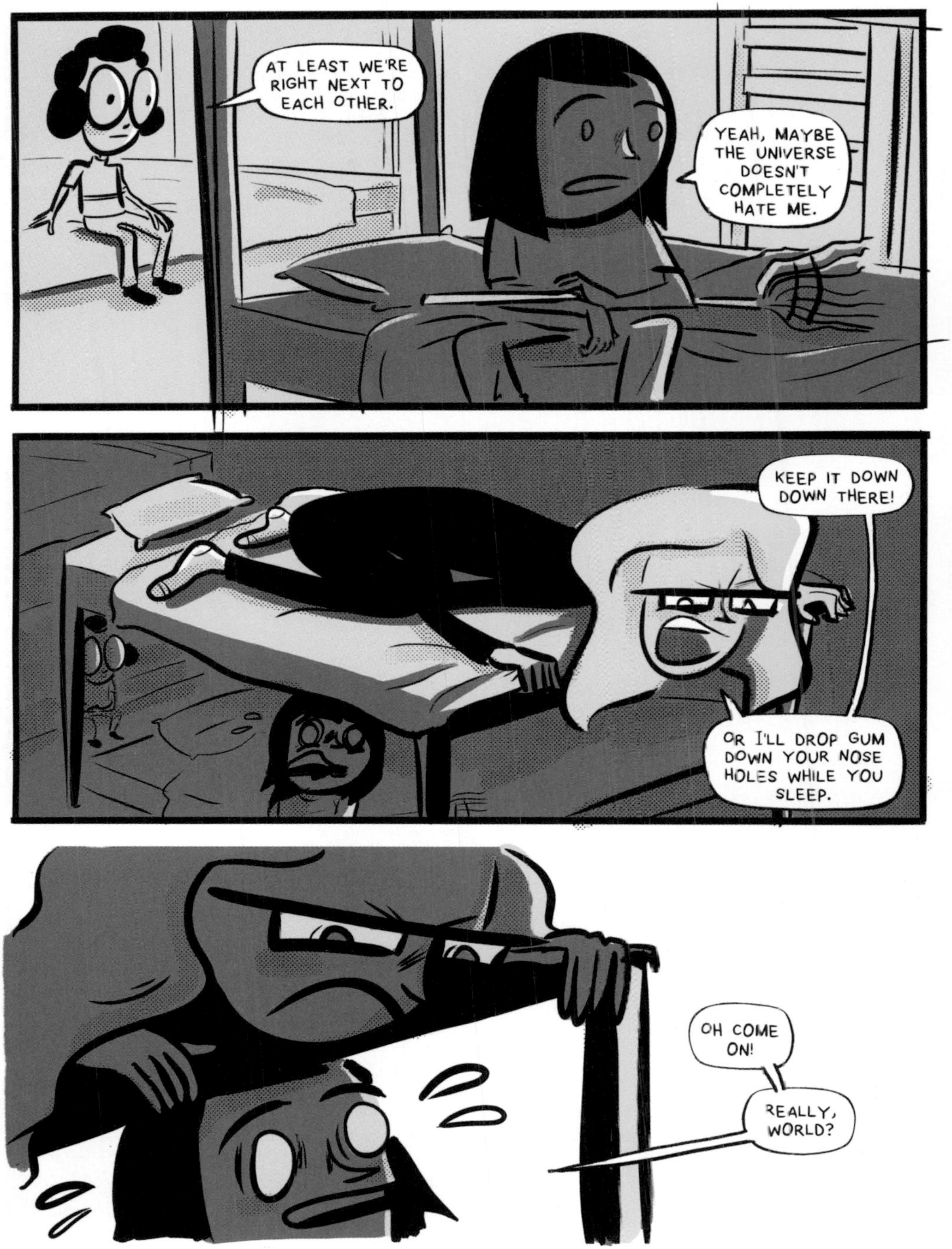
AT LEAST WE'RE RIGHT NEXT TO EACH OTHER.
YEAH, MAYBE THE UNIVERSE DOESN'T COMPLETELY HATE ME.
KEEP IT DOWN DOWN THERE!
OR I'LL DROP GUM DOWN YOUR NOSE HOLES WHILE YOU SLEEP.
OH COME ON!
REALLY, WORLD?

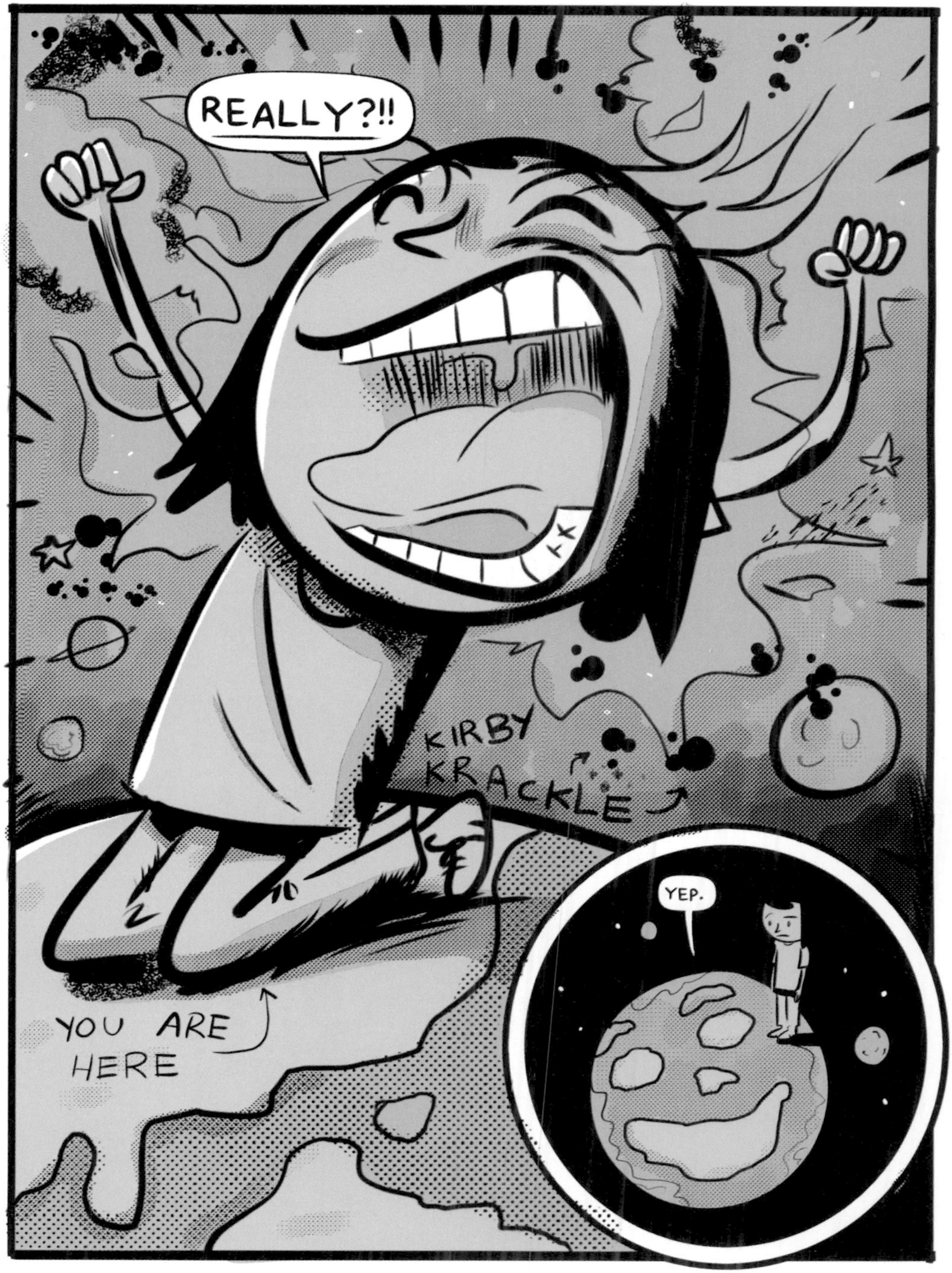
REALLY?!!
KIRBY KRACKLE
YOU ARE HERE
YEP.

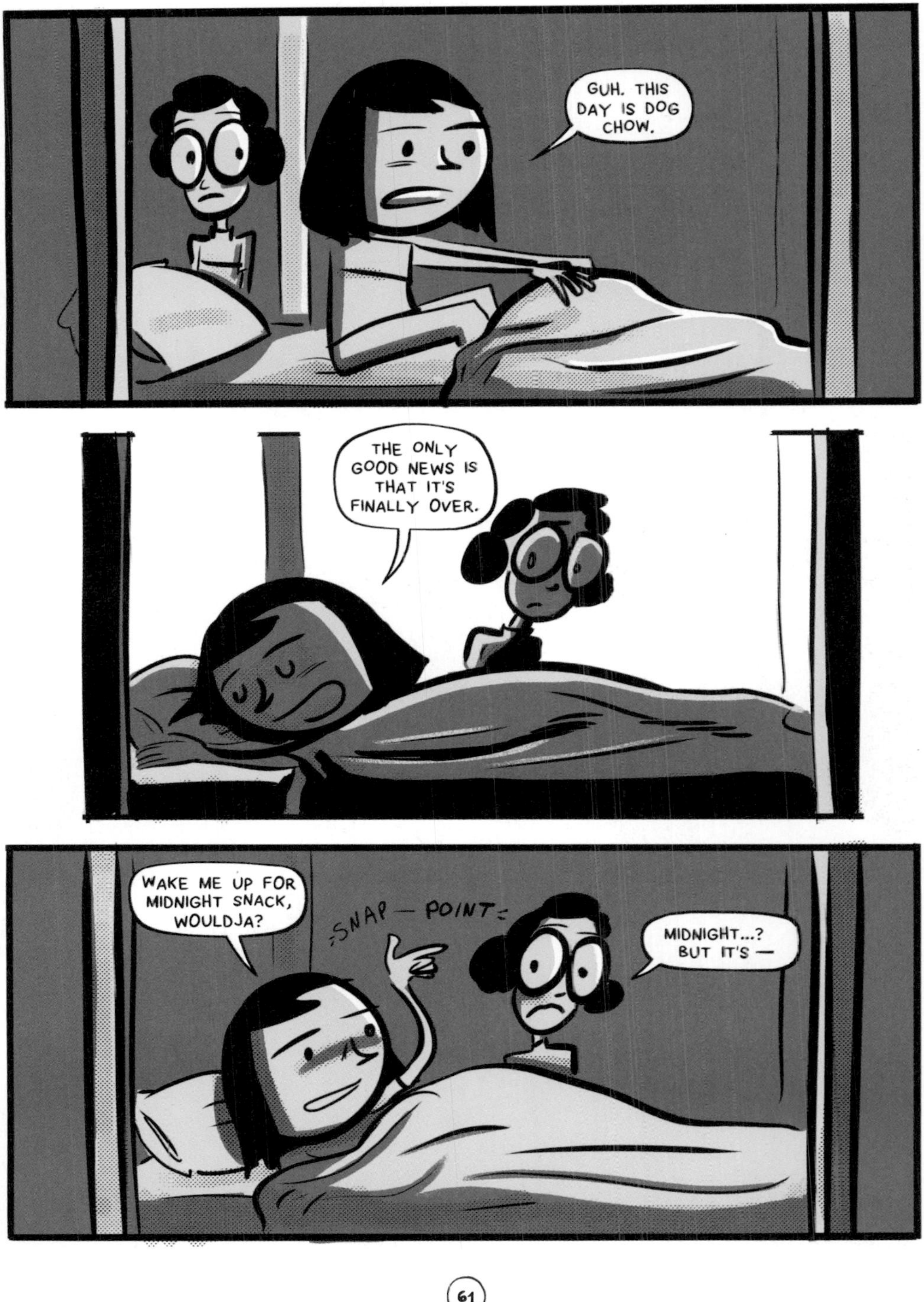
GUH. THIS DAY IS DOG CHOW.
THE ONLY GOOD NEWS IS THAT IT'S FINALLY OVER.
WAKE ME UP FOR MIDNIGHT SNACK, WOULDJA?
SNAP — POINT
MIDNIGHT...? BUT IT'S —

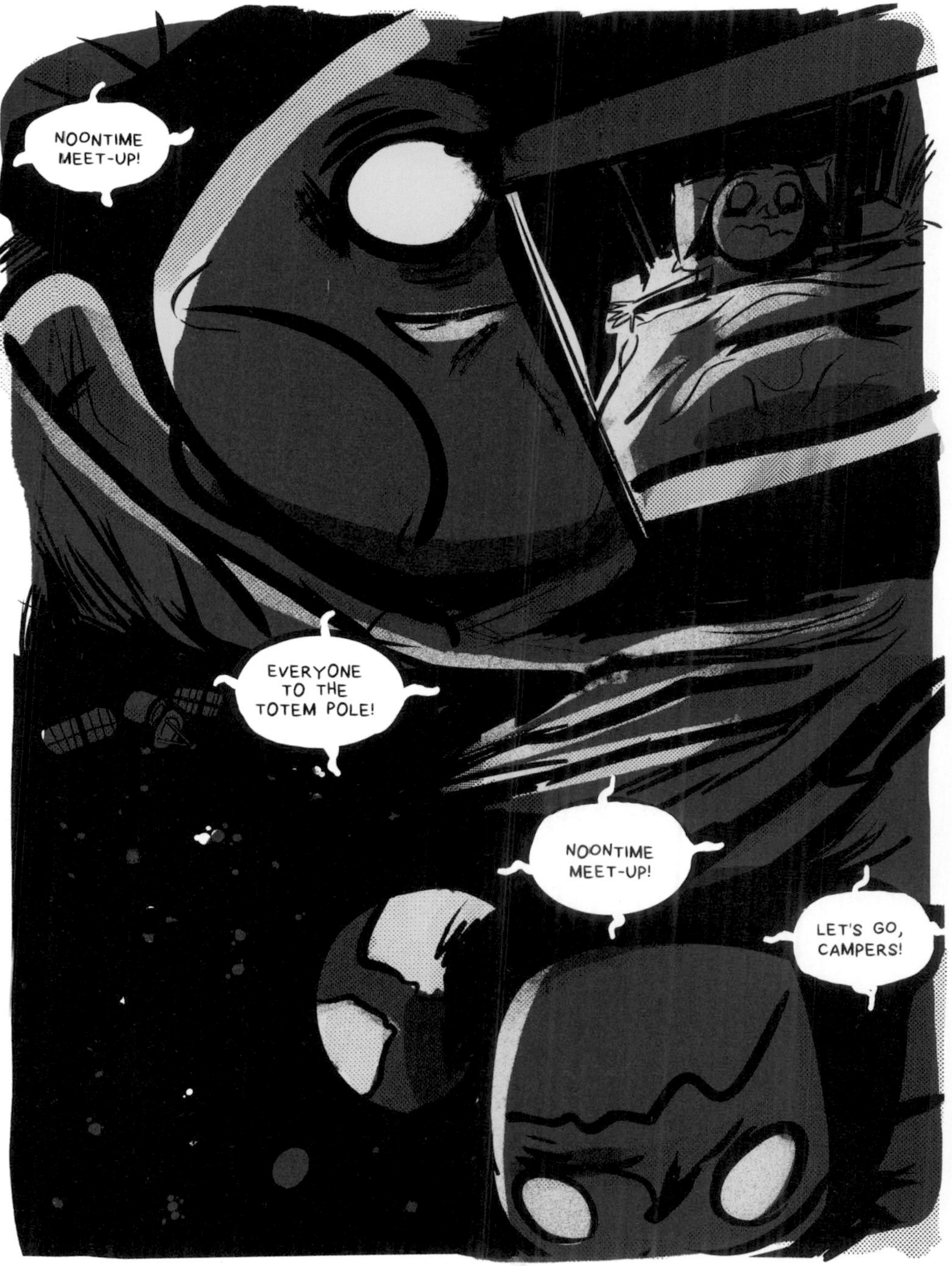
NOONTIME MEET-UP!
EVERYONE TO THE TOTEM POLE!
NOONTIME MEET-UP!
LET'S GO, CAMPERS!

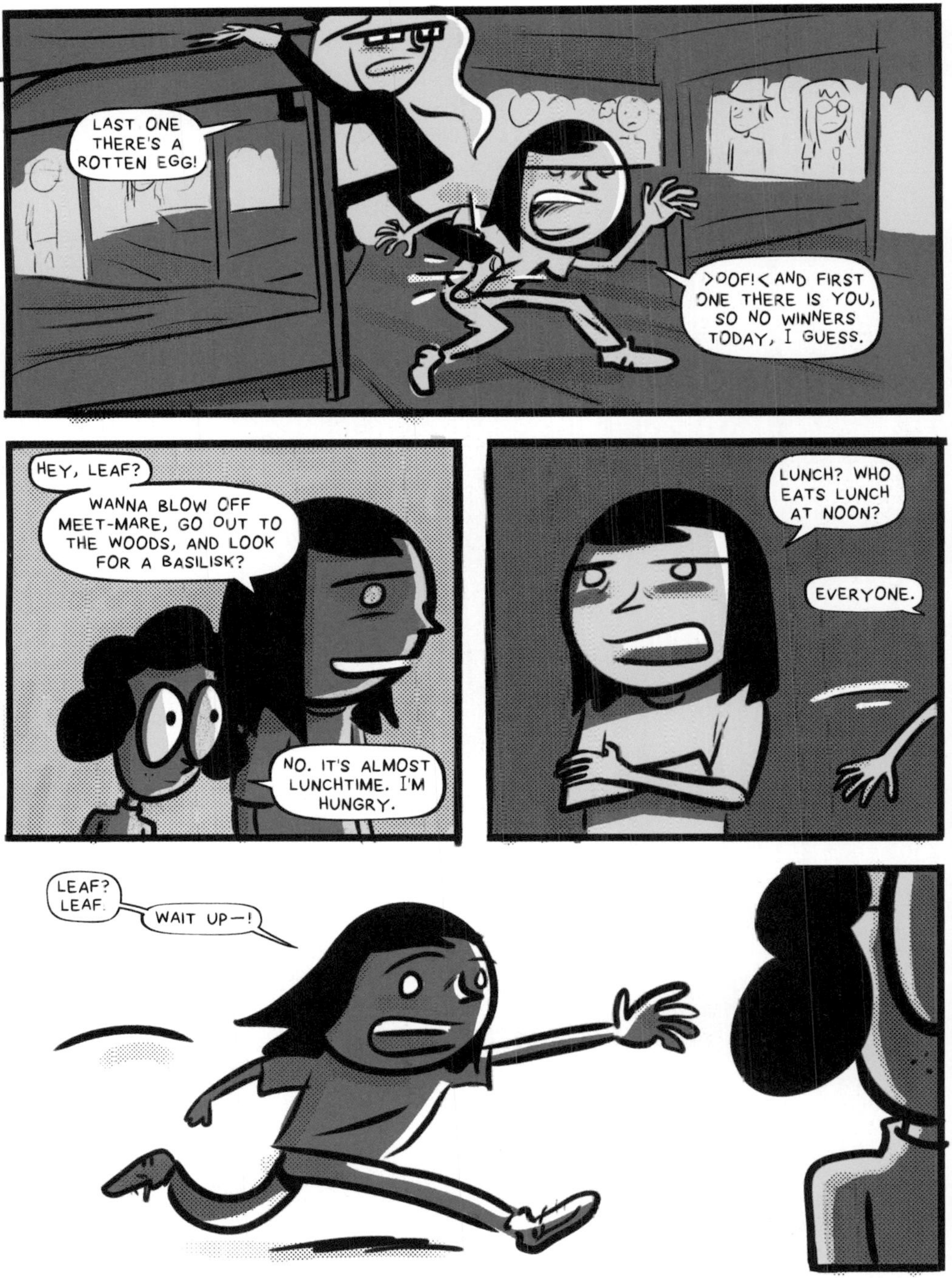
LAST ONE THERE'S A ROTTEN EGG!
>OOF!< AND FIRST ONE THERE IS YOU, SO NO WINNERS TODAY, I GUESS.
HEY, LEAF?
WANNA BLOW OFF MEET-MARE, GO OUT TO THE WOODS, AND LOOK FOR A BASILISK?
NO. IT'S ALMOST LUNCHTIME. I'M HUNGRY.
LUNCH? WHO EATS LUNCH AT NOON?
EVERYONE.
LEAF? LEAF.
WAIT UP—!

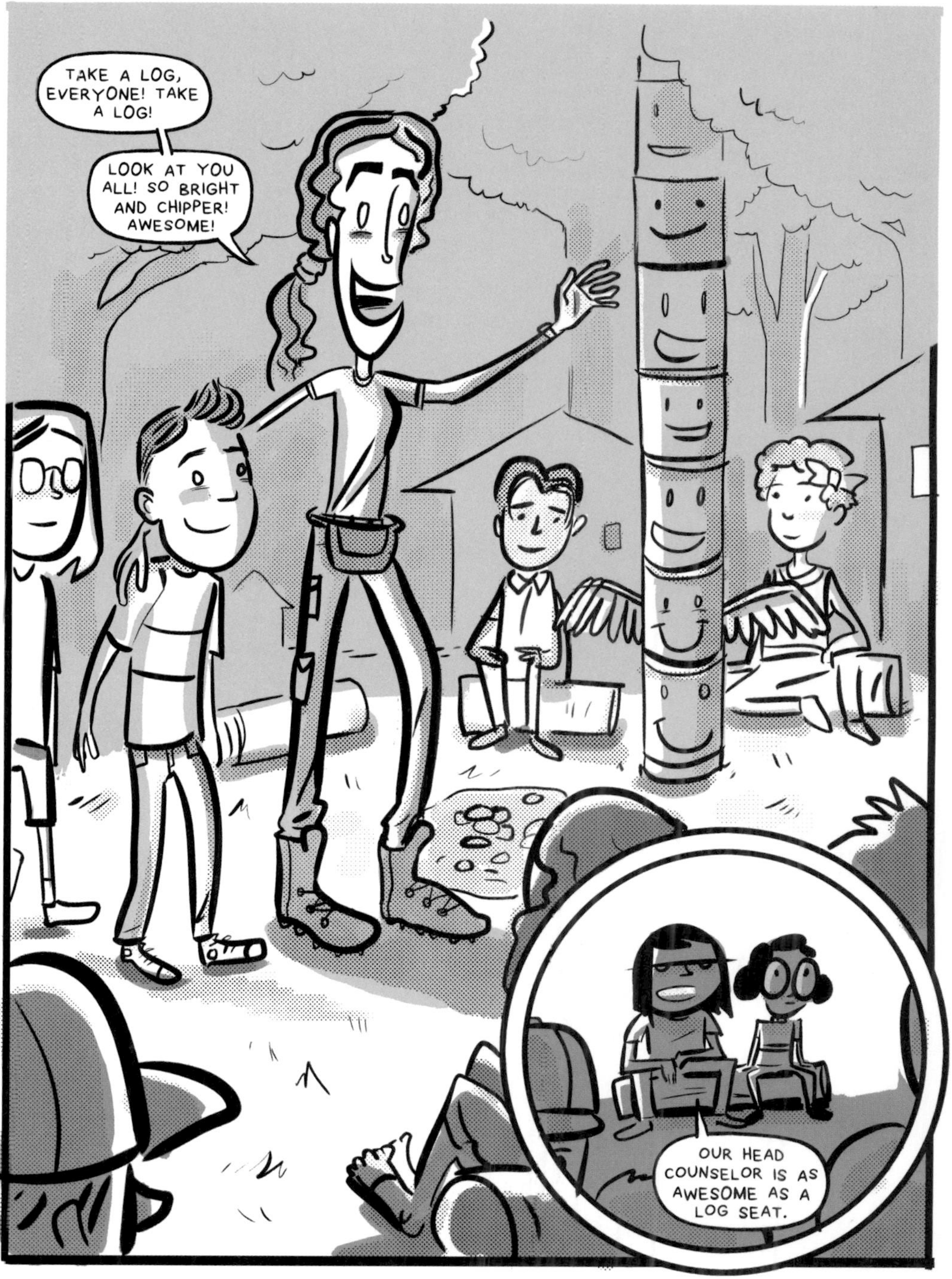
TAKE A LOG, EVERYONE! TAKE A LOG!
LOOK AT YOU ALL! SO BRIGHT AND CHIPPER! AWESOME!
OUR HEAD COUNSELOR IS AS AWESOME AS A LOG SEAT.

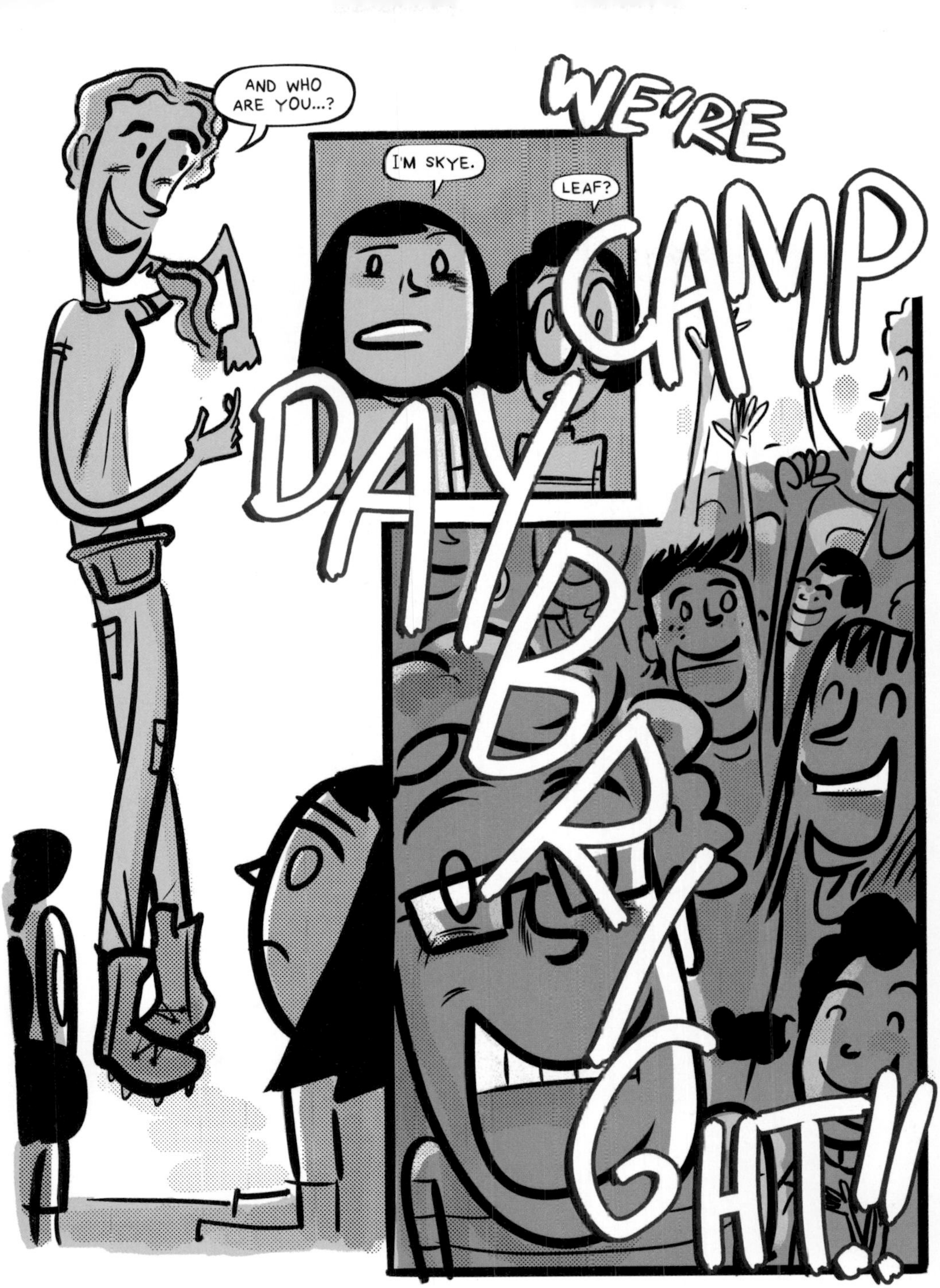
AND WHO ARE YOU...?
I'M SKYE.
LEAF?
WE'RE CAMP DAYBRIGHT!!

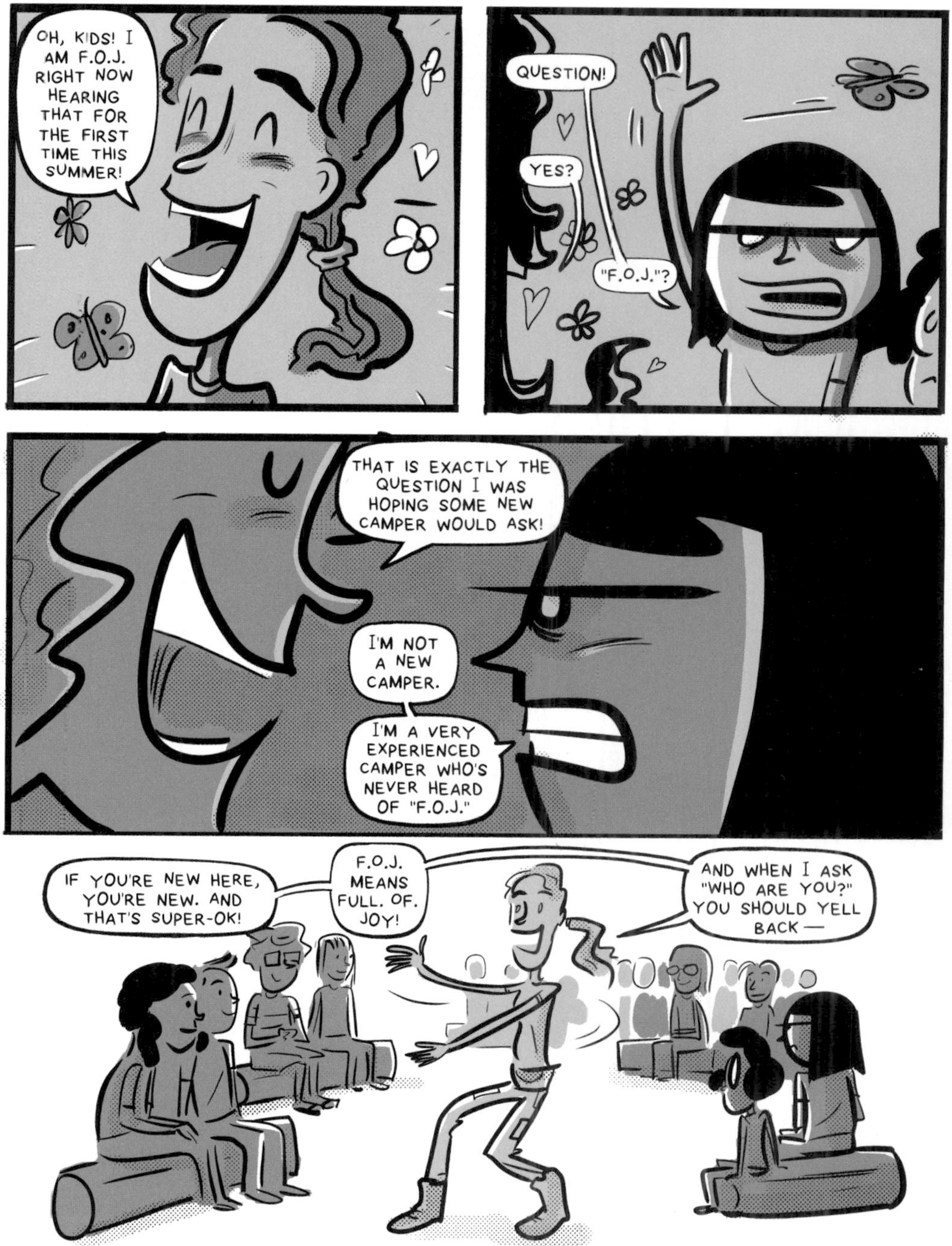
OH, KIDS! I AM F.O.J. RIGHT NOW HEARING THAT FOR THE FIRST TIME THIS SUMMER!
QUESTION!
YES?
"F.O.J."?
THAT IS EXACTLY THE QUESTION I WAS HOPING SOME NEW CAMPER WOULD ASK!
I'M NOT A NEW CAMPER.
I'M A VERY EXPERIENCED CAMPER WHO'S NEVER HEARD OF "F.O.J."
IF YOU'RE NEW HERE, YOU'RE NEW. AND THAT'S SUPER-OK!
F.O.J. MEANS FULL. OF. JOY!
AND WHEN I ASK "WHO ARE YOU?" YOU SHOULD YELL BACK—

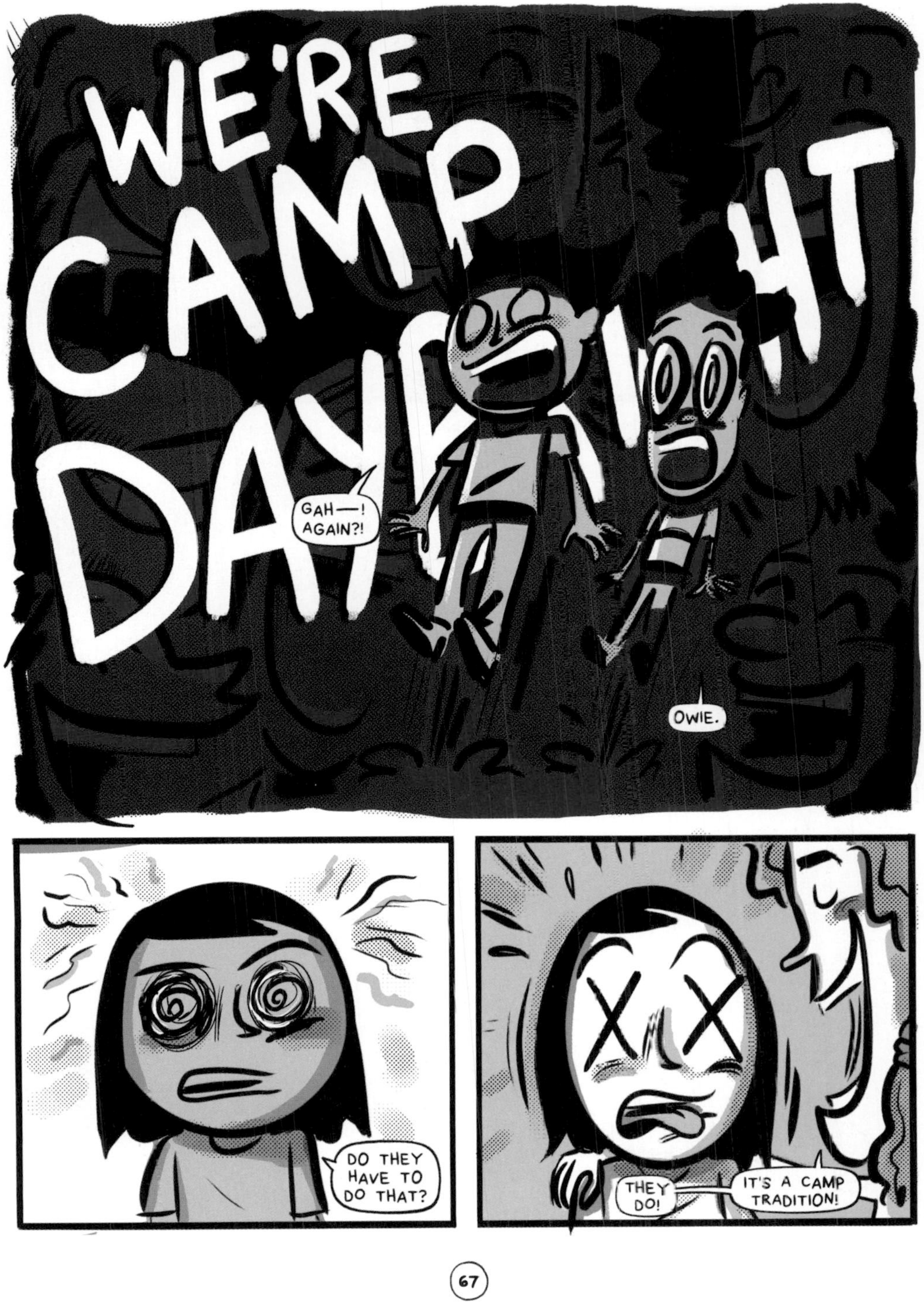

WE'RE
CAMP
GAH—! AGAIN?!
OWIE.
DO THEY HAVE TO DO THAT?
THEY DO!
IT'S A CAMP TRADITION!

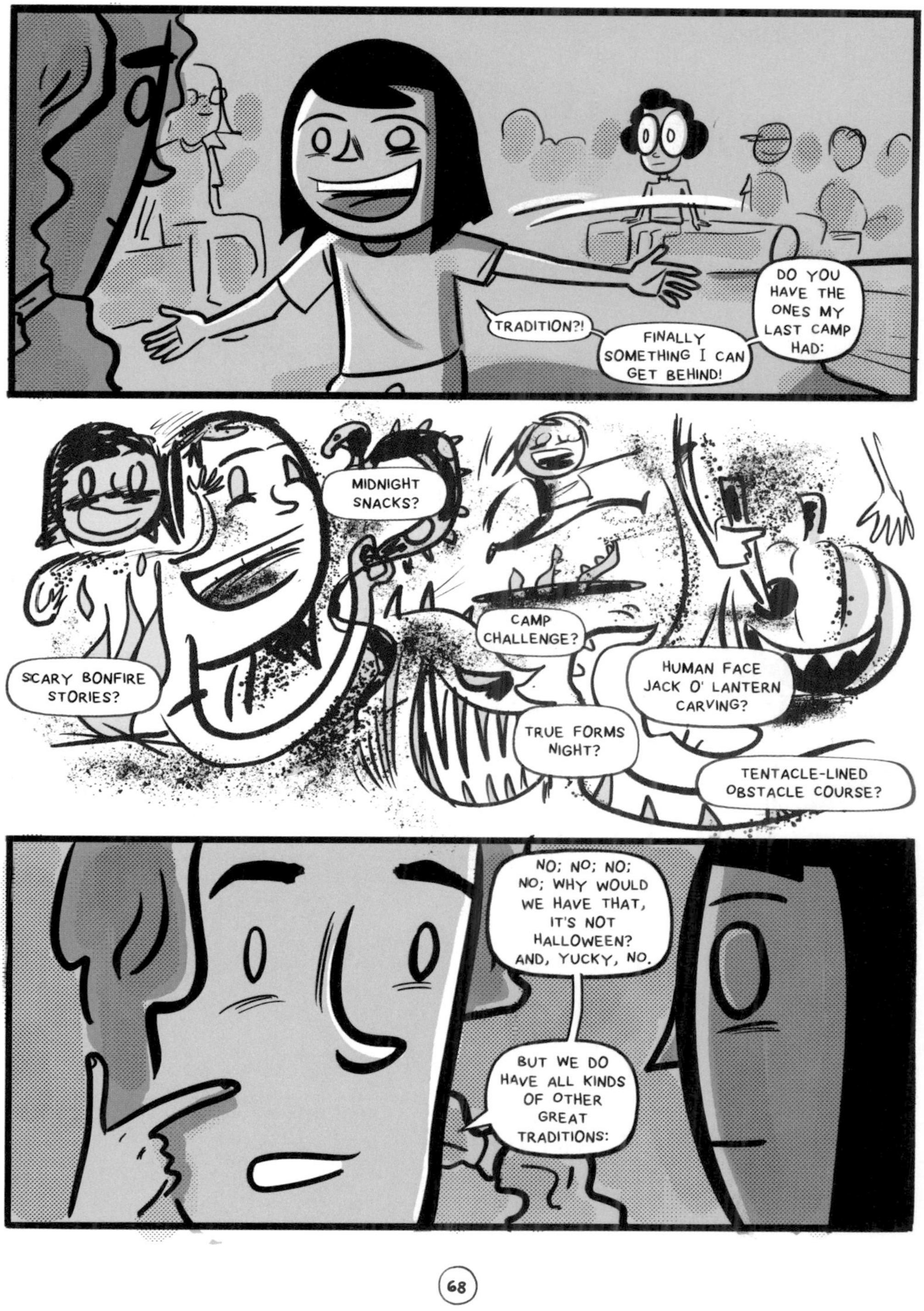
TRADITION?!
FINALLY SOMETHING I CAN GET BEHIND!
DO YOU HAVE THE ONES MY LAST CAMP HAD:
MIDNIGHT SNACKS?
CAMP CHALLENGE?
SCARY BONFIRE STORIES?
HUMAN FACE JACK O' LANTERN CARVING?
TRUE FORMS NIGHT?
TENTACLE-LINED OBSTACLE COURSE?
NO; NO; NO; NO; WHY WOULD WE HAVE THAT, IT'S NOT HALLOWEEN? AND, YUCKY, NO.
BUT WE DO HAVE ALL KINDS OF OTHER GREAT TRADITIONS:

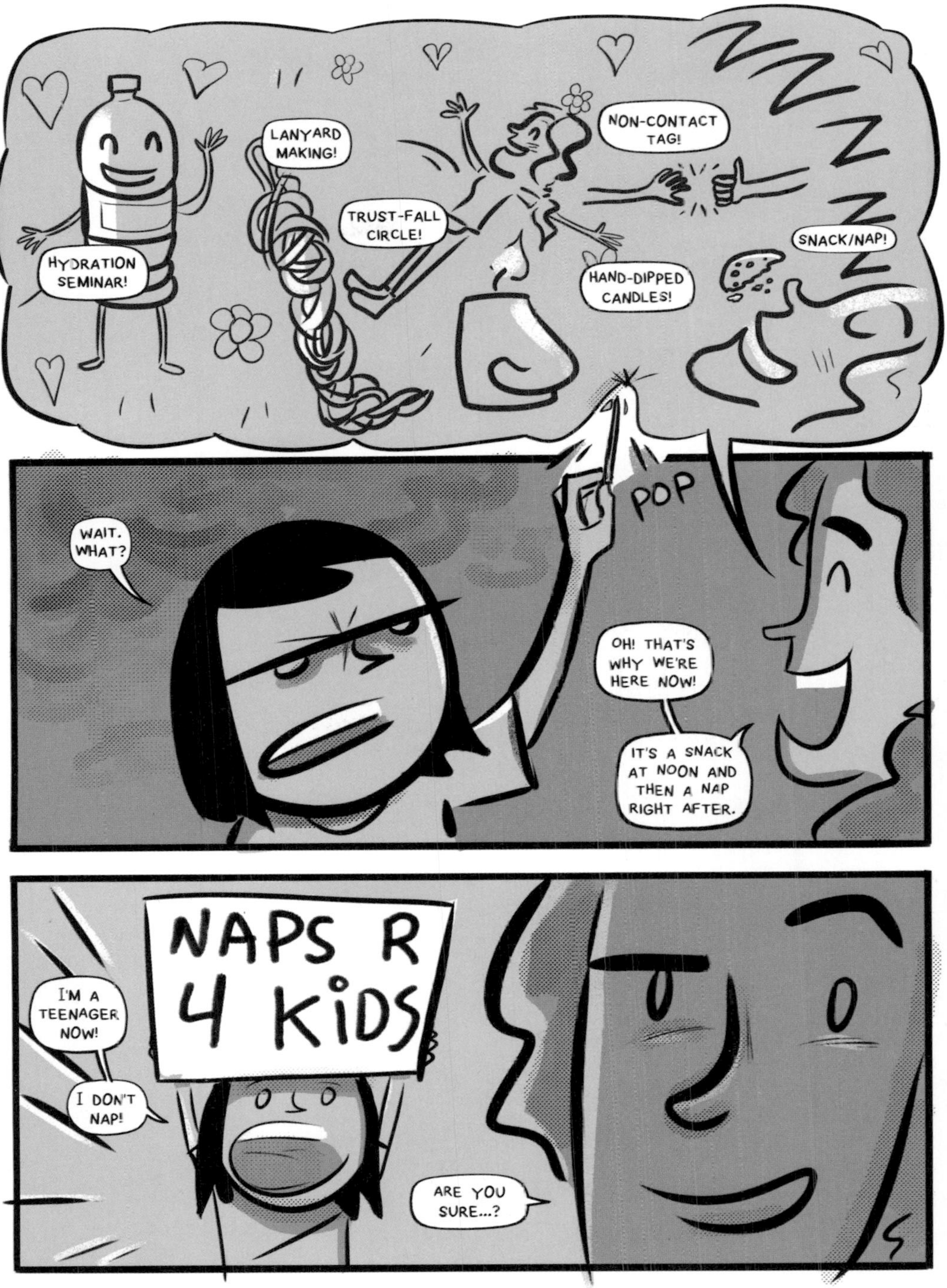
HYDRATION SEMINAR!
LANYARD MAKING!
TRUST-FALL CIRCLE!
NON-CONTACT TAG!
HAND-DIPPED CANDLES!
SNACK/NAP!
POP
WAIT. WHAT?
OH! THAT'S WHY WE'RE HERE NOW!
IT'S A SNACK AT NOON AND THEN A NAP RIGHT AFTER.
NAPS R 4 KIDS
I'M A TEENAGER NOW!
I DON'T NAP!
ARE YOU SURE...?

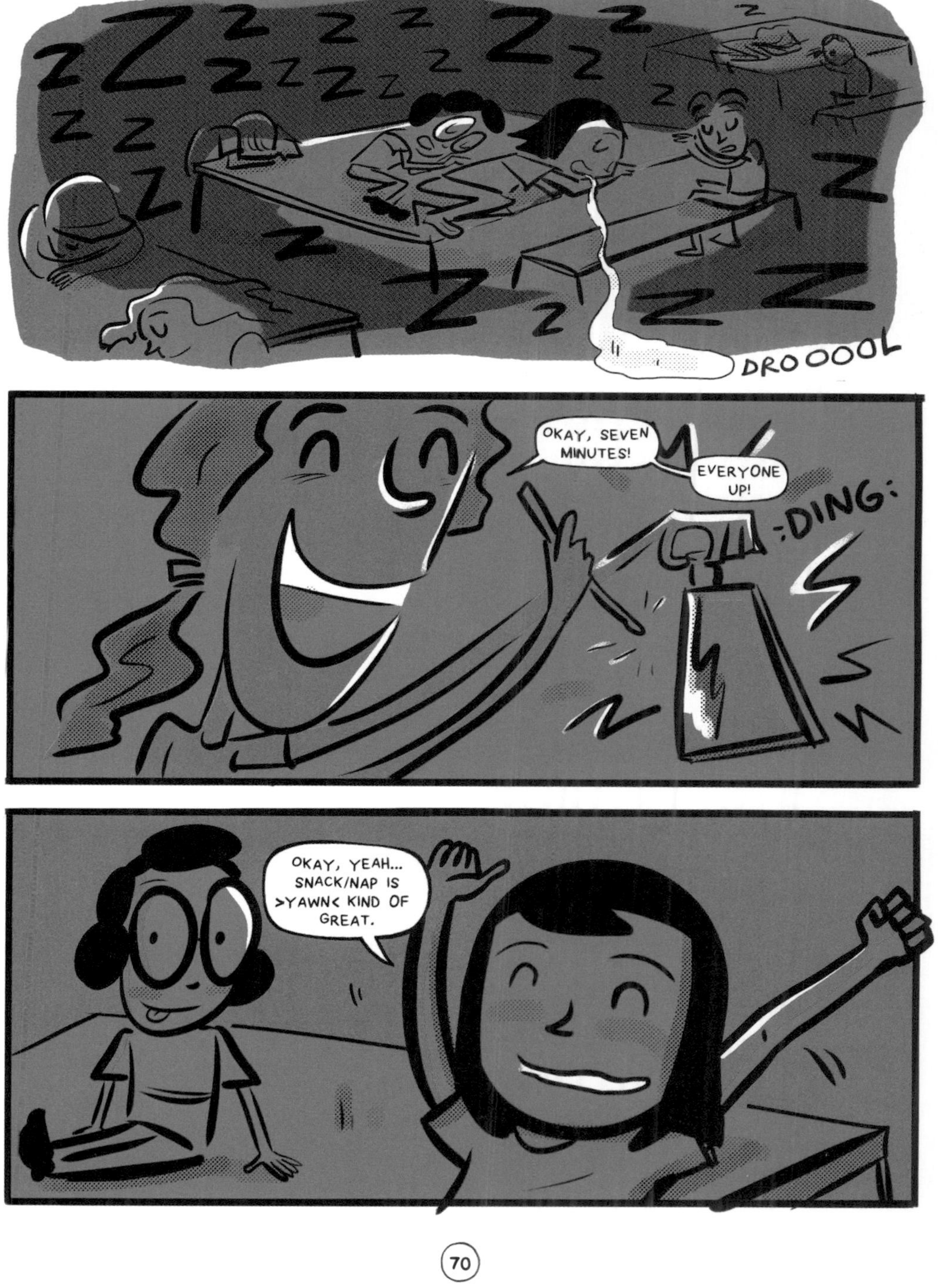
DROOOOL
OKAY, SEVEN MINUTES!
EVERYONE UP!
:DING:
OKAY, YEAH... SNACK/NAP IS >YAWN< KIND OF GREAT.

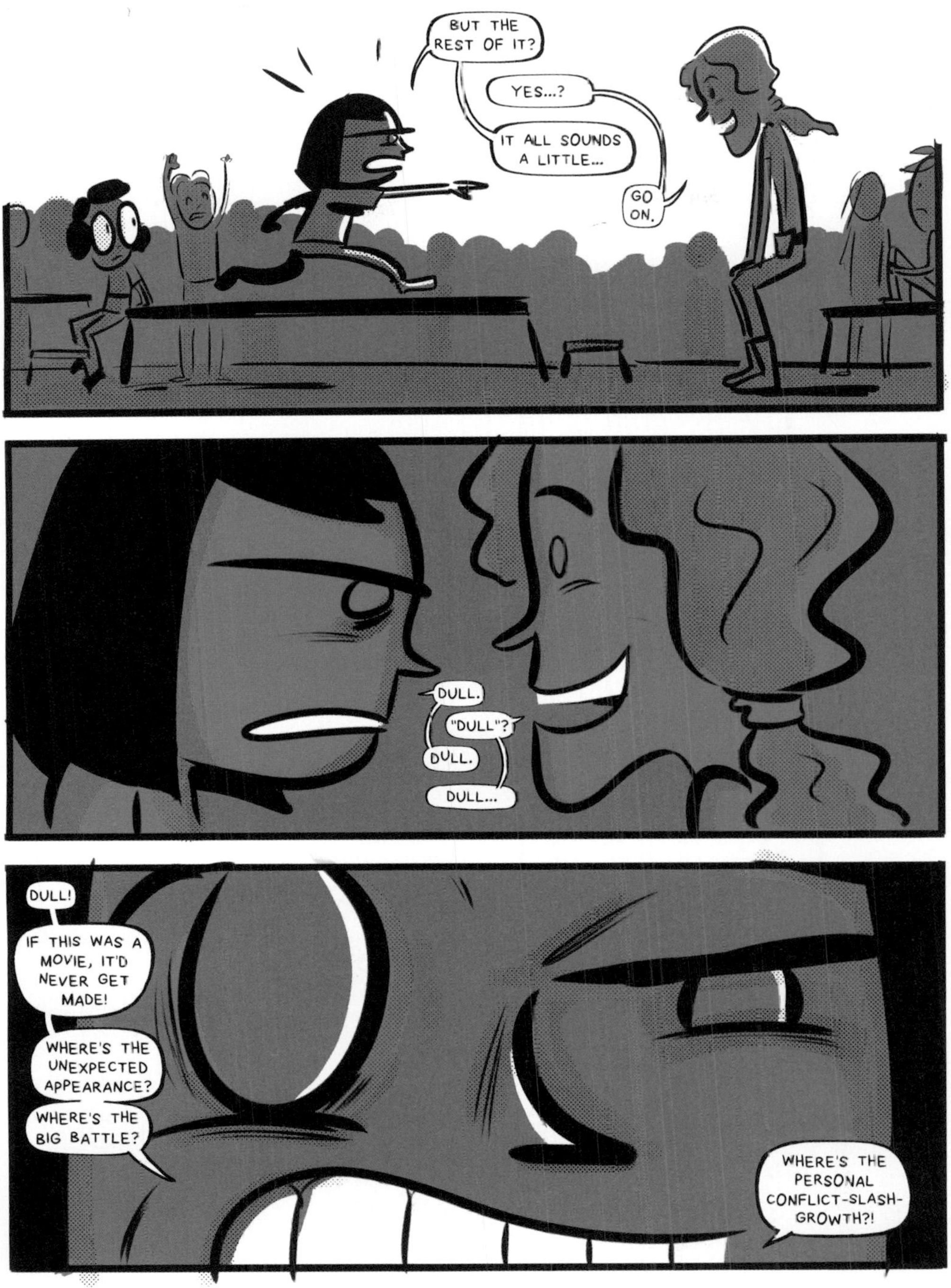
BUT THE REST OF IT?
YES...?
IT ALL SOUNDS A LITTLE...
GO ON.
DULL.
"DULL"?
DULL.
DULL...
DULL!
IF THIS WAS A MOVIE, IT'D NEVER GET MADE!
WHERE'S THE UNEXPECTED APPEARANCE?
WHERE'S THE BIG BATTLE?
WHERE'S THE PERSONAL CONFLICT-SLASH-GROWTH?!

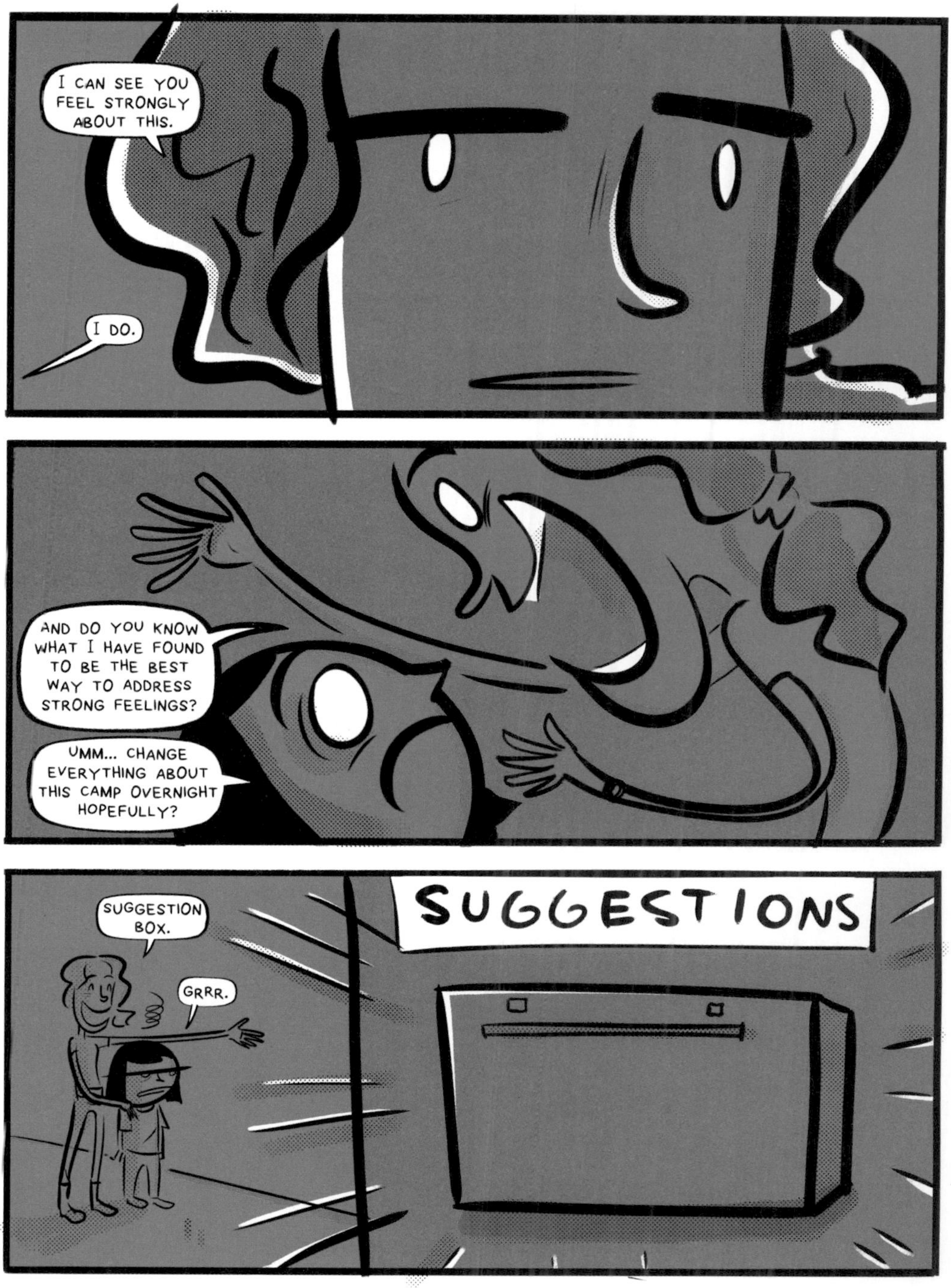
I CAN SEE YOU FEEL STRONGLY ABOUT THIS.
I DO.
AND DO YOU KNOW WHAT I HAVE FOUND TO BE THE BEST WAY TO ADDRESS STRONG FEELINGS?
UMM... CHANGE EVERYTHING ABOUT THIS CAMP OVERNIGHT HOPEFULLY?
SUGGESTION BOX.
GRRR.
SUGGESTIONS

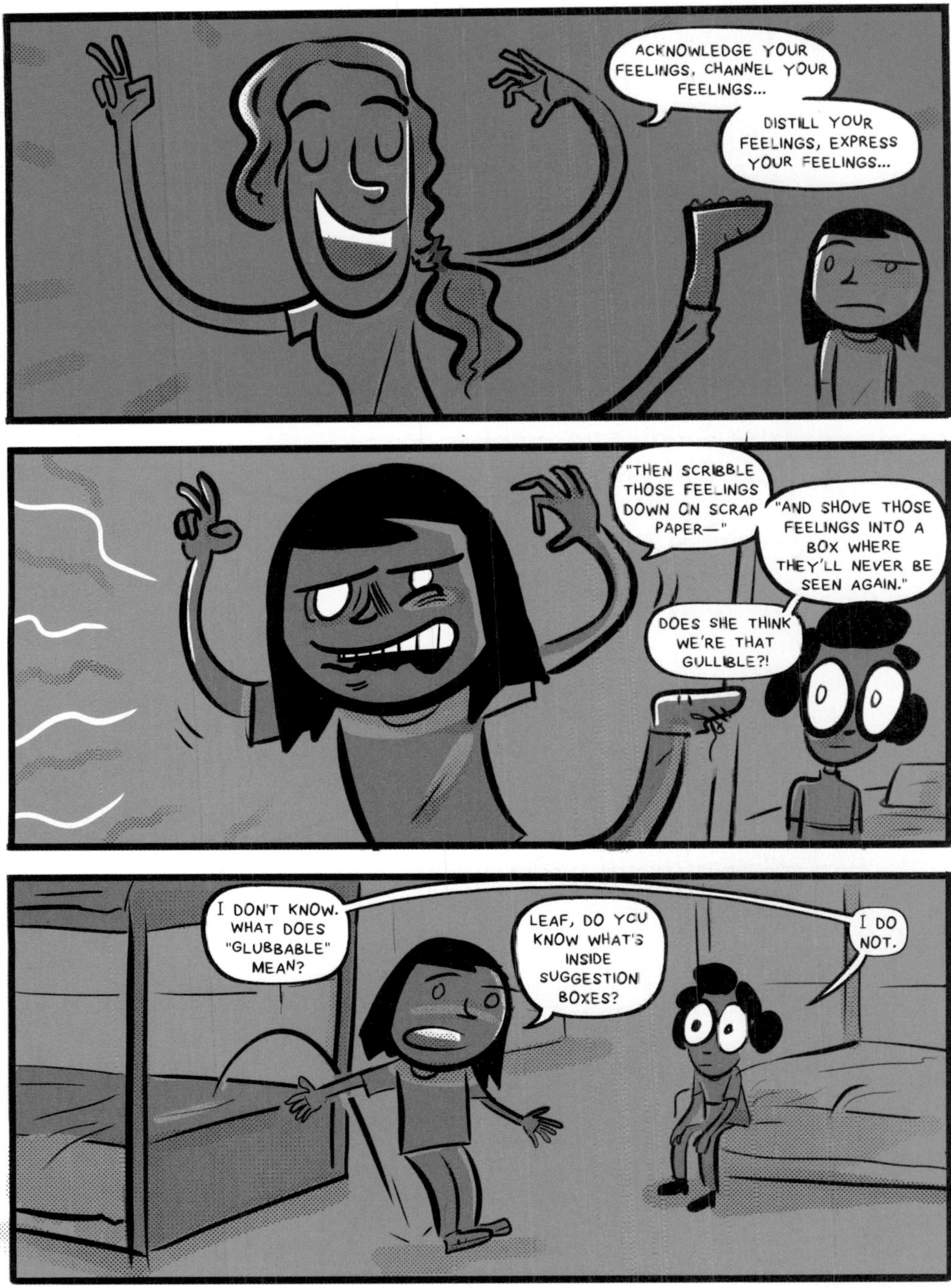
ACKNOWLEDGE YOUR FEELINGS, CHANNEL YOUR FEELINGS...
DISTILL YOUR FEELINGS, EXPRESS YOUR FEELINGS...
"THEN SCRIBBLE THOSE FEELINGS DOWN ON SCRAP PAPER—"
"AND SHOVE THOSE FEELINGS INTO A BOX WHERE THEY'LL NEVER BE SEEN AGAIN."
DOES SHE THINK WE'RE THAT GULLIBLE?!
LEAF, DO YOU KNOW WHAT'S INSIDE SUGGESTION BOXES?
I DO NOT.
I DON'T KNOW. WHAT DOES "GLUBBABLE" MEAN?

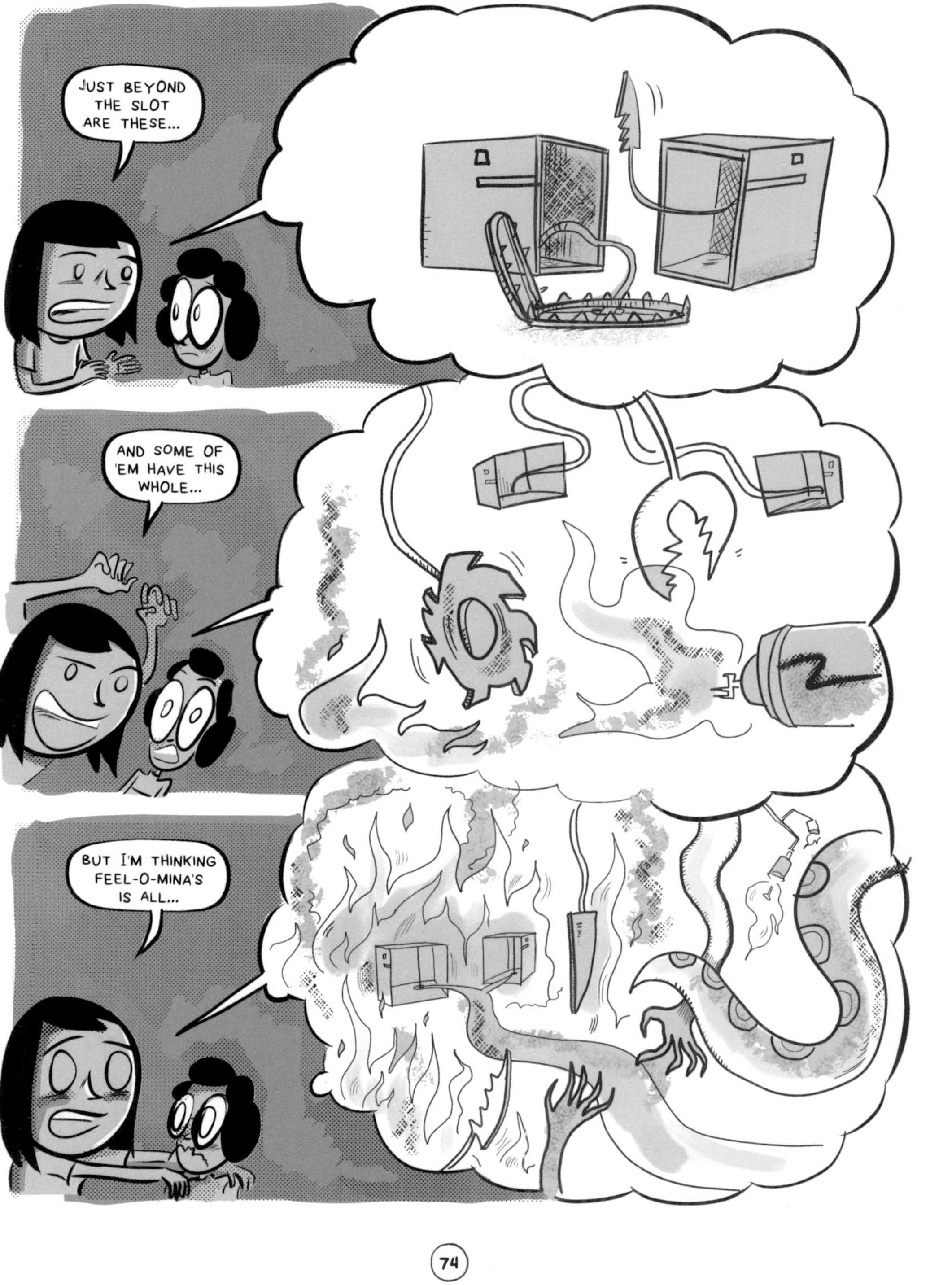
JUST BEYOND THE SLOT ARE THESE...
AND SOME OF 'EM HAVE THIS WHOLE...
BUT I'M THINKING FEEL-O-MINA'S IS ALL...

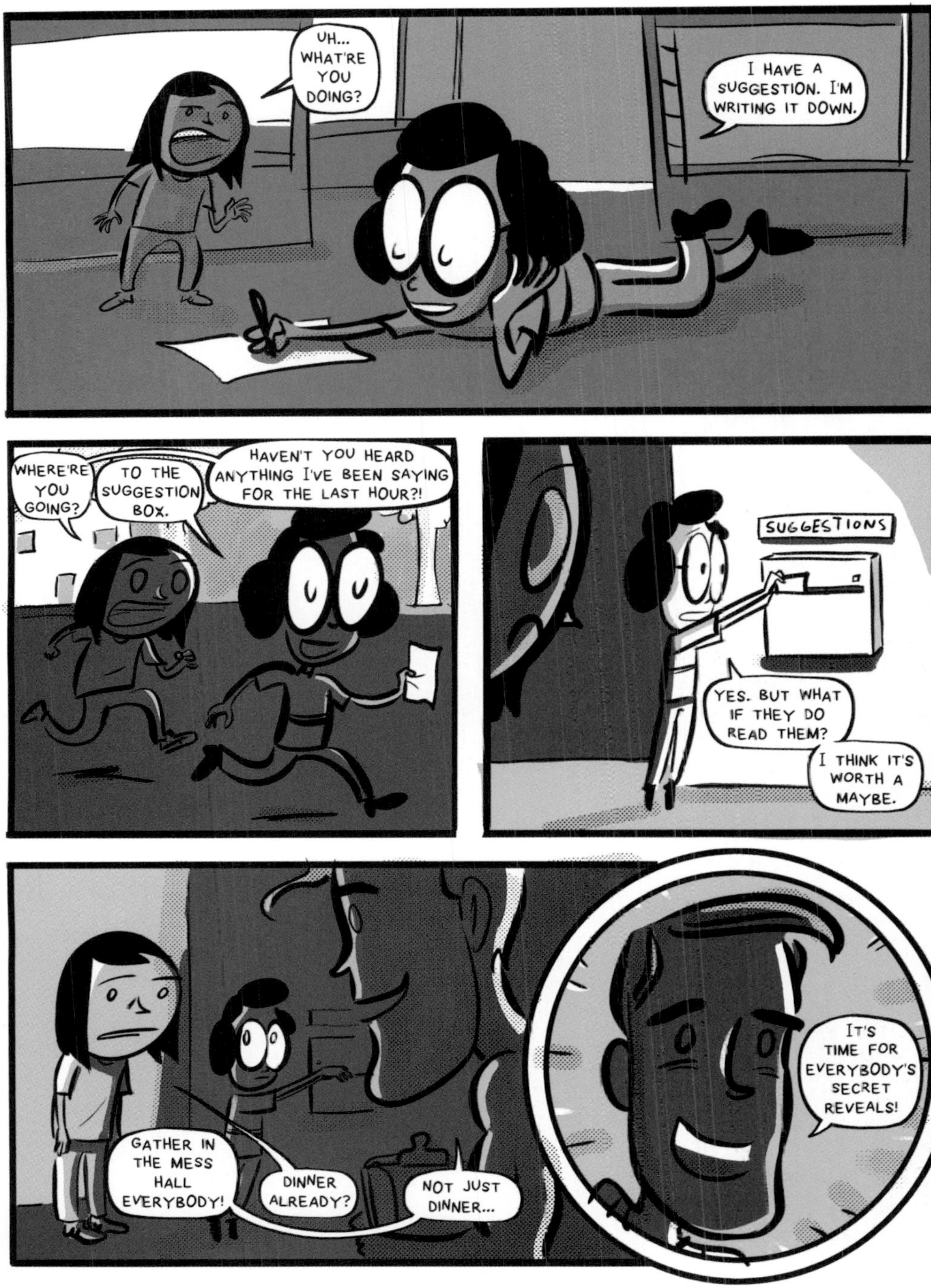
UH... WHAT'RE YOU DOING?
I HAVE A SUGGESTION. I'M WRITING IT DOWN.
WHERE'RE YOU GOING?
TO THE SUGGESTION BOX.
HAVEN'T YOU HEARD ANYTHING I'VE BEEN SAYING FOR THE LAST HOUR?!
SUGGESTIONS
YES. BUT WHAT IF THEY DO READ THEM?
I THINK IT'S WORTH A MAYBE.
GATHER IN THE MESS HALL EVERYBODY!
DINNER ALREADY?
NOT JUST DINNER...
IT'S TIME FOR EVERYBODY'S SECRET REVEALS!

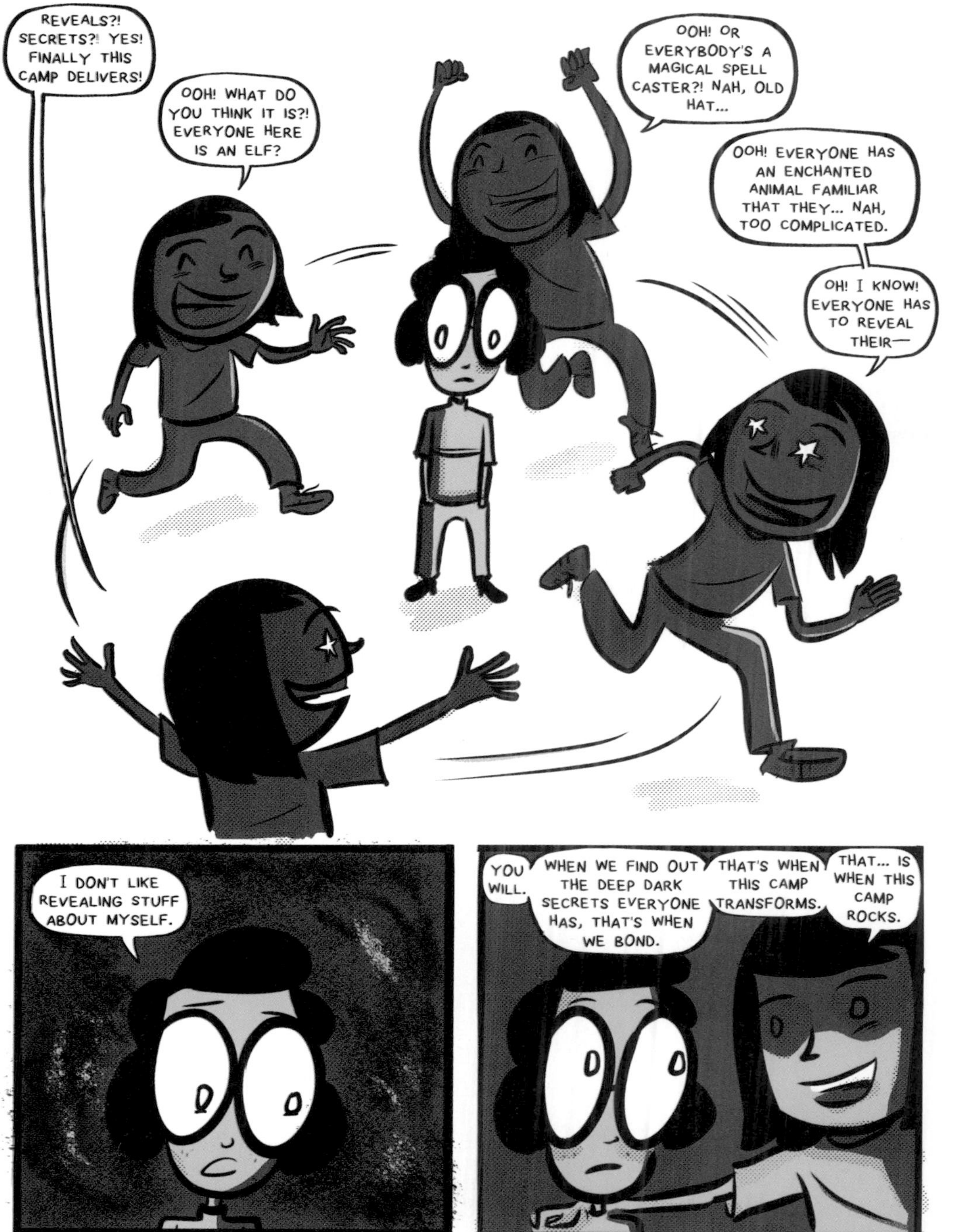
REVEALS?! SECRETS?! YES! FINALLY THIS CAMP DELIVERS!
OOH! WHAT DO YOU THINK IT IS?! EVERYONE HERE IS AN ELF?
OOH! OR EVERYBODY'S A MAGICAL SPELL CASTER?! NAH, OLD HAT...
OOH! EVERYONE HAS AN ENCHANTED ANIMAL FAMILIAR THAT THEY... NAH, TOO COMPLICATED.
OH! I KNOW! EVERYONE HAS TO REVEAL THEIR—
I DON'T LIKE REVEALING STUFF ABOUT MYSELF.
YOU WILL.
WHEN WE FIND OUT THE DEEP DARK SECRETS EVERYONE HAS, THAT'S WHEN WE BOND.
THAT'S WHEN THIS CAMP TRANSFORMS.
THAT... IS WHEN THIS CAMP ROCKS.

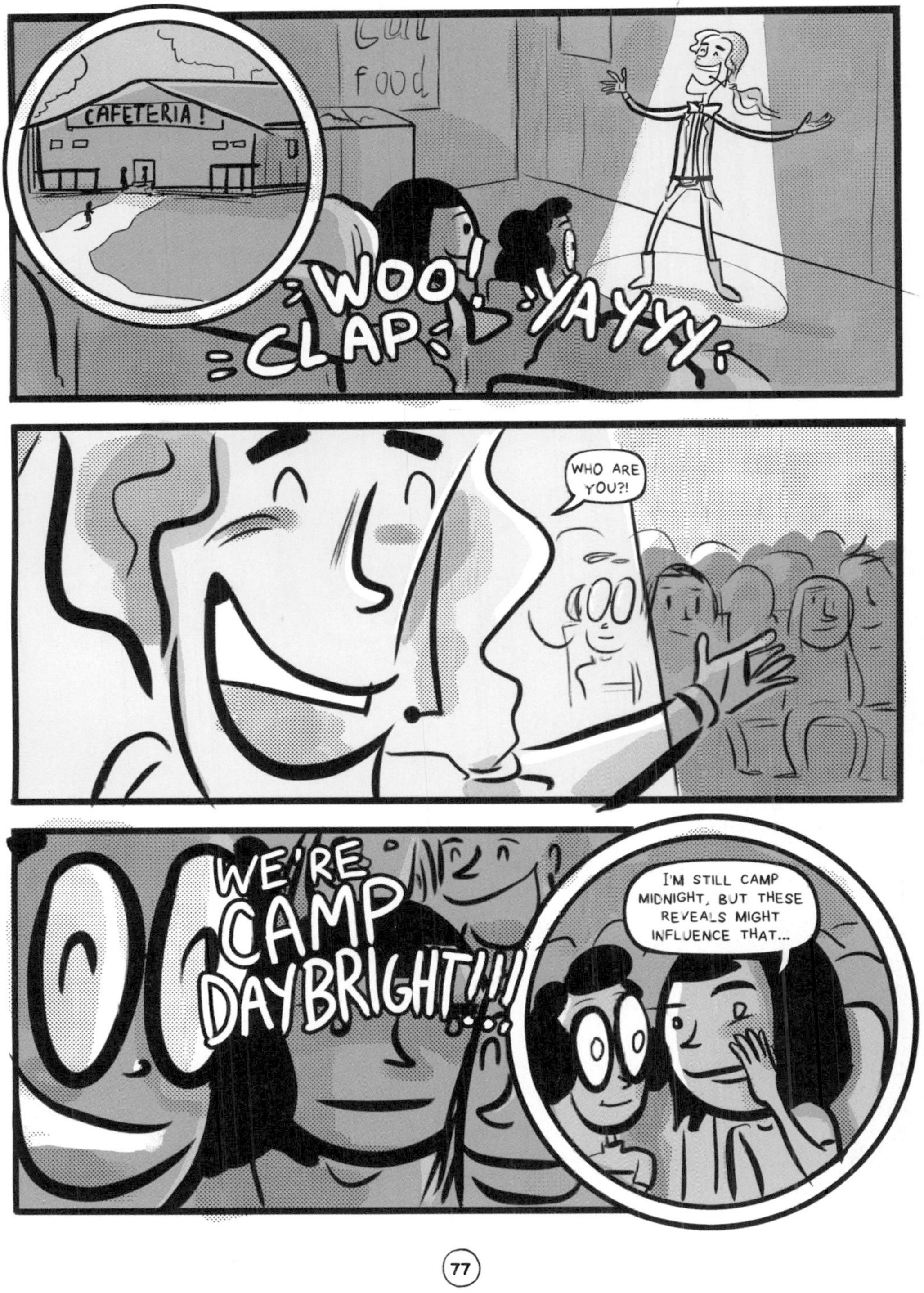
CAFETERIA!
food
WOO!
YAYYY
CLAP
WHO ARE YOU?!
WE'RE CAMP DAYBRIGHT!!!!
I'M STILL CAMP MIDNIGHT, BUT THESE REVEALS MIGHT INFLUENCE THAT...

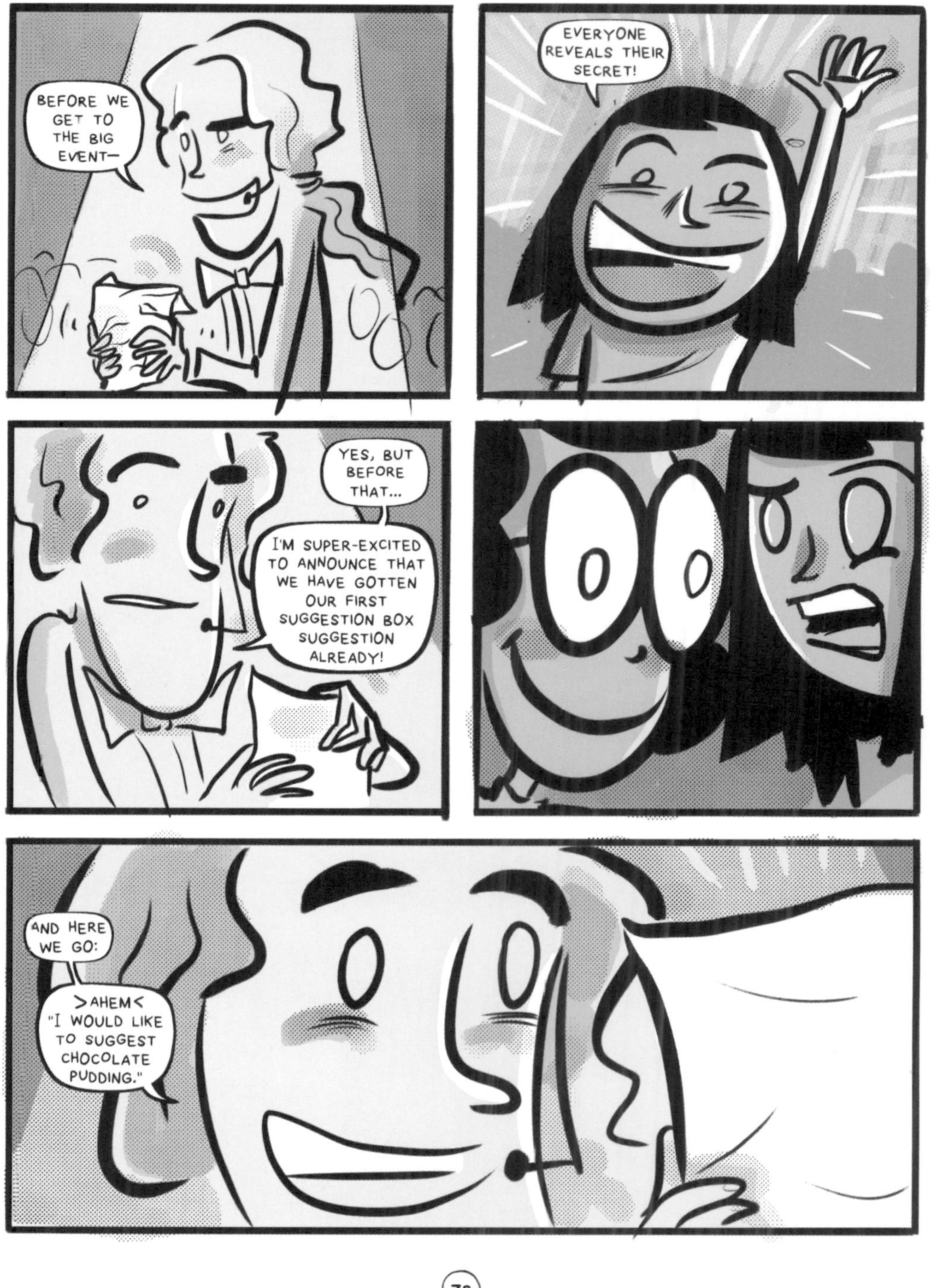
BEFORE WE GET TO THE BIG EVENT—
EVERYONE REVEALS THEIR SECRET!
YES, BUT BEFORE THAT...
I'M SUPER-EXCITED TO ANNOUNCE THAT WE HAVE GOTTEN OUR FIRST SUGGESTION BOX SUGGESTION ALREADY!
AND HERE WE GO:
>AHEM< "I WOULD LIKE TO SUGGEST CHOCOLATE PUDDING."

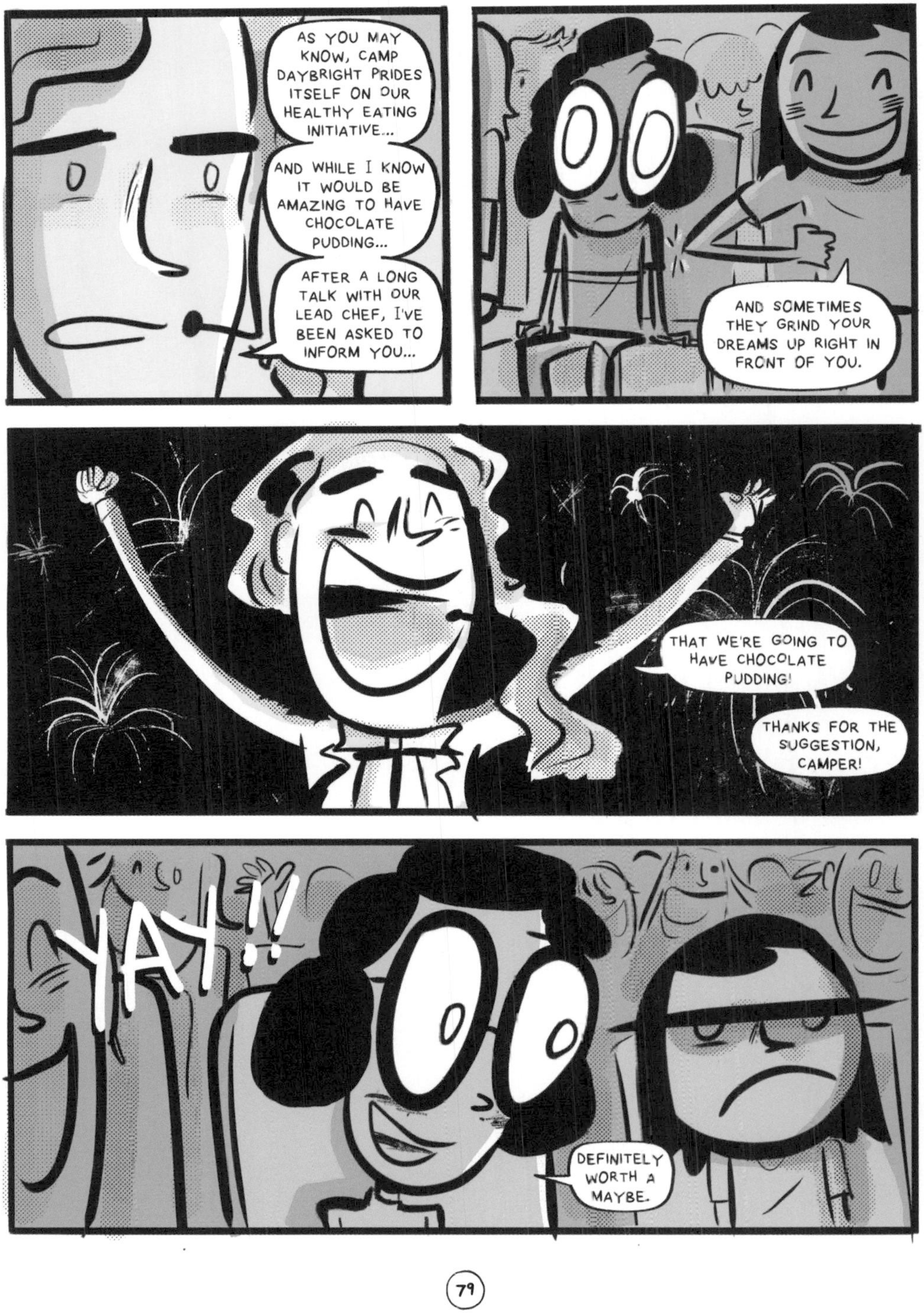

AS YOU MAY KNOW, CAMP DAYBRIGHT PRIDES ITSELF ON OUR HEALTHY EATING INITIATIVE...
AND WHILE I KNOW IT WOULD BE AMAZING TO HAVE CHOCOLATE PUDDING...
AFTER A LONG TALK WITH OUR LEAD CHEF, I'VE BEEN ASKED TO INFORM YOU...
AND SOMETIMES THEY GRIND YOUR DREAMS UP RIGHT IN FRONT OF YOU.
THAT WE'RE GOING TO HAVE CHOCOLATE PUDDING!
THANKS FOR THE SUGGESTION, CAMPER!
YAY!!
DEFINITELY WORTH A MAYBE.

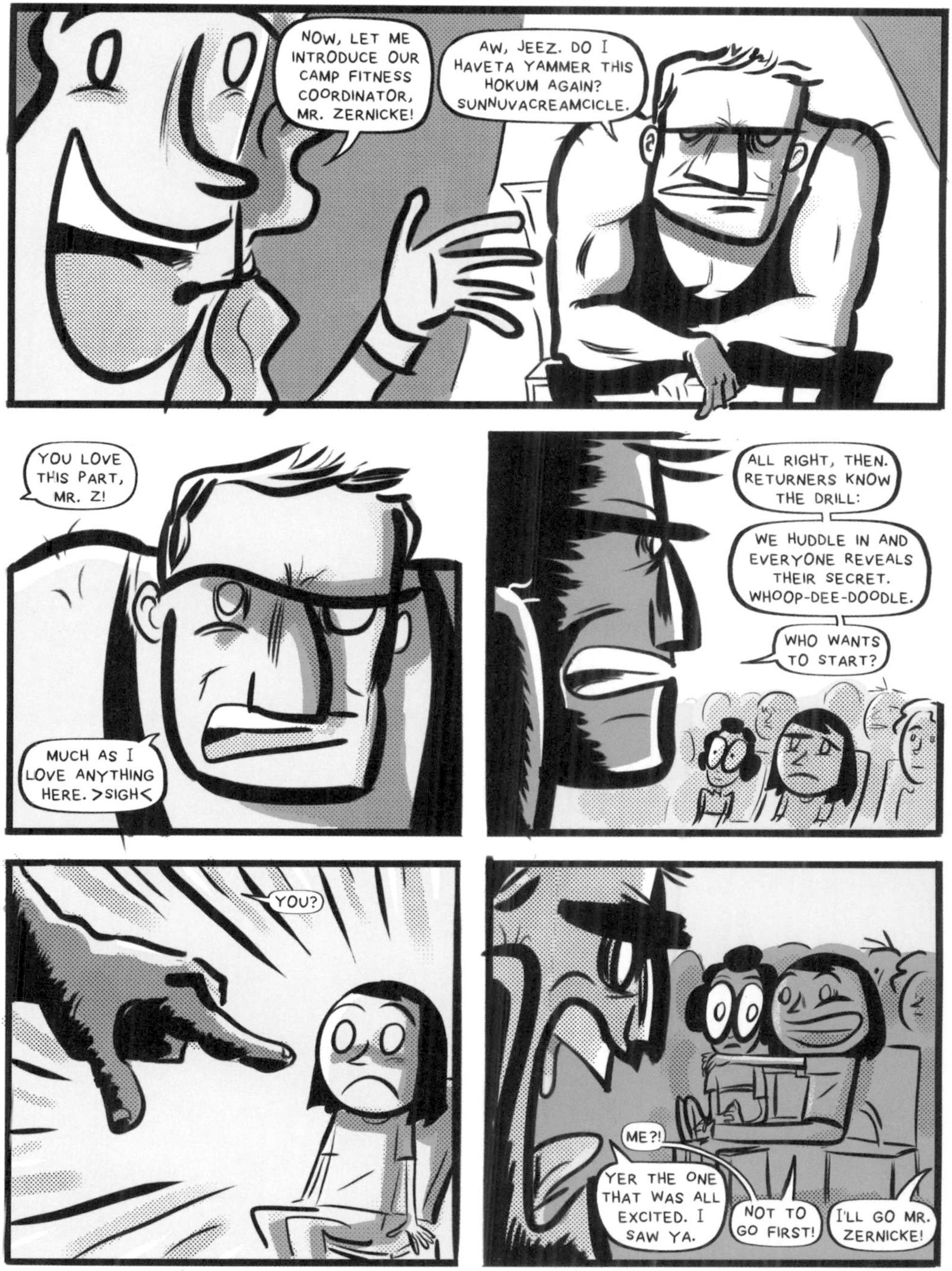
NOW, LET ME INTRODUCE OUR CAMP FITNESS COORDINATOR, MR. ZERNICKE!
AW, JEEZ. DO I HAVETA YAMMER THIS HOKUM AGAIN? SUNNUVACREAMCICLE.
YOU LOVE THIS PART, MR. Z!
MUCH AS I LOVE ANYTHING HERE. >SIGH<
ALL RIGHT, THEN. RETURNERS KNOW THE DRILL:
WE HUDDLE IN AND EVERYONE REVEALS THEIR SECRET. WHOOP-DEE-DOODLE.
WHO WANTS TO START?
YOU?
ME?!
YER THE ONE THAT WAS ALL EXCITED. I SAW YA.
NOT TO GO FIRST!
I'LL GO MR. ZERNICKE!

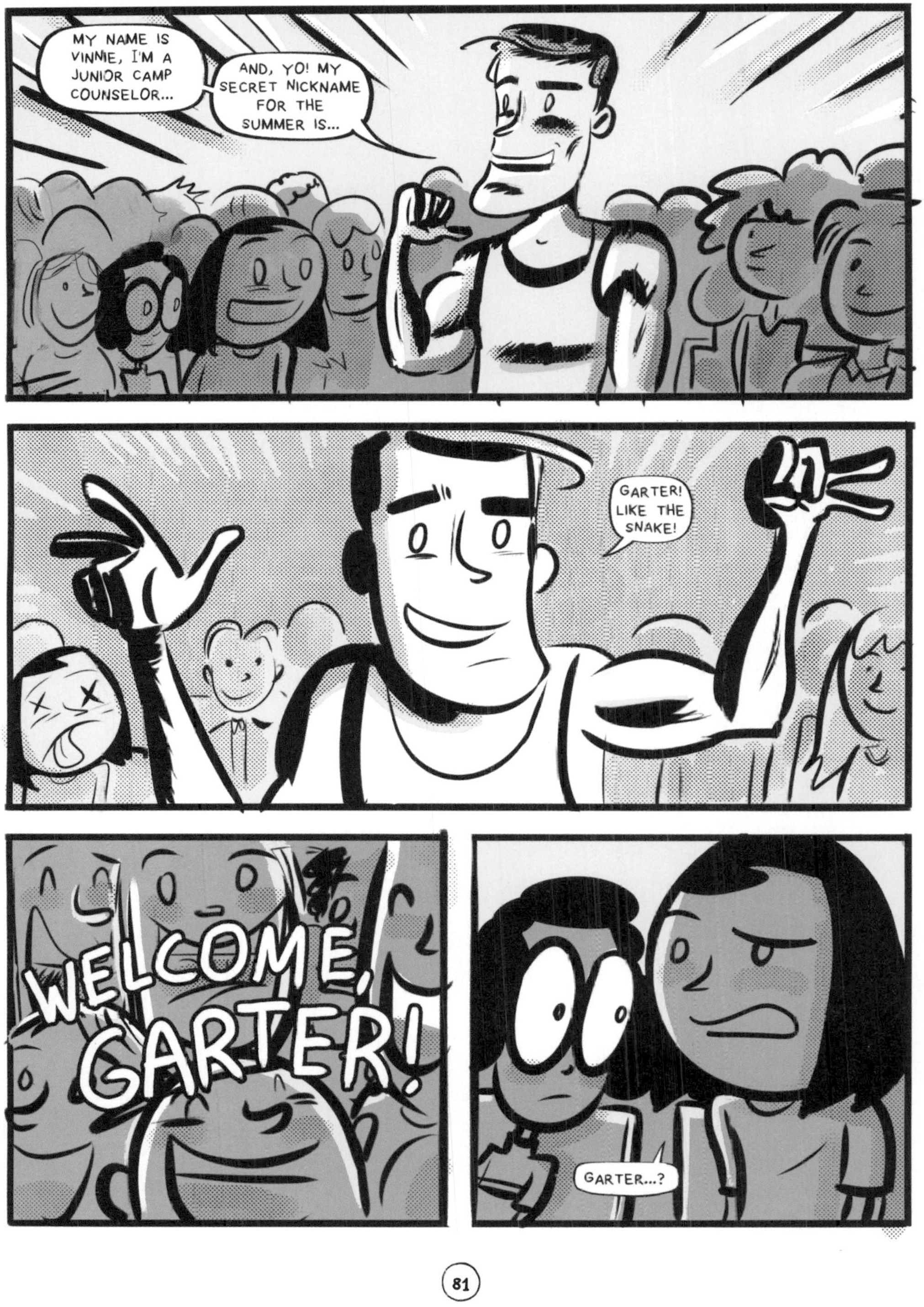
MY NAME IS VINNIE, I'M A JUNIOR CAMP COUNSELOR...
AND, YO! MY SECRET NICKNAME FOR THE SUMMER IS...
GARTER! LIKE THE SNAKE!
WELCOME, GARTER!
GARTER...?

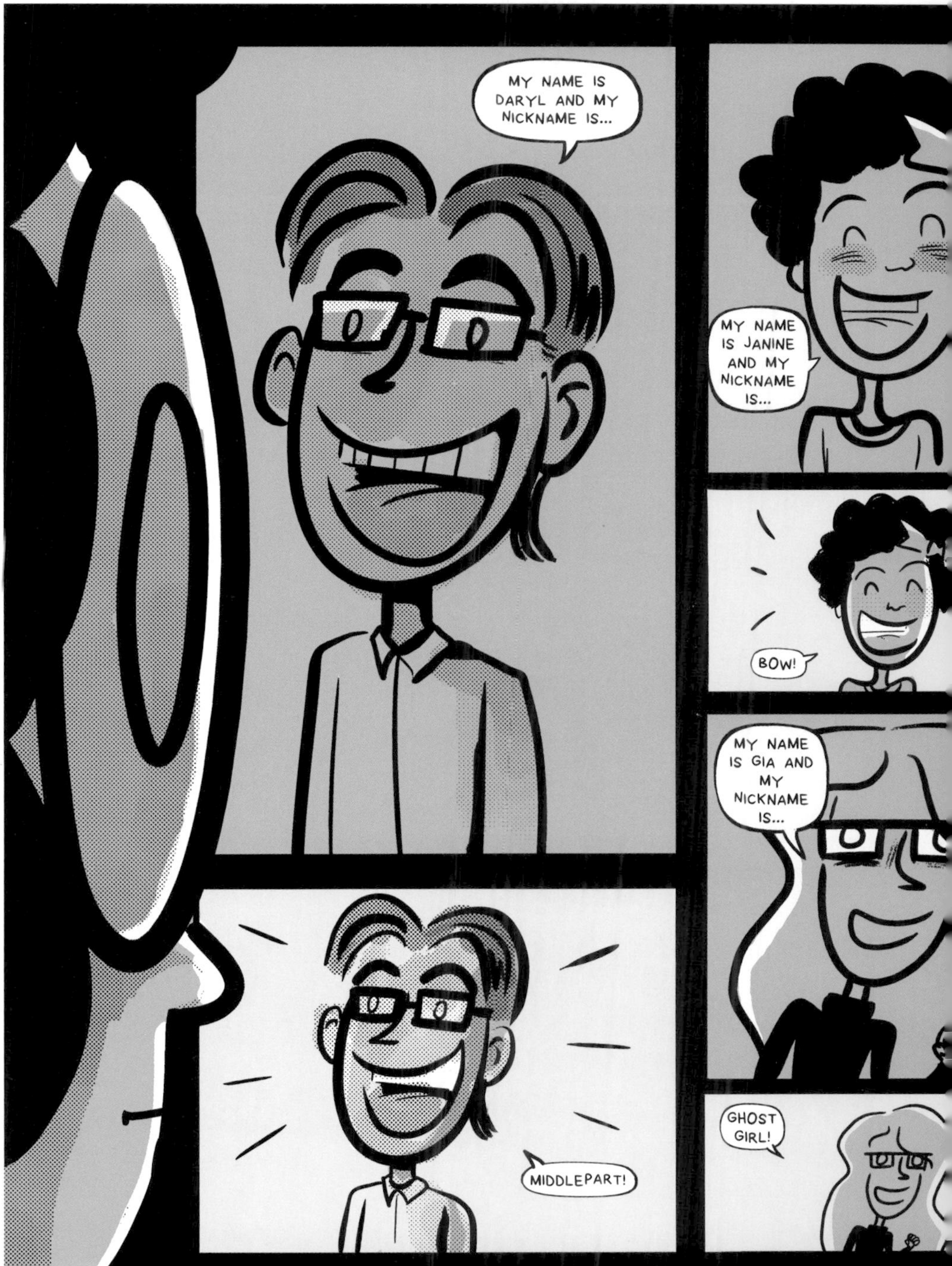

MY NAME IS DARYL AND MY NICKNAME IS...
MIDDLEPART!
MY NAME IS JANINE AND MY NICKNAME IS...
BOW!
MY NAME IS GIA AND MY NICKNAME IS...
GHOST GIRL!

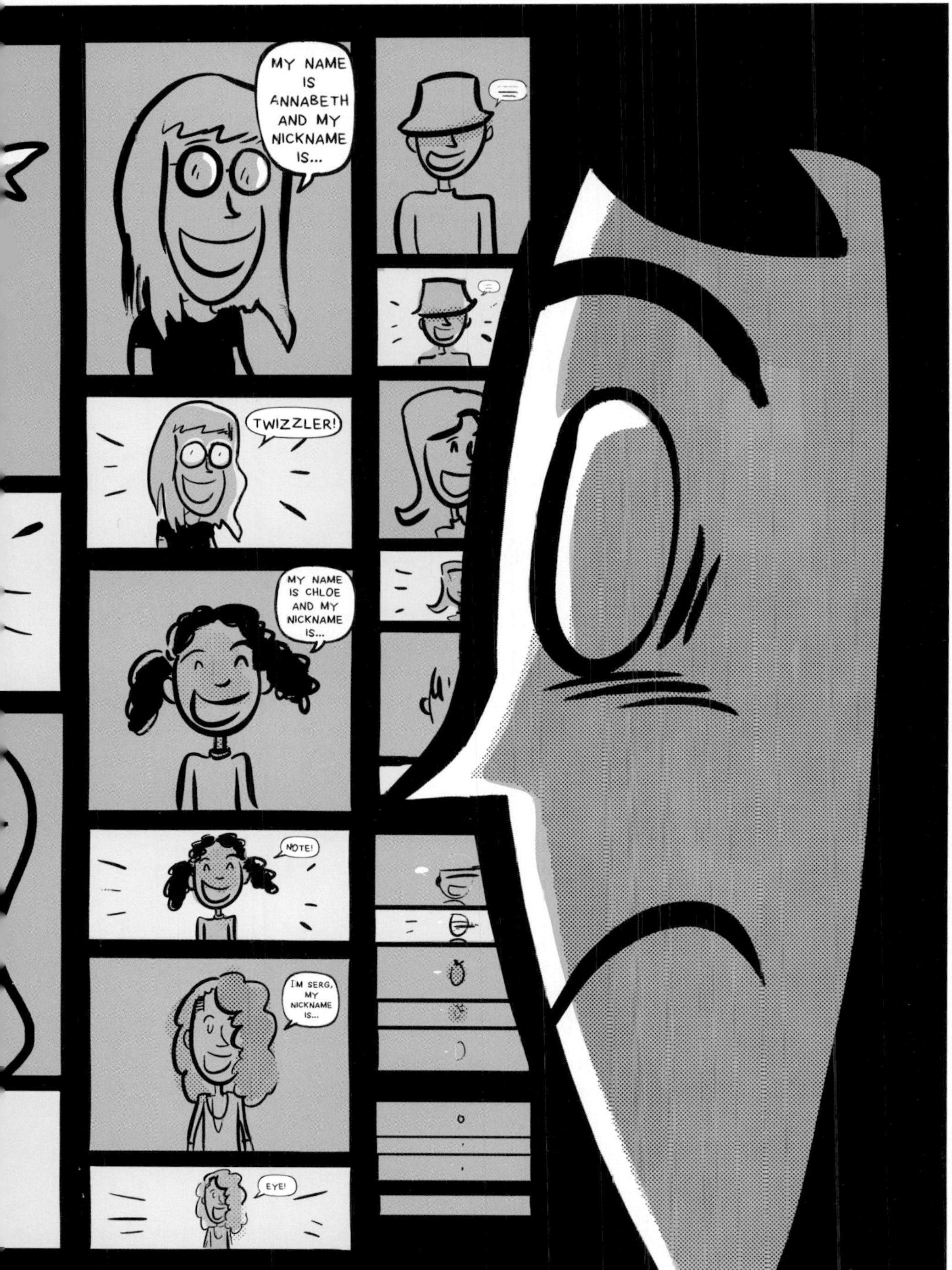
MY NAME IS ANNABETH AND MY NICKNAME IS...
TWIZZLER!
MY NAME IS CHLOE AND MY NICKNAME IS...
NOTE!
I'M SERG, MY NICKNAME IS...
EYE!

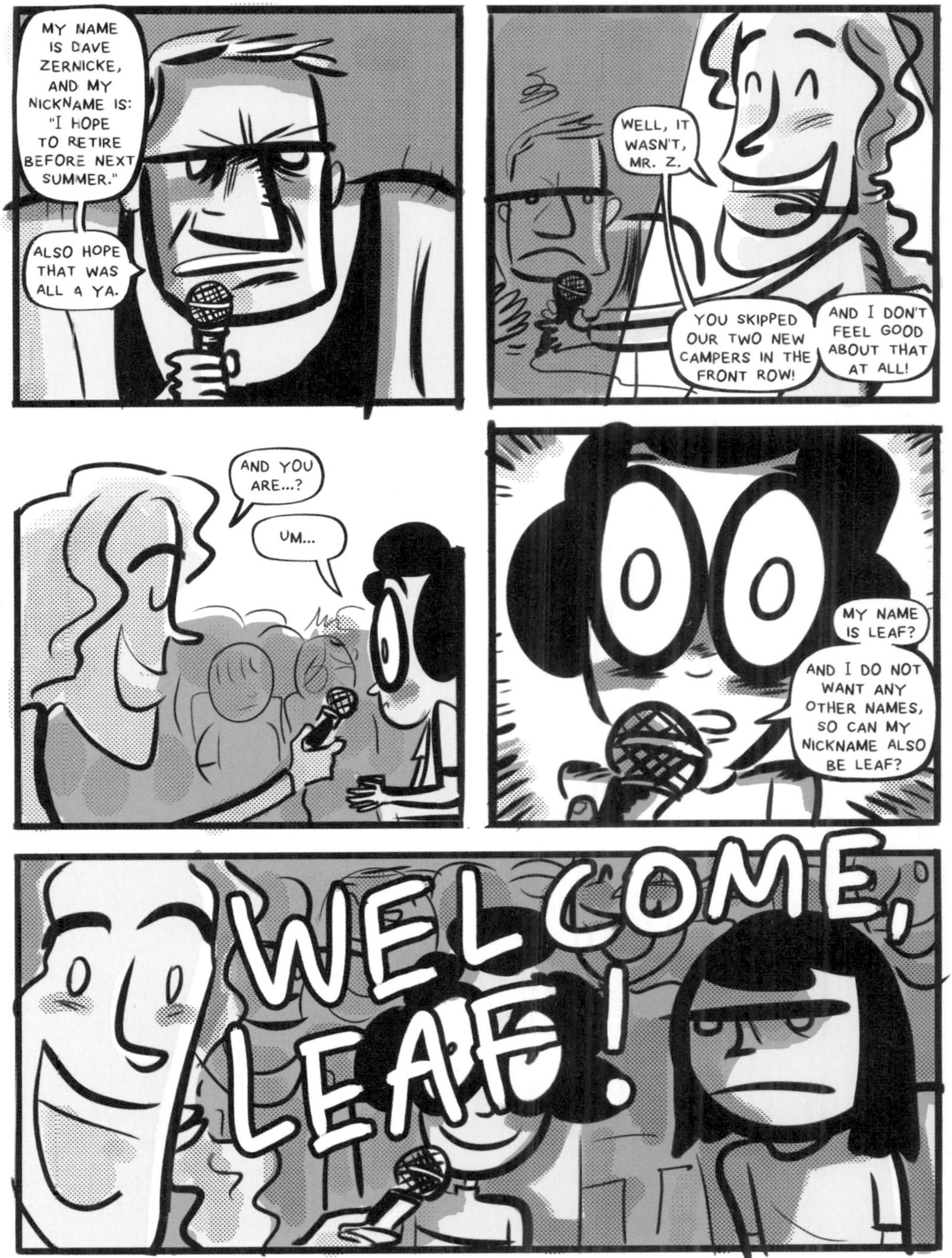
MY NAME IS DAVE ZERNICKE, AND MY NICKNAME IS: "I HOPE TO RETIRE BEFORE NEXT SUMMER."
ALSO HOPE THAT WAS ALL 4 YA.
WELL, IT WASN'T, MR. Z.
YOU SKIPPED OUR TWO NEW CAMPERS IN THE FRONT ROW!
AND I DON'T FEEL GOOD ABOUT THAT AT ALL!
AND YOU ARE...?
UM...
MY NAME IS LEAF?
AND I DO NOT WANT ANY OTHER NAMES, SO CAN MY NICKNAME ALSO BE LEAF?
WELCOME, LEAF!

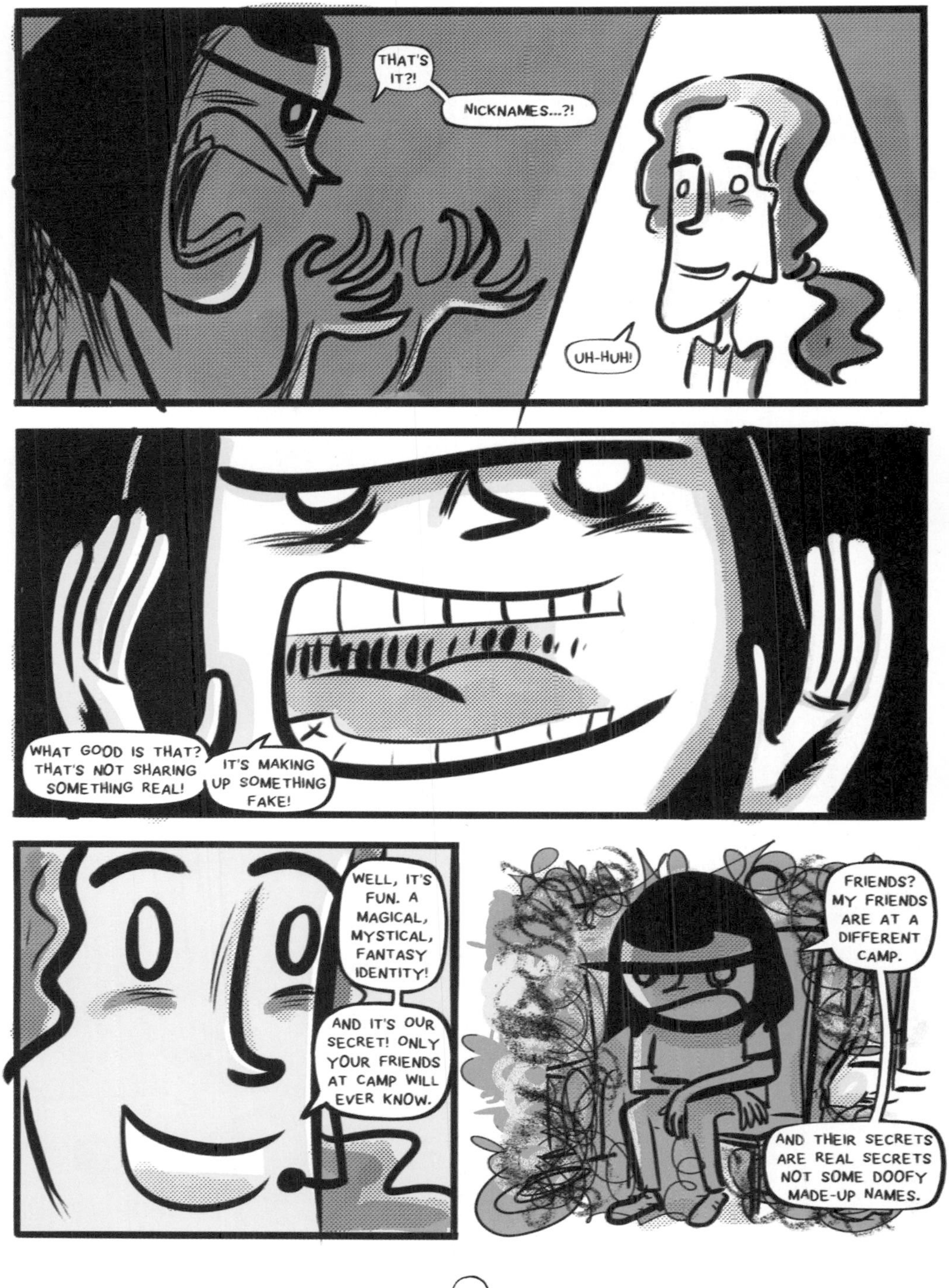
THAT'S IT?!
NICKNAMES...?!
UH-HUH!
WHAT GOOD IS THAT? THAT'S NOT SHARING SOMETHING REAL!
IT'S MAKING UP SOMETHING FAKE!
WELL, IT'S FUN. A MAGICAL, MYSTICAL, FANTASY IDENTITY!
AND IT'S OUR SECRET! ONLY YOUR FRIENDS AT CAMP WILL EVER KNOW.
FRIENDS? MY FRIENDS ARE AT A DIFFERENT CAMP.
AND THEIR SECRETS ARE REAL SECRETS NOT SOME DOOFY MADE-UP NAMES.

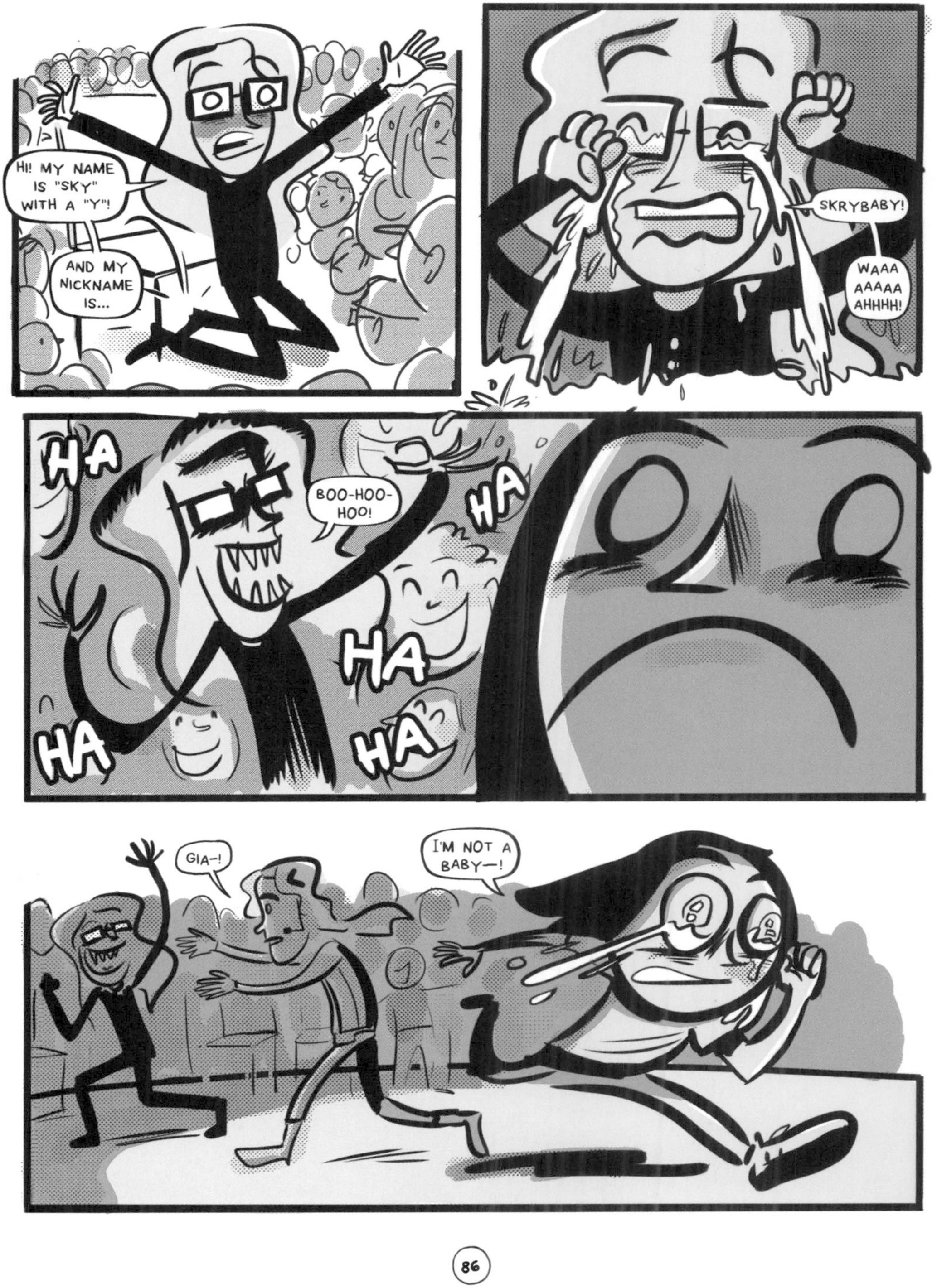

HI! MY NAME IS "SKY" WITH A "Y"!
AND MY NICKNAME IS...
SKRYBABY!
WAAA AAAAA AHHHH!
HA
BOO-HOO-HOO!
HA
HA
HA
HA
GIA-!
I'M NOT A BABY—!

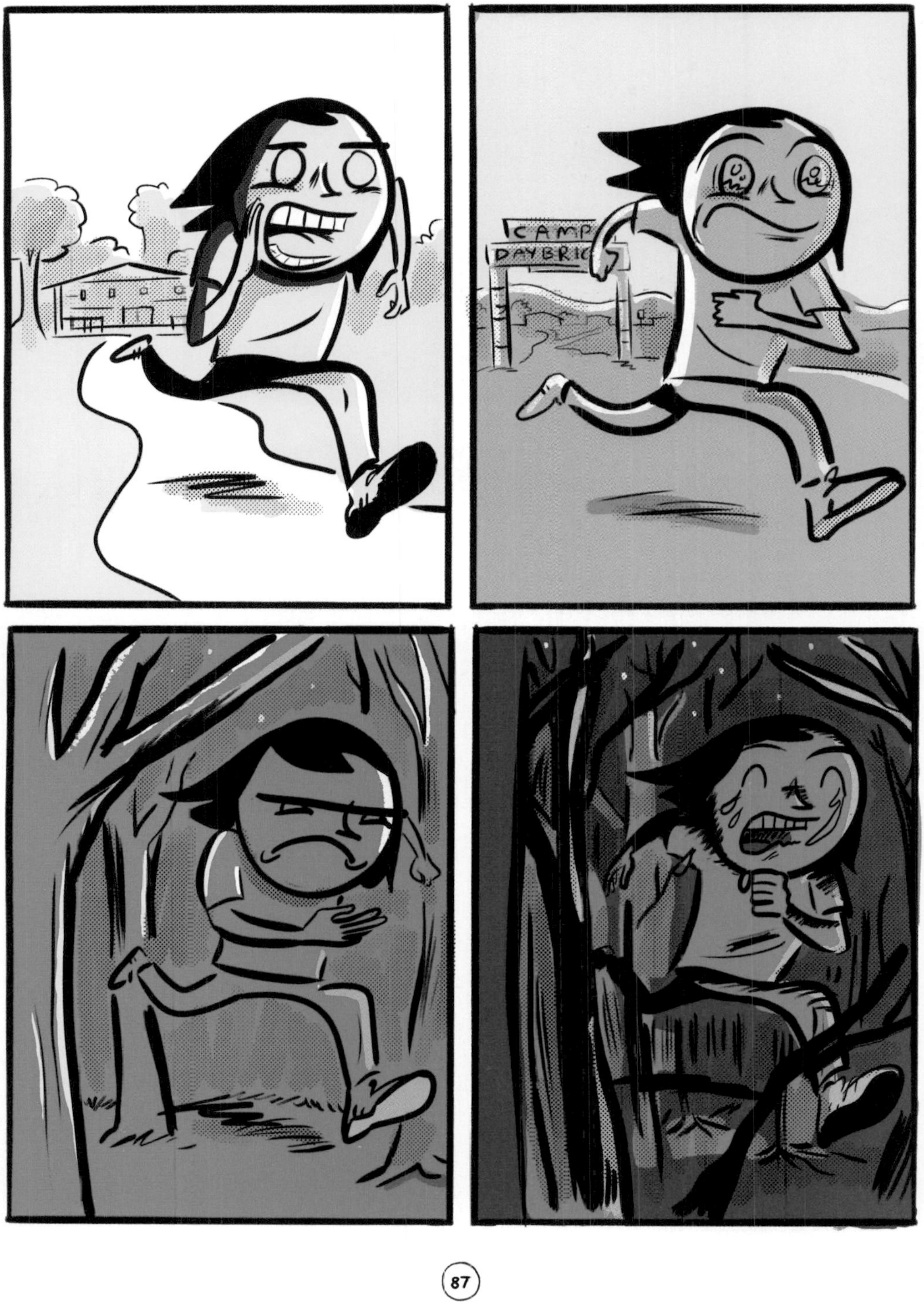
CAMP
DAYBRIG

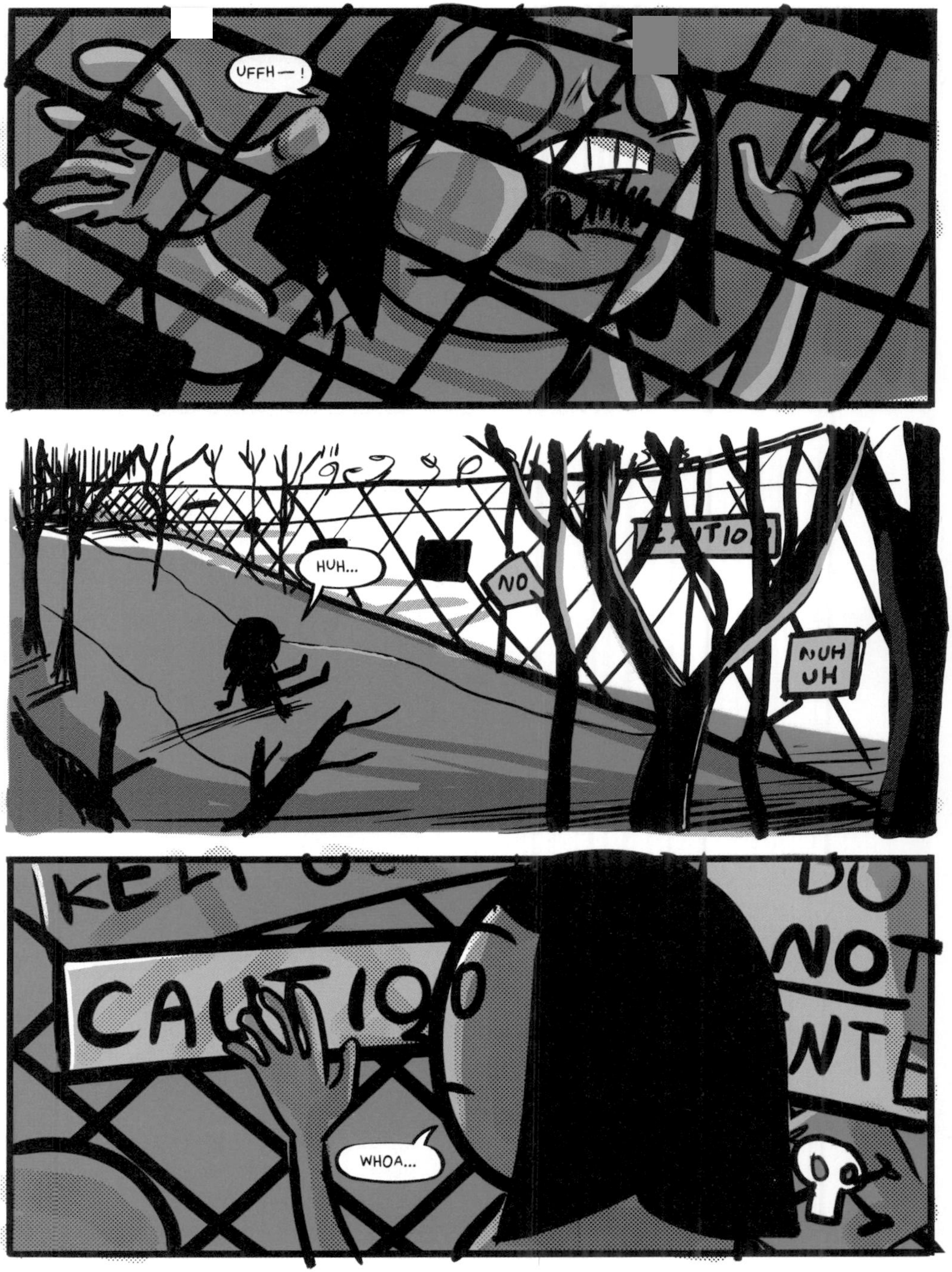
UFFH—!
HUH...
NO
NUH UH
WHOA...

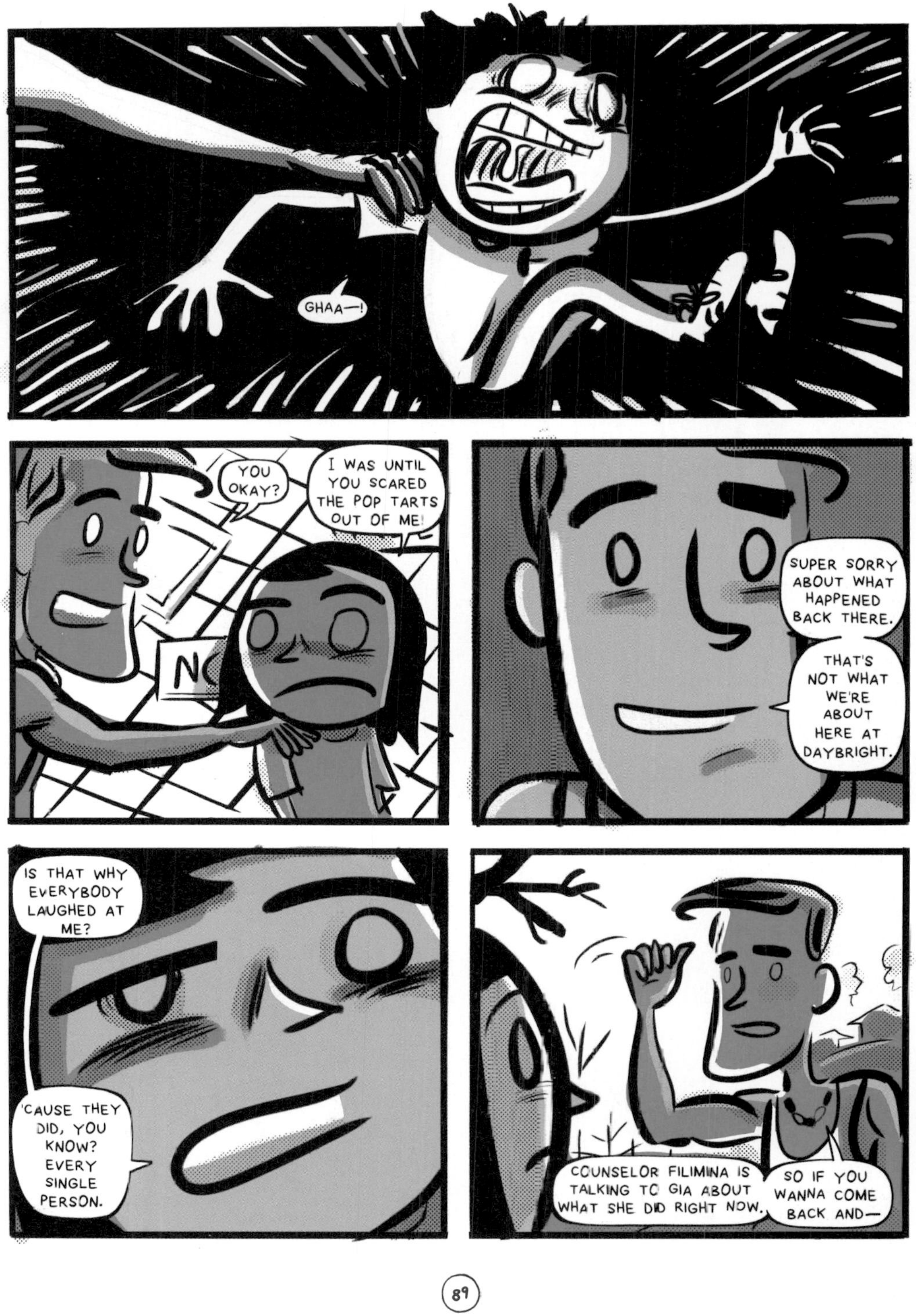

GHAA—!
YOU OKAY?
I WAS UNTIL YOU SCARED THE POP TARTS OUT OF ME!
NO
SUPER SORRY ABOUT WHAT HAPPENED BACK THERE.
THAT'S NOT WHAT WE'RE ABOUT HERE AT DAYBRIGHT.
IS THAT WHY EVERYBODY LAUGHED AT ME?
'CAUSE THEY DID, YOU KNOW? EVERY SINGLE PERSON.
COUNSELOR FILIMINA IS TALKING TO GIA ABOUT WHAT SHE DID RIGHT NOW.
SO IF YOU WANNA COME BACK AND—

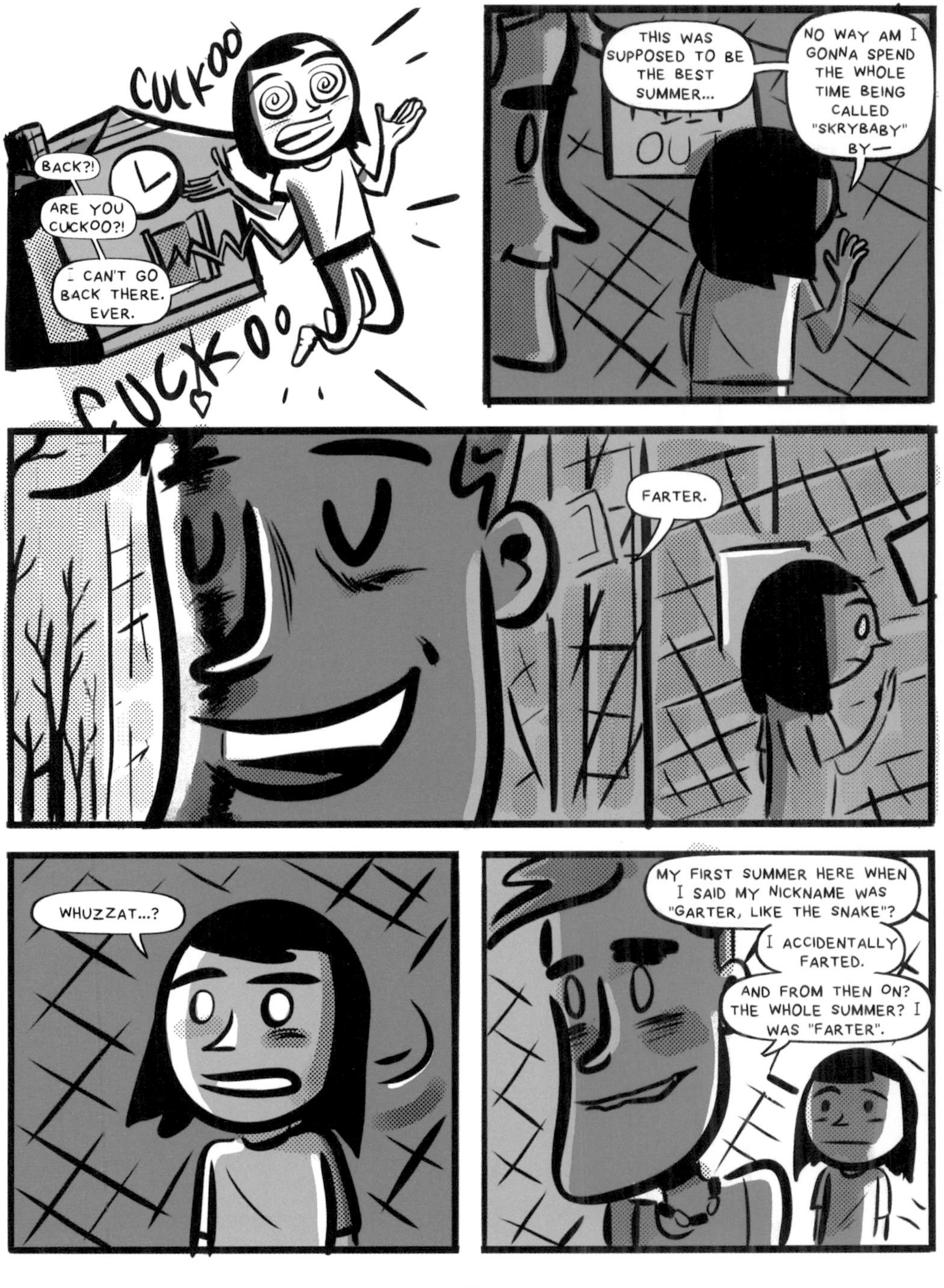
CUCKOO
BACK?!
ARE YOU CUCKOO?!
I CAN'T GO BACK THERE. EVER.
CUCKOO
THIS WAS SUPPOSED TO BE THE BEST SUMMER...
NO WAY AM I GONNA SPEND THE WHOLE TIME BEING CALLED "SKRYBABY" BY—
FARTER.
WHUZZAT...?
MY FIRST SUMMER HERE WHEN I SAID MY NICKNAME WAS "GARTER, LIKE THE SNAKE"?
I ACCIDENTALLY FARTED.
AND FROM THEN ON? THE WHOLE SUMMER? I WAS "FARTER".

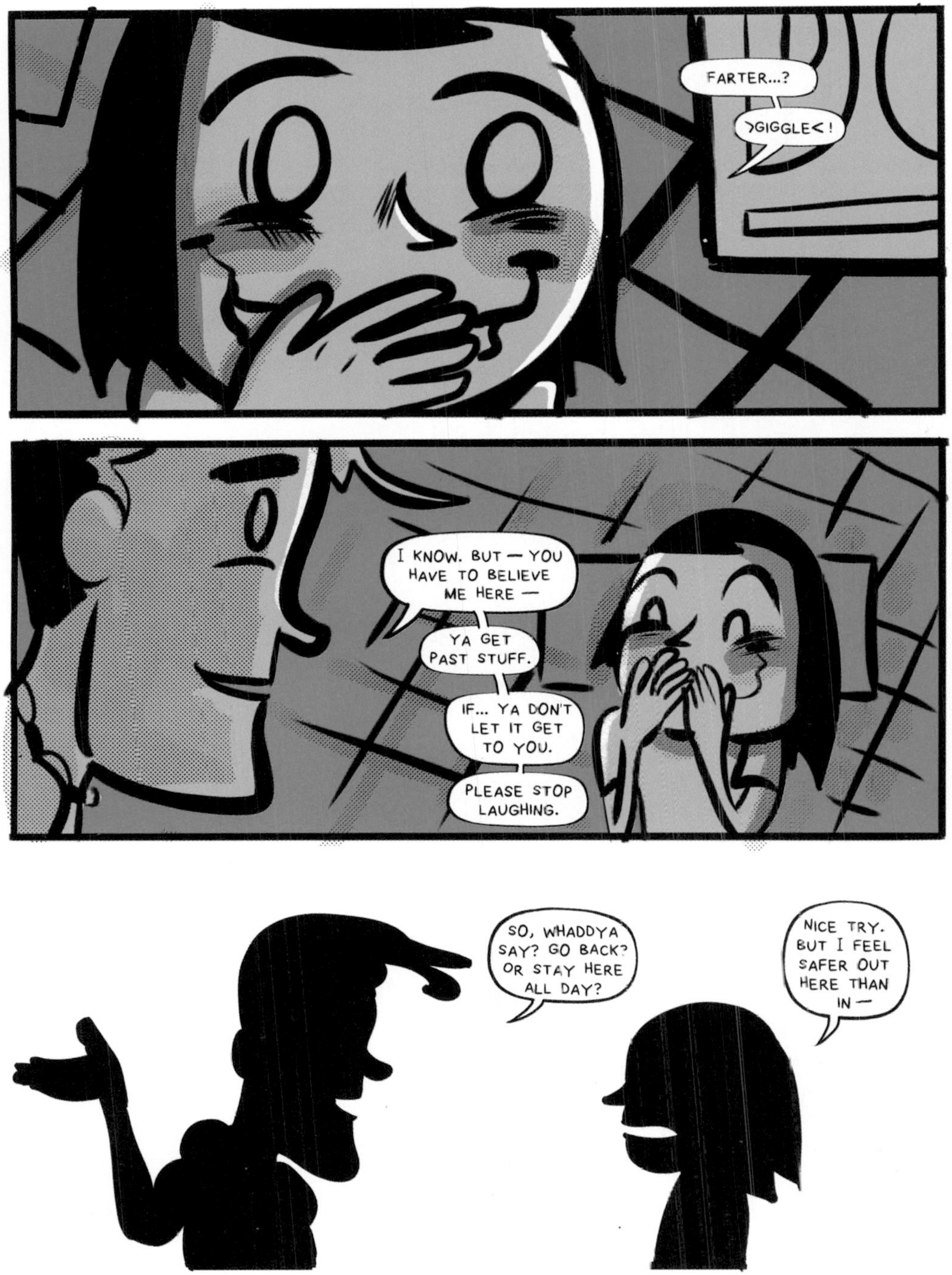
FARTER...?
>GIGGLE<!
I KNOW. BUT — YOU HAVE TO BELIEVE ME HERE —
YA GET PAST STUFF.
IF... YA DON'T LET IT GET TO YOU.
PLEASE STOP LAUGHING.
SO, WHADDYA SAY? GO BACK? OR STAY HERE ALL DAY?
NICE TRY. BUT I FEEL SAFER OUT HERE THAN IN —

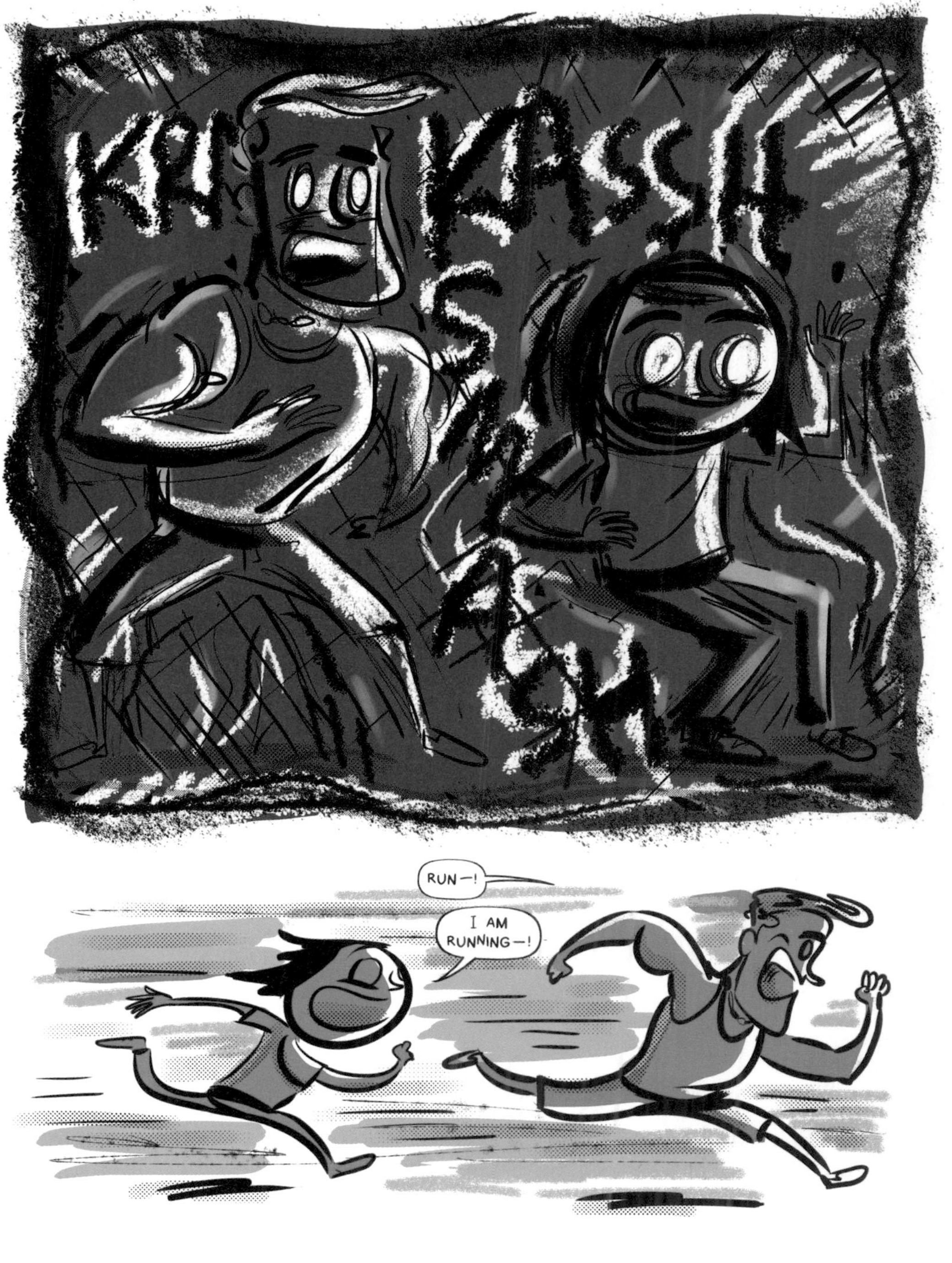
RUN—!
I AM RUNNING—!

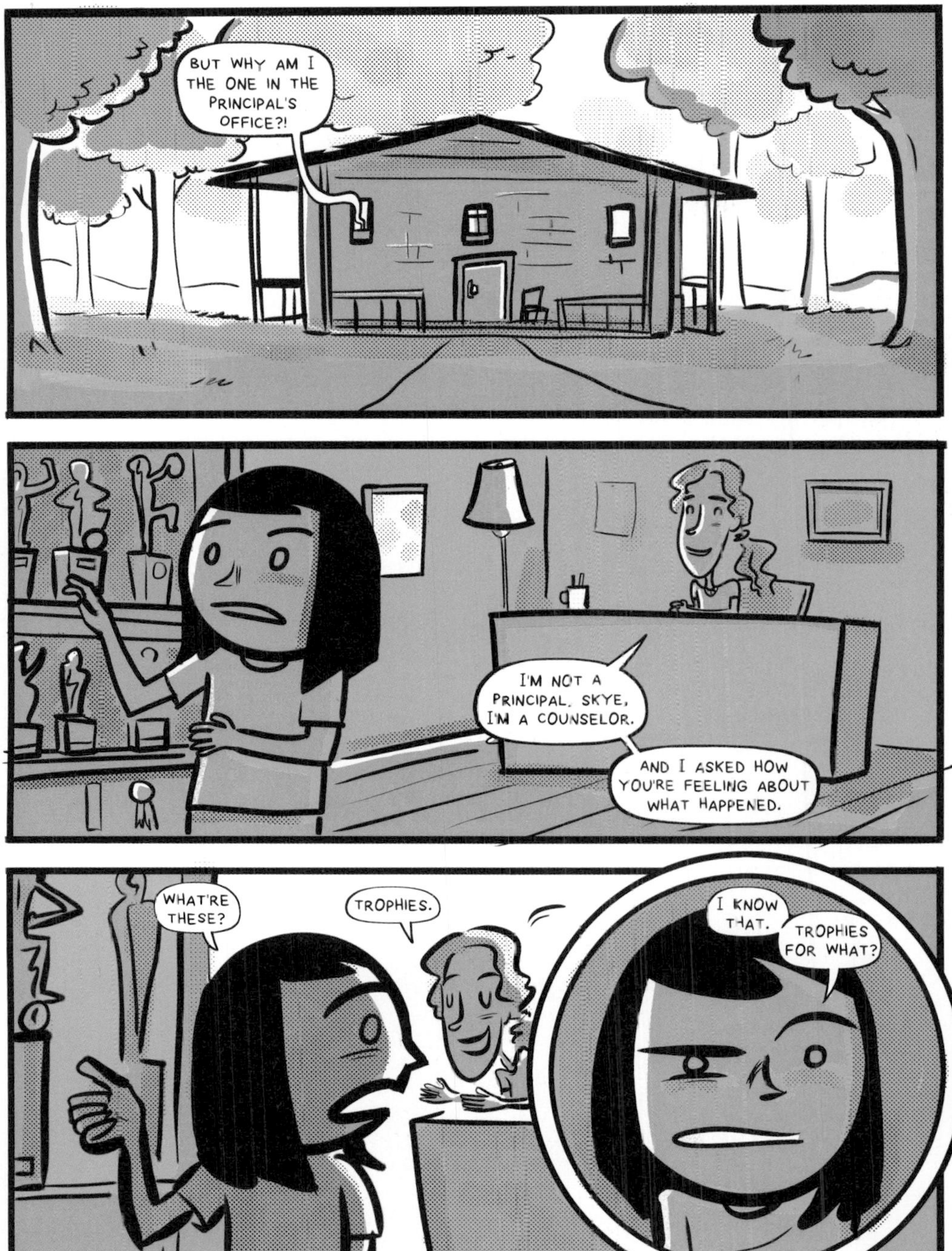

BUT WHY AM I THE ONE IN THE PRINCIPAL'S OFFICE?!
I'M NOT A PRINCIPAL, SKYE, I'M A COUNSELOR.
AND I ASKED HOW YOU'RE FEELING ABOUT WHAT HAPPENED.
WHAT'RE THESE?
TROPHIES.
I KNOW THAT.
TROPHIES FOR WHAT?

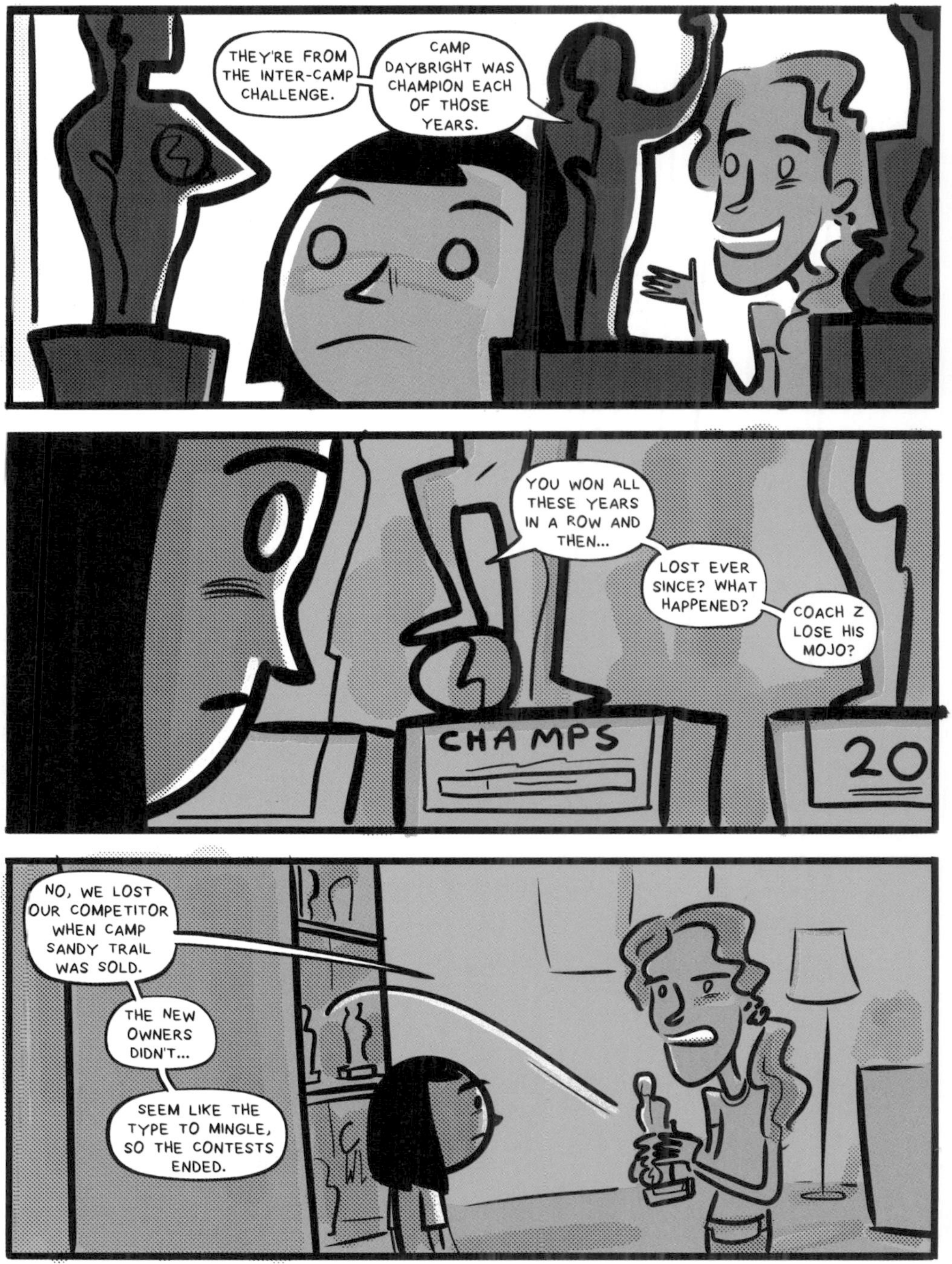
THEY'RE FROM THE INTER-CAMP CHALLENGE.
CAMP DAYBRIGHT WAS CHAMPION EACH OF THOSE YEARS.
YOU WON ALL THESE YEARS IN A ROW AND THEN...
LOST EVER SINCE? WHAT HAPPENED?
COACH Z LOSE HIS MOJO?
CHAMPS
20
NO, WE LOST OUR COMPETITOR WHEN CAMP SANDY TRAIL WAS SOLD.
THE NEW OWNERS DIDN'T...
SEEM LIKE THE TYPE TO MINGLE, SO THE CONTESTS ENDED.

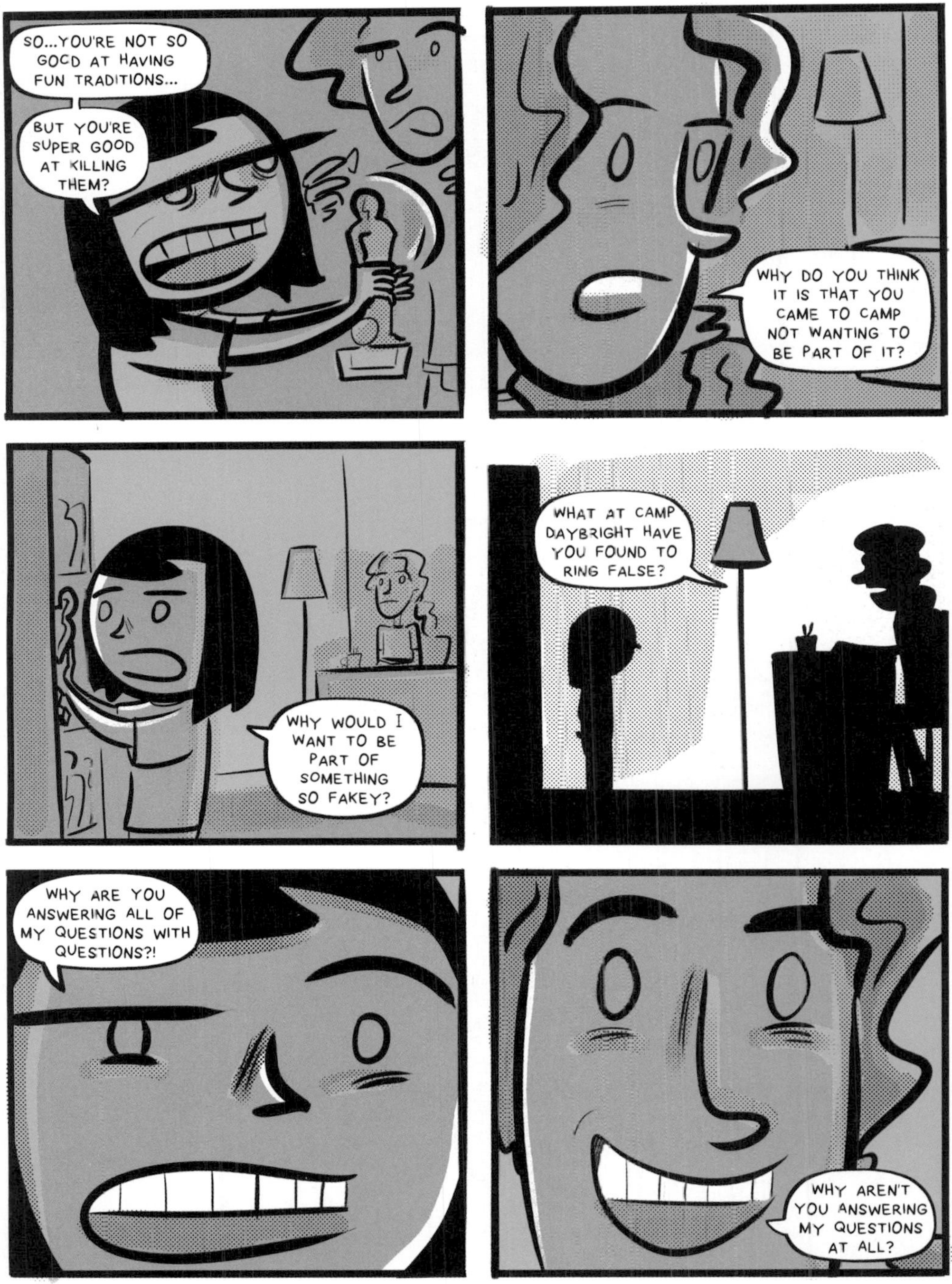
SO...YOU'RE NOT SO GOOD AT HAVING FUN TRADITIONS...
BUT YOU'RE SUPER GOOD AT KILLING THEM?
WHY DO YOU THINK IT IS THAT YOU CAME TO CAMP NOT WANTING TO BE PART OF IT?
WHY WOULD I WANT TO BE PART OF SOMETHING SO FAKEY?
WHAT AT CAMP DAYBRIGHT HAVE YOU FOUND TO RING FALSE?
WHY ARE YOU ANSWERING ALL OF MY QUESTIONS WITH QUESTIONS?!
WHY AREN'T YOU ANSWERING MY QUESTIONS AT ALL?

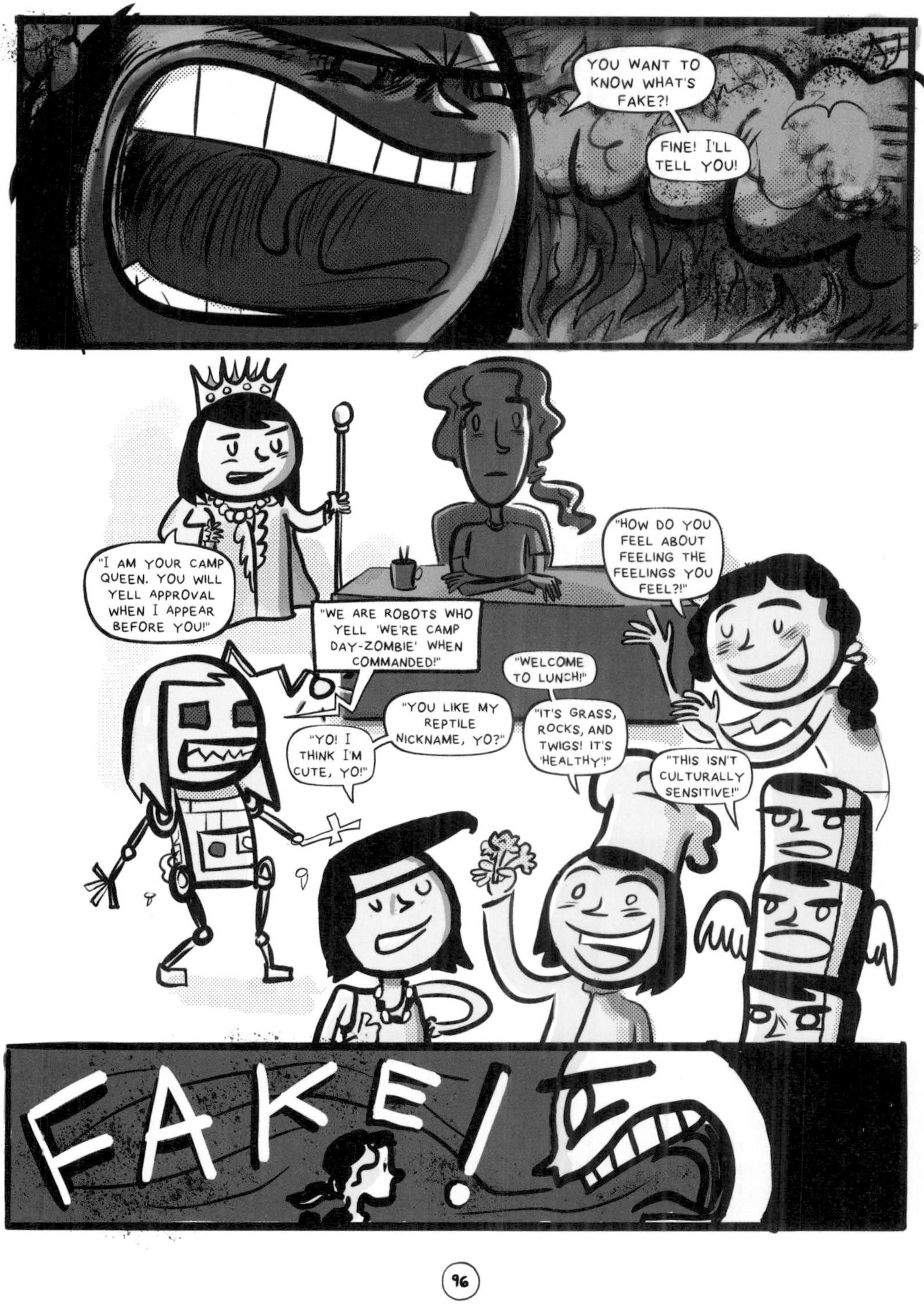
YOU WANT TO KNOW WHAT'S FAKE?!
FINE! I'LL TELL YOU!
"I AM YOUR CAMP QUEEN. YOU WILL YELL APPROVAL WHEN I APPEAR BEFORE YOU!"
"WE ARE ROBOTS WHO YELL 'WE'RE CAMP DAY-ZOMBIE' WHEN COMMANDED!"
"HOW DO YOU FEEL ABOUT FEELING THE FEELINGS YOU FEEL?!"
"WELCOME TO LUNCH!"
"YOU LIKE MY REPTILE NICKNAME, YO?"
"YO! I THINK I'M CUTE, YO!"
"IT'S GRASS, ROCKS, AND TWIGS! IT'S 'HEALTHY'!"
"THIS ISN'T CULTURALLY SENSITIVE!"
FAKE!

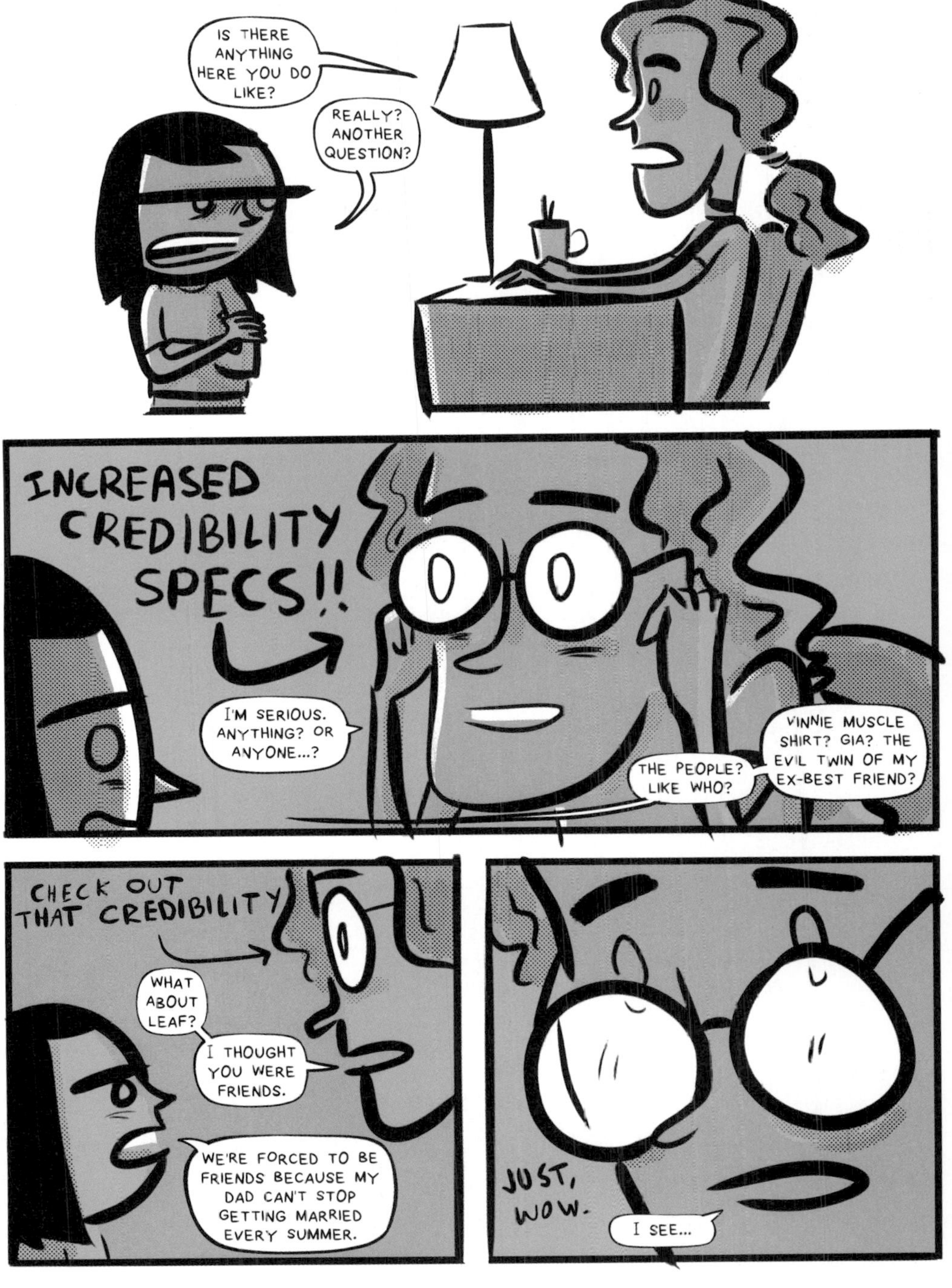
IS THERE ANYTHING HERE YOU DO LIKE?
REALLY? ANOTHER QUESTION?
INCREASED CREDIBILITY SPECS!!
I'M SERIOUS. ANYTHING? OR ANYONE...?
THE PEOPLE? LIKE WHO?
VINNIE MUSCLE SHIRT? GIA? THE EVIL TWIN OF MY EX-BEST FRIEND?
CHECK OUT THAT CREDIBILITY
WHAT ABOUT LEAF?
I THOUGHT YOU WERE FRIENDS.
WE'RE FORCED TO BE FRIENDS BECAUSE MY DAD CAN'T STOP GETTING MARRIED EVERY SUMMER.
JUST, WOW.
I SEE...

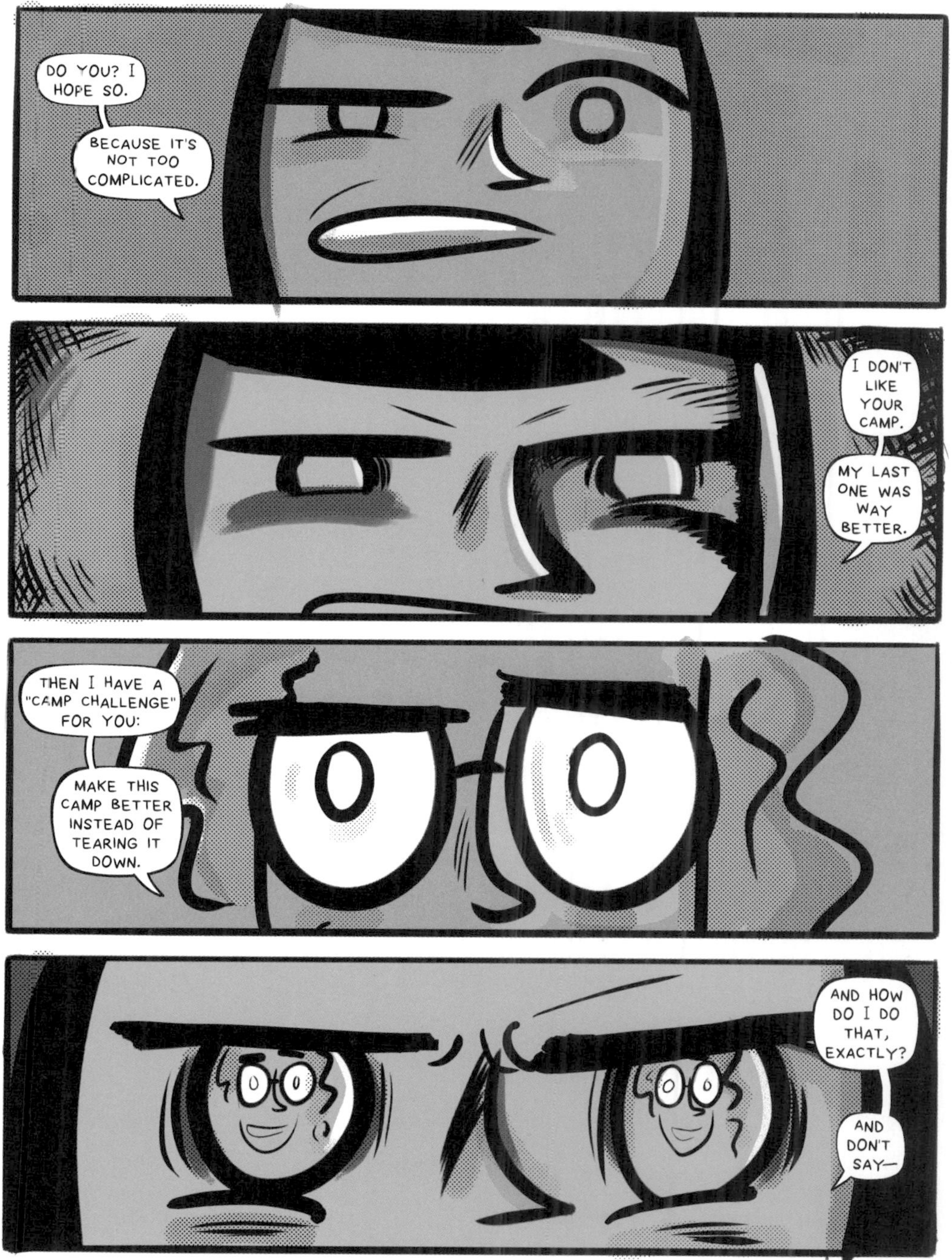
DO YOU? I HOPE SO.
BECAUSE IT'S NOT TOO COMPLICATED.
I DON'T LIKE YOUR CAMP.
MY LAST ONE WAS WAY BETTER.
THEN I HAVE A "CAMP CHALLENGE" FOR YOU:
MAKE THIS CAMP BETTER INSTEAD OF TEARING IT DOWN.
AND HOW DO I DO THAT, EXACTLY?
AND DON'T SAY—

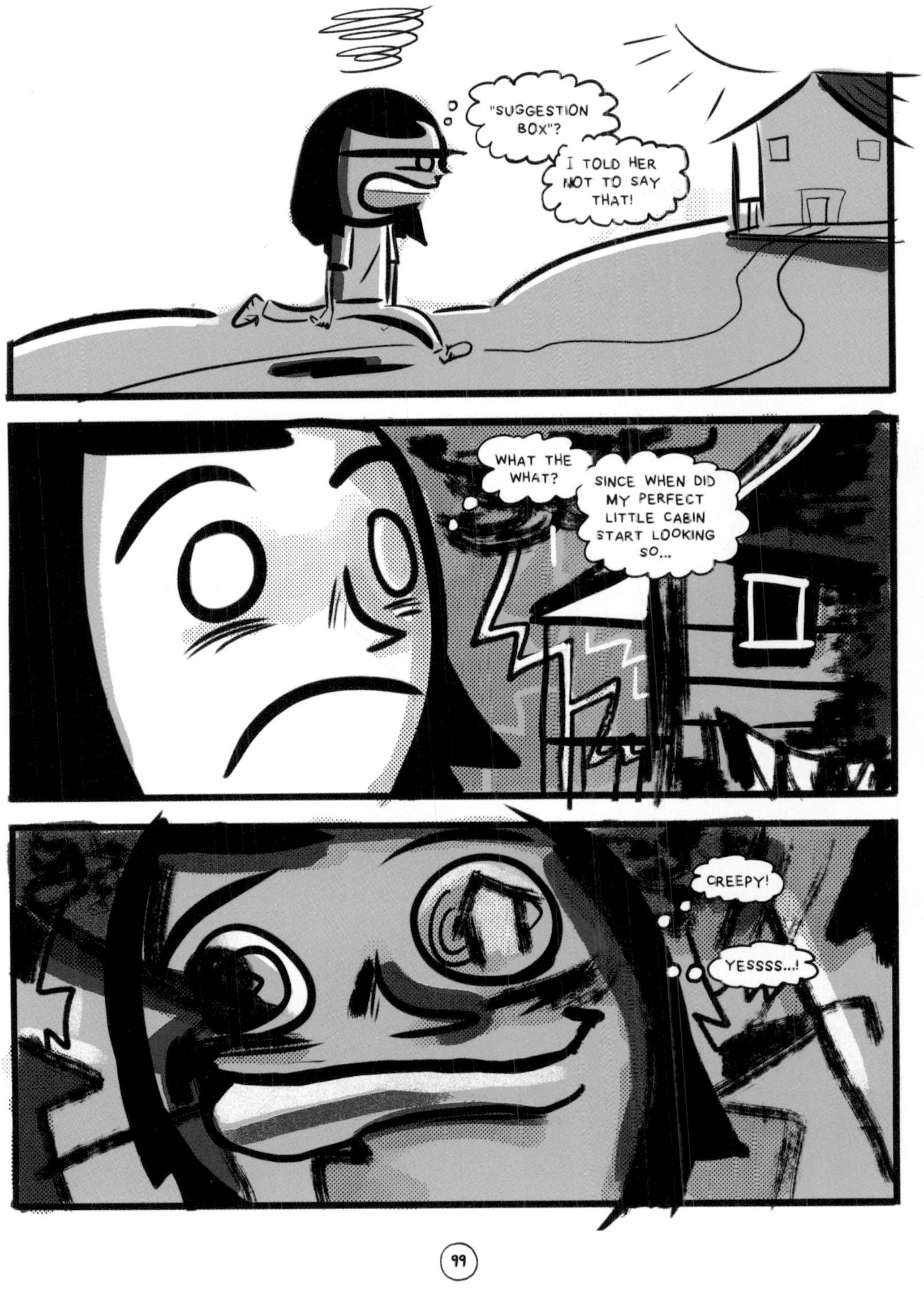
"SUGGESTION BOX"?
I TOLD HER NOT TO SAY THAT!
WHAT THE WHAT?
SINCE WHEN DID MY PERFECT LITTLE CABIN START LOOKING SO...
CREEPY!
YESSSS...!

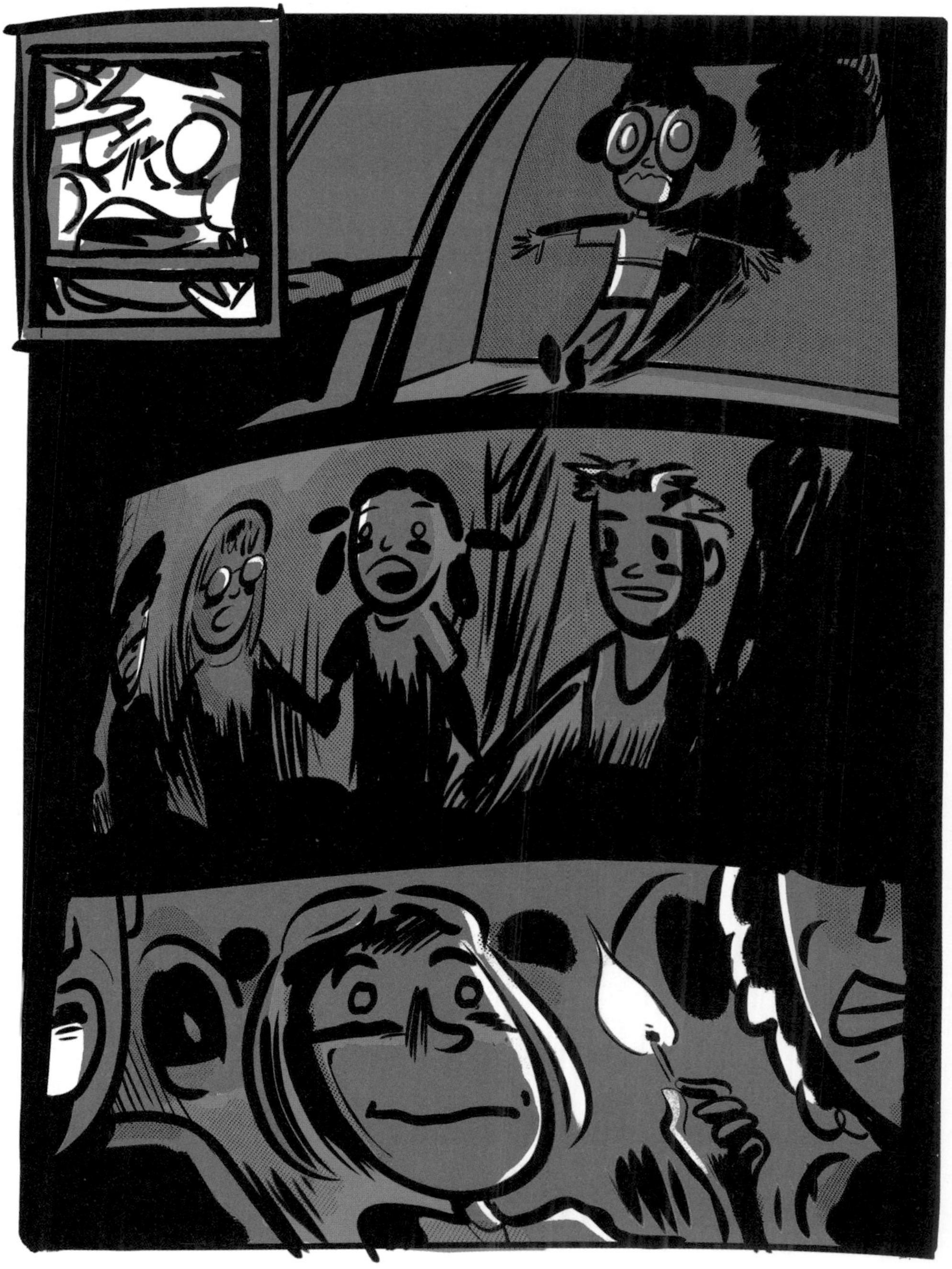

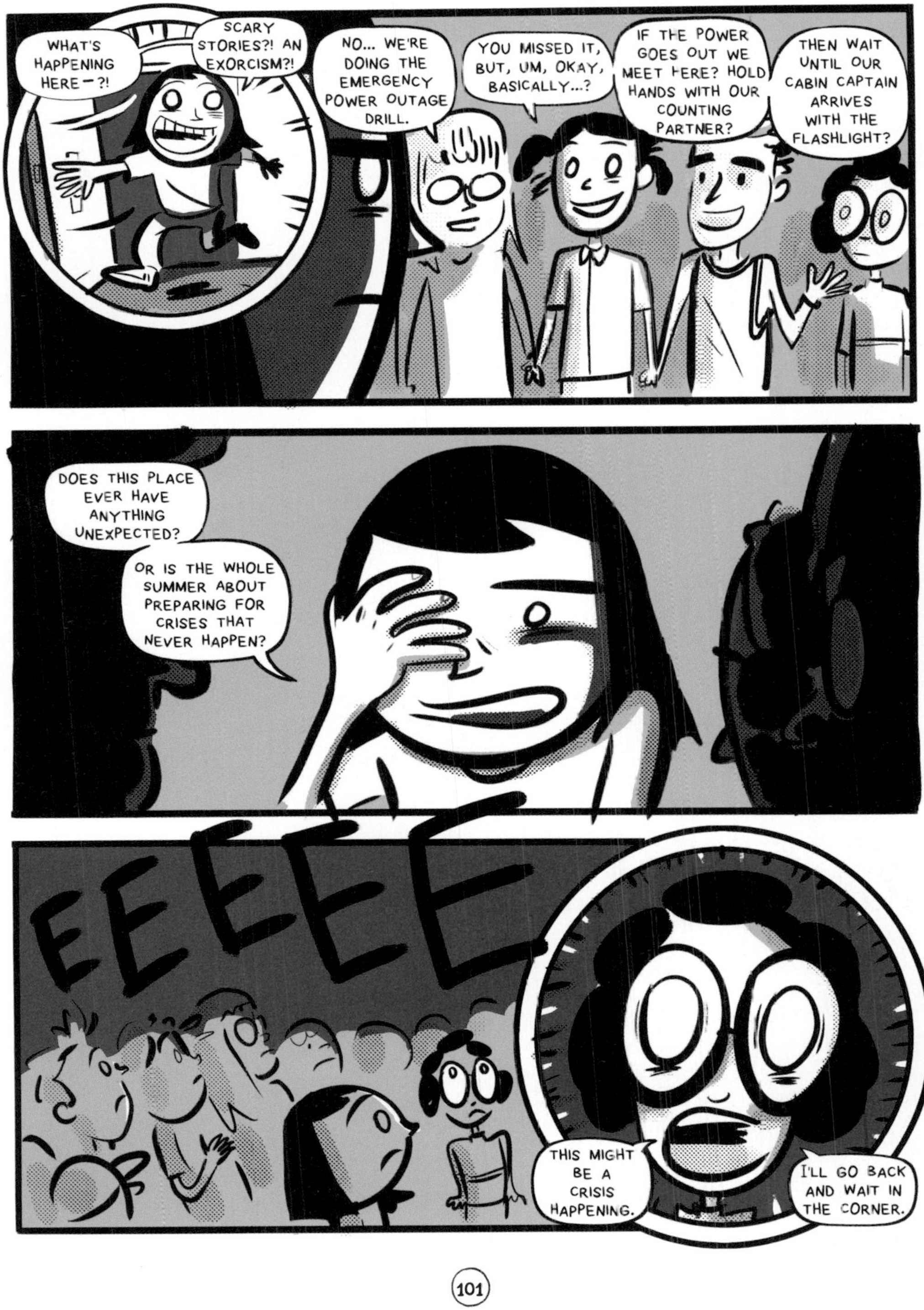
WHAT'S HAPPENING HERE—?!
SCARY STORIES?! AN EXORCISM?!
NO... WE'RE DOING THE EMERGENCY POWER OUTAGE DRILL.
YOU MISSED IT, BUT, UM, OKAY, BASICALLY...?
IF THE POWER GOES OUT WE MEET HERE? HOLD HANDS WITH OUR COUNTING PARTNER?
THEN WAIT UNTIL OUR CABIN CAPTAIN ARRIVES WITH THE FLASHLIGHT?
DOES THIS PLACE EVER HAVE ANYTHING UNEXPECTED?
OR IS THE WHOLE SUMMER ABOUT PREPARING FOR CRISES THAT NEVER HAPPEN?
EEEEE
THIS MIGHT BE A CRISIS HAPPENING.
I'LL GO BACK AND WAIT IN THE CORNER.

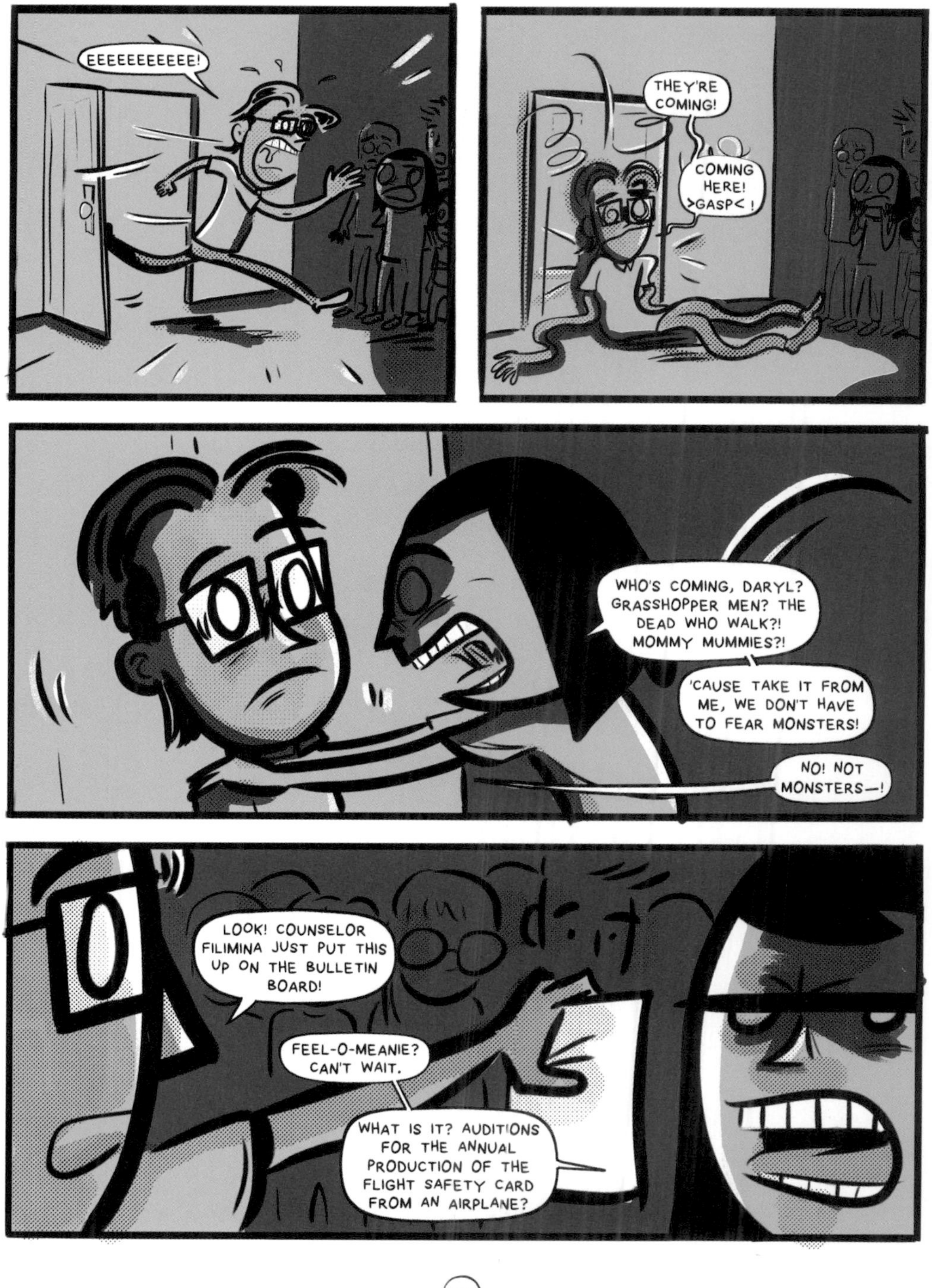
EEEEEEEEEEE!
THEY'RE COMING!
COMING HERE! >GASP< !
WHO'S COMING, DARYL? GRASSHOPPER MEN? THE DEAD WHO WALK?! MOMMY MUMMIES?!
'CAUSE TAKE IT FROM ME, WE DON'T HAVE TO FEAR MONSTERS!
NO! NOT MONSTERS—!
LOOK! COUNSELOR FILIMINA JUST PUT THIS UP ON THE BULLETIN BOARD!
FEEL-O-MEANIE? CAN'T WAIT.
WHAT IS IT? AUDITIONS FOR THE ANNUAL PRODUCTION OF THE FLIGHT SAFETY CARD FROM AN AIRPLANE?

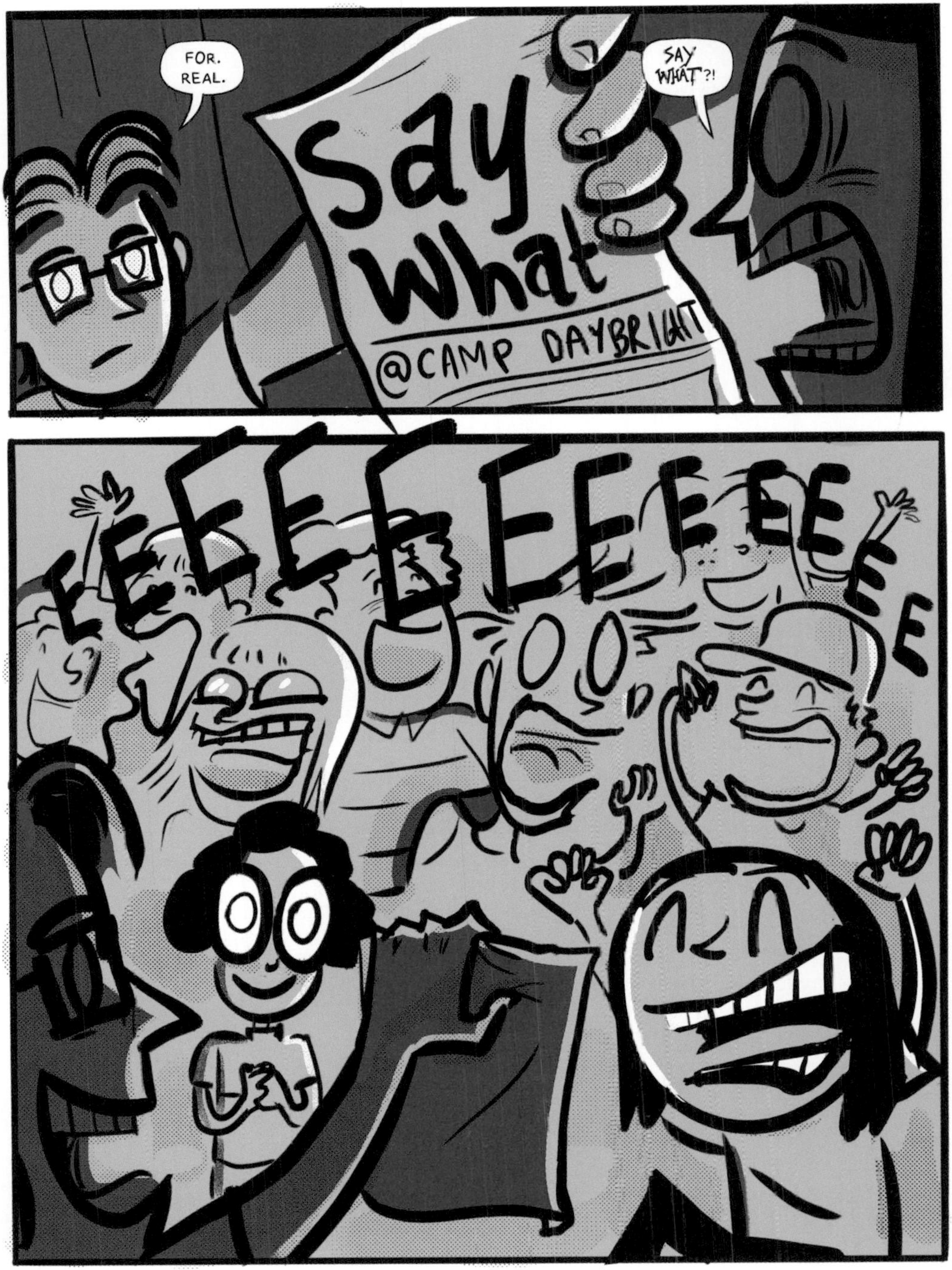
FOR. REAL.
Say What
@CAMP DAYBRIGHT
SAY WHAT?!
EEEEEEEEEEEE

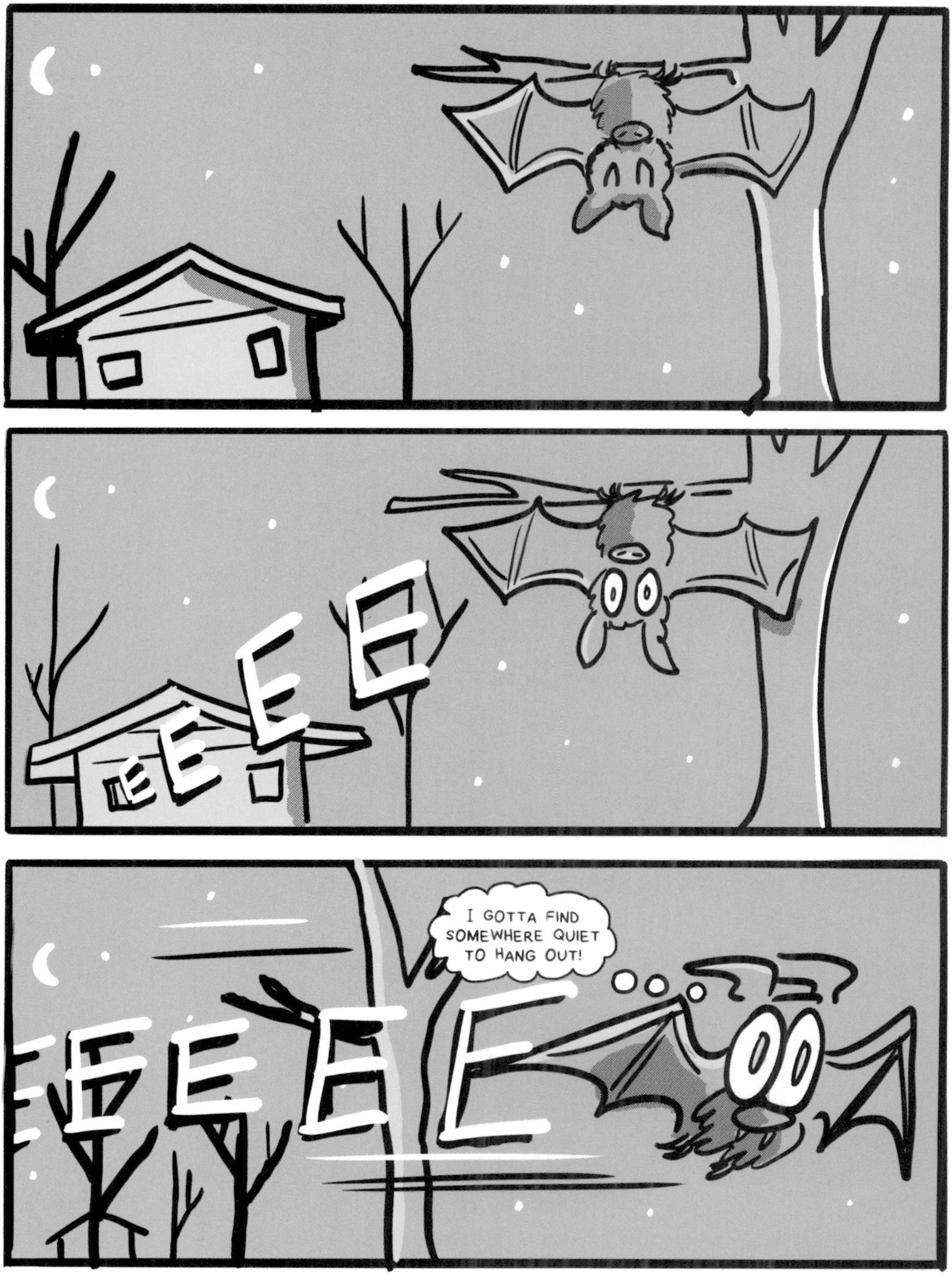
EEEEE
I GOTTA FIND SOMEWHERE QUIET TO HANG OUT!
EEEEEE

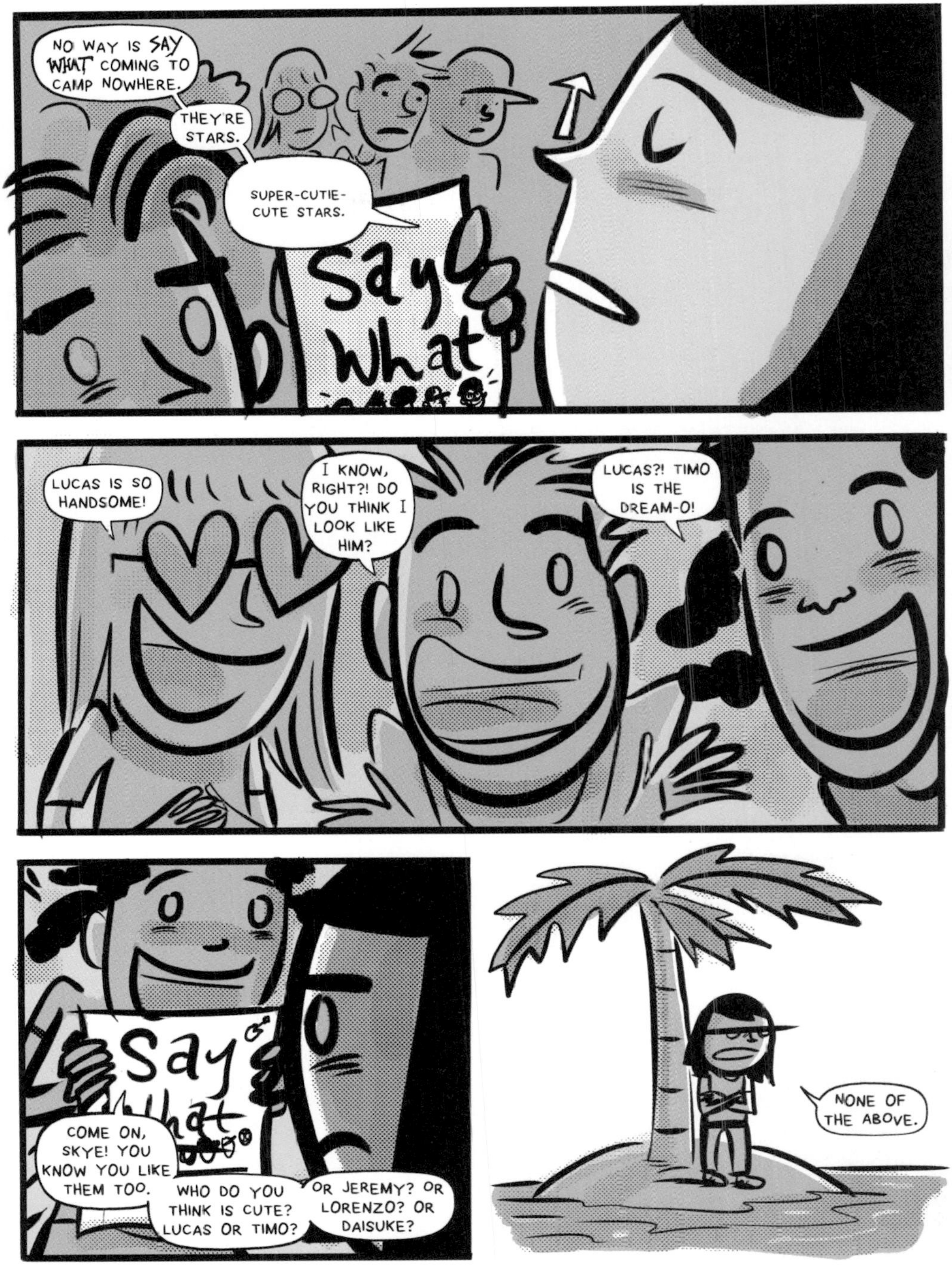
NO WAY IS SAY WHAT COMING TO CAMP NOWHERE.
THEY'RE STARS.
SUPER-CUTIE-CUTE STARS.
Say What
LUCAS IS SO HANDSOME!
I KNOW, RIGHT?! DO YOU THINK I LOOK LIKE HIM?
LUCAS?! TIMO IS THE DREAM-O!
Say What
COME ON, SKYE! YOU KNOW YOU LIKE THEM TOO.
WHO DO YOU THINK IS CUTE? LUCAS OR TIMO?
OR JEREMY? OR LORENZO? OR DAISUKE?
NONE OF THE ABOVE.

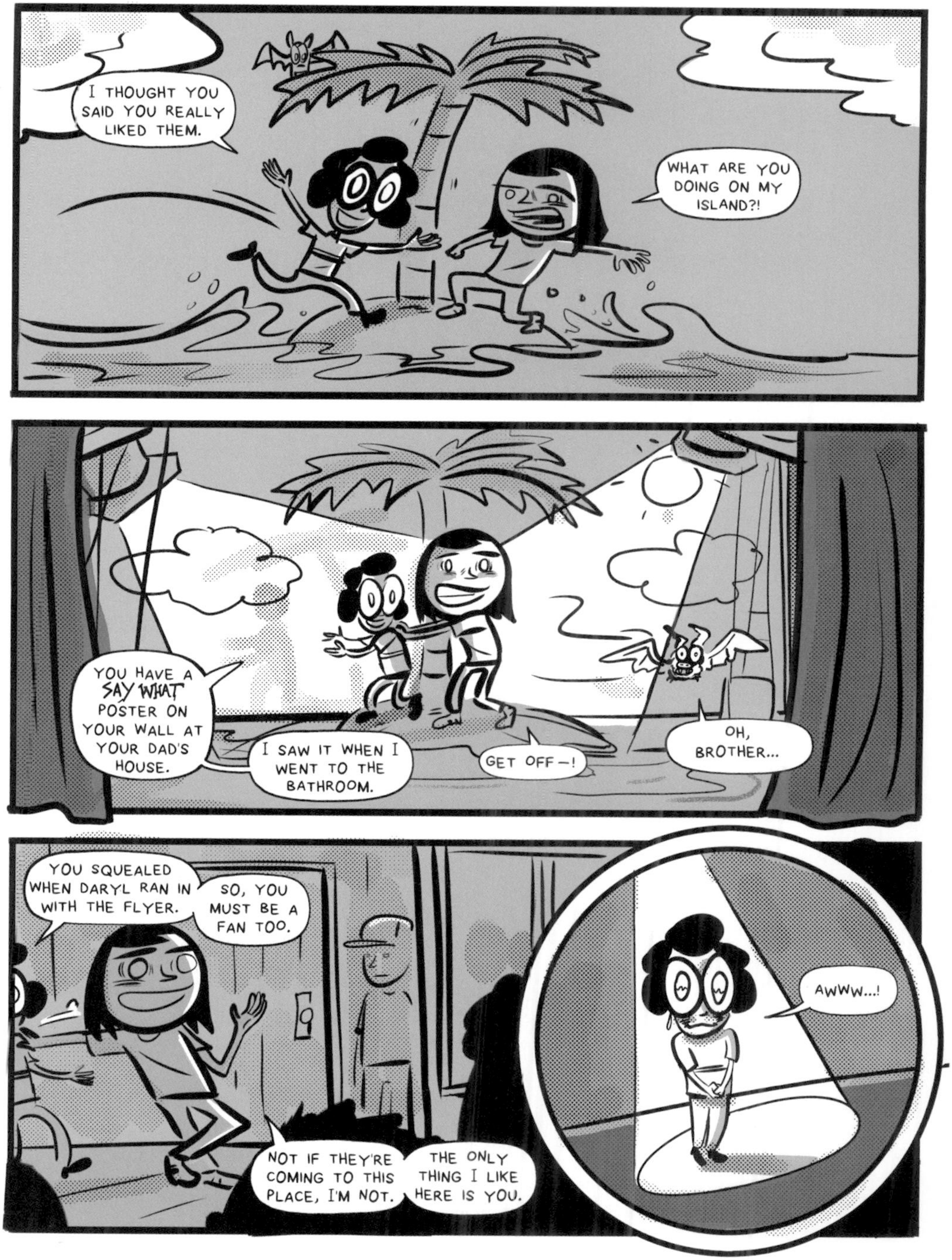
I THOUGHT YOU SAID YOU REALLY LIKED THEM.
WHAT ARE YOU DOING ON MY ISLAND?!
YOU HAVE A SAY WHAT POSTER ON YOUR WALL AT YOUR DAD'S HOUSE.
I SAW IT WHEN I WENT TO THE BATHROOM.
GET OFF—!
OH, BROTHER...
YOU SQUEALED WHEN DARYL RAN IN WITH THE FLYER.
SO, YOU MUST BE A FAN TOO.
NOT IF THEY'RE COMING TO THIS PLACE, I'M NOT.
THE ONLY THING I LIKE HERE IS YOU.
AWWW...!

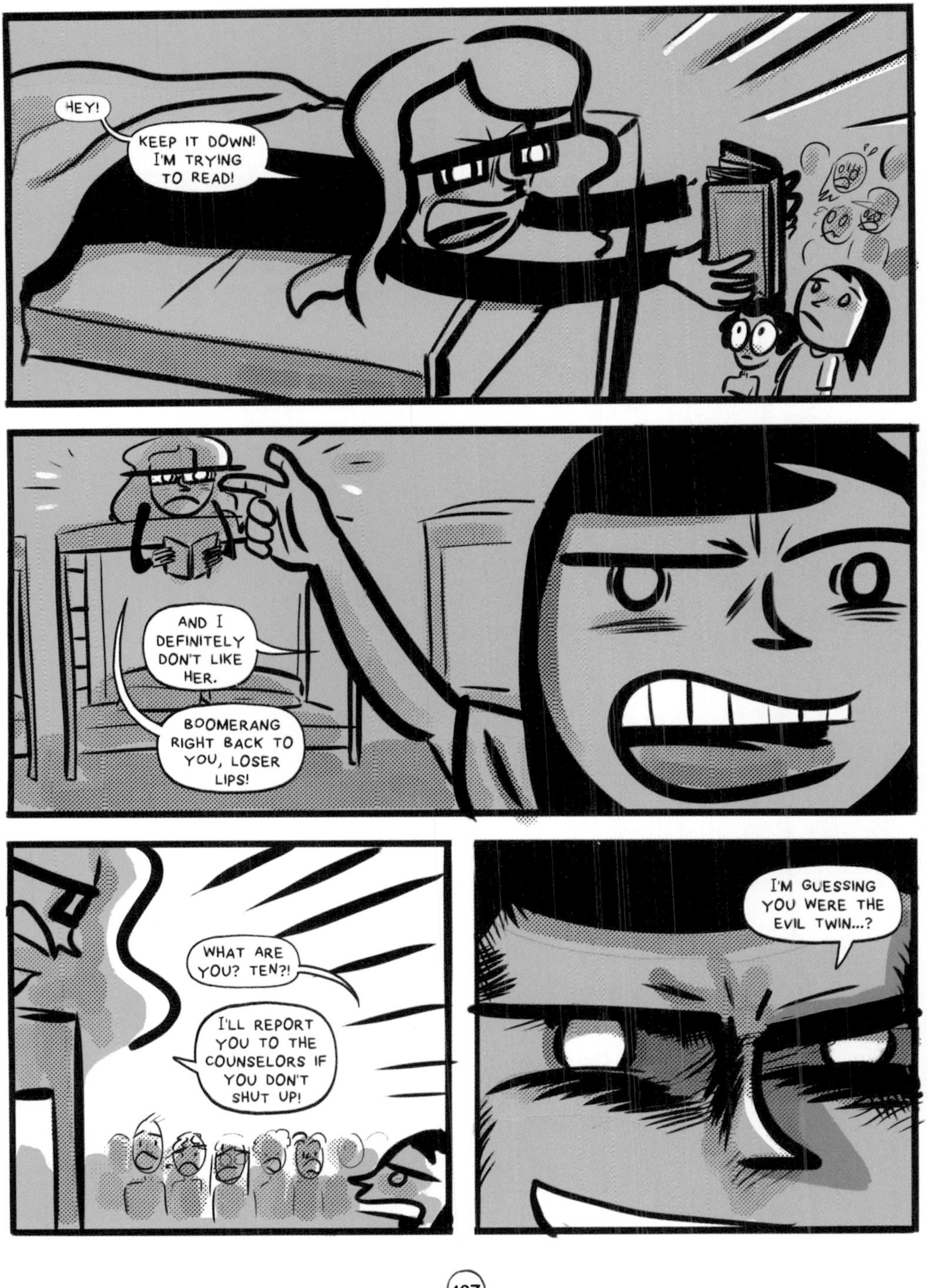
HEY!
KEEP IT DOWN! I'M TRYING TO READ!
AND I DEFINITELY DON'T LIKE HER.
BOOMERANG RIGHT BACK TO YOU, LOSER LIPS!
WHAT ARE YOU? TEN?!
I'LL REPORT YOU TO THE COUNSELORS IF YOU DON'T SHUT UP!
I'M GUESSING YOU WERE THE EVIL TWIN...?

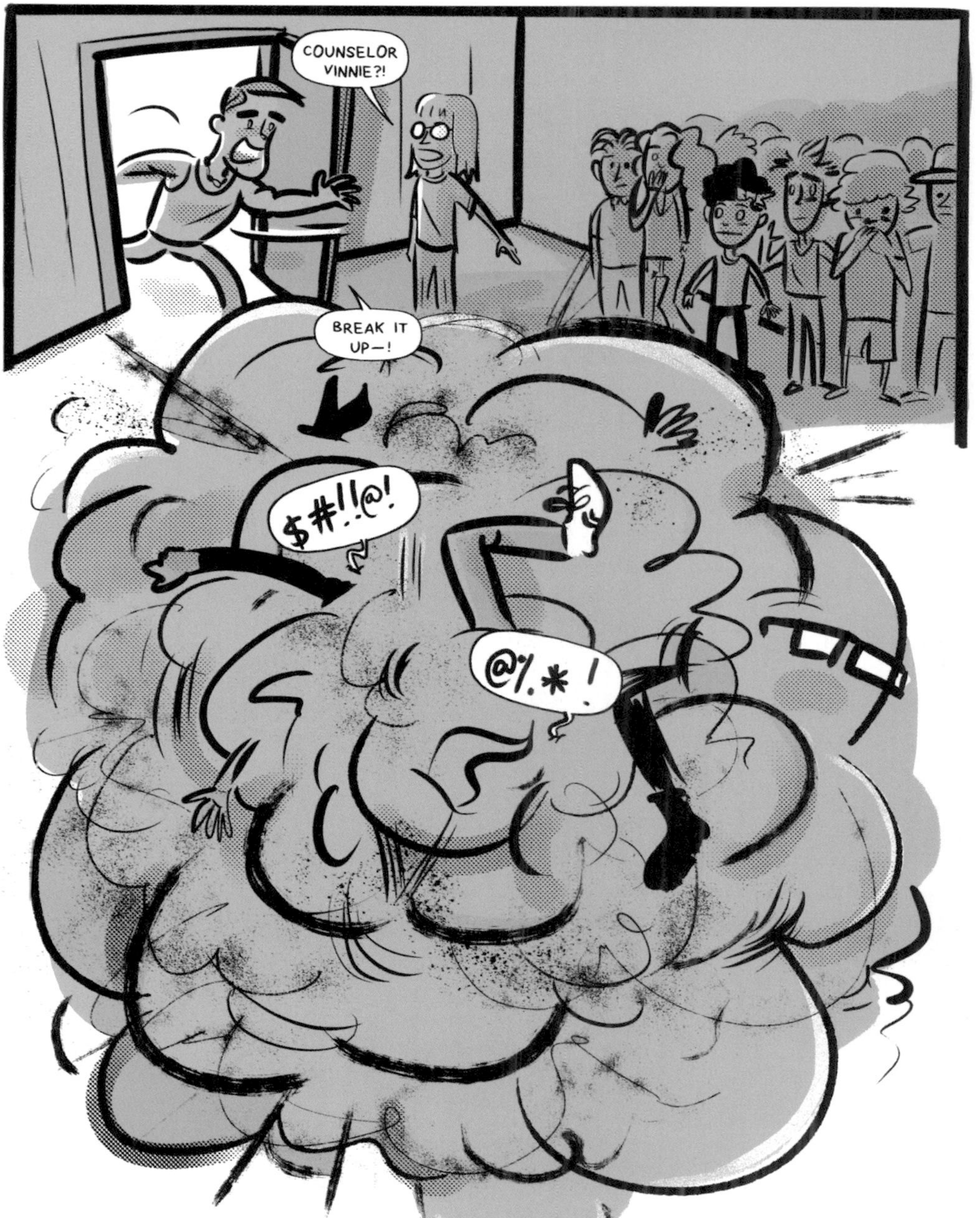
COUNSELOR VINNIE?!
BREAK IT UP—!
$#!!@!
@%.*!

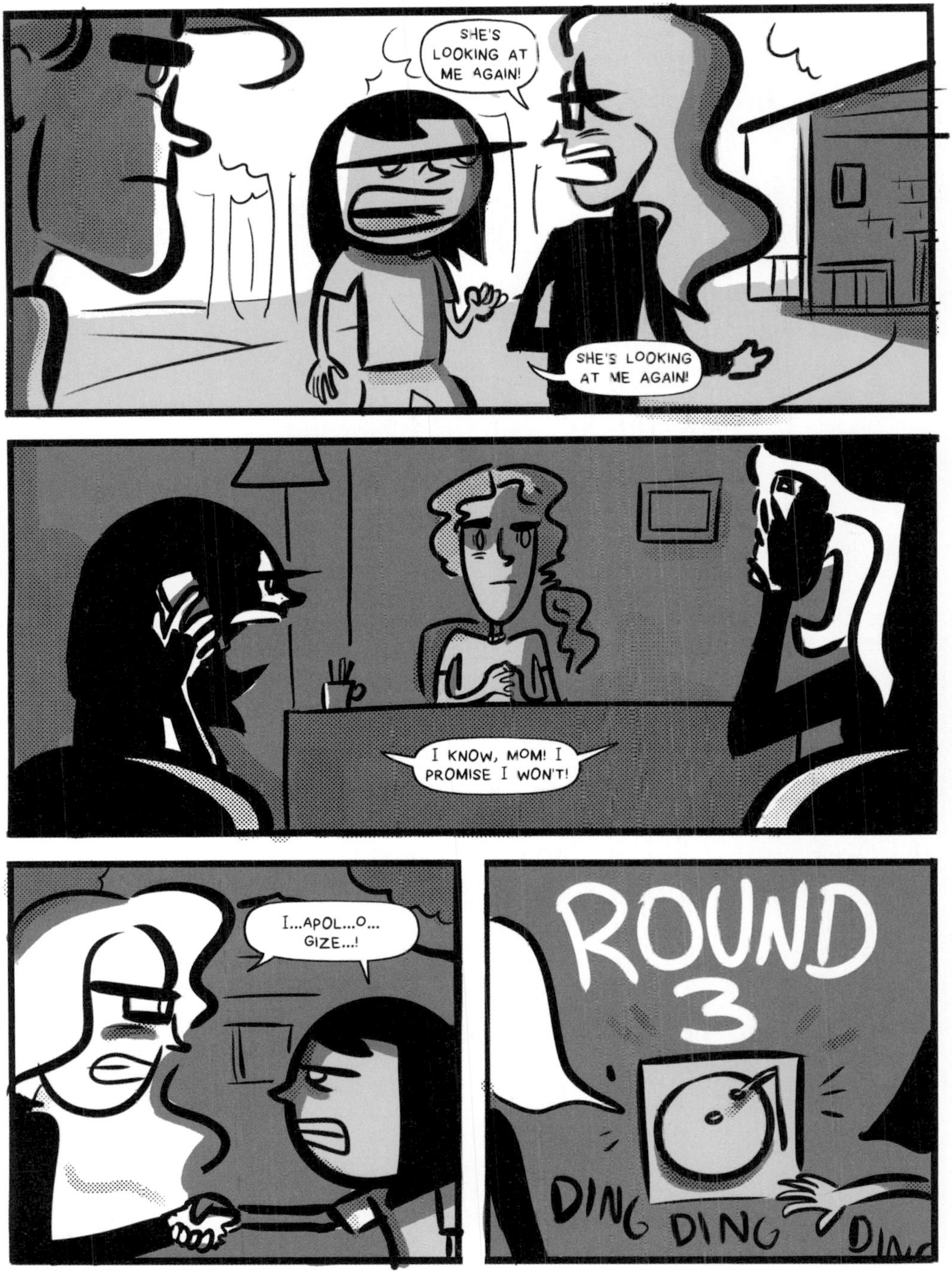
SHE'S LOOKING AT ME AGAIN!
SHE'S LOOKING AT ME AGAIN!
I KNOW, MOM! I PROMISE I WON'T!
I...APOL...O... GIZE...!
ROUND 3
DING DING DING

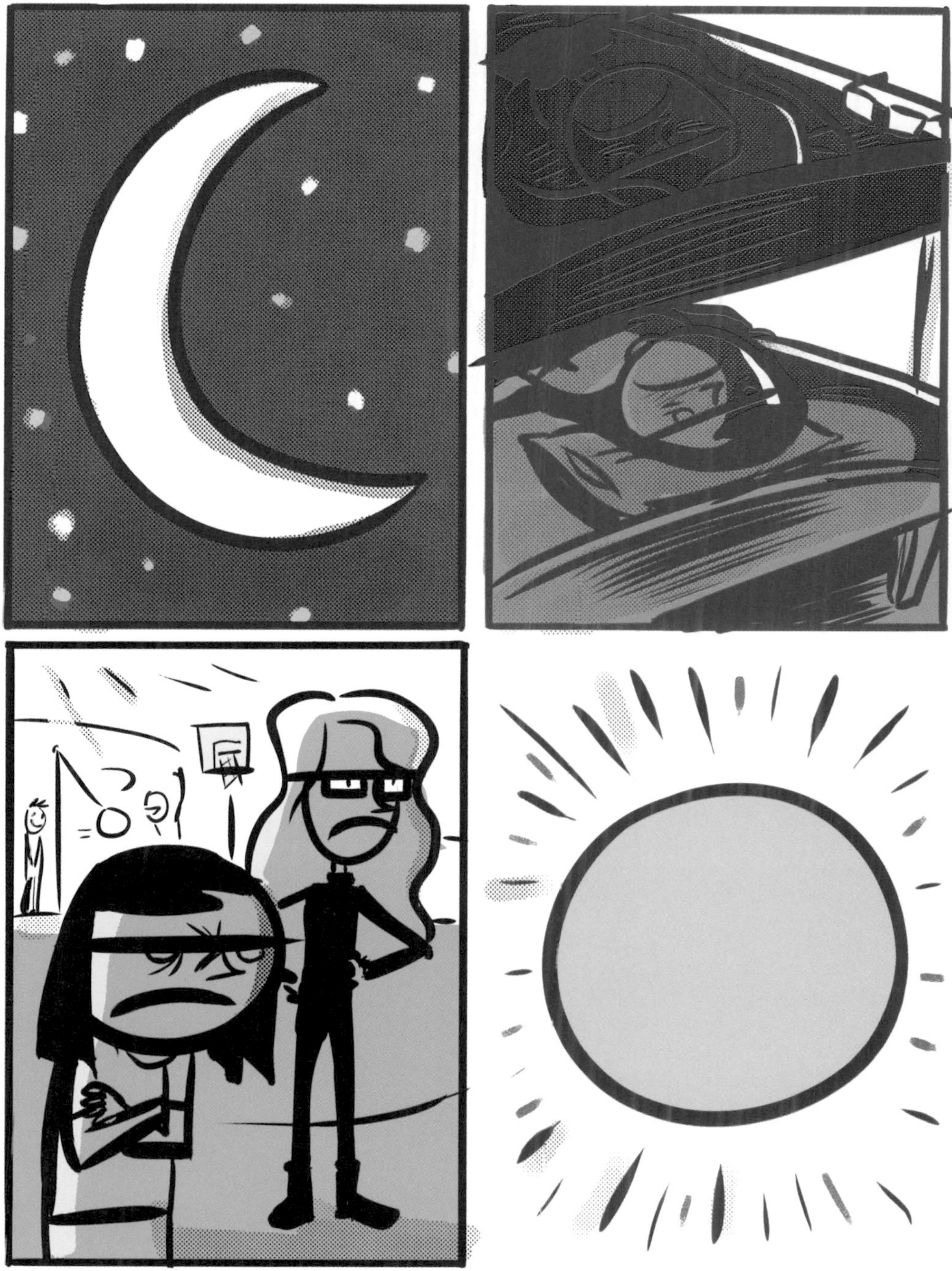

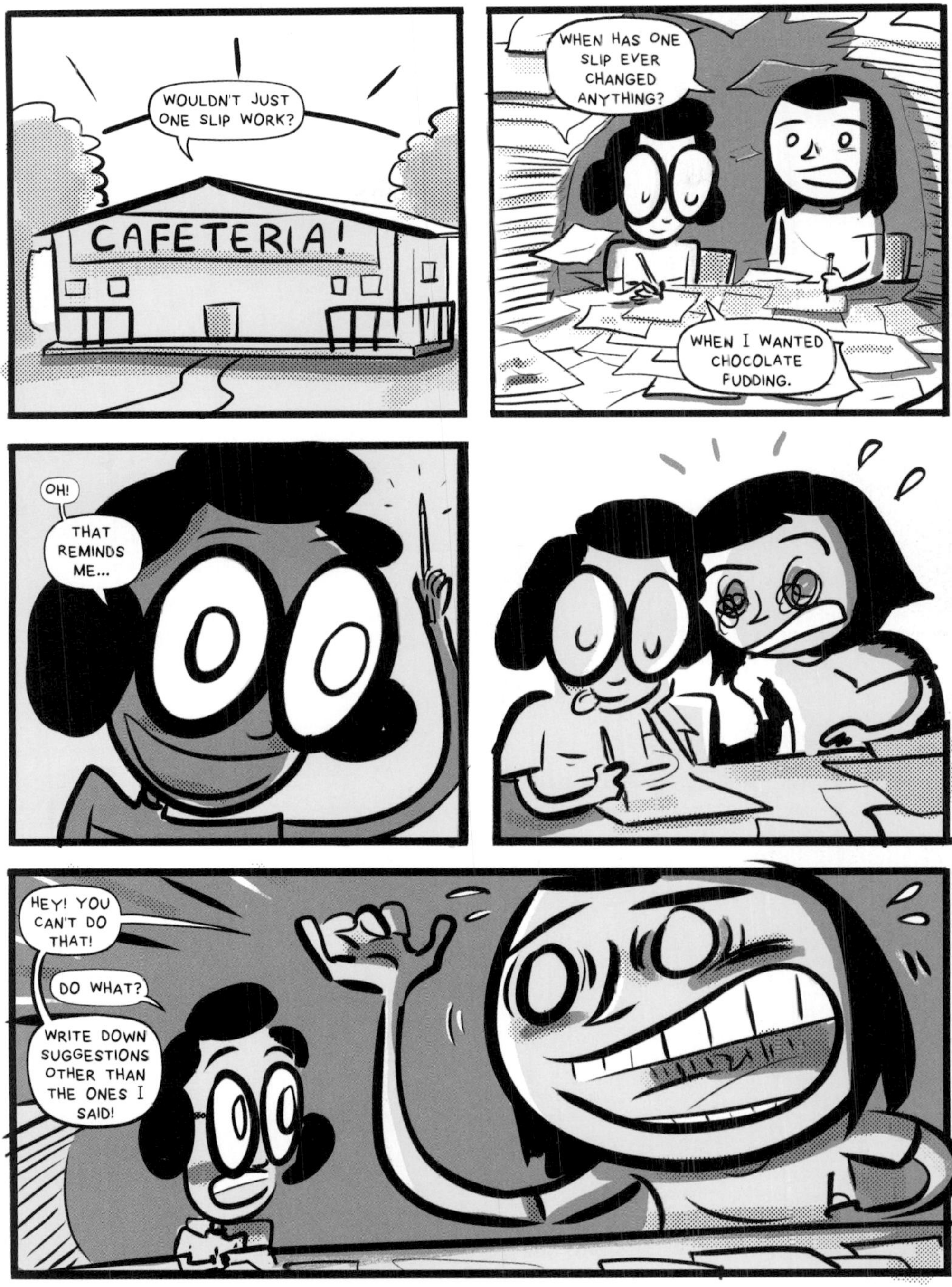
WOULDN'T JUST ONE SLIP WORK?
CAFETERIA!
WHEN HAS ONE SLIP EVER CHANGED ANYTHING?
WHEN I WANTED CHOCOLATE PUDDING.
OH!
THAT REMINDS ME...
HEY! YOU CAN'T DO THAT!
DO WHAT?
WRITE DOWN SUGGESTIONS OTHER THAN THE ONES I SAID!

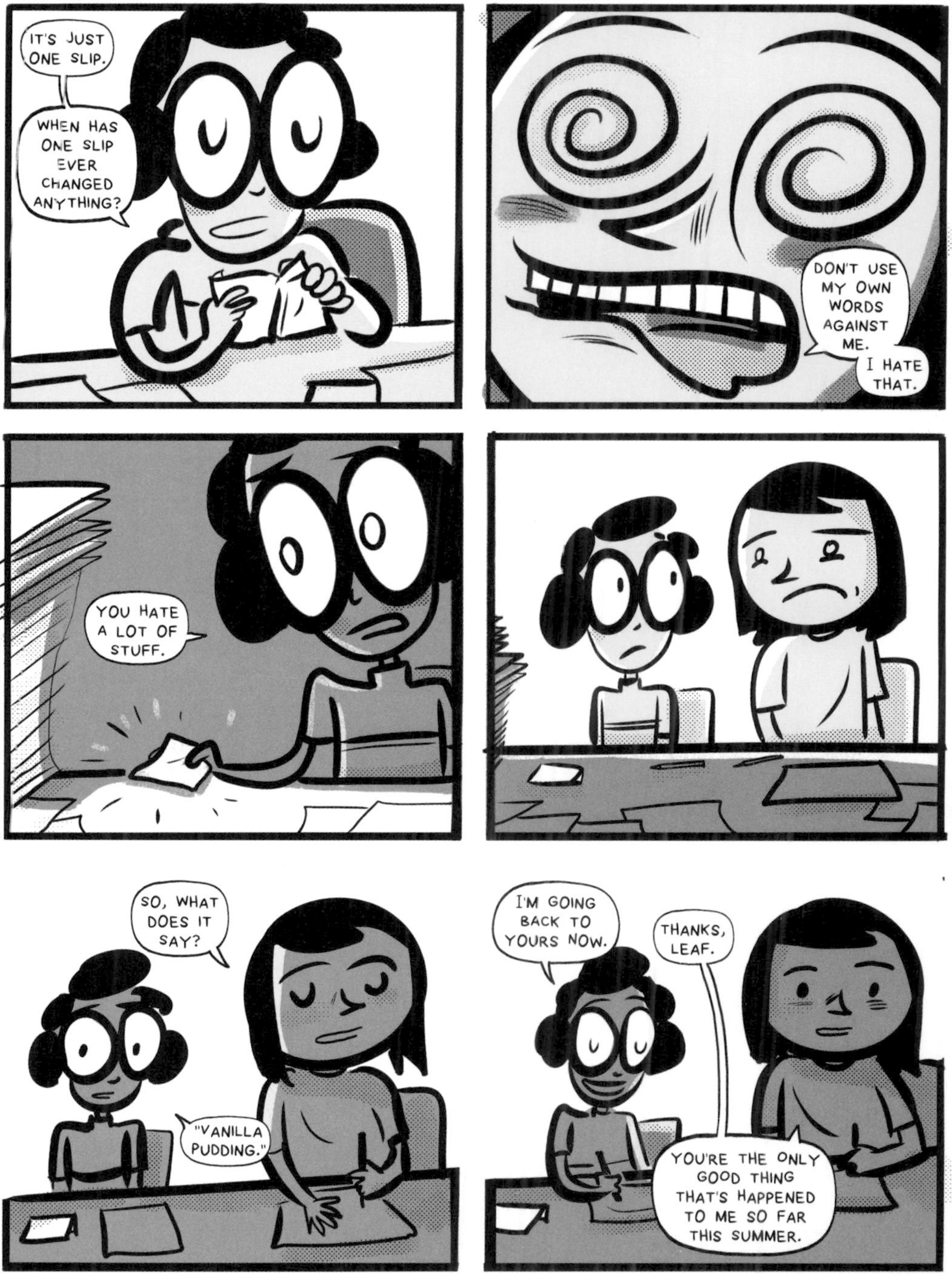
IT'S JUST ONE SLIP.
WHEN HAS ONE SLIP EVER CHANGED ANYTHING?
DON'T USE MY OWN WORDS AGAINST ME.
I HATE THAT.
YOU HATE A LOT OF STUFF.
SO, WHAT DOES IT SAY?
"VANILLA PUDDING."
I'M GOING BACK TO YOURS NOW.
THANKS, LEAF.
YOU'RE THE ONLY GOOD THING THAT'S HAPPENED TO ME SO FAR THIS SUMMER.

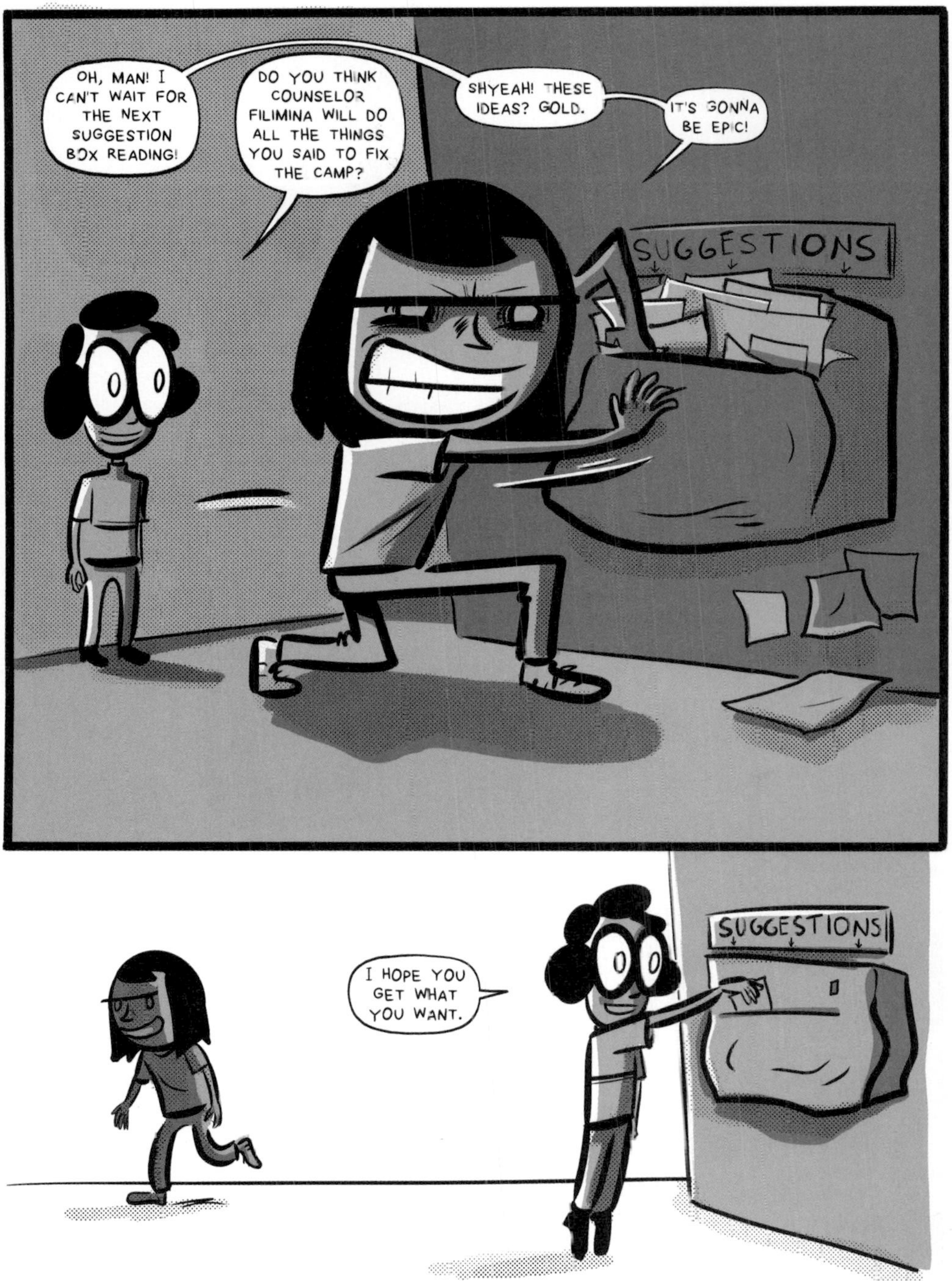
OH, MAN! I CAN'T WAIT FOR THE NEXT SUGGESTION BOX READING!
DO YOU THINK COUNSELOR FILIMINA WILL DO ALL THE THINGS YOU SAID TO FIX THE CAMP?
SHYEAH! THESE IDEAS? GOLD.
IT'S GONNA BE EPIC!
SUGGESTIONS
SUGGESTIONS
I HOPE YOU GET WHAT YOU WANT.

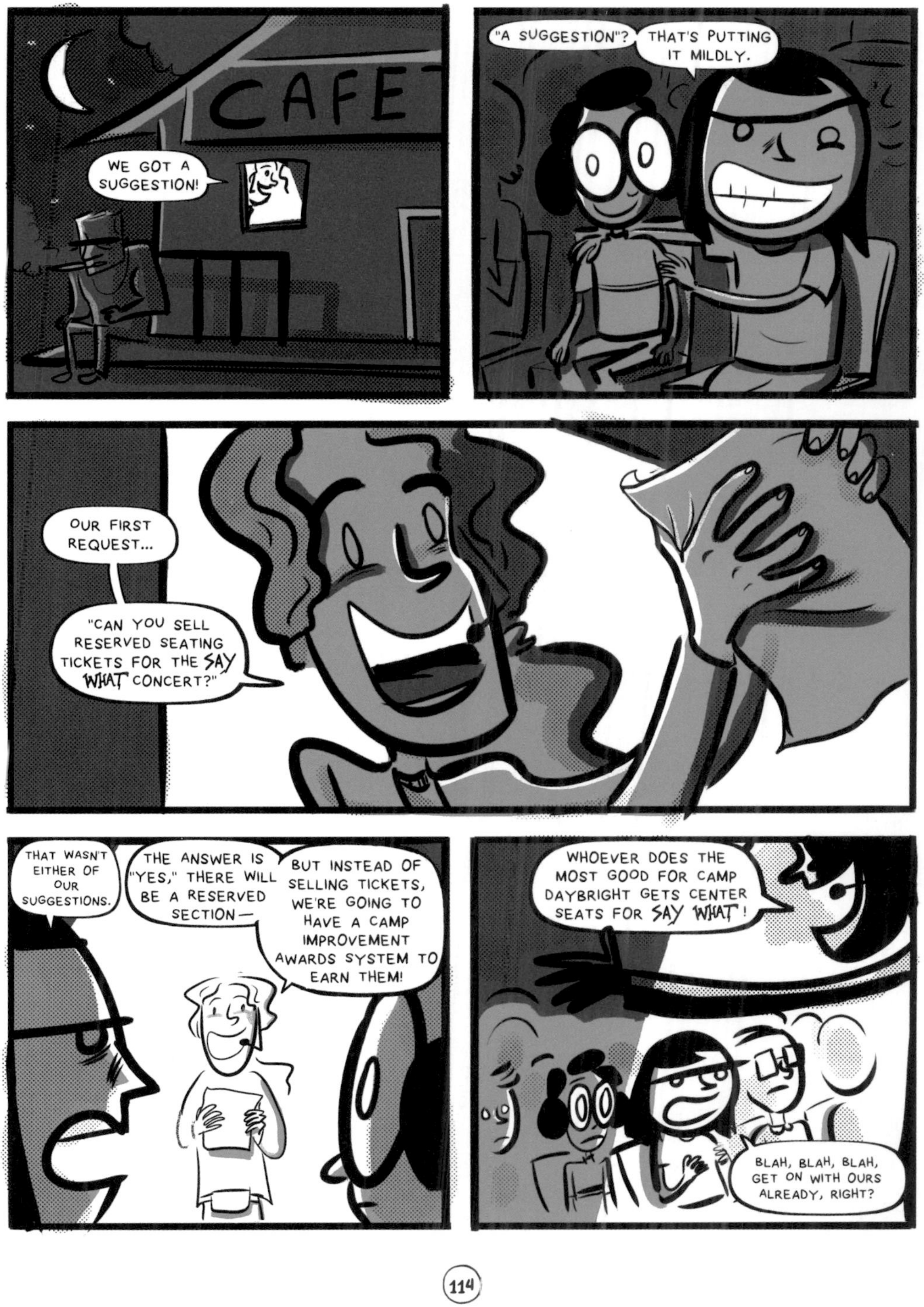
CAFE
WE GOT A SUGGESTION!
"A SUGGESTION"?
THAT'S PUTTING IT MILDLY.
OUR FIRST REQUEST...
"CAN YOU SELL RESERVED SEATING TICKETS FOR THE SAY WHAT CONCERT?"
THAT WASN'T EITHER OF OUR SUGGESTIONS.
THE ANSWER IS "YES," THERE WILL BE A RESERVED SECTION—
BUT INSTEAD OF SELLING TICKETS, WE'RE GOING TO HAVE A CAMP IMPROVEMENT AWARDS SYSTEM TO EARN THEM!
WHOEVER DOES THE MOST GOOD FOR CAMP DAYBRIGHT GETS CENTER SEATS FOR SAY WHAT!
BLAH, BLAH, BLAH, GET ON WITH OURS ALREADY, RIGHT?

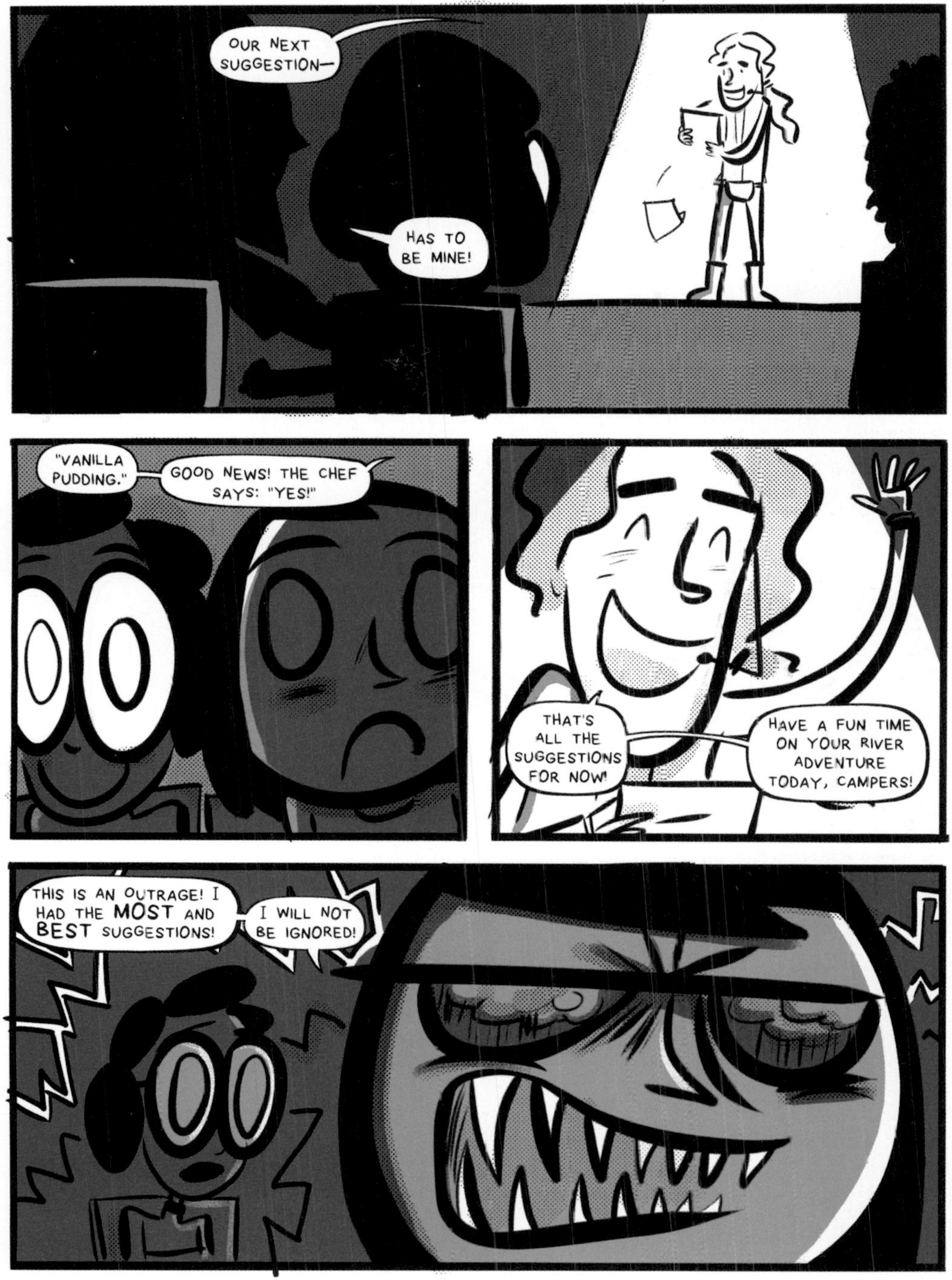

OUR NEXT SUGGESTION—
HAS TO BE MINE!
"VANILLA PUDDING."
GOOD NEWS! THE CHEF SAYS: "YES!"
THAT'S ALL THE SUGGESTIONS FOR NOW!
HAVE A FUN TIME ON YOUR RIVER ADVENTURE TODAY, CAMPERS!
THIS IS AN OUTRAGE! I HAD THE MOST AND BEST SUGGESTIONS!
I WILL NOT BE IGNORED!

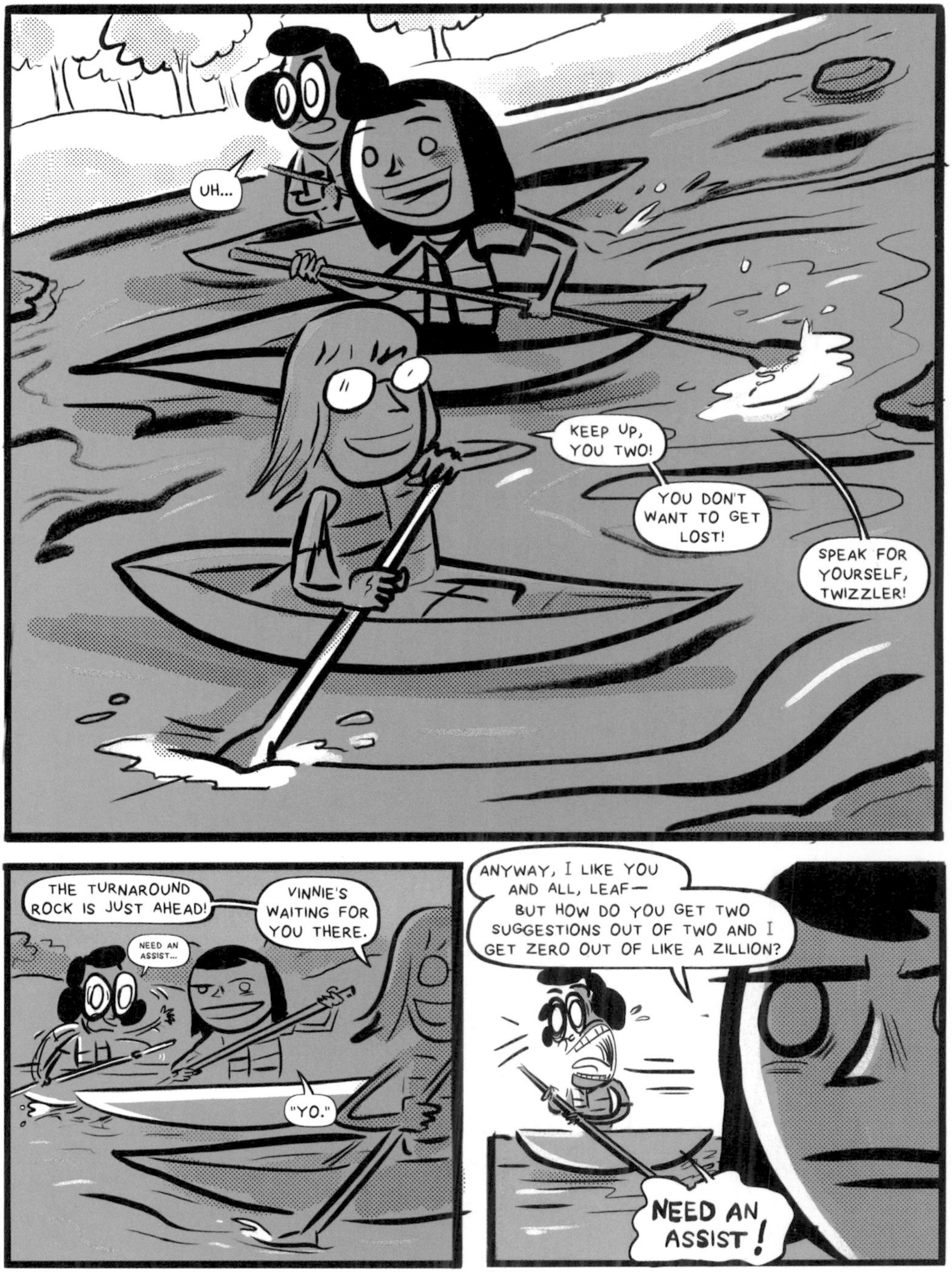
UH...
KEEP UP, YOU TWO!
YOU DON'T WANT TO GET LOST!
SPEAK FOR YOURSELF, TWIZZLER!
THE TURNAROUND ROCK IS JUST AHEAD!
VINNIE'S WAITING FOR YOU THERE.
NEED AN ASSIST...
"YO."
ANYWAY, I LIKE YOU AND ALL, LEAF—
BUT HOW DO YOU GET TWO SUGGESTIONS OUT OF TWO AND I GET ZERO OUT OF LIKE A ZILLION?
NEED AN ASSIST!

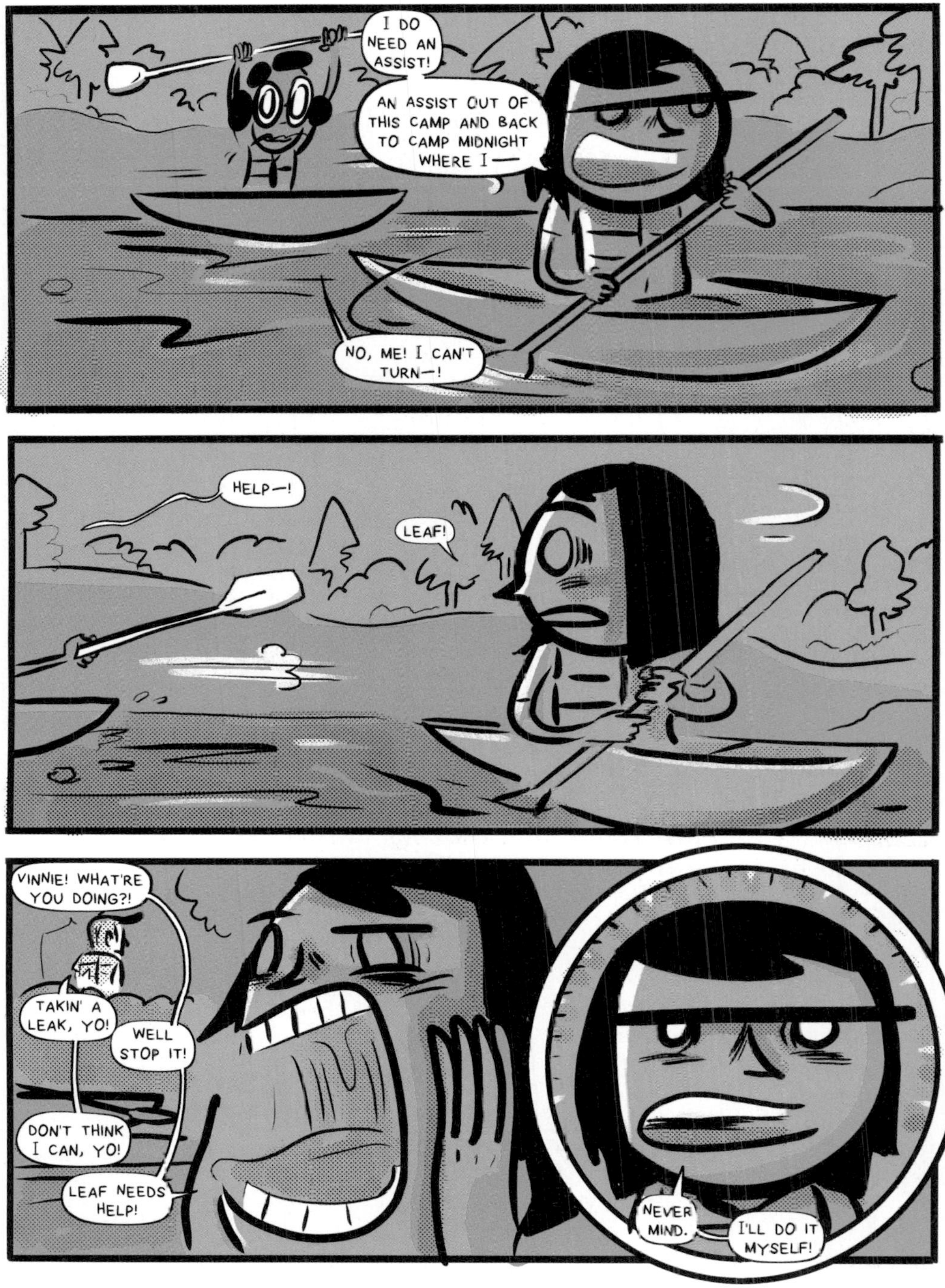
I DO NEED AN ASSIST!
AN ASSIST OUT OF THIS CAMP AND BACK TO CAMP MIDNIGHT WHERE I—
NO, ME! I CAN'T TURN—!
HELP—!
LEAF!
VINNIE! WHAT'RE YOU DOING?!
TAKIN' A LEAK, YO!
WELL STOP IT!
DON'T THINK I CAN, YO!
LEAF NEEDS HELP!
NEVER MIND.
I'LL DO IT MYSELF!

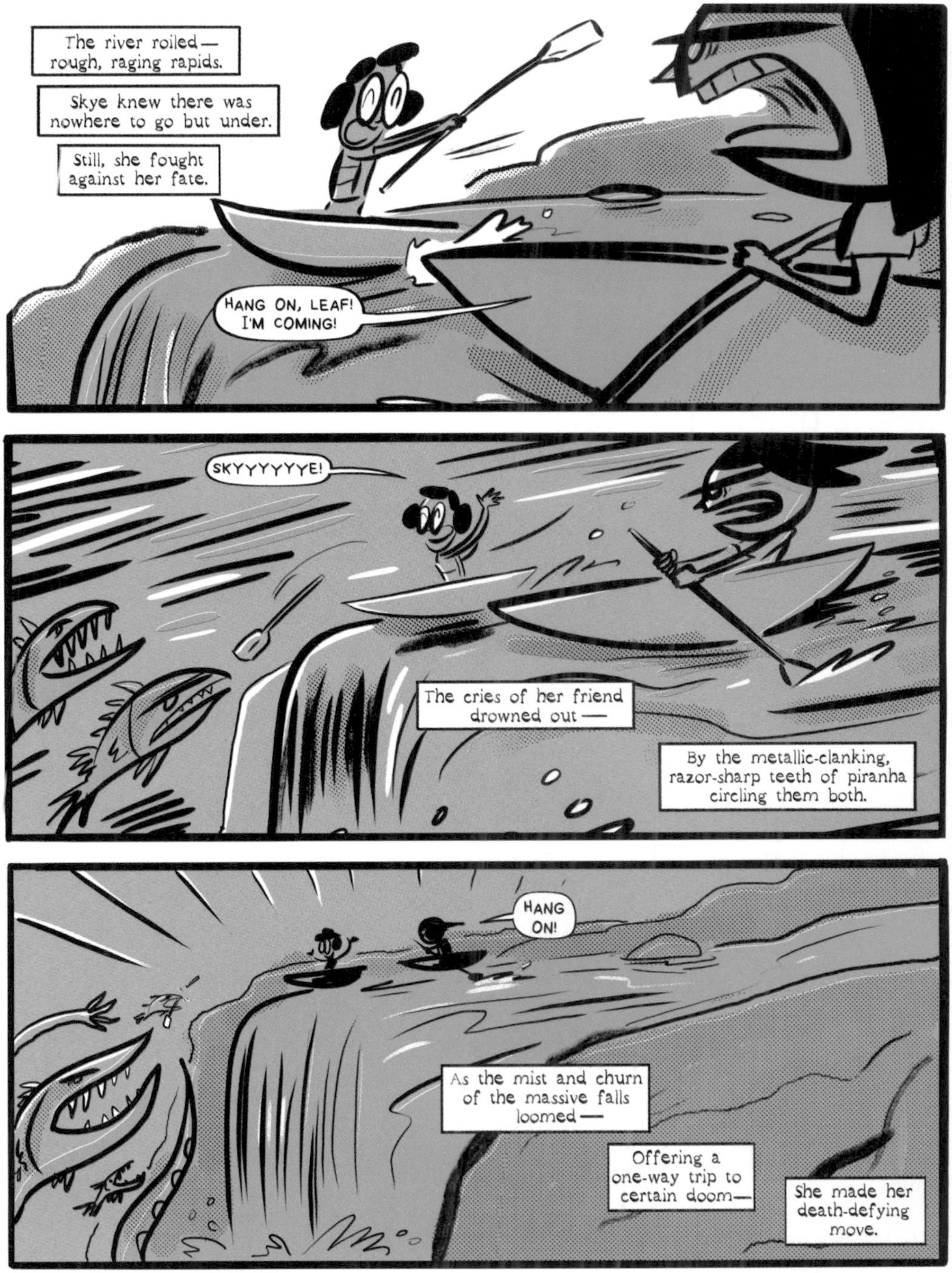
The river roiled— rough, raging rapids.
Skye knew there was nowhere to go but under.
Still, she fought against her fate.
HANG ON, LEAF! I'M COMING!
SKYYYYYYE!
The cries of her friend drowned out—
By the metallic-clanking, razor-sharp teeth of piranha circling them both.
HANG ON!
As the mist and churn of the massive falls loomed—
Offering a one-way trip to certain doom—
She made her death-defying move.

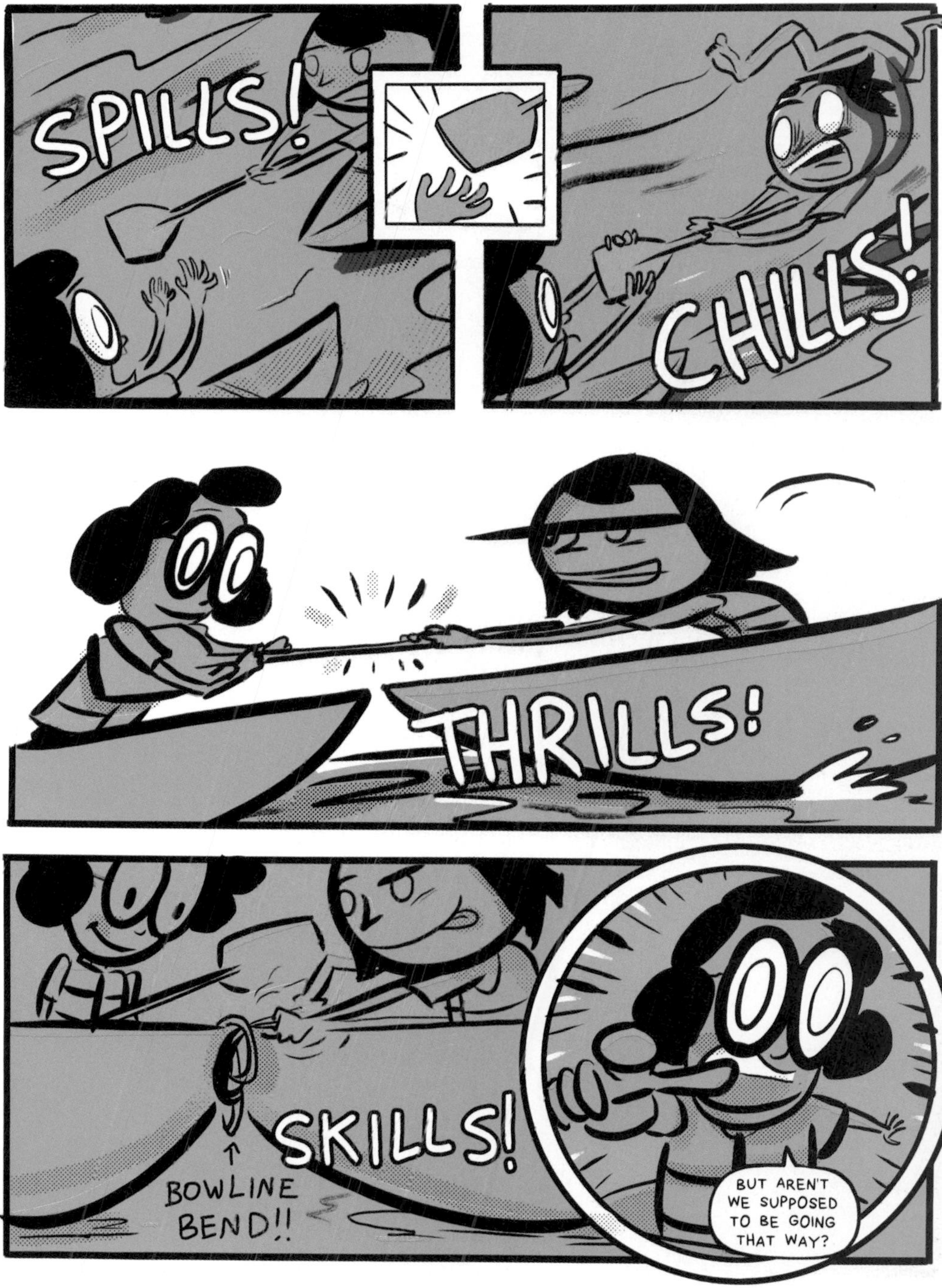
SPILLS!
CHILLS!
THRILLS!
SKILLS!
BOWLINE BEND!!
BUT AREN'T WE SUPPOSED TO BE GOING THAT WAY?

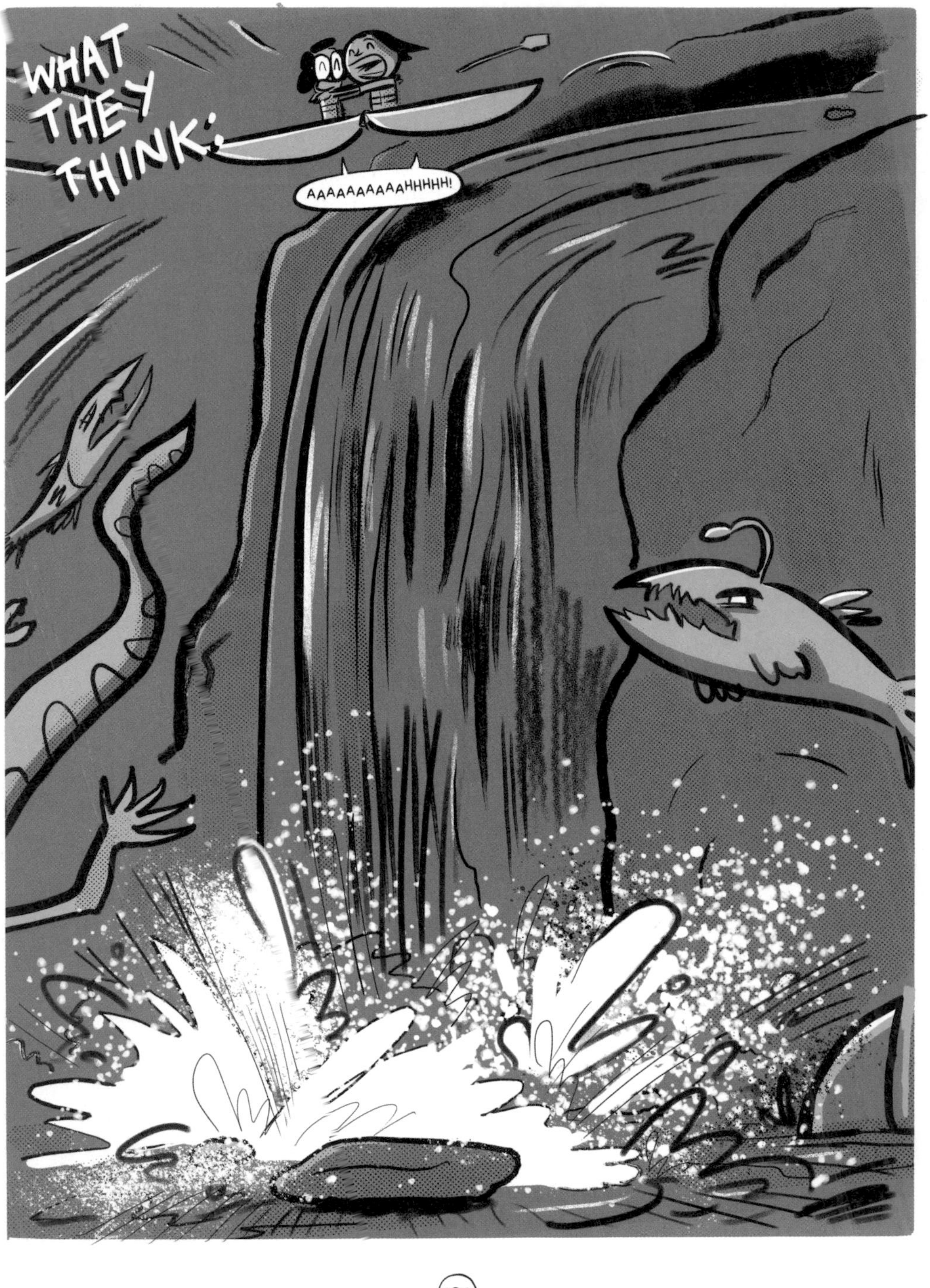
WHAT THEY THINK:
AAAAAAAAAAHHHHHH!

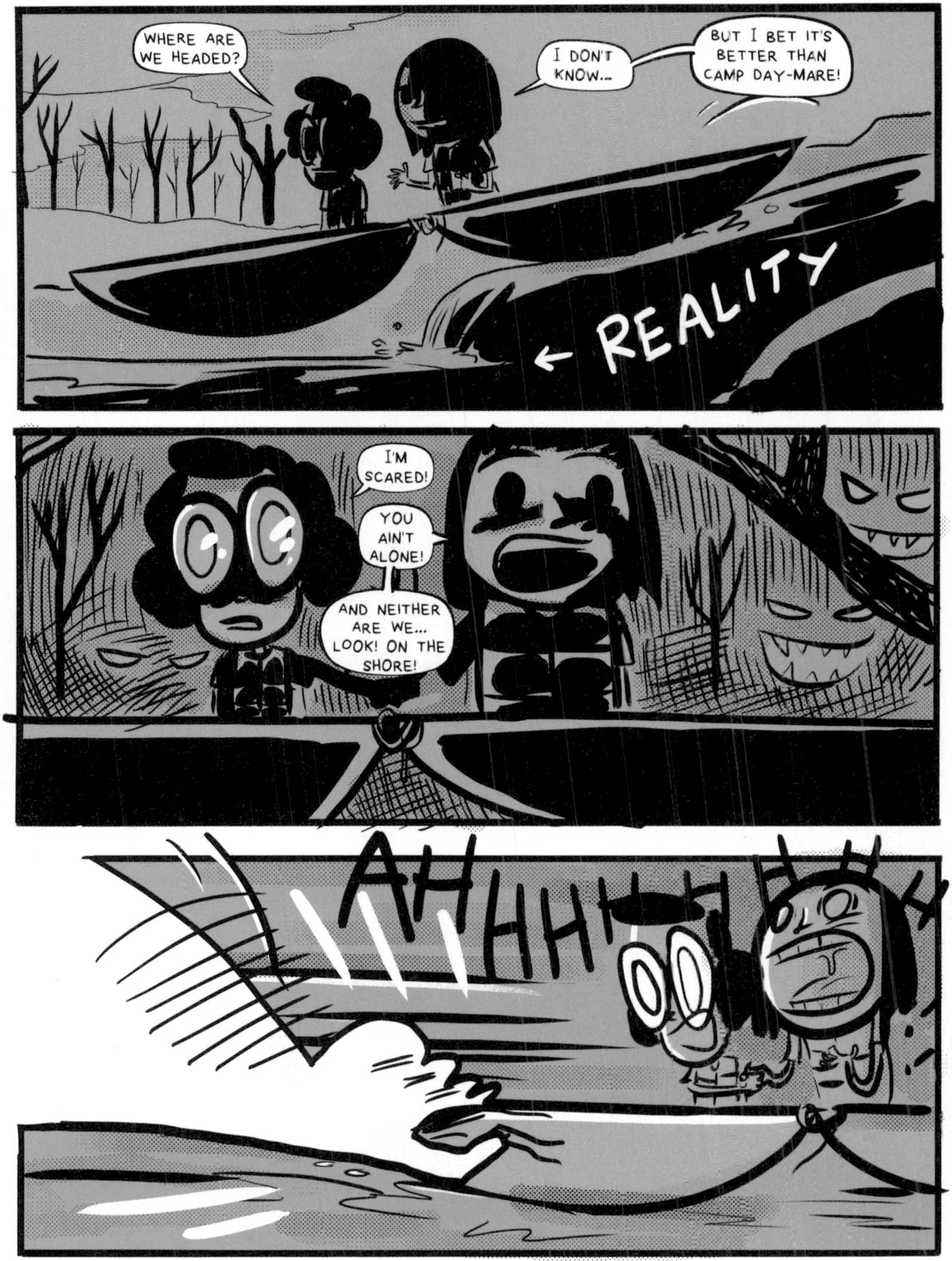
WHERE ARE WE HEADED?
I DON'T KNOW...
BUT I BET IT'S BETTER THAN CAMP DAY-MARE!
← REALITY
I'M SCARED!
YOU AIN'T ALONE!
AND NEITHER ARE WE... LOOK! ON THE SHORE!
AHHHHHH

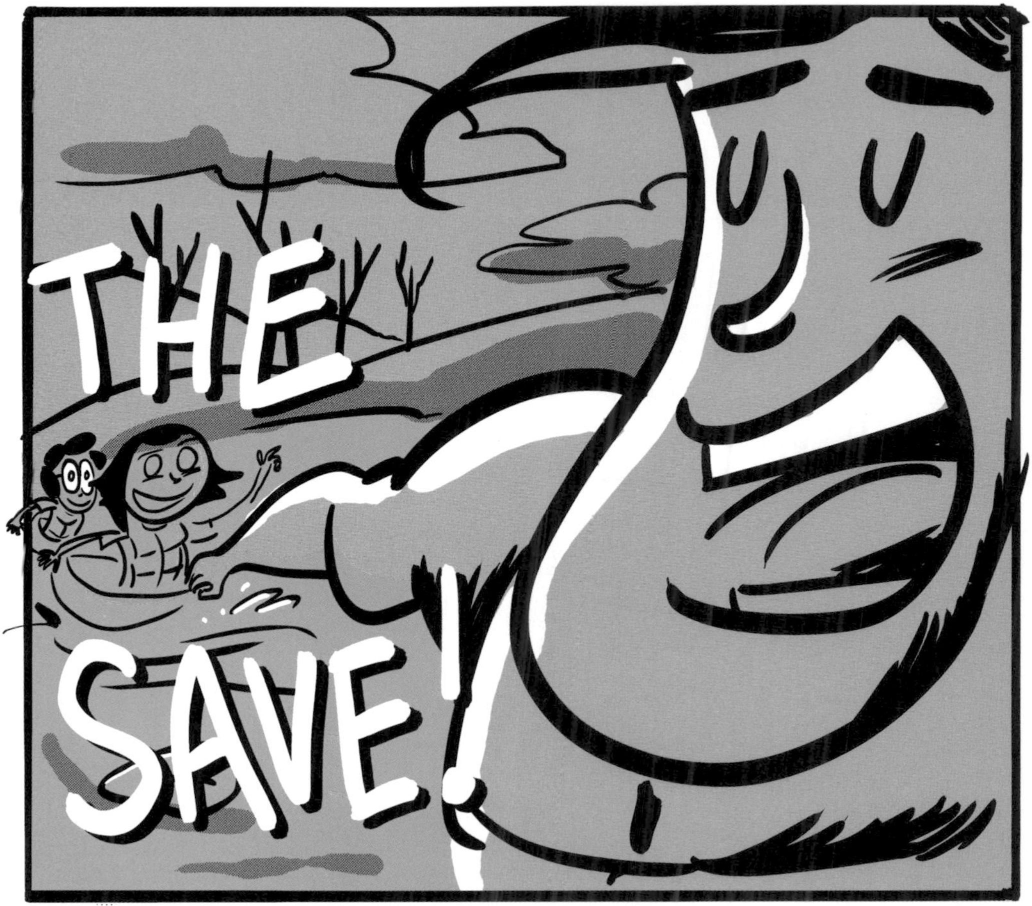
THE SAVE!

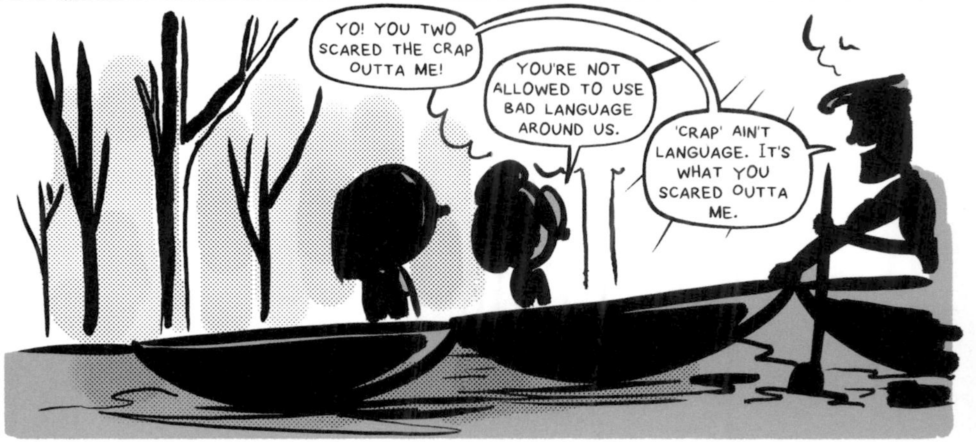
YO! YOU TWO SCARED THE CRAP OUTTA ME!
YOU'RE NOT ALLOWED TO USE BAD LANGUAGE AROUND US.
'CRAP' AIN'T LANGUAGE. IT'S WHAT YOU SCARED OUTTA ME.

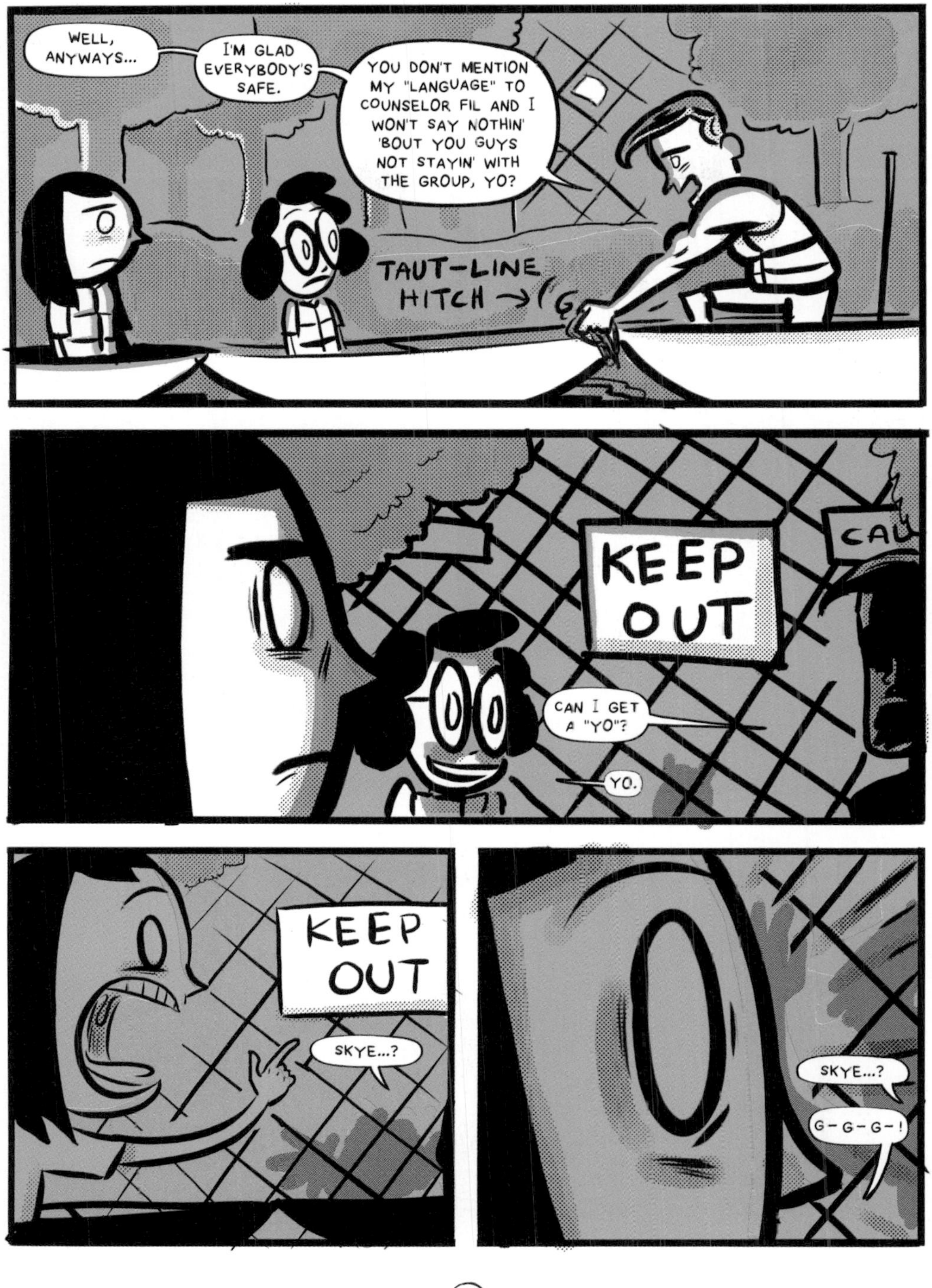
WELL, ANYWAYS...
I'M GLAD EVERYBODY'S SAFE.
YOU DON'T MENTION MY "LANGUAGE" TO COUNSELOR FIL AND I WON'T SAY NOTHIN' 'BOUT YOU GUYS NOT STAYIN' WITH THE GROUP, YO?
TAUT-LINE HITCH →
KEEP OUT
CAN I GET A "YO"?
YO.
KEEP OUT
SKYE...?
SKYE...?
G-G-G-!

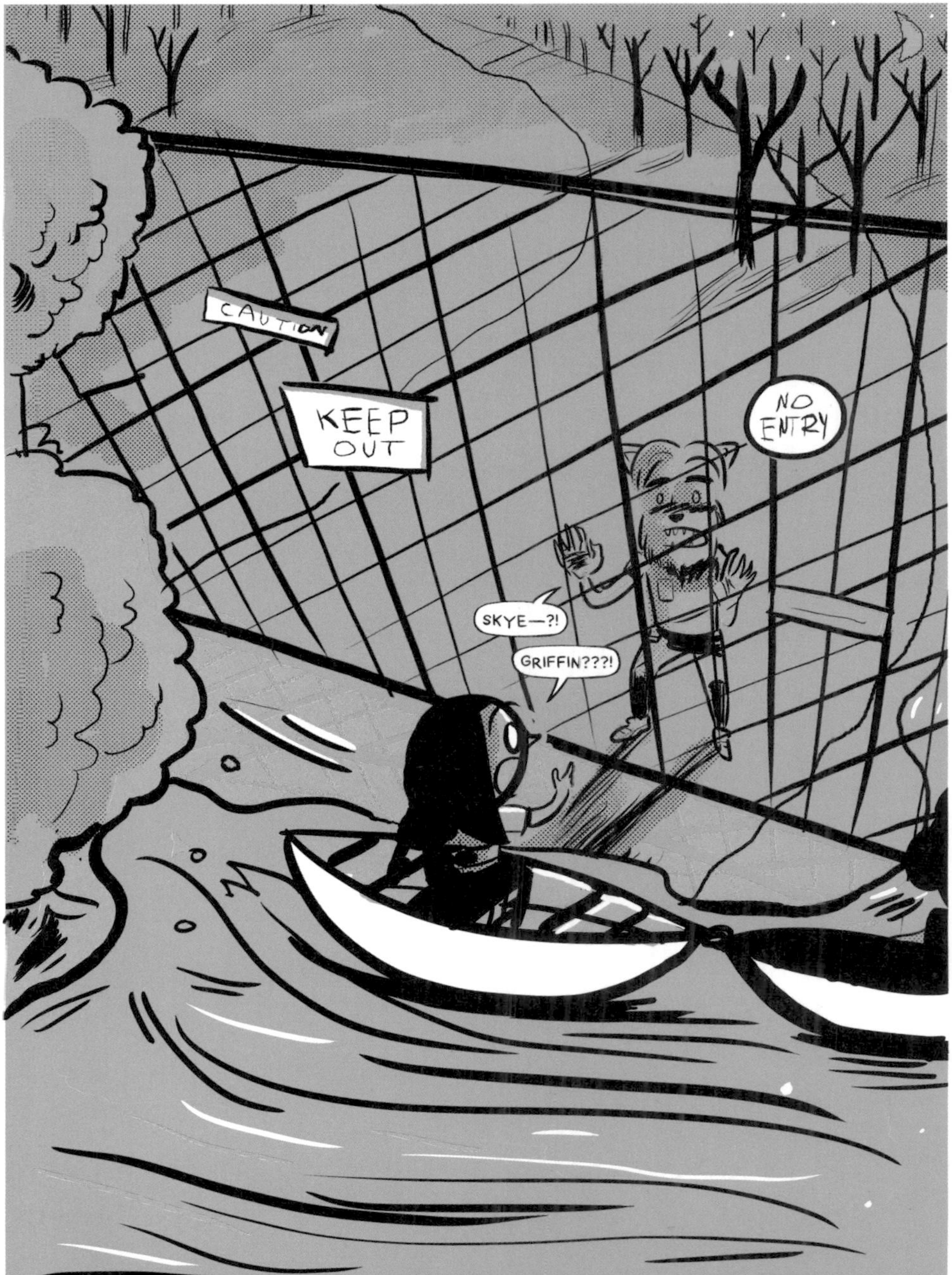
CAUTION
KEEP OUT
NO ENTRY
SKYE—?!
GRIFFIN???!

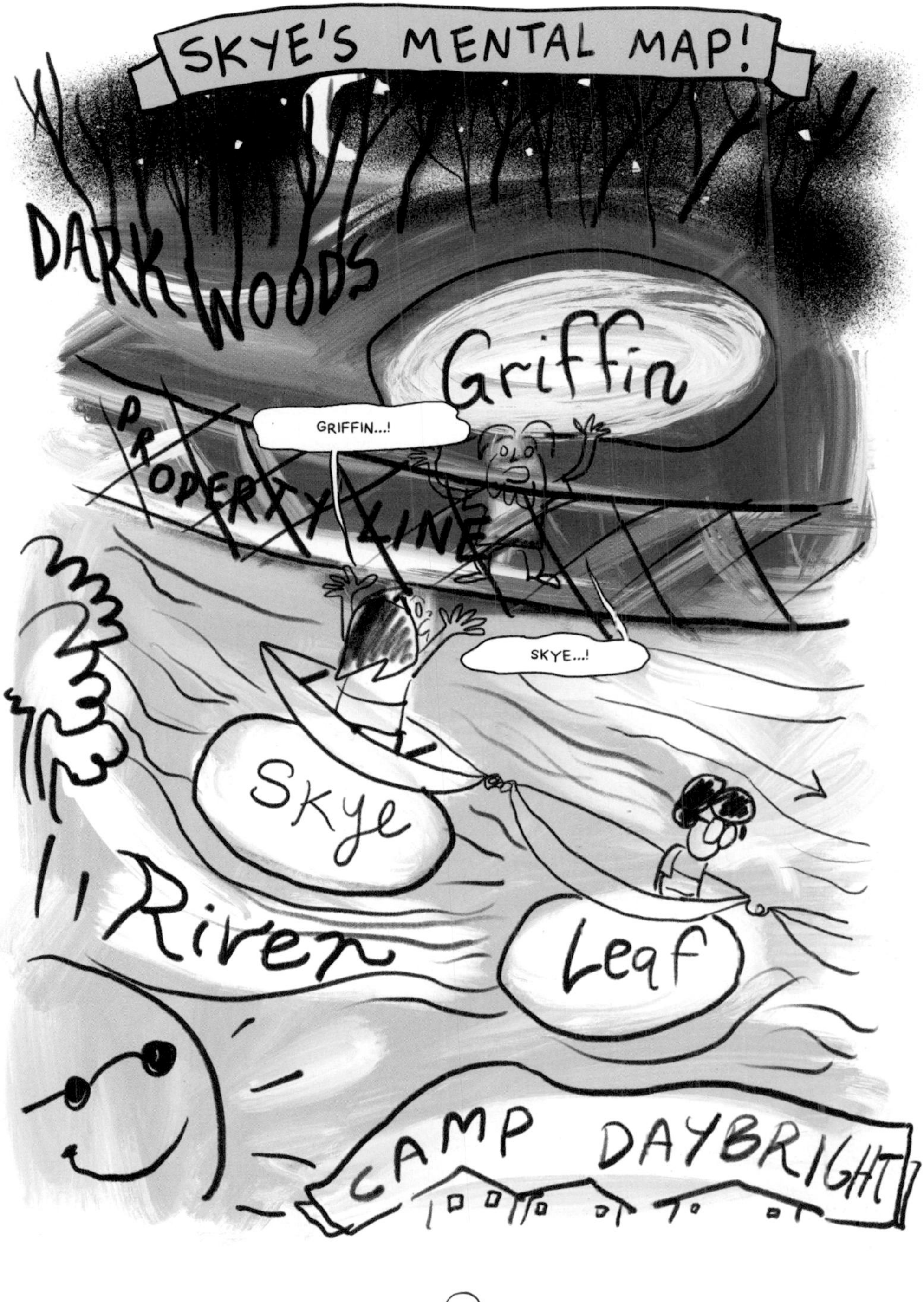
SKYE'S MENTAL MAP!
DARK WOODS
Griffin
PROPERTY LINE
GRIFFIN...!
SKYE...!
Skye
River
Leaf
CAMP DAYBRIGHT

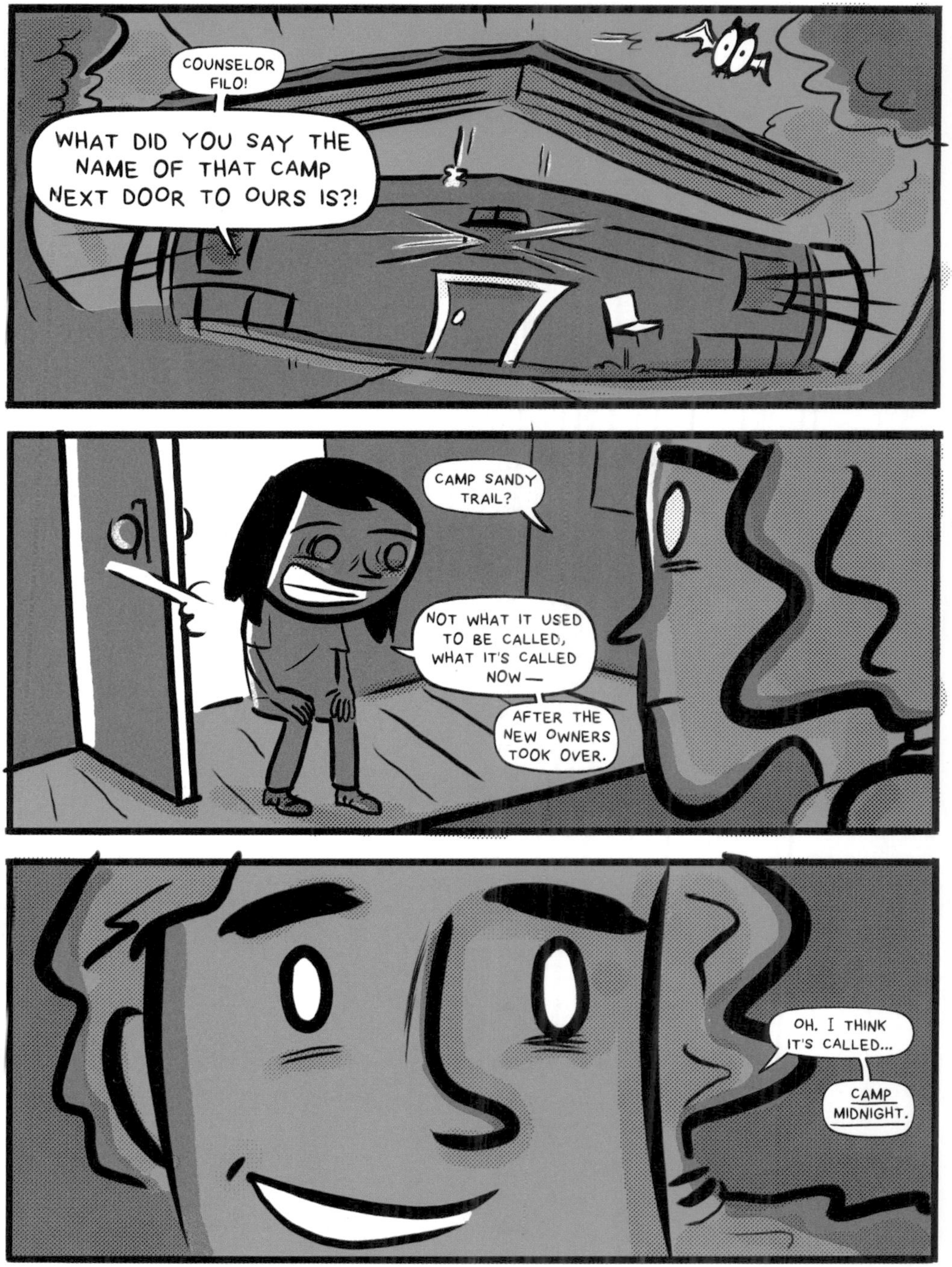
COUNSELOR FILO!
WHAT DID YOU SAY THE NAME OF THAT CAMP NEXT DOOR TO OURS IS?!
CAMP SANDY TRAIL?
NOT WHAT IT USED TO BE CALLED, WHAT IT'S CALLED NOW—
AFTER THE NEW OWNERS TOOK OVER.
OH. I THINK IT'S CALLED...
CAMP MIDNIGHT.

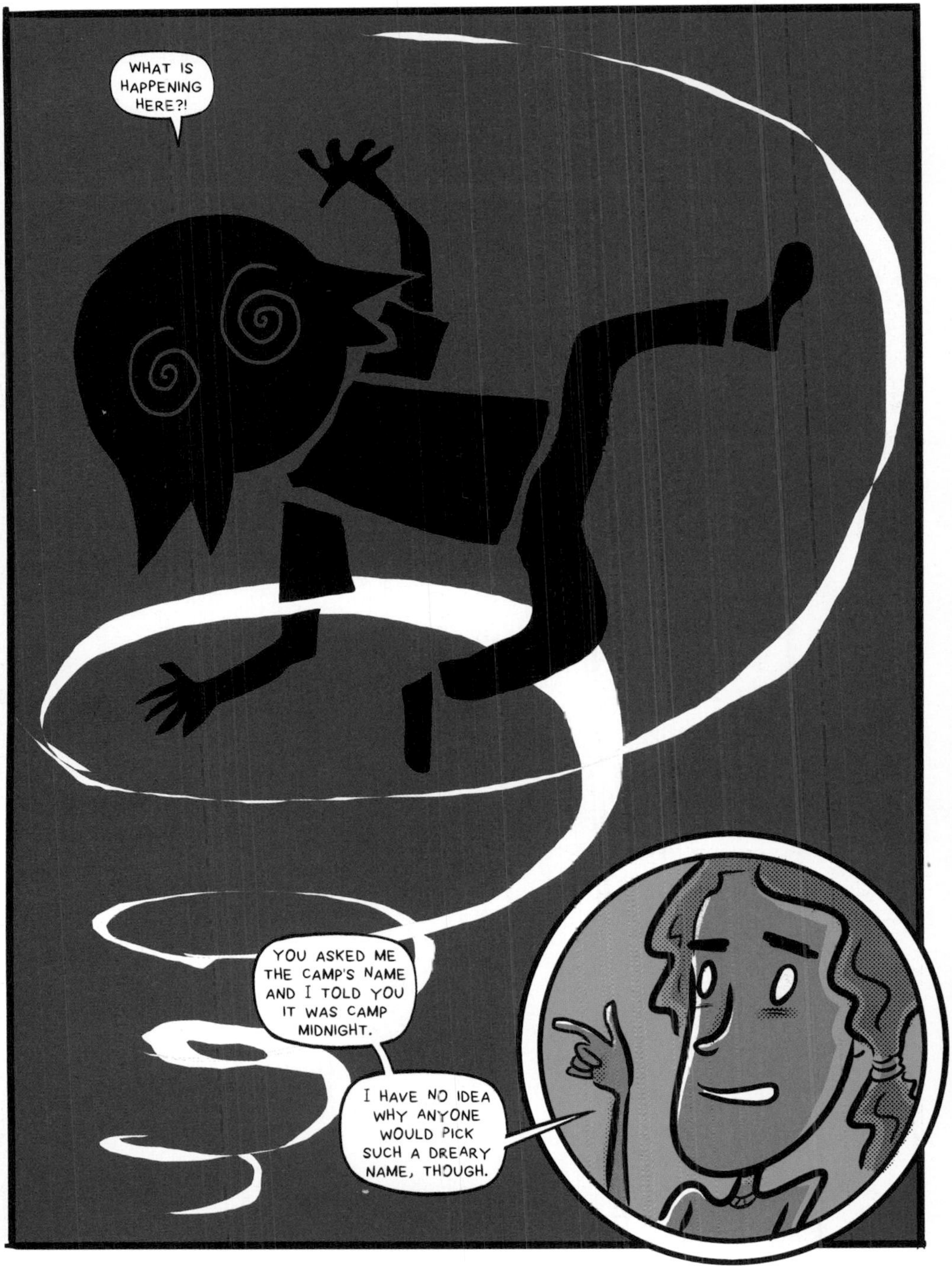
WHAT IS HAPPENING HERE?!
YOU ASKED ME THE CAMP'S NAME AND I TOLD YOU IT WAS CAMP MIDNIGHT.
I HAVE NO IDEA WHY ANYONE WOULD PICK SUCH A DREARY NAME, THOUGH.

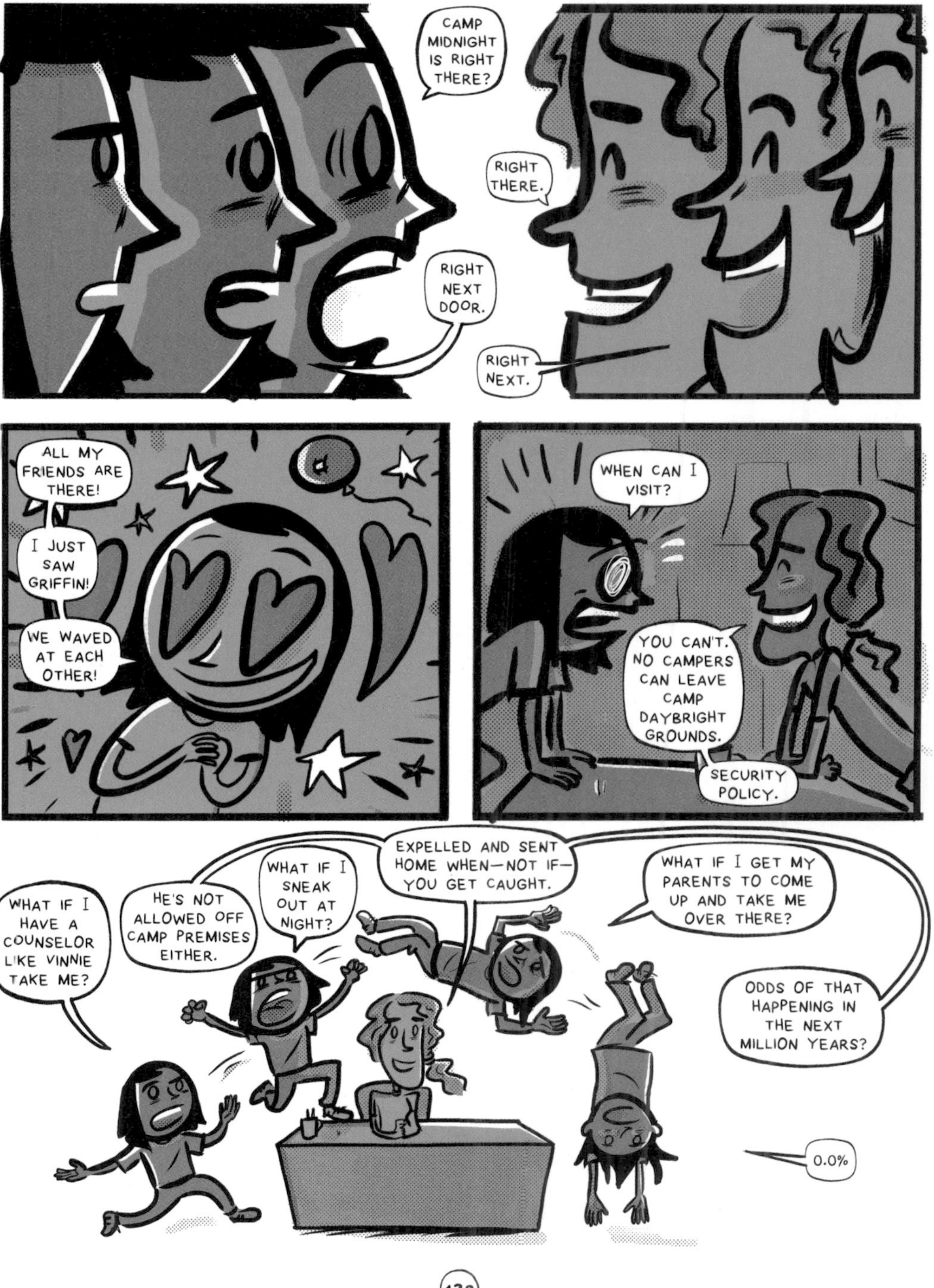
CAMP MIDNIGHT IS RIGHT THERE?
RIGHT THERE.
RIGHT NEXT DOOR.
RIGHT NEXT.
ALL MY FRIENDS ARE THERE!
I JUST SAW GRIFFIN!
WE WAVED AT EACH OTHER!
WHEN CAN I VISIT?
YOU CAN'T. NO CAMPERS CAN LEAVE CAMP DAYBRIGHT GROUNDS.
SECURITY POLICY.
WHAT IF I HAVE A COUNSELOR LIKE VINNIE TAKE ME?
HE'S NOT ALLOWED OFF CAMP PREMISES EITHER.
WHAT IF I SNEAK OUT AT NIGHT?
EXPELLED AND SENT HOME WHEN—NOT IF—YOU GET CAUGHT.
WHAT IF I GET MY PARENTS TO COME UP AND TAKE ME OVER THERE?
ODDS OF THAT HAPPENING IN THE NEXT MILLION YEARS?
0.0%

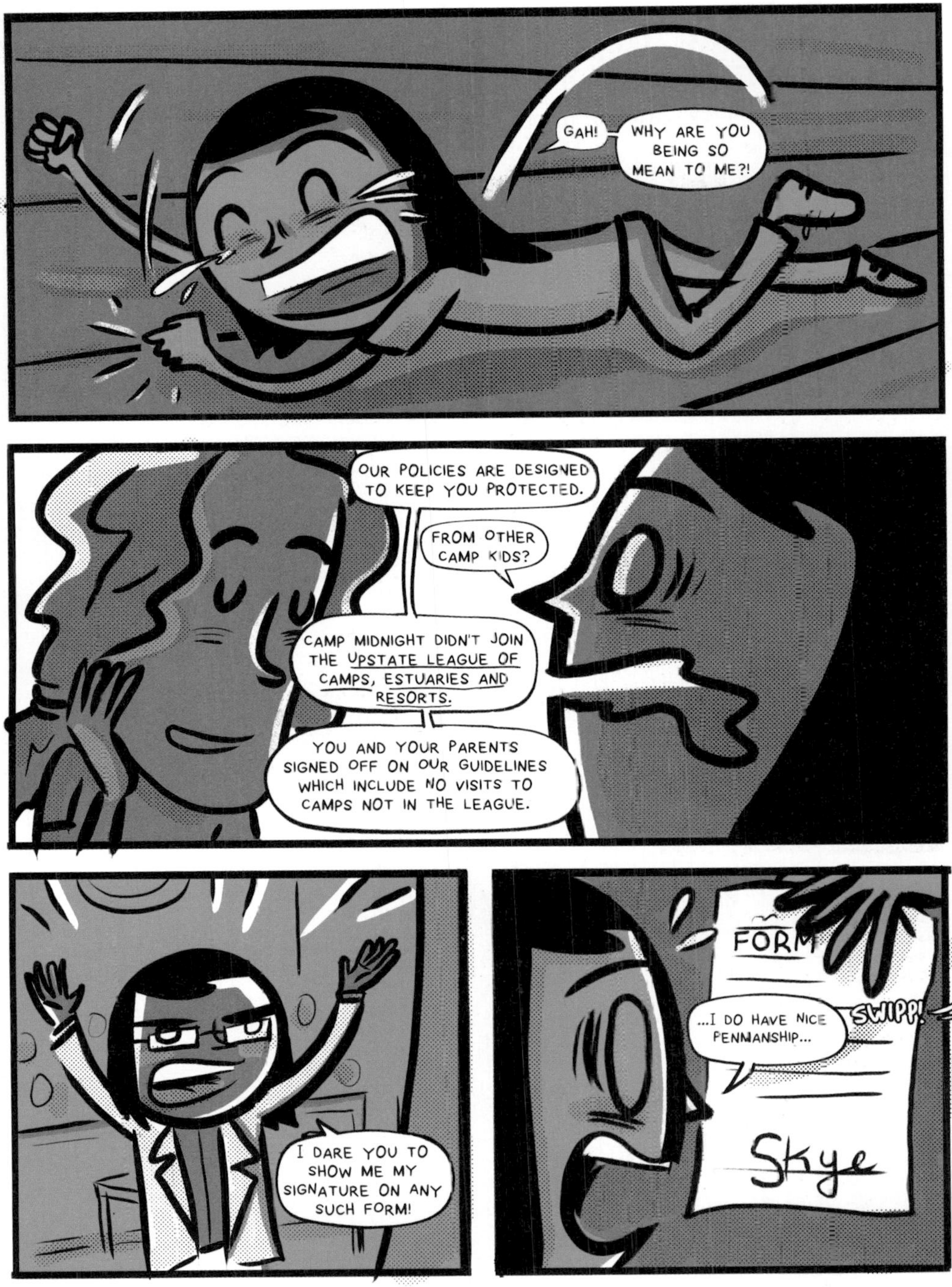
GAH!
WHY ARE YOU BEING SO MEAN TO ME?!
OUR POLICIES ARE DESIGNED TO KEEP YOU PROTECTED.
FROM OTHER CAMP KIDS?
CAMP MIDNIGHT DIDN'T JOIN THE UPSTATE LEAGUE OF CAMPS, ESTUARIES AND RESORTS.
YOU AND YOUR PARENTS SIGNED OFF ON OUR GUIDELINES WHICH INCLUDE NO VISITS TO CAMPS NOT IN THE LEAGUE.
I DARE YOU TO SHOW ME MY SIGNATURE ON ANY SUCH FORM!
FORM
SWIPP!
...I DO HAVE NICE PENMANSHIP...
Skye

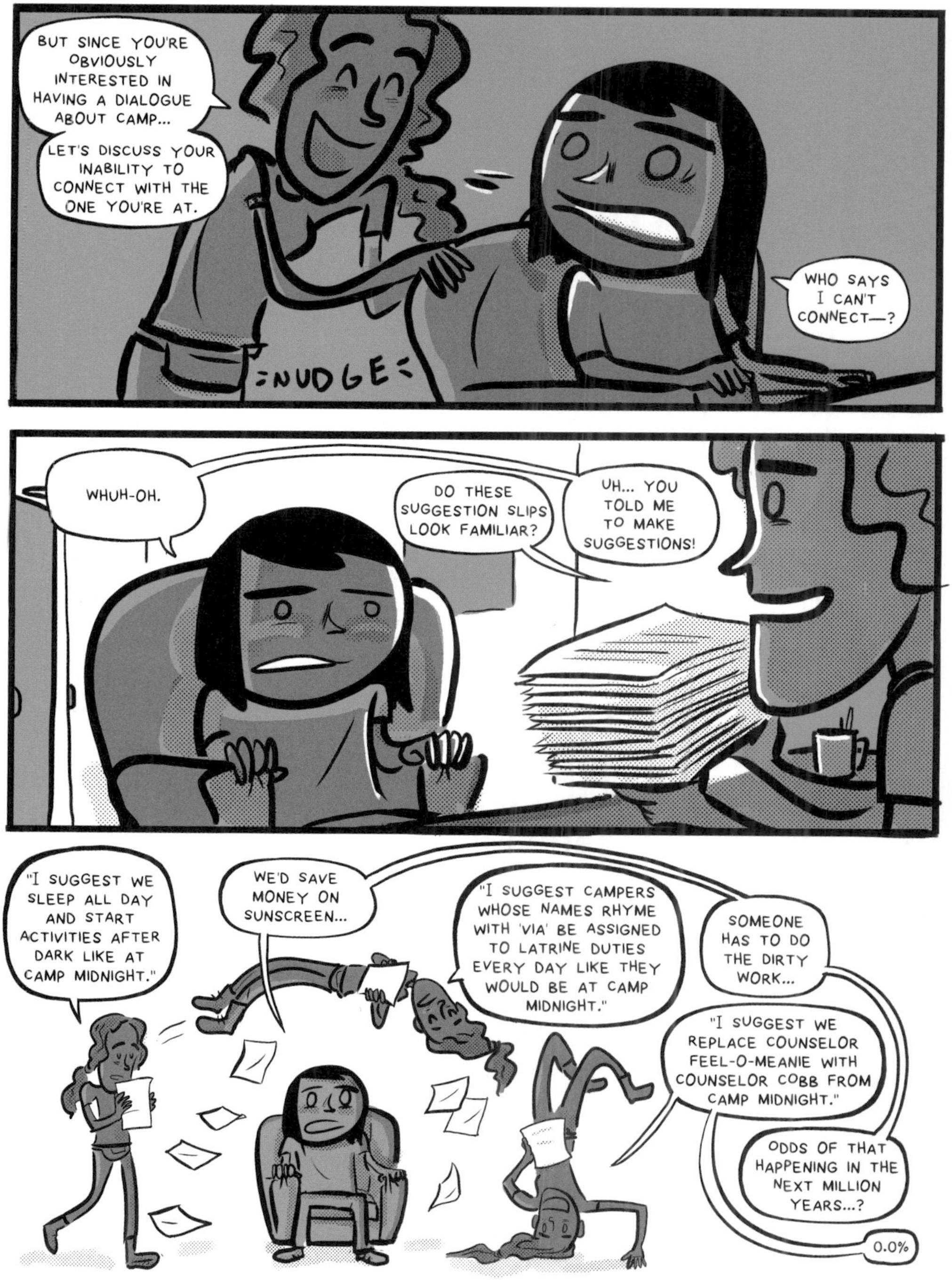
BUT SINCE YOU'RE OBVIOUSLY INTERESTED IN HAVING A DIALOGUE ABOUT CAMP...
LET'S DISCUSS YOUR INABILITY TO CONNECT WITH THE ONE YOU'RE AT.
WHO SAYS I CAN'T CONNECT—?
=NUDGE=
WHUH-OH.
DO THESE SUGGESTION SLIPS LOOK FAMILIAR?
UH... YOU TOLD ME TO MAKE SUGGESTIONS!
"I SUGGEST WE SLEEP ALL DAY AND START ACTIVITIES AFTER DARK LIKE AT CAMP MIDNIGHT."
WE'D SAVE MONEY ON SUNSCREEN...
"I SUGGEST CAMPERS WHOSE NAMES RHYME WITH 'VIA' BE ASSIGNED TO LATRINE DUTIES EVERY DAY LIKE THEY WOULD BE AT CAMP MIDNIGHT."
SOMEONE HAS TO DO THE DIRTY WORK...
"I SUGGEST WE REPLACE COUNSELOR FEEL-O-MEANIE WITH COUNSELOR COBB FROM CAMP MIDNIGHT."
ODDS OF THAT HAPPENING IN THE NEXT MILLION YEARS...?
0.0%

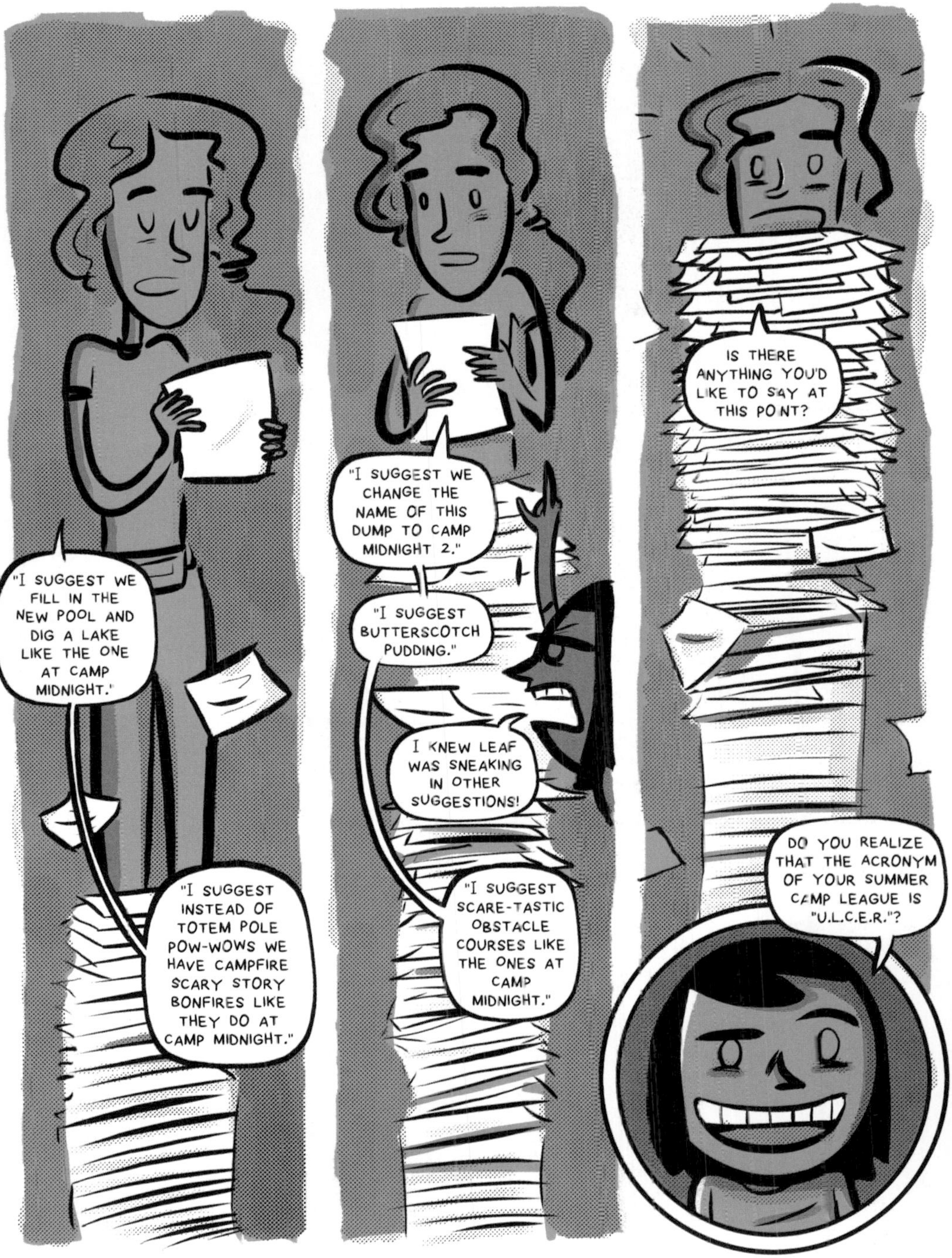
"I SUGGEST WE FILL IN THE NEW POOL AND DIG A LAKE LIKE THE ONE AT CAMP MIDNIGHT."
"I SUGGEST INSTEAD OF TOTEM POLE POW-WOWS WE HAVE CAMPFIRE SCARY STORY BONFIRES LIKE THEY DO AT CAMP MIDNIGHT."
"I SUGGEST WE CHANGE THE NAME OF THIS DUMP TO CAMP MIDNIGHT 2."
"I SUGGEST BUTTERSCOTCH PUDDING."
I KNEW LEAF WAS SNEAKING IN OTHER SUGGESTIONS!
"I SUGGEST SCARE-TASTIC OBSTACLE COURSES LIKE THE ONES AT CAMP MIDNIGHT."
IS THERE ANYTHING YOU'D LIKE TO SAY AT THIS POINT?
DO YOU REALIZE THAT THE ACRONYM OF YOUR SUMMER CAMP LEAGUE IS "U.L.C.E.R."?

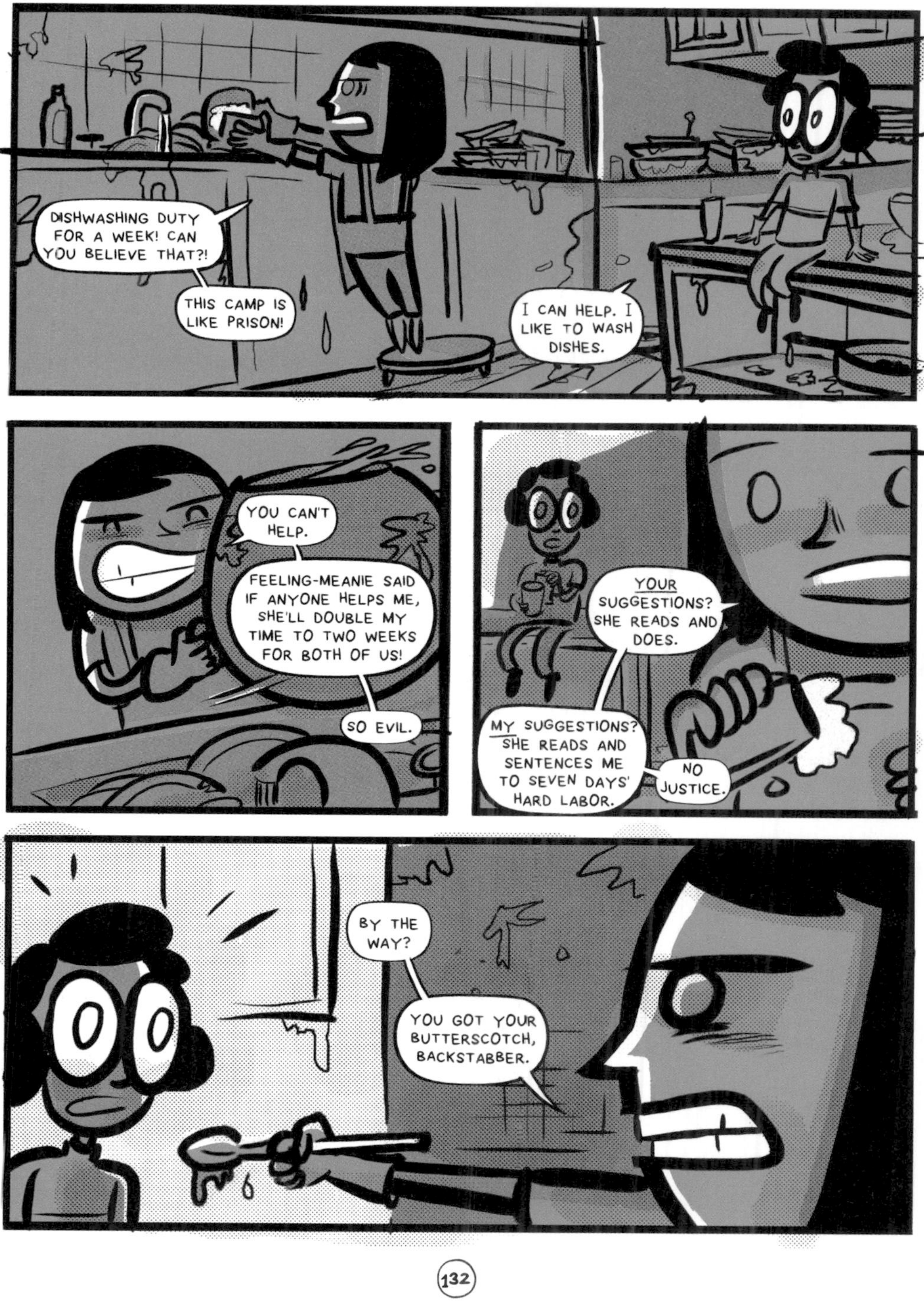
DISHWASHING DUTY FOR A WEEK! CAN YOU BELIEVE THAT?!
THIS CAMP IS LIKE PRISON!
I CAN HELP. I LIKE TO WASH DISHES.
YOU CAN'T HELP.
FEELING-MEANIE SAID IF ANYONE HELPS ME, SHE'LL DOUBLE MY TIME TO TWO WEEKS FOR BOTH OF US!
SO EVIL.
YOUR SUGGESTIONS? SHE READS AND DOES.
MY SUGGESTIONS? SHE READS AND SENTENCES ME TO SEVEN DAYS' HARD LABOR.
NO JUSTICE.
BY THE WAY?
YOU GOT YOUR BUTTERSCOTCH, BACKSTABBER.

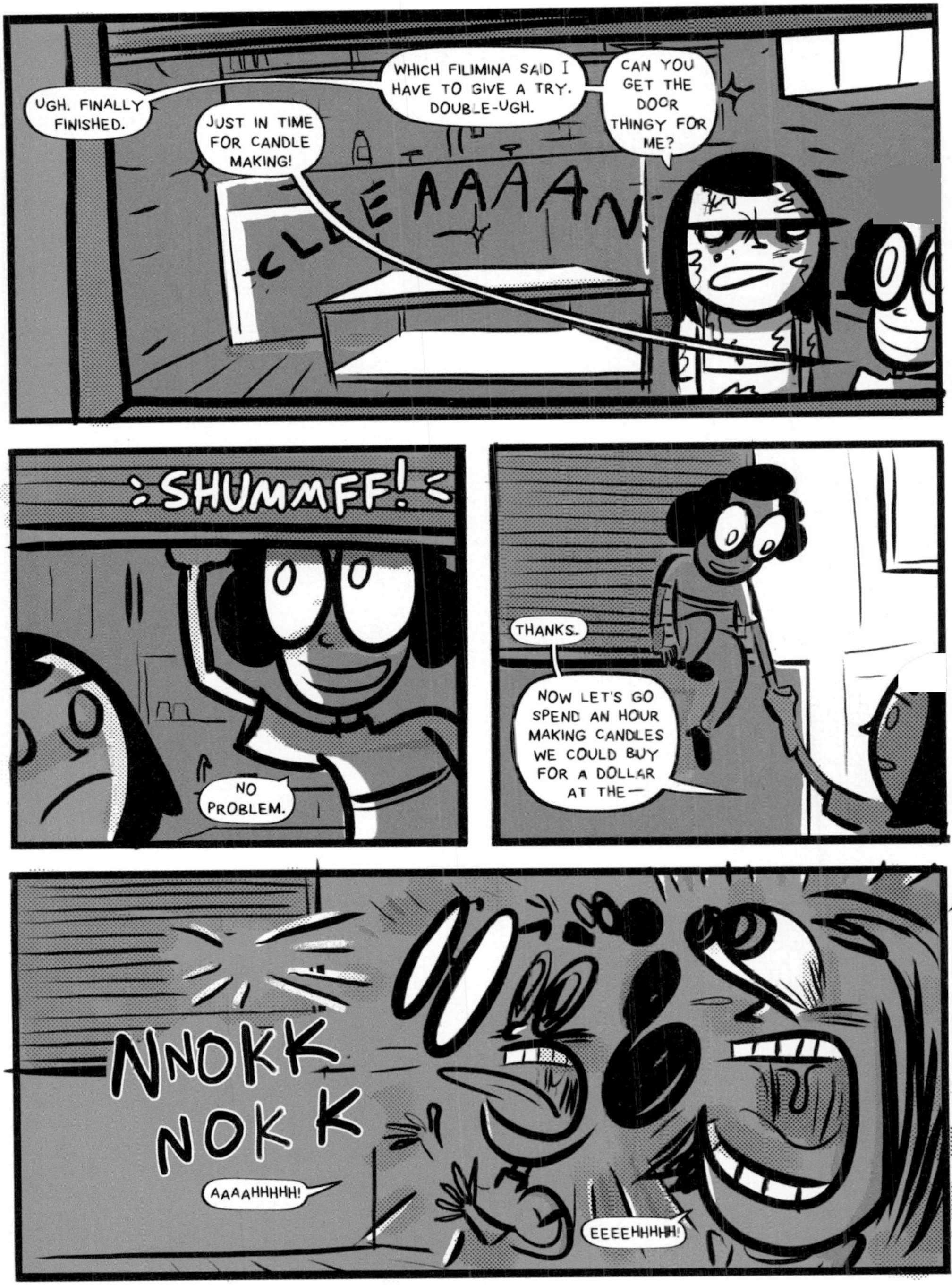

UGH. FINALLY FINISHED.
JUST IN TIME FOR CANDLE MAKING!
WHICH FILIMINA SAID I HAVE TO GIVE A TRY. DOUBLE-UGH.
CAN YOU GET THE DOOR THINGY FOR ME?
CLEEAAAAAN
SHUMMFF!
NO PROBLEM.
THANKS.
NOW LET'S GO SPEND AN HOUR MAKING CANDLES WE COULD BUY FOR A DOLLAR AT THE—
NNOKK NOK K
AAAAHHHHH!
EEEEHHHHH!

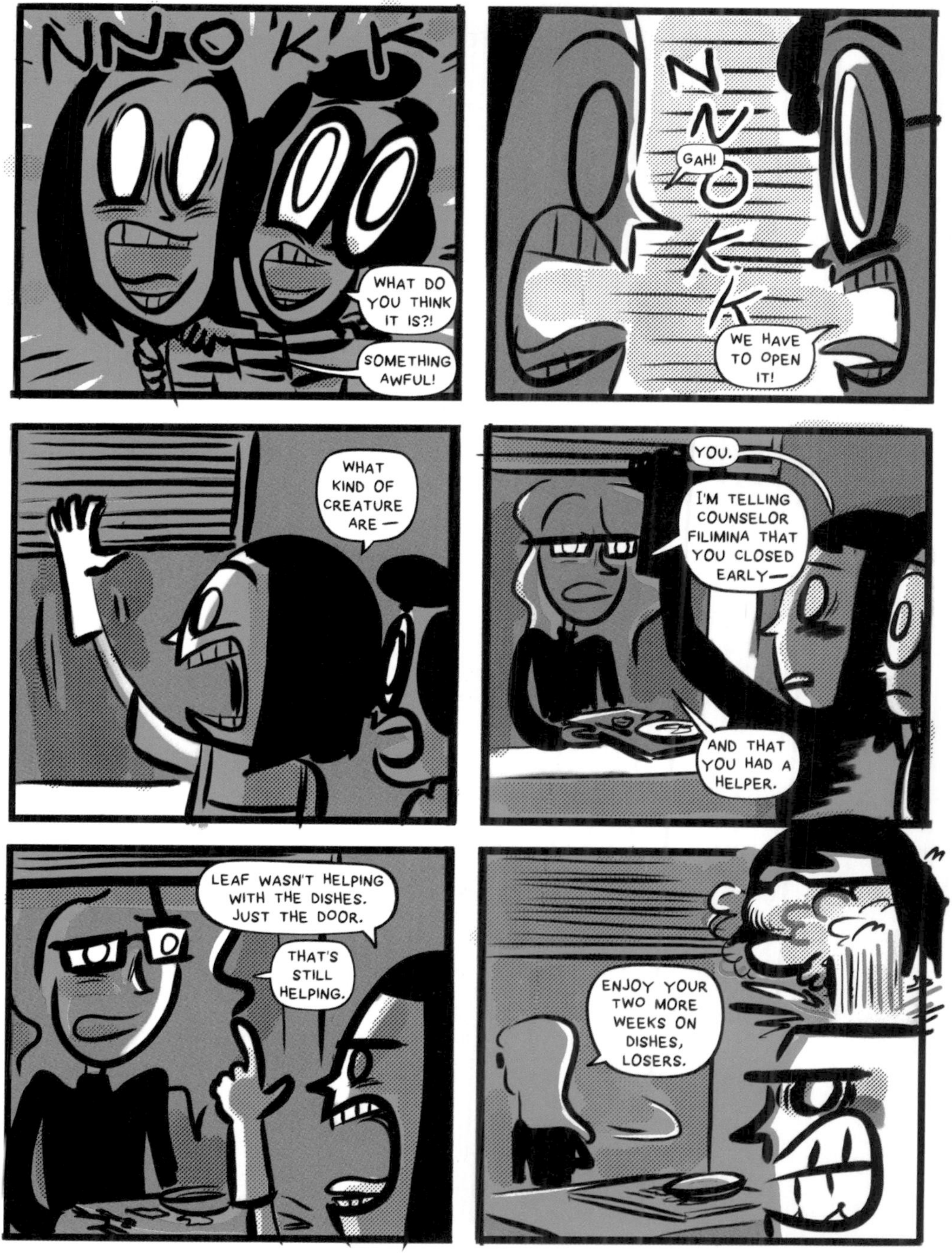
NNOKK
WHAT DO YOU THINK IT IS?!
SOMETHING AWFUL!
NNOKK
GAH!
WE HAVE TO OPEN IT!
WHAT KIND OF CREATURE ARE—
YOU.
I'M TELLING COUNSELOR FILIMINA THAT YOU CLOSED EARLY—
AND THAT YOU HAD A HELPER.
LEAF WASN'T HELPING WITH THE DISHES. JUST THE DOOR.
THAT'S STILL HELPING.
ENJOY YOUR TWO MORE WEEKS ON DISHES, LOSERS.

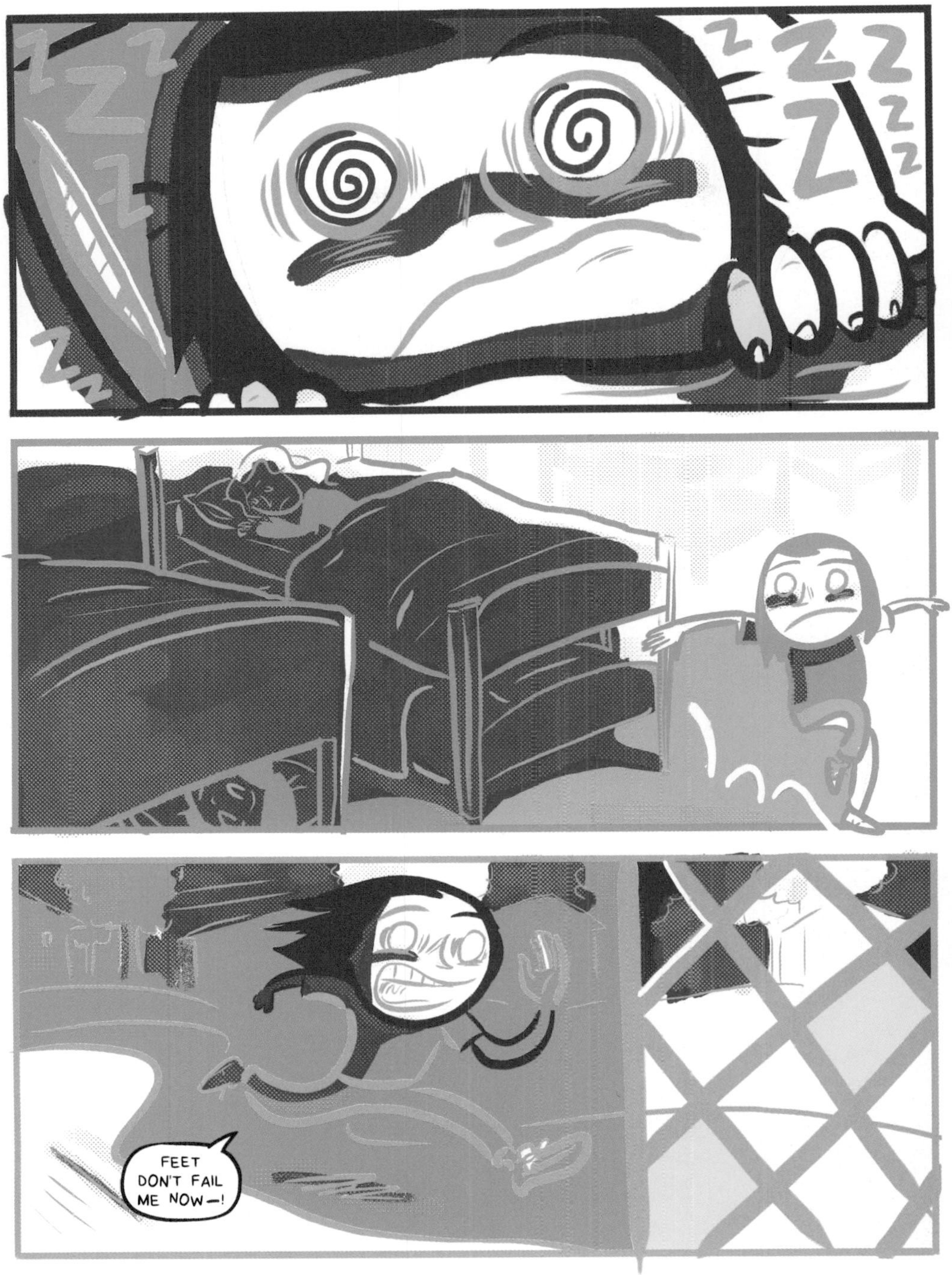
FEET DON'T FAIL ME NOW—!

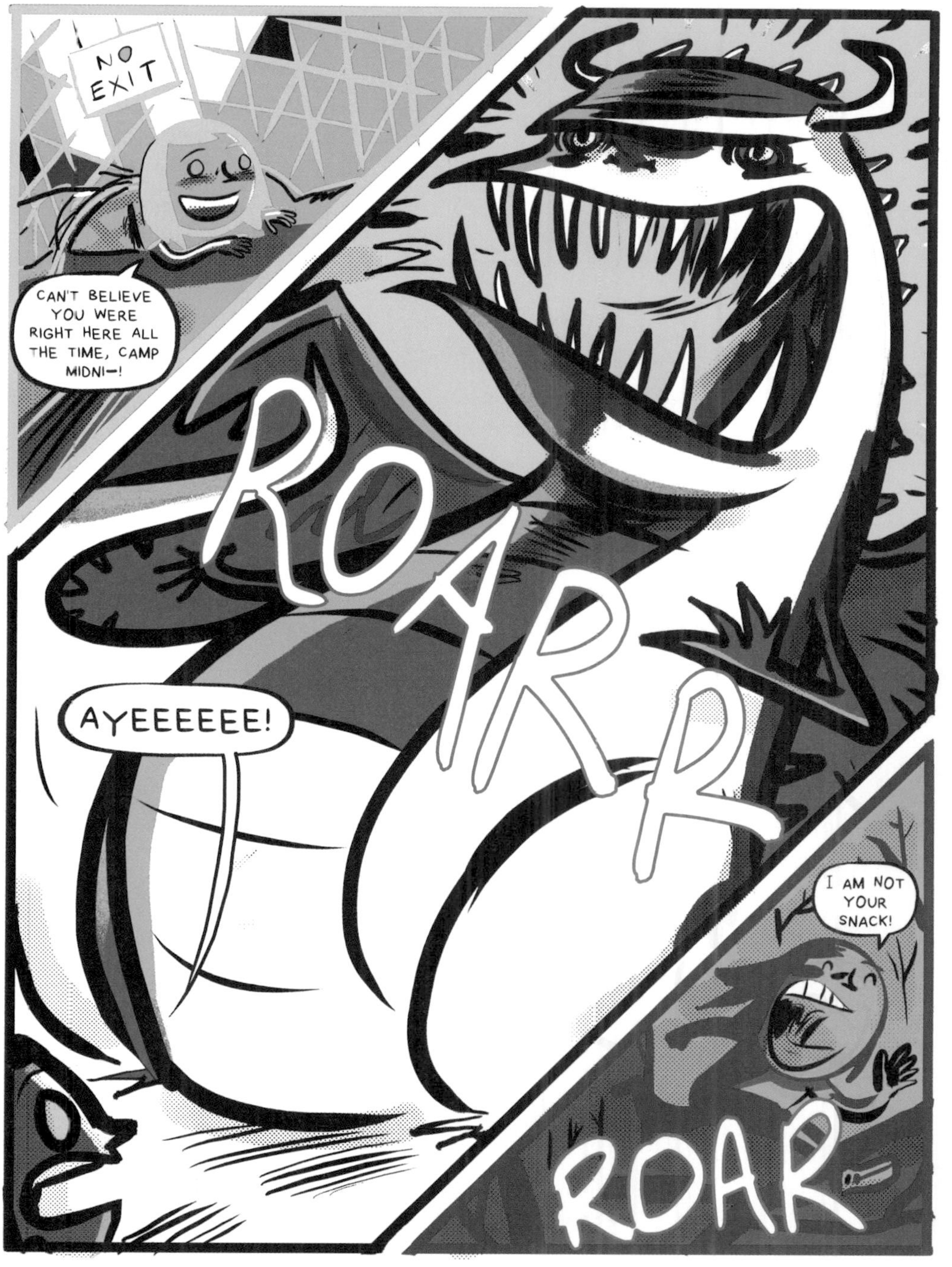
NO EXIT
CAN'T BELIEVE YOU WERE RIGHT HERE ALL THE TIME, CAMP MIDNI—!
ROARR
AYEEEEEE!
I AM NOT YOUR SNACK!
ROAR

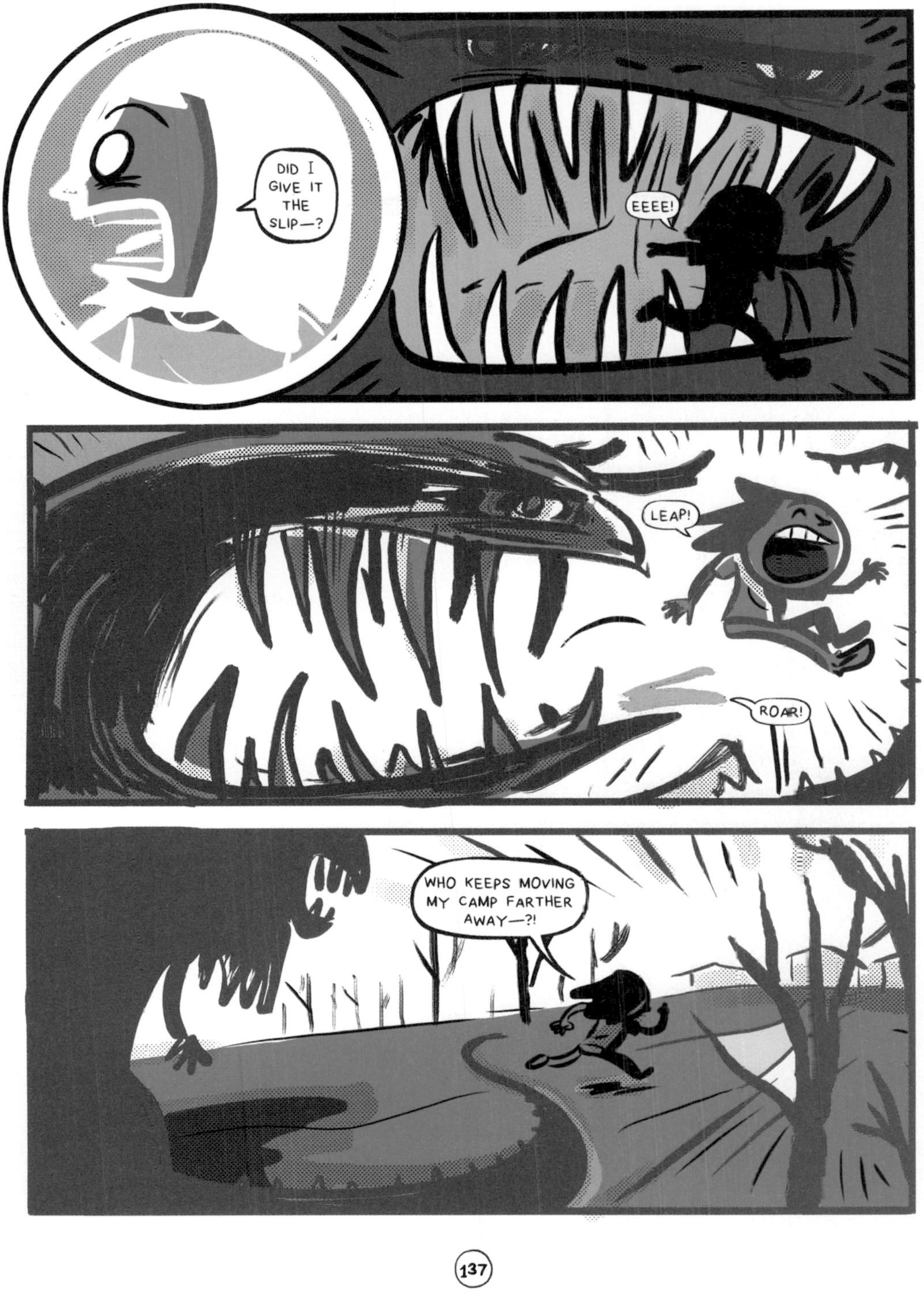
DID I GIVE IT THE SLIP—?
EEEE!
LEAP!
ROAR!
WHO KEEPS MOVING MY CAMP FARTHER AWAY—?!

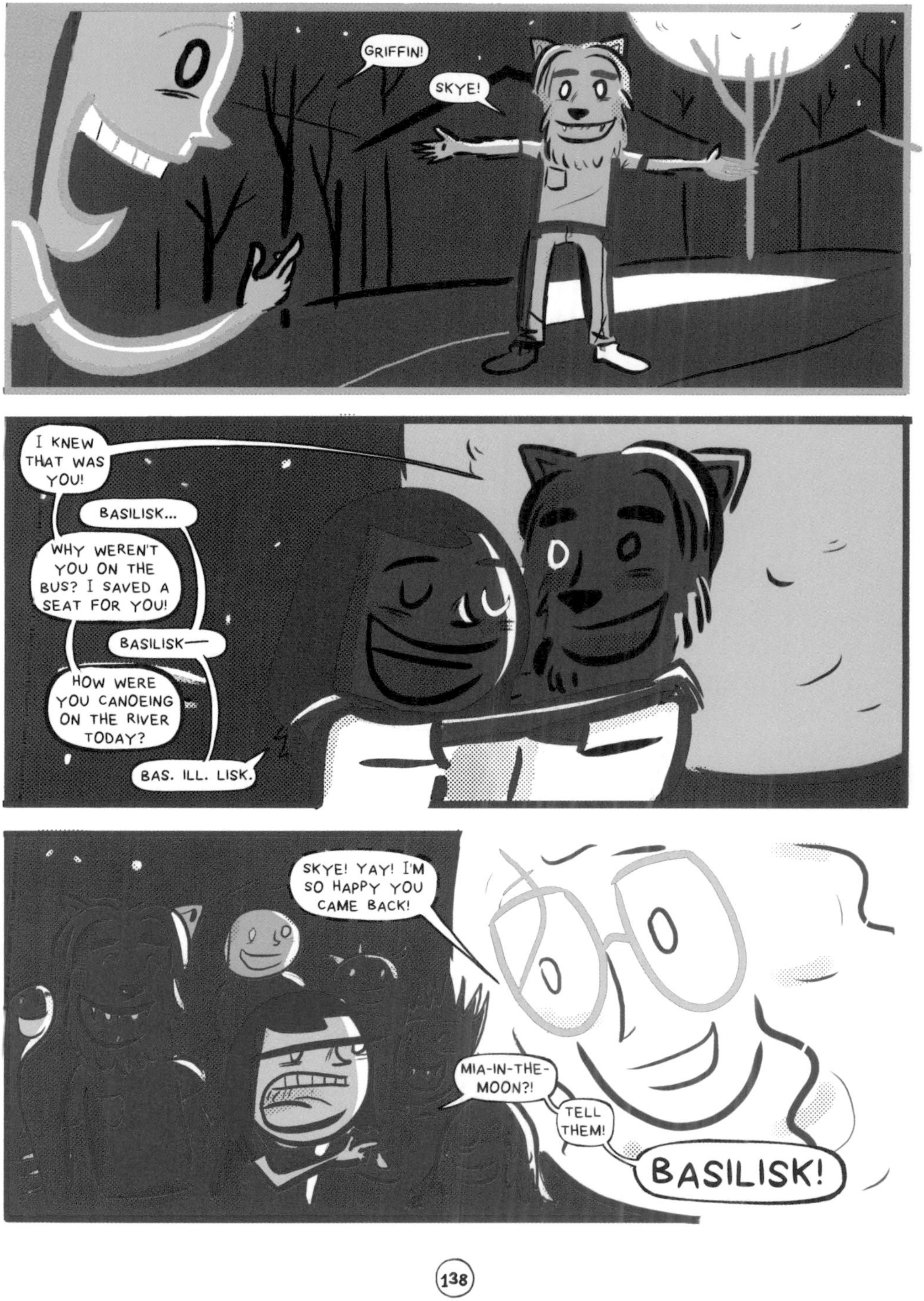
GRIFFIN!
SKYE!
I KNEW THAT WAS YOU!
BASILISK...
WHY WEREN'T YOU ON THE BUS? I SAVED A SEAT FOR YOU!
BASILISK—
HOW WERE YOU CANOEING ON THE RIVER TODAY?
BAS. ILL. LISK.
SKYE! YAY! I'M SO HAPPY YOU CAME BACK!
MIA-IN-THE-MOON?!
TELL THEM!
BASILISK!

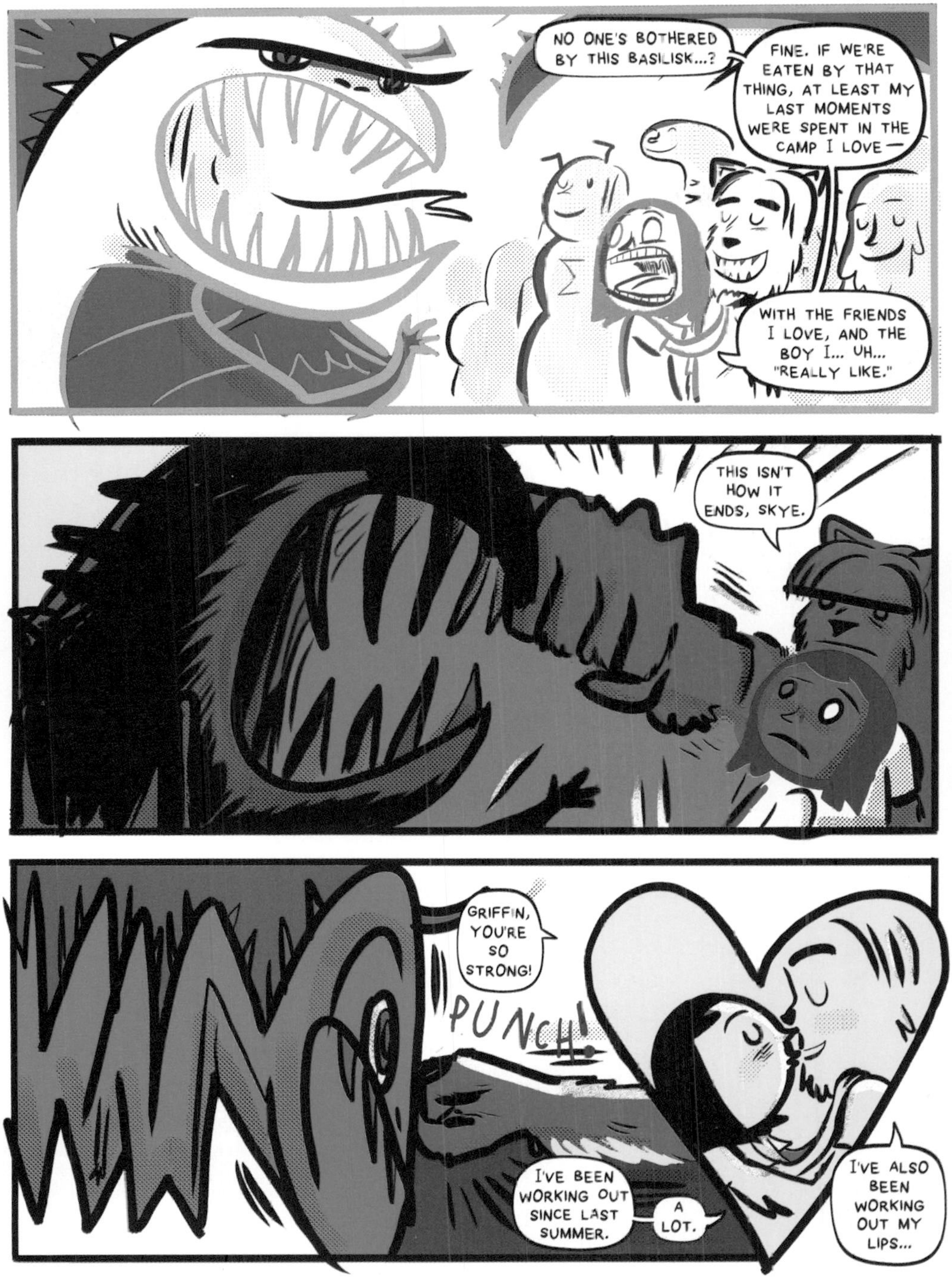
NO ONE'S BOTHERED BY THIS BASILISK...?
FINE. IF WE'RE EATEN BY THAT THING, AT LEAST MY LAST MOMENTS WERE SPENT IN THE CAMP I LOVE—
WITH THE FRIENDS I LOVE, AND THE BOY I... UH... "REALLY LIKE."
THIS ISN'T HOW IT ENDS, SKYE.
GRIFFIN, YOU'RE SO STRONG!
PUNCH!
I'VE BEEN WORKING OUT SINCE LAST SUMMER.
A LOT.
I'VE ALSO BEEN WORKING OUT MY LIPS...

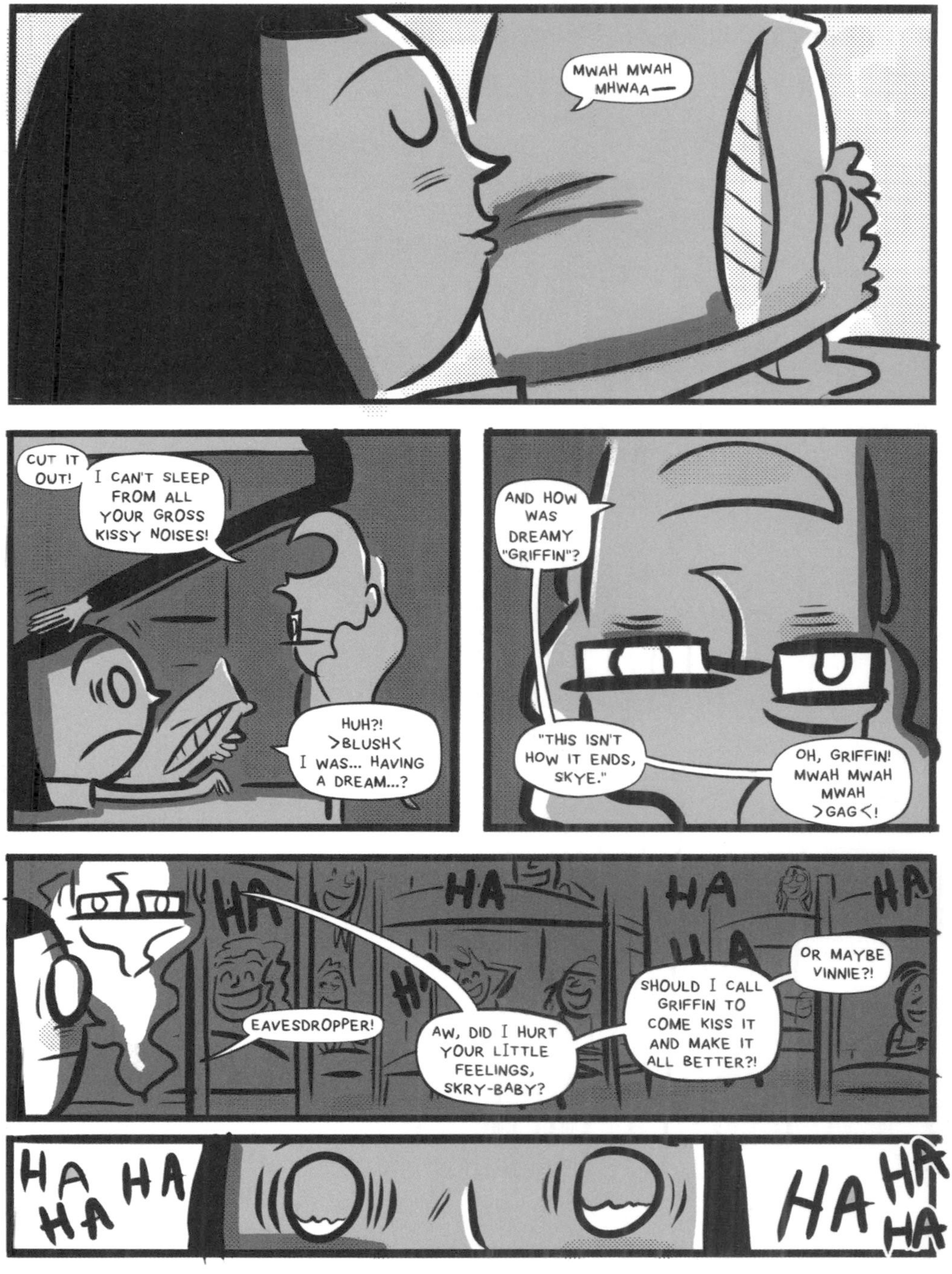
MWAH MWAH MHWAA—
CUT IT OUT!
I CAN'T SLEEP FROM ALL YOUR GROSS KISSY NOISES!
HUH?! >BLUSH< I WAS... HAVING A DREAM...?
AND HOW WAS DREAMY "GRIFFIN"?
"THIS ISN'T HOW IT ENDS, SKYE."
OH, GRIFFIN! MWAH MWAH MWAH >GAG<!
HA HA HA HA HA
EAVESDROPPER!
AW, DID I HURT YOUR LITTLE FEELINGS, SKRY-BABY?
SHOULD I CALL GRIFFIN TO COME KISS IT AND MAKE IT ALL BETTER?!
OR MAYBE VINNIE?!
HA HA HA HA
HA HA HA HA

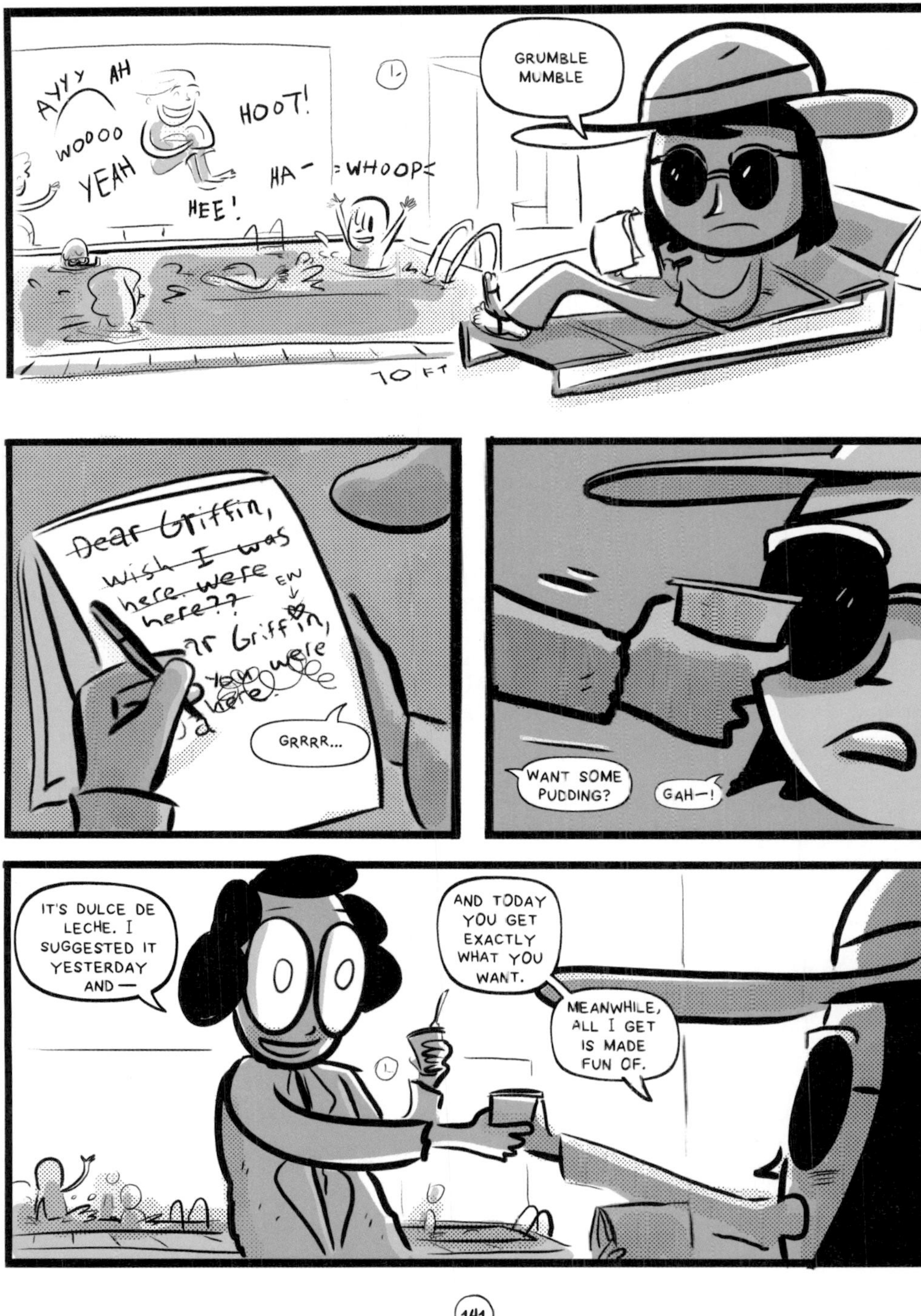
AYYY AH
WOOOO
YEAH
HOOT!
HA-
=WHOOP=
HEE!
GRUMBLE MUMBLE
10 FT
Dear Griffin,
wish I was
here. were
here??
EW
GRRRR...
WANT SOME PUDDING?
GAH—!
IT'S DULCE DE LECHE. I SUGGESTED IT YESTERDAY AND—
AND TODAY YOU GET EXACTLY WHAT YOU WANT.
MEANWHILE, ALL I GET IS MADE FUN OF.

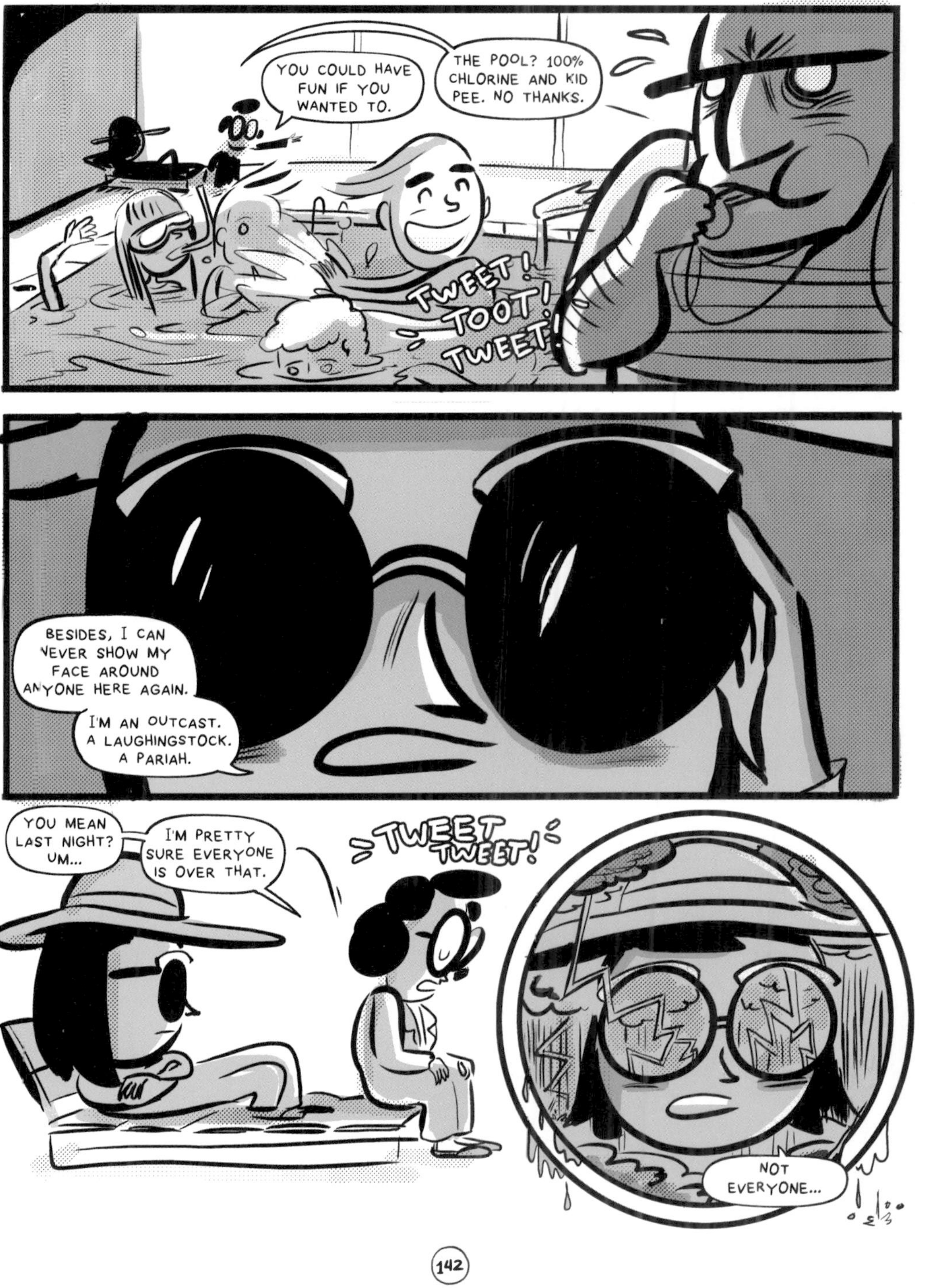
YOU COULD HAVE FUN IF YOU WANTED TO.
THE POOL? 100% CHLORINE AND KID PEE. NO THANKS.
TWEET! TOOT! TWEET!
BESIDES, I CAN NEVER SHOW MY FACE AROUND ANYONE HERE AGAIN.
I'M AN OUTCAST. A LAUGHINGSTOCK. A PARIAH.
YOU MEAN LAST NIGHT? UM...
I'M PRETTY SURE EVERYONE IS OVER THAT.
TWEET TWEET!
NOT EVERYONE...

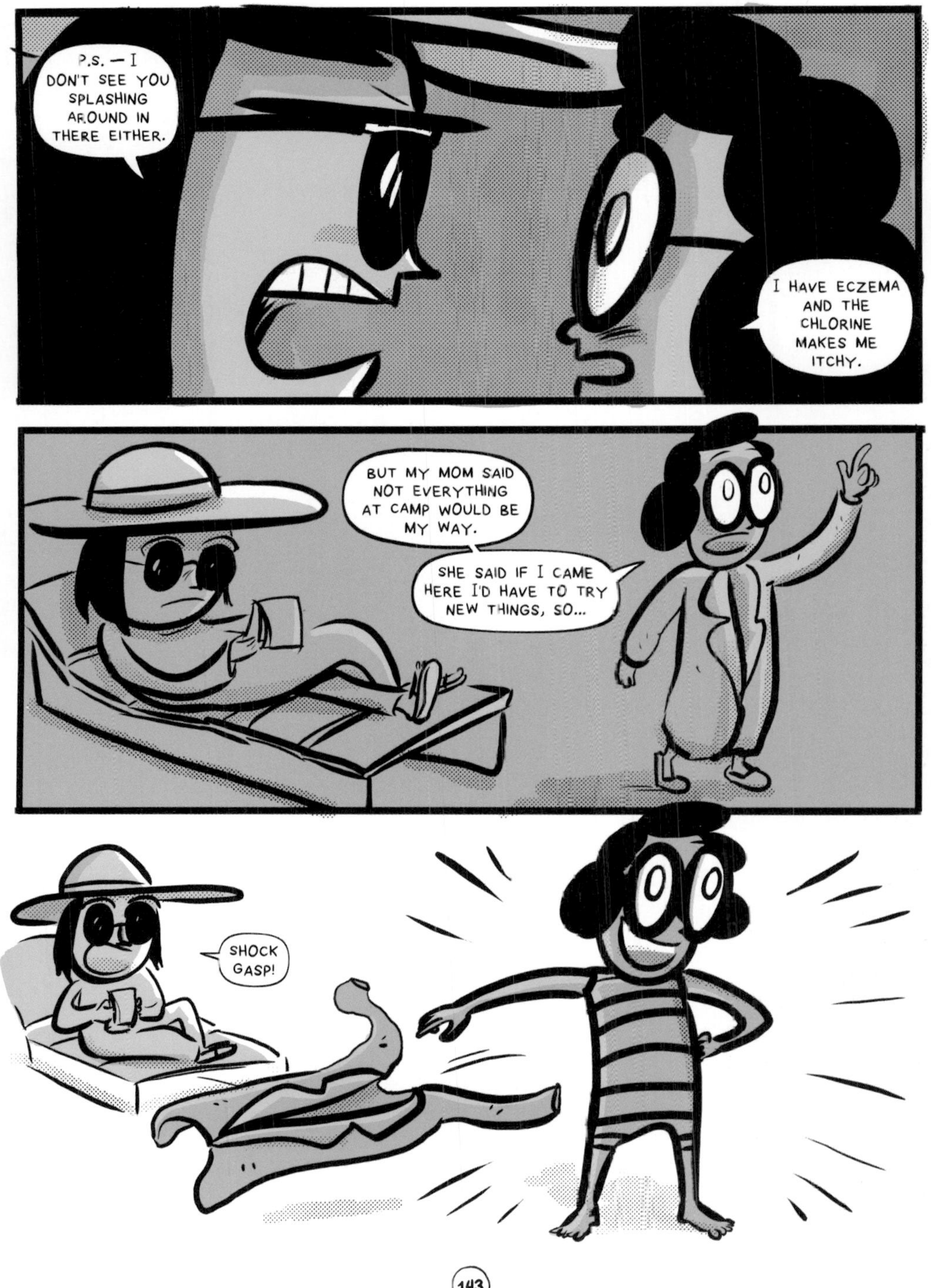
P.S. — I DON'T SEE YOU SPLASHING AROUND IN THERE EITHER.
I HAVE ECZEMA AND THE CHLORINE MAKES ME ITCHY.
BUT MY MOM SAID NOT EVERYTHING AT CAMP WOULD BE MY WAY.
SHE SAID IF I CAME HERE I'D HAVE TO TRY NEW THINGS, SO...
SHOCK GASP!

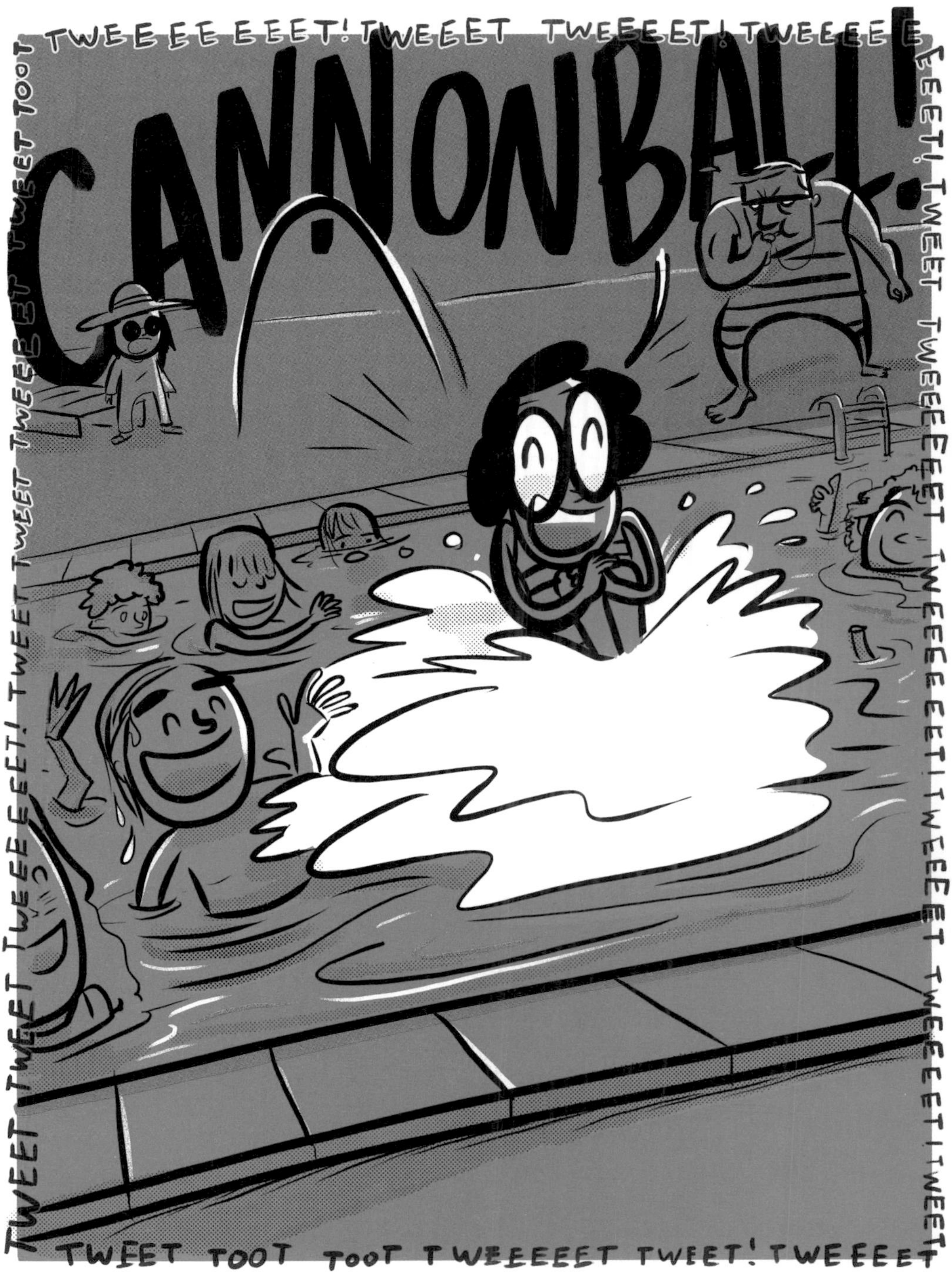
TWEEEEE EEET! TWEEET TWEEEET! TWEEEEE
CANNONBALL!
EEEET! TWEET TWEEEEEEEET TWEEEEEE EET! TWEEEEEET TWEEEEEET! TWEET
TWEET TOOT TOOT TWEEEEEET TWEET! TWEEEEET
TWEET TWEET TWEEEEEEEET! TWEET TWEEEEET TWEET TWEET TOOT

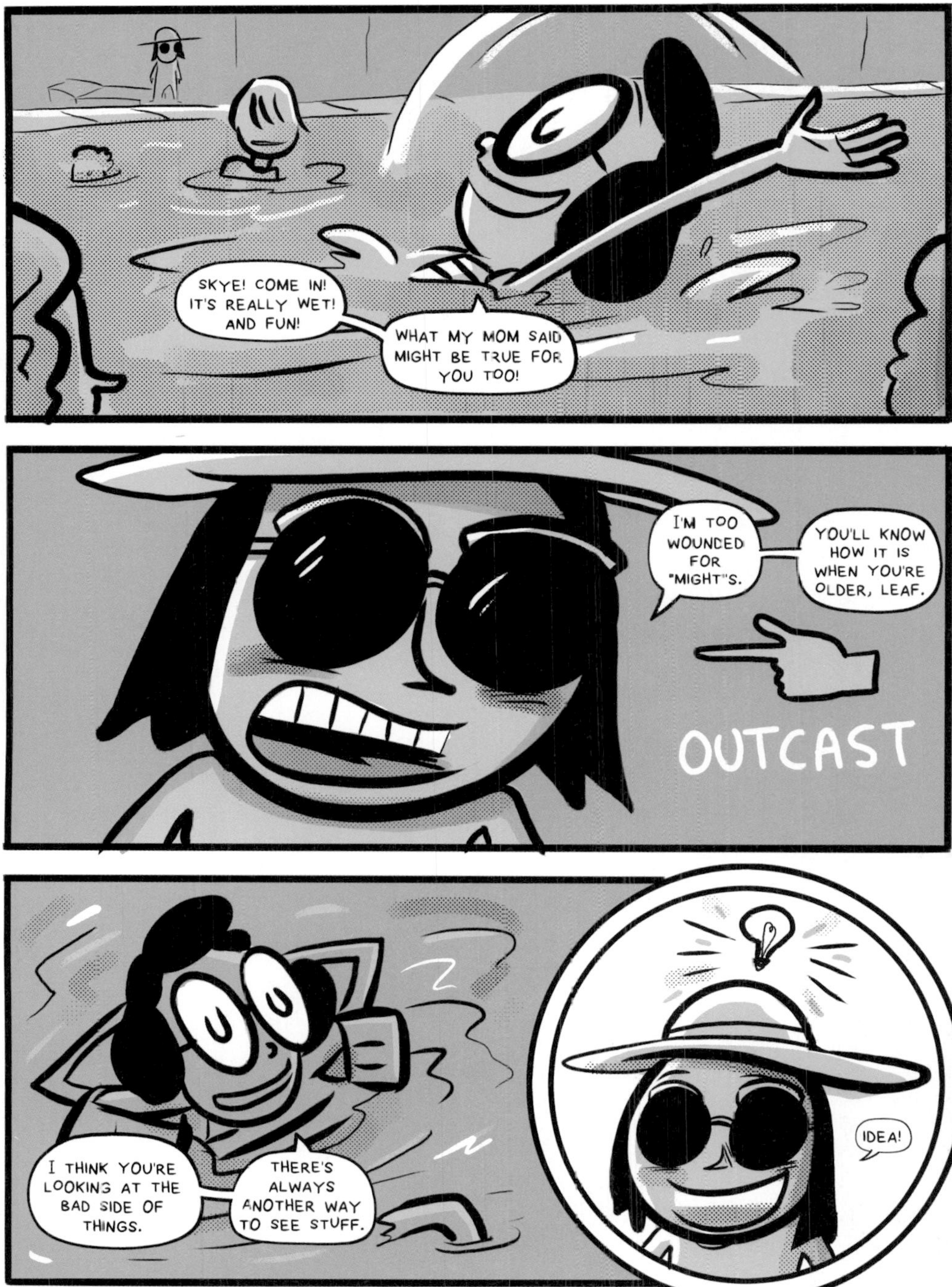
SKYE! COME IN! IT'S REALLY WET! AND FUN!
WHAT MY MOM SAID MIGHT BE TRUE FOR YOU TOO!
I'M TOO WOUNDED FOR "MIGHT"S.
YOU'LL KNOW HOW IT IS WHEN YOU'RE OLDER, LEAF.
OUTCAST
I THINK YOU'RE LOOKING AT THE BAD SIDE OF THINGS.
THERE'S ALWAYS ANOTHER WAY TO SEE STUFF.
IDEA!

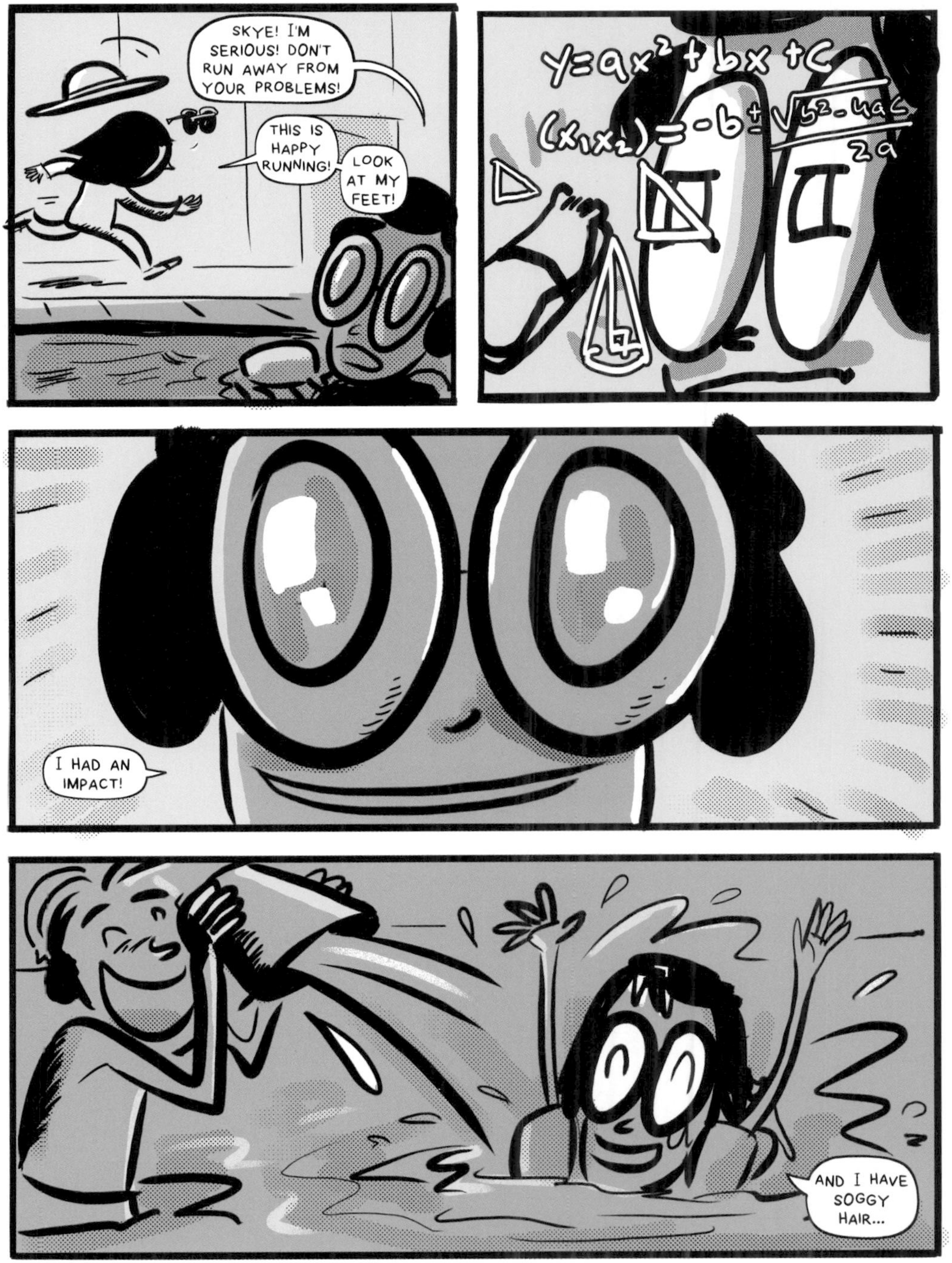
SKYE! I'M SERIOUS! DON'T RUN AWAY FROM YOUR PROBLEMS!
THIS IS HAPPY RUNNING!
LOOK AT MY FEET!
$y=ax^2+bx+c$
$(x_1x_2)=\frac{-b\pm\sqrt{b^2-4ac}}{2a}$
I HAD AN IMPACT!
AND I HAVE SOGGY HAIR...

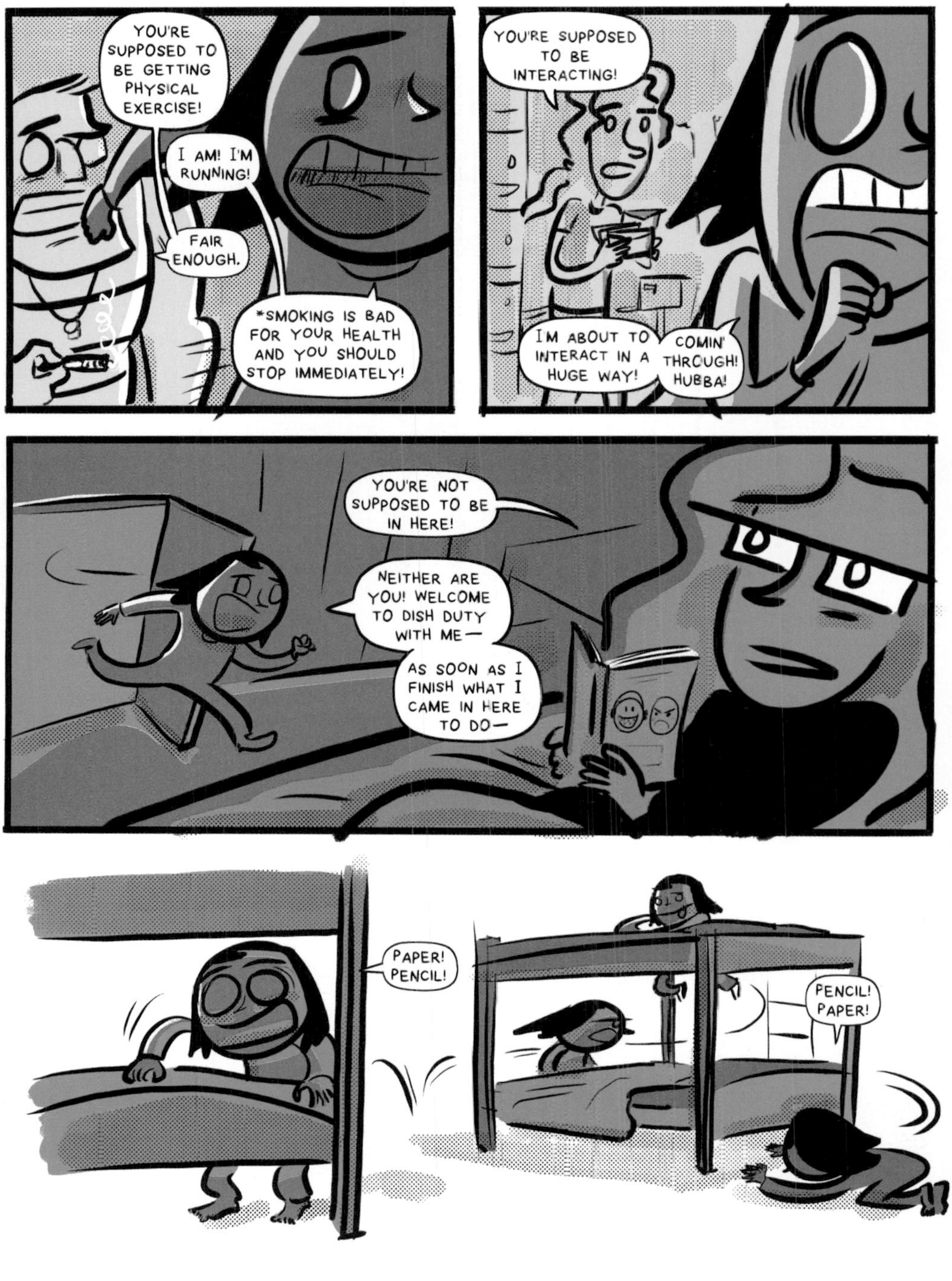
YOU'RE SUPPOSED TO BE GETTING PHYSICAL EXERCISE!
I AM! I'M RUNNING!
FAIR ENOUGH.
*SMOKING IS BAD FOR YOUR HEALTH AND YOU SHOULD STOP IMMEDIATELY!
YOU'RE SUPPOSED TO BE INTERACTING!
I'M ABOUT TO INTERACT IN A HUGE WAY!
COMIN' THROUGH! HUBBA!
YOU'RE NOT SUPPOSED TO BE IN HERE!
NEITHER ARE YOU! WELCOME TO DISH DUTY WITH ME—
AS SOON AS I FINISH WHAT I CAME IN HERE TO DO—
PAPER! PENCIL!
PENCIL! PAPER!

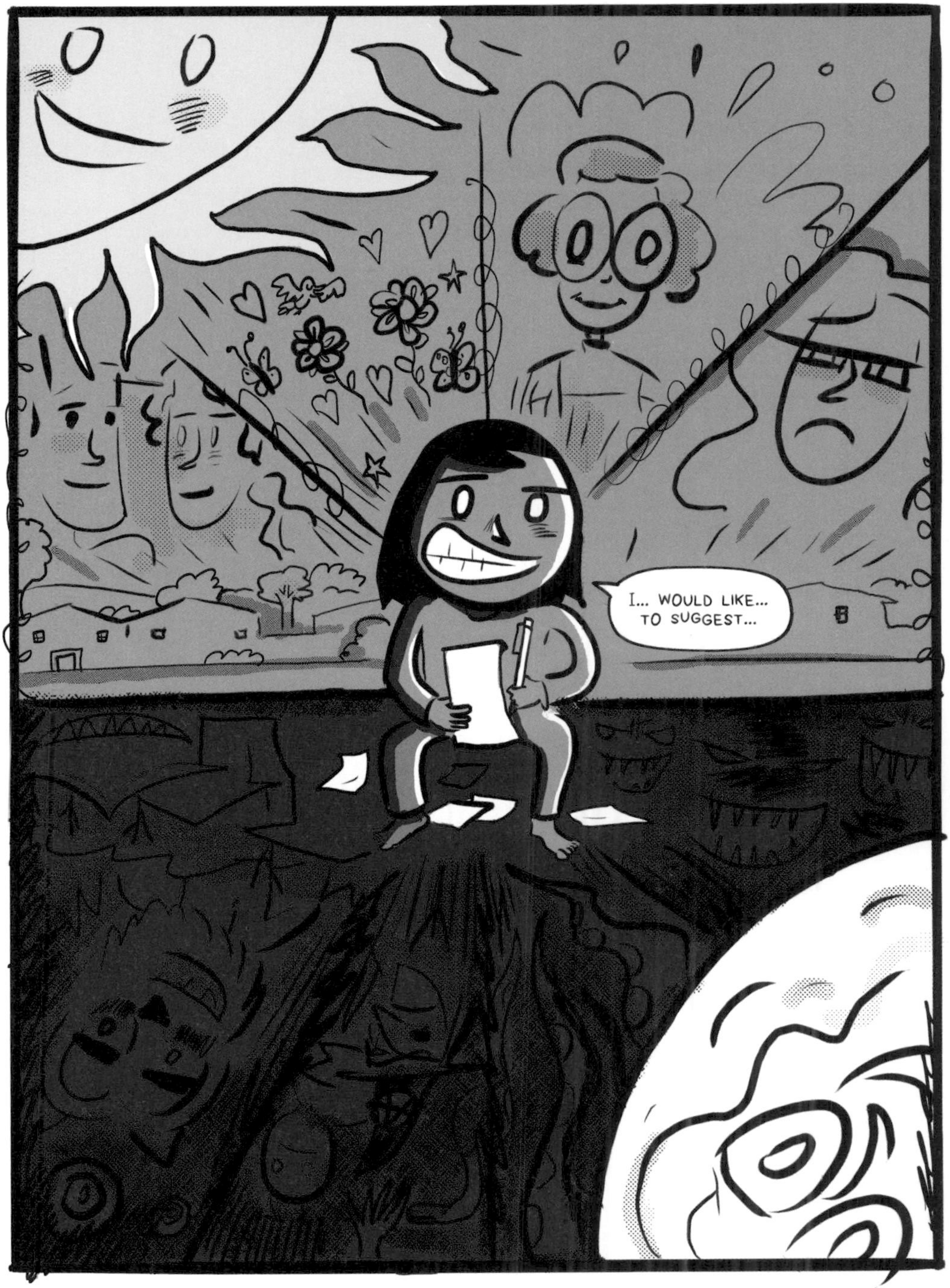
I... WOULD LIKE... TO SUGGEST...

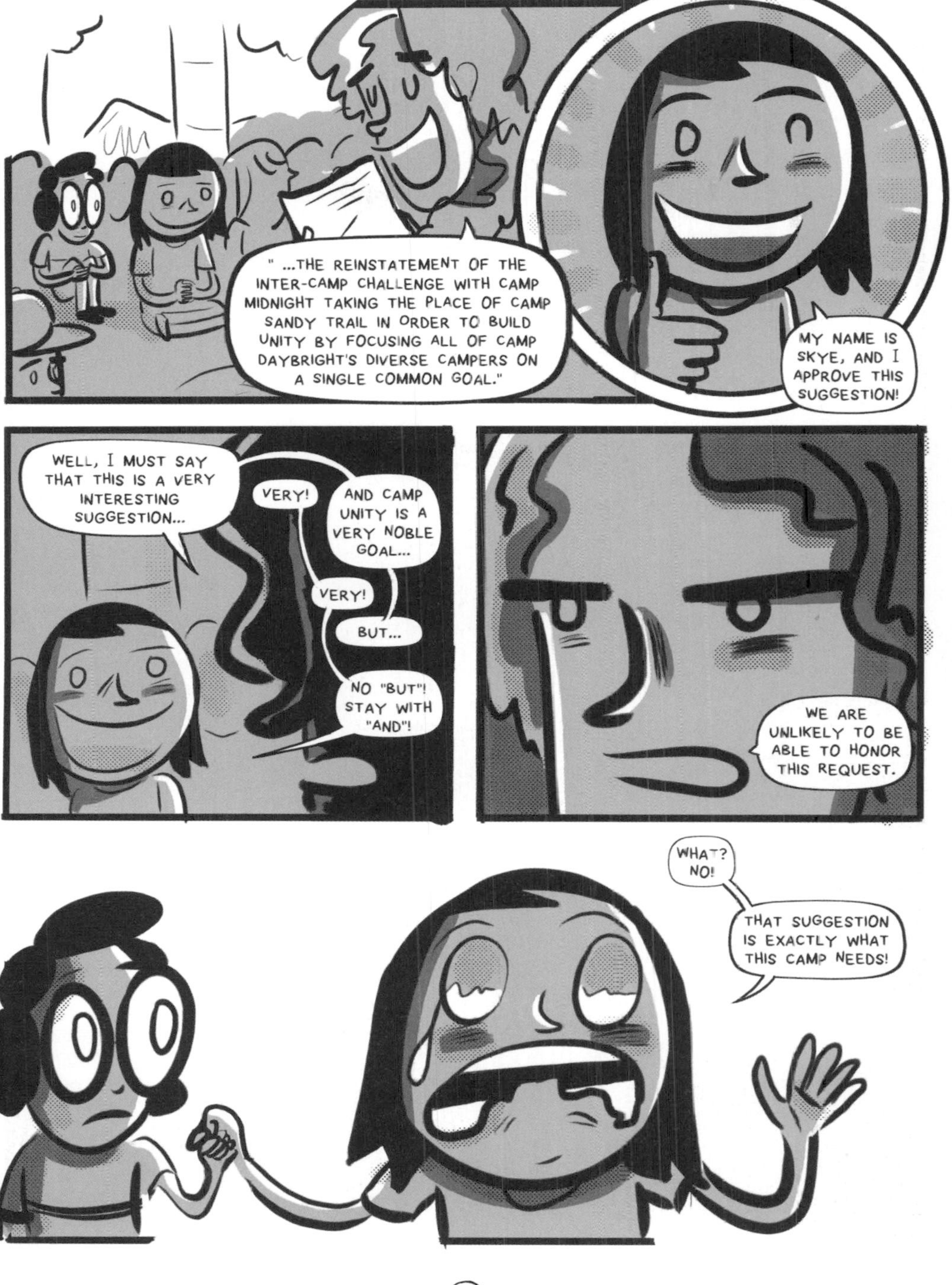

" ...THE REINSTATEMENT OF THE INTER-CAMP CHALLENGE WITH CAMP MIDNIGHT TAKING THE PLACE OF CAMP SANDY TRAIL IN ORDER TO BUILD UNITY BY FOCUSING ALL OF CAMP DAYBRIGHT'S DIVERSE CAMPERS ON A SINGLE COMMON GOAL."
MY NAME IS SKYE, AND I APPROVE THIS SUGGESTION!
WELL, I MUST SAY THAT THIS IS A VERY INTERESTING SUGGESTION...
VERY!
AND CAMP UNITY IS A VERY NOBLE GOAL...
VERY!
BUT...
NO "BUT"! STAY WITH "AND"!
WE ARE UNLIKELY TO BE ABLE TO HONOR THIS REQUEST.
WHAT? NO!
THAT SUGGESTION IS EXACTLY WHAT THIS CAMP NEEDS!

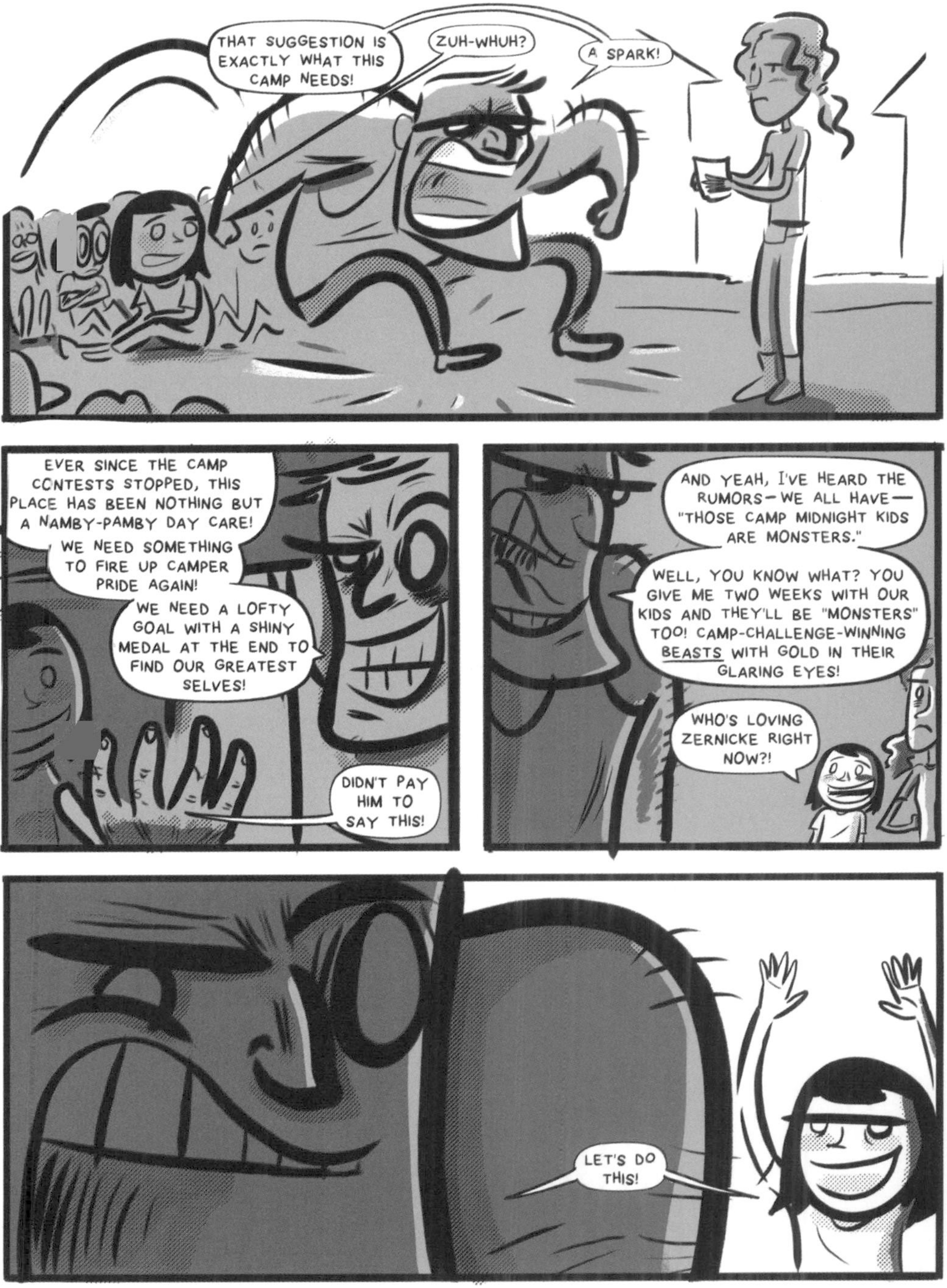
THAT SUGGESTION IS EXACTLY WHAT THIS CAMP NEEDS!
ZUH-WHUH?
A SPARK!
EVER SINCE THE CAMP CONTESTS STOPPED, THIS PLACE HAS BEEN NOTHING BUT A NAMBY-PAMBY DAY CARE!
WE NEED SOMETHING TO FIRE UP CAMPER PRIDE AGAIN!
WE NEED A LOFTY GOAL WITH A SHINY MEDAL AT THE END TO FIND OUR GREATEST SELVES!
DIDN'T PAY HIM TO SAY THIS!
AND YEAH, I'VE HEARD THE RUMORS—WE ALL HAVE—"THOSE CAMP MIDNIGHT KIDS ARE MONSTERS."
WELL, YOU KNOW WHAT? YOU GIVE ME TWO WEEKS WITH OUR KIDS AND THEY'LL BE "MONSTERS" TOO! CAMP-CHALLENGE-WINNING BEASTS WITH GOLD IN THEIR GLARING EYES!
WHO'S LOVING ZERNICKE RIGHT NOW?!
LET'S DO THIS!

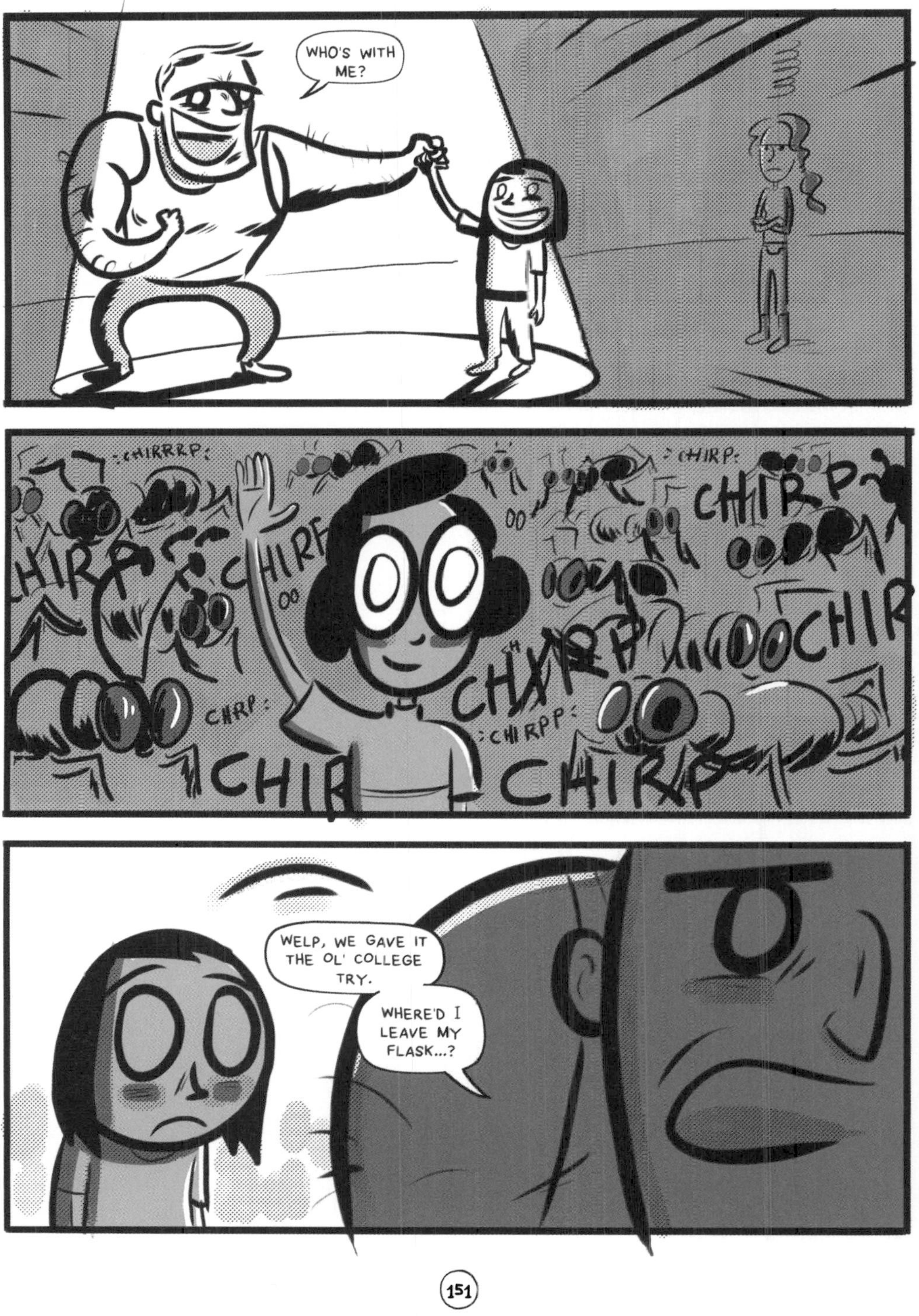
WHO'S WITH ME?
:CHIRRRP:
:CHIRP:
CHIRP
CHIRP
CHIRP
CHIRP:
:CHIRPP:
CHIRP
WELP, WE GAVE IT THE OL' COLLEGE TRY.
WHERE'D I LEAVE MY FLASK...?

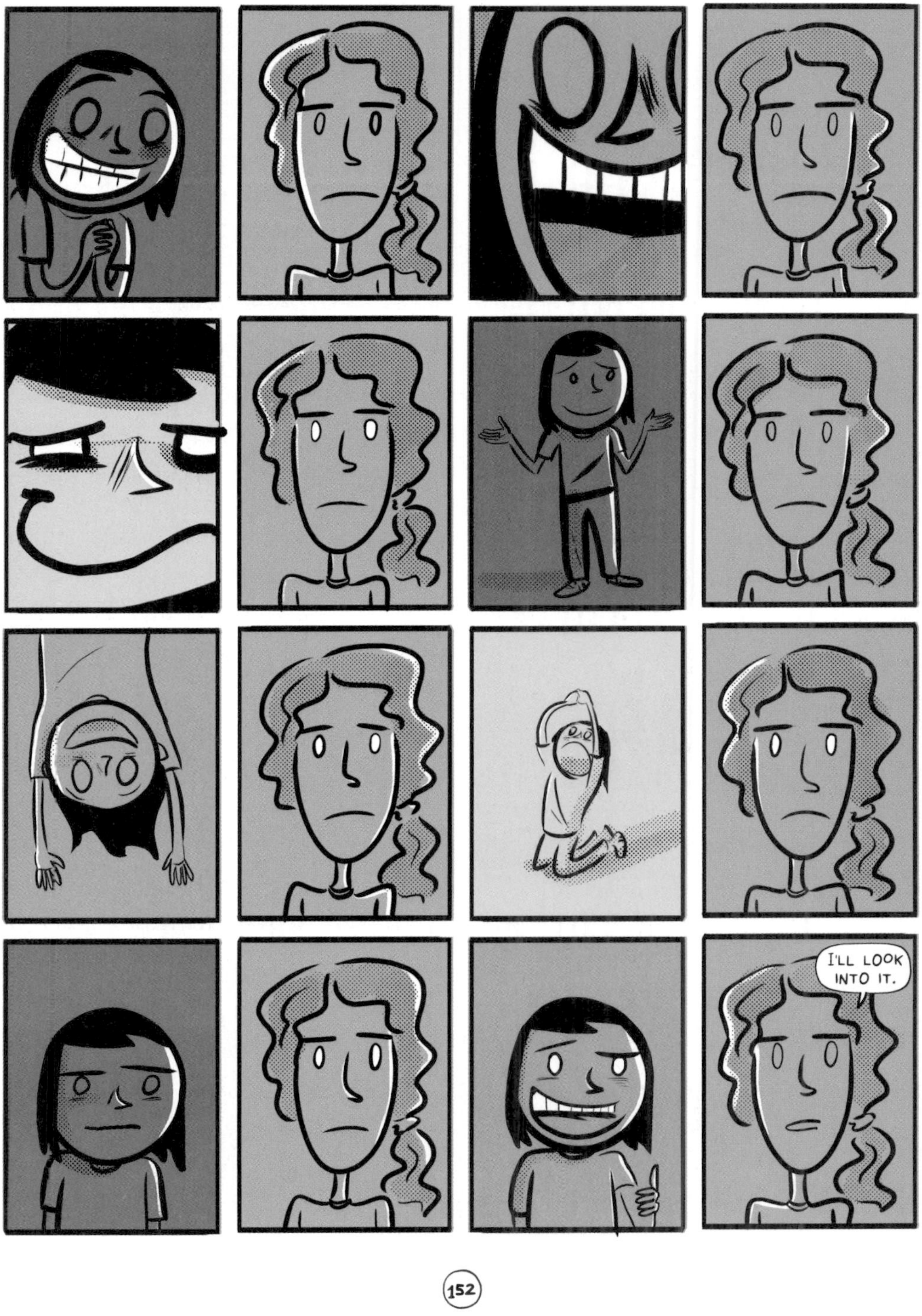
I'LL LOOK INTO IT.

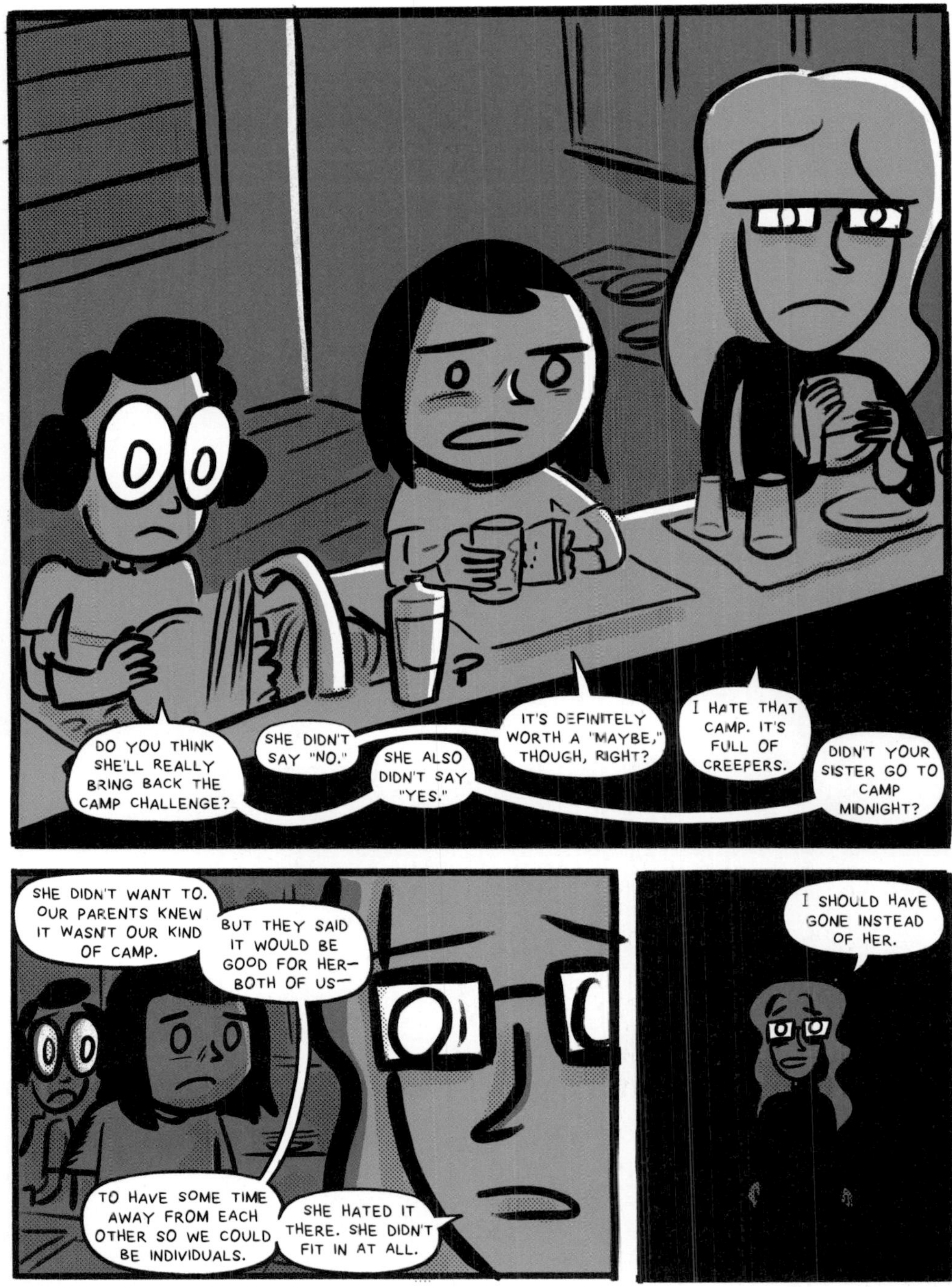
DO YOU THINK SHE'LL REALLY BRING BACK THE CAMP CHALLENGE?
SHE DIDN'T SAY "NO."
SHE ALSO DIDN'T SAY "YES."
IT'S DEFINITELY WORTH A "MAYBE," THOUGH, RIGHT?
I HATE THAT CAMP. IT'S FULL OF CREEPERS.
DIDN'T YOUR SISTER GO TO CAMP MIDNIGHT?
SHE DIDN'T WANT TO. OUR PARENTS KNEW IT WASN'T OUR KIND OF CAMP.
BUT THEY SAID IT WOULD BE GOOD FOR HER— BOTH OF US—
TO HAVE SOME TIME AWAY FROM EACH OTHER SO WE COULD BE INDIVIDUALS.
SHE HATED IT THERE. SHE DIDN'T FIT IN AT ALL.
I SHOULD HAVE GONE INSTEAD OF HER.

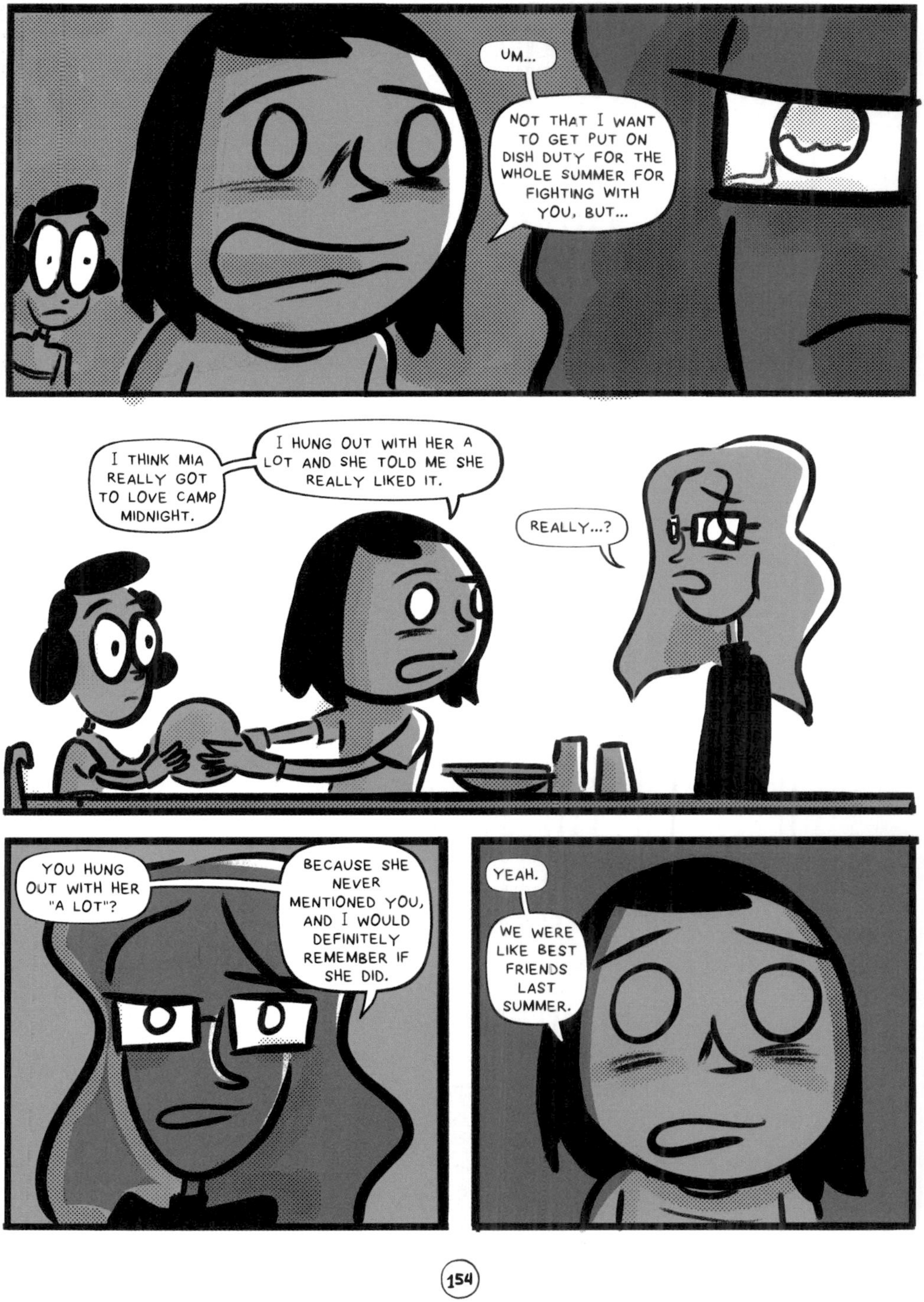
UM...
NOT THAT I WANT TO GET PUT ON DISH DUTY FOR THE WHOLE SUMMER FOR FIGHTING WITH YOU, BUT...
I THINK MIA REALLY GOT TO LOVE CAMP MIDNIGHT.
I HUNG OUT WITH HER A LOT AND SHE TOLD ME SHE REALLY LIKED IT.
REALLY...?
YOU HUNG OUT WITH HER "A LOT"?
BECAUSE SHE NEVER MENTIONED YOU, AND I WOULD DEFINITELY REMEMBER IF SHE DID.
YEAH.
WE WERE LIKE BEST FRIENDS LAST SUMMER.

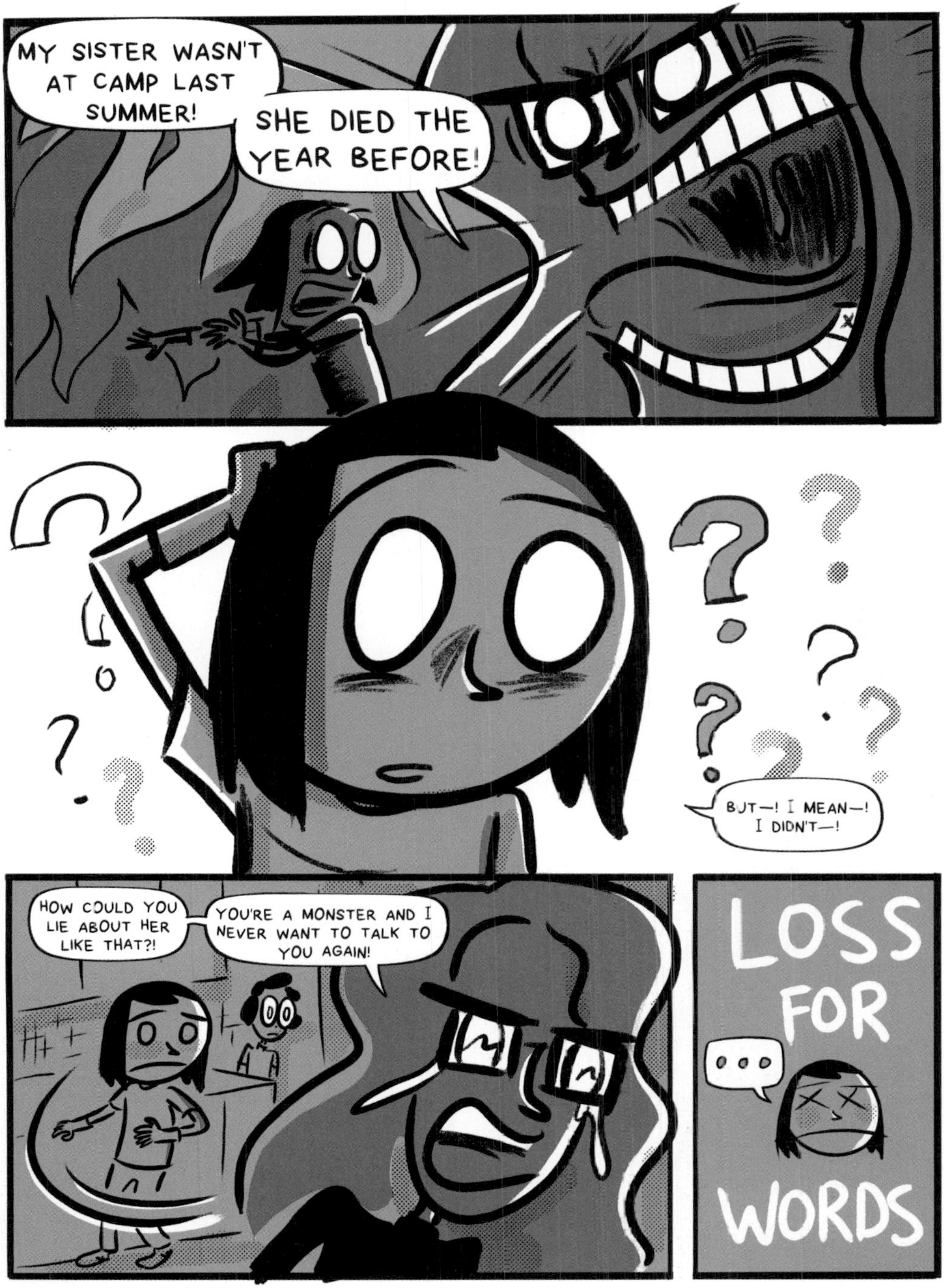
MY SISTER WASN'T AT CAMP LAST SUMMER!
SHE DIED THE YEAR BEFORE!
BUT—! I MEAN—! I DIDN'T—!
HOW COULD YOU LIE ABOUT HER LIKE THAT?!
YOU'RE A MONSTER AND I NEVER WANT TO TALK TO YOU AGAIN!
LOSS FOR WORDS
...

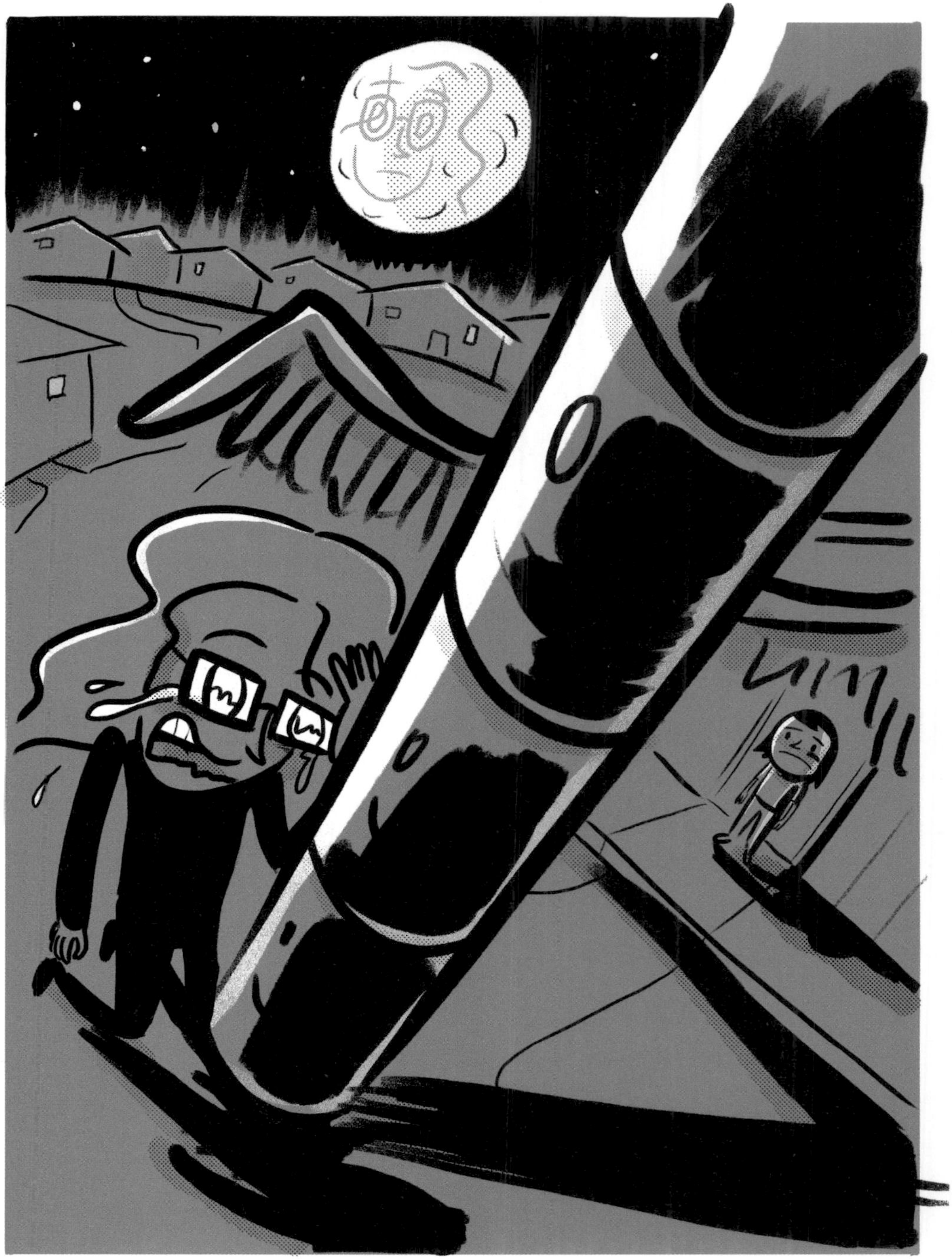

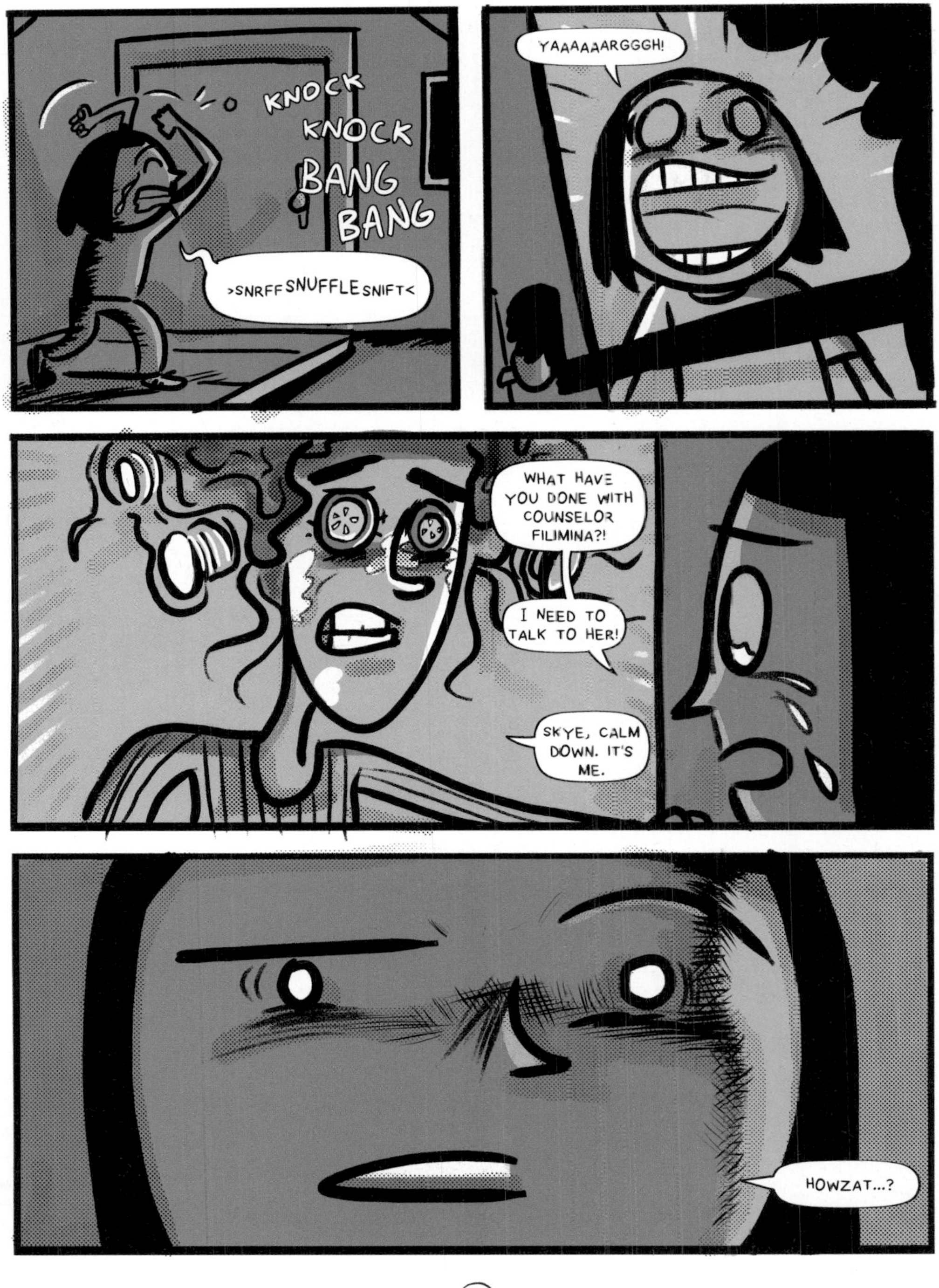
KNOCK
KNOCK
BANG
BANG
>SNRFF SNUFFLE SNIFT<
YAAAAAARGGGH!
WHAT HAVE YOU DONE WITH COUNSELOR FILIMINA?!
I NEED TO TALK TO HER!
SKYE, CALM DOWN. IT'S ME.
HOWZAT...?

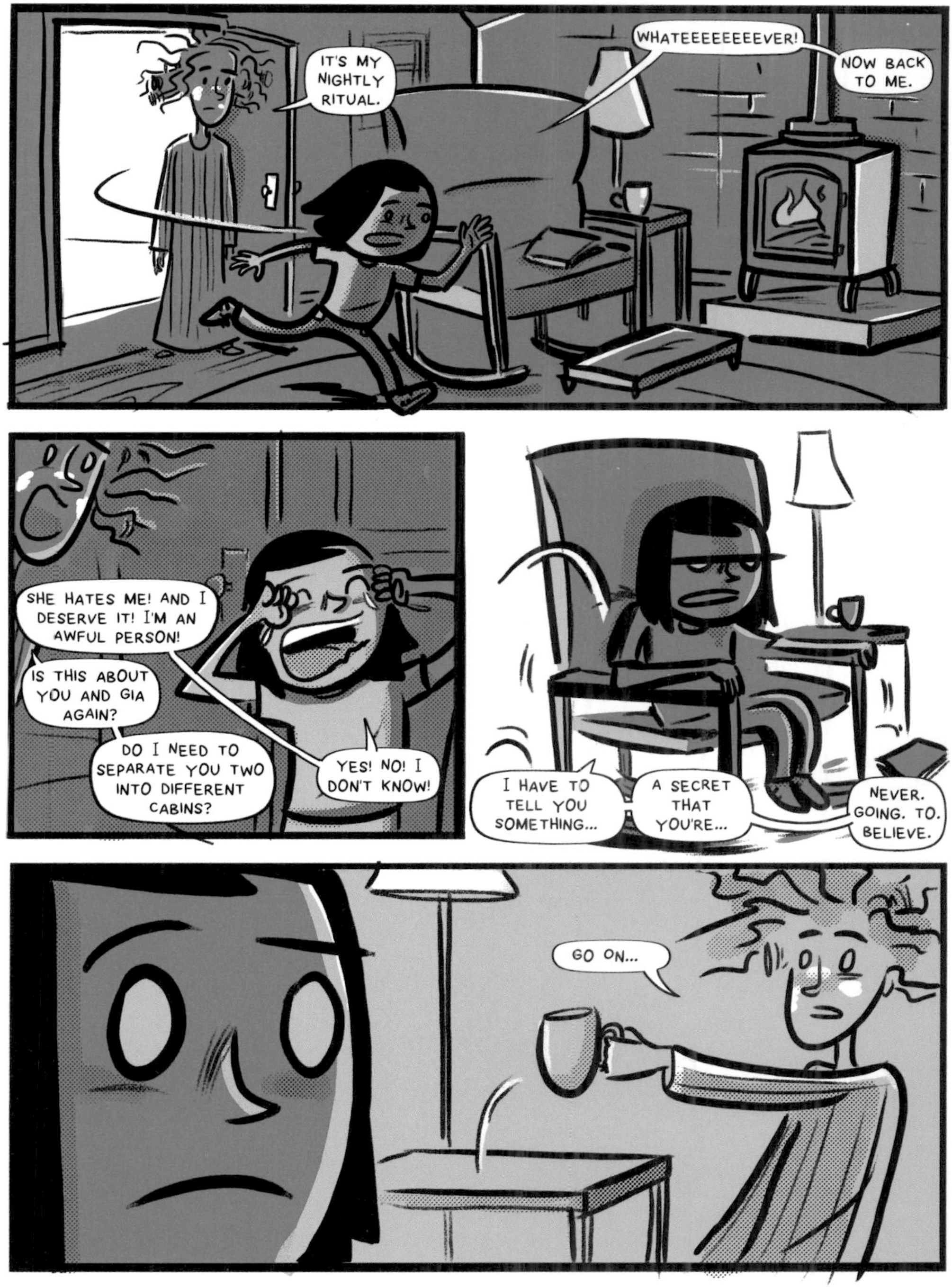
IT'S MY NIGHTLY RITUAL.
WHATEEEEEEEEEVER!
NOW BACK TO ME.
SHE HATES ME! AND I DESERVE IT! I'M AN AWFUL PERSON!
IS THIS ABOUT YOU AND GIA AGAIN?
DO I NEED TO SEPARATE YOU TWO INTO DIFFERENT CABINS?
YES! NO! I DON'T KNOW!
I HAVE TO TELL YOU SOMETHING...
A SECRET THAT YOU'RE...
NEVER. GOING. TO. BELIEVE.
GO ON...

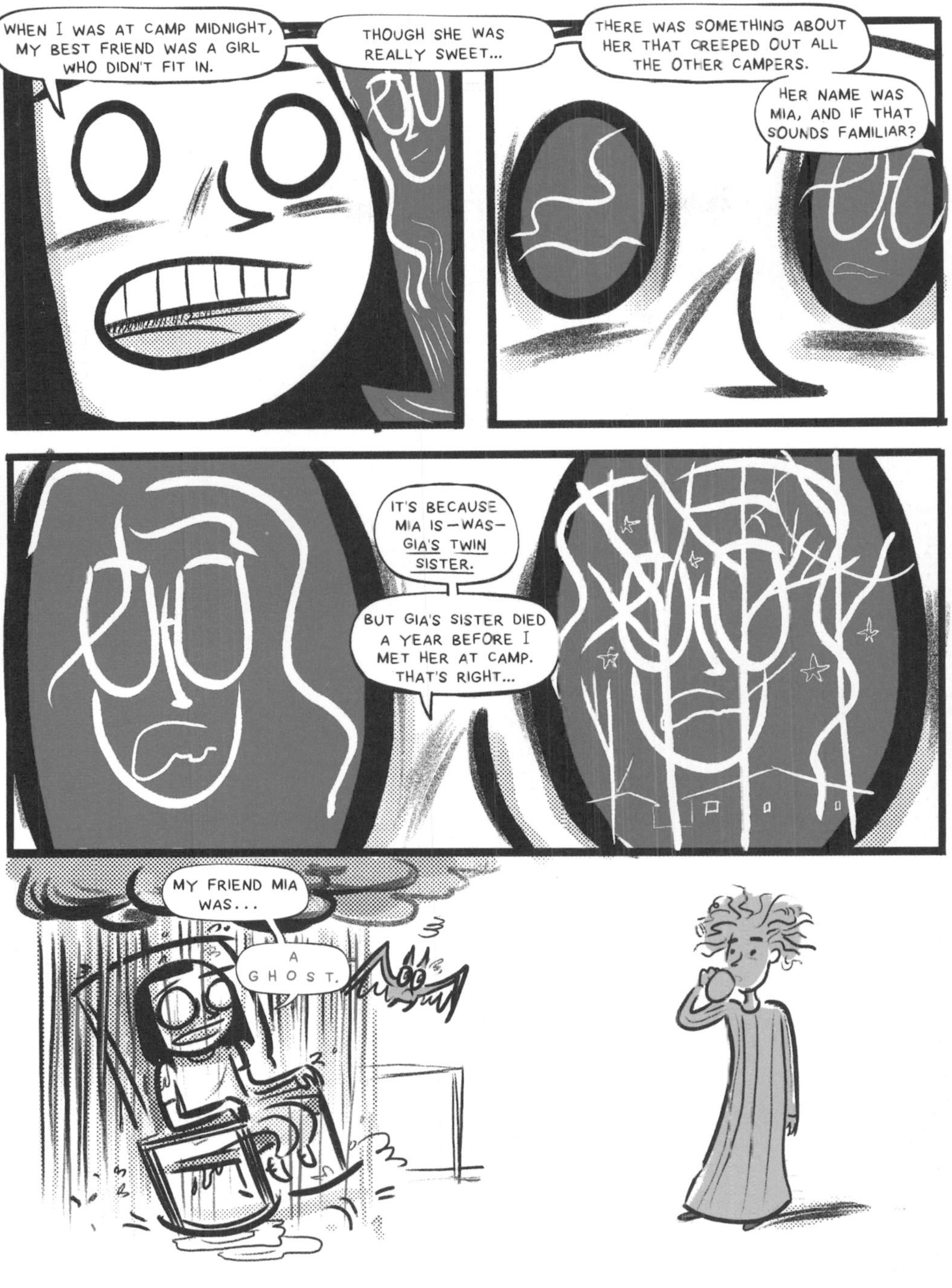
WHEN I WAS AT CAMP MIDNIGHT, MY BEST FRIEND WAS A GIRL WHO DIDN'T FIT IN.
THOUGH SHE WAS REALLY SWEET...
THERE WAS SOMETHING ABOUT HER THAT CREEPED OUT ALL THE OTHER CAMPERS.
HER NAME WAS MIA, AND IF THAT SOUNDS FAMILIAR?
IT'S BECAUSE MIA IS—WAS—GIA'S TWIN SISTER.
BUT GIA'S SISTER DIED A YEAR BEFORE I MET HER AT CAMP. THAT'S RIGHT...
MY FRIEND MIA WAS...
A GHOST.

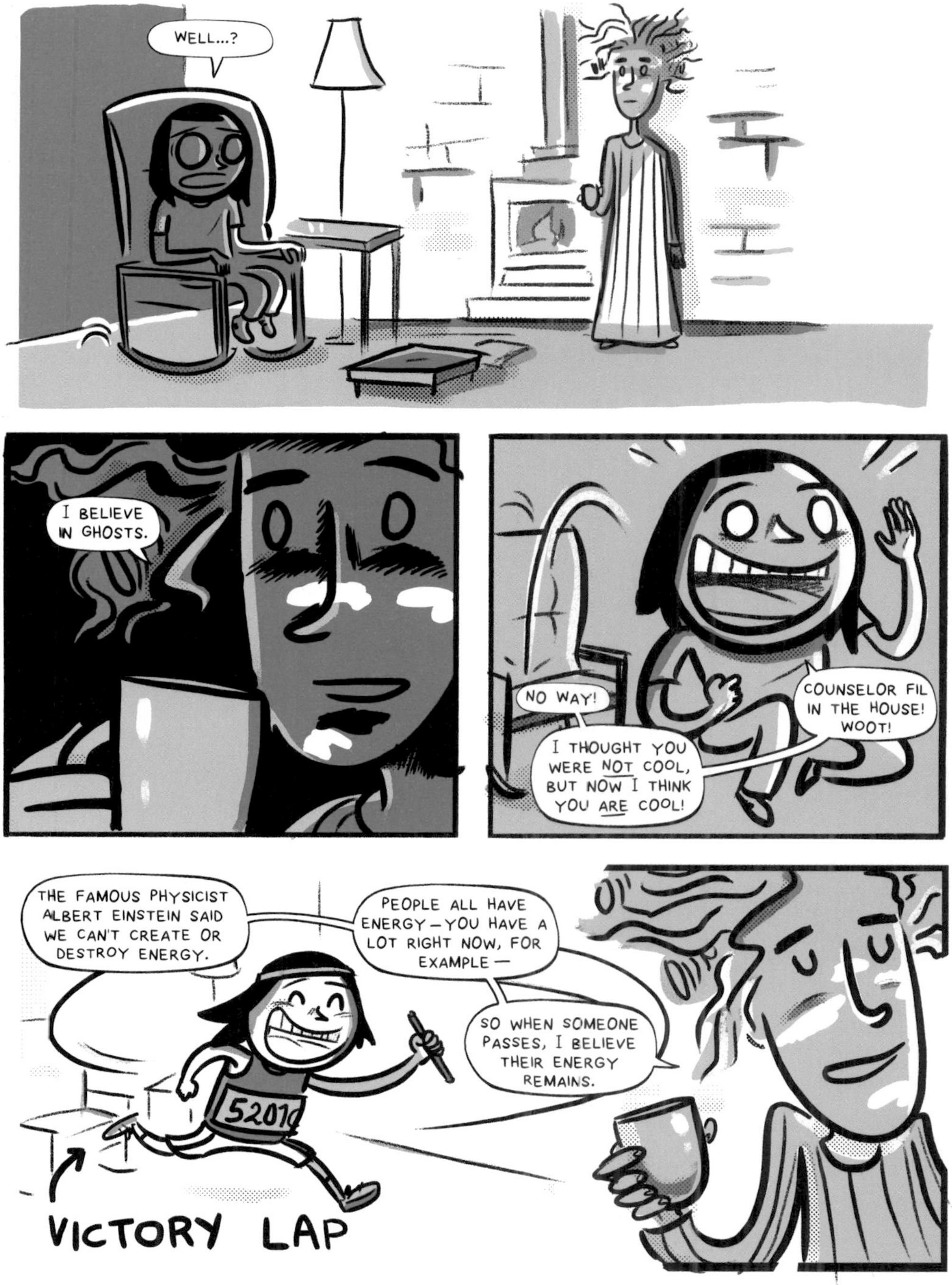
WELL...?
I BELIEVE IN GHOSTS.
NO WAY!
I THOUGHT YOU WERE NOT COOL, BUT NOW I THINK YOU ARE COOL!
COUNSELOR FIL IN THE HOUSE! WOOT!
THE FAMOUS PHYSICIST ALBERT EINSTEIN SAID WE CAN'T CREATE OR DESTROY ENERGY.
PEOPLE ALL HAVE ENERGY—YOU HAVE A LOT RIGHT NOW, FOR EXAMPLE—
SO WHEN SOMEONE PASSES, I BELIEVE THEIR ENERGY REMAINS.
5201
VICTORY LAP

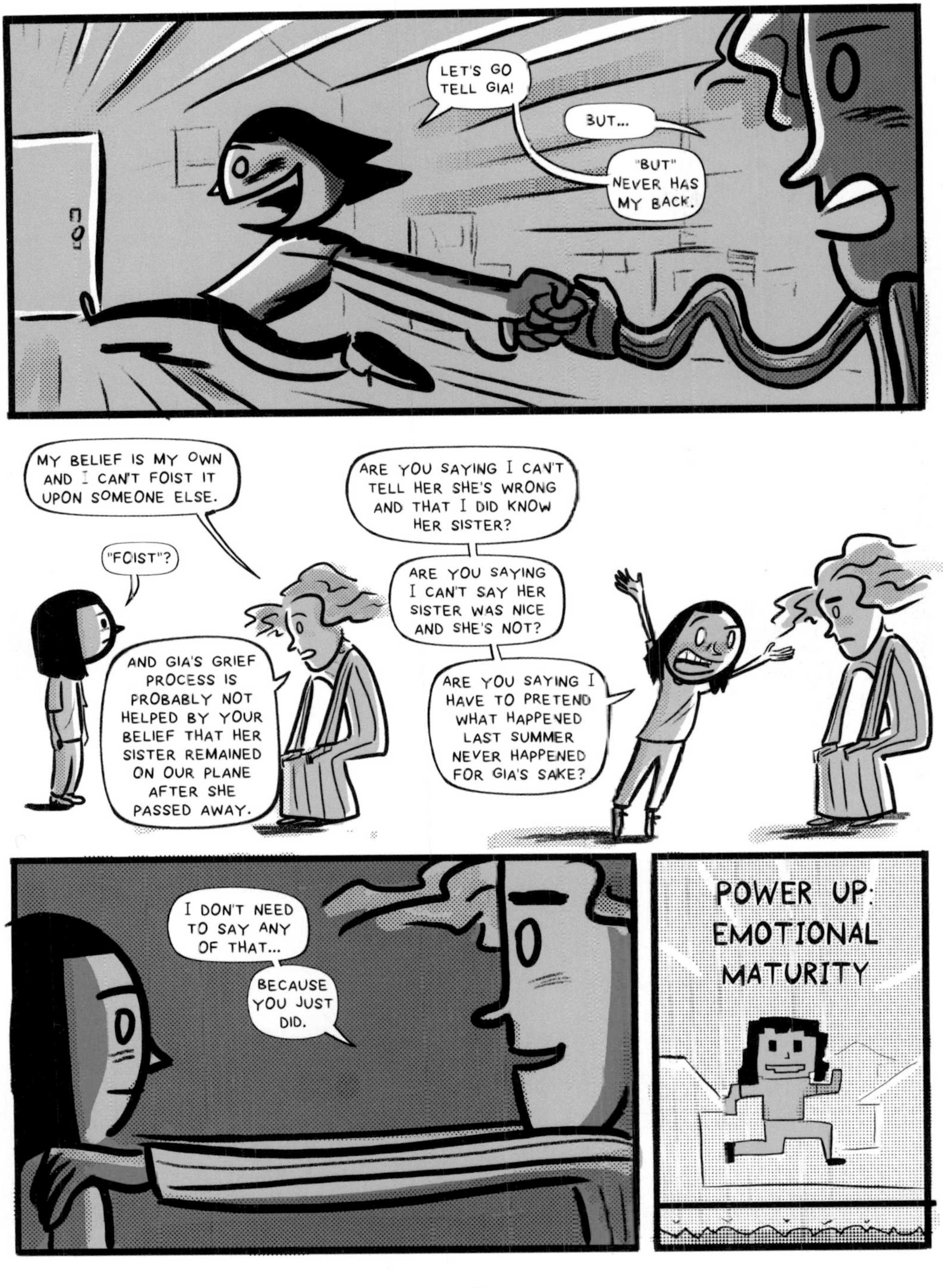
LET'S GO TELL GIA!
BUT...
"BUT" NEVER HAS MY BACK.
MY BELIEF IS MY OWN AND I CAN'T FOIST IT UPON SOMEONE ELSE.
"FOIST"?
AND GIA'S GRIEF PROCESS IS PROBABLY NOT HELPED BY YOUR BELIEF THAT HER SISTER REMAINED ON OUR PLANE AFTER SHE PASSED AWAY.
ARE YOU SAYING I CAN'T TELL HER SHE'S WRONG AND THAT I DID KNOW HER SISTER?
ARE YOU SAYING I CAN'T SAY HER SISTER WAS NICE AND SHE'S NOT?
ARE YOU SAYING I HAVE TO PRETEND WHAT HAPPENED LAST SUMMER NEVER HAPPENED FOR GIA'S SAKE?
I DON'T NEED TO SAY ANY OF THAT...
BECAUSE YOU JUST DID.
POWER UP: EMOTIONAL MATURITY

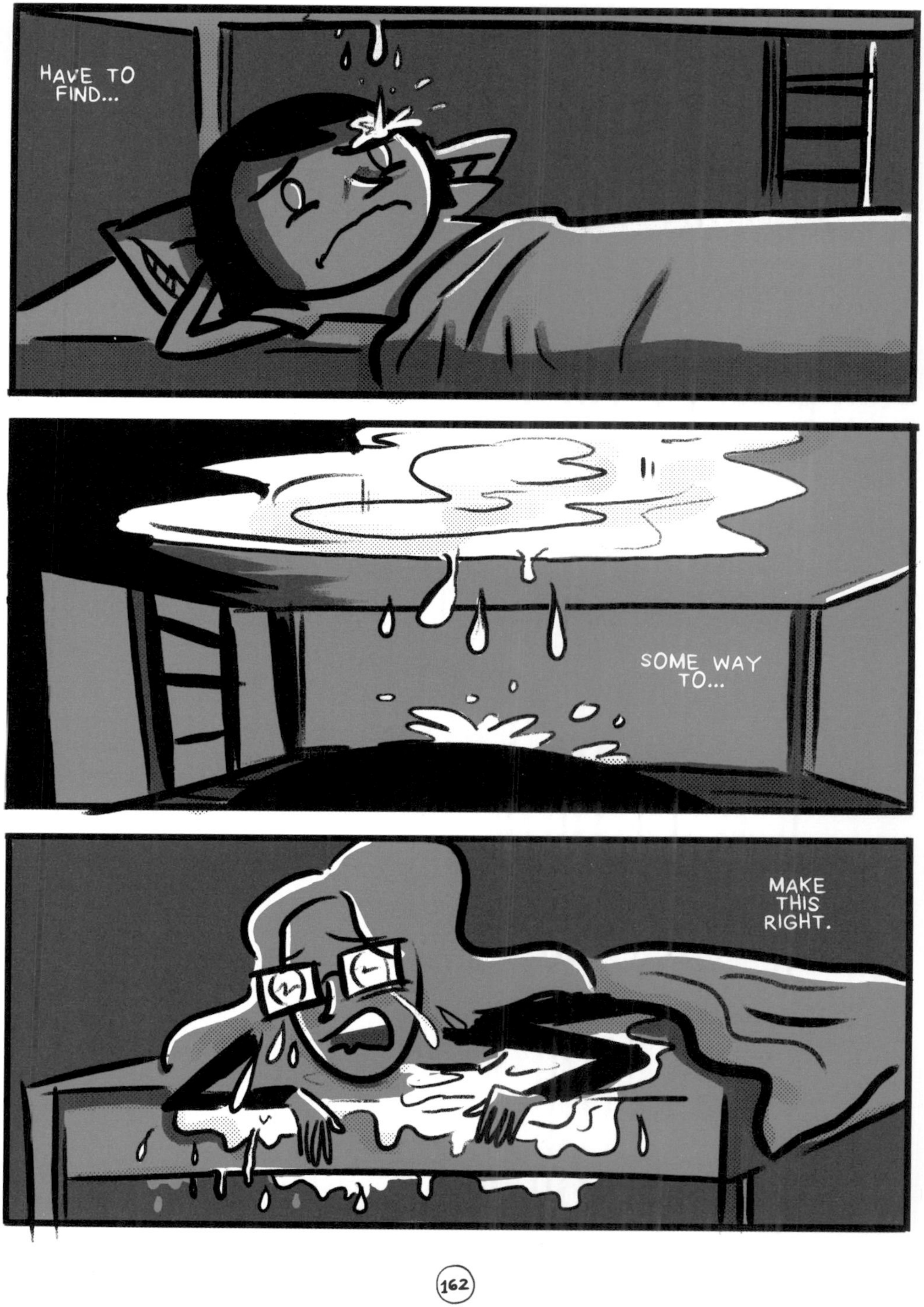
HAVE TO FIND...
SOME WAY TO...
MAKE THIS RIGHT.

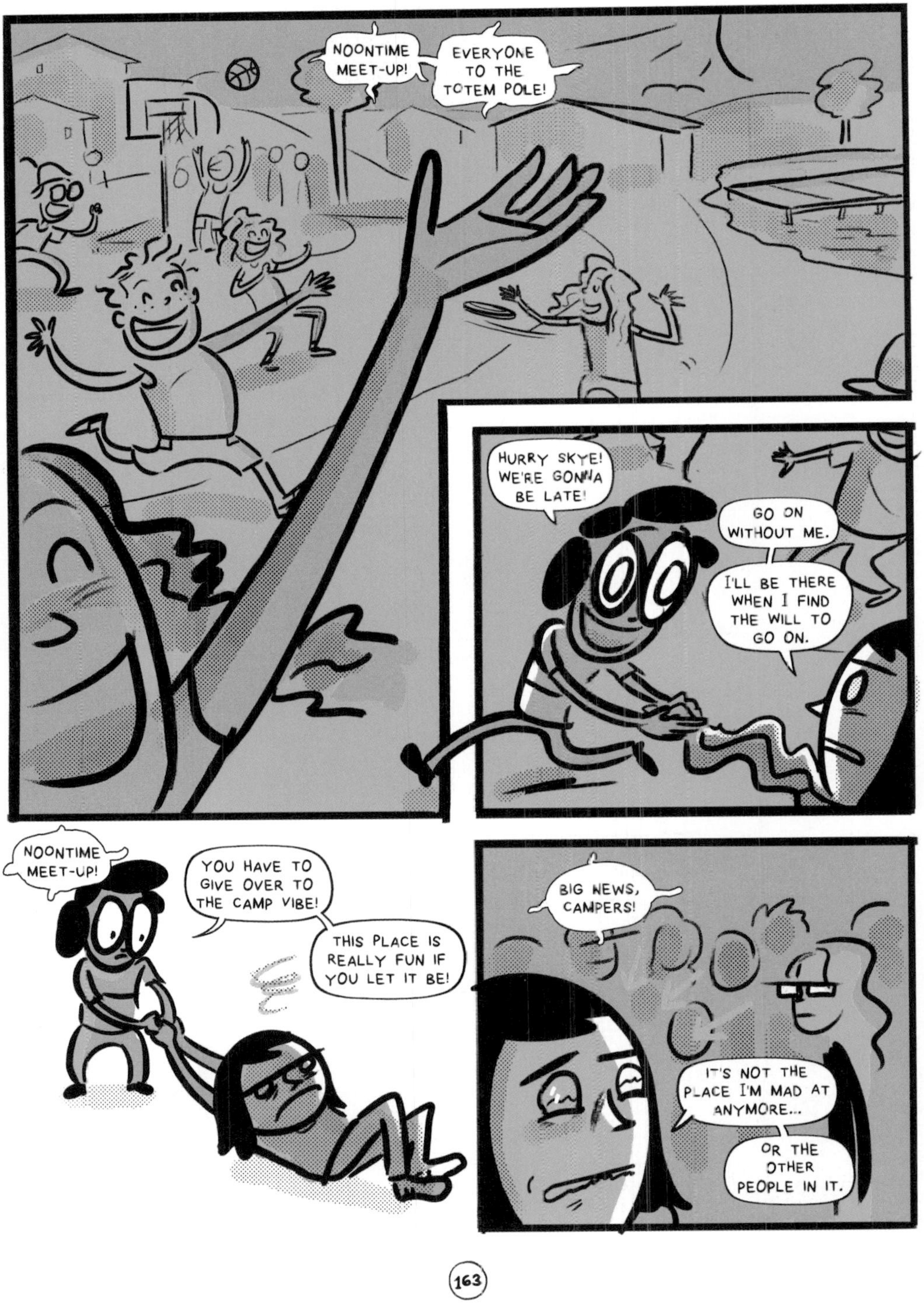
NOONTIME MEET-UP!
EVERYONE TO THE TOTEM POLE!
HURRY SKYE! WE'RE GONNA BE LATE!
GO ON WITHOUT ME.
I'LL BE THERE WHEN I FIND THE WILL TO GO ON.
NOONTIME MEET-UP!
YOU HAVE TO GIVE OVER TO THE CAMP VIBE!
THIS PLACE IS REALLY FUN IF YOU LET IT BE!
BIG NEWS, CAMPERS!
IT'S NOT THE PLACE I'M MAD AT ANYMORE...
OR THE OTHER PEOPLE IN IT.

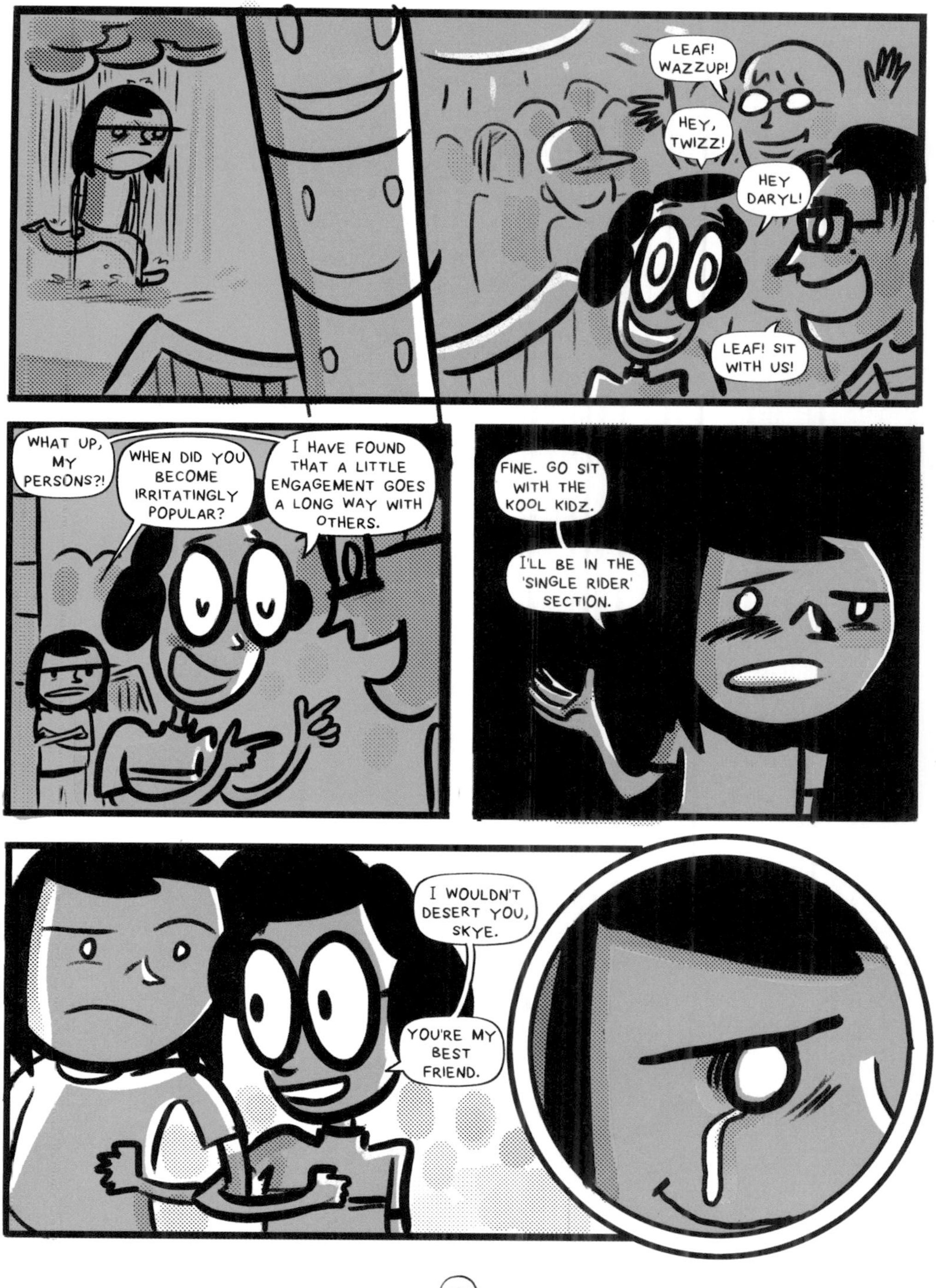
LEAF! WAZZUP!
HEY, TWIZZ!
HEY DARYL!
LEAF! SIT WITH US!
WHAT UP, MY PERSONS?!
WHEN DID YOU BECOME IRRITATINGLY POPULAR?
I HAVE FOUND THAT A LITTLE ENGAGEMENT GOES A LONG WAY WITH OTHERS.
FINE. GO SIT WITH THE KOOL KIDZ.
I'LL BE IN THE 'SINGLE RIDER' SECTION.
I WOULDN'T DESERT YOU, SKYE.
YOU'RE MY BEST FRIEND.

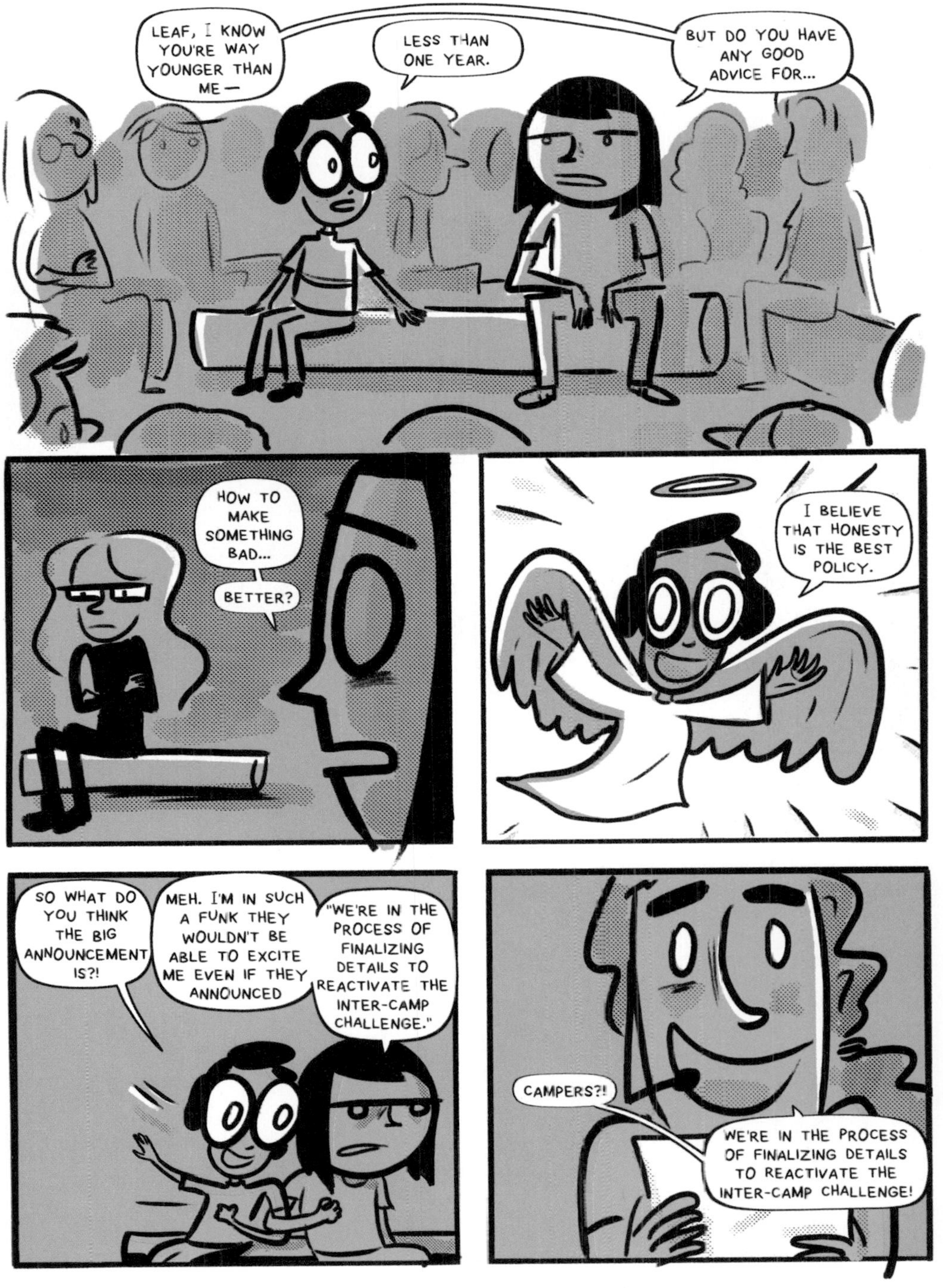
LEAF, I KNOW YOU'RE WAY YOUNGER THAN ME—
LESS THAN ONE YEAR.
BUT DO YOU HAVE ANY GOOD ADVICE FOR...
HOW TO MAKE SOMETHING BAD...
BETTER?
I BELIEVE THAT HONESTY IS THE BEST POLICY.
SO WHAT DO YOU THINK THE BIG ANNOUNCEMENT IS?!
MEH. I'M IN SUCH A FUNK THEY WOULDN'T BE ABLE TO EXCITE ME EVEN IF THEY ANNOUNCED
"WE'RE IN THE PROCESS OF FINALIZING DETAILS TO REACTIVATE THE INTER-CAMP CHALLENGE."
CAMPERS?!
WE'RE IN THE PROCESS OF FINALIZING DETAILS TO REACTIVATE THE INTER-CAMP CHALLENGE!

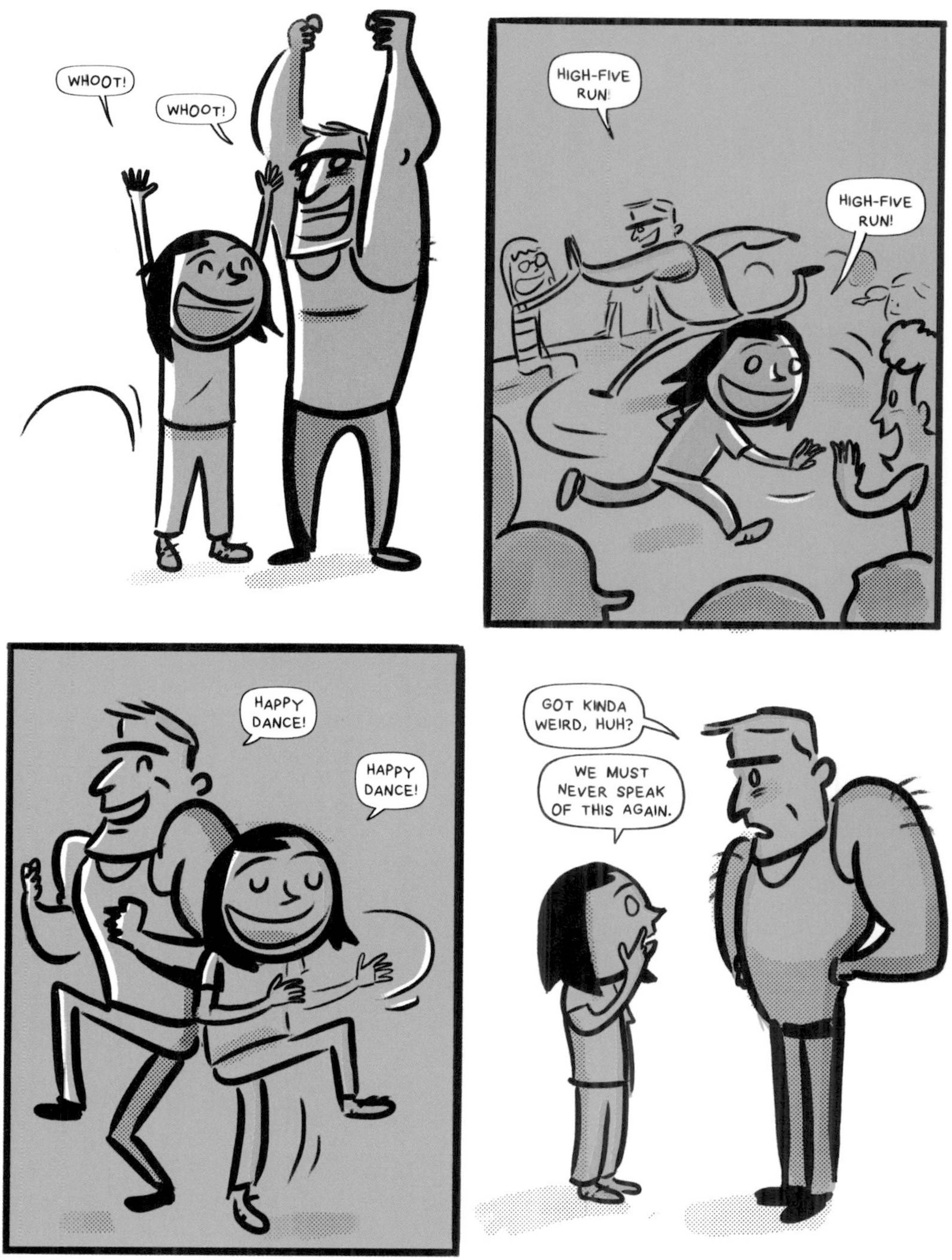
WHOOT!
WHOOT!
HIGH-FIVE RUN!
HIGH-FIVE RUN!
HAPPY DANCE!
HAPPY DANCE!
GOT KINDA WEIRD, HUH?
WE MUST NEVER SPEAK OF THIS AGAIN.

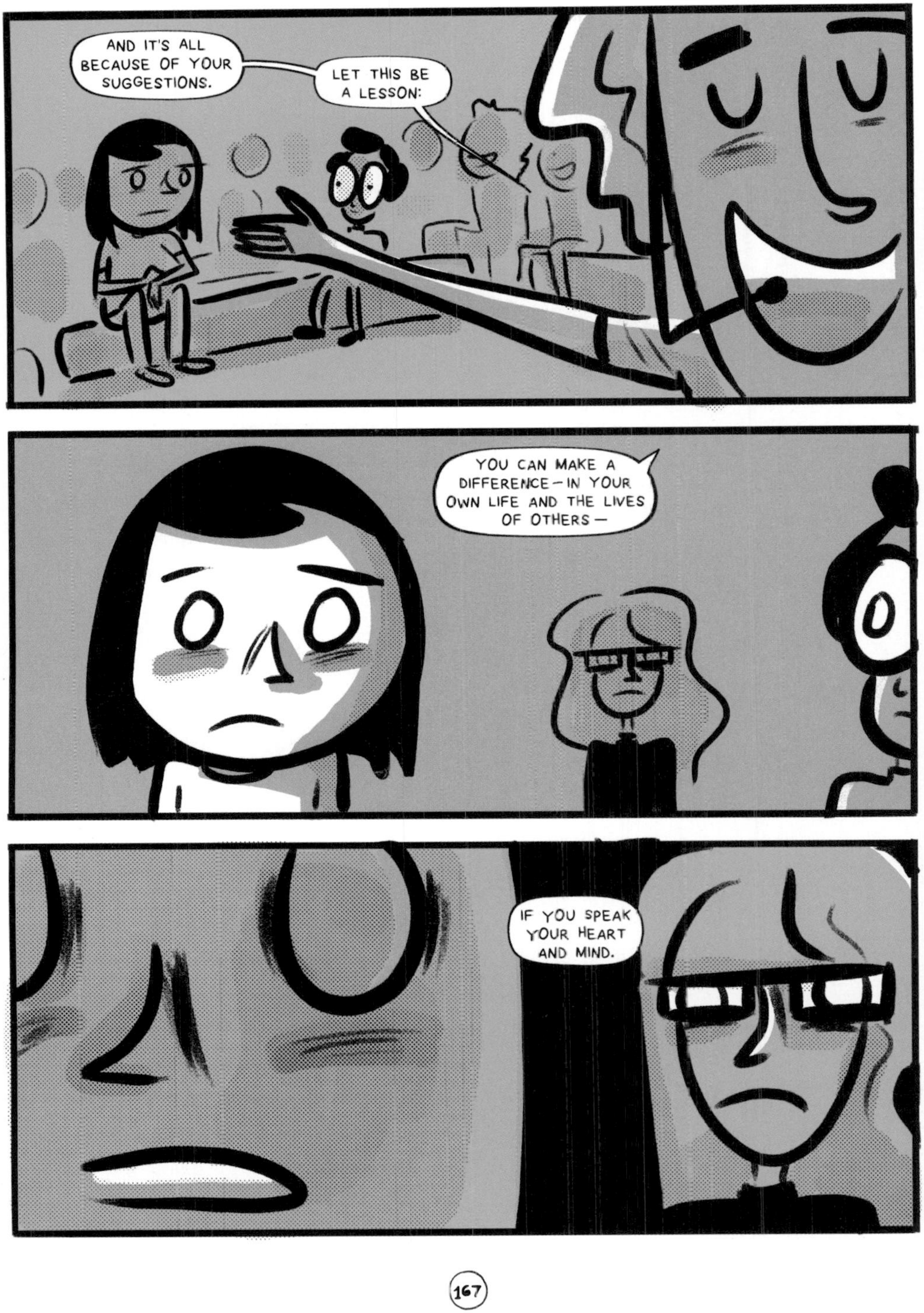
AND IT'S ALL BECAUSE OF YOUR SUGGESTIONS.
LET THIS BE A LESSON:
YOU CAN MAKE A DIFFERENCE—IN YOUR OWN LIFE AND THE LIVES OF OTHERS—
IF YOU SPEAK YOUR HEART AND MIND.

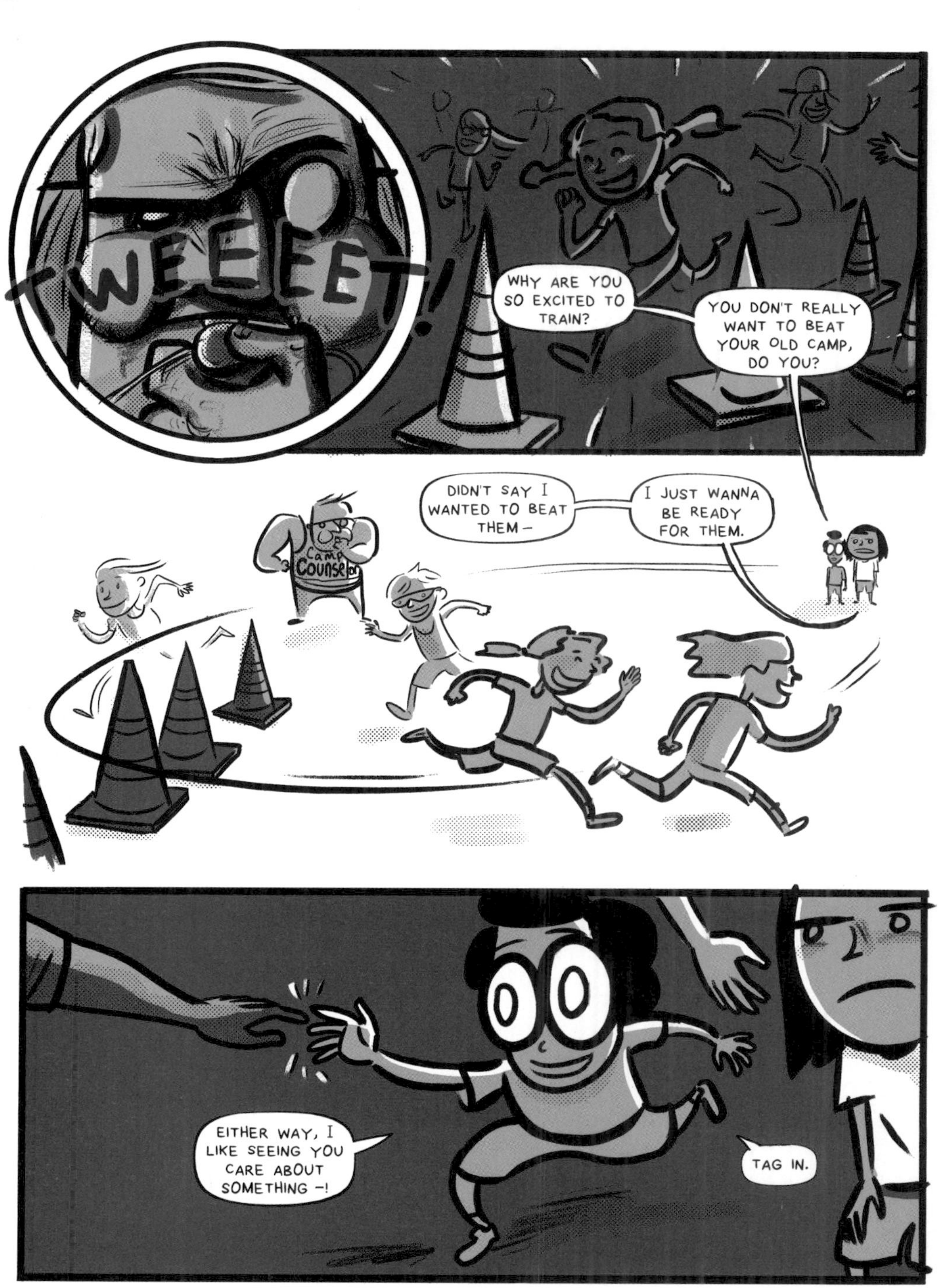
WEEEET!
WHY ARE YOU SO EXCITED TO TRAIN?
YOU DON'T REALLY WANT TO BEAT YOUR OLD CAMP, DO YOU?
Camp Counselor
DIDN'T SAY I WANTED TO BEAT THEM—
I JUST WANNA BE READY FOR THEM.
EITHER WAY, I LIKE SEEING YOU CARE ABOUT SOMETHING —!
TAG IN.

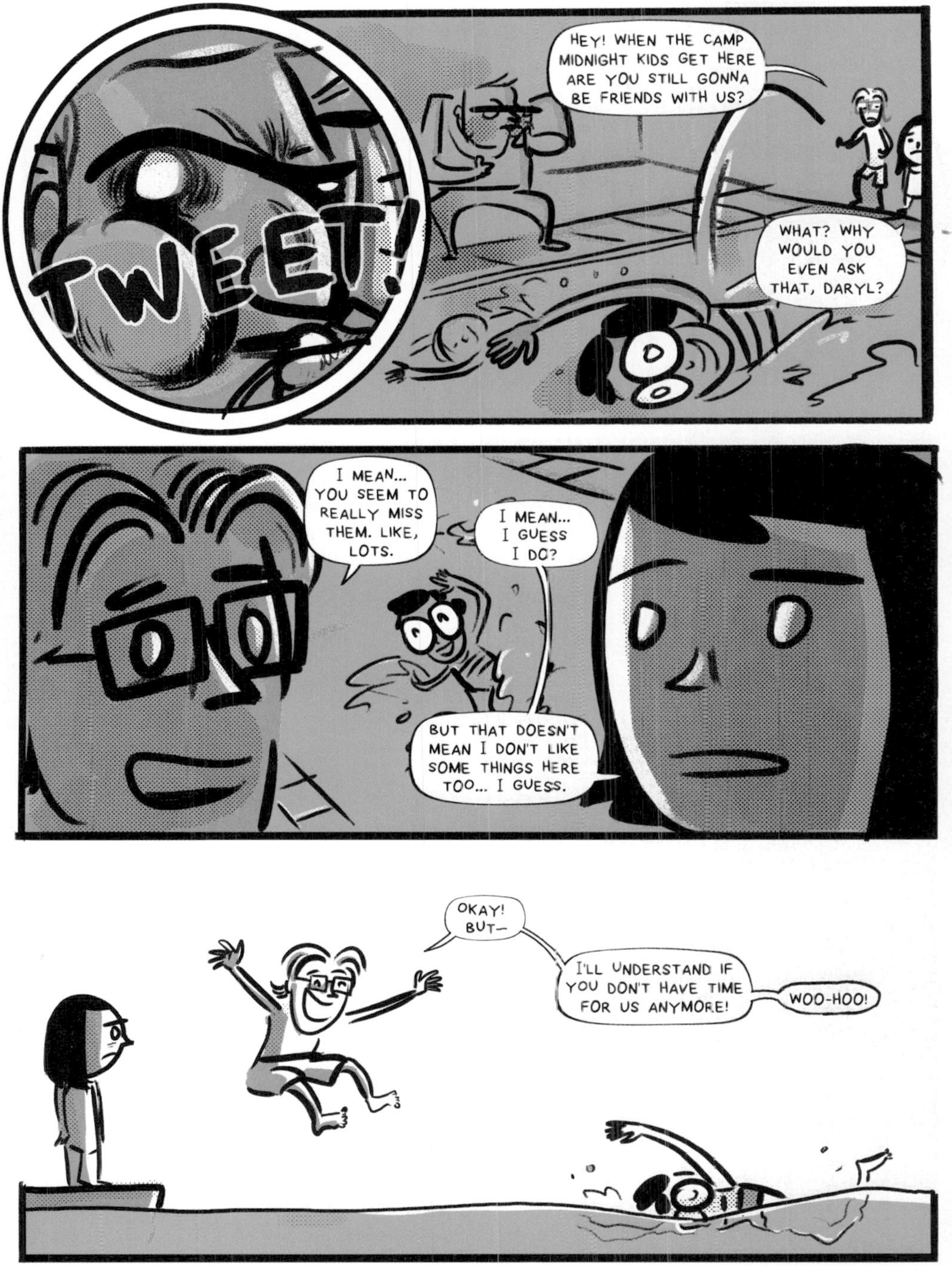
TWEET!
HEY! WHEN THE CAMP MIDNIGHT KIDS GET HERE ARE YOU STILL GONNA BE FRIENDS WITH US?
WHAT? WHY WOULD YOU EVEN ASK THAT, DARYL?
I MEAN... YOU SEEM TO REALLY MISS THEM. LIKE, LOTS.
I MEAN... I GUESS I DO?
BUT THAT DOESN'T MEAN I DON'T LIKE SOME THINGS HERE TOO... I GUESS.
OKAY! BUT—
I'LL UNDERSTAND IF YOU DON'T HAVE TIME FOR US ANYMORE!
WOO-HOO!

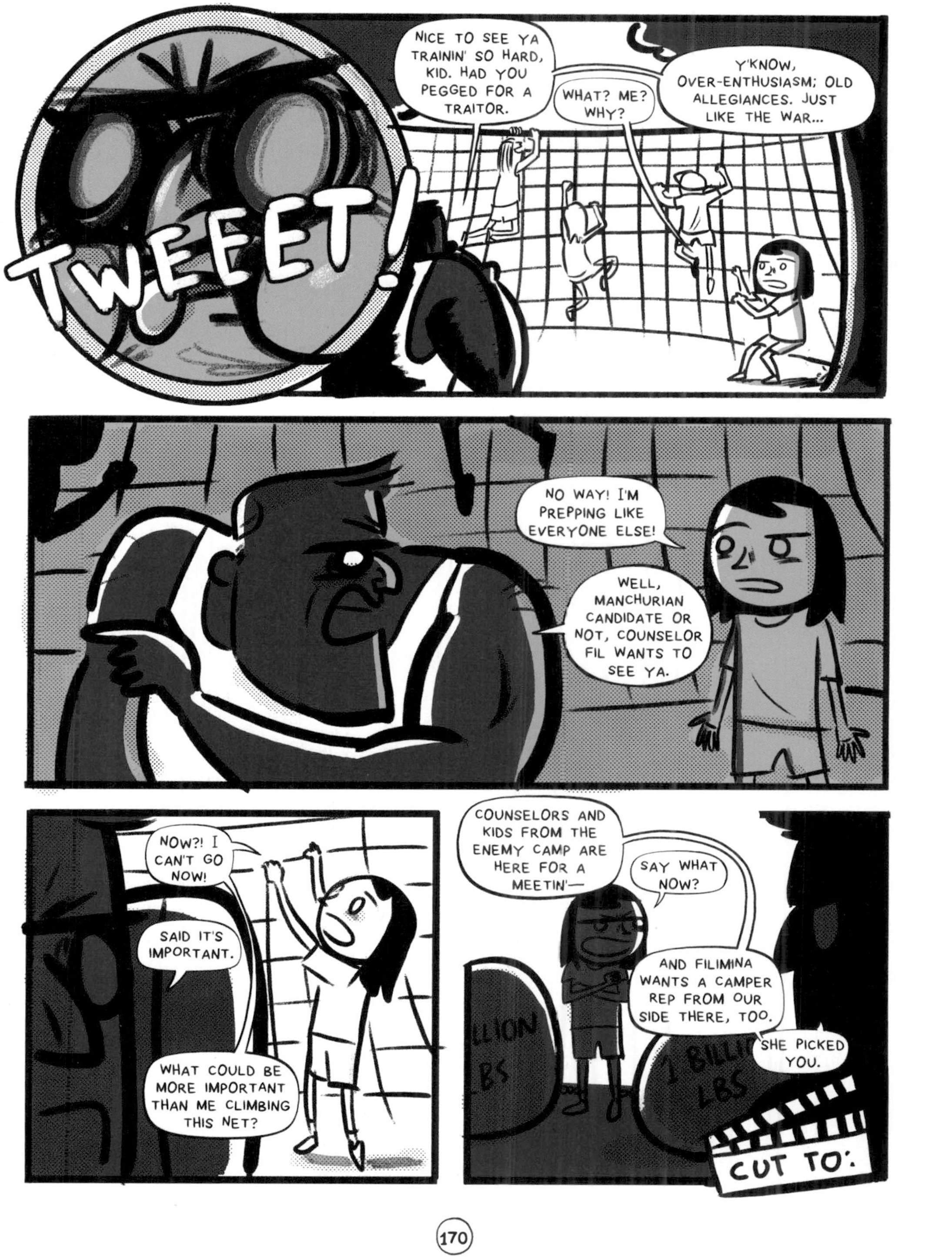

TWEEET!
NICE TO SEE YA TRAININ' SO HARD, KID. HAD YOU PEGGED FOR A TRAITOR.
WHAT? ME? WHY?
Y'KNOW, OVER-ENTHUSIASM; OLD ALLEGIANCES. JUST LIKE THE WAR...
NO WAY! I'M PREPPING LIKE EVERYONE ELSE!
WELL, MANCHURIAN CANDIDATE OR NOT, COUNSELOR FIL WANTS TO SEE YA.
NOW?! I CAN'T GO NOW!
SAID IT'S IMPORTANT.
WHAT COULD BE MORE IMPORTANT THAN ME CLIMBING THIS NET?
COUNSELORS AND KIDS FROM THE ENEMY CAMP ARE HERE FOR A MEETIN'—
SAY WHAT NOW?
AND FILIMINA WANTS A CAMPER REP FROM OUR SIDE THERE, TOO.
SHE PICKED YOU.
1 BILLION LBS
CUT TO:

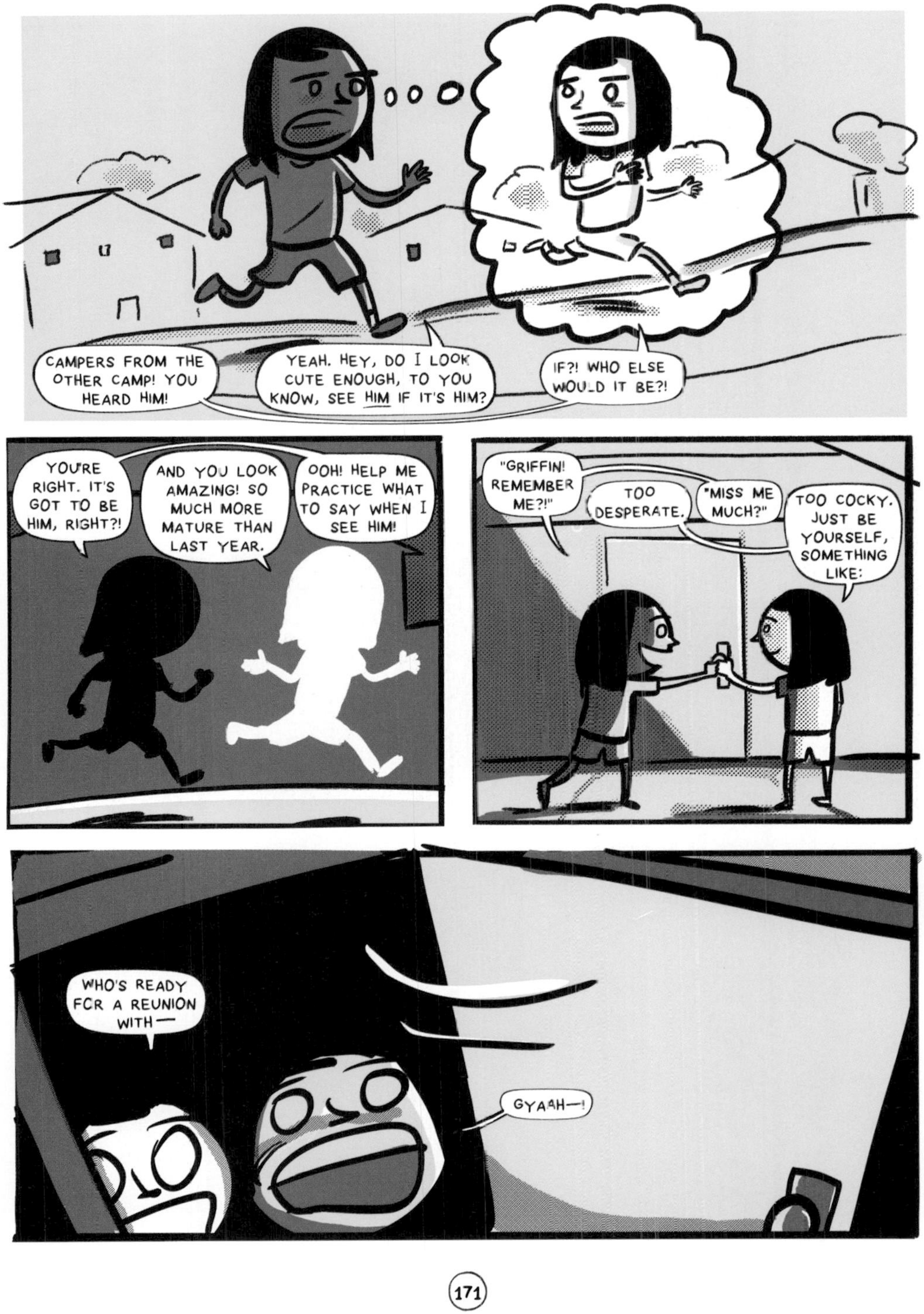

CAMPERS FROM THE OTHER CAMP! YOU HEARD HIM!
YEAH. HEY, DO I LOOK CUTE ENOUGH, TO YOU KNOW, SEE HIM IF IT'S HIM?
IF?! WHO ELSE WOULD IT BE?!
YOU'RE RIGHT. IT'S GOT TO BE HIM, RIGHT?!
AND YOU LOOK AMAZING! SO MUCH MORE MATURE THAN LAST YEAR.
OOH! HELP ME PRACTICE WHAT TO SAY WHEN I SEE HIM!
"GRIFFIN! REMEMBER ME?!"
TOO DESPERATE.
"MISS ME MUCH?"
TOO COCKY. JUST BE YOURSELF, SOMETHING LIKE:
WHO'S READY FOR A REUNION WITH—
GYAAH—!

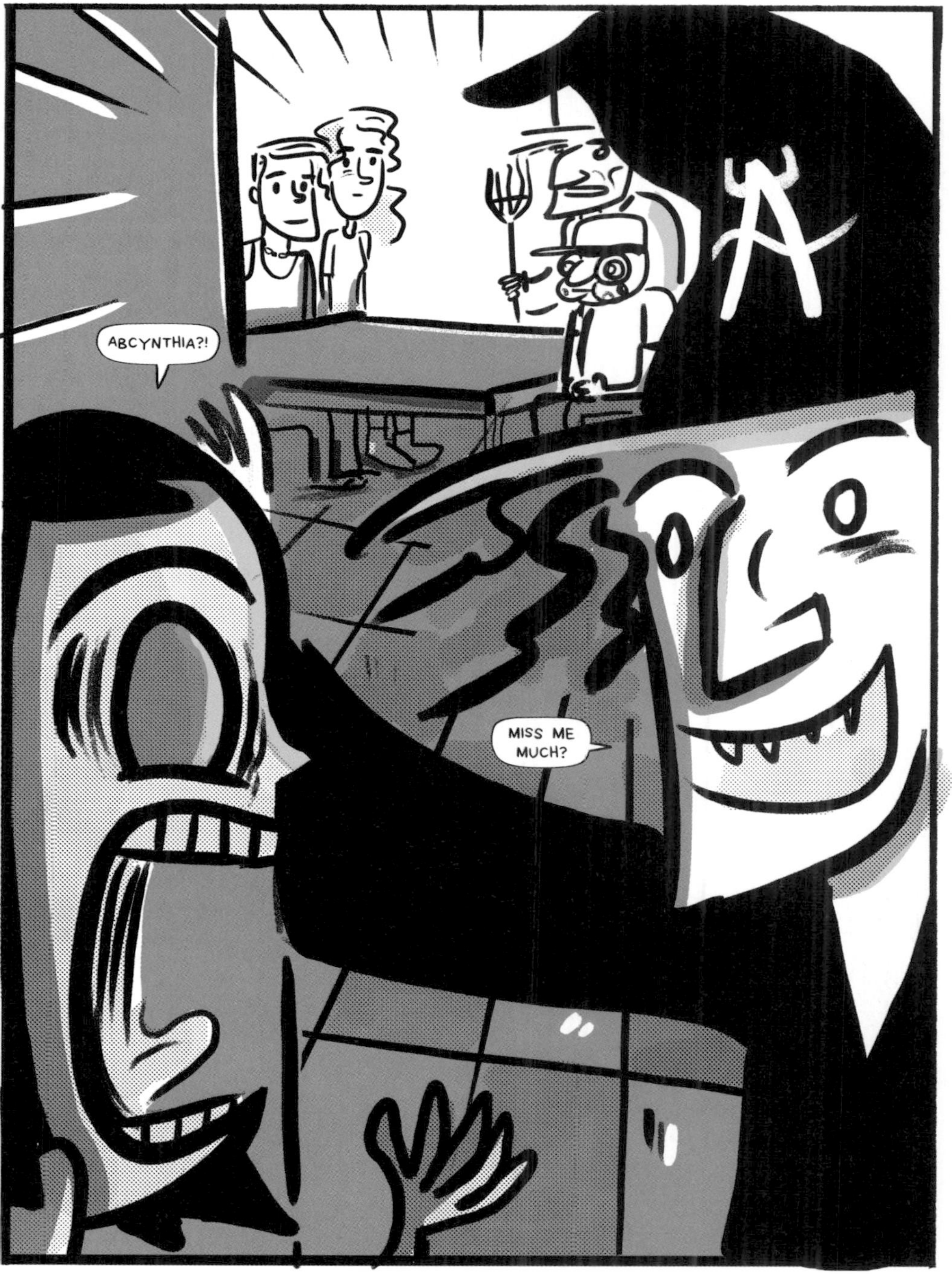
ABCYNTHIA?!
MISS ME MUCH?

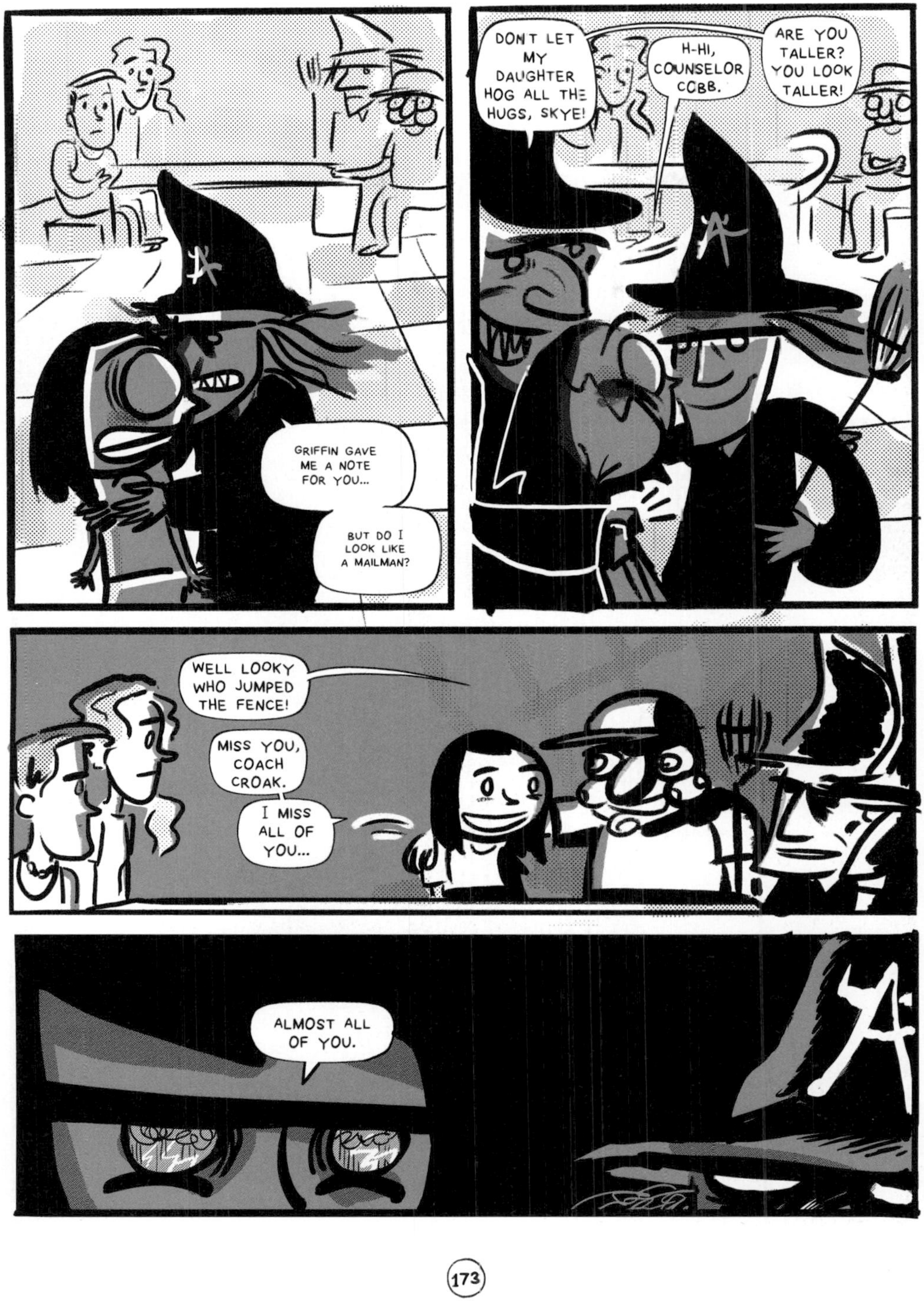
GRIFFIN GAVE ME A NOTE FOR YOU...
BUT DO I LOOK LIKE A MAILMAN?
DON'T LET MY DAUGHTER HOG ALL THE HUGS, SKYE!
H-HI, COUNSELOR COBB.
ARE YOU TALLER? YOU LOOK TALLER!
WELL LOOKY WHO JUMPED THE FENCE!
MISS YOU, COACH CROAK.
I MISS ALL OF YOU...
ALMOST ALL OF YOU.

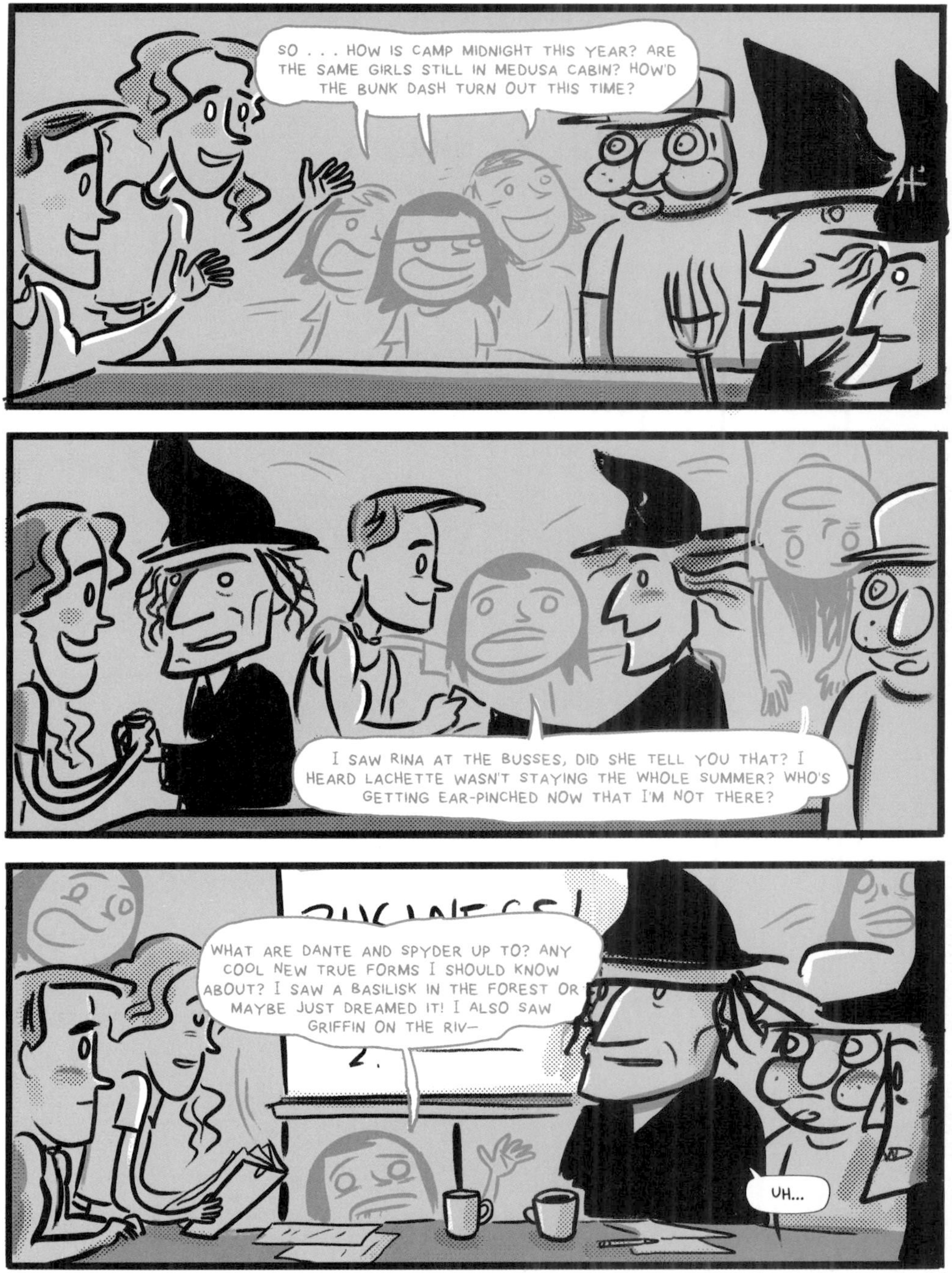
SO . . . HOW IS CAMP MIDNIGHT THIS YEAR? ARE THE SAME GIRLS STILL IN MEDUSA CABIN? HOW'D THE BUNK DASH TURN OUT THIS TIME?
I SAW RINA AT THE BUSSES, DID SHE TELL YOU THAT? I HEARD LACHETTE WASN'T STAYING THE WHOLE SUMMER? WHO'S GETTING EAR-PINCHED NOW THAT I'M NOT THERE?
WHAT ARE DANTE AND SPYDER UP TO? ANY COOL NEW TRUE FORMS I SHOULD KNOW ABOUT? I SAW A BASILISK IN THE FOREST OR MAYBE JUST DREAMED IT! I ALSO SAW GRIFFIN ON THE RIV—
UH...

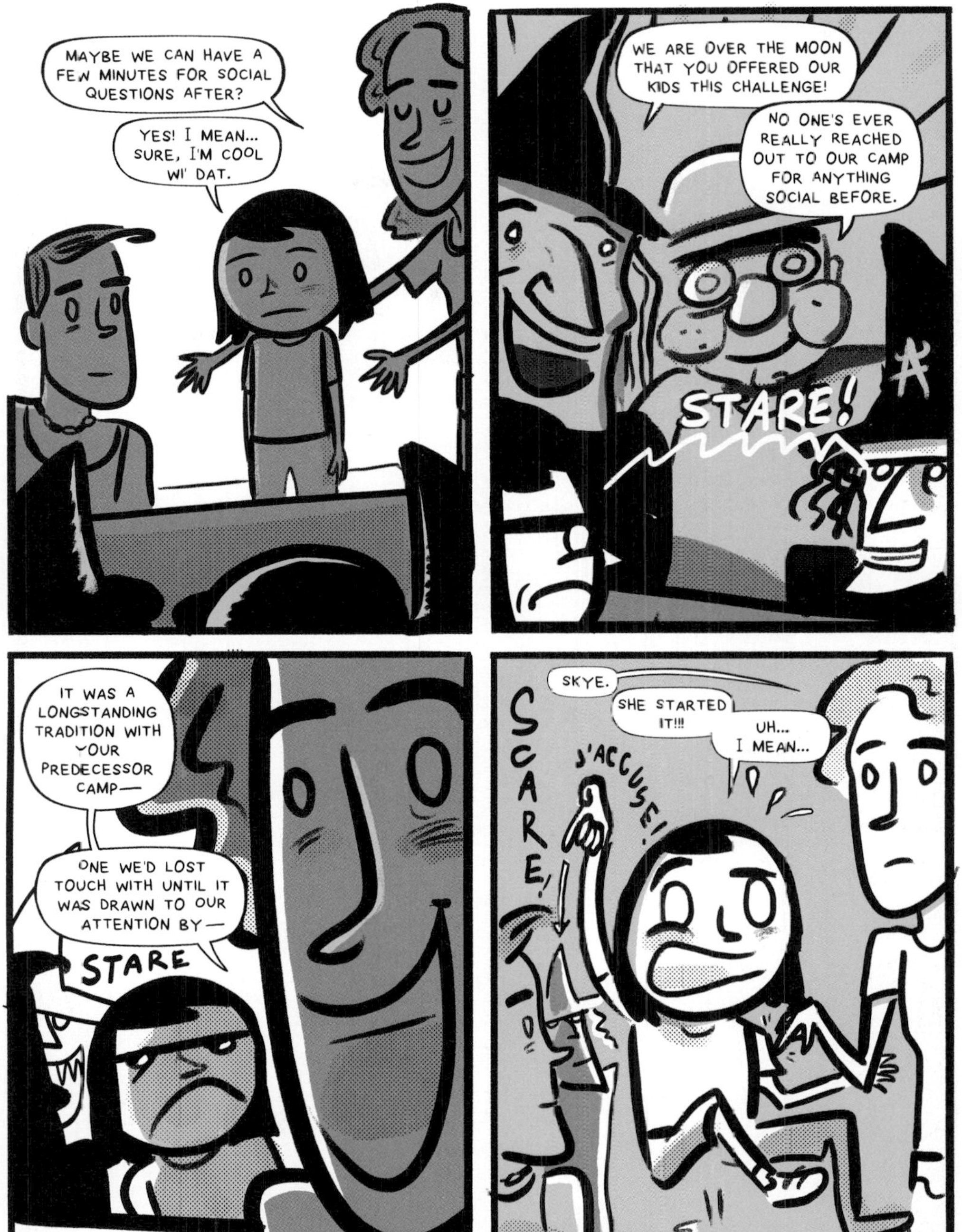
MAYBE WE CAN HAVE A FEW MINUTES FOR SOCIAL QUESTIONS AFTER?
YES! I MEAN... SURE, I'M COOL WI' DAT.
WE ARE OVER THE MOON THAT YOU OFFERED OUR KIDS THIS CHALLENGE!
NO ONE'S EVER REALLY REACHED OUT TO OUR CAMP FOR ANYTHING SOCIAL BEFORE.
STARE!
IT WAS A LONGSTANDING TRADITION WITH YOUR PREDECESSOR CAMP—
ONE WE'D LOST TOUCH WITH UNTIL IT WAS DRAWN TO OUR ATTENTION BY—
STARE
SKYE.
SHE STARTED IT!!!
UH... I MEAN...
SCARE!
J'ACCUSE!

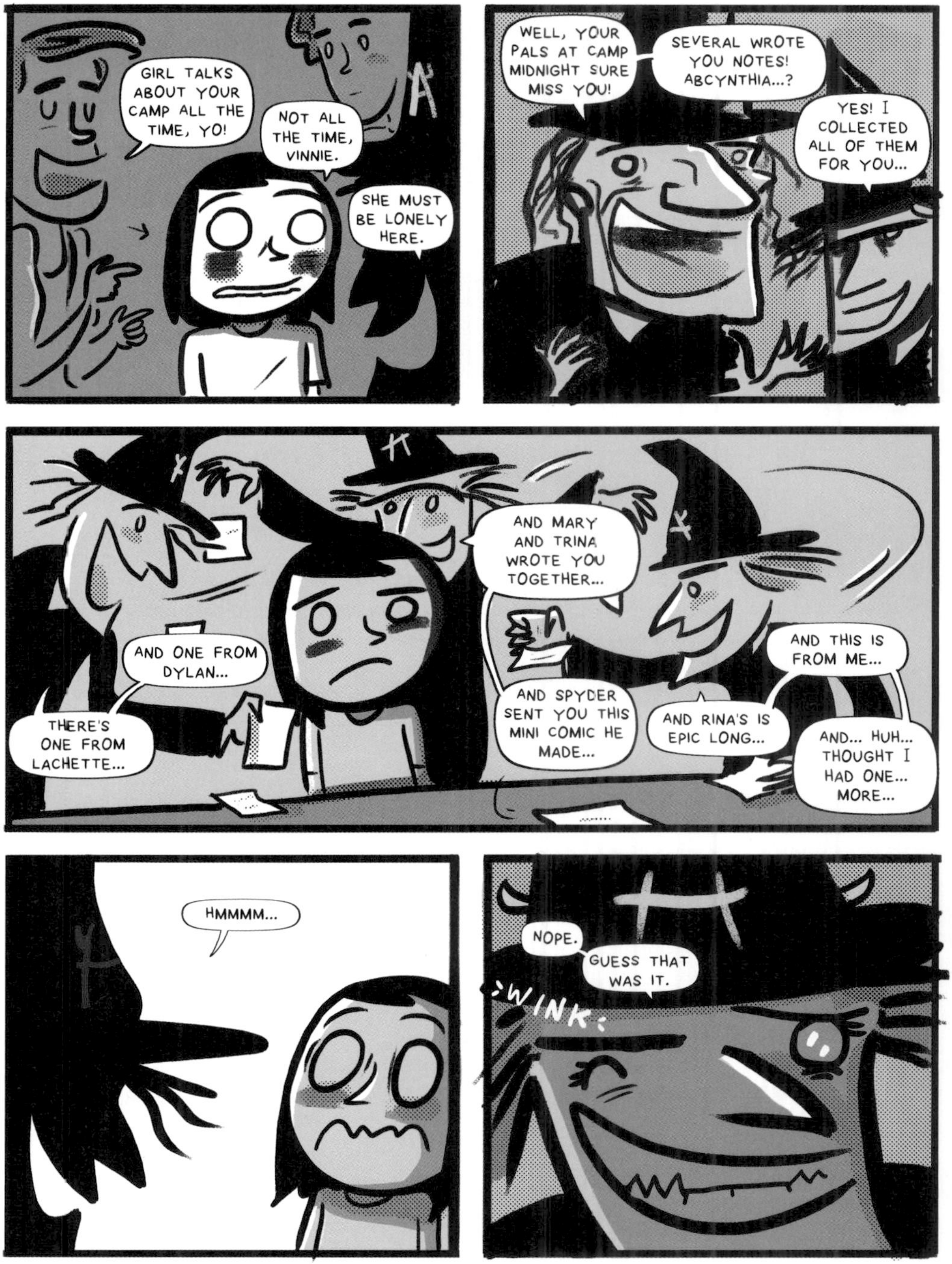
GIRL TALKS ABOUT YOUR CAMP ALL THE TIME, YO!
NOT ALL THE TIME, VINNIE.
SHE MUST BE LONELY HERE.
WELL, YOUR PALS AT CAMP MIDNIGHT SURE MISS YOU!
SEVERAL WROTE YOU NOTES! ABCYNTHIA...?
YES! I COLLECTED ALL OF THEM FOR YOU...
THERE'S ONE FROM LACHETTE...
AND ONE FROM DYLAN...
AND MARY AND TRINA WROTE YOU TOGETHER...
AND SPYDER SENT YOU THIS MINI COMIC HE MADE...
AND RINA'S IS EPIC LONG...
AND THIS IS FROM ME...
AND... HUH... THOUGHT I HAD ONE... MORE...
HMMMM...
NOPE.
GUESS THAT WAS IT.
WINK

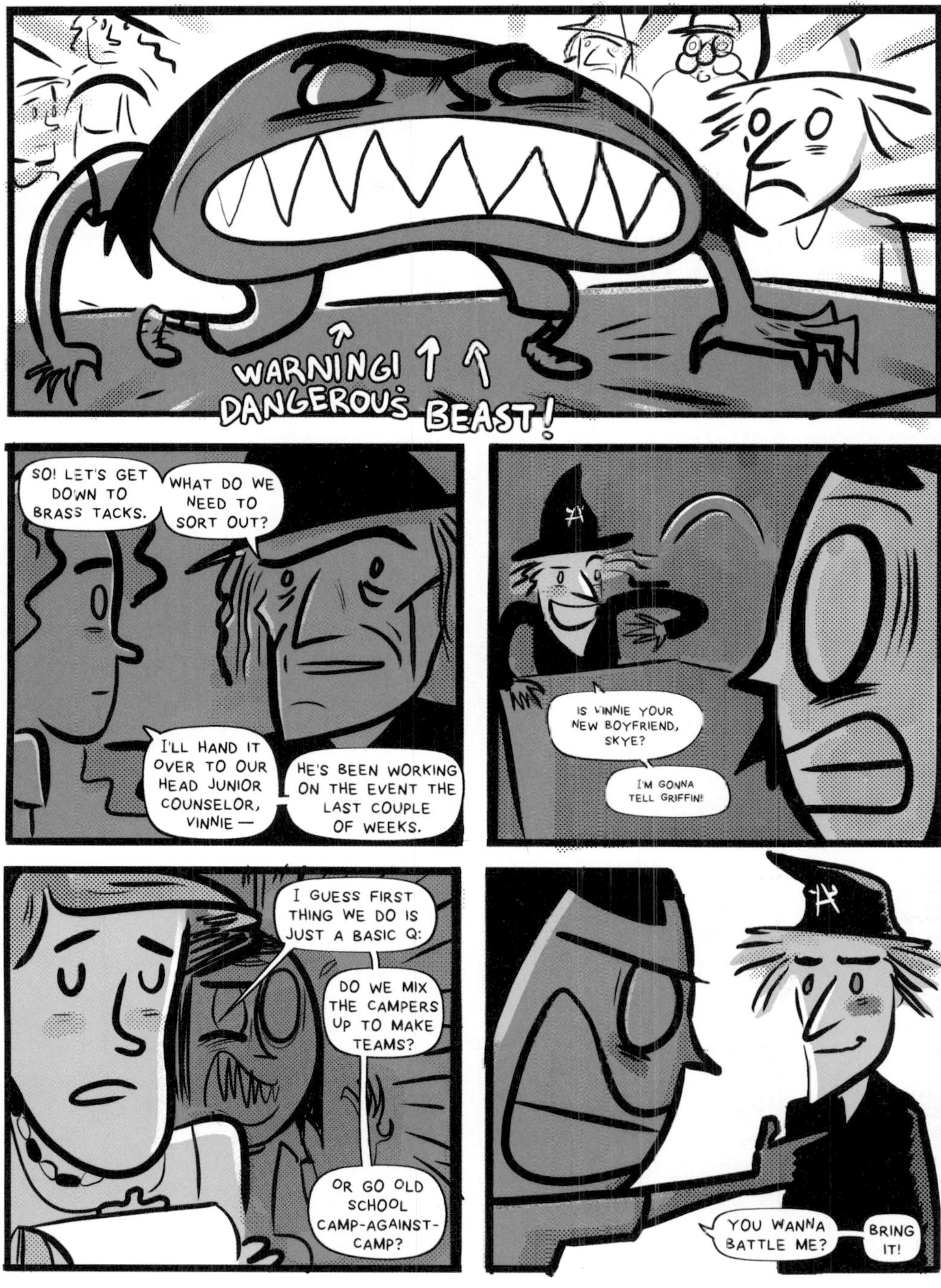
WARNING! DANGEROUS BEAST!
SO! LET'S GET DOWN TO BRASS TACKS.
WHAT DO WE NEED TO SORT OUT?
I'LL HAND IT OVER TO OUR HEAD JUNIOR COUNSELOR, VINNIE —
HE'S BEEN WORKING ON THE EVENT THE LAST COUPLE OF WEEKS.
IS VINNIE YOUR NEW BOYFRIEND, SKYE?
I'M GONNA TELL GRIFFIN!
I GUESS FIRST THING WE DO IS JUST A BASIC Q:
DO WE MIX THE CAMPERS UP TO MAKE TEAMS?
OR GO OLD SCHOOL CAMP-AGAINST-CAMP?
YOU WANNA BATTLE ME?
BRING IT!

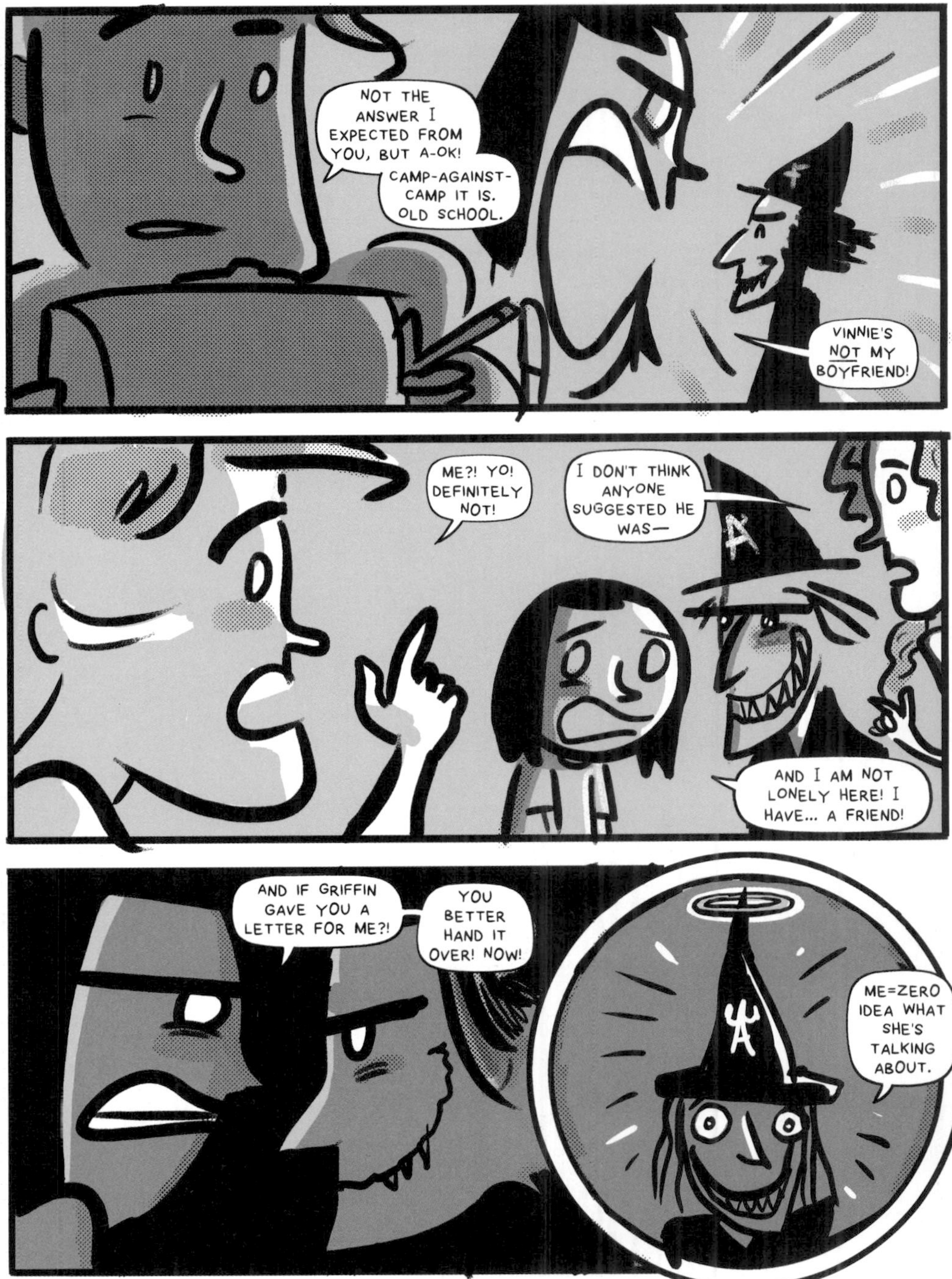
NOT THE ANSWER I EXPECTED FROM YOU, BUT A-OK!
CAMP-AGAINST-CAMP IT IS. OLD SCHOOL.
VINNIE'S NOT MY BOYFRIEND!
ME?! YO! DEFINITELY NOT!
I DON'T THINK ANYONE SUGGESTED HE WAS—
AND I AM NOT LONELY HERE! I HAVE... A FRIEND!
AND IF GRIFFIN GAVE YOU A LETTER FOR ME?!
YOU BETTER HAND IT OVER! NOW!
ME=ZERO IDEA WHAT SHE'S TALKING ABOUT.

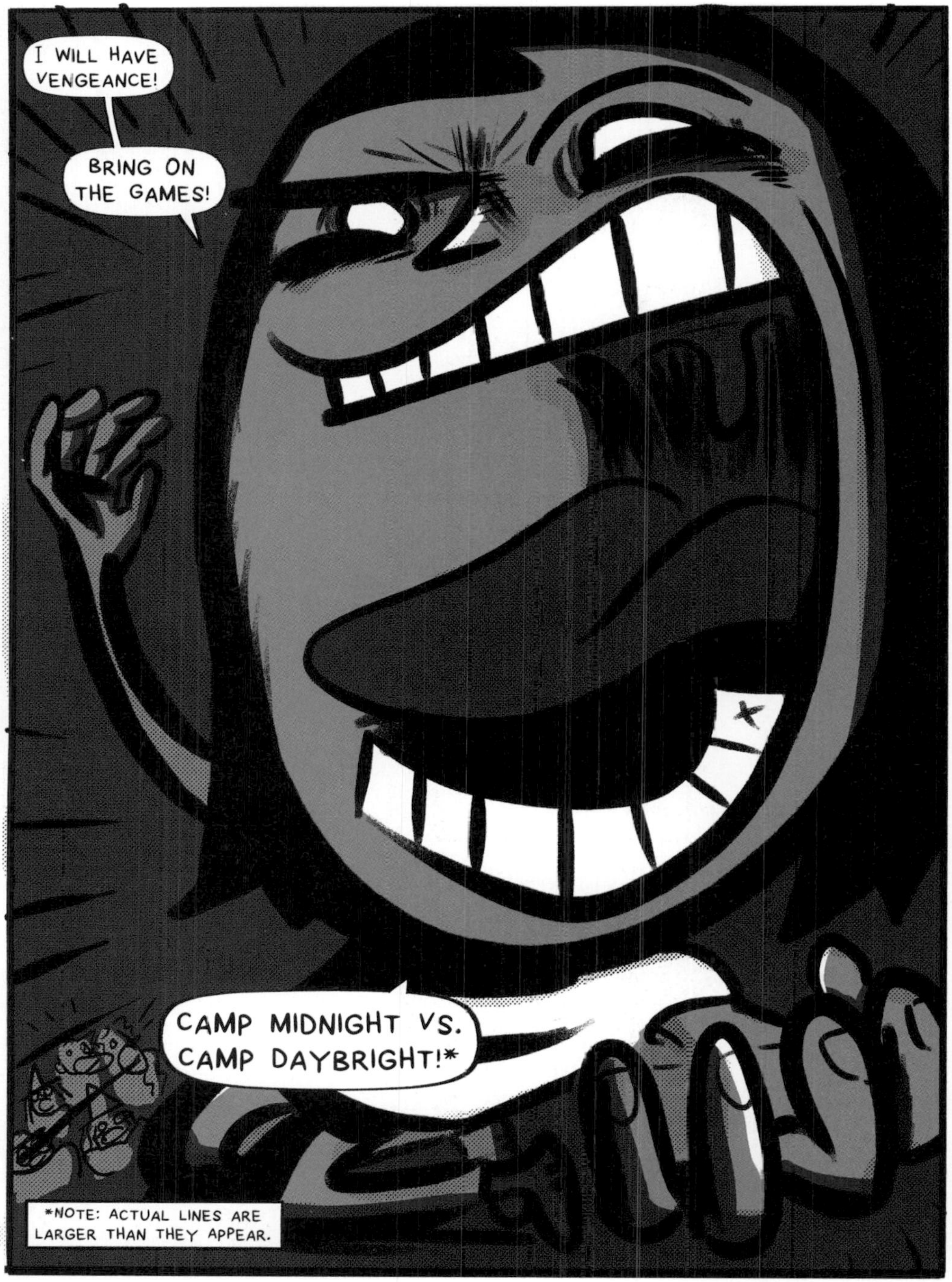
I WILL HAVE VENGEANCE!
BRING ON THE GAMES!
CAMP MIDNIGHT VS. CAMP DAYBRIGHT!*
*NOTE: ACTUAL LINES ARE LARGER THAN THEY APPEAR.

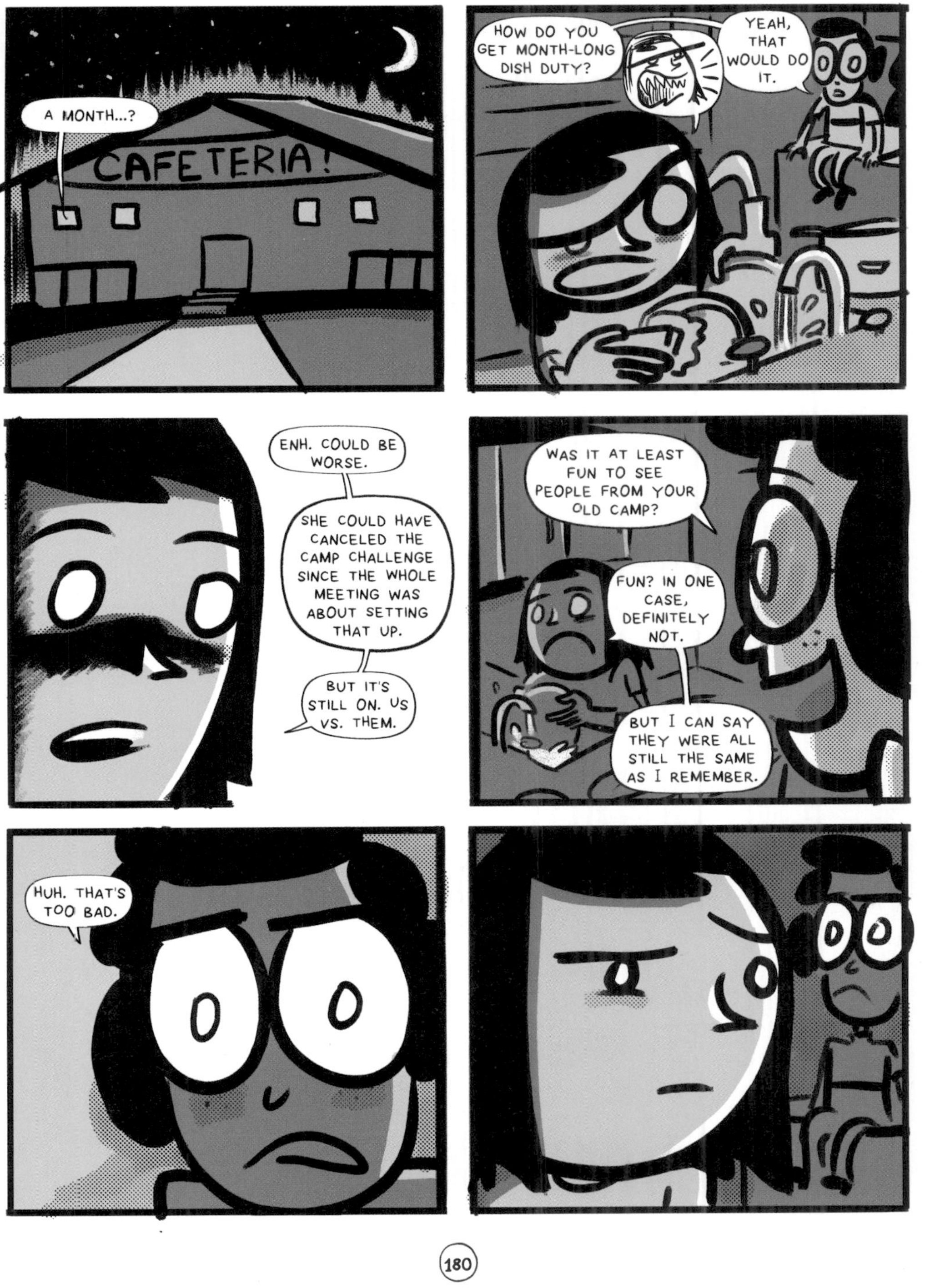
A MONTH...?
CAFETERIA!
HOW DO YOU GET MONTH-LONG DISH DUTY?
YEAH, THAT WOULD DO IT.
ENH. COULD BE WORSE.
SHE COULD HAVE CANCELED THE CAMP CHALLENGE SINCE THE WHOLE MEETING WAS ABOUT SETTING THAT UP.
BUT IT'S STILL ON. US VS. THEM.
WAS IT AT LEAST FUN TO SEE PEOPLE FROM YOUR OLD CAMP?
FUN? IN ONE CASE, DEFINITELY NOT.
BUT I CAN SAY THEY WERE ALL STILL THE SAME AS I REMEMBER.
HUH. THAT'S TOO BAD.

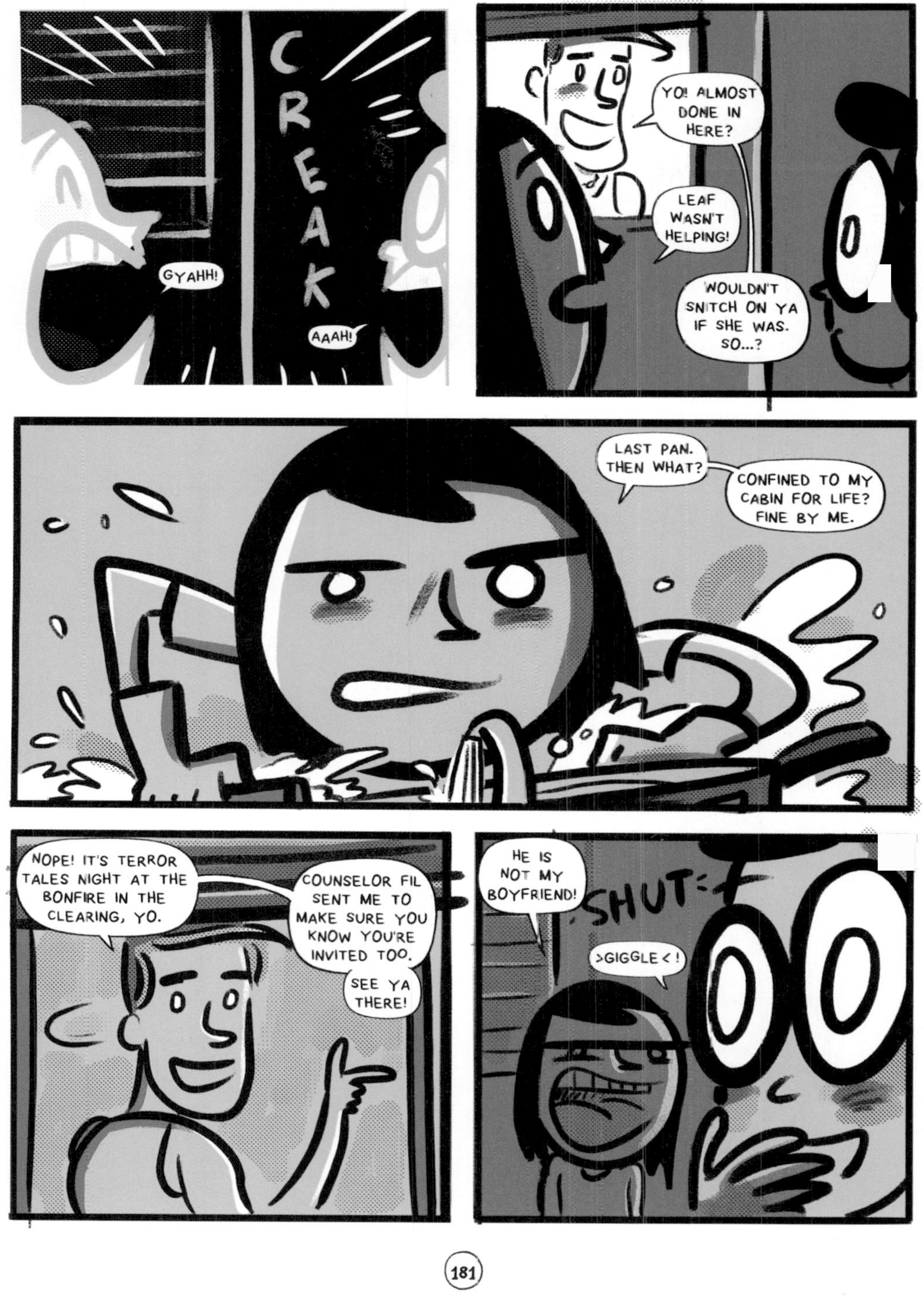
CREAK
GYAHH!
AAAH!
YO! ALMOST DONE IN HERE?
LEAF WASN'T HELPING!
WOULDN'T SNITCH ON YA IF SHE WAS. SO...?
LAST PAN. THEN WHAT?
CONFINED TO MY CABIN FOR LIFE? FINE BY ME.
NOPE! IT'S TERROR TALES NIGHT AT THE BONFIRE IN THE CLEARING, YO.
COUNSELOR FIL SENT ME TO MAKE SURE YOU KNOW YOU'RE INVITED TOO.
SEE YA THERE!
HE IS NOT MY BOYFRIEND!
SHUT
>GIGGLE<!

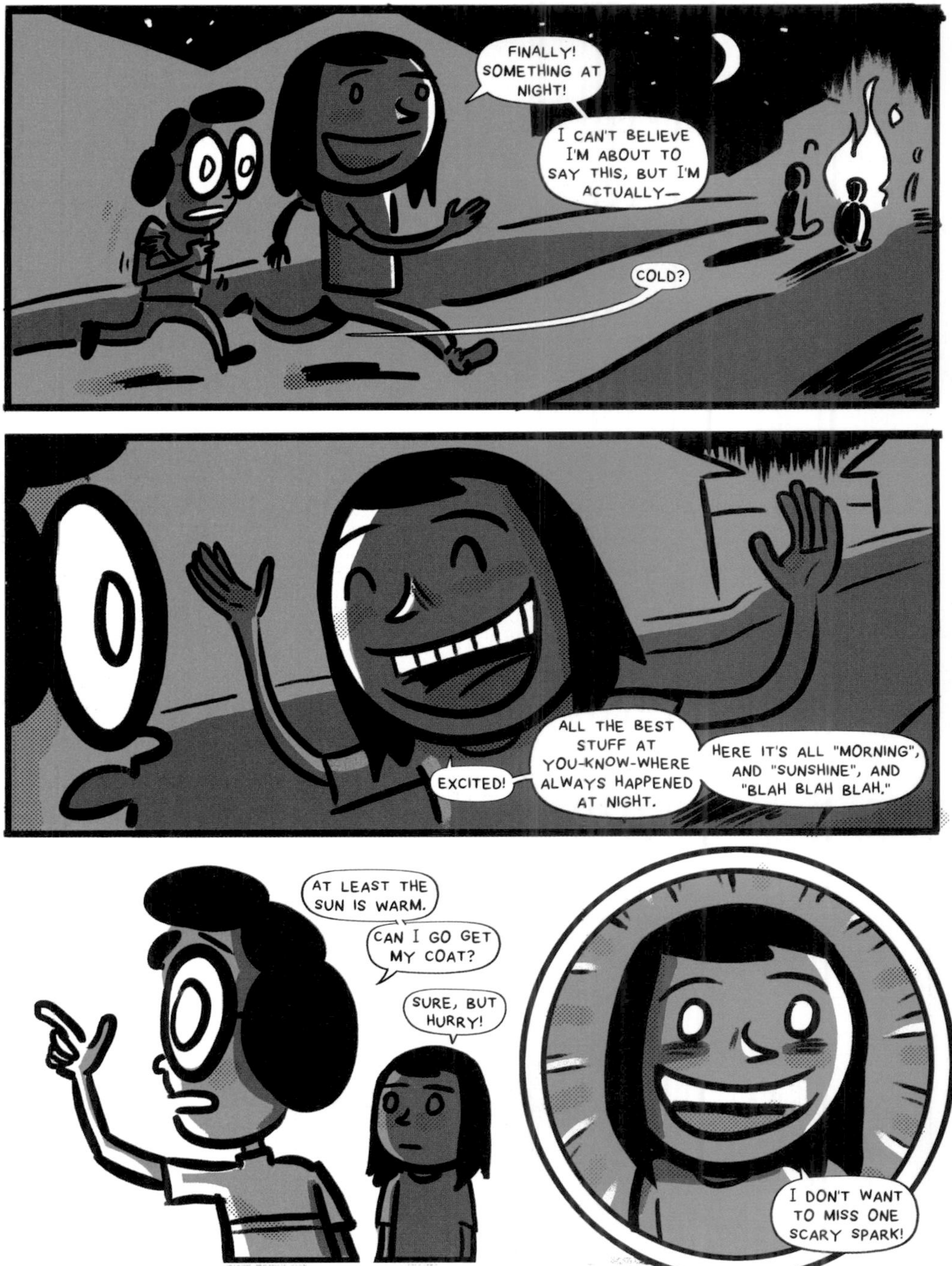
FINALLY! SOMETHING AT NIGHT!
I CAN'T BELIEVE I'M ABOUT TO SAY THIS, BUT I'M ACTUALLY—
COLD?
EXCITED!
ALL THE BEST STUFF AT YOU-KNOW-WHERE ALWAYS HAPPENED AT NIGHT.
HERE IT'S ALL "MORNING", AND "SUNSHINE", AND "BLAH BLAH BLAH."
AT LEAST THE SUN IS WARM.
CAN I GO GET MY COAT?
SURE, BUT HURRY!
I DON'T WANT TO MISS ONE SCARY SPARK!

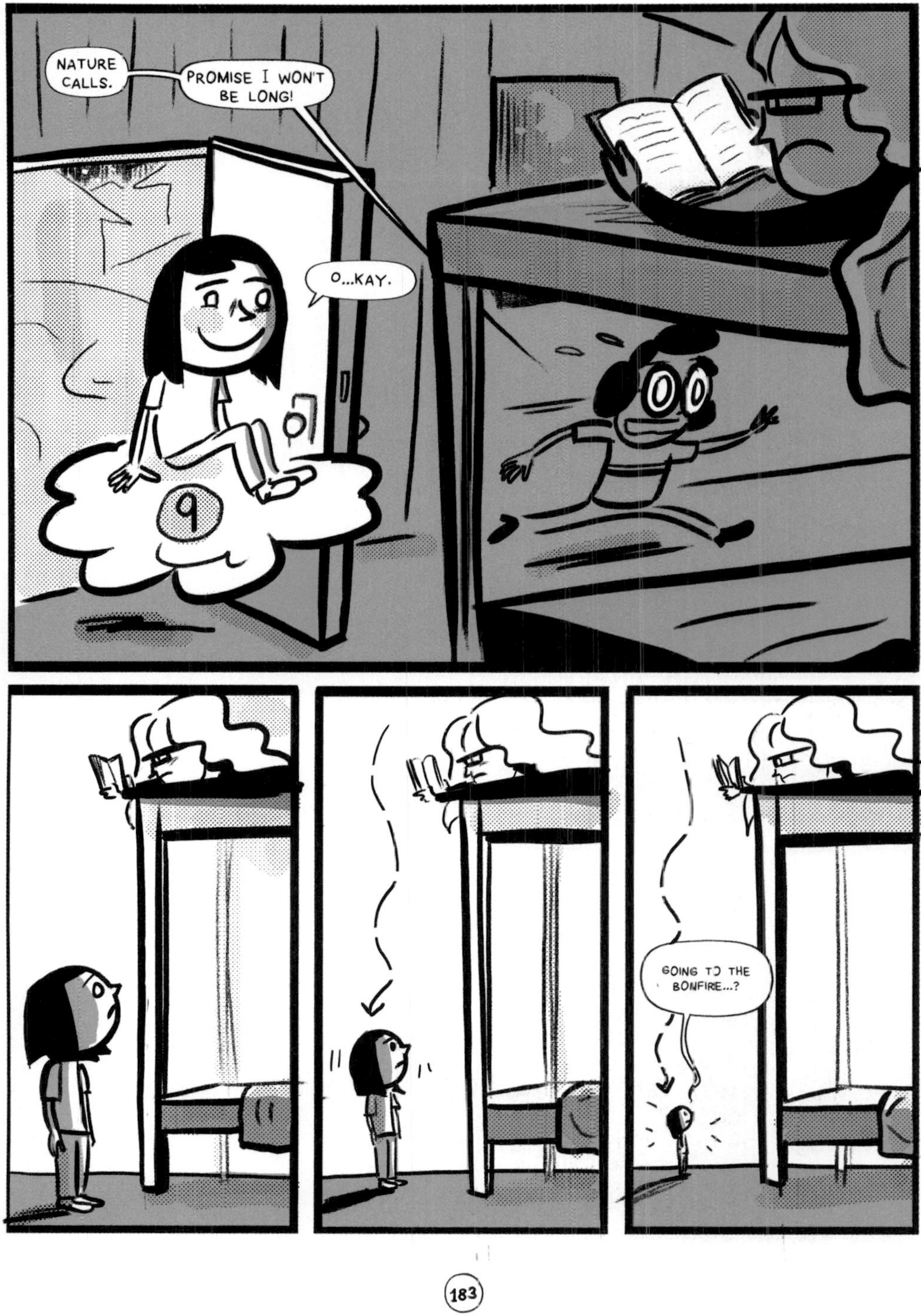
NATURE CALLS.
PROMISE I WON'T BE LONG!
O...KAY.
GOING TO THE BONFIRE...?

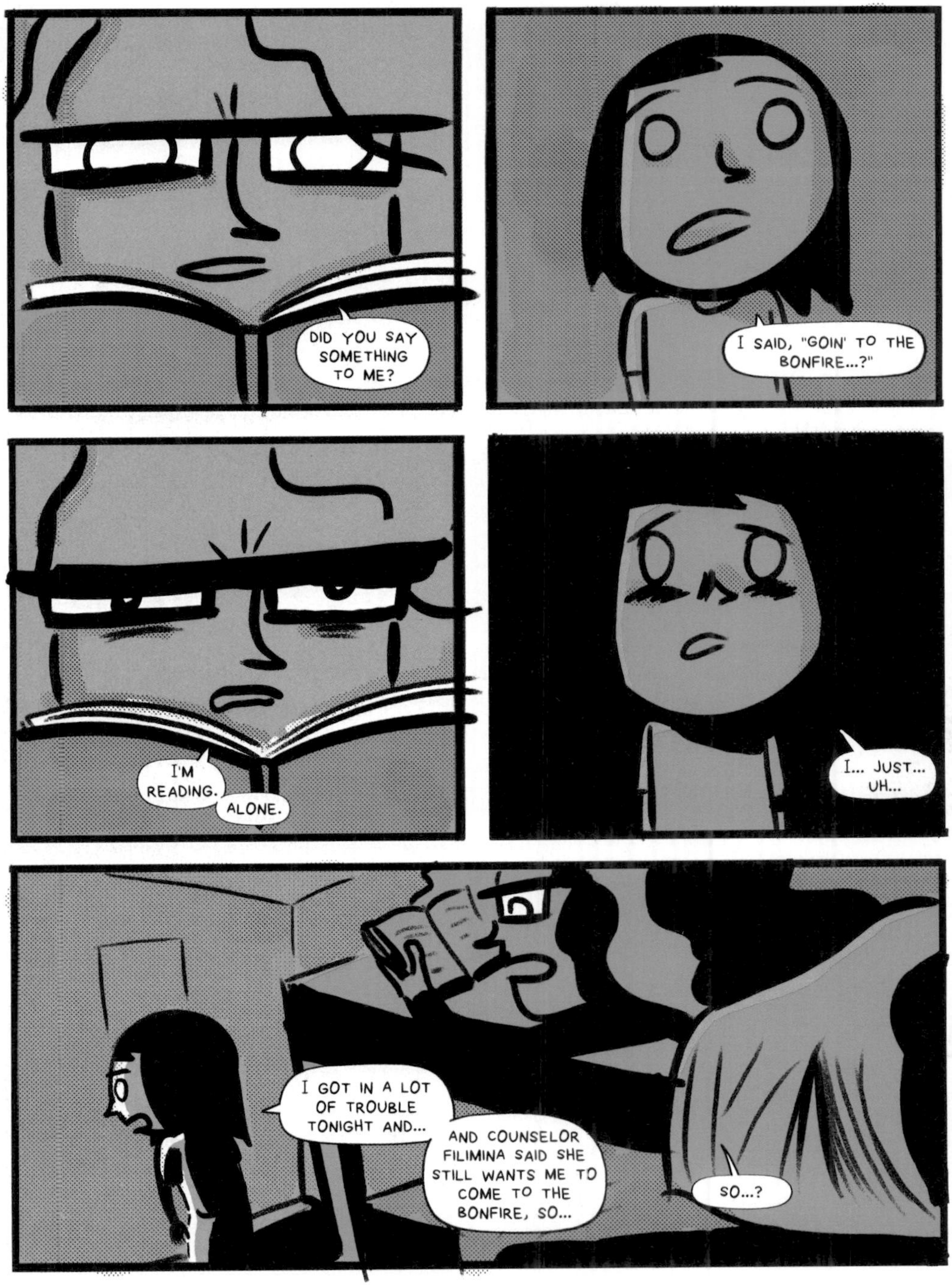
DID YOU SAY SOMETHING TO ME?
I SAID, "GOIN' TO THE BONFIRE...?"
I'M READING.
ALONE.
I... JUST... UH...
I GOT IN A LOT OF TROUBLE TONIGHT AND...
AND COUNSELOR FILIMINA SAID SHE STILL WANTS ME TO COME TO THE BONFIRE, SO...
SO...?

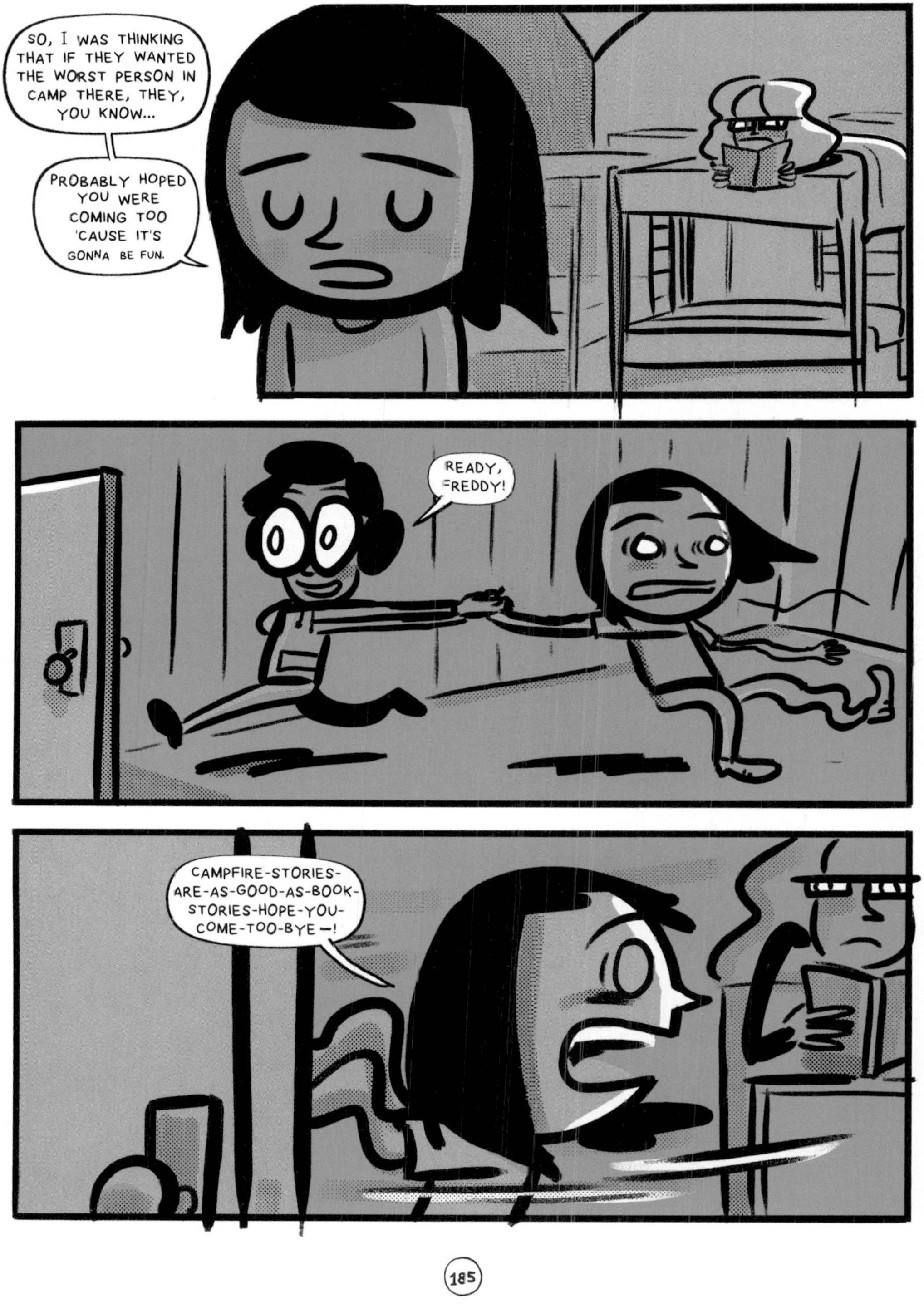
SO, I WAS THINKING THAT IF THEY WANTED THE WORST PERSON IN CAMP THERE, THEY, YOU KNOW...
PROBABLY HOPED YOU WERE COMING TOO 'CAUSE IT'S GONNA BE FUN.
READY, FREDDY!
CAMPFIRE-STORIES-ARE-AS-GOOD-AS-BOOK-STORIES-HOPE-YOU-COME-TOO-BYE—!

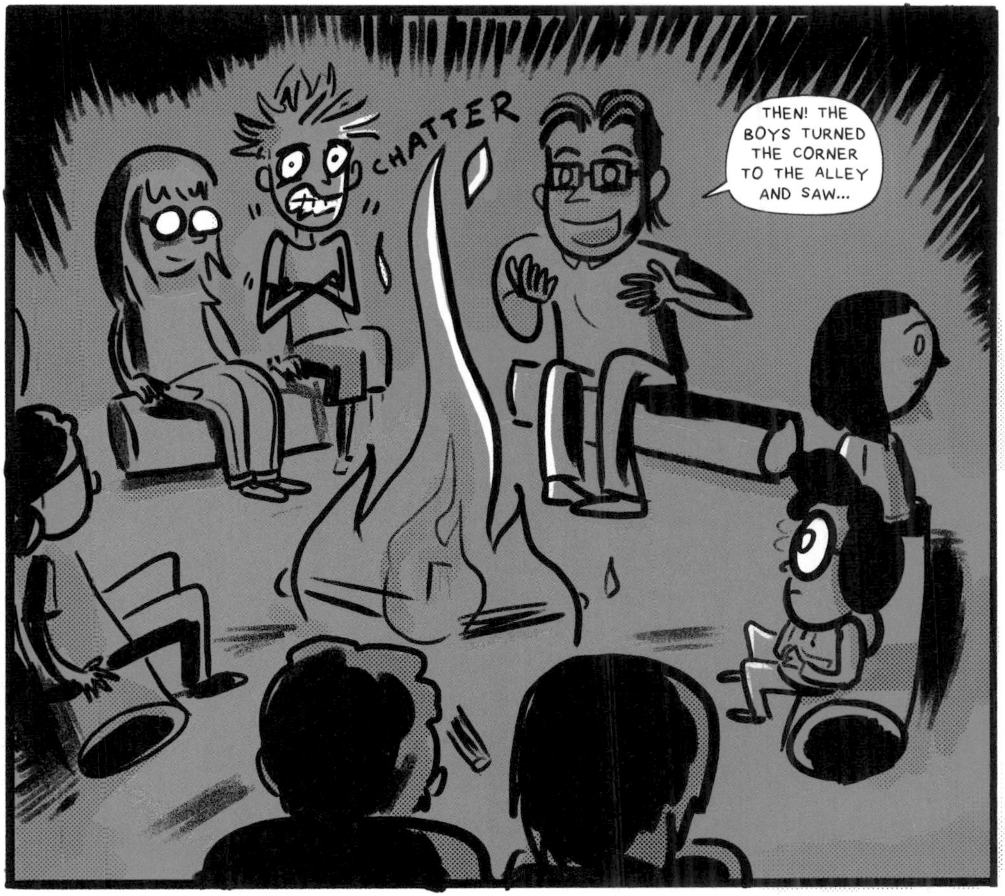
CHATTER
THEN! THE BOYS TURNED THE CORNER TO THE ALLEY AND SAW...

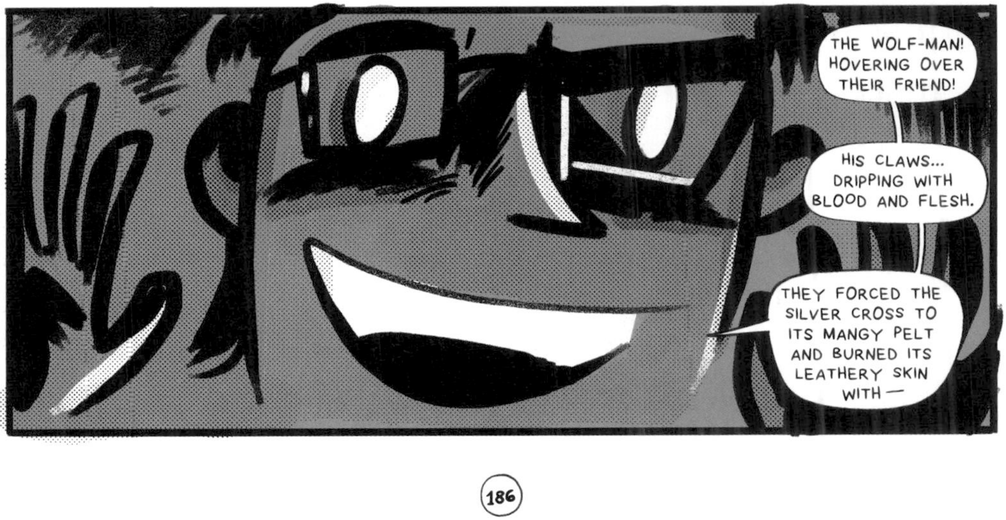
THE WOLF-MAN! HOVERING OVER THEIR FRIEND!
HIS CLAWS... DRIPPING WITH BLOOD AND FLESH.
THEY FORCED THE SILVER CROSS TO ITS MANGY PELT AND BURNED ITS LEATHERY SKIN WITH—

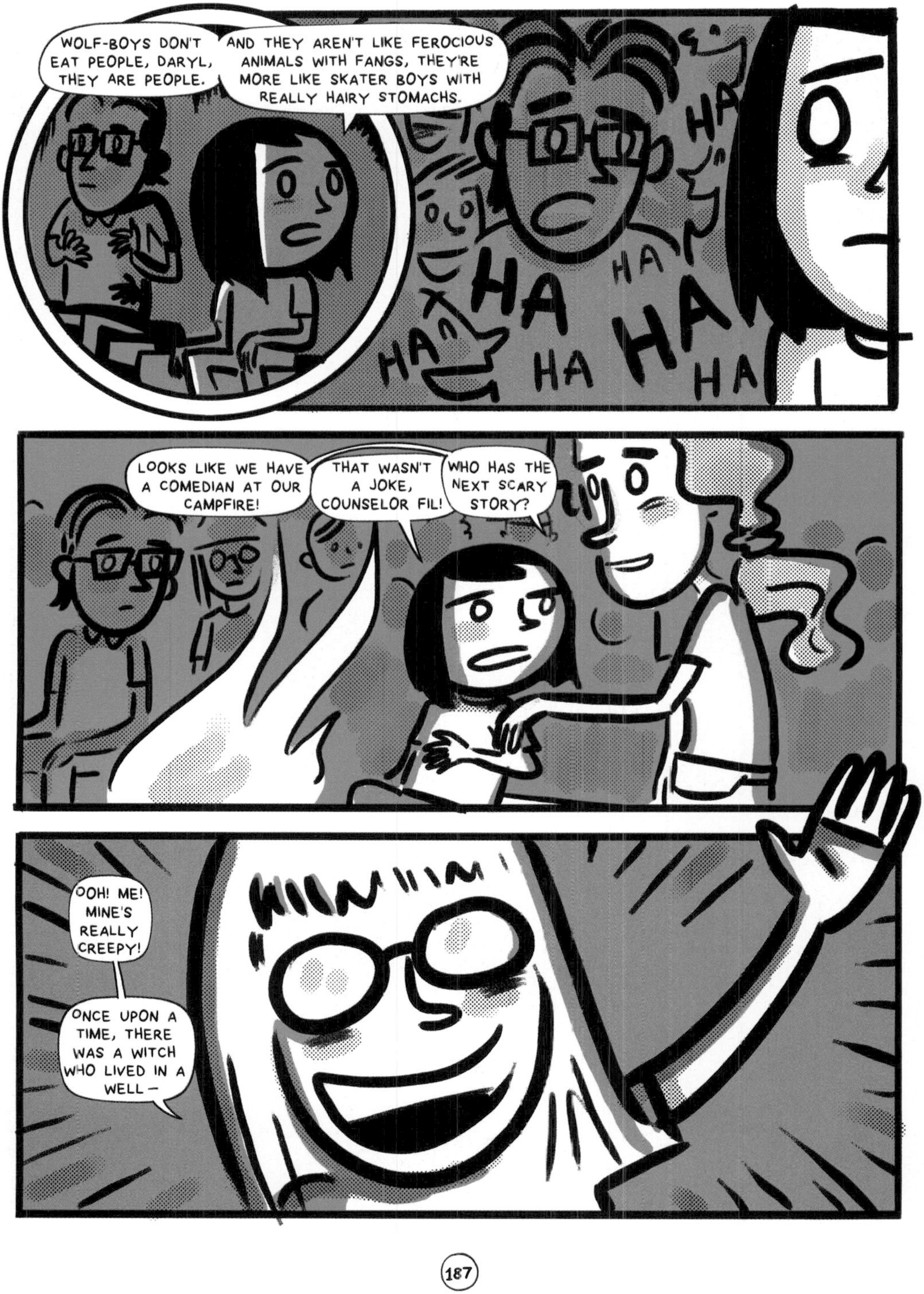
WOLF-BOYS DON'T EAT PEOPLE, DARYL, THEY ARE PEOPLE.
AND THEY AREN'T LIKE FEROCIOUS ANIMALS WITH FANGS, THEY'RE MORE LIKE SKATER BOYS WITH REALLY HAIRY STOMACHS.
HA HA HA HA HA HA HA HA
LOOKS LIKE WE HAVE A COMEDIAN AT OUR CAMPFIRE!
THAT WASN'T A JOKE, COUNSELOR FIL!
WHO HAS THE NEXT SCARY STORY?
OOH! ME! MINE'S REALLY CREEPY!
ONCE UPON A TIME, THERE WAS A WITCH WHO LIVED IN A WELL—

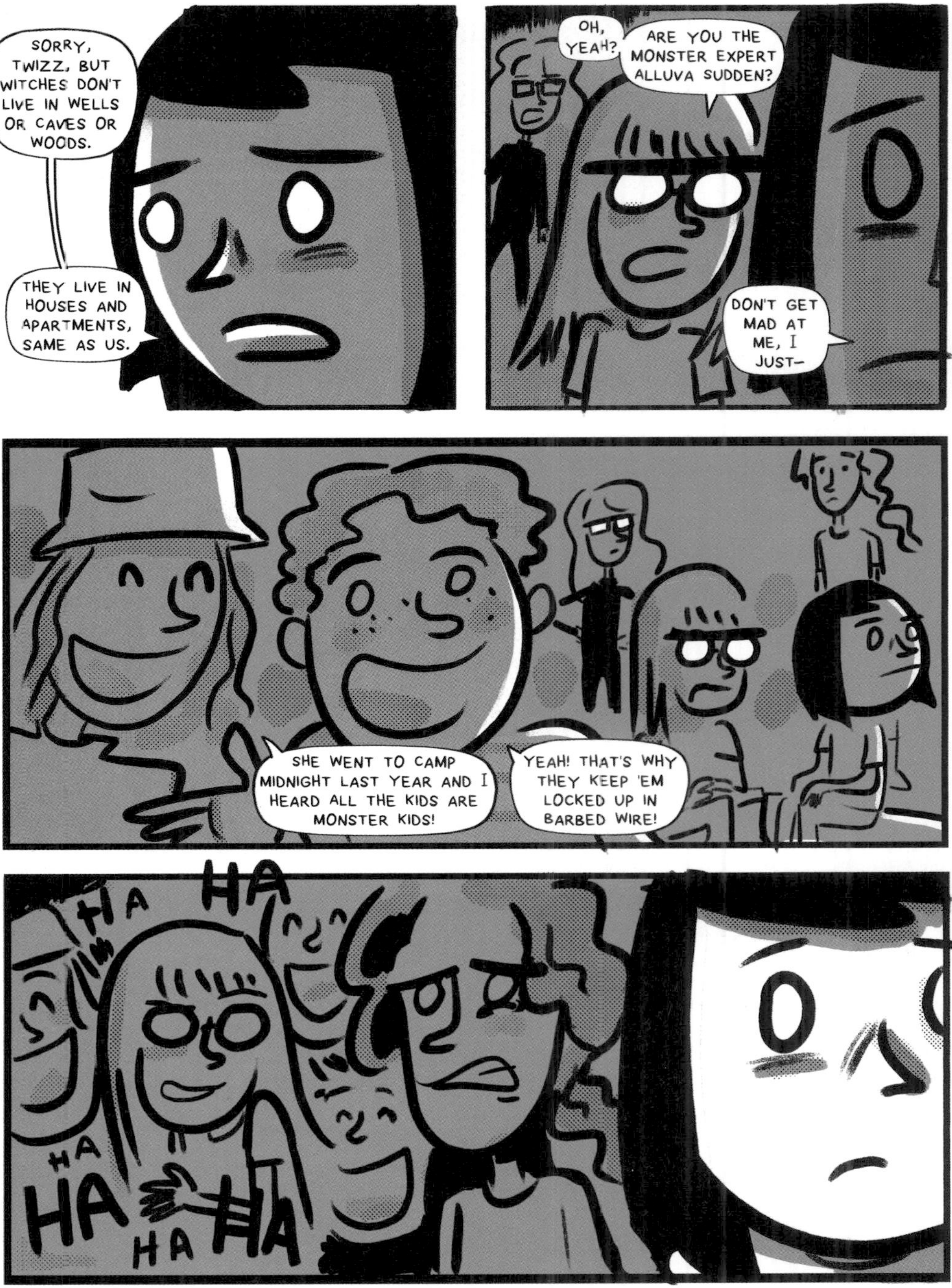
SORRY, TWIZZ, BUT WITCHES DON'T LIVE IN WELLS OR CAVES OR WOODS.
THEY LIVE IN HOUSES AND APARTMENTS, SAME AS US.
OH, YEAH?
ARE YOU THE MONSTER EXPERT ALLUVA SUDDEN?
DON'T GET MAD AT ME, I JUST–
SHE WENT TO CAMP MIDNIGHT LAST YEAR AND I HEARD ALL THE KIDS ARE MONSTER KIDS!
YEAH! THAT'S WHY THEY KEEP 'EM LOCKED UP IN BARBED WIRE!
HA HA HA HA HA HA HA HA

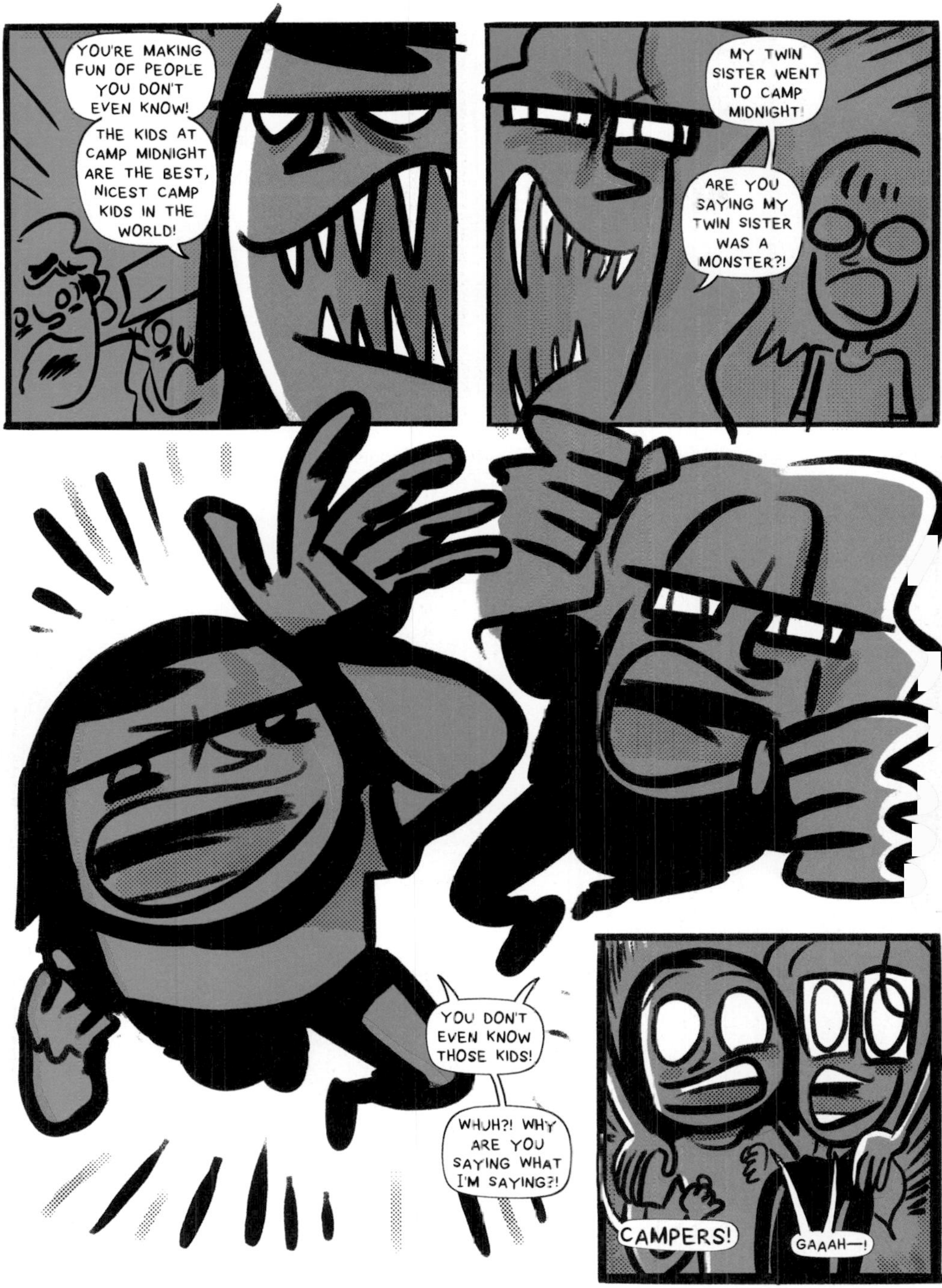
YOU'RE MAKING FUN OF PEOPLE YOU DON'T EVEN KNOW!
THE KIDS AT CAMP MIDNIGHT ARE THE BEST, NICEST CAMP KIDS IN THE WORLD!
MY TWIN SISTER WENT TO CAMP MIDNIGHT!
ARE YOU SAYING MY TWIN SISTER WAS A MONSTER?!
YOU DON'T EVEN KNOW THOSE KIDS!
WHUH?! WHY ARE YOU SAYING WHAT I'M SAYING?!
CAMPERS!
GAAAH—!

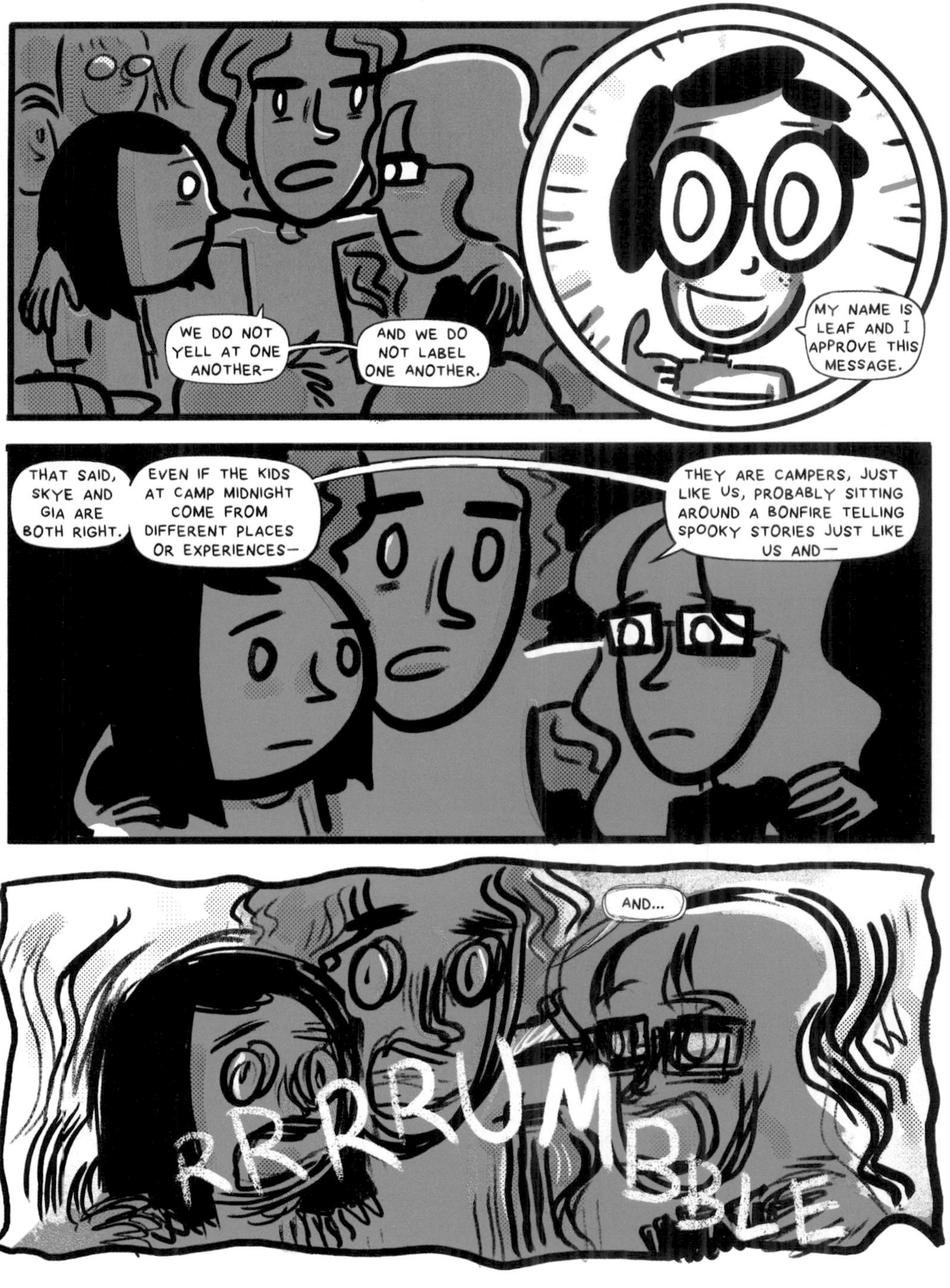

WE DO NOT YELL AT ONE ANOTHER—
AND WE DO NOT LABEL ONE ANOTHER.
MY NAME IS LEAF AND I APPROVE THIS MESSAGE.
THAT SAID, SKYE AND GIA ARE BOTH RIGHT.
EVEN IF THE KIDS AT CAMP MIDNIGHT COME FROM DIFFERENT PLACES OR EXPERIENCES—
THEY ARE CAMPERS, JUST LIKE US, PROBABLY SITTING AROUND A BONFIRE TELLING SPOOKY STORIES JUST LIKE US AND—
AND...
RRRRUMBBLE

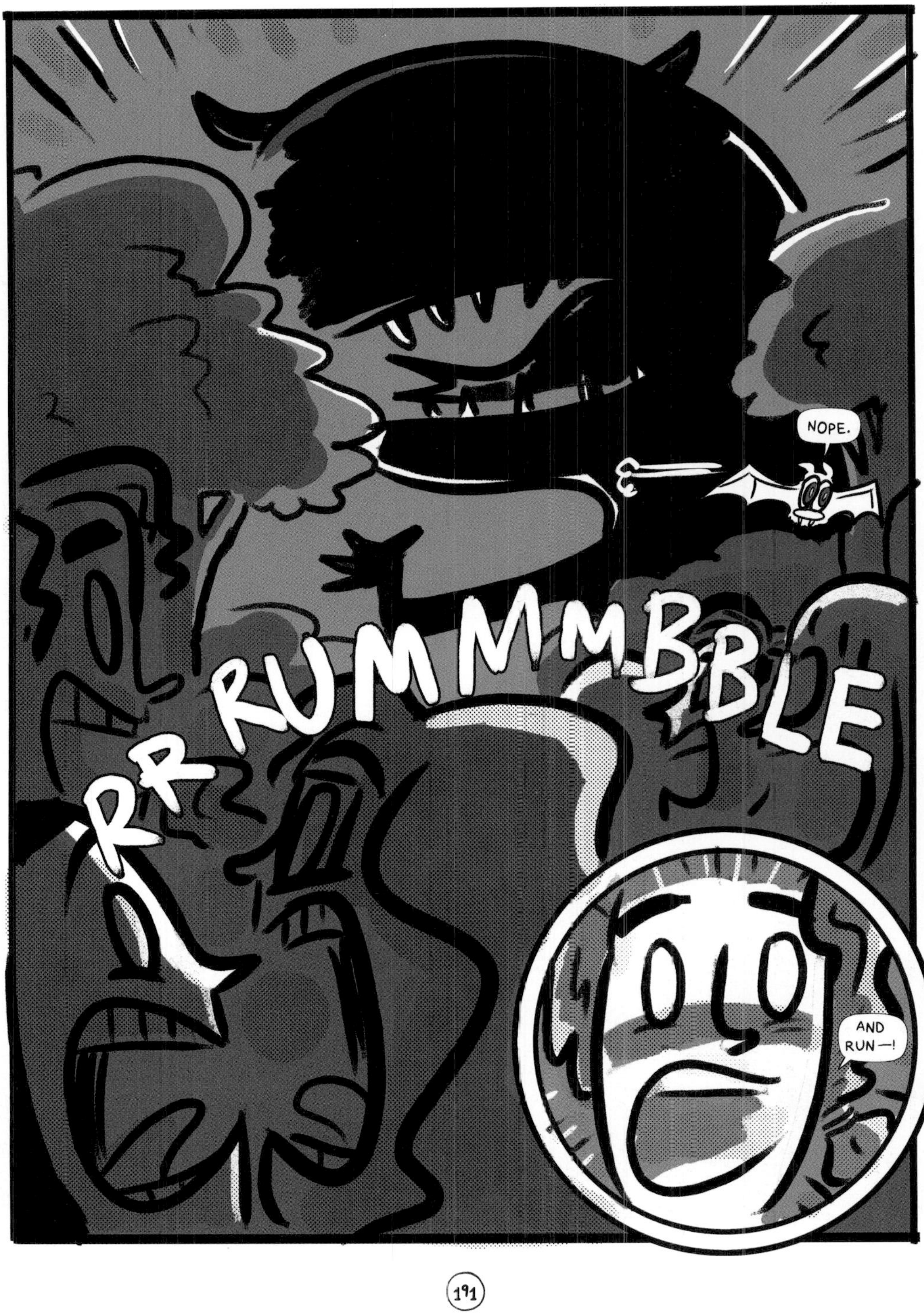
NOPE.
RRRUMMMBBLE
AND RUN—!

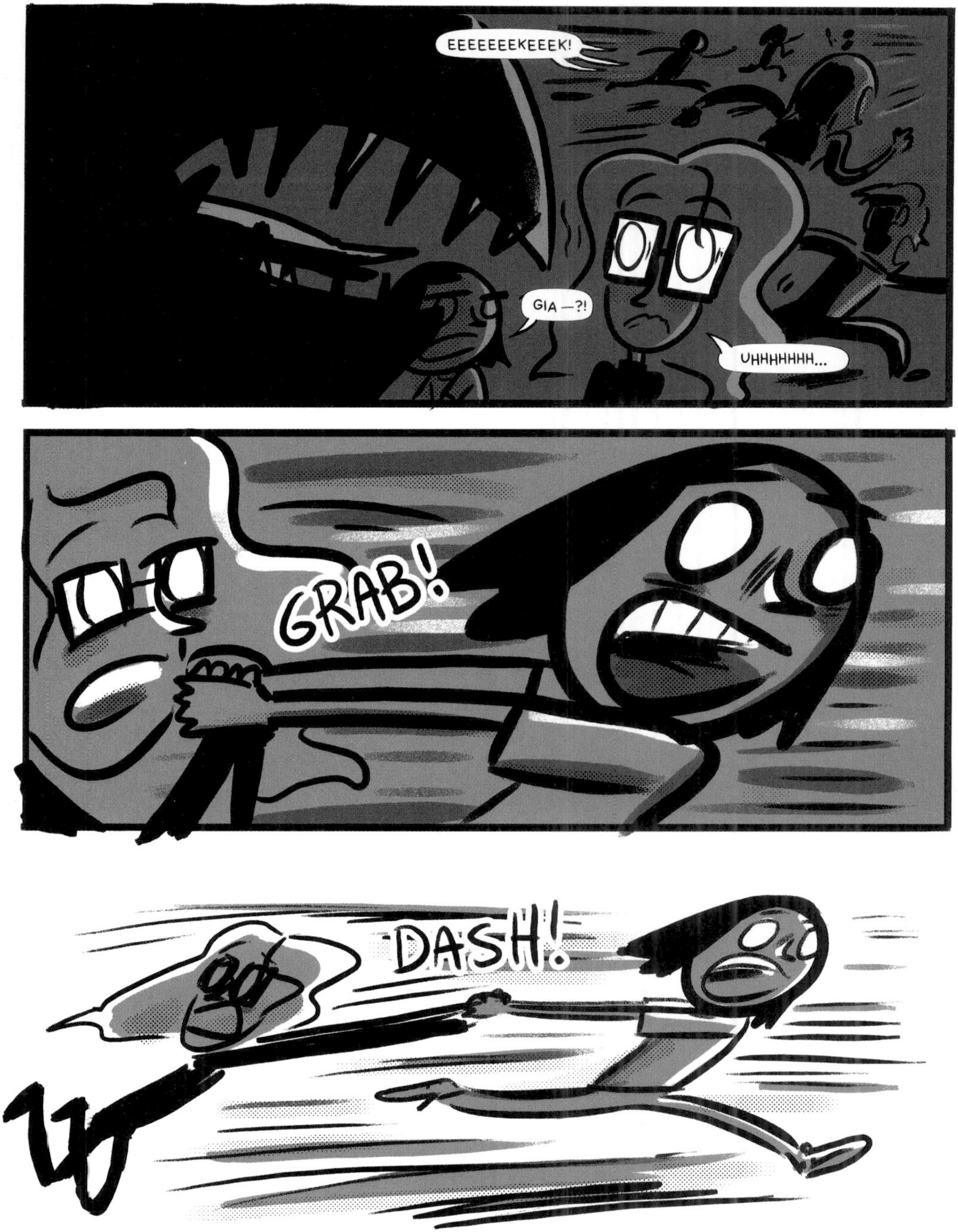
EEEEEEEKEEEK!
GIA —?!
UHHHHHHH...
GRAB!
DASH!

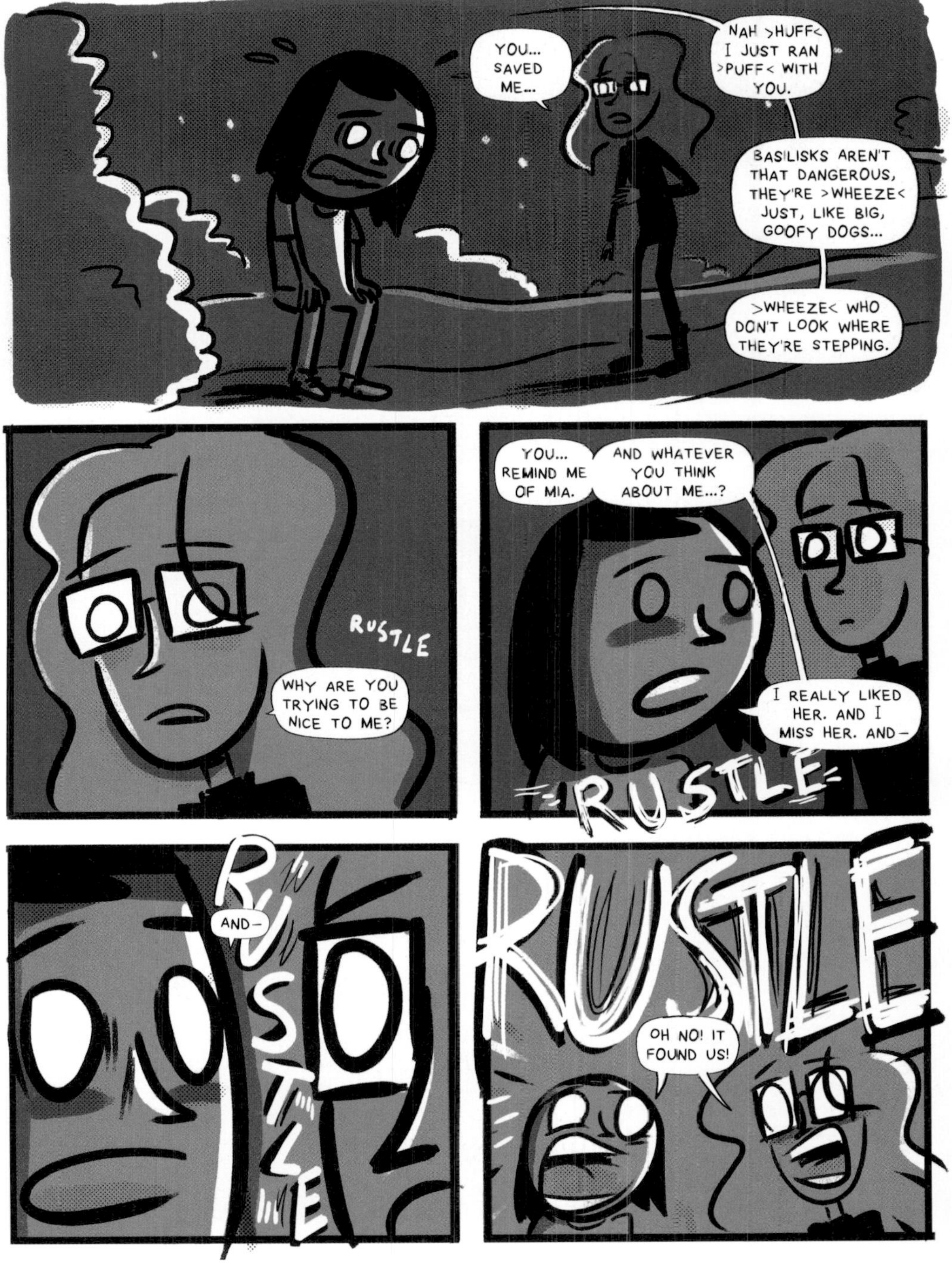
YOU... SAVED ME...
NAH >HUFF< I JUST RAN >PUFF< WITH YOU.
BASILISKS AREN'T THAT DANGEROUS, THEY'RE >WHEEZE< JUST, LIKE BIG, GOOFY DOGS...
>WHEEZE< WHO DON'T LOOK WHERE THEY'RE STEPPING.
RUSTLE
WHY ARE YOU TRYING TO BE NICE TO ME?
YOU... REMIND ME OF MIA.
AND WHATEVER YOU THINK ABOUT ME...?
I REALLY LIKED HER. AND I MISS HER. AND—
RUSTLE
RUSTLE
AND—
RUSTLE
OH NO! IT FOUND US!

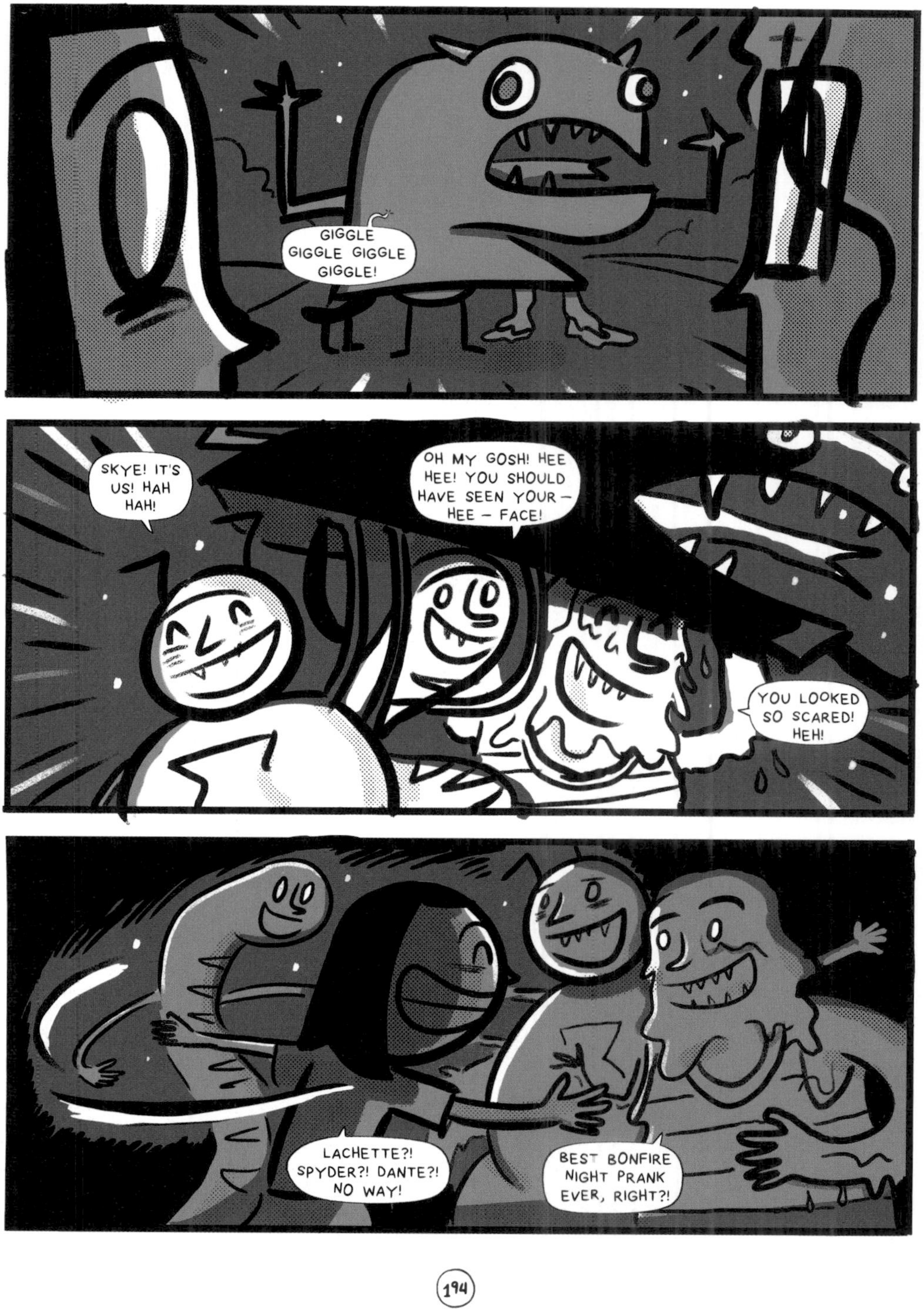
GIGGLE GIGGLE GIGGLE GIGGLE!
SKYE! IT'S US! HAH HAH!
OH MY GOSH! HEE HEE! YOU SHOULD HAVE SEEN YOUR— HEE — FACE!
YOU LOOKED SO SCARED! HEH!
LACHETTE?! SPYDER?! DANTE?! NO WAY!
BEST BONFIRE NIGHT PRANK EVER, RIGHT?!

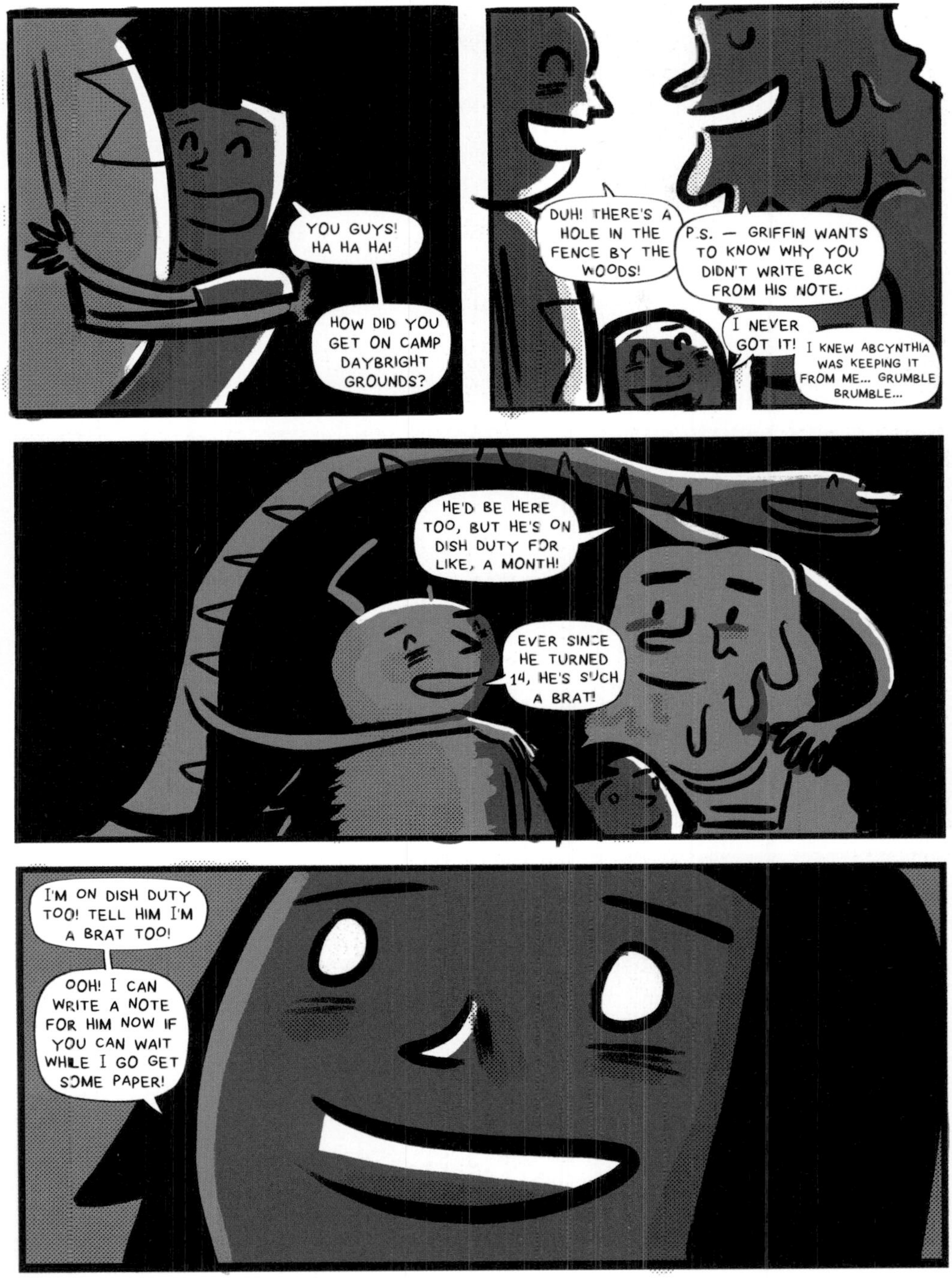
YOU GUYS! HA HA HA!
HOW DID YOU GET ON CAMP DAYBRIGHT GROUNDS?
DUH! THERE'S A HOLE IN THE FENCE BY THE WOODS!
P.S. — GRIFFIN WANTS TO KNOW WHY YOU DIDN'T WRITE BACK FROM HIS NOTE.
I NEVER GOT IT!
I KNEW ABCYNTHIA WAS KEEPING IT FROM ME... GRUMBLE BRUMBLE...
HE'D BE HERE TOO, BUT HE'S ON DISH DUTY FOR LIKE, A MONTH!
EVER SINCE HE TURNED 14, HE'S SUCH A BRAT!
I'M ON DISH DUTY TOO! TELL HIM I'M A BRAT TOO!
OOH! I CAN WRITE A NOTE FOR HIM NOW IF YOU CAN WAIT WHILE I GO GET SOME PAPER!

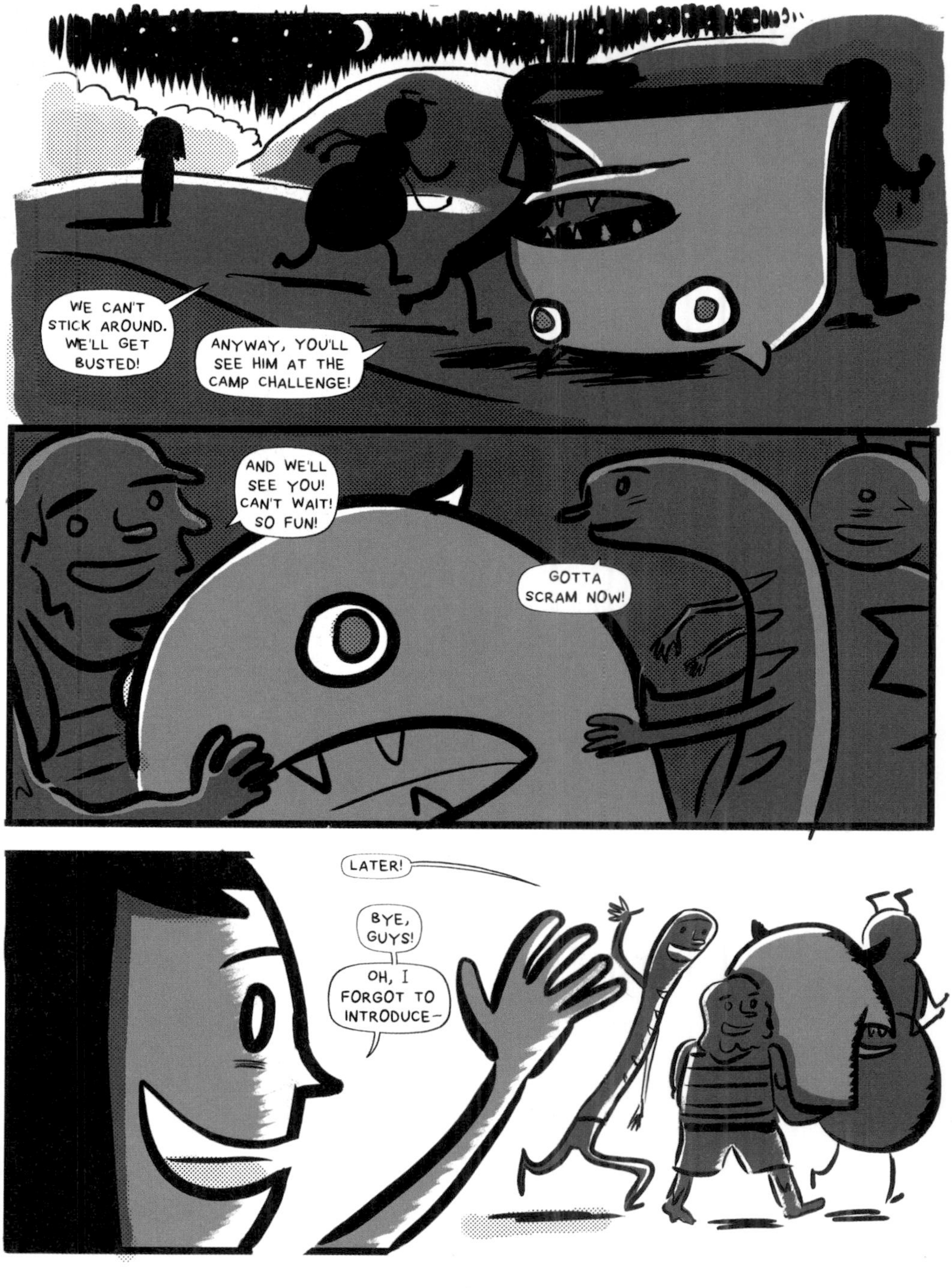
WE CAN'T STICK AROUND. WE'LL GET BUSTED!
ANYWAY, YOU'LL SEE HIM AT THE CAMP CHALLENGE!
AND WE'LL SEE YOU! CAN'T WAIT! SO FUN!
GOTTA SCRAM NOW!
LATER!
BYE, GUYS!
OH, I FORGOT TO INTRODUCE—

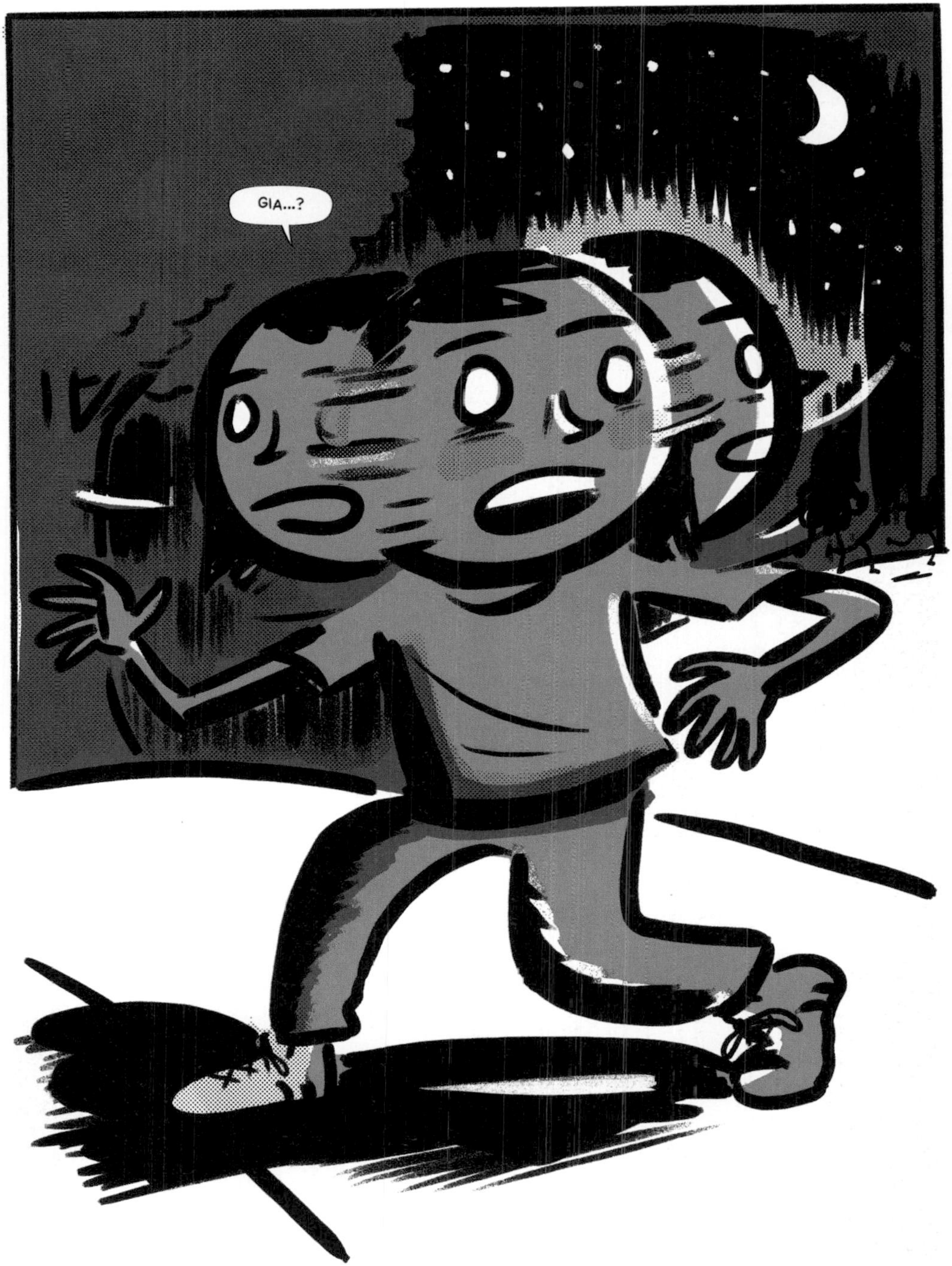
GIA...?

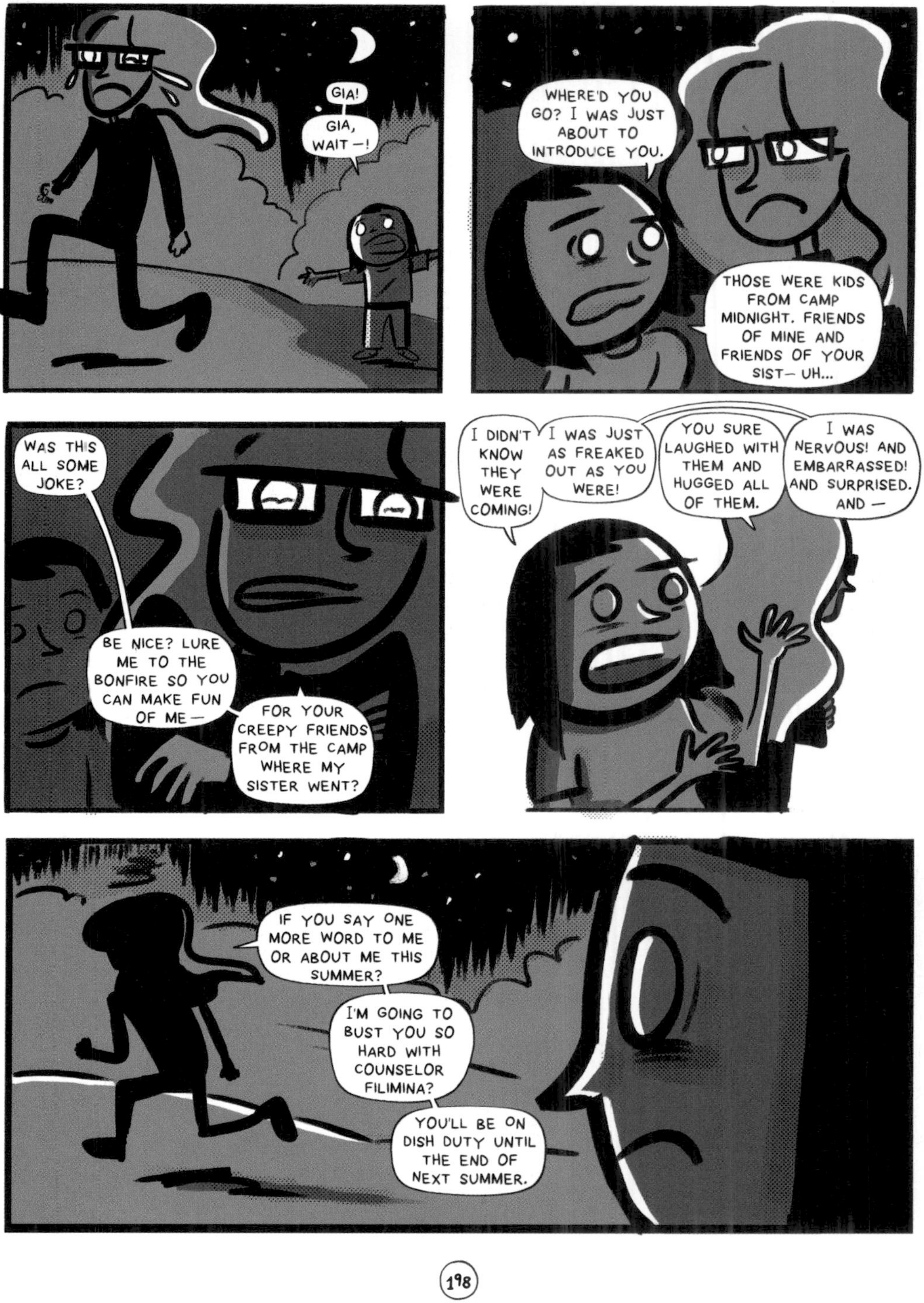
GIA!
GIA, WAIT—!
WHERE'D YOU GO? I WAS JUST ABOUT TO INTRODUCE YOU.
THOSE WERE KIDS FROM CAMP MIDNIGHT. FRIENDS OF MINE AND FRIENDS OF YOUR SIST— UH...
WAS THIS ALL SOME JOKE?
BE NICE? LURE ME TO THE BONFIRE SO YOU CAN MAKE FUN OF ME—
FOR YOUR CREEPY FRIENDS FROM THE CAMP WHERE MY SISTER WENT?
I DIDN'T KNOW THEY WERE COMING!
I WAS JUST AS FREAKED OUT AS YOU WERE!
YOU SURE LAUGHED WITH THEM AND HUGGED ALL OF THEM.
I WAS NERVOUS! AND EMBARRASSED! AND SURPRISED. AND—
IF YOU SAY ONE MORE WORD TO ME OR ABOUT ME THIS SUMMER?
I'M GOING TO BUST YOU SO HARD WITH COUNSELOR FILIMINA?
YOU'LL BE ON DISH DUTY UNTIL THE END OF NEXT SUMMER.

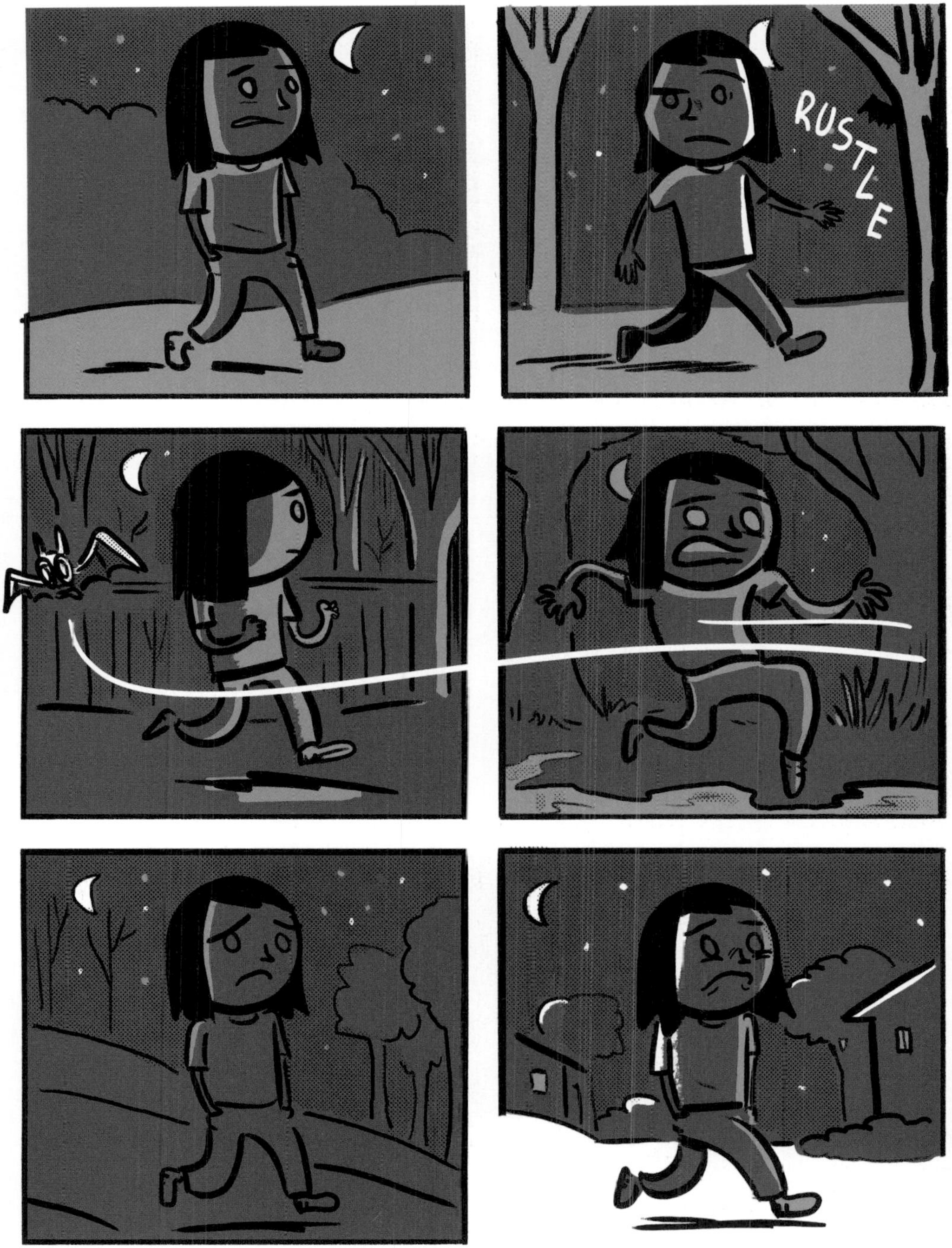
RUSTLE

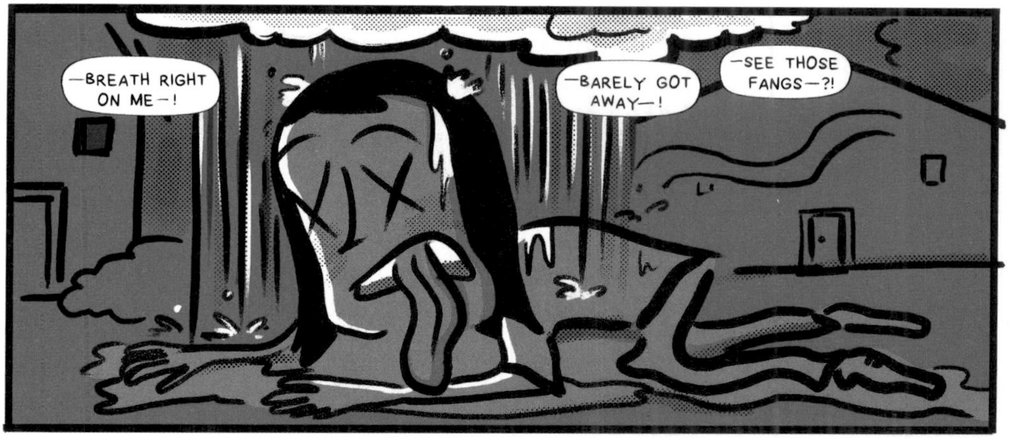
—BREATH RIGHT ON ME—!
—BARELY GOT AWAY—!
—SEE THOSE FANGS—?!

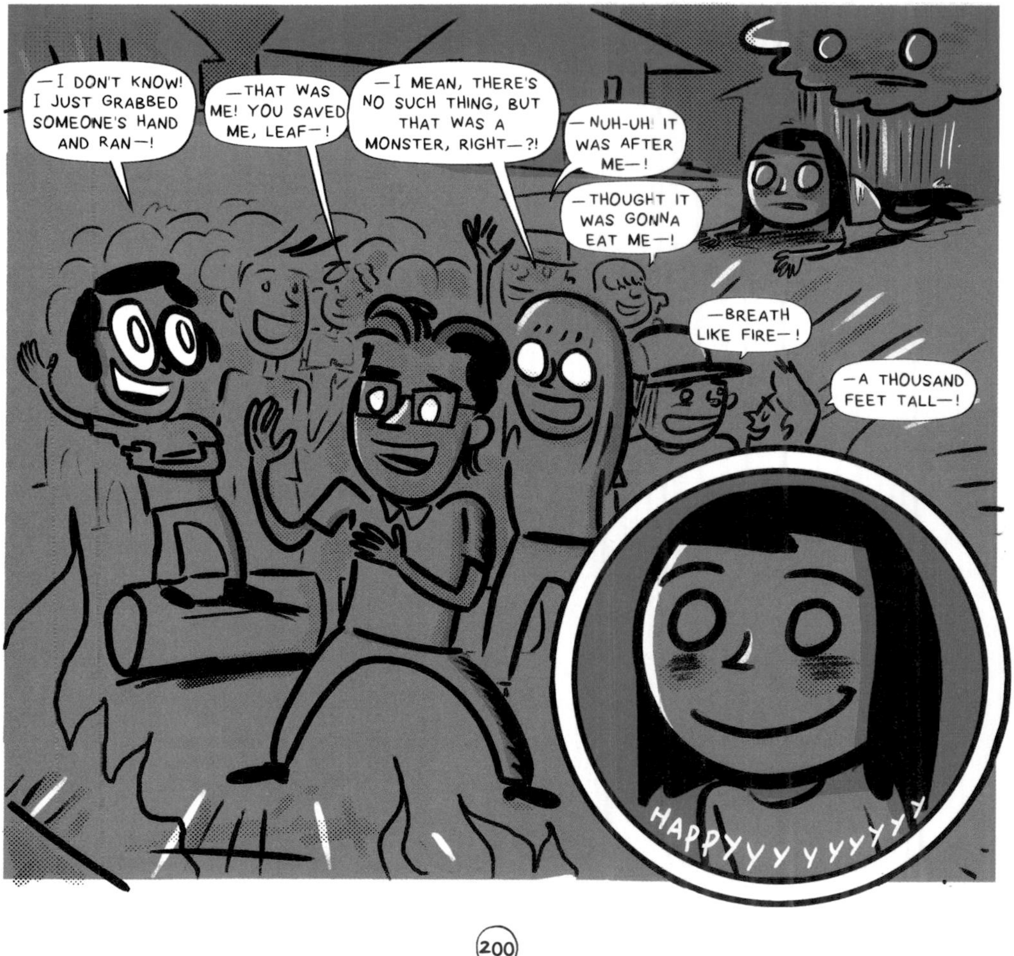
—I DON'T KNOW! I JUST GRABBED SOMEONE'S HAND AND RAN—!
—THAT WAS ME! YOU SAVED ME, LEAF—!
—I MEAN, THERE'S NO SUCH THING, BUT THAT WAS A MONSTER, RIGHT—?!
—NUH-UH! IT WAS AFTER ME—!
—THOUGHT IT WAS GONNA EAT ME—!
—BREATH LIKE FIRE—!
—A THOUSAND FEET TALL—!
HAPPYYYYYYYYY

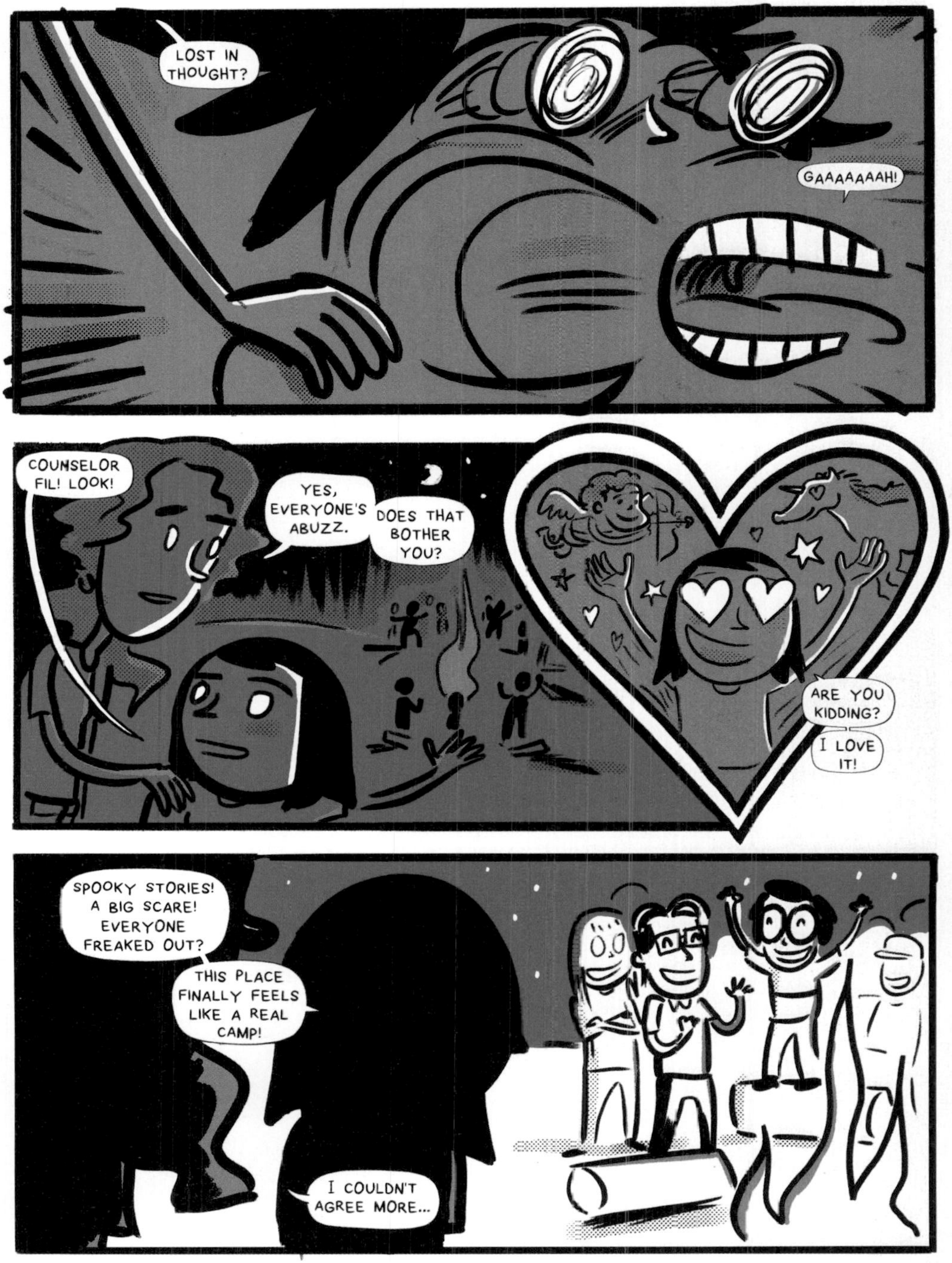
LOST IN THOUGHT?
GAAAAAAAH!
COUNSELOR FIL! LOOK!
YES, EVERYONE'S ABUZZ.
DOES THAT BOTHER YOU?
ARE YOU KIDDING?
I LOVE IT!
SPOOKY STORIES! A BIG SCARE! EVERYONE FREAKED OUT?
THIS PLACE FINALLY FEELS LIKE A REAL CAMP!
I COULDN'T AGREE MORE...

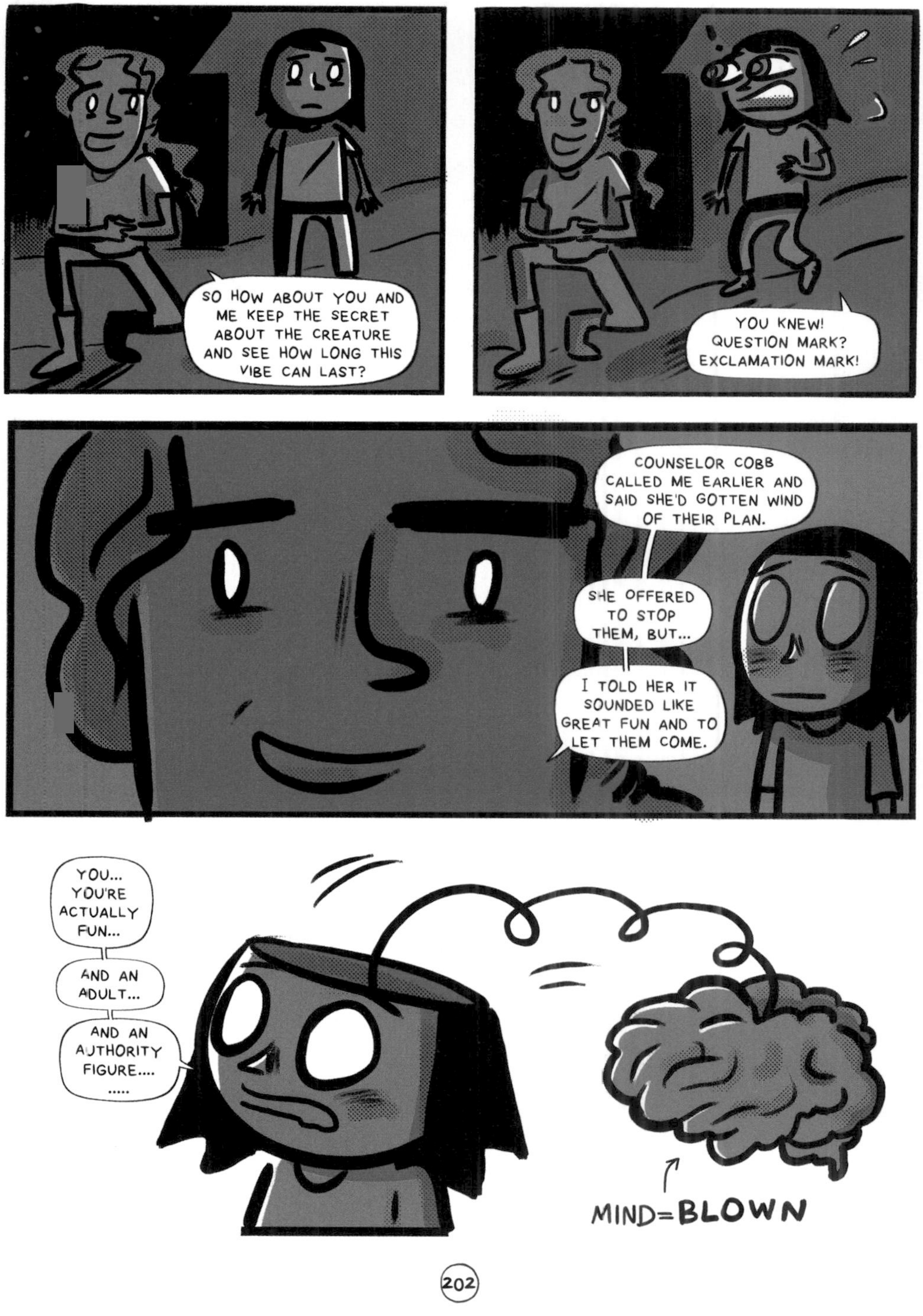
SO HOW ABOUT YOU AND ME KEEP THE SECRET ABOUT THE CREATURE AND SEE HOW LONG THIS VIBE CAN LAST?
YOU KNEW! QUESTION MARK? EXCLAMATION MARK!
COUNSELOR COBB CALLED ME EARLIER AND SAID SHE'D GOTTEN WIND OF THEIR PLAN.
SHE OFFERED TO STOP THEM, BUT...
I TOLD HER IT SOUNDED LIKE GREAT FUN AND TO LET THEM COME.
YOU... YOU'RE ACTUALLY FUN...
AND AN ADULT...
AND AN AUTHORITY FIGURE.... .....
MIND=BLOWN

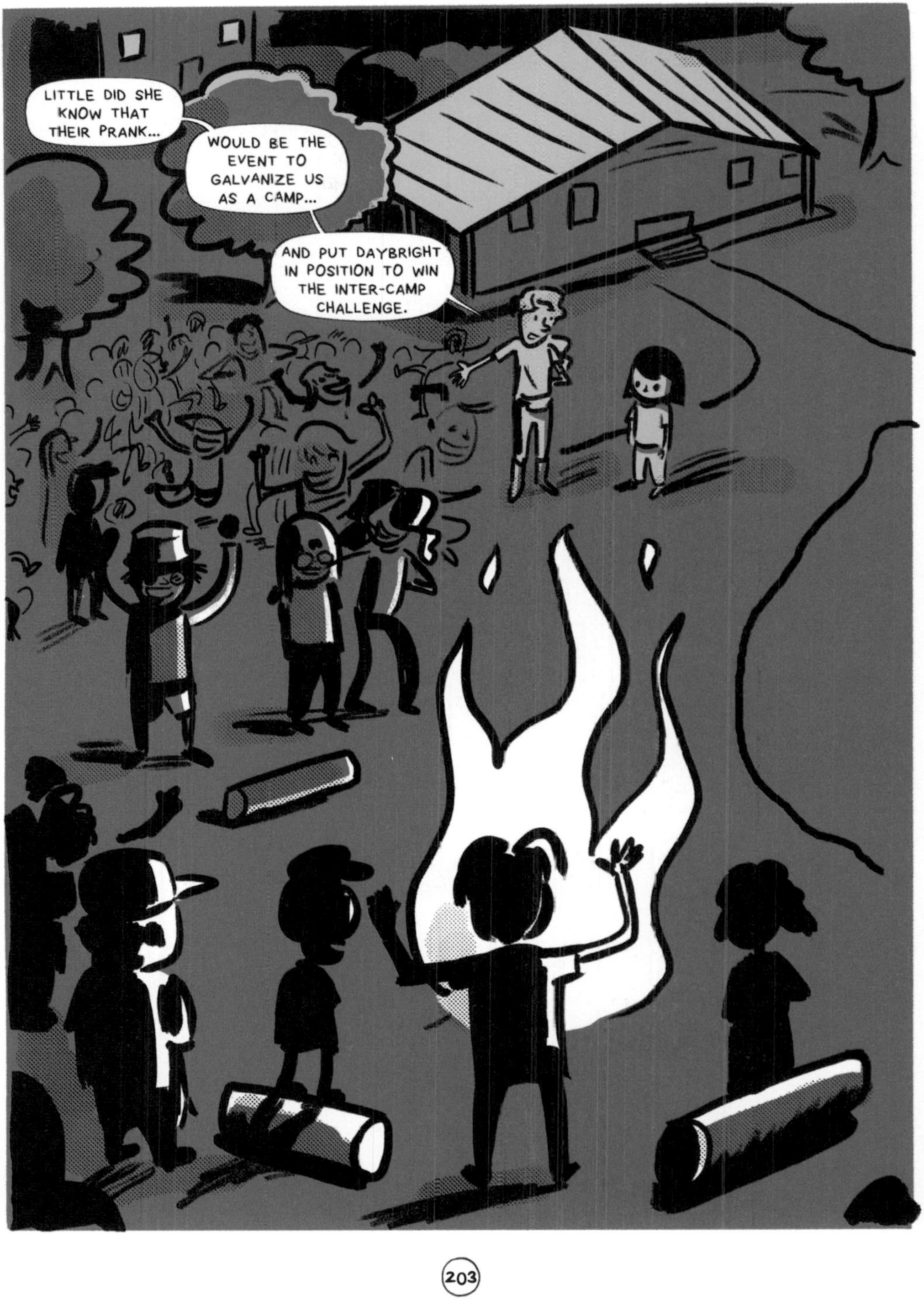
LITTLE DID SHE KNOW THAT THEIR PRANK...
WOULD BE THE EVENT TO GALVANIZE US AS A CAMP...
AND PUT DAYBRIGHT IN POSITION TO WIN THE INTER-CAMP CHALLENGE.

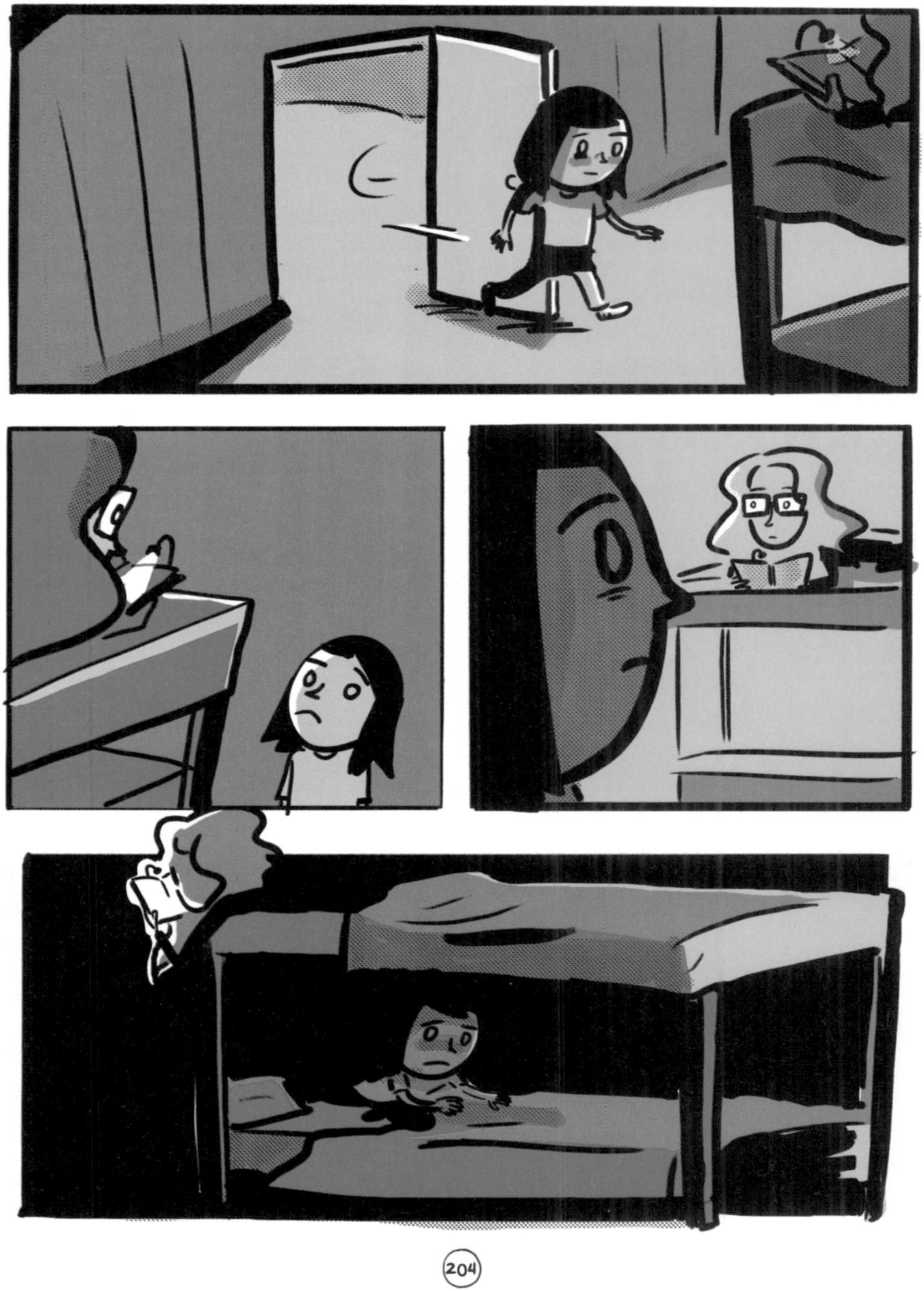

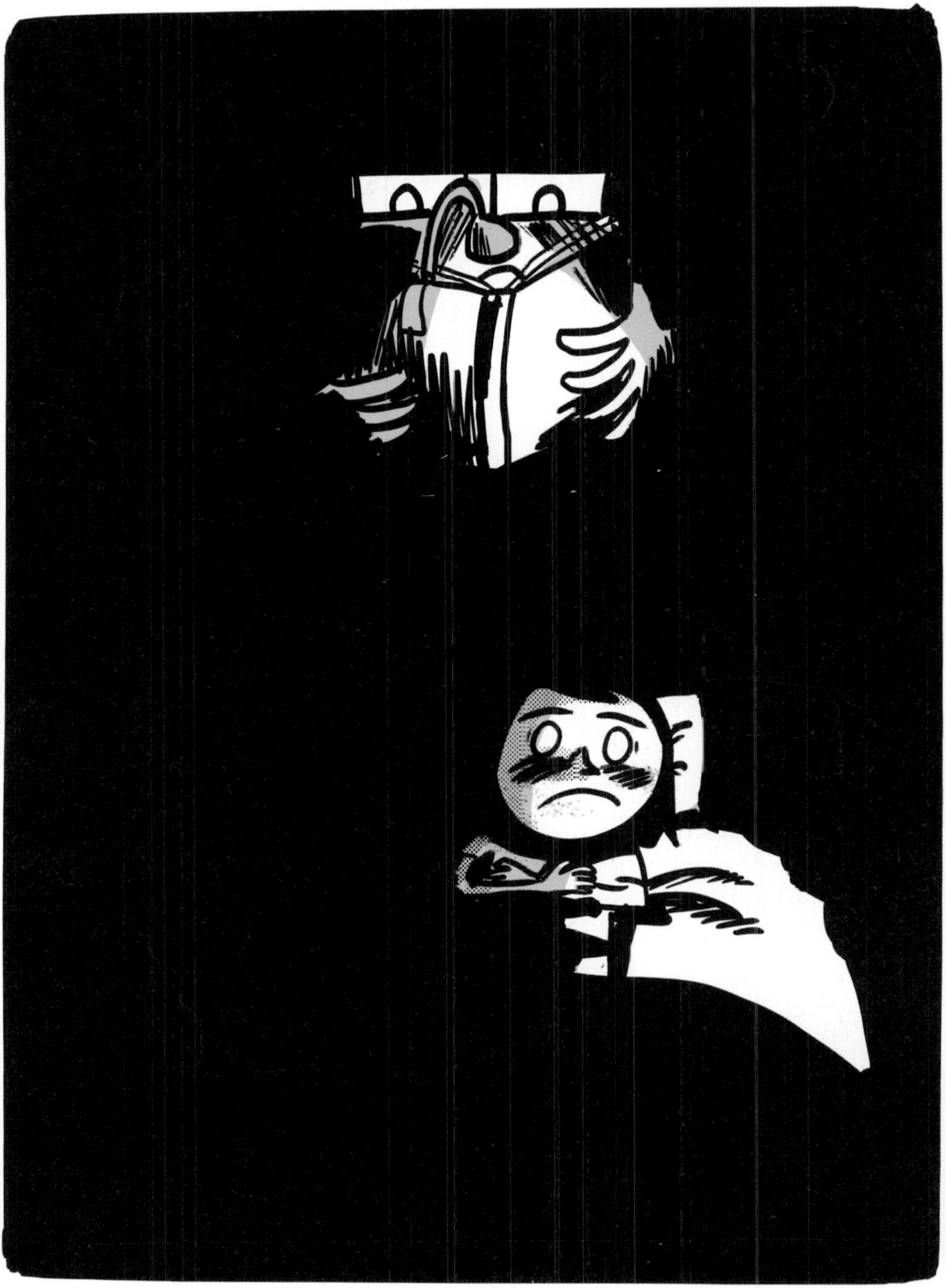

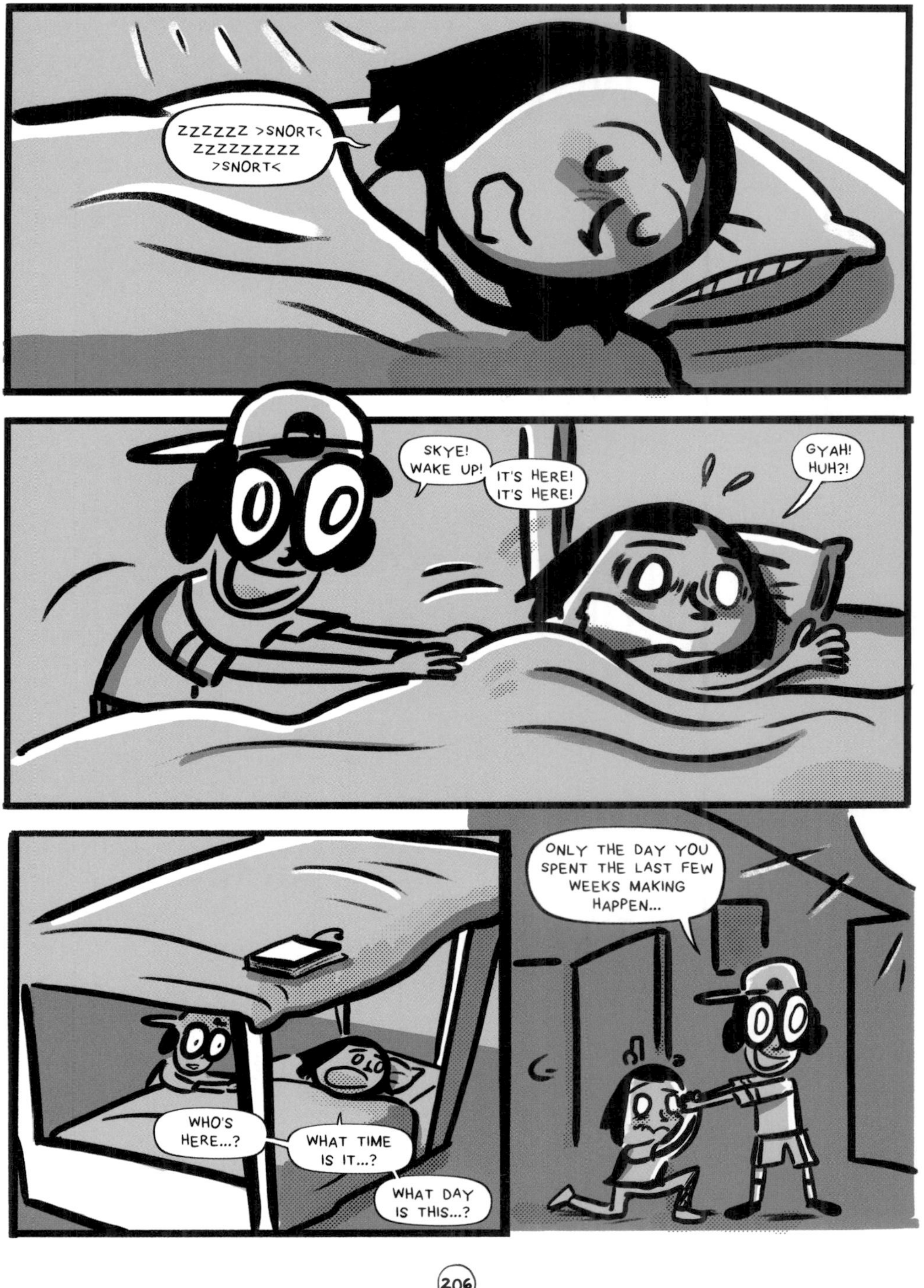
ZZZZZZ >SNORT<
ZZZZZZZZZ
>SNORT<
SKYE! WAKE UP!
IT'S HERE! IT'S HERE!
GYAH! HUH?!
WHO'S HERE...?
WHAT TIME IS IT...?
WHAT DAY IS THIS...?
ONLY THE DAY YOU SPENT THE LAST FEW WEEKS MAKING HAPPEN...

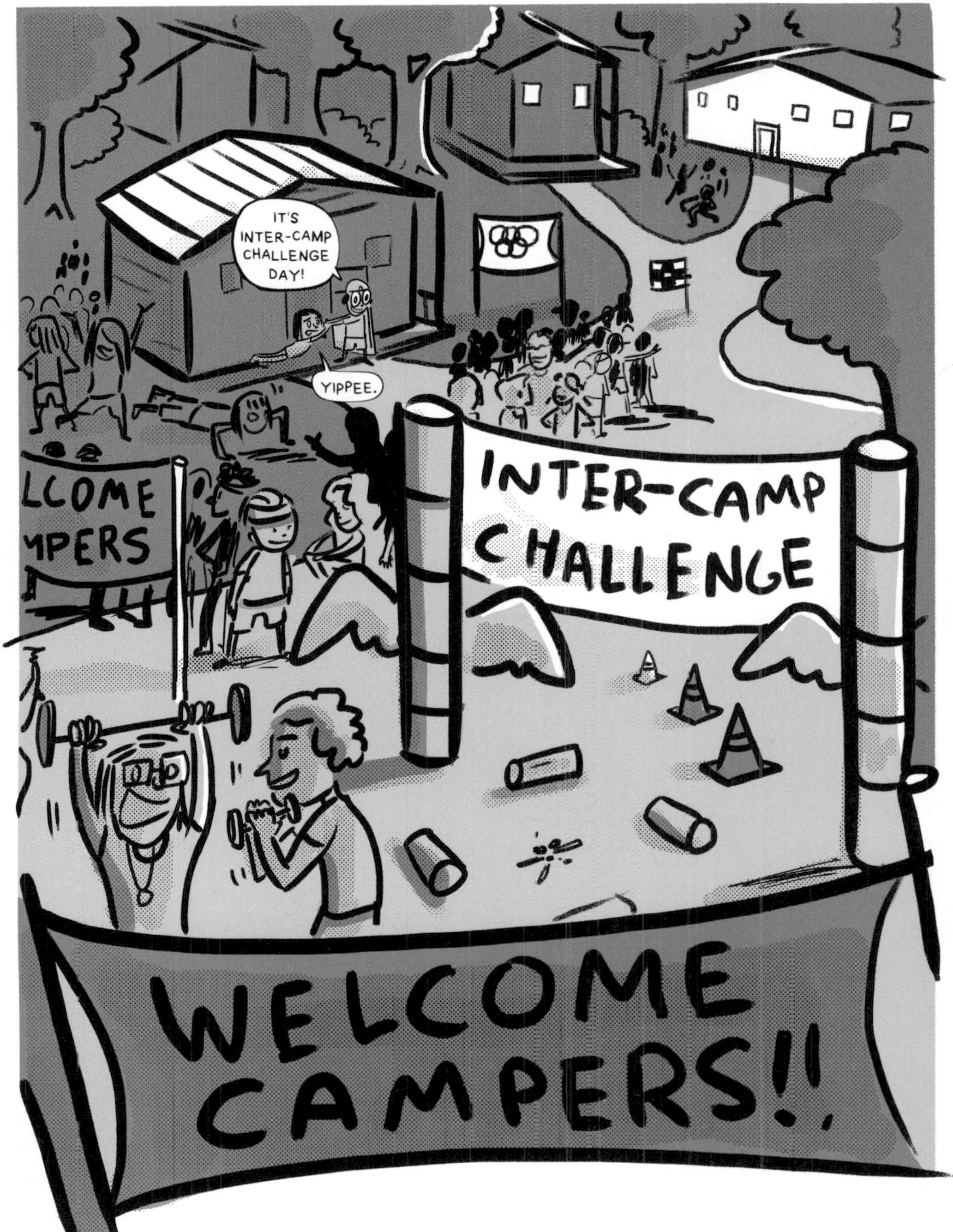
IT'S INTER-CAMP CHALLENGE DAY!
YIPPEE.
INTER-CAMP CHALLENGE
LCOME
MPERS
WELCOME CAMPERS!!

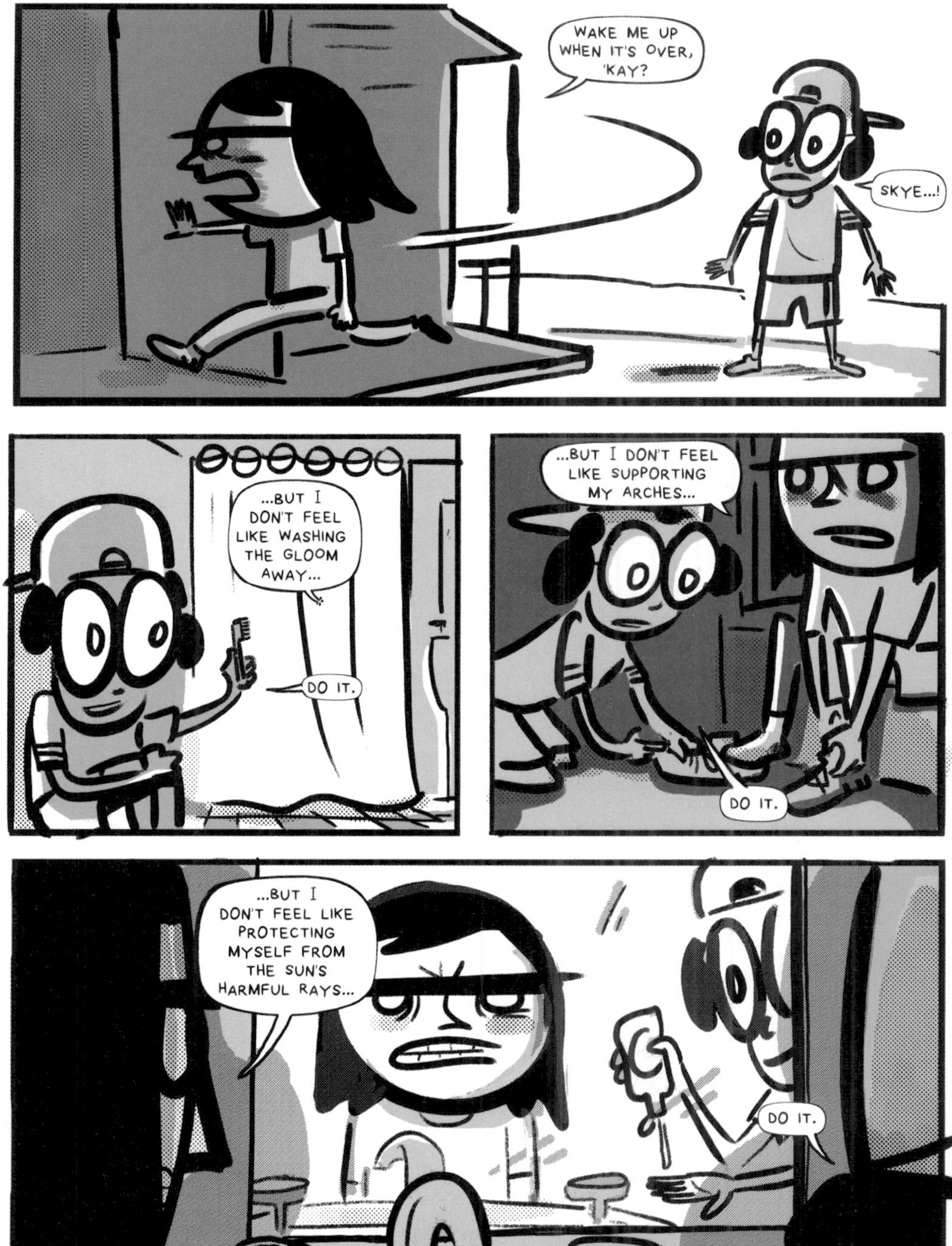

WAKE ME UP WHEN IT'S OVER, 'KAY?
SKYE...!
...BUT I DON'T FEEL LIKE WASHING THE GLOOM AWAY...
DO IT.
...BUT I DON'T FEEL LIKE SUPPORTING MY ARCHES...
DO IT.
...BUT I DON'T FEEL LIKE PROTECTING MYSELF FROM THE SUN'S HARMFUL RAYS...
DO IT.

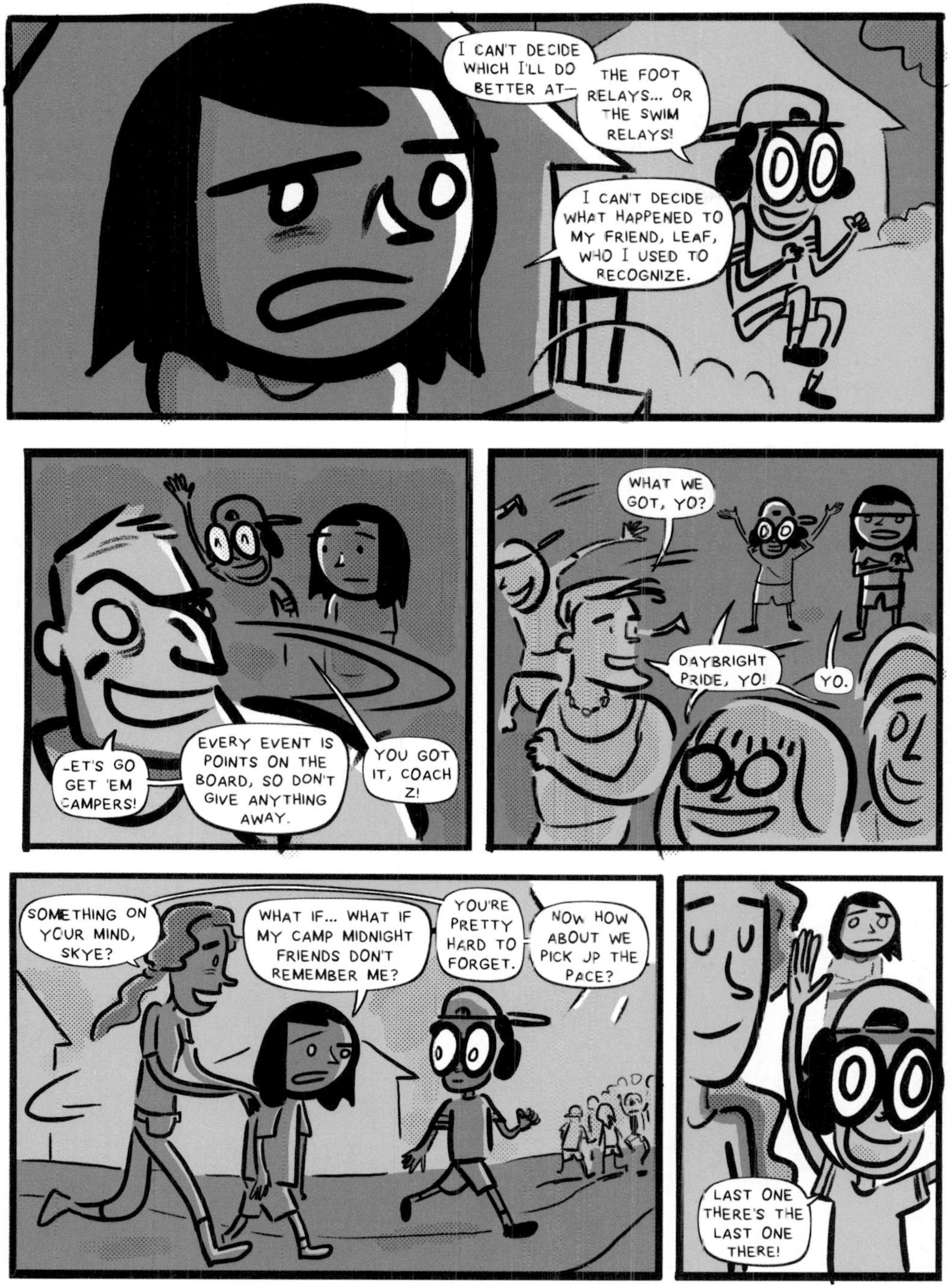
I CAN'T DECIDE WHICH I'LL DO BETTER AT—
THE FOOT RELAYS... OR THE SWIM RELAYS!
I CAN'T DECIDE WHAT HAPPENED TO MY FRIEND, LEAF, WHO I USED TO RECOGNIZE.
LET'S GO GET 'EM CAMPERS!
EVERY EVENT IS POINTS ON THE BOARD, SO DON'T GIVE ANYTHING AWAY.
YOU GOT IT, COACH Z!
WHAT WE GOT, YO?
DAYBRIGHT PRIDE, YO!
YO.
SOMETHING ON YOUR MIND, SKYE?
WHAT IF... WHAT IF MY CAMP MIDNIGHT FRIENDS DON'T REMEMBER ME?
YOU'RE PRETTY HARD TO FORGET.
NOW HOW ABOUT WE PICK UP THE PACE?
LAST ONE THERE'S THE LAST ONE THERE!

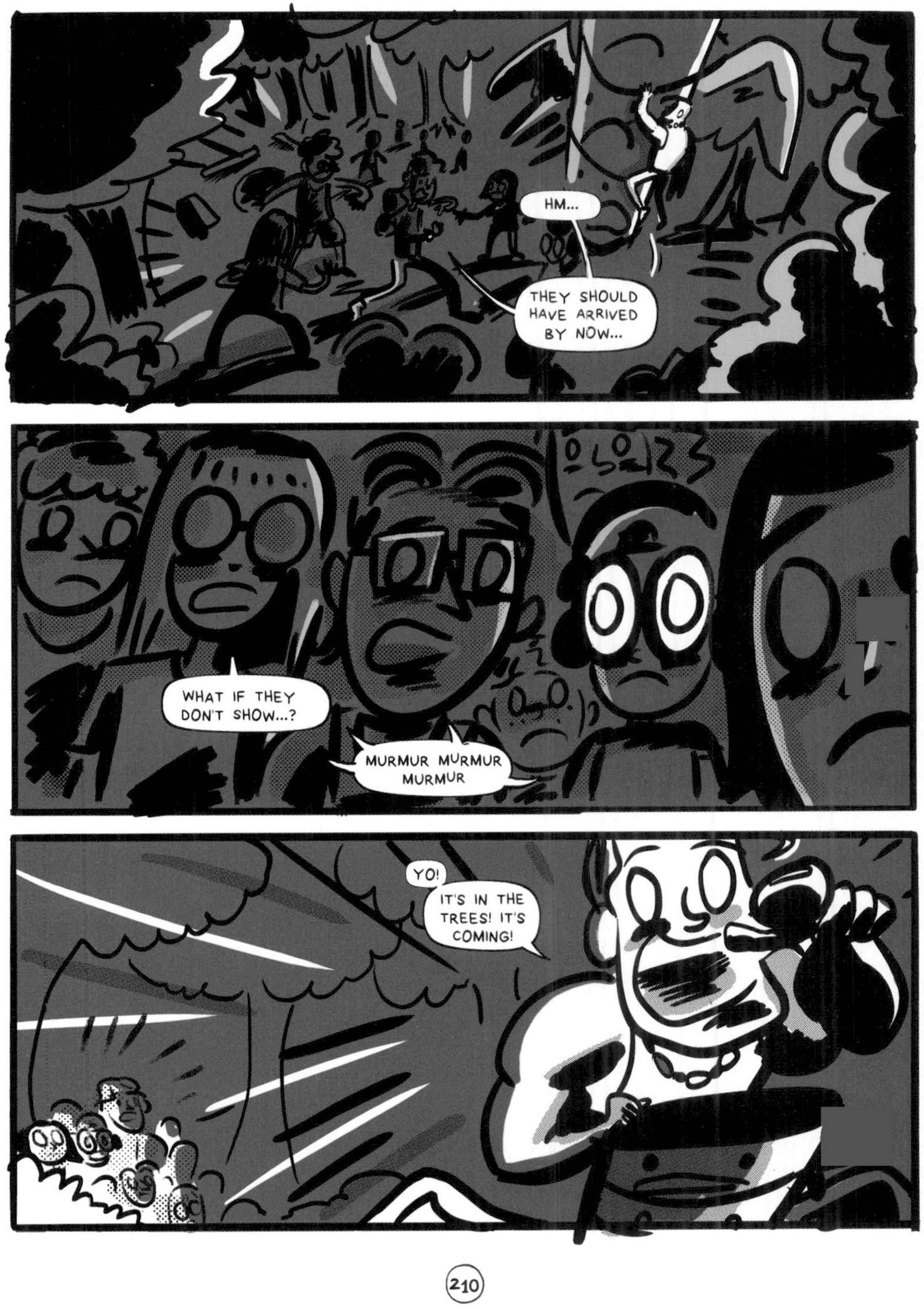
HM...
THEY SHOULD HAVE ARRIVED BY NOW...
WHAT IF THEY DON'T SHOW...?
MURMUR MURMUR MURMUR
YO!
IT'S IN THE TREES! IT'S COMING!

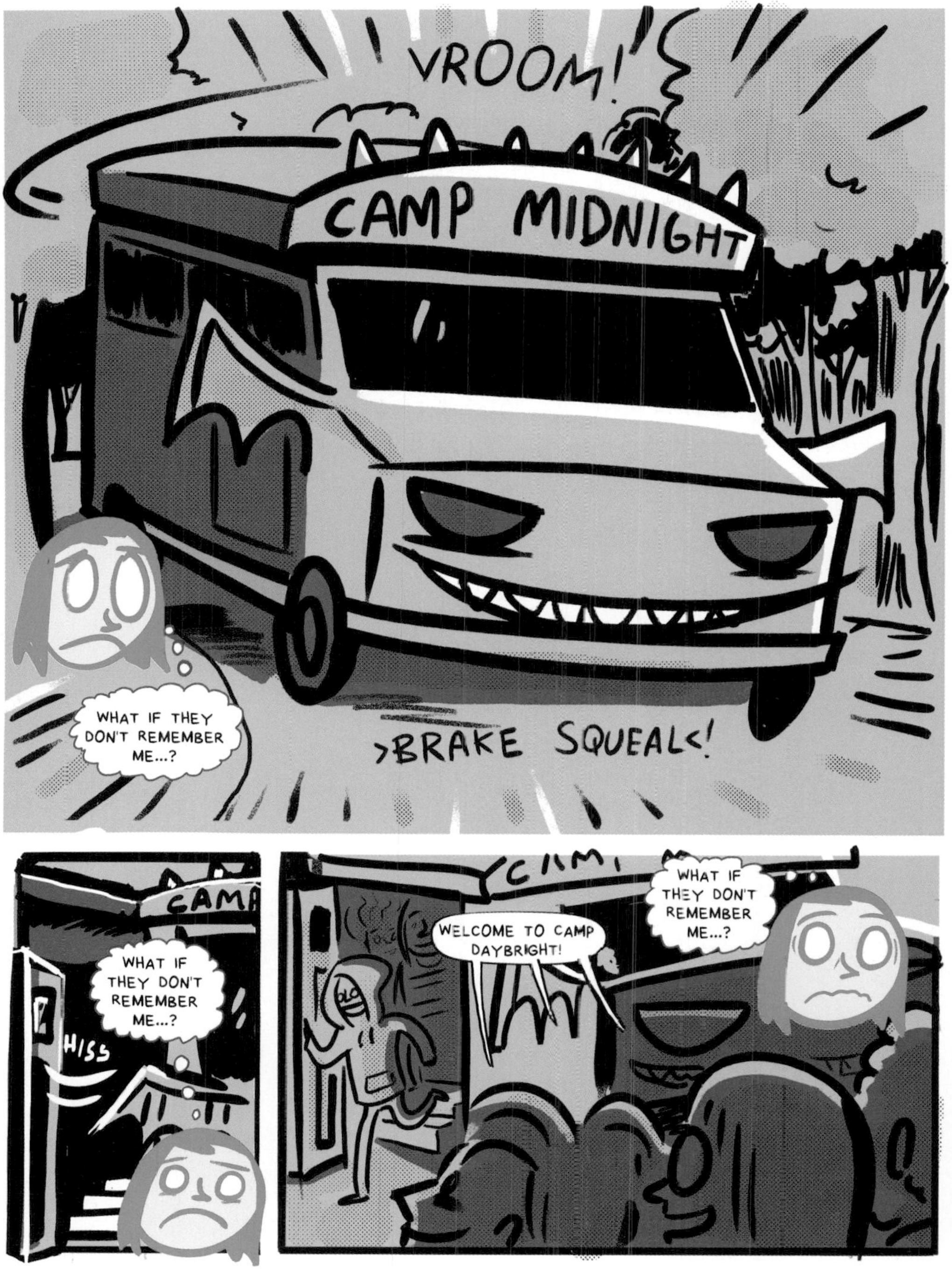
VROOM!
CAMP MIDNIGHT
WHAT IF THEY DON'T REMEMBER ME...?
>BRAKE SQUEAL<!
WHAT IF THEY DON'T REMEMBER ME...?
HISS
WELCOME TO CAMP DAYBRIGHT!
WHAT IF THEY DON'T REMEMBER ME...?

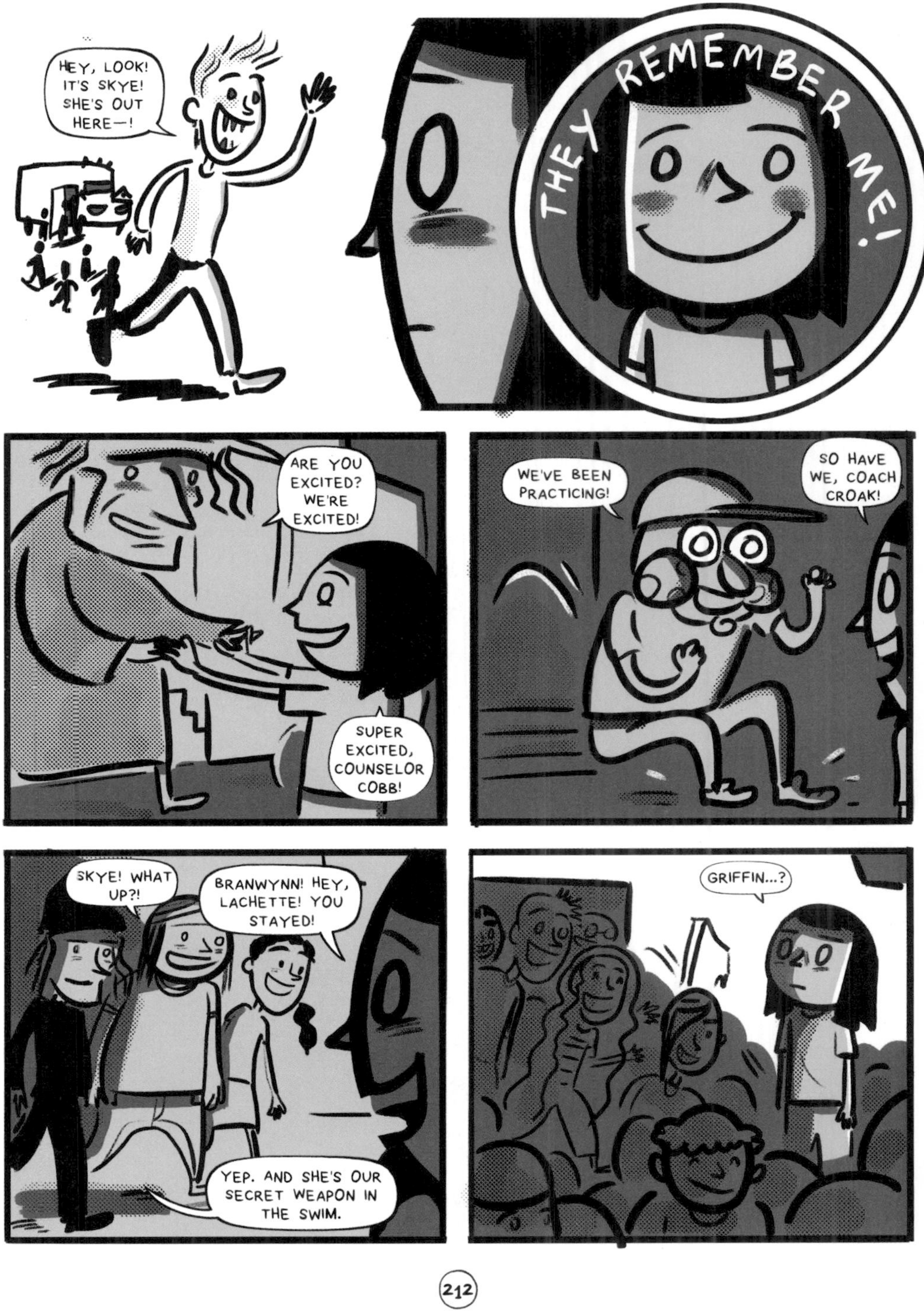
HEY, LOOK! IT'S SKYE! SHE'S OUT HERE—!
THEY REMEMBER ME!
ARE YOU EXCITED? WE'RE EXCITED!
SUPER EXCITED, COUNSELOR COBB!
WE'VE BEEN PRACTICING!
SO HAVE WE, COACH CROAK!
SKYE! WHAT UP?!
BRANWYNN! HEY, LACHETTE! YOU STAYED!
YEP. AND SHE'S OUR SECRET WEAPON IN THE SWIM.
GRIFFIN...?

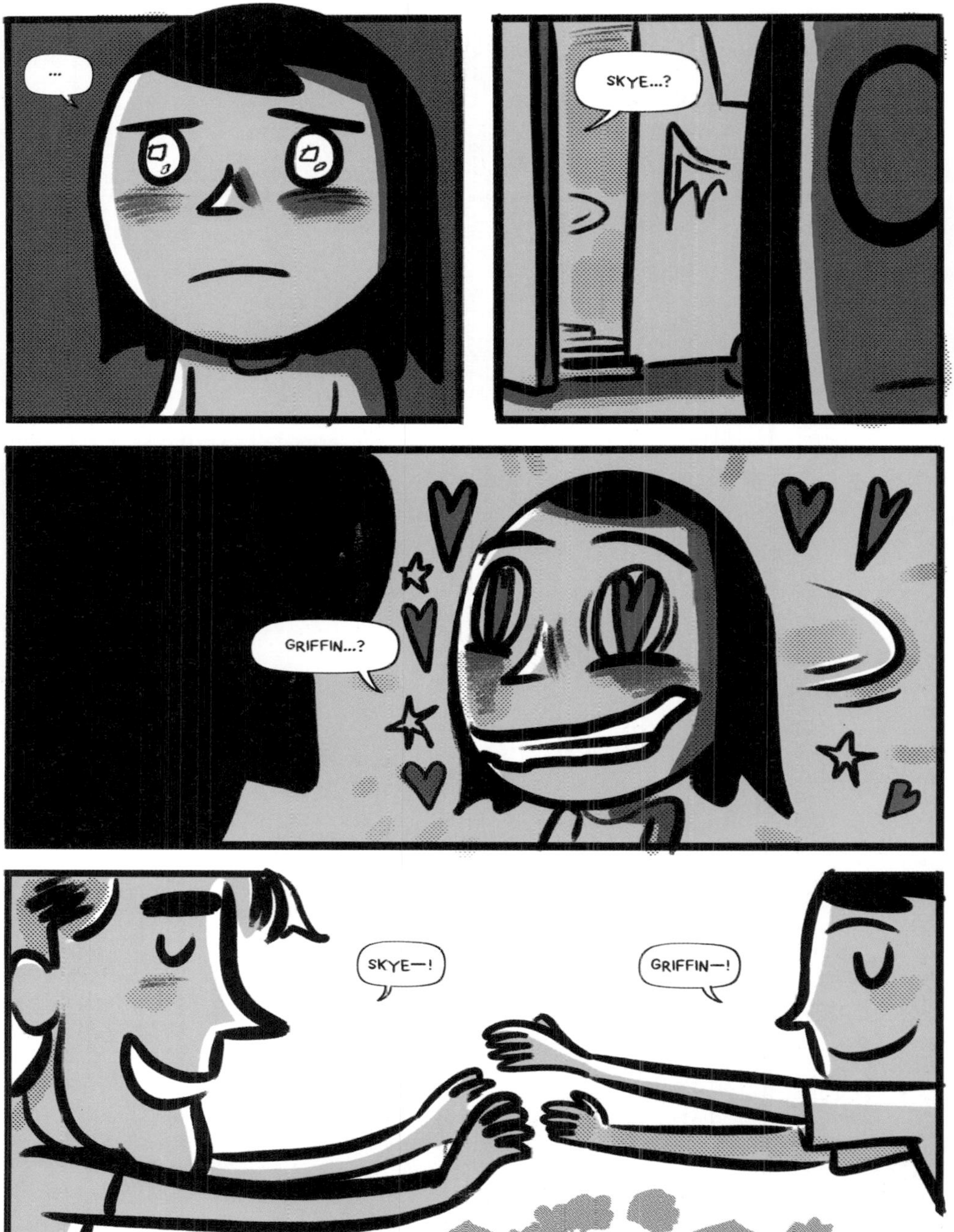
...
SKYE...?
GRIFFIN...?
SKYE—!
GRIFFIN—!

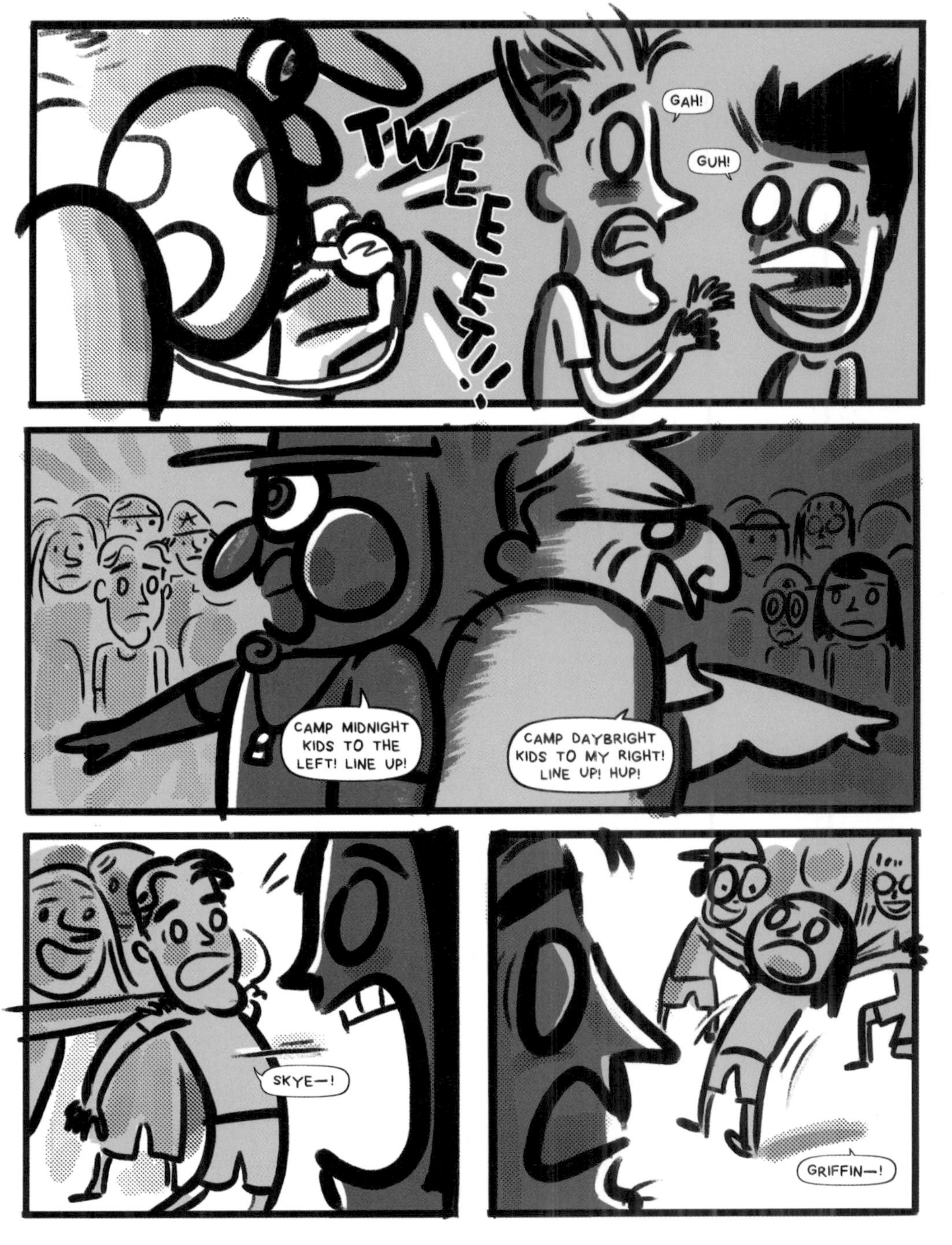
TWEEEET!!
GAH!
GUH!
CAMP MIDNIGHT KIDS TO THE LEFT! LINE UP!
CAMP DAYBRIGHT KIDS TO MY RIGHT! LINE UP! HUP!
SKYE—!
GRIFFIN—!

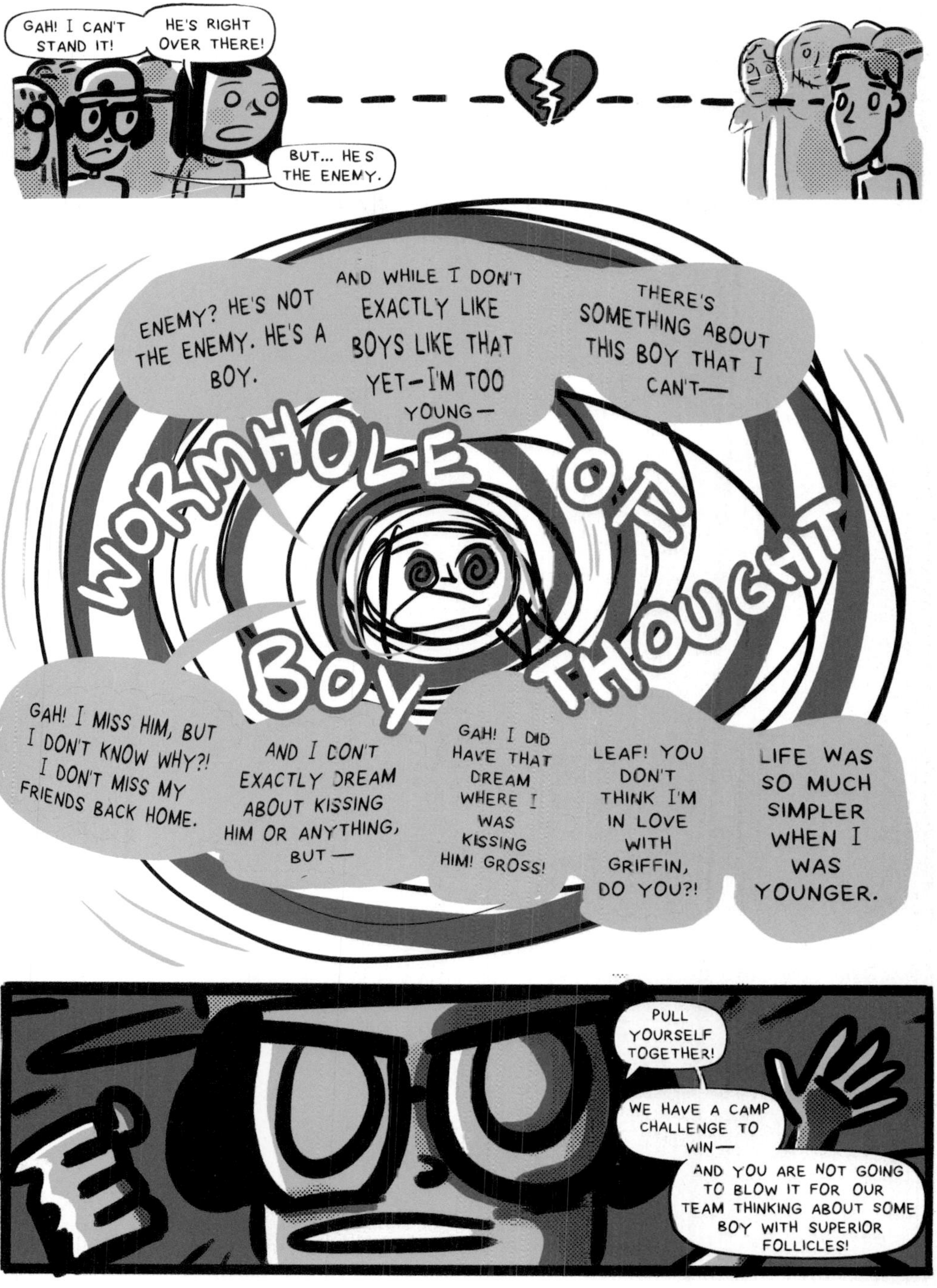
GAH! I CAN'T STAND IT!
HE'S RIGHT OVER THERE!
BUT... HE'S THE ENEMY.
ENEMY? HE'S NOT THE ENEMY. HE'S A BOY.
AND WHILE I DON'T EXACTLY LIKE BOYS LIKE THAT YET—I'M TOO YOUNG—
THERE'S SOMETHING ABOUT THIS BOY THAT I CAN'T—
WORMHOLE OF BOY THOUGHT
GAH! I MISS HIM, BUT I DON'T KNOW WHY?! I DON'T MISS MY FRIENDS BACK HOME.
AND I DON'T EXACTLY DREAM ABOUT KISSING HIM OR ANYTHING, BUT—
GAH! I DID HAVE THAT DREAM WHERE I WAS KISSING HIM! GROSS!
LEAF! YOU DON'T THINK I'M IN LOVE WITH GRIFFIN, DO YOU?!
LIFE WAS SO MUCH SIMPLER WHEN I WAS YOUNGER.
PULL YOURSELF TOGETHER!
WE HAVE A CAMP CHALLENGE TO WIN—
AND YOU ARE NOT GOING TO BLOW IT FOR OUR TEAM THINKING ABOUT SOME BOY WITH SUPERIOR FOLLICLES!

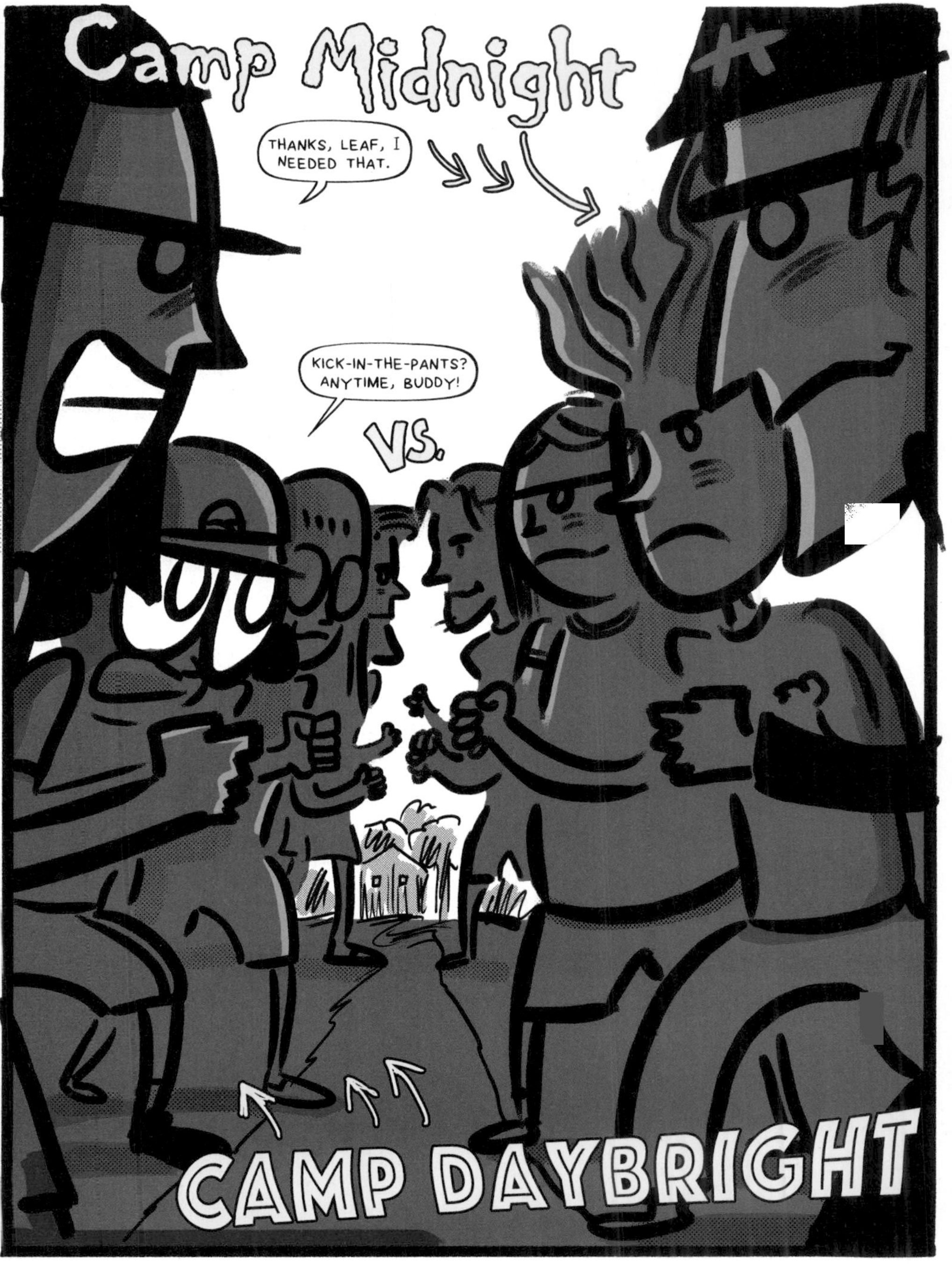
Camp Midnight
THANKS, LEAF, I NEEDED THAT.
KICK-IN-THE-PANTS? ANYTIME, BUDDY!
VS.
CAMP DAYBRIGHT

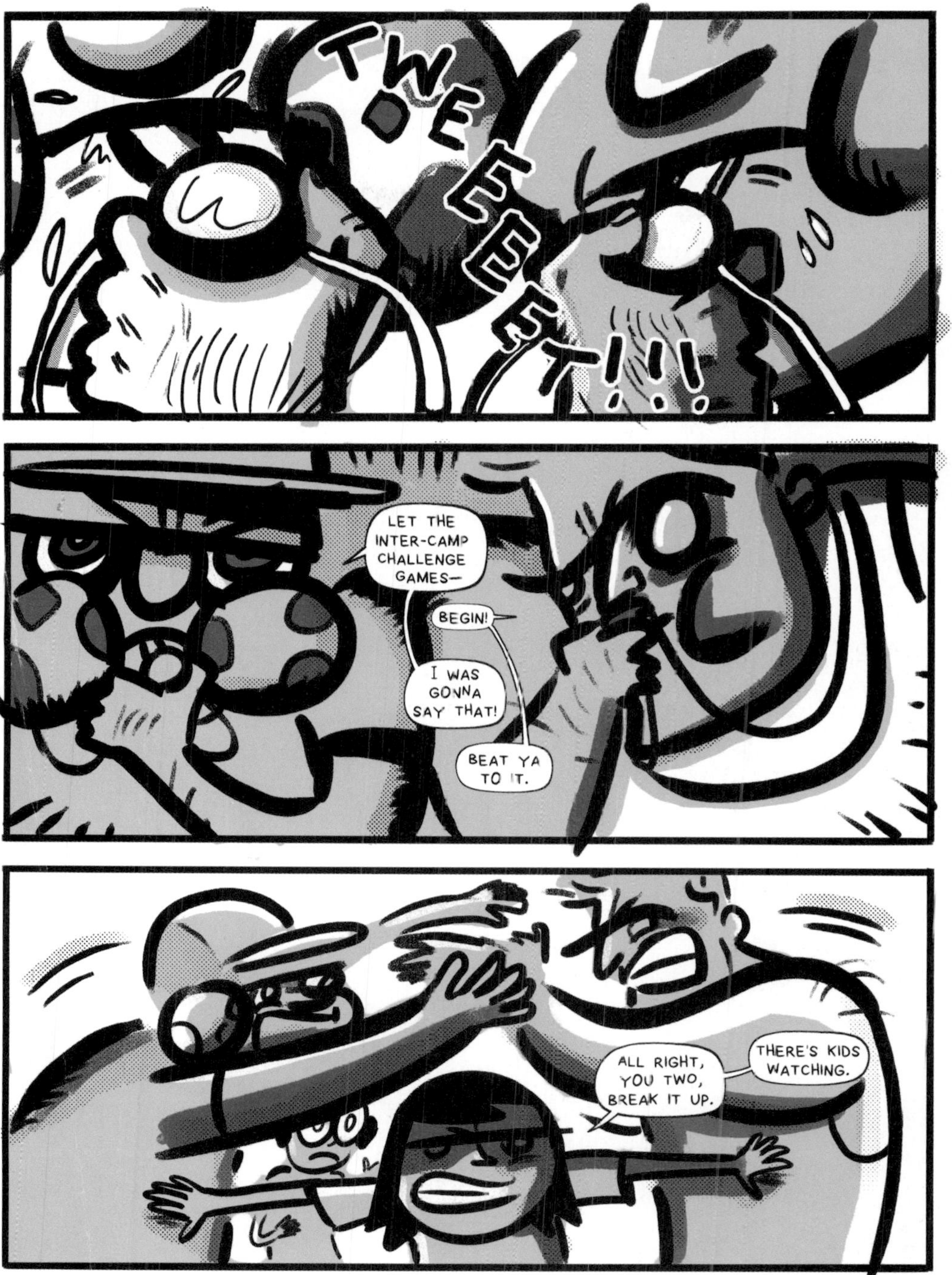
TWEEEEEET!!!
LET THE INTER-CAMP CHALLENGE GAMES—
BEGIN!
I WAS GONNA SAY THAT!
BEAT YA TO IT.
ALL RIGHT, YOU TWO, BREAK IT UP.
THERE'S KIDS WATCHING.

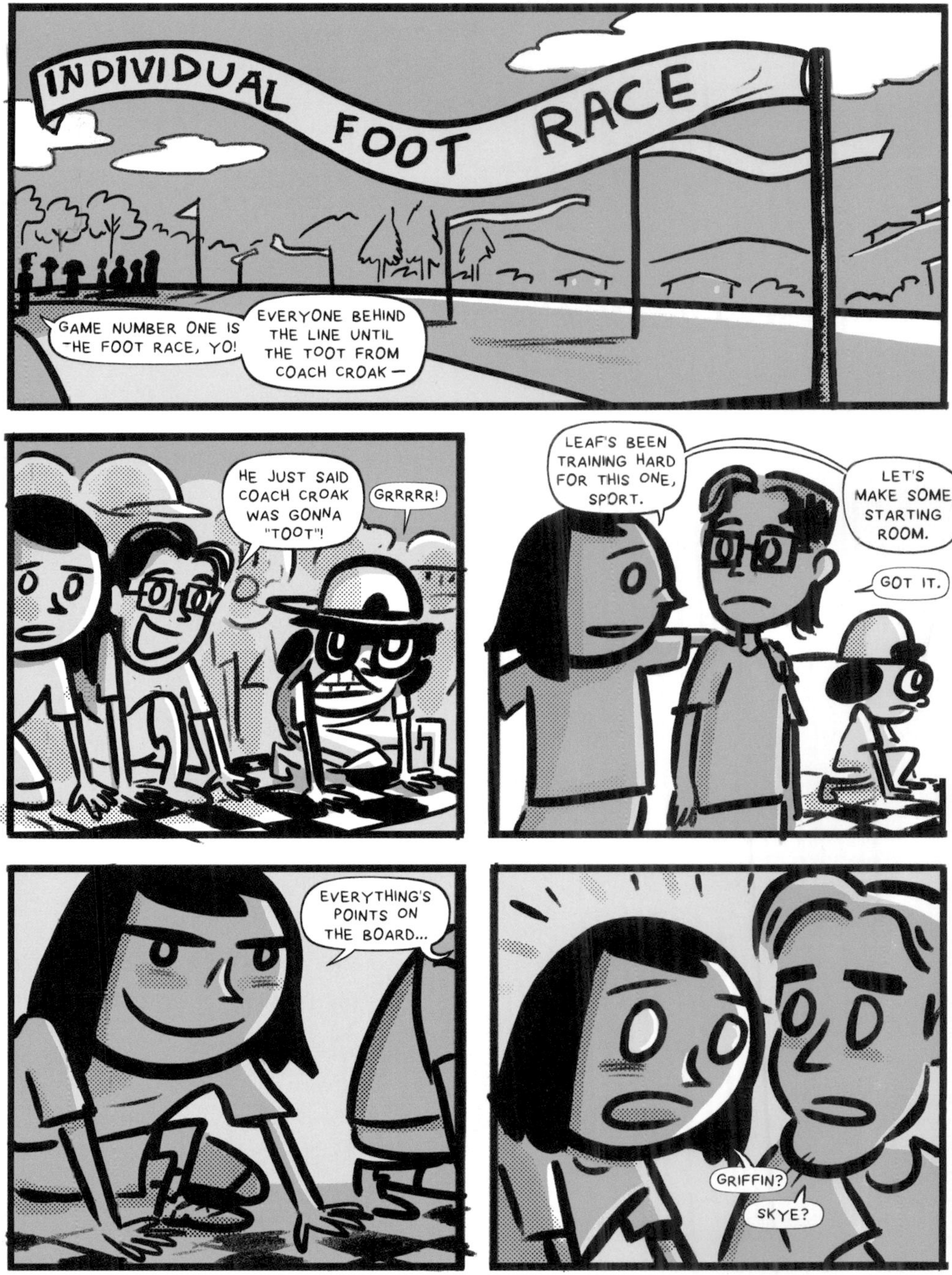

INDIVIDUAL FOOT RACE
GAME NUMBER ONE IS THE FOOT RACE, YO!
EVERYONE BEHIND THE LINE UNTIL THE TOOT FROM COACH CROAK—
HE JUST SAID COACH CROAK WAS GONNA "TOOT"!
GRRRRR!
LEAF'S BEEN TRAINING HARD FOR THIS ONE, SPORT.
LET'S MAKE SOME STARTING ROOM.
GOT IT.
EVERYTHING'S POINTS ON THE BOARD...
GRIFFIN?
SKYE?

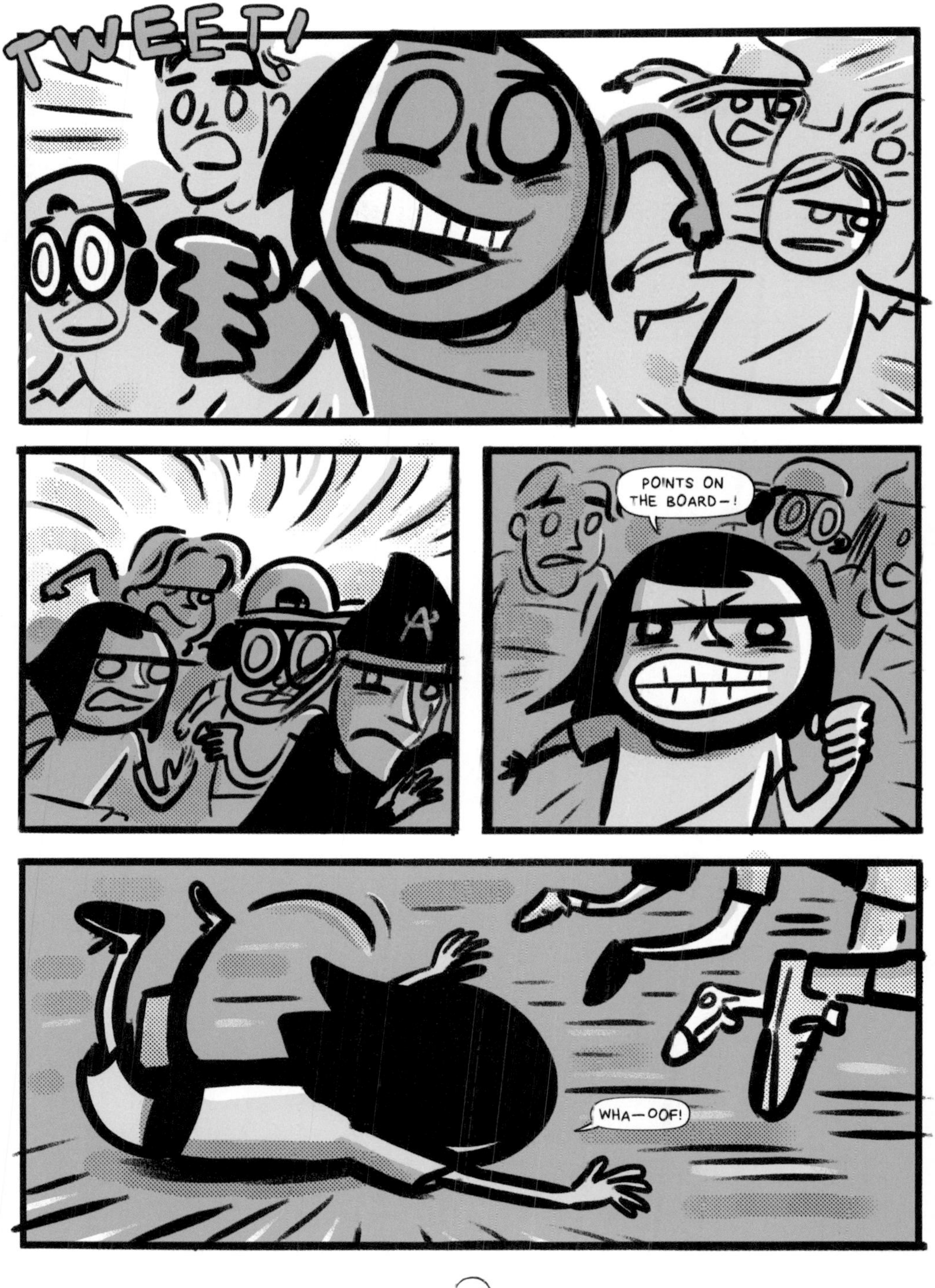
TWEET!
POINTS ON THE BOARD—!
WHA—OOF!

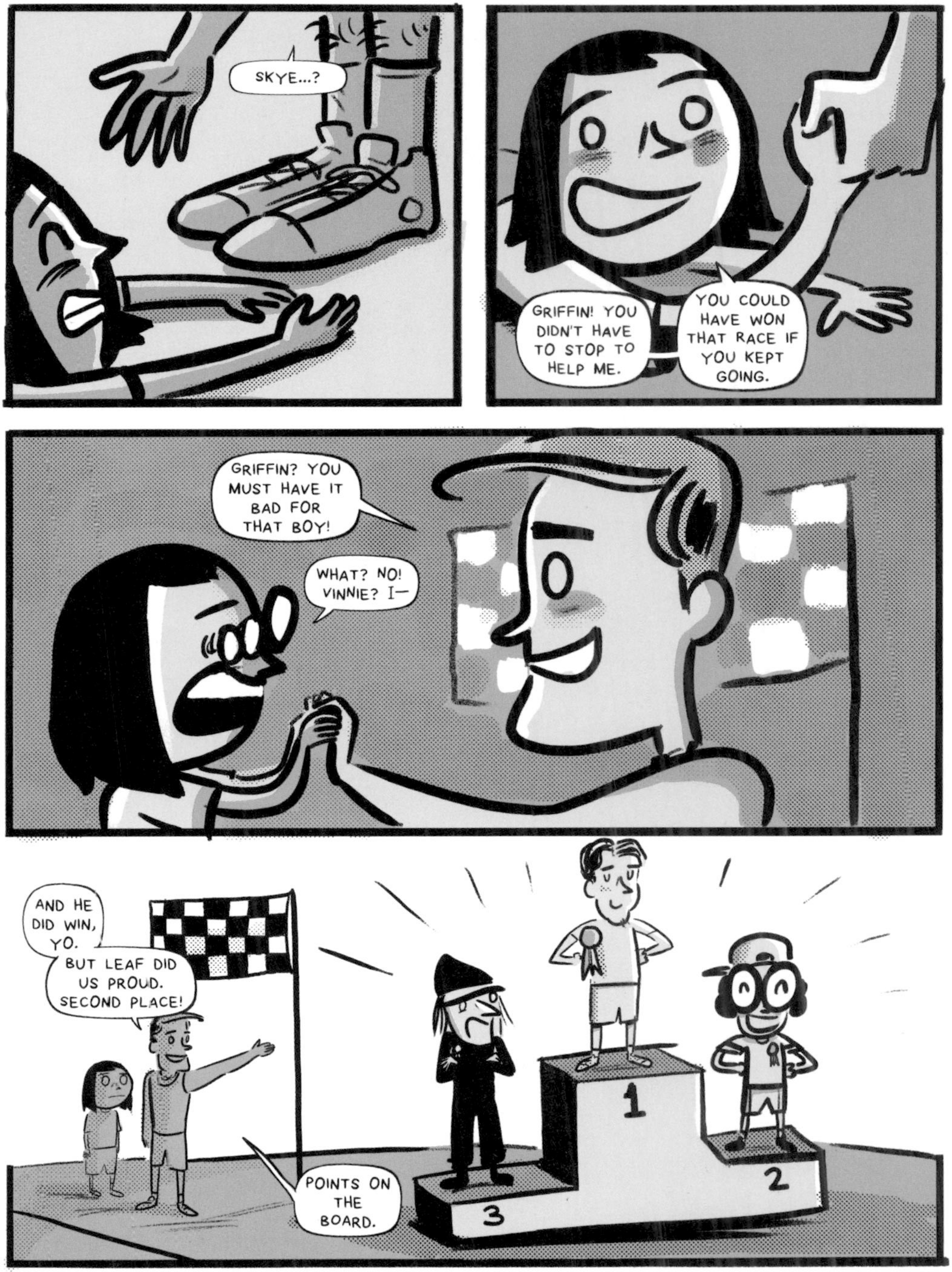
SKYE...?
GRIFFIN! YOU DIDN'T HAVE TO STOP TO HELP ME.
YOU COULD HAVE WON THAT RACE IF YOU KEPT GOING.
GRIFFIN? YOU MUST HAVE IT BAD FOR THAT BOY!
WHAT? NO! VINNIE? I—
AND HE DID WIN, YO.
BUT LEAF DID US PROUD. SECOND PLACE!
POINTS ON THE BOARD.
1
2
3

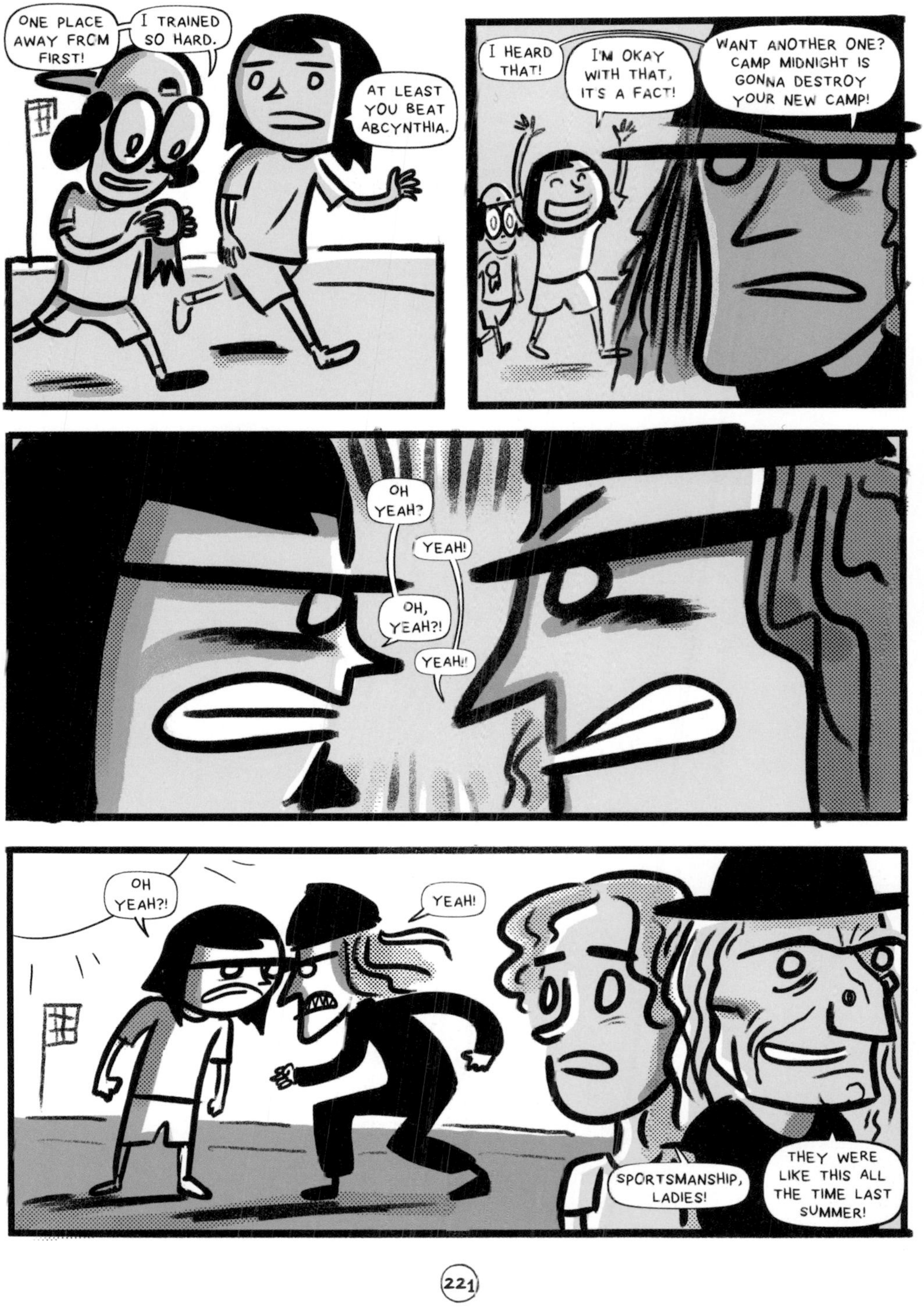
ONE PLACE AWAY FROM FIRST!
I TRAINED SO HARD.
AT LEAST YOU BEAT ABCYNTHIA.
I HEARD THAT!
I'M OKAY WITH THAT, IT'S A FACT!
WANT ANOTHER ONE? CAMP MIDNIGHT IS GONNA DESTROY YOUR NEW CAMP!
OH YEAH?
YEAH!
OH, YEAH?!
YEAH!!
OH YEAH?!
YEAH!
SPORTSMANSHIP, LADIES!
THEY WERE LIKE THIS ALL THE TIME LAST SUMMER!

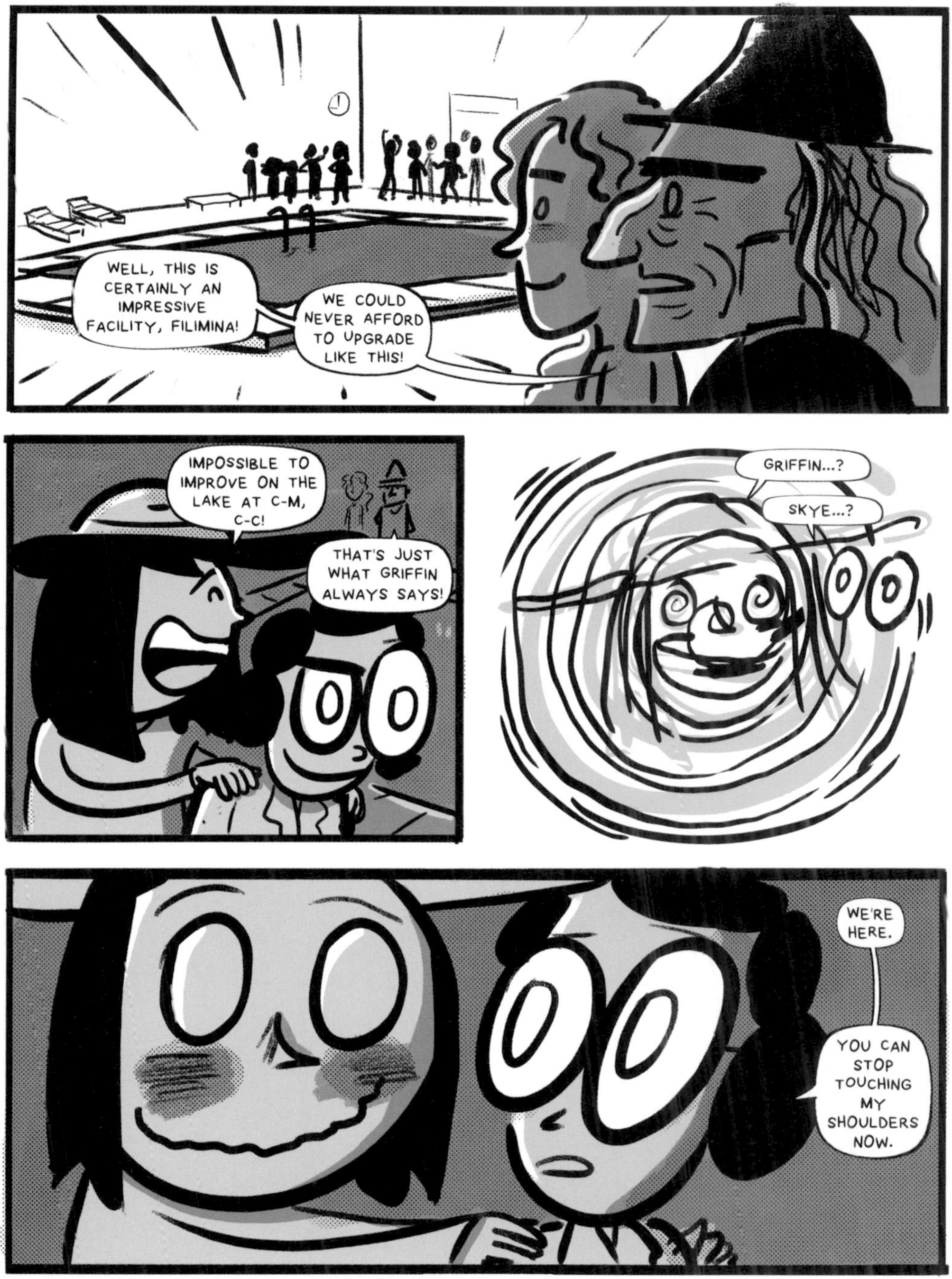
WELL, THIS IS CERTAINLY AN IMPRESSIVE FACILITY, FILIMINA!
WE COULD NEVER AFFORD TO UPGRADE LIKE THIS!
IMPOSSIBLE TO IMPROVE ON THE LAKE AT C-M, C-C!
THAT'S JUST WHAT GRIFFIN ALWAYS SAYS!
GRIFFIN...?
SKYE...?
WE'RE HERE.
YOU CAN STOP TOUCHING MY SHOULDERS NOW.

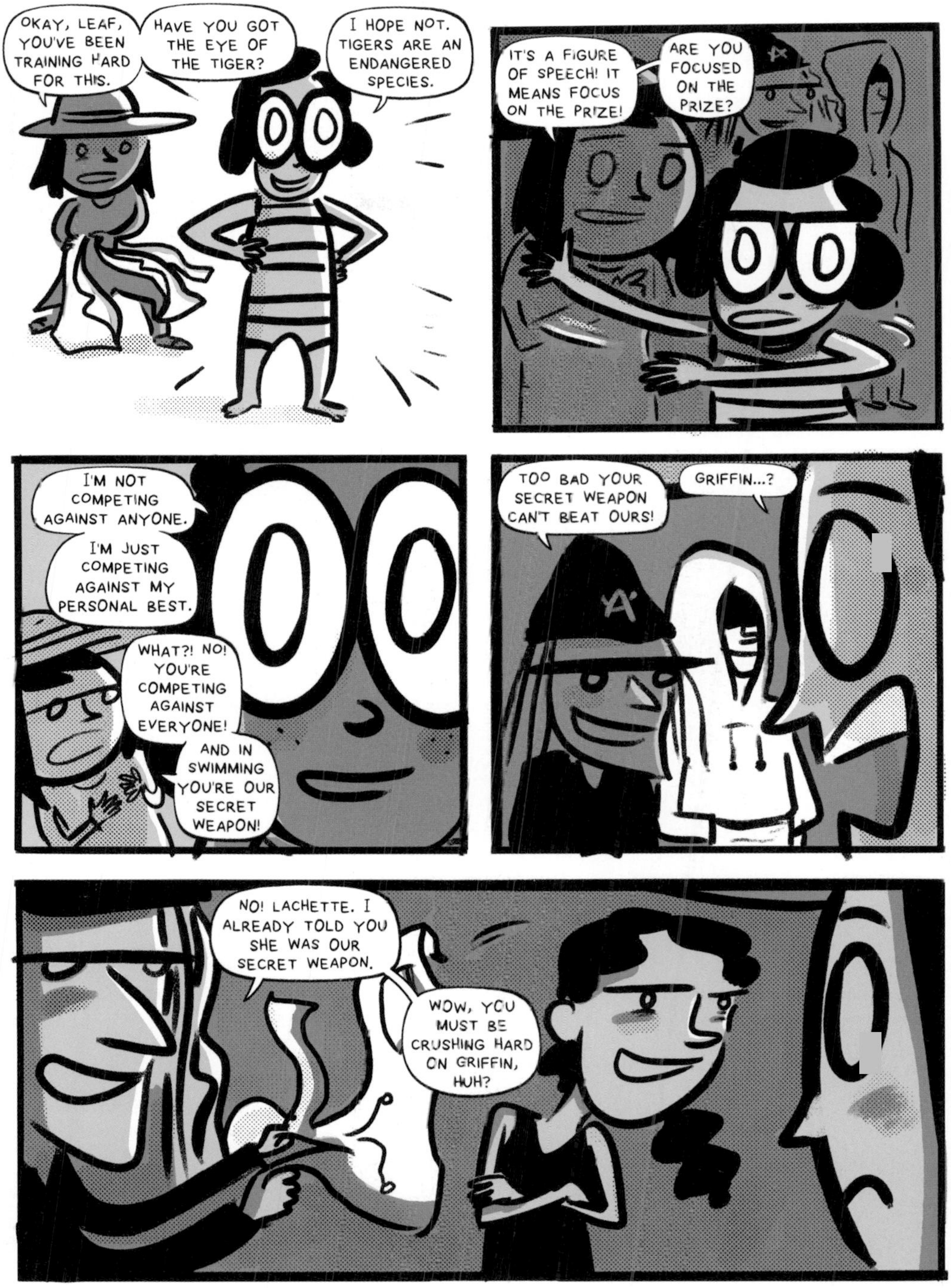
OKAY, LEAF, YOU'VE BEEN TRAINING HARD FOR THIS.
HAVE YOU GOT THE EYE OF THE TIGER?
I HOPE NOT. TIGERS ARE AN ENDANGERED SPECIES.
IT'S A FIGURE OF SPEECH! IT MEANS FOCUS ON THE PRIZE!
ARE YOU FOCUSED ON THE PRIZE?
I'M NOT COMPETING AGAINST ANYONE.
I'M JUST COMPETING AGAINST MY PERSONAL BEST.
WHAT?! NO! YOU'RE COMPETING AGAINST EVERYONE!
AND IN SWIMMING YOU'RE OUR SECRET WEAPON!
TOO BAD YOUR SECRET WEAPON CAN'T BEAT OURS!
GRIFFIN...?
NO! LACHETTE. I ALREADY TOLD YOU SHE WAS OUR SECRET WEAPON.
WOW, YOU MUST BE CRUSHING HARD ON GRIFFIN, HUH?

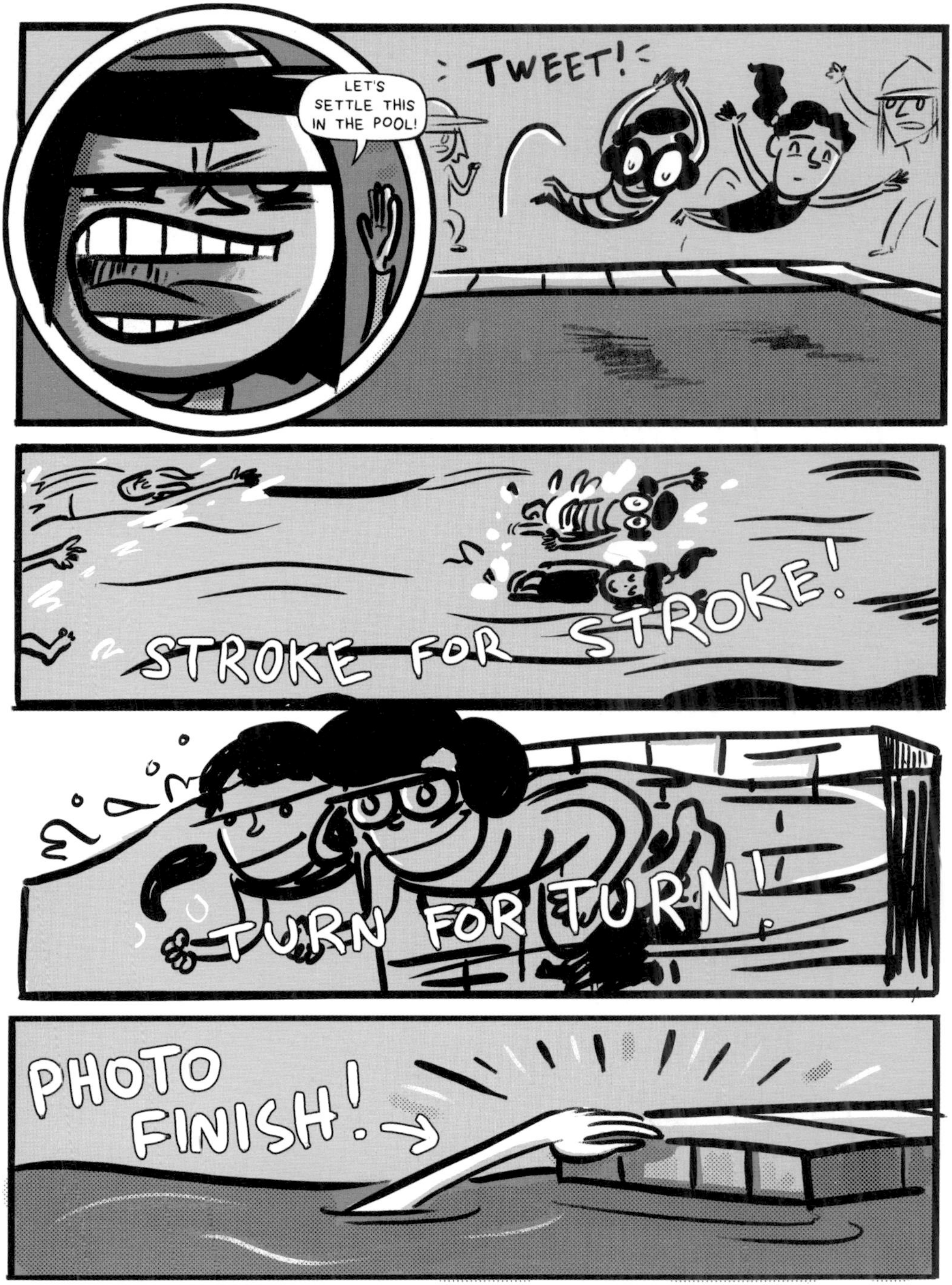
LET'S SETTLE THIS IN THE POOL!
TWEET!
STROKE FOR STROKE!
TURN FOR TURN!
PHOTO FINISH!

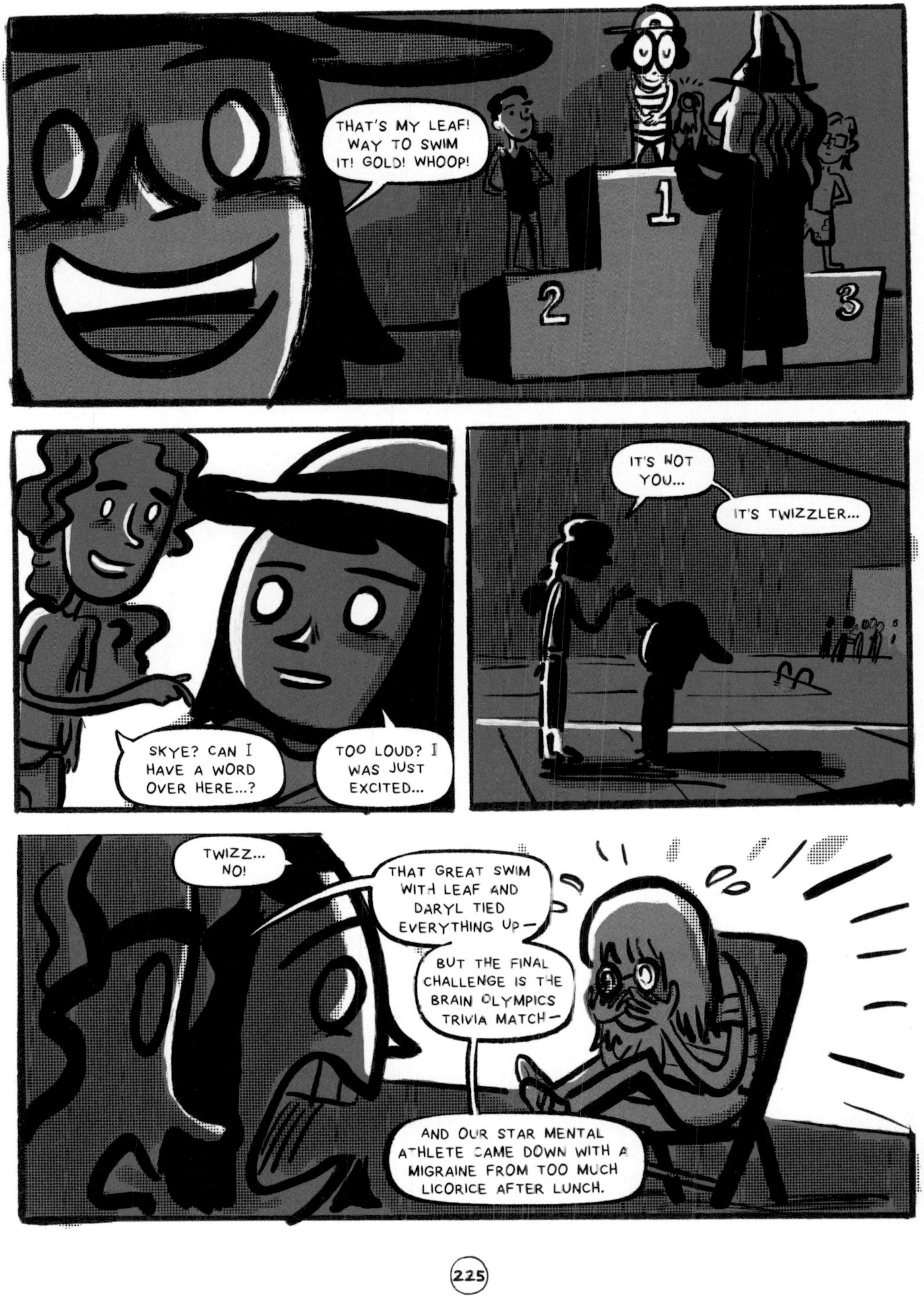
THAT'S MY LEAF! WAY TO SWIM IT! GOLD! WHOOP!
1
2
3
SKYE? CAN I HAVE A WORD OVER HERE...?
TOO LOUD? I WAS JUST EXCITED...
IT'S NOT YOU...
IT'S TWIZZLER...
TWIZZ... NO!
THAT GREAT SWIM WITH LEAF AND DARYL TIED EVERYTHING UP—
BUT THE FINAL CHALLENGE IS THE BRAIN OLYMPICS TRIVIA MATCH—
AND OUR STAR MENTAL ATHLETE CAME DOWN WITH A MIGRAINE FROM TOO MUCH LICORICE AFTER LUNCH.

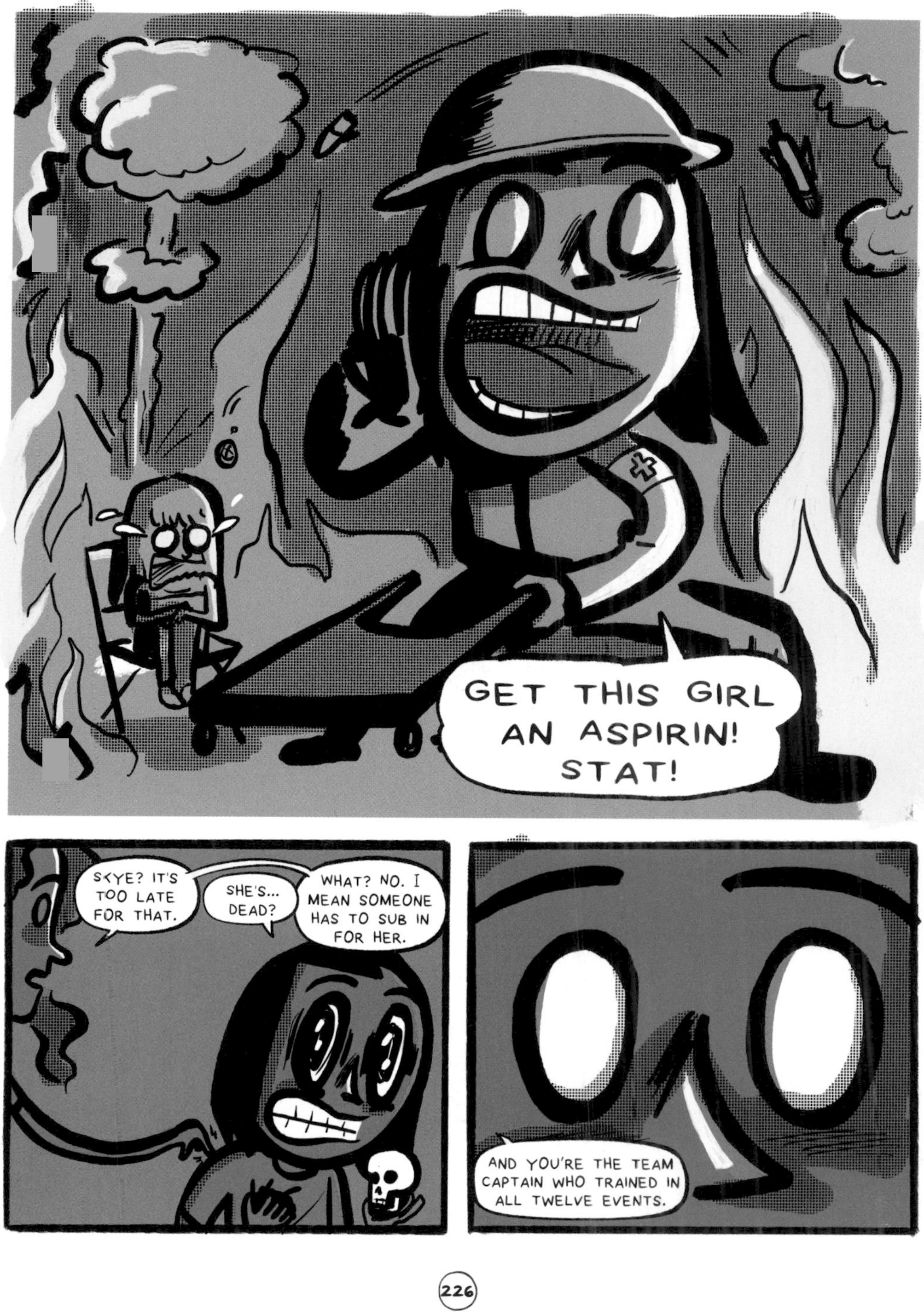
GET THIS GIRL AN ASPIRIN! STAT!
SKYE? IT'S TOO LATE FOR THAT.
SHE'S... DEAD?
WHAT? NO. I MEAN SOMEONE HAS TO SUB IN FOR HER.
AND YOU'RE THE TEAM CAPTAIN WHO TRAINED IN ALL TWELVE EVENTS.

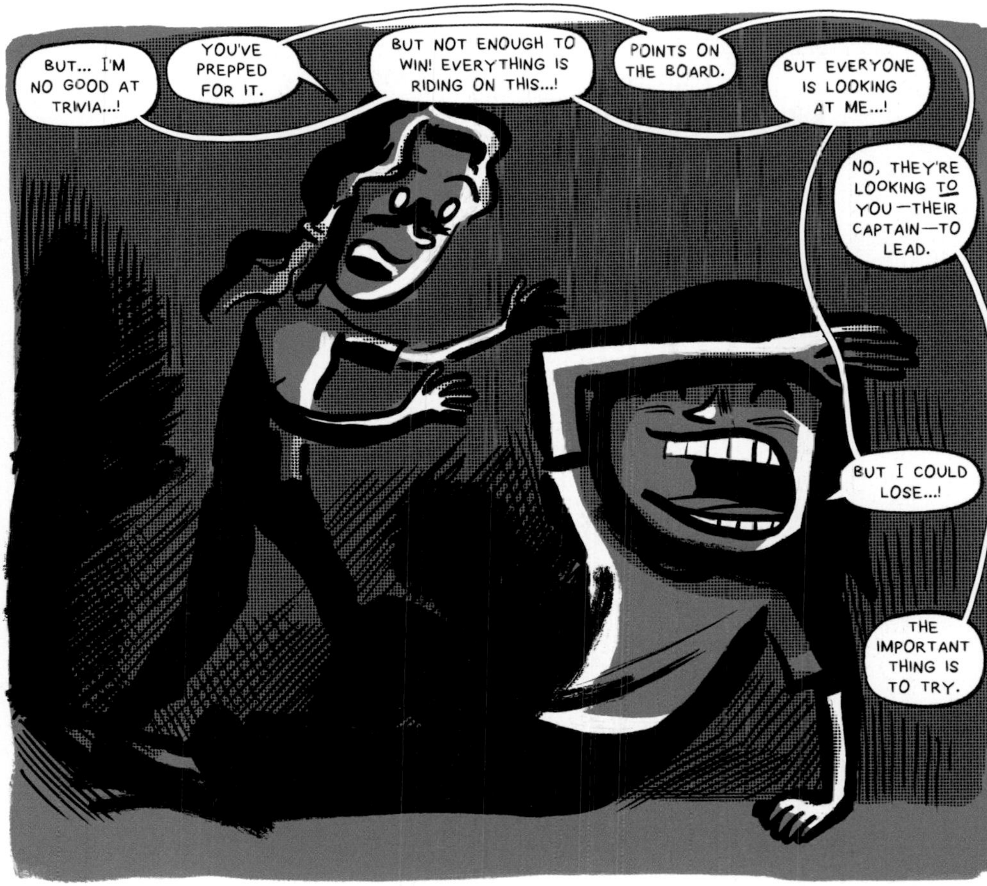
BUT... I'M NO GOOD AT TRIVIA...!
YOU'VE PREPPED FOR IT.
BUT NOT ENOUGH TO WIN! EVERYTHING IS RIDING ON THIS...!
POINTS ON THE BOARD.
BUT EVERYONE IS LOOKING AT ME...!
NO, THEY'RE LOOKING TO YOU—THEIR CAPTAIN—TO LEAD.
BUT I COULD LOSE...!
THE IMPORTANT THING IS TO TRY.

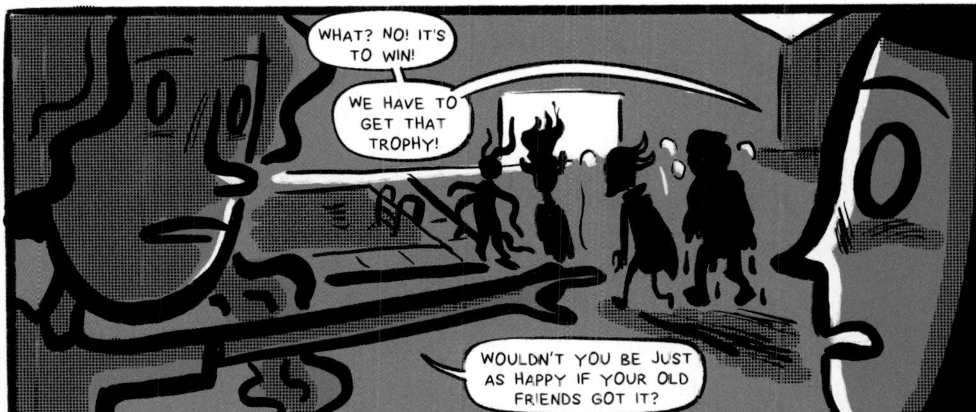
WHAT? NO! IT'S TO WIN!
WE HAVE TO GET THAT TROPHY!
WOULDN'T YOU BE JUST AS HAPPY IF YOUR OLD FRIENDS GOT IT?

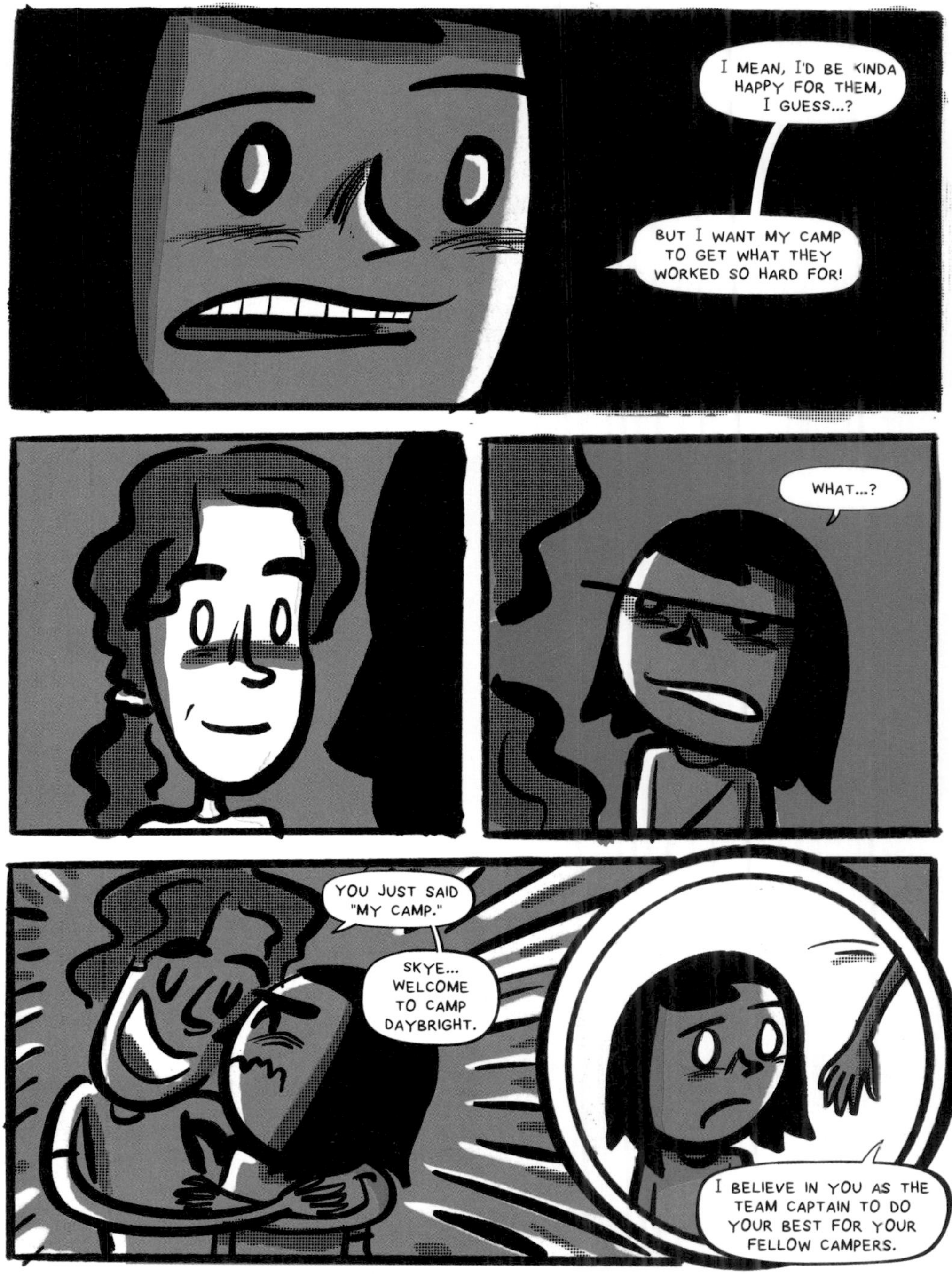
I MEAN, I'D BE KINDA HAPPY FOR THEM, I GUESS...?
BUT I WANT MY CAMP TO GET WHAT THEY WORKED SO HARD FOR!
WHAT...?
YOU JUST SAID "MY CAMP."
SKYE... WELCOME TO CAMP DAYBRIGHT.
I BELIEVE IN YOU AS THE TEAM CAPTAIN TO DO YOUR BEST FOR YOUR FELLOW CAMPERS.

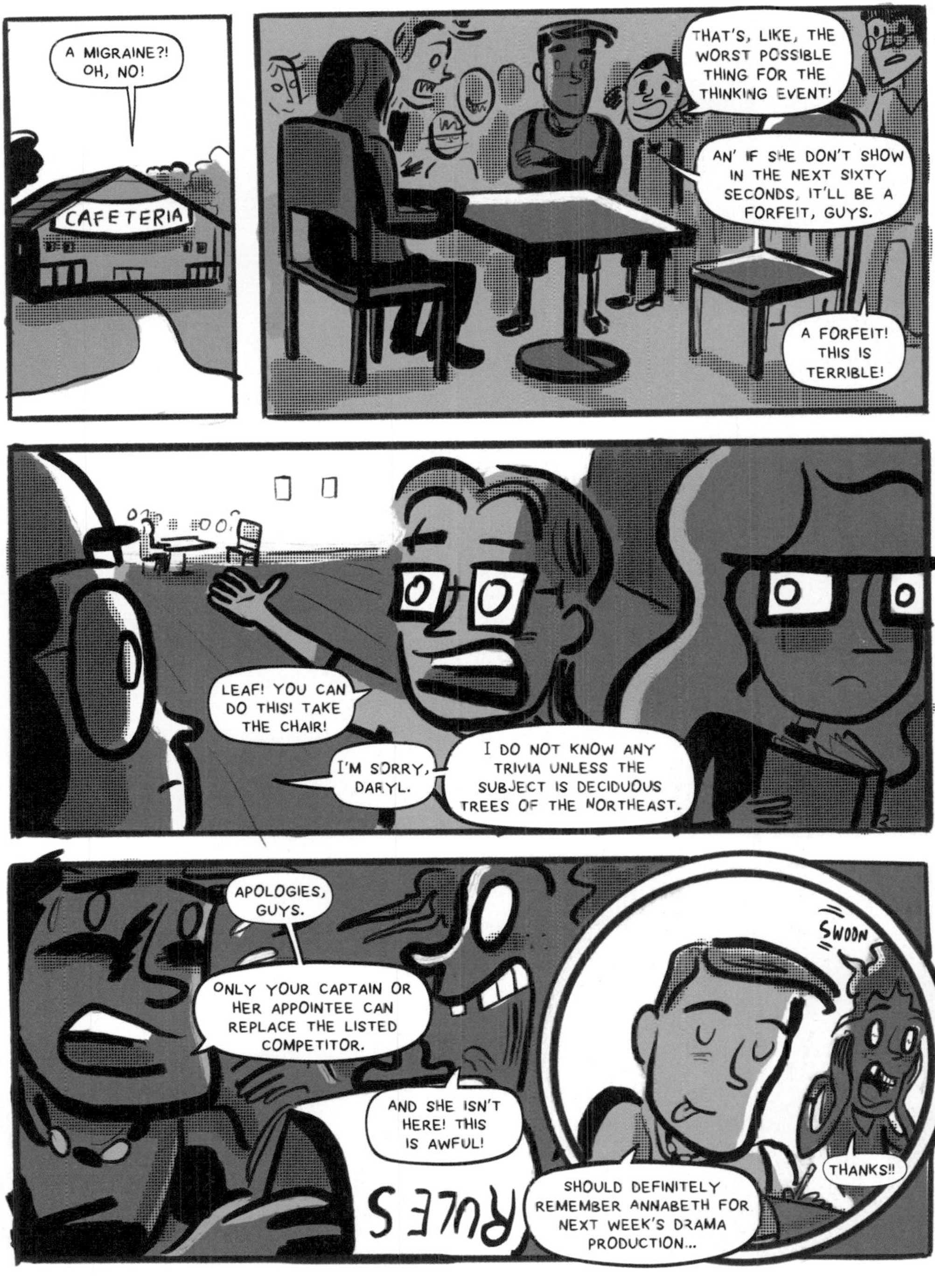
A MIGRAINE?! OH, NO!
CAFETERIA
THAT'S, LIKE, THE WORST POSSIBLE THING FOR THE THINKING EVENT!
AN' IF SHE DON'T SHOW IN THE NEXT SIXTY SECONDS, IT'LL BE A FORFEIT, GUYS.
A FORFEIT! THIS IS TERRIBLE!
LEAF! YOU CAN DO THIS! TAKE THE CHAIR!
I'M SORRY, DARYL.
I DO NOT KNOW ANY TRIVIA UNLESS THE SUBJECT IS DECIDUOUS TREES OF THE NORTHEAST.
APOLOGIES, GUYS.
ONLY YOUR CAPTAIN OR HER APPOINTEE CAN REPLACE THE LISTED COMPETITOR.
AND SHE ISN'T HERE! THIS IS AWFUL!
RULES
SWOON
SHOULD DEFINITELY REMEMBER ANNABETH FOR NEXT WEEK'S DRAMA PRODUCTION...
THANKS!!

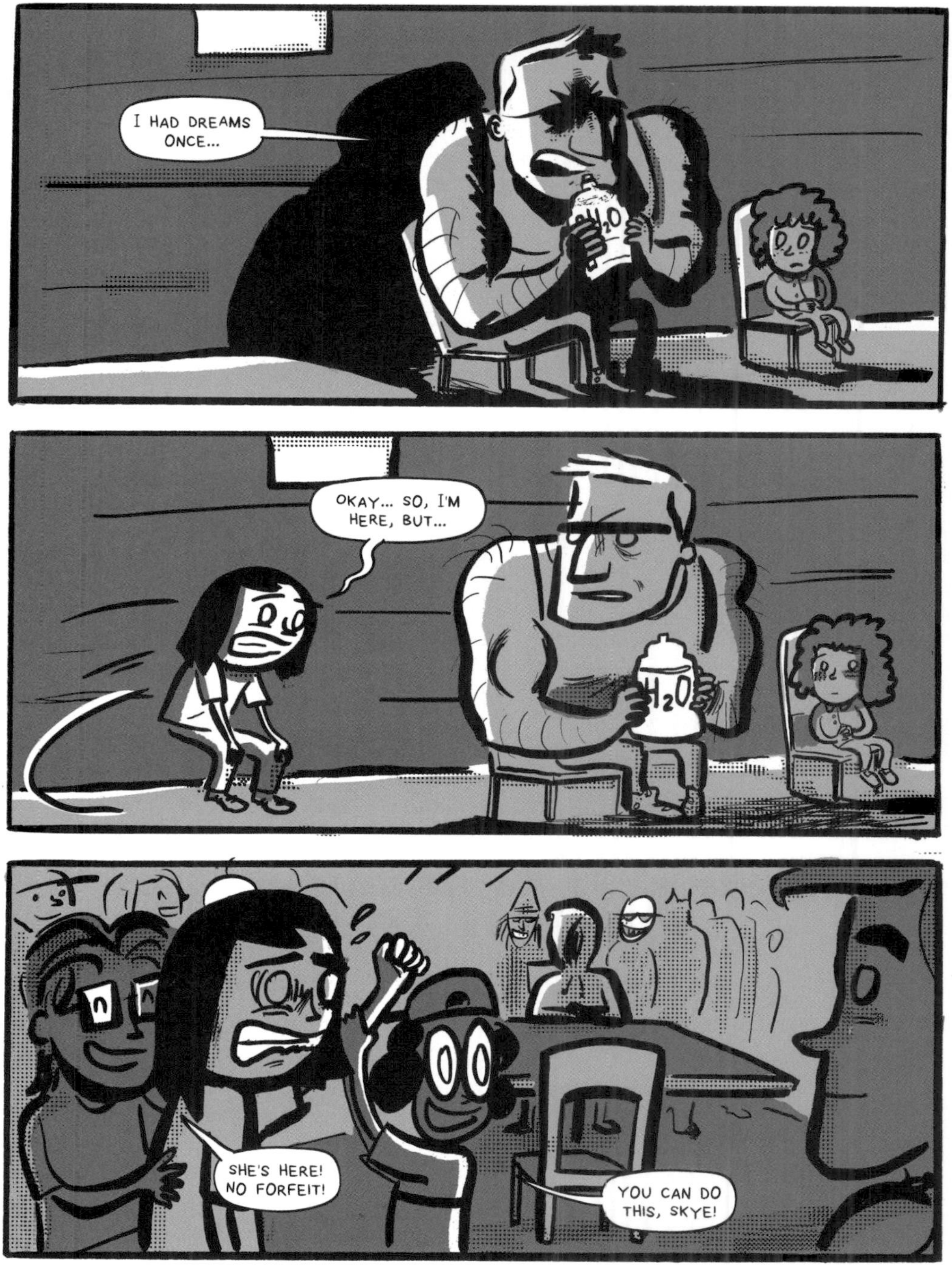
I HAD DREAMS ONCE...
H_2O
OKAY... SO, I'M HERE, BUT...
H_2O
SHE'S HERE! NO FORFEIT!
YOU CAN DO THIS, SKYE!

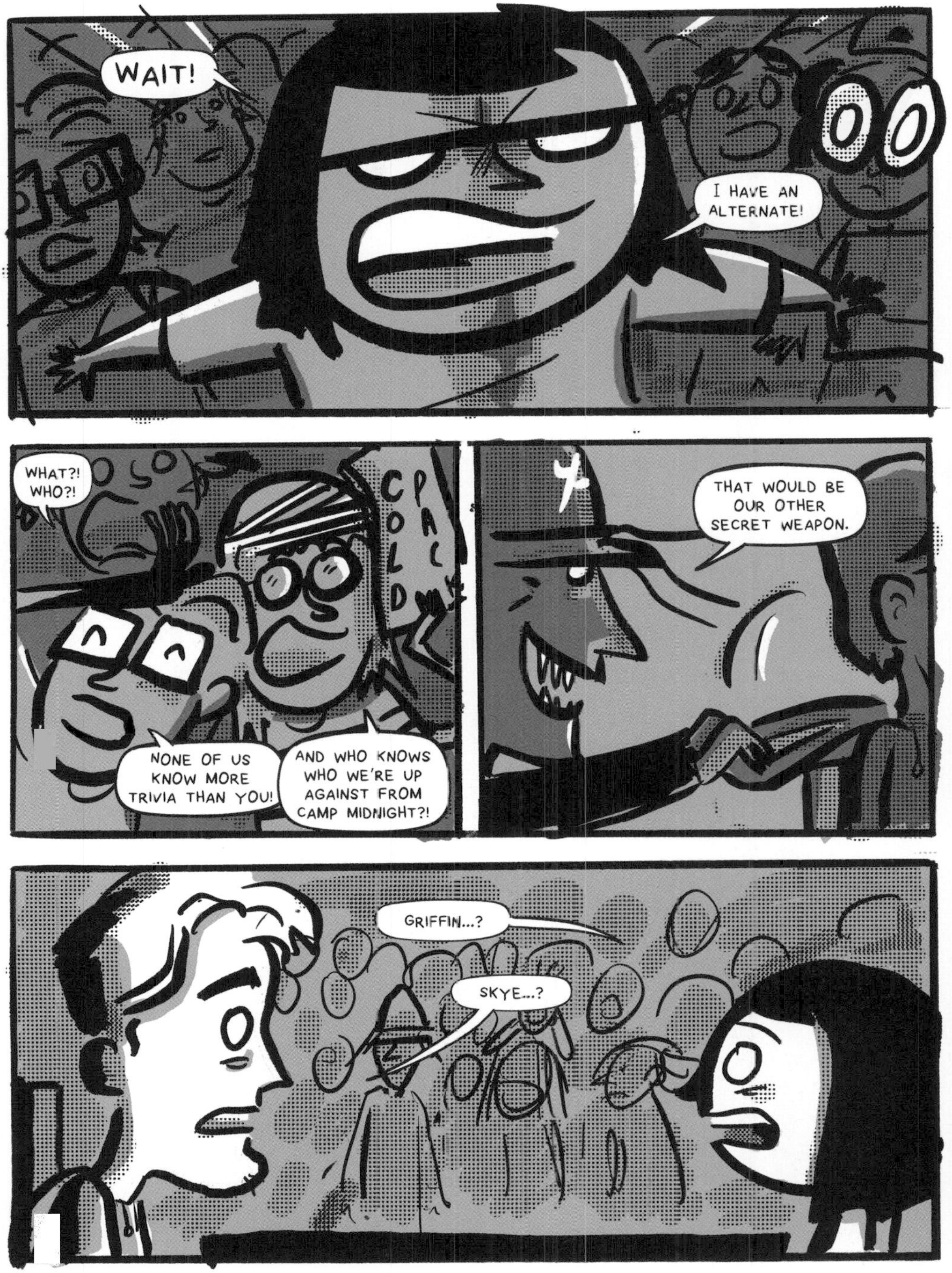
WAIT!
I HAVE AN ALTERNATE!
WHAT?! WHO?!
COLD PACK
NONE OF US KNOW MORE TRIVIA THAN YOU!
AND WHO KNOWS WHO WE'RE UP AGAINST FROM CAMP MIDNIGHT?!
THAT WOULD BE OUR OTHER SECRET WEAPON.
GRIFFIN...?
SKYE...?

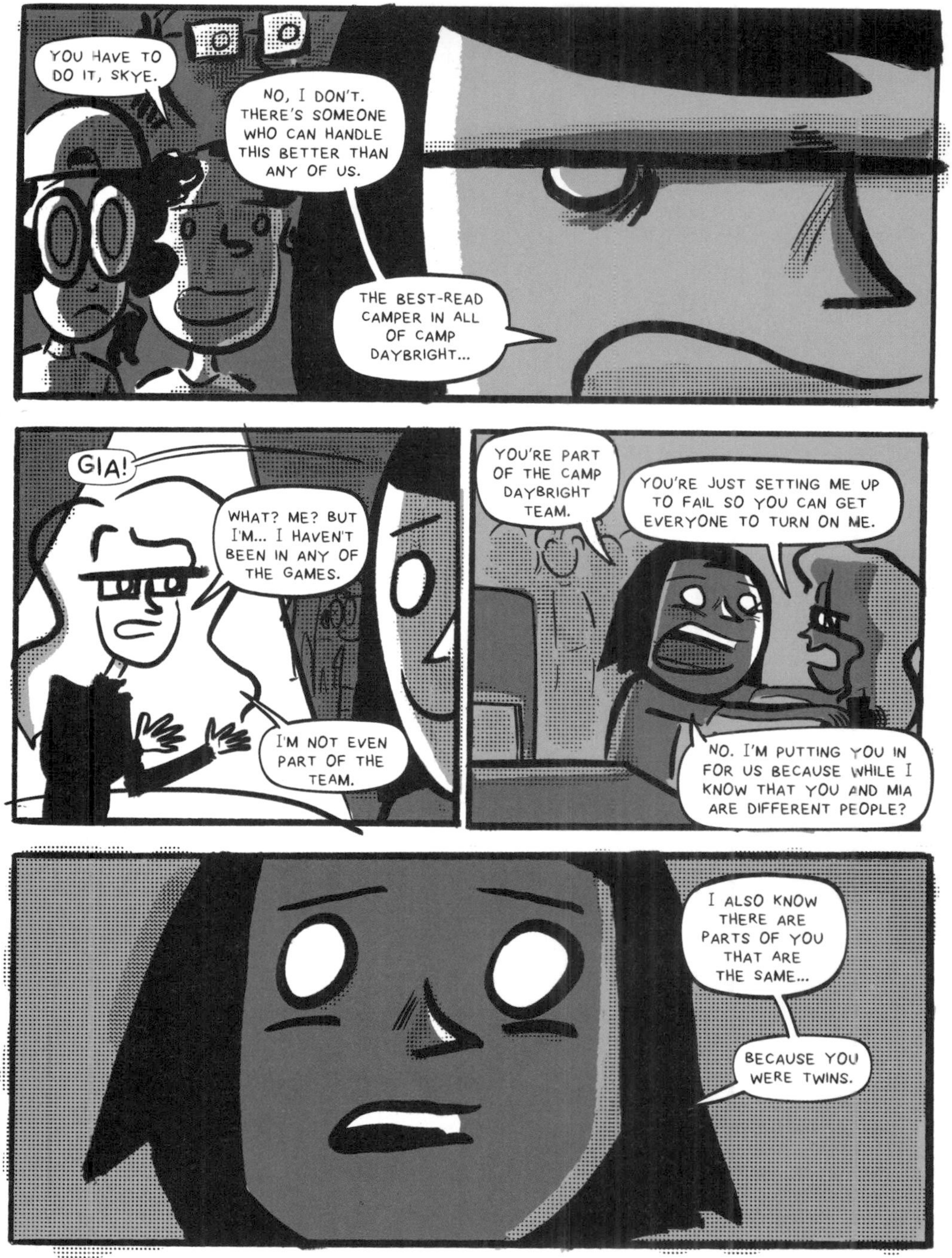
YOU HAVE TO DO IT, SKYE.
NO, I DON'T. THERE'S SOMEONE WHO CAN HANDLE THIS BETTER THAN ANY OF US.
THE BEST-READ CAMPER IN ALL OF CAMP DAYBRIGHT...
GIA!
WHAT? ME? BUT I'M... I HAVEN'T BEEN IN ANY OF THE GAMES.
I'M NOT EVEN PART OF THE TEAM.
YOU'RE PART OF THE CAMP DAYBRIGHT TEAM.
YOU'RE JUST SETTING ME UP TO FAIL SO YOU CAN GET EVERYONE TO TURN ON ME.
NO. I'M PUTTING YOU IN FOR US BECAUSE WHILE I KNOW THAT YOU AND MIA ARE DIFFERENT PEOPLE?
I ALSO KNOW THERE ARE PARTS OF YOU THAT ARE THE SAME...
BECAUSE YOU WERE TWINS.

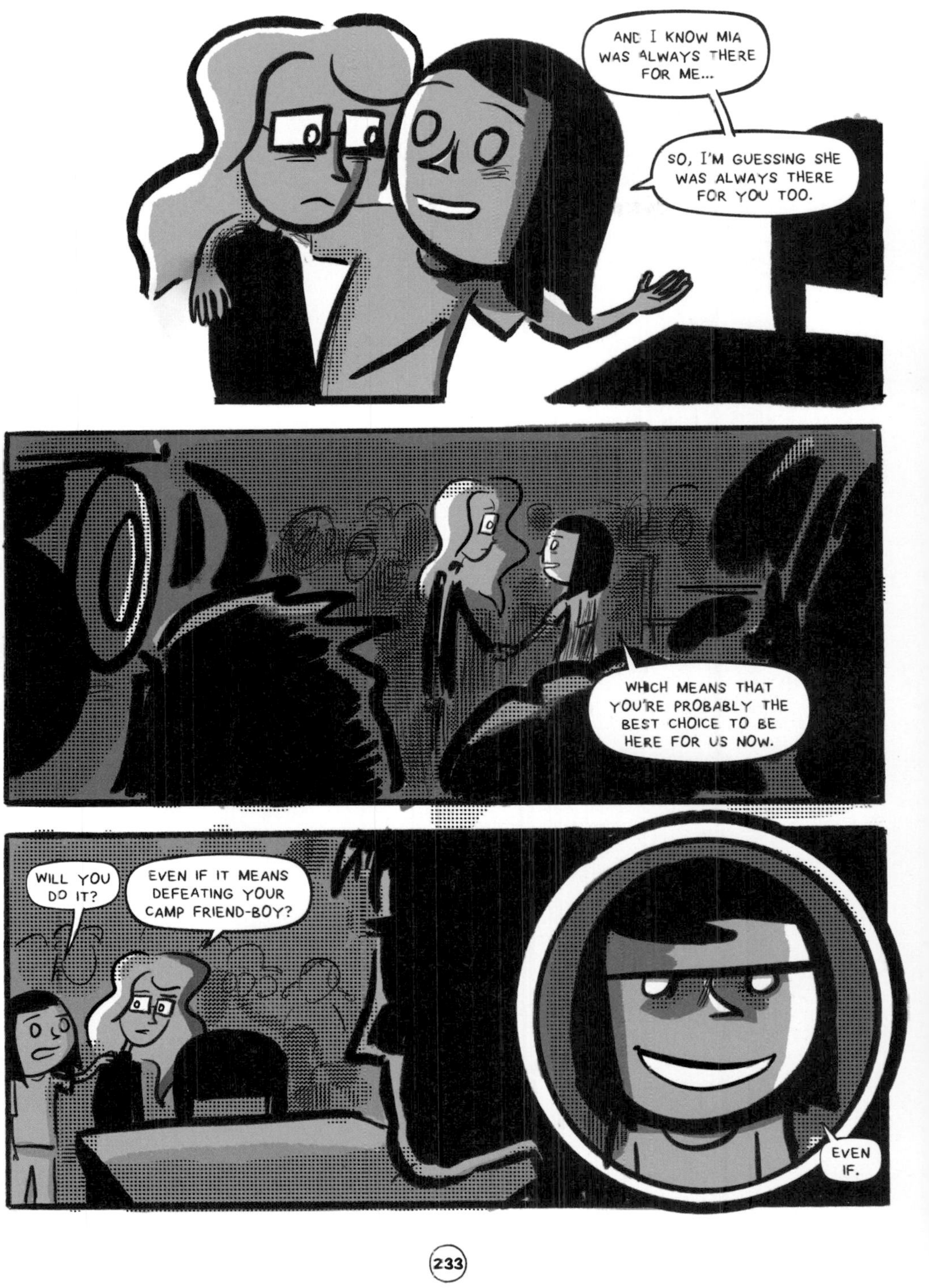
AND I KNOW MIA WAS ALWAYS THERE FOR ME...
SO, I'M GUESSING SHE WAS ALWAYS THERE FOR YOU TOO.
WHICH MEANS THAT YOU'RE PROBABLY THE BEST CHOICE TO BE HERE FOR US NOW.
WILL YOU DO IT?
EVEN IF IT MEANS DEFEATING YOUR CAMP FRIEND-BOY?
EVEN IF.

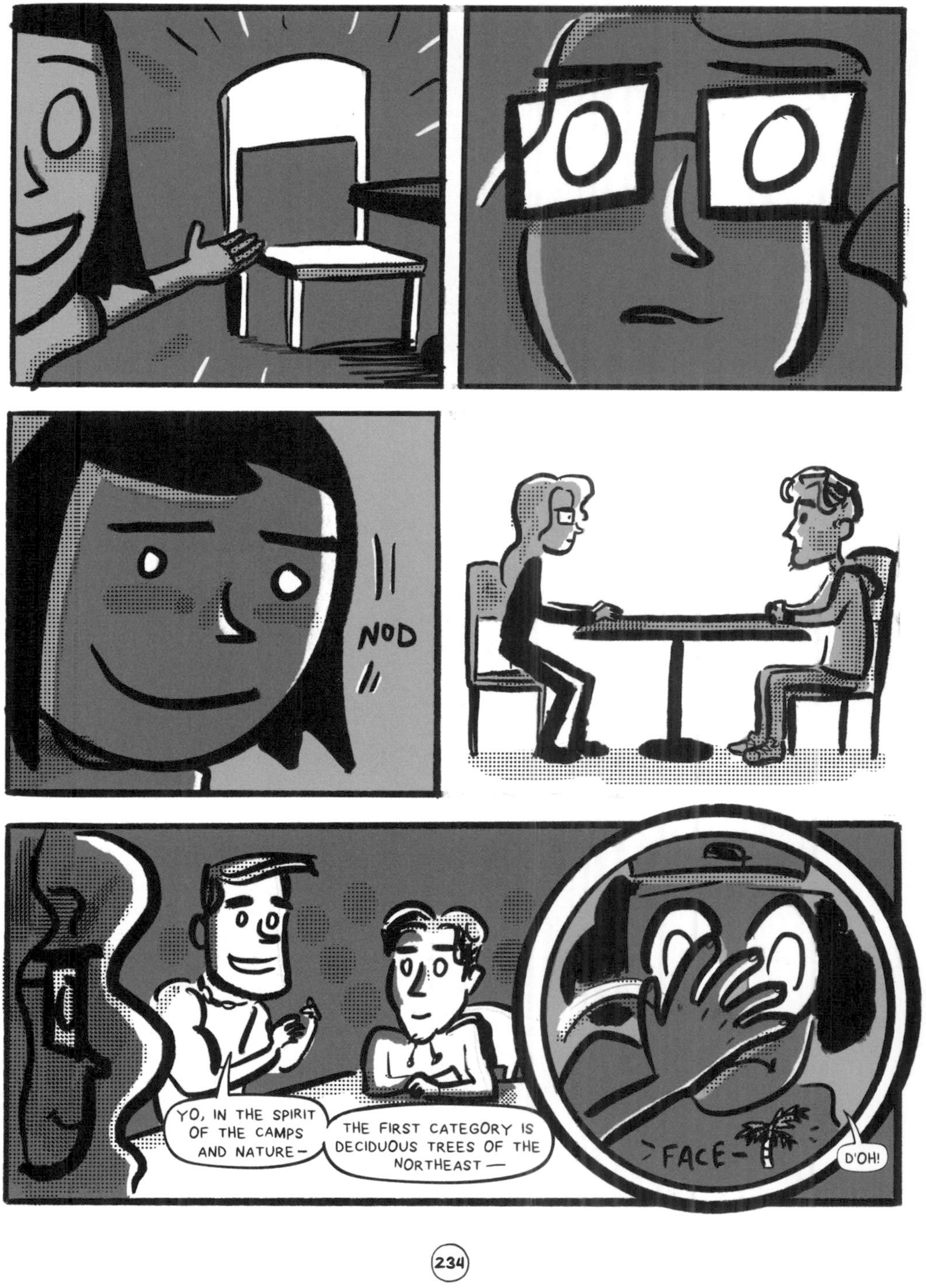
NOD
YO, IN THE SPIRIT OF THE CAMPS AND NATURE—
THE FIRST CATEGORY IS DECIDUOUS TREES OF THE NORTHEAST—
FACE-
D'OH!

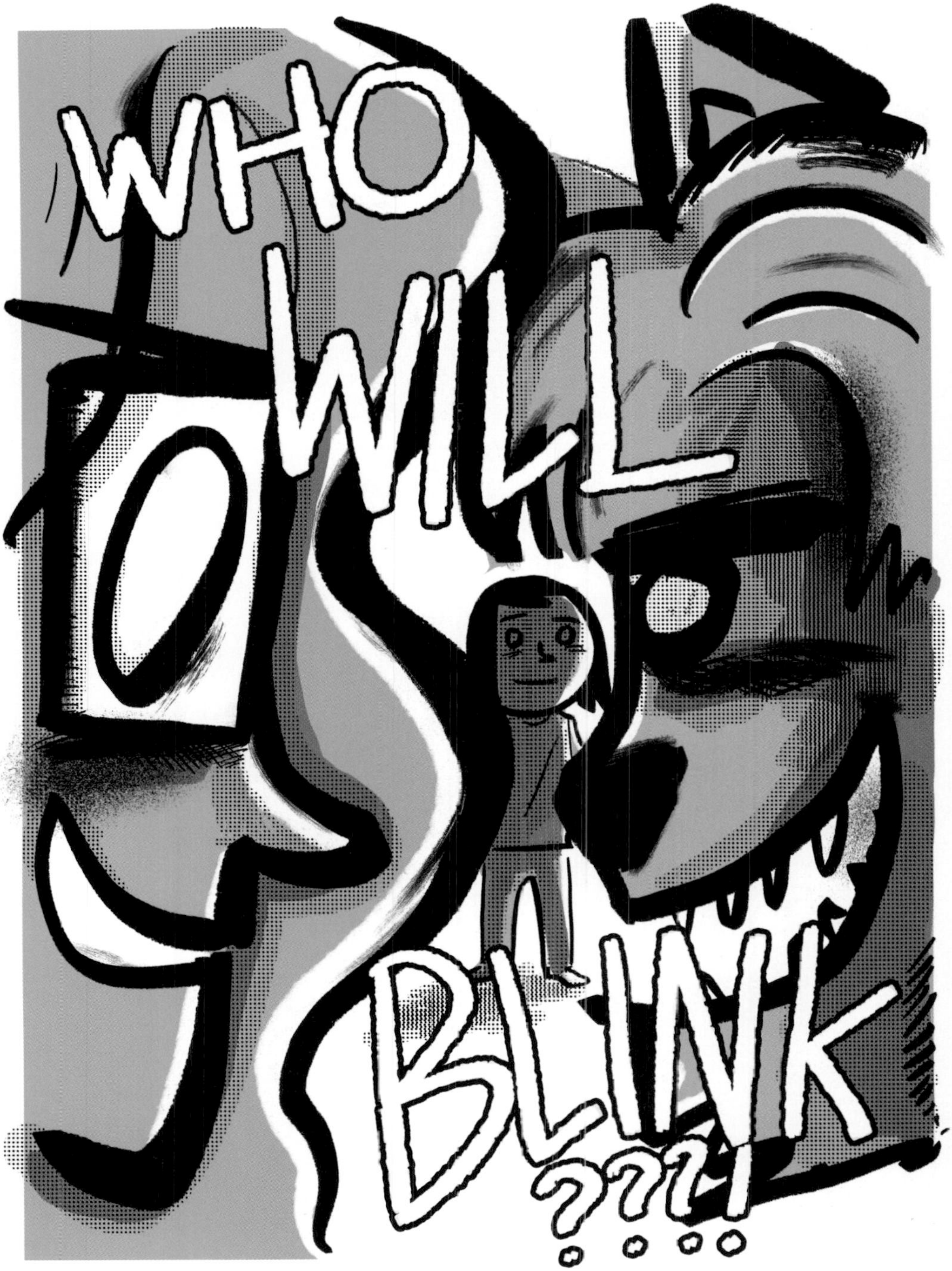
WHO WILL BLINK???!

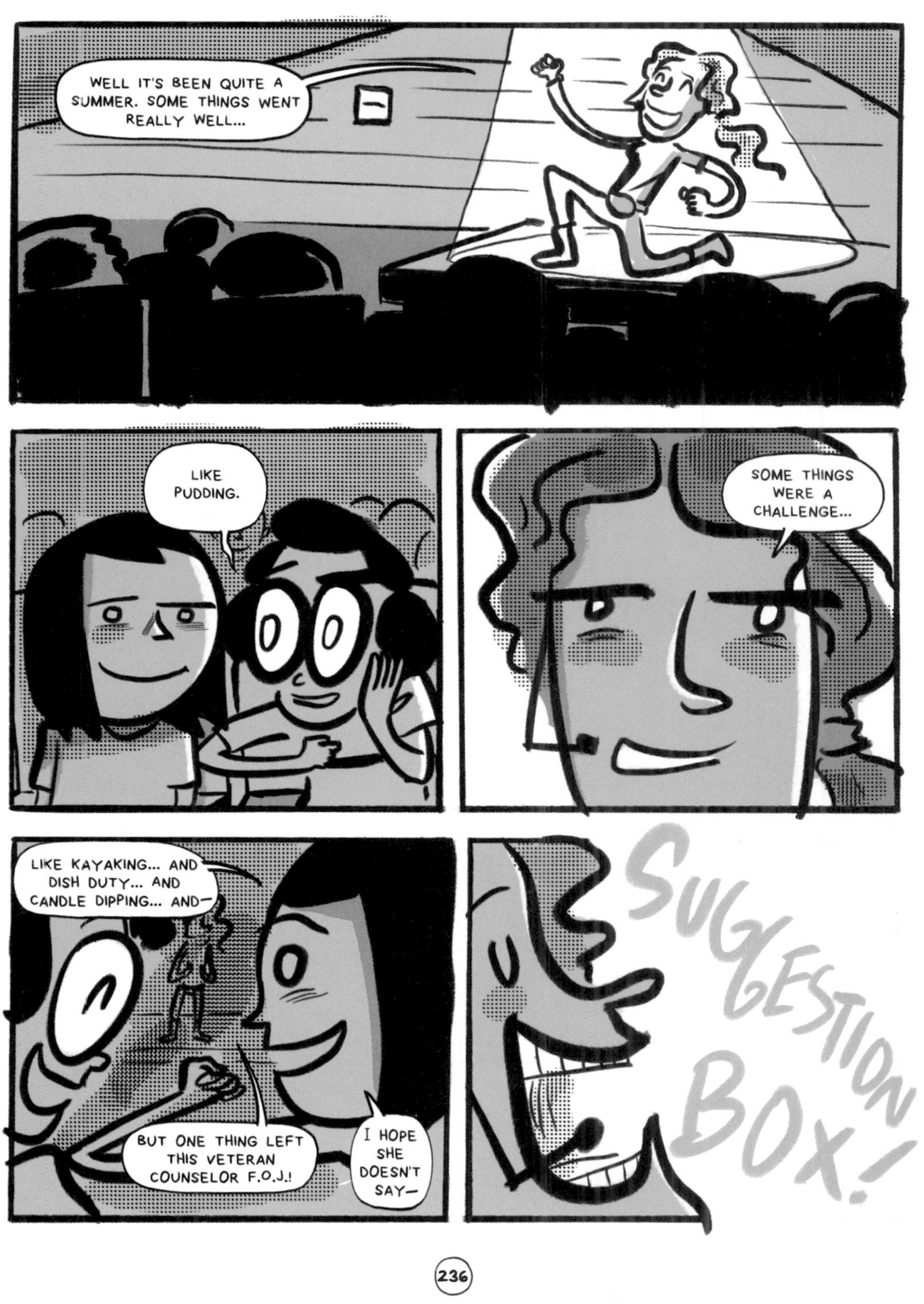
WELL IT'S BEEN QUITE A SUMMER. SOME THINGS WENT REALLY WELL...
LIKE PUDDING.
SOME THINGS WERE A CHALLENGE...
LIKE KAYAKING... AND DISH DUTY... AND CANDLE DIPPING... AND—
BUT ONE THING LEFT THIS VETERAN COUNSELOR F.O.J.!
I HOPE SHE DOESN'T SAY—
SUGGESTION BOX!

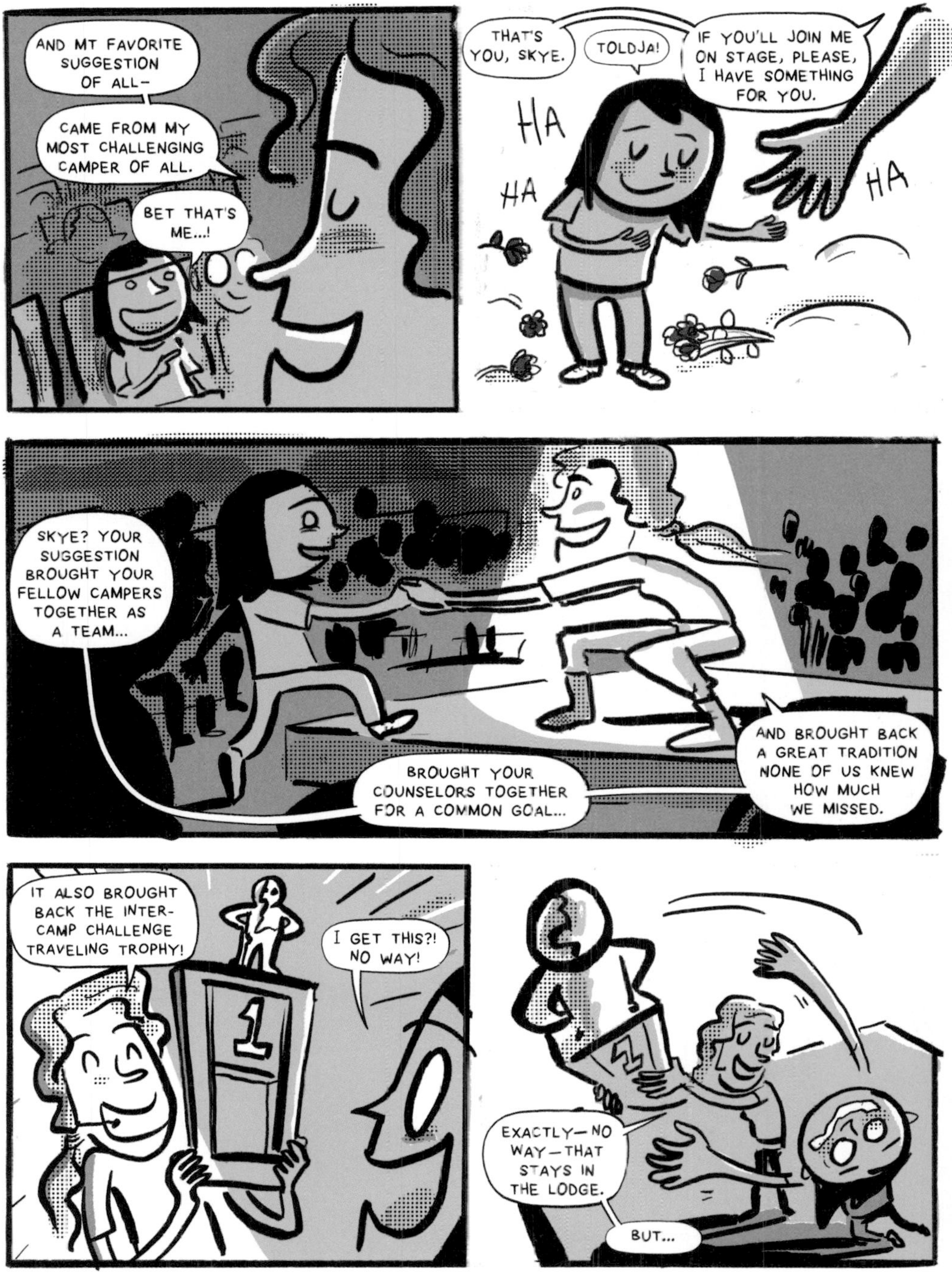
AND MT FAVORITE SUGGESTION OF ALL-
CAME FROM MY MOST CHALLENGING CAMPER OF ALL.
BET THAT'S ME...!
THAT'S YOU, SKYE.
TOLDJA!
IF YOU'LL JOIN ME ON STAGE, PLEASE, I HAVE SOMETHING FOR YOU.
HA
HA
HA
SKYE? YOUR SUGGESTION BROUGHT YOUR FELLOW CAMPERS TOGETHER AS A TEAM...
BROUGHT YOUR COUNSELORS TOGETHER FOR A COMMON GOAL...
AND BROUGHT BACK A GREAT TRADITION NONE OF US KNEW HOW MUCH WE MISSED.
IT ALSO BROUGHT BACK THE INTER-CAMP CHALLENGE TRAVELING TROPHY!
1
I GET THIS?! NO WAY!
EXACTLY—NO WAY—THAT STAYS IN THE LODGE.
BUT...

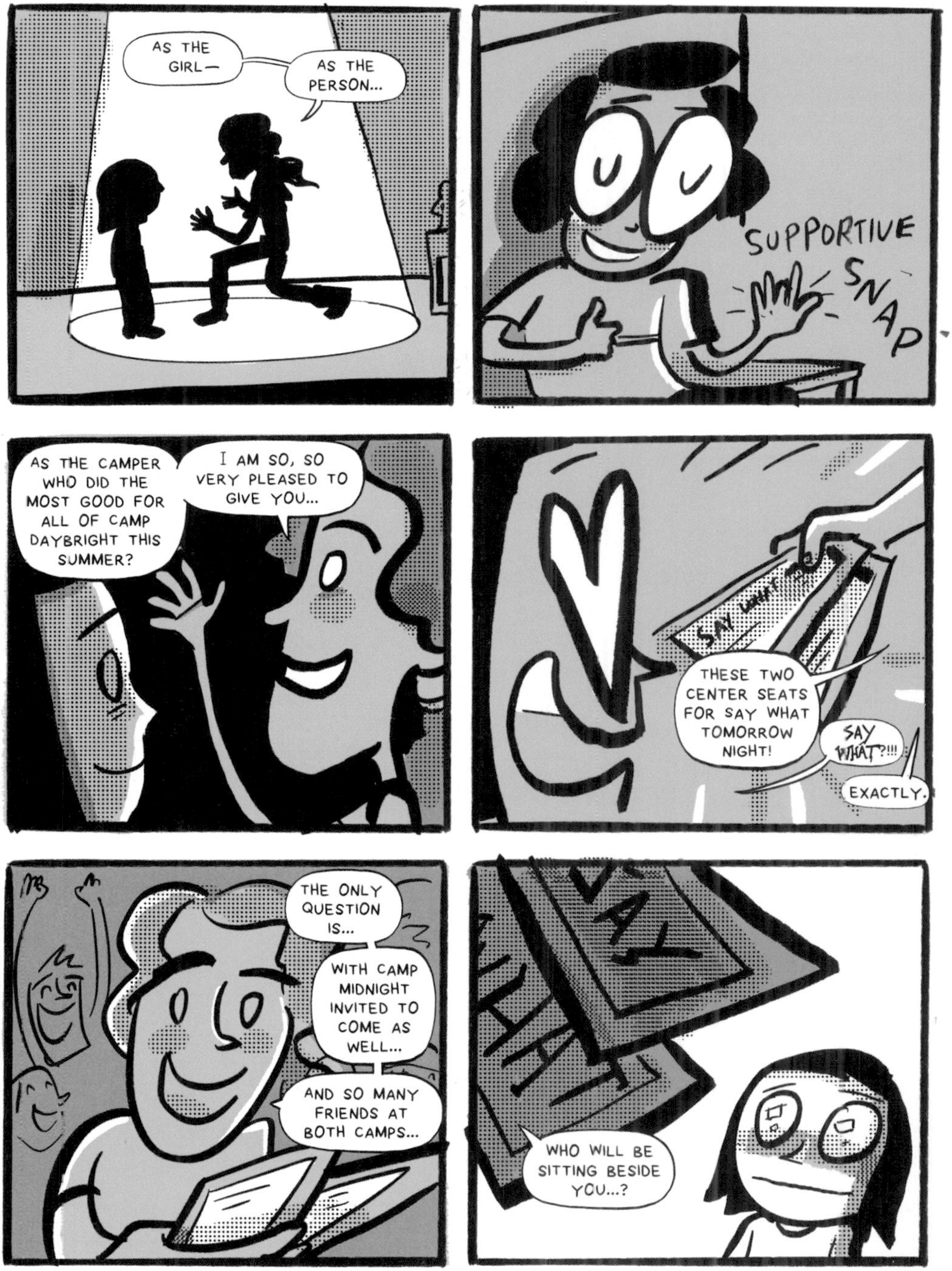
AS THE GIRL—
AS THE PERSON...
SUPPORTIVE SNAP
AS THE CAMPER WHO DID THE MOST GOOD FOR ALL OF CAMP DAYBRIGHT THIS SUMMER?
I AM SO, SO VERY PLEASED TO GIVE YOU...
THESE TWO CENTER SEATS FOR SAY WHAT TOMORROW NIGHT!
SAY WHAT?!!!
EXACTLY.
THE ONLY QUESTION IS...
WITH CAMP MIDNIGHT INVITED TO COME AS WELL...
AND SO MANY FRIENDS AT BOTH CAMPS...
WHO WILL BE SITTING BESIDE YOU...?

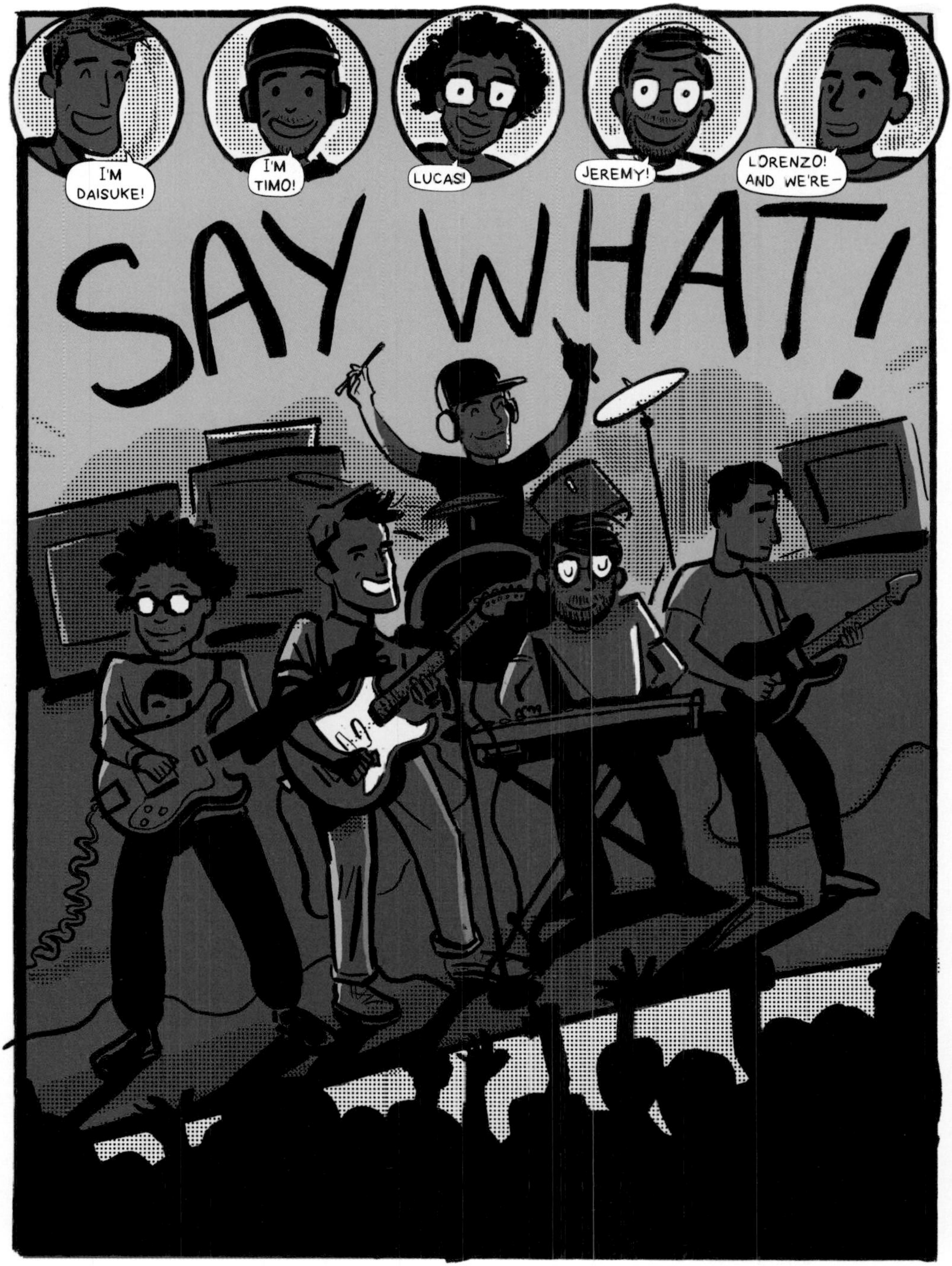
I'M DAISUKE!
I'M TIMO!
LUCAS!
JEREMY!
LORENZO! AND WE'RE-
SAY WHAT!

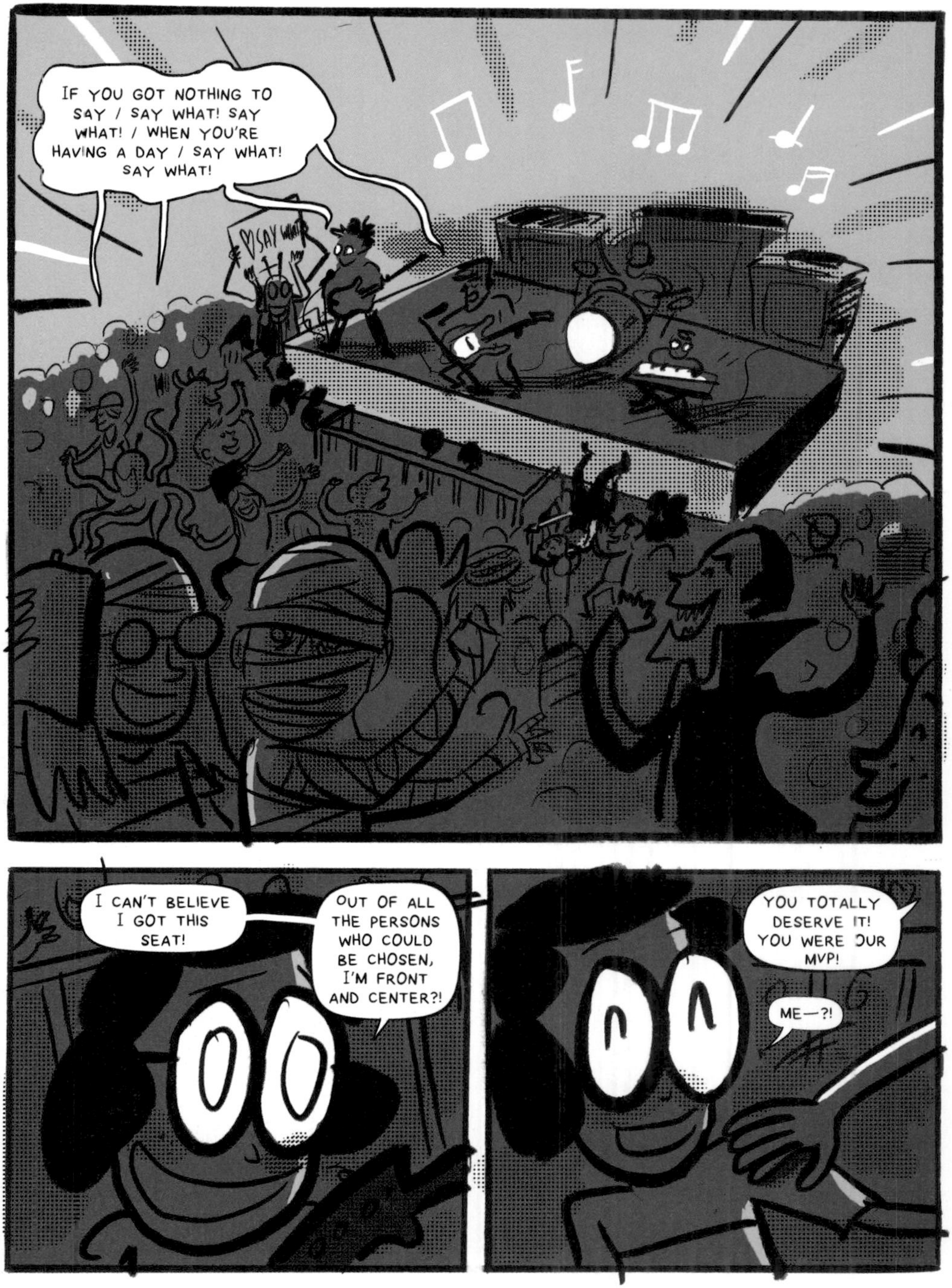
IF YOU GOT NOTHING TO SAY / SAY WHAT! SAY WHAT! / WHEN YOU'RE HAVING A DAY / SAY WHAT! SAY WHAT!
♡SAY WHAT
I CAN'T BELIEVE I GOT THIS SEAT!
OUT OF ALL THE PERSONS WHO COULD BE CHOSEN, I'M FRONT AND CENTER?!
YOU TOTALLY DESERVE IT! YOU WERE OUR MVP!
ME—?!

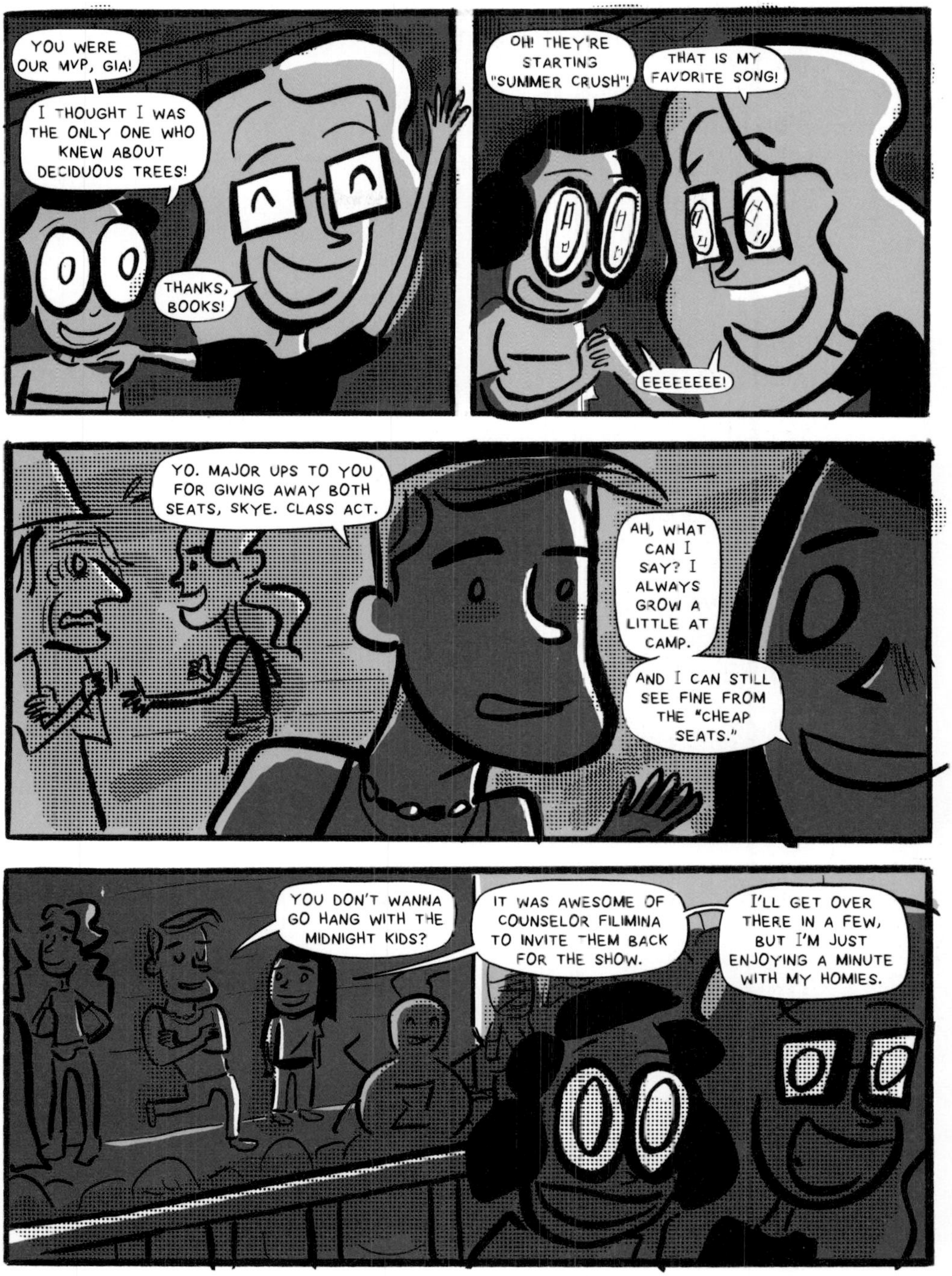

YOU WERE OUR MVP, GIA!
I THOUGHT I WAS THE ONLY ONE WHO KNEW ABOUT DECIDUOUS TREES!
THANKS, BOOKS!
OH! THEY'RE STARTING "SUMMER CRUSH"!
THAT IS MY FAVORITE SONG!
EEEEEEEE!
YO. MAJOR UPS TO YOU FOR GIVING AWAY BOTH SEATS, SKYE. CLASS ACT.
AH, WHAT CAN I SAY? I ALWAYS GROW A LITTLE AT CAMP.
AND I CAN STILL SEE FINE FROM THE "CHEAP SEATS."
YOU DON'T WANNA GO HANG WITH THE MIDNIGHT KIDS?
IT WAS AWESOME OF COUNSELOR FILIMINA TO INVITE THEM BACK FOR THE SHOW.
I'LL GET OVER THERE IN A FEW, BUT I'M JUST ENJOYING A MINUTE WITH MY HOMIES.

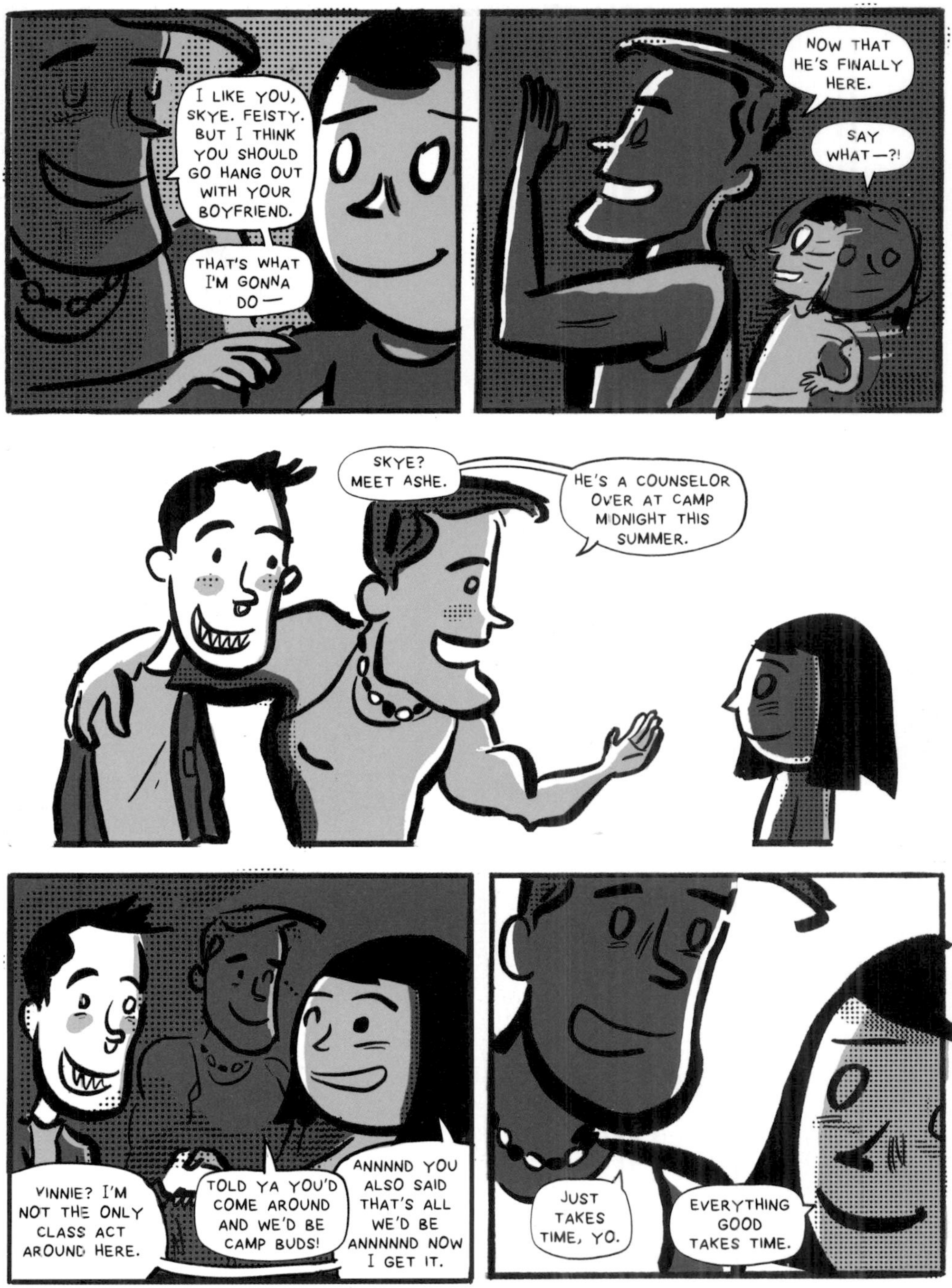
I LIKE YOU, SKYE. FEISTY. BUT I THINK YOU SHOULD GO HANG OUT WITH YOUR BOYFRIEND.
THAT'S WHAT I'M GONNA DO—
NOW THAT HE'S FINALLY HERE.
SAY WHAT—?!
SKYE? MEET ASHE.
HE'S A COUNSELOR OVER AT CAMP MIDNIGHT THIS SUMMER.
VINNIE? I'M NOT THE ONLY CLASS ACT AROUND HERE.
TOLD YA YOU'D COME AROUND AND WE'D BE CAMP BUDS!
ANNNND YOU ALSO SAID THAT'S ALL WE'D BE ANNNNND NOW I GET IT.
JUST TAKES TIME, YO.
EVERYTHING GOOD TAKES TIME.

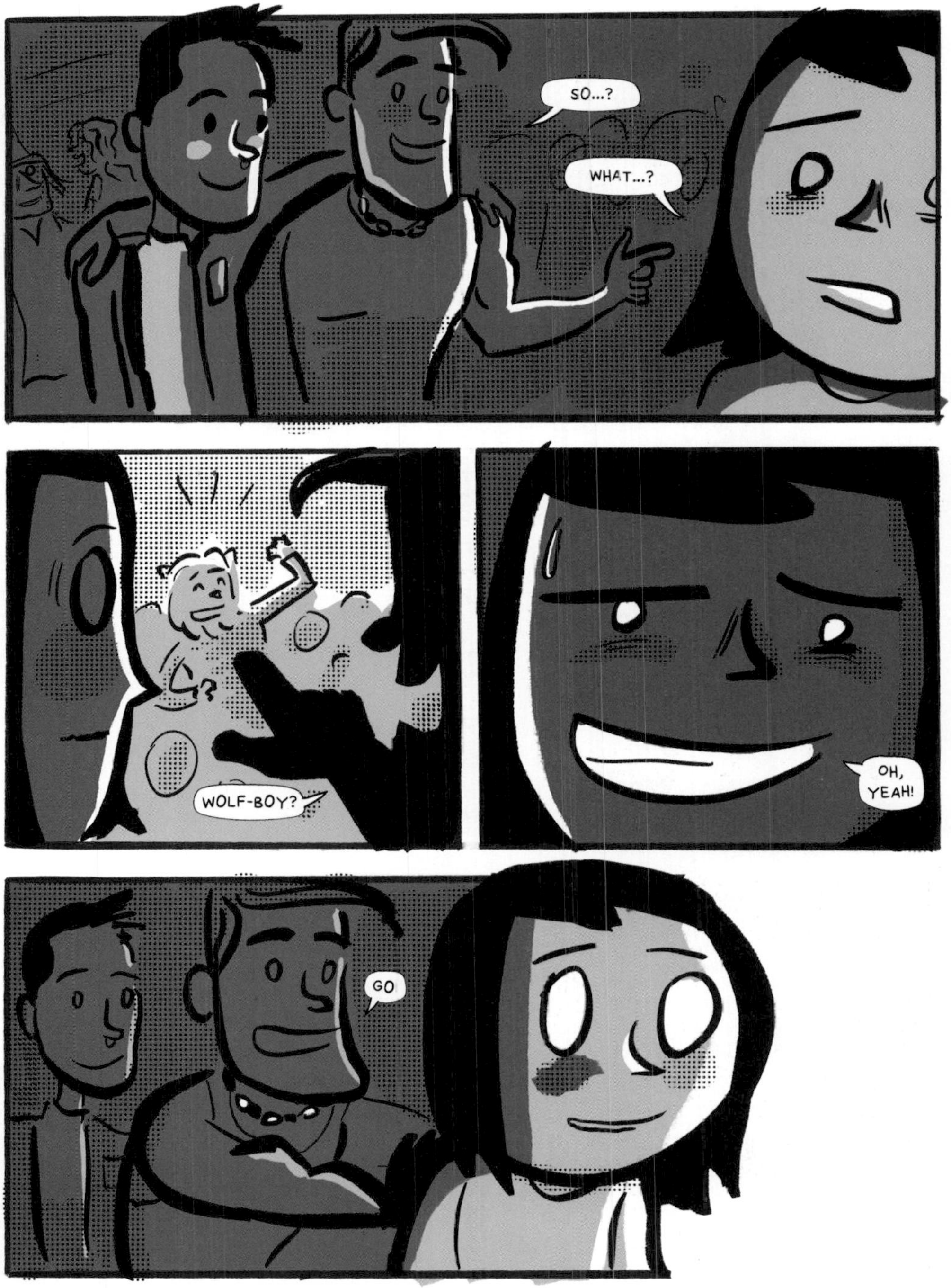
SO...?
WHAT...?
WOLF-BOY?
OH, YEAH!
GO

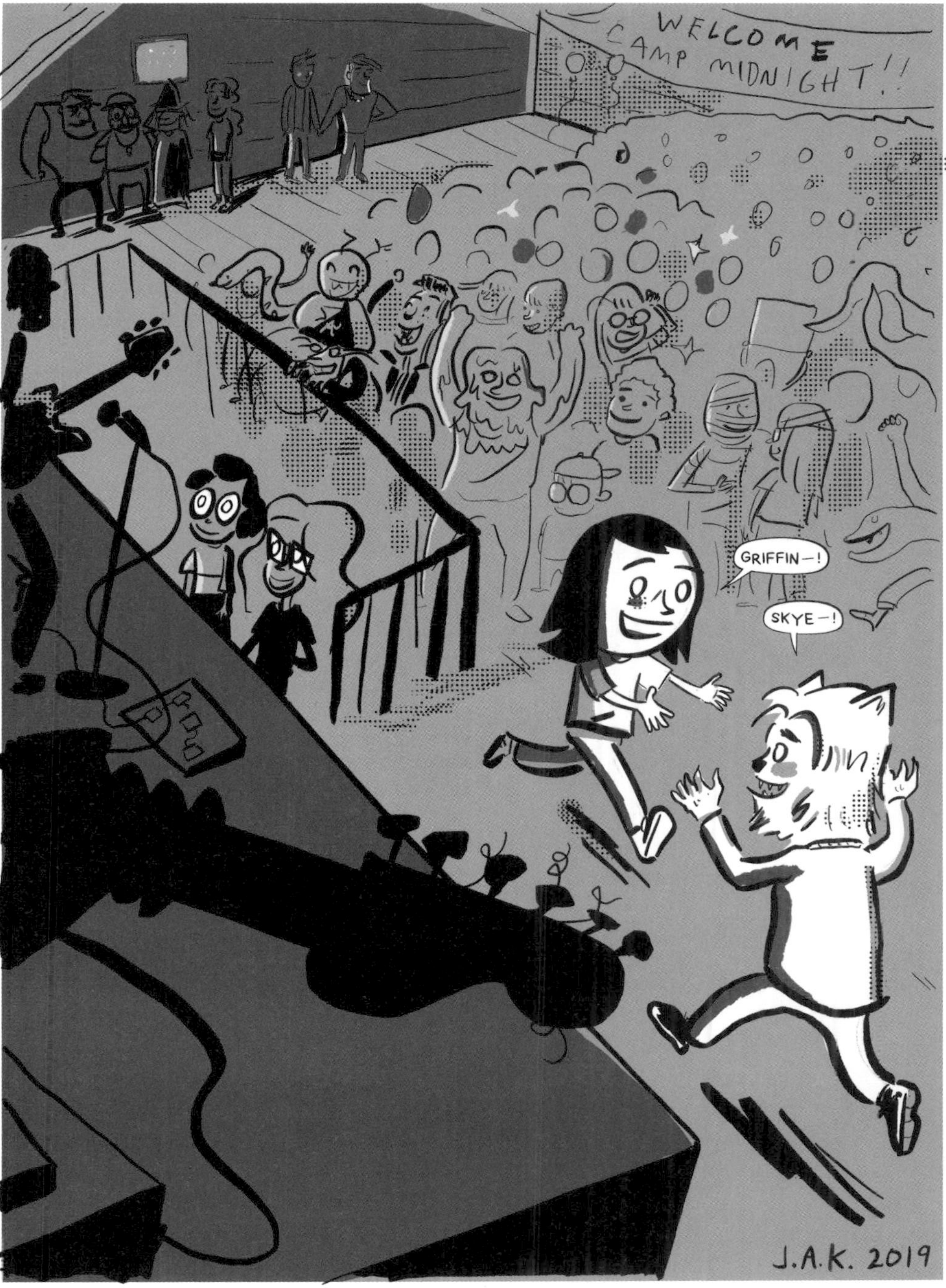
WELCOME CAMP MIDNIGHT!!
GRIFFIN—!
SKYE—!
J.A.K. 2019

The End

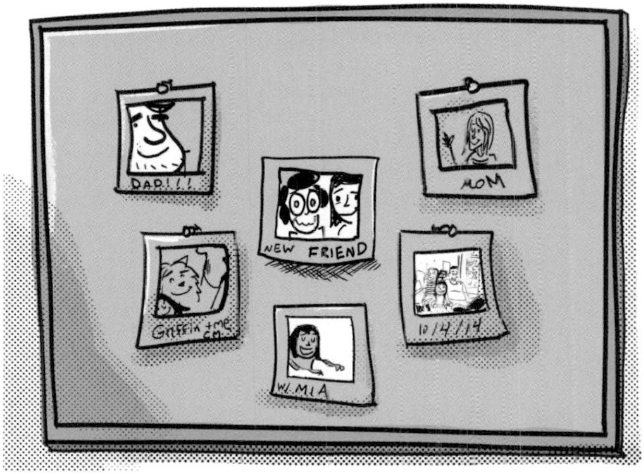
DAD!!!
MOM
NEW FRIEND
Griffin + me
W/ MIA
10/4/14

STEVEN T. SEAGLE IS A FOUNDING PARTNER OF MAN OF ACTION ENTERTAINMENT — CREATORS OF BEN 10 AND BIG HERO 6. HIS COMIC BOOKS HAVE BEEN NOMINATED FOR 10 EISNER AWARDS, NONE OF WHICH WERE WON BUT HE ISN'T HAUNTED BY THAT. HE COULDN'T MAKE THIS BOOK WITHOUT DARYL SABARA INTRODUCING HIM TO JASON IN THE FIRST PLACE; NOR COULD HE MAKE THIS BOOK WITHOUT JASON HIMSELF; NOR COULD HE MAKE THIS BOOK WITHOUT HIS WIFE, CATS, EVERYONE AT IMAGE COMICS, OR THE TONS OF READERS WHO LIKED THE FIRST BOOK!

JASON ADAM KATZENSTEIN IS A CARTOONIST AND WRITER FOR COMICS, MAGAZINES AND TV. HIS CARTOONS APPEAR IN THE NEW YORKER, AND STEVE MOSTLY GETS THEM. JASON PLAYS IN A BAND CALLED WET LEATHER, WHO, INCIDENTALLY, LOOK A LOT LIKE "SAY WHAT". HE COULDN'T MAKE THIS BOOK WITHOUT THE LOVE AND SUPPORT OF HIS FRIENDS AND FAMILY, BUT IN PARTICULAR THIS ONE'S FOR SOFIA WARREN, WHOSE WORK MAKES HIM WANT TO BE BETTER, AND DARYL SABARA, WHO ONCE SAID, "YOU MAKE COMICS? YOU GOTTA MEET STEVE!"

SEE WHERE IT ALL BEGAN!

STEVEN T. SEAGLE·
JASON ADAM KATZENSTEIN

Camp Midnight

CAMP MIDNIGHT VOLUME 1

CAN SKYE KEEP HER SECRET IDENTITY AS THE ONLY HUMAN IN A CAMP FOR MONSTER KIDS? ALONGSIDE FELLOW CAMPER AND FAST-FRIEND, MIA, SKYE LEARNS WHAT HAPPENS WHEN WE STOP TRYING TO BE SOMETHING WE'RE NOT AND LEARN HOW TO BE EXACTLY WHAT — AND WHO — WE ARE.

PRAISE FOR CAMP MIDNIGHT VOL 1:
"A DEVILISHLY FUN SUMMER CAMP STORY" — PUBLISHERS WEEKLY
"FROM COVER TO COVER CAMP MIDNIGHT IS A VISUAL JOY" — COMICSVERSE
"PERFECTLY BLENDS THE CREEPY WITH THE HUMOROUS" — SCHOOL LIBRARY JOURNAL
"WILD, FUN, AND INFINITELY RE-READABLE" — SPOOKY KIDLIT
"CREATIVE. CREEPY. HILARIOUS." — DIAMOND BOOKSHELF

248 PAGES/FULL COLOR
PUBLISHED BY IMAGE COMICS
AVAILABLE AT YOUR LOCAL COMIC BOOK STORE, BETTER BOOKSTORES, AND AMAZON.COM.

WWW.MANOFACTION.TV

IMAGE COMICS, INC.

Robert Kirkman: Chief Operating Officer

Erik Larsen: Chief Financial Officer

Todd McFarlane: President

Marc Silvestri: Chief Executive Officer

Jim Valentino: Vice President

Eric Stephenson: Publisher / Chief Creative Officer

Jeff Boison: Director of Publishing Planning & Book Trade Sales

Chris Ross: Director of Digital Sales

Jeff Stang: Director of Direct Market Sales

Kat Salazar: Director of PR & Marketing

Drew Gill: Cover Editor

Heather Doornink: Production Director

Nicole Lapalme: Controller

IMAGECOMICS.COM

CAMP MIDNIGHT VOLUME 2: CAMP MIDNIGHT VS. CAMP DAYBRIGHT. First printing. October 2019. Published by Image Comics, Inc. Office of publication: 2701 NW Vaughn St., Suite 780, Portland, OR 97210. Copyright © 2019 Steven T. Seagle & Jason Adam Katzenstein. All rights reserved. "Camp Midnight," its logos, and the likenesses of all characters herein are trademarks of Steven T. Seagle & Jason Adam Katzenstein, unless otherwise noted. "Image" and the Image Comics logos are registered trademarks of Image Comics, Inc. No part of this publication may be reproduced or transmitted, in any form or by any means (except for short excerpts for journalistic or review purposes), without the express written permission of Steven T. Seagle & Jason Adam Katzenstein or Image Comics, Inc. All names, characters, events, and locales in this publication are entirely fictional. Any resemblance to actual persons (living or dead), events, or places, without satirical intent, is coincidental. Printed in the USA. For information regarding the CPSIA on this printed material call: 203-595-3636. For international rights, contact: foreignlicensing@imagecomics.com. ISBN: 978-1-5343-1341-5.